D1292590

THE I TATTI
RENAISSANCE LIBRARY

James Hankins, General Editor

FOLENGO

BALDO

VOLUME 2

ITRL 36

TEOFILO FOLENGO
✦ ✦ ✦
BALDO
VOLUME 2 · BOOKS XIII–XV

TRANSLATED BY

ANN E. MULLANEY

THE I TATTI RENAISSANCE LIBRARY
HARVARD UNIVERSITY PRESS
CAMBRIDGE, MASSACHUSETTS
LONDON, ENGLAND
2008

Copyright © 2008 by the President and Fellows of Harvard College
Printed in the United States of America

Series design by Dean Bornstein

Library of Congress Control Number 2006052943

CIP data available from the Library of Congress

ISBN 978-0-674-02521-9 (vol. 1)
ISBN 978-0-674-03124-1 (vol. 2)

Contents

ॐ⸱ॐ

Introduction

ॐ⸮ॐ

We last saw Baldo and his friends coping with a frightening but comical storm at sea. The second volume of Teofilo Folengo's *Baldo* begins with a melodramatic council of the gods, after which Aeolus is persuaded to withdraw his winds. Our heroes reach land safely and enjoy a brief period of camaraderie and learning, but then the focus of the epic shifts from real people, their roles in society and traditional scenes of combat, to mutating creatures, self-referencing elements and unresolved struggles.

The narrative line which had been so direct in Books 1–12 becomes convoluted in Books 13–25: the men are forever going down into yet another black cavern; we sense meaning just beyond our grasp. The violence, which crescendos steadily throughout the epic, reaches a ghoulish climax in Book 21 when Baldo dismembers demonic animals with his bare hands as his giant friend, Fracasso, tears the beasts apart with his teeth and soaks himself thoroughly in their warm blood. Happily, Merlin the bard pops in to save the day (21.378–461). He empowers his protagonists with the armor and weapons of classical heroes and sends them off to kill witches and demons (22.1–368). After his intervention, the rest of the epic flows along, alternating playful antics with sharp criticism of the Catholic Church and scholasticism. The poem ends, innovatively, in a huge Pumpkin which all must enter, to have a tooth pulled repeatedly for every lie they've ever told.

Early enthusiasts, including François Rabelais, seem to have been captivated by Folengo's works in all their complexity. *Baldo* went through four quite different editions and countless reprints, many of which feature striking illustrations. A popular French translation was published in 1606 as the *Histoire macaronique de Merlin Coccaie, prototype de Rablais* [*sic*]. Later readers may come away from a first reading with questions: Why does that relentless eel-like dragon which gets between the men's legs suddenly turn into a pretty woman? What should we make of Baldo and his friends riding an eel-like whale for hours while brutally assaulting it? And what prompted Folengo to split himself into so many pieces? In Book 19, for instance, an exemplary character who bears the author's religious name (Philotheus for Teofilo) uncovers his pseudonym's tomb and unleashes a devil both hideous and hilarious; the devil then proceeds to read out loud about a wizard who forced howling spirits to put on an enchanted cape and become invisible.[1] The clues are slippery, but too numerous to ignore.

Possible answers appear in the middle of Folengo's autobiographical *Chaos del Triperuno* (1527), where two authorial selves (Merlino and Limerno) tell of having been molested as children:

> *Limerno:* . . . I won't hold back from reciting to you some verses composed by me when I was still a young boy, finding myself in a certain villa in that area around Ferrara, sent there by my father to learn letters at the home of a priest, who held many students subject, and more the handsome than the homely ones; in which place, due to a corruption of the filthy air, there abounded so many snakes, frogs, mosquitoes, and bats that it seemed an inferno of tormentors. Therefore, finding myself every night like a mendicant Lazarus, wounded all over by the punctures of those little flying creatures, to my master I recited childishly:

> Thus, I invoke my Muses: Behold, instead of Muses,
> a swarm of gnats rises up and brands me about the face.
> While I prepare to sing, my eyes flood with tears,
> and the wounds made by the gnats drip with dew.
> Here, too, night-flying birds screech and howl,
> and black birds threaten misfortunes to come.

> What shall I say of the fleas, who jump with agile bodies?
> And by now both my hands lack nails for stabbing.[2]

Merlino acknowledges the truth in Limerno's verses and offers his own poem, in which a personified Ferrara says to him, "Come . . . be ours; accept our rites as well. / We live on human blood, surrender food!"

This revelation may elucidate certain episodes in the *Baldo*, and may also explain certain word choices, for example, all the strategic things that are pierced: the Folengazzo coat of arms (*sbusata* from *buso*, Italian *buco*, hole, dent, 5.407); Moon Mountain, where a carnivorous pirate brother plows the waters, and where Baldo and his friends fight the *ferrari* and the dragon (*busa. . . tota*, 20.301–10, 692–5, 815–7); the *busis* (grottoes) where Merlin waits for his heroes (22.142); and the great Pumpkin, described as *sbusata* and rattling with *semina sicca* (25.621–2). Renaissance scholars might remind us that Folengo, like other writers of his day, may have achieved "self-fashioning" in relation to "something perceived as alien, strange, or hostile. This threatening other — heretic, savage, witch, adulteress, traitor, Antichrist — [had to] be discovered or invented in order to be attacked and destroyed."[3] But whether the menacing Other originated inside or outside our poet, we need to read what Folengo has written. In 1924, perhaps fresh from his reading of *Baldo*, Carlo Emilio Gadda seemed comfortable with Folengo's chaotic world: when considering an overall tone for the prize-winning novel he was planning, after enumerating the logical-rational, humorous-ironic, serio-comic and emphatic-tragic-baroque, Gadda added a fifth way, "the moronic way, which is fresh, childish, mythical, Homeric, with traces of symbolism, with stupefaction-innocence-ingenuousness. It is the style of a child who sees the world (and who would already know how to write)."[4] Now, in the third millennium, with increasing knowledge of how the mind works, we can shed light on Book 21 and on the rest of Folengo's dark places — just as Seraphus, one of his character-doubles, lit a torch to guide Gilberto.

I would like to acknowledge all of Folengo's readers, especially those who contributed to the present volume: ever-generous Mario Chiesa, who added to his other acts of kindness by providing newly corrected files of the Latin text, resourceful David Marsh, and the intrepid General Editor, James Hankins. And my first readers, especially Sarah Knox Armstrong, Mollie Mishek DeCoster, Ronald Martinez, John McLucas, and Maggie Tacheny.

Ann E. Mullaney
Minneapolis, Minnesota
March 2008

NOTES

1. There are many significant revisions from edition to edition: the name Philotheus is changed to Philoforno ("Beloved of God" to "Oven-lover"); the tomb he opens no longer belongs to Merlin but to two other magicians; the wizard (Zoroaster) who enchants the cape of invisibility and designs a magic ship which earlier was conjured by a Merlin double, Seraphus, who used it to sail away with handsome young Gilberto. The principal revisions are indicated in the notes to this edition.

2. Merlino insists that Limerno can perceive the truth under his fiction, "That courtly Ferrara is bothersome to me, not for its houseflies and horseflies, but because there they harvest their wines on the backs of frogs" (*ivi raccoglionsi lor vini su le groppe de le rane*). See *Chaos del Triperuno*, in *Opere italiane* (Scrittori d'Italia), vol. 1, ed. Umberto Renda (Bari: Laterza, 1911), 276–8, currently available at www.bibliotecaitaliana.it.

3. Stephen Greenblatt, *Renaissance Self-fashioning: From More to Shakespeare* (Chicago: Chicago University Press, 1980), 9.

4. *Racconto italiano di ignoto del novecento, Cahiers d'études* 1 in *Opere di Carlo Emilio Gadda: Scritti vari e postumi*, ed. Dante Isella et al. (Milan: Garzanti, 1993), 395–6.

• Mantua and Vicinity •

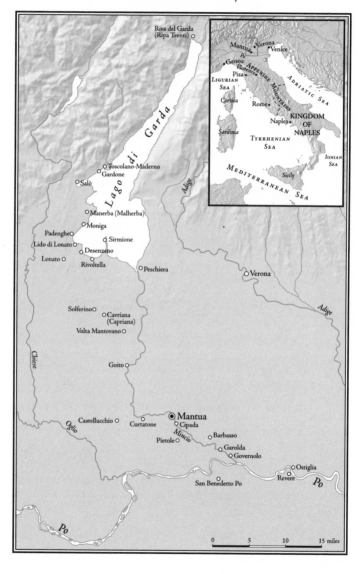

Riva del Garda
(Ripa Trenti)

Lago di Garda

Toscolano-Maderno
Gardone
Salò
Manerba (Malherba)
Moniga
Padenghe
Lido di Lonato
Desenzano
Lonato
Rivoltella
Sirmione
Peschiera

Adige

Verona

Adige

Solferino
Cavriana
(Capriana)
Volta Mantovano

Chiese

Goito

Castellucchio
Curtatone
Cipada
Pietole
Mincio
Barbasso
Garolda
Governolo
San Benedetto Po
Revere
Ostiglia
Po

Oglio

Po

Mantua

0   5   10   15 miles

KINGDOM OF NAPLES inset:
Mantua Verona Venice
Po
Genoa Florence
Pisa APPENNINE MOUNTAINS
LIGURIAN SEA
ADRIATIC SEA
Corsica Rome
Naples
KINGDOM OF NAPLES
Sardinia TYRRHENIAN SEA
IONIAN SEA
MEDITERRANEAN SEA
Sicily

BALDO

Liber tertius decimus

Stabat Neptunus scragna reposatus in alta,
qui sua sub pelagi fundamine regna governat,
inque maris centro locat urbes, castra, palazzos.
Chors ibi continuo populis bandita tenetur,
5 pars it, pars tornat semper casamenta per illa,
in quibus albergant nymphae divique bagnati,
fluminaque atque lacus veniunt ad iura tyranni.
Stabat honorevolos, inquam, deus intra barones,
dispensans varias, conseio adstante, facendas,
10 quando super piscem Triton infretta cavalcans,
Triton Oceani bastardus et Anguillinae,
improvisus adest trottatque sperone batuto.
Quisque facit largum, nescitur causa viaggi,
unde quis affrettat verunam scire novellam.
15 Protinus a curvo delphini tergore saltat,
inde, cavans brettam duro de cortice conchae,
ante pedes regis Neptuni crura pigavit:
'Quonam', proclamans inquit, 'rex magne profundi,
quo novus hic fastus, quo tanta superbia nascit?
20 magnane sub vili praesumptio pectore bravat?
Ergo Iovis cum sis fratellus et aequoris alti
rector et imperium super omnia flumina portes,
quod tua guastentur patieris regna per unum
furfantum, sguatarum, boiam plenumque pedocchis,
25 indignumque tibi, dicam?, leccare dedretum?
Aeolus is ipse est proprius, de quo tibi parlo;
qui quia Iunonis fantescam Deiopaeam
(ex illis siquidem, quibus est data cura lavandi
cantara, pignattas porcisque recare brodaiam)
30 stentavit sposare diu, manigolditer altam

2

Book XIII

Neptune sat comfortably on his high throne, he who governs his 1
kingdom on the ocean floor and builds cities, fortresses and pal-
aces in the middle of the sea. A continual open court is held down
there for everyone: someone is always coming and going in those
abodes where nymphs and soaked divinities dwell, and where
rivers and lakes gather by command of their sovereign.

This god, as I was saying, together with his honorable barons, 8
was arranging various matters in the presence of the council, when
Triton, riding in haste on a fish, suddenly approached at a full gal-
lop—Triton, the bastard son of Oceanus and Lady Eel. Everyone
makes way for him; no one knows the cause of his journey so ev-
eryone rushes to hear his news. Swiftly he jumps down from the
curved back of the dolphin. Then, doffing his cap of hard conch
shell, he bows at the feet of King Neptune. "Whence, O great
King of the Sea," he queries loudly, "comes this strange contempt?
Whence such haughtiness? Can great presumption thunder in a
coward's breast? So even though you are the brother of Jupiter and
ruler of the high seas and hold command over all the rivers, you
are going to allow your kingdom to be devastated by a rascal, a va-
grant, a delinquent riddled with lice? By someone who is unwor-
thy (shall I say it?) of licking your backside? It is Aeolus himself
I am talking about, the very one who pined for a long time,
then married Deiopea, Juno's maid, one of those servant girls
whose job it is to wash cups and pots and to slop the pigs. Now he

3

fert cristam et sese gravibus talvolta facendis
ingerit hic ipsis, quas nec tu fare calares.
Aeolus est, dico, qui nescio qualia saxa,
saxa polita herbis strinataque solis ab igne,
35 possedisse godit fumumque annasat arosti,
castigatque suos ventos de more pedanti,
moreque cozzoni magris dat fraina cavallis.
Hic fuit arditus, asinus temerarius, absque,
absque tuo imperio, rex o grandissime ponti,
40 grottas montagnae vastas aperire busatae,
atque, scadenatis pedibus manibusque Libecchi,
ventorumque simul cunctorum carcere fracto,
tot slanzavit aquas totque undas totque procellas,
quod superi metuere diu metuuntque negari;
45 mancavitque pocum quin strabuccaret ab arce
Iuppiter aetherea, credens anchora gigantes
velle, superpositis montagnis montibus altis,
tollere per forzam summi regnamina coeli.
En quoque nunc nostras audent intrare masones,
50 atque ruinarunt, tutaviaque nostra ruinant
attria, giardinos, stallas, casamenta, palazzos;
et nisi providcas, o rex, te certus aviso:
quod tu nosque tuis nunc nunc afogabimur undis'.
    Talia dum scoltat Neptunus, totus abrasat
55 terque tridentino sbattivit littora rasco.
Trombettam subito, trombettam voce comandat
chiamari ad sese, quem praestiter atque debottum
drizzat ad Aeolios scoios rupesque pelatas.
Hic trovet hunc regem talqualem, cui data cura est
60 a Iove striggiandi ventos stallasque sgurandi;
huic de parte sua convitia talia dicat,
qualia conveniunt poltronibus atque dapochis,
qualia fameio quadrant scalzoque regazzo.

brashly lifts his crest up high and at times takes on serious matters that even you wouldn't dare to tackle.

"It is Aeolus, I say, who enjoys possessing I don't know what sort of rocks, rocks cleansed of moss and scorched by the sun's fires; he sniffs in the fumes of the roast. He castigates his winds like a schoolmaster, and like a groom, gives darnel to his scrawny horses. This bold ass had the audacity without your authorization — without it! — O great King of the Oceans, to open the vast grottoes of his hollow mountain. After unchaining the hands and feet of Libeccio and unleashing all the winds from their prison, he released so much water, so many waves and so many storms that the gods above feared, and still fear, they would drown. Jupiter nearly tumbled from his heavenly fortress, thinking that the giants once again wanted to stack mountains on top of high peaks and take the kingdom of the high heavens by force. And now these storms even dare to enter our homes. They have wrecked and continue to wreck our halls, our gardens, our stables, our dwellings and our palaces. If you do not intervene, O King, I warn you that all of us and you yourself soon will be drowned in your very own waves."

While Neptune listens to these words, he becomes completely enflamed and strikes the ocean bottom three times with his trident. A herald — at once! He commands in a loud voice that a herald be summoned and sent directly and at once to Aeolus' reefs and scoured cliffs. There, he should find this so-called king, who was appointed by Jupiter to rein in the winds and clean the stables, and shower him with such insults in Neptune's name as befits bums and good-for-nothings, like those suited to a servant or a barefoot boy.

33

54

Non trombetta sibi cosam bis dicere fecit:
65   it via, festinus veluti staffetta galoppat;
      fert humero trombam buso de dente balenae
      perque maris fundum campagna trottat in ampla.
      Mox susum drizzans cursum, qua summa travaiant
      aequora bagnanturque pedes aspergine Lunae,
70   ipse quoque undarum danza danzare comenzat,
      ut facit ocha nodans, seu mergus, sive nedrottus.
      Undique fluctisonis hinc inde butatur ab undis
      atque sonans trombam chiamat procul Aeola regem.
      Aeolus ascoltat, subito descendit ab alpa,
75   cuius ab excelso mirabat vertice ludum
      undarumque giocum ventosque insemma tacatos:
      laudabat forzam nunc Borrae nuncve Sirocchi,
      nunc Tramontanae possam rabiemque Libecchi.
      En tandem trombetta venit, coleraque brasatus
80   ambassariam facit ira et fulmine plenam.
      Aeolus, ut minimus divum stronzusque deorum,
      formidat regem cui flumina et aequora parent.
      'Nil dubita', dixit: 'facio quae Iuno comandat.
      Nunc nunc in montis chiavabo carcere ventos.
85   I celer atque sona bis terque per aequora cornu.
      Altera fratantum per me provisio fiet'.
      Dixerat, et rupis testam repetivit aguzzam,
      ingrediensque busam, ventum disgardinat illum,
      quem Zephirum dicunt multi multique Maëstrum,
90   qui rabidos valeat ponto distollere fratres
      ad primamque maris fluctus tornare bonazzam.
      Ergo Maëstralis vultu se scoprit alegro,
      ghirlandamque ferens vario de flore cositam,
      tranquillat proprios blando sermone fradellos;
95   hinc magna illorum cito controversia cessat
      atque tumor pelagi sese nihilare comenzat.

The herald does not have to be told twice: he departs and gal- 64
lops as quickly as a courier. He carries on his shoulder a trumpet
made from a hollow whale's tooth and trots across the vast plain of
the ocean's bottom. Next, directing his course upward where the
surface of the water is turbulent and the Moon's feet get soaked
with spray, he too begins to dance the dance of the waves, just like
a swimming goose or a merganser or a duckling. Thrown here and
there by the rushing waves and sounding his trumpet, from afar he
summons the Aeolian king.

Aeolus hears him and comes down at once from his peak, from 74
whose exalted summit he was admiring the spectacle of the waves
and the play of the winds coming together. First he praised the
strength of Boreas, then of Sirocco, then the power of Tramon-
tana, and the fury of Libeccio. Now at last the herald arrives, and
burning with anger delivers his message full of thunderbolts and
wrath.

Aeolus, as the least of the deities and the turd of the gods, is 81
afraid of the king whom the rivers and oceans obey. "Have no
doubt," he says, "I will do as Juno commands. Right now I will
lock up the winds in their mountain prison. Go quickly and sound
your trumpet on the sea, two or three times. In the meantime I
will take other precautions as well." Having said this, Aeolus re-
turned to the craggy mountaintop. Entering the cavern, he un-
leashes the wind, whom many call Zephyr and many Mistral, so
that he can drive his rabid brothers from the sea and return the
marine swells to their former calm. So then, Mistral emerges with
a smiling face, wearing garlands woven of various flowers and
calming his brothers with a soothing speech. Their great contro-
versy thus ends quickly and the tumult of the sea begins to cancel

Incipit et sonitum trombae trombetta sonorae,
quo monitu scapolant venti nettantque paësum.
    Fugerat ergo ingens rabies maris atque bagordus;
100   ecce procul scoium Baldus discoprit aguzzum,
qui fert sicut Atlas in collo pondera coeli.
Huc nochierus agit navem (si dicere navem
iam liceat), quae rocca paret, vel bastio muri,
cui dederit dudum in costis bataria canonum.
105   Hic non herba viret, non spuntat rupibus arbor,
nemo pascit oves, nemo dat gramina bobus;
tantum nuda patent grossissima saxa ruinis,
sub quibus albergant falco, sparaverus et uncis
cum griffis aquilae, smerli gavinellaque proles.
110   Huc tamen acclinat spennatam nauta galaeam
solis ut ad radios possint sugare camisas
et pegola et stuppa legni renovare galones.
Cingar se prora saltu despiccat ab alta:
tangere gaudet humum gestisque solazzat alegris
115   votaque post humeros peradessum facta butantur.
Baldus eum sequitur, sequitur Leonardus et ille. . .
ille galantus homo, qui nuper in aequora bruttam
iecerat uxorem dicens non esse fagottum
fardellumque homini plus laidum plusque pesentum
120   quam sibi moieram lateri mirare tacatam,
quae sit oca ingenio, quae vultu spazzacaminus.
Is erat e Berghem patria, descesus ab illa
stirpe maronorum, quam menzonare pudemus
vergognantque illam fomnae nomare fameiam.
125   Huic nomen Boccalus erat, quo doctior alter
arte bufonandi numquam fuit intra Gonellas.
Succedunt alii, saltantes extra caraccam;
quisque locum cercat, quo soli corpore curent.
Cingar ubique suam rugando servat usanzam

itself. The trumpeter starts to sound his sonorous trumpet; at this warning the winds run away and clear out of there.

Thus the monstrous fury and frenzy of the seas had retreated; 99 suddenly in the distance Baldo sights a sharp rock that, like Atlas, bears on its back the weight of the skies. The captain steers the ship (if one can call it a ship) to the place which appears to be a . fortress or a walled bastion whose belly has just taken a battery of cannon fire. Here no green grass grows, no tree sticks out of the cliffs, no one is pasturing sheep, no one is grazing cattle — only immense naked rocks lie open on the precipice, harboring various falcons, sparrow hawks, sharp-clawed eagles, merlins and broods of seagulls. But nevertheless, the mariner guides his battered ship here so that she can dry her shirts in the rays of the sun and shore up her sides with pitch and sticks.

Cingar launches himself off the high prow with a leap; he is de- 113 lighted to touch the earth and happily gambols about, the vows he'd made are thrown over his shoulder for now. Baldo follows him, then Leonardo and that man, that gallant man who had just tossed his ugly wife into the sea, saying that there is no heavier or more unsightly load or burden for a man than to see stuck to his side a wife who has the wits of a goose and the face of a chimney-sweep.

This man was from the country of Bergamo, born of the 122 Chestnut family, which we blush to name: women are ashamed to say "nuts." His name is Boccalo; he is more skilled at the comic arts than any of the Gonellas. Others follow suit, jumping off the galleon and each looking for a spot where they can heal their bodies in the sun. Cingar observes his custom of poking around.

130 donec ad obscuram pervenit denique grottam,
quam intrare timet, sed apertam porgit orecchiam
si quemquam strepitum valeat sentire ladentrum.
Quale per artificum botegas murmur habetur,
cum pars martellat, pars limat parsque nigrantes
135 mantice carbones reddit plus gambare tostos,
seu voias Bressae, seu voias dire Milano,
tale per inventam sentit resonare cavernam.
Nil tamen aspectat, nullo huc intrante lusoro;
accennat socios, currunt, placet ire dedrentum.
140 Itur; coeca domus fuligine tota nigrescit,
cernere quam possunt, stizzum portante Bocalo.
Quo magis introëunt magis illa sonatio tich toch
fit martellorum nec non sofiatio buf bof.
Post centum passus quadram catavere piazzam,
145 cui quaevis trenta est quadratio longa cavezzos.
Porticus intornum, octo sustentata colonnis
qualibet in banda, format mirabile claustrum,
quod rotat incercum velut omnis sphera polorum,
seu sicut Modenae, seu sicut magna Bolognae
150 filatoia gravi circum gyramine vadunt,
per circumque strepunt de seta mille canones.
Quaeque colonna duplex de bronzi facta metallo est,
archi de argento facti voltaeque musaico,
in quibus hoeroum fortissima gesta leguntur.
155 Pinxerat hic pictor pictorum, magnus Apelles,
quidquid fada sibi comisit pingere Manto;
Manto, Thyresiae proles uxorque Foletti.
Cernitur hic illic semper memorabile bellum,
quando Barigazzum Pompeius ab arce Cipadae
160 compulit et, missis raptim squadronibus, ipsum
stravit Alexandrum Magnum Xersisque canaiam,
sub duce Grandonio mazzavit ad oppida Nini.

Eventually he comes to a dark grotto that he is afraid to enter, but he tilts his open ear to see if he can hear some sound from inside. Just like the hubbub that is heard in an artisan's workshop, let's say in Brescia or, if you prefer, in Milan, where one group hammers, another files and yet another works the bellows and makes the black carbon glow redder than a lobster, such is the din he hears resounding in the cavern he has found. Yet with no light entering there, he sees nothing. He signals to his companions; they come running and decide to go inside.

They proceed; the gloomy place is completely black with soot; 140 they are able to see it because Boccalo is carrying a torch. The further in they go, the louder grows the tick-tock sound of the hammers and the puff-paff of the blowing. After a hundred paces, they find a square piazza, nine rods long on each side. A portico runs all around, supported by eight columns on each side, forming a remarkable cloister that rotates like the stars around the North Pole, or like the great looms of Modena or Bologna that turn around with heavy gyrations, while all around resound a thousand spools of silk.

Each double column is made of bronze; the arches are made of 152 silver; and the vaults, in which one can read the magnanimous deeds of heroes, are made of mosaics. Here that painter of painters, Apelles, has painted everything that the Fate Manto commissioned (Manto, the offspring of Tiresias, and his wife Folletto). Here and there one could see the always memorable war in which Pompey forced Barigazzo from the fortress of Cipada and, having speedily sent off his squadrons, defeated Alexander the Great and slew the rabble of Xerxes led by Grandonio near the city of

Armiger Orlandus furit hic, dum fortis avanzat
Hanibalem nec non capelettum buttat Achillem
165   cum caput avantum magni de arzone Bufalchi.
Parte alia Caesar, secum veniente Rinaldo,
alpibus in vastis Ferrarae, iuxta Folignum,
diripit armatam de fustis deque galaeis,
quam Darius, princeps mundi mediique Milani,
170   miserat in punto propter ruinare Cipadam.
Haec ea cum multis aliis depinxerat illic
pictorum columen, lux lunaque solque penelli.
In medio claustri, super octo alzata pilastros,
arca sedet, quam tunda coprit testudo piombi.
175   Illa decem brazzos est longa, sed alta triginta
pyramidisque instar surgens sibi culmen aguzzat.
Tota lavoratur nitido sculptoribus auro,
per quam distinctae lissato in marmore zoiae
stralucent tamquam per coeli marmora stellae.
180   Quisque pilastronus crystallo conditur albo,
cuius in interno sberlucet ventre rubinus,
ceu cum fare solet lanterna moccus in una.
Porphida non desunt alabastraque lucida muris,
nec calcidonium, nec vulsa coralia ponto.
185   Hic ascoltantur gyramina plura rotarum,
quas velut orlogii vaga contrapesia guidant.
Ista pro causa currit fabricatio circum
ad formam naspi, cum foemina fila volutat;
arca manet solum rutilis imposta pilastris,
190   atque inter septem ceu tellus pendula coelos
eminet et semper moles it spherica circum.
    Constiterant ergo stupefacta mente barones,
cuncta palesa vident, claro splendente lusoro,
quem pretiosarum fundit lumera petrarum.
195   Hi quoque ridentes a circum circa menantur,

Nineveh. On one side, Orlando in arms rages and staunchly advances against Hannibal and throws the mercenary Achilles headfirst off great Buffalco's saddle. On the other, in the great mountains of Ferrara near Foligno, Caesar (Rinaldo coming with him) destroys a fleet of vessels and galleys which Darius, ruler of all the world and half of Milan, had gathered together in order to defeat Cipada. These things and many others had been depicted here by Apelles, that crown, that light, that moon and sun of the paintbrush.

In the middle of the cloister, held up by eight pilasters, stands   173
an ark covered with a round lead shell. It is ten arms long and thirty high; rising up like a pyramid, it narrows to a point. It has been worked all over by sculptors in shining gold; precious jewels glow on its smooth marble, just as stars glow in the marble of the heavens. Each of the large pilasters is made of transparent crystal and in the belly of each glows a ruby just as a wick glows in a lantern. The walls do not lack porphyry, brilliant alabaster, chalcedony, and coral extracted from the sea. Here are heard the gyrations of many wheels which are turned by swinging counterweights, like those in clocks. And this is why the entire structure revolves like a spool when a woman winds thread on it. Only the ark remains still—set on its glowing red pilasters, standing out just like the earth suspended amid the seven heavens—and the spherical orb goes around continually.

So the barons, utterly stupefied, had stopped moving. They see   192
everything distinctly in the clear shining light given off by the lanterns of precious stones. They too are being carried in a circle, laughing as the whole structure gallops around. But when they come to the center, to the fixed umbilical point where the ark

namque per intornum fabricatio tota galoppat;
sed quando ad centrum veniunt bigolumque posadae,
arca ubi firmatur stabilique in sede repossat,
stant firmi cerchiosque vident rotolare theatri.
200 Tum sibi praeterea maior maravilia nascit,
quod cernuntur ibi circum pirlare solari
ireque dattornum velut omnis machina mundi,
quam dentata menat moles diversa rotarum.
Non huc comparet neque vir neque parvula musca;
205 tantum sentitur, generat quem fabrica, rumor.
Ad martellorum sonitum vult pergere Baldus,
unde videns scalam, quae scandit more limachae,
hanc montat gradibus; tamen it velut ante datornum,
ac sua fit duplex rotolatio: namque movetur
210 omne opus incircum, scalam quoque tirat apressum,
ipsaque per sese circumfert scala scalinos.
Post multos gradulos, tandem reperere masonem,
quae crebris stantem gyris intorniat arcam.
Septem sunt sperae varia de sorte metalli,
215 quarum derdana est cunctis angustior altris,
quarum suprema est cunctis spatiosior altris.
Extrema argentum est; fissatum sulphur et album
mercurio mixtum facit hoc buliente bodega;
hoc valet in finum argentum convertere stagnum.
220 Hic plenas athalac et aceto mille burinas
effumare vident, quo fumo argentea blancam
materies perdit spetiem coelique colorem
vestit, ut ad vistas hominum sit gratior illa.
Circuit haec igitur de argento machina puro,
225 in qua sculpita est facies cornuta Dianae.
Post haec ascendunt alios cinquanta scalinos
atque ibi Mercurii fabricam invenere gelatam:
alphatar instabilis flueret faceretque nientum,

stands firm and rests in a stationary position, they stand still and watch the rings of the theater turning. And then, an even greater marvel arises for them because they see the heavens whirling and going around just like the entire machinery of the universe, driven by a diverse mass of cogged wheels. Not one person, not one little fly, appears. One can hear only the noise made by the machinery.

Baldo wants to get to the pounding of the hammers. Therefore, 206 seeing a staircase that ascends in the form of a snail, he starts up step by step, although he is still rotating as before, so that now he makes a double rotation—for the whole structure moves in a circle and pulls the staircase around with it as well, and the stairway itself carries its stairs around. After many steps, they finally come to the building whose constant gyrations encircle the fixed ark.

There are seven spheres of various metals: the last one is smaller 214 than all the others, the highest one is the largest. The lowest one is of silver, made of solid white sulfur mixed with mercury in a boiling vat; this has the power to convert tin to fine silver. Here they see a thousand glass vials smoking, filled with salt and vinegar, and in these vapors the silver matter loses its white appearance and takes on a sky-blue color so that it will be more pleasing to human sight. And surrounding these things there is an apparatus of pure silver, on which the horned face of Diana is sculpted.

After this, they ascend another fifty steps and there discover 226 Mercury's frigid edifice: the unstable quicksilver would dissolve and be worthless if it were not mixed with tragacanth gum and tartar and thoroughly distilled in an alembic over a burner. This

ni simul admixtum dragantum salque liei
230   esset et ad furnum cuncta haec stillaret aludel.
Voltatur finum servus fugitivus in aurum,
si bene iuncta suos cohibet medicina vapores.
Non sine Mercurio valeas mutare metalla,
unde canunt vates quod nuncius ille deorum est,
235   quo sine nulla quidem vel pax vel guerra movetur.
Ascendunt iterum Veneris solaria rubrae;
rammus ibi fulvum tandem voltatur in aurum,
ast opus est centos carbonum spendere saccos;
argenti et auri naturam rammus aquistat,
240   at numquam horumdem, Gebber testante, colorem;
unde minor spesa est, at rerum maior aquistus,
ut rammus maneat rammus formetque pignattas,
sive bagatinos praestet quantumque legeros,
quam cercare aurum tot afannis totque malhoris,
245   nec reperire umquam nisi post ter mille pacias.
De Venere ascendunt ad cerchium Solis et auri;
aureus est cerchius Phoeboque simillimus ipso.
Author earumdem rerum, post mille fadigas
in cassum spesas, post persum tempus et annos,
250   hanc fecit veram finaliter improbus artem:
verbitrium lapidem retrovavit philosophorum.
Multicolor lapis est, elementis quatribus extat:
igneus, aëreus, terrenus, aquaticus; unde
siccus in occulto caldusque, sed in manifesto
255   humidus et gelidus, naturave querna fit una.
Spiritus hic lapis est, qui transmutatur in unum
nobile, adustivum pariterque volatile corpus.
Non fugit a flammis, liquidi fluit instar olivi,
multiplicat, solidat, praeservat tempore longo,
260   atque potest mortos primaiae rendere vitae.
Hoc tribus in verbis consistit munus, ab alto

fugitive slave can be transformed into fine gold if a chemical is carefully added to it to condense its vapors. You cannot mutate metals without Mercury; for this reason the poets proclaim him the messenger of the gods, for indeed without him neither war nor peace can be made.

Next they ascend to the dome of ruddy Venus. Here copper is 236 eventually turned into yellow gold; however, it is necessary to spend a hundred sacks of rubies. Copper acquires the nature of silver and gold, but according to Geber, never their colors. Hence it costs less and yields more to let copper remain copper, and just make pots out of it or pennies, however light in weight, than it does to pursue gold despite all the hardships and suffering, since it is never found without three thousand slip-ups.

From Venus, they ascend to the circle of the Sun and of gold, a 246 circle that is golden and most like Apollo himself. The creator of these things, after thousands of efforts expended in vain, after having lost time and years, unflagging to the end, finally created the true art, and found the three-worded Philosopher's stone. It is a multicolored stone, composed of four elements — fire, air, earth and water — so that internally it is dry and hot but externally damp and cold; and from four natures makes one. This stone is spirit, which is transmuted into a noble body, burning and volatile. It does not flee from flames; it flows like olive oil; it multiplies, solidifies and preserves for a long time and can bring the dead back to their former lives. In three words this gift resides, bestowed by

quod Iove donatur sapientibus atque beatis.
Ingravidat semet, de semet concipit, inde
parturit et sibimet vivit sibimetque necatur.
265 Suscitat hinc semet, nam sic Deus ordinat illum.
Est tinctura rubens lapis iste biancaque, vivax,
concipiens aurum si fumo iungitur albo.
Numquid elithropia est? adamas? calamita? lypercol?
Absit! nam fluitat, seu sit cum corpore, seu non.
270 Est VI (num dicam tandem manifestius?) est A,
qua vita fruimur, qua verum acquiritur aurum.
Ad Martis veniunt, post Solis clymata, ballam:
ferrea quae tota est nitidoque azzale finatur.
Hac sine materia nostras nihil esse fadigas
275 iudico; quapropter ferrum est magis utile quod sit
ferrum quam quod sit seu stagnum sive latonum.
Sunt ferrum vanghae, sunt ferrum rastra, badili,
sunt ferrum falces, zappae centumque ricettae,
cum quibus et vini bonitas et panis habetur.
280 Commodius nihil est ferro, nihil aptius, inquam.
Non opus artificum quorumlibet esse catatur,
quod fieri duro sine ferro denique possit.
Ecce: marangones operant lignamina ferro,
ferro taiantur calzae variaeque gonellae;
285 pistat mortaro speciarius omnia ferro,
cum gucchis ferri brettas brettarus agucchiat;
ferro zavattas gens scarpazina repezzat,
calcinat et ferro muros murator et albat;
non radit barbam barberius absque rasoro,
290 non herbolattus dentes cavat absque tenaia,
nec porcos castrat sine ferro conzalavezus.
His bene discussis, Iovis ascendere biancam
materiam stagni, quod corpora nigra dealbat;
sed peccat buliens, nam corpus deterit omne,

Jupiter on the wise and the holy. It impregnates itself, conceives by itself, then gives birth and lives and dies by itself. Afterwards it resuscitates itself because God wills it to. This stone is tinted red and white, it conceives gold if it is joined to white vapor. Is it then heliotrope? diamond? lodestone? lypercol? Far from it, because it flows whether it is in a solid state or not. It is the "WA" (shall I not speak more clearly at last?), the "Y," by which we enjoy life, and by which we acquire gold.

After the region of the sun, the group comes to the ball of 272 Mars, which is all made of iron and finished with shiny steel. Without this element I believe our labors would come to naught. It is thus more useful that iron be iron, rather than tin or bronze. Plowshares are made of iron, as are rakes and shovels. Of iron are the scythes, the hoes and a hundred receptacles that hold the goodness of wine and bread. Nothing is more convenient than iron, I say, nor more adaptable. No work can be found by any artisan whatsoever that is achieved without durable iron. Carpenters work wood with iron; shoes and all kinds of skirts are cut with iron; the apothecary pounds everything in his mortar with iron; the hat maker sews hats with iron needles; the cobbler repairs shoes with iron; the bricklayer builds brick walls and stuccoes with iron; the barber cannot shave a beard without a razor; the herbalist cannot pull teeth without pliers; the tinker cannot castrate pigs without iron.

After discussing these matters at length, they ascended to the 292 white material of Jupiter's tin, which brightens black objects. But it goes wrong when it boils, for it destroys all objects unless they

295 praeter Saturni et Solis; tum firmius haeret
et Soli et Lunae, nec ab illis nempe recedit.
Cuius peccatum (ne corpora scilicet ipsa
frangat) quisquis enim cognoscet tollere, felix!
Oh felix nimium, qui travos, saxa, quadrellos,
300 ac sua quaeque cito fulvum cangiabit in aurum!
Sed quia nescitur mortalibus ista recetta,
felix! o felix qui scit stagnare padellas,
atque repezzandi cum stagno praestat in arte!
Post spheram stagni, Saturni ad fluxile plumbum
305 itur et artifices illic reperere dosentos.
Illico pulchra, gravis leggiadraque donna resurgit
contraque barones vultu veniebat alegro.
Baldus eam, curvando genu, cortesus honorat;
mox veniam chiedit, nimium si forte protervi
310 tecta subintrassent et sacra et sancta dearum.
Subrisit matrona illi, dehinc talia dixit:
'Sumne ego tam grandem dignata videre guererum,
quem coeli, terrae, ponti venerantur et Orci?
Urbs mea te genuit talem cortesa baronem
315 qualem non generat totum natura per orbem.
Illa ego sum Manto, de cuius nomine nomen
Mantua suscepit, quam condidit Ocnus in undis,
tempore quo Troiam ruinavit panza cavalli.
Nec penitus vestros animos stupor occupet ullus,
320 si nunc usque meam potui traducere vitam,
nam datur aeterno me tempore vivere fadam,
donec ab aethereo guastetur iudice mundus.
Hactenus ingemuit sub acerbo nostra tyranno
Mantua, quo mores cortesos perdidit omnes.
325 At praeclara modo, regalis et alma fameia
Gonziadum venit atque aquilas spigat undique nigras.
Haec, quam vidistis, miro fabricata lavoro

are of the Sun or Saturn. It adheres firmly to the Sun and Moon and never detaches from them. Anyone who knows how to remove this fault (that is, so it does not shatter bodies) indeed is happy! O so happy he who may quickly turn beams, rocks, bricks, and all his things into yellow gold! But since this recipe is unknown to mortals, happy, oh happy the man who knows how to patch pots and who excels in the art of tinkering with tin.

After the sphere of tin, they travel to the meltable lead of Sat- 304 urn where they find two hundred artisans. Here a beautiful, dignified and graceful woman rises up and approaches the barons with a cheerful countenance. Baldo honors her courteously on bended knee, then begs her pardon if they have entered too boldly into the sacred and holy place of the goddesses. The lady smiled at him, then said, "Am I so worthy as to behold such a great warrior, whom the heavens venerate and the earth, the seas and the netherworld? My noble city gave birth to you, such a baron that nature has not created your equal anywhere in the world. I am Manto, from whose name Mantua derives her name, which Ocno founded on the sea, in the era when Troy was ruined by the belly of a horse. Nor should you be at all surprised if I have been able to prolong my life up until now, for as a Fate, I have been given eternal life, until the heavenly judge shall demolish the world. Up to now, our Mantua has bewailed her bitter tyrant, on account of whom she has lost all her courteous customs.

"Yet the illustrious, regal and glorious Gonzaga family now 325 appears, flying their black eagles everywhere. This palace you have seen, constructed with marvelous workmanship, is completely dedi-

stancia, Francisco Gonzagae tota dicatur.
Post centum guerrae palmas, post mille trophaeos,
330 post vitae laudes, post vecchi Nestoris annos,
illius huic magno donabimus ossa sepulchro.
His ego divitiis praesum facioque magistros
aurifices doceoque aurum formare, catatum
ex virtute trium verborum; nomina quorum
335 auribus admotis audite, quod illa docebo'.
His dictis Thebana parens nutrixque Cipadae,
multa susurrando per eorum fixit orecchias,
quae toccare manu faciunt genitalia rerum,
herbarum forzas, stellarum facta, petrarum
340 effectus varios et habendi denique plenam
semper ducatis borsam donavit avisum;
quod magis importat, magis altum recat honorem,
quam studiando libros et stellis perdere sennum.
    Nauta sed interea non poca foramina barchae
345 conzarat rursumque parat tentare diablos.
Baldus ab aurificum, sociis comitantibus, antro
se portat caricatque suo cum corpore lignum.
Tunc dare vela iubet, Zephyri velamina boffant,
Mantoaeque magae spallis casamenta relinquunt.
350   Forte alios inter peregrinos atque romeros,
quos omnes pariter barca illa in ventre ferebat,
vir vivax oculis aderat vultuque galantus,
tam respettosus, tam sequestratus ab altris,
ut totum per iter non dixerit octo parolas;
355 quippe habitu proprio genioque suopte tacendo
vergognosus erat stabatque in parte solettus.
Huic nomen Giubertus erat, qui voce lyraque
Orpheus in sylvis, inter delphinas Arion,
saxorum ad sese nemorumque tirabat orecchias.

cated to Francesco Gonzaga. After a hundred wartime victories, a thousand trophies, after a laudable life, after he has reached the age of Nestor, we will consign his bones to this great sepulcher. I preside over these riches, I train these goldsmiths and teach them how to make gold as revealed by the virtue of the three words. Listen with your ears brought close, because I will teach you their names."

Having said this, the Theban mother and nurse of Cipada in a soft voice drove many things into their ears which let them grasp the means of procreation: the power of herbs, the accomplishments of the stars, the various effects of stones, and lastly she gave them advice on always having their purses full of ducats, which is more important, which brings greater honor, than studying books and losing your mind on the stars.   336

The captain, meanwhile, has repaired not a few holes in the boat and prepares to face the devils again. Baldo returns from the cavern of the goldsmiths, accompanied by his comrades, and loads the ship with his own body. He then commands that the sails be raised; the zephyrs blow into the sails and they depart from the abodes of the Mantuan mage.   344

By chance, among the pilgrims and hermits which that ship carries all together in her belly, there was a man with lively eyes and a gallant mien, so reserved, so isolated from the others, that during the entire voyage he hadn't said eight words. He was in fact timid both by habit and nature and kept to himself. His name was Gilberto, and by his voice and lyre (an Orpheus in the woods, an Arion among the dolphins) he charmed the ears of the stones and the trees.   350

360 Baldus eum pridem tacitis guardabat ochiadis.
Ille, viri tanti cernens sibi lumina flecti,
fronte rubescebat bassosque tenebat ocellos.
Captus ob id, Baldus penitus moruisset alhoram,
ni prius agnosset qui sit, quo vadat et unde
365 adveniat, mentemque suam studiumque suorum.
Ergo, ubi cognovit cythara cantare peritum,
hunc rogat ut tantam voiat recreare brigatam,
voceque dulciloqua longum nihilare caminum.
Ille statim censet tanto magis esse barono
370 parendum, quanto se noscit in arte magistrum.
Expedit e panno sedae mirabile plectrum,
sive lyram dicas potius, quae concinit arcu,
concentuque suo facit omnes stare balordos.
Iam rectas longasque arcu menat ille tiratas
375 taliaque altandem modulando carmina coepit:
'Infidum arridet saepe imprudentibus aequor
mentiturque leves Zephiros, Aquilone parato.
Hinc veniunt homines cupidi, quos plura videndi
cura subit, seu forte Deas in gurgite nantes,
380 sive Tridentiferi verrentes caerula currus.
Verum ubi subducto ventum est qua littore circum
misceri aspiciunt coelum aequore et aequora coelo,
en miseri avulso singultant viscere proni
hinc atque hinc nautae, nigraeque urgente vomuntur
385 bile dapes foedatque acidus Nereidas humor;
unde indignantes venti tam audacter amicas
commaculare suas genus hoc mortale, caducum
atque procax, ne sic evadat crimen inultum
concurrunt, sonituque ingenti obnixa profundo
390 tergora subiciunt pelago totumque revellunt.
Heu stulti, quos nulla monet iactura priorum!
Tunc ea tempestas, ea tunc asperrima rerum

Baldo had been watching him silently for some time. Gilberto,   360
seeing the eyes of such a man turned on him, blushed openly and
kept his eyes lowered. Fascinated, Baldo felt he would surely die if
he could not discover who this man is, where he is going and
where he comes from, and know his thoughts and his endeavors.
Therefore, when he learned that Gilberto was an expert at singing
to the cithara, he asked him if he would like to entertain the whole
crowd with his sweet-toned voice and thereby obliterate the long
voyage. The man deems it best to obey this great baron at once,
especially since he knows himself to be a master in this art. From a
silk cloth he takes a wonderful harp, or you might call it a lyre,
which he plays with a bow, and his harmonies leave everyone
dumbstruck. For a while he guides the bow in long, straight
strokes and then begins to intone the following song:

The faithless sea sometimes smiles at the unwary and de-   376
ceives them with light breezes while the north wind lies in
wait. Curious men come here, moved by the desire to see
many things, perhaps goddesses swimming in the swells or
Neptune's chariots skimming the blue sea. But once far from
shore, they observe the wind all around them mixing sky
with sea and sea with sky; behold, the wretched sailors wail
with their insides turned out, bent over this way and that,
they vomit blackened food impelled by bile, and their acidic
humor befouls the Nereides; whence the winds, indignant
that this mortal race, this impudent, fallen race is polluting
their girlfriends so brashly, lest such a crime go unpunished,
rush forth and with a tremendous clamor thrust their robust
backs under the deep sea and completely overturn it. O foo-
lish men, who have learnt nothing from prior sacrifices! It
was *then* that the tempest, *then* the harsh face of reality
should have been foreseen by the mind, before the brash

debuerat facies animo spectarier ante,
quam nauta insultans Fortunae solveret audax;
395   mox frustra insani vellent contingere portus'.
    Talia cantando Giubertus, talia plectrum
pulsando, sic sic hominum stupefecerat aures
ut nisi Boccalus cito providisset ad illos
non homines certe navis carigata menasset,
400   sed tot pignattas, tot zoccos totque colonnas.
Bergamascus erat, ut diximus ante, Bocalus.
Protinus accurrens, trat de cantone sacozzas
quasdam pezzatas, recusitas plusque bisuntas
quam gremiale coghi numquam savone lavantis.
405   Hinc sibi de medio strazzarum tasca cavatur,
quam cito praecingit dextro gallone cadentem.
Mox positis trespis, mensam sibi praeparat ante,
ac si bancherus vellet numerare monetam.
Praestiter hic brazzos tunica manicisque camisae
410   liberat ad cubitos, ut fitur quando parecchiat
fluminis ad ripam fantesca lavare bugadam
atque bretarolis grossas ostendere gambas.
Giubertus cytharam rursus velamine coprit,
inde, sedens iuxta Baldum, ghignare comenzat;
415   namque Bocalus habet iam tractos extra besazzam
quosdam de latta, vel tres, vel quinque becheros,
insemmamque leves balotellas nescio quantas,
maiores pilulis illis, quas Mesue dixit:
'Recipe pro capite, anna, tria scropola, fiat'.
420   His bagatellandi tantum gallantiter artem
incipit ut numquam melius Zaramella giocavit
ante ducam Borsum solitus manegiare balottas.
Mirum quam subitis manibus de suque de giuque
stravoltat zaynos ut tres cinquanta parerent.
425   Nunc unum ponit super altrum, nuncve roversos

captain, challenging Fate, had set sail. Later these crazy
people in vain desire to reach port.

Singing of these things and strumming the plectrum, Gilberto   396
has utterly stupefied the men's ears, so that if Boccalo had not
quickly succored them, the ship would have been laden not with
men, but with so many pots, logs and columns. Boccalo was a
Bergamasco, as we said before. Running up promptly, he pulls
some old sacks from the corner — raggedy, patched and greasier
than a cook's apron never washed with soap. From the middle of
all these rags, Boccalo pulls out a pouch and quickly attaches it to
hang from his right side. Then, arranging some trestles, he sets up
a table in front of him, as if he were a banker wishing to count
money. Swiftly he frees his arms from his cloak and shirtsleeves up
to his elbows, just as a maid does when she gets ready to wash the
laundry at the river's edge and shows off her fat legs to boys in
caps. Gilberto covers his harp back up and sitting next to Baldo,
begins to chuckle — for Boccalo has already pulled out of his bag
three or five tin cups together with some little balls (I don't know
how many), slightly larger than the pills mentioned by Masawayh,
who said, "Take three scruples each, in equal parts. *Fiat.*"

He began doing sleight of hand with such polished skill that   420
Zaramella, who used to play at maneuvering little balls for Duke
Borso d'Este, was never better. It is amazing how he turns the
beakers up, then down, with his hands moving so rapidly that
three look like fifty. First he puts one on top of another, then he
instantly separates them, turned over butt end up, and now three,

dividit antrattum, stantes culamine coelo,
atque super fundos modo tres, modo quinque balottae
apparent ac una modo soletta videtur.
His bene completis positisque dabanda moiolis,
430 maius asaltat opus: facit huc portare caraffam,
non malvasiae garbae, sed dulcis afattum,
dicens non aliter fieri quod fare parecchiat.
Hanc bibit ad fundum veniens, trat in aequora zuccam.
Mox aperit boccam, monstrat nihil esse dedentrum,
435 inde serans dentes grignantes atque scopertos,
soffiat et risum, dum soffiat, excitat illis,
cernere qui monam bertuzzam nempe parebant,
quae tenet in testa scufiam dentesque righignat.
Sopiat et vulgum sberlato lumine sgognat.
440 Verum quis credat? dum soffiat, ecce farina,
ecce farina venit largo de gutture, quae iam
imbrattando omnes cogit scampare brigatam.
Oh puta, si strepitat plebs hic grossera cachinnis!
Nil tamen a Baldo valuit plus ducere risum,
445 quam quod in hoc ipso medemo tempore zucca,
zucca gitata viam Boccalo nuper in undas,
Cingaris ad collum subito sprovista pependit.
Dumque illi stesso Boccalus buttat in ora
bocconem panis, dumque ocyus inde comandat
450 hunc spudare foras, o res mirabilis! ecce
non ultra est panis, sed merda rodunda cavalli.
Omnia corteso tolerat costumine Cingar,
dum sic schrizzetur ne schrizzum doia sequatur.
Quid plura? ex oculis coram tot gente Lonardi
455 absque nocimento gucchias striccavit acutas;
inque sinu Baldi mandat cercare Gibertum:
hinc trahit oh quantas qualesque con ordine robbas!
scilicet ampollam, specchium, calamare, sonaium,

now five little balls appear on their bottoms; then, it looks like just one.

Having performed this part well and having set aside the tumblers, he launches into a more difficult trick: he asks that he be given a carafe, not of harsh Malvasia, but of a really sweet wine, saying that this is the only way he can do what he plans to do. He drinks the wine straight down to the bottom and throws the gourd into the sea. Next he opens his mouth and shows that he has nothing inside it, then clenching his teeth, he bares them in a grimace; he blows and, while blowing, excites laughter in the others since they seemed to be looking at a macaque monkey with a bonnet on its head and baring its teeth. He blows and makes faces at the crowd with wild eyes. Well, who could believe this? While he is blowing, behold! flour — yes, flour — comes out of his wide gullet and, soiling everyone, drives the crowd away. You can imagine how this rustic crew burst into laughter! 429

Nothing could have caused Baldo to laugh any harder, except that at that same moment the gourd, the very gourd Boccalo had just tossed into the waves, all of a sudden hung unexpectedly from Cingar's neck. And then, while Boccalo starts throwing pieces of bread into Cingar's mouth and just as speedily commanding him to spit them out, such a marvel! look! it's no longer bread, but round horse turds. Cingar tolerates all this with the graciousness demanded by etiquette, as long as one jokes so that joking does no harm. What's next? While everyone is watching, Boccalo pulls sharp needles out of Leonardo's eyes, without causing any damage. And he tells Gilberto to search Baldo's chest, and he extracts all sorts of stuff from it in the following order: a bulb, a mirror, an 444

chiappam piatelli, strigiam pezzumque bragheri
460 et quos ad missam mocolos zaghettus avanzat.
Obstupet his Baldus, nec scit pensare qualhora
iverit ad feram Lanzani seu Recanatae,
has comprare cosas non soldos quinque valentes.
Denique Giuberto nasum sopiare comandat;
465 non negat hoc cantor; bis, ter, quater ille stranudat;
evolat ecce foras magno rumore tavanus,
quem seguitat grillus, post grillum trenta pedocchi,
quos mage compitos non dat sguarnazza pitocchi.
    Et iam finis erat, cum Phoebus giunsit acasam
470 chiamavitque suos alta cum voce fameios.
Ptous adest, Horius, Pythius, Phos, Mitra, Myrinus
patronemque volant de carro tollere giusum;
disfangat pars una rotas nettatque lavacchio,
altera pars disfrenat equos stallaque reponit,
475 ac ibi cum paia sudantia tergora fregat,
mox beverat solitasque orzi butat ante prevendas.

Liber quartus decimus

Memnon, ab Aurora iam missus matre, fugabat
cum scutica Chiozzam, Capram Braccumque baiantem
innumerasque alias stellas de tramite coeli,
per quam nunc debet transire caretta parentis;
5 noxque viam scapolat, visis splendoribus albae.
Baldus, Apollineos cernens uscire cavallos
extra orizontem carrumque tirare brasatum,
talia contemplat, mox sic cum Cingare parlat:
'O Cingar, grandis me nunc maravilia brancat,
10 nec scio qua guisa possunt, quae cernimus, esse.

inkwell, a bell, a shard of a plate, a bridle, part of a truss and the bits of candle which are left for the altar boy to gather after Mass. Baldo is amazed at these things; he doesn't know when Boccalo went to the fair in Lanciano or in Recanati to buy these things that aren't worth five cents.

Finally, he tells Gilberto to blow his nose. The singer does not   464
refuse: twice, thrice, four times he sneezes and behold, with a great noise, out darts a horsefly, then a cricket, and after the cricket come thirty lice—a beggar's coat does not offer a better choice of lice.

The end had already come when Phoebus got back home and   469
called his servants in a loud voice. Ptous appears, and Horus, Pythias, Phos, Mithras and Myrinus, and they fly up to get their master down from his cart. Some of the servants clear the mud off the wheels and wash off the grime; others unhitch the horses and return them to their stall, where they rub the beasts' sweaty backs with straw, then water them and throw before them their regular ration of barley.

Book XIV

Memnon, sent by his mother Aurora, was using a whip to chase   1
the Pleiades, Capricorn, the barking Dog and countless other stars from the celestial road, through which his mother's cart must now pass. And Night, having seen the splendors of dawn, runs off. Baldo contemplates such doings while observing Apollo's horses rise above the horizon, pulling the fiery chariot. He then speaks to Cingar thus, "O Cingar, at this moment great wonder grips me: I do not understand how these things that we observe can exist.

Nonne vides solem plus largum plusque rotundum
quando foras exit nascens quandove tramontat,
quam cum sustollit per coeli culmina carrum?
Praeterea nunc fert tam rossum ille visazzum
15 quod mihi barrillam Corsi trincasse videtur'.
Cingar ait: 'Magnas cosas mihi, Balde, rechiedis,
quas nimis astrologi dudum schiarire fadigant,
nam super humanos sensus ea facta provantur.
Sed tamen insigni quidam de semine Gregus,
20 cuius (si memini) Piationi nomen habetur,
astronomusque alius Tolomellus, Iona propheta,
Solon, Aristotel, Melchisedech, Oga Magoga,
talia tractarunt per magnos sparsa librazzos'.
Quando Leonardus sic audit nomine grosso
25 Cingara philosophos Ogamque referre Magogam,
corripitur tanto grigno strepituque risaiae
ut prostratus humi iam iam crepare videtur.
Baldus at, usanzam qui norat Cingaris ante
millibus in cosis, tantum soghignat et inquit:
30 'Cingar, es astrologus? numeras num sydera, Cingar?
Oh! si te nossem has ipsas studiasse facendas,
me fortasse ista fecisses arte magistrum!'
Nil ridet Cingar, sed stat gravitudine tanta,
quanta Pytagoras non staret supra cadregam.
35 Mox ait: 'Oh quoties olim te, Balde, gabavi!
Oh!, inquam, quoties oselatus, Balde, fuisti!
Me de nocte quidem pensabas ire robatum,
seu sbusare ussos seu rampegare fenestras,
sed (cancar veniat mihi nunc, si dico bosiam!)
40 nocte ibam stellas ad contemplare fogatas.
Montabam intenta super altas mente pioppas
ut possem melius coelum guardare propinquum.
 'Cernebam Lunam, macchiata fronte, biancam

Don't you see that the sun is larger and rounder when it emerges while rising or setting than when its chariot ascends to the heavenly zenith? Besides, the sun has such a big red face now that it looks to me as though it has just guzzled a barrel of Corsican wine."

Cingar answers, "You are asking me great things, Baldo, which astrologers have long wearied themselves in explaining, for they prove to be beyond human reason. But be that as it may, a certain Greek from a distinguished family, whose name (if memory serves me) is Playtoe, and another astronomer, Tolomello, as well as Jonah the prophet, Solon, Aristotel, Melchisedech, and Oga Magoga discussed these matters here and there in great big books." 16

When Leonardo hears Cingar refer to philosophers with rustic names, and to Oga and Magoga, he is so convulsed by guffaws and raucous laughter that he falls prostrate on the ground and seems about to burst. But Baldo, who was already familiar with Cingar's habits in a thousand things, only smirks and says, "Cingar, you're an astrologer? Do you count the stars, Cingar? If I'd known you'd studied these matters, maybe you could have made me a professor in this subject!" 24

Cingar does not laugh at all, but rather stands there with as much solemnity as Pythagoras himself would have stood at his lectern. Then he speaks: "O how many times in the past, Baldo, did I trick you! O, I say, how many times were you hoodwinked, Baldo! Indeed, you thought that I went out at night to rob, to break down doors or to climb into windows, but instead—and may cancer strike me now if I am telling a lie—I went out at night to contemplate the fiery stars. I deliberately climbed the highest poplars so that I could view the sky better up close. I watched the white Moon with her spotty face dispel shadows from the shoals of the sea and the lands of the earth. With her horns pointed, she 33

distenebrare maris scoios terraeque paësos.

45   Cornibus aguzzis, nunc paret scorza melonis;
cornibus impletis, nunc est pars meza taieri;
cornibus aggiuntis, nunc fundamenta tinazzi.
Haec in cervello non lassat stare legeros,
namque illam sentit cerebros picigare Valenza,

50   quae urbs in Spagna stultorum millia pascit.
Villani, quamvis sint de lignamine grosso,
hanc tamen observant quando est taiabilis arbor,
namque solent gigni sub cortice saepe caroles.
Hanc servant medici, quando medicina malato

55   danda sit: haec faceret quandoque cagare budellas.
Hac lucente, stryae godunt saltantque stryones,
qui tunc se spoliant nudos ad cornua Lunae,
moxque diabolicis ungunt sibi membra cirottis,
inde super gramolas, trespos et guindala, zoccos,

60   supraque cadregas tota illa nocte cavalcant.
Desperare facit nocturnos luna ladrones,
nam contrabandos retegit mostratque palesos.
Nunciat haec pluvias, vultum nigrefacta rotundum,
nunciat et nautis rubea cum fronte procellam.

65   Continet hoc bassum freddi regnamen olympi,
atque lusentatur Phoebeis nocte cavallis;
hanc tamen interdum Pluto strassinat ad Orcum,
quae pomgranati fuit aggabbata granellis.
'Te quoque, Mercuri, pochinas cerno fiatas,

70   qui fur es et latro et primus in arte robandi.
Namque times ne cum per coeli rura caminas,
teque fretolosis adiungat Apollo carettis
teque giusum burlans faciat spezzare colengum.
Tu tua supra casas Lunae casamenta locasti,

75   sunt ubi sex centum pegorae cridantque bebeum
mille caprae, totidemque boves asinique, somari,

looks at times like a melon rind; at other times, with her horns filled in, she looks like half a plate; when the horns meet, then she looks like the bottom of a vat. The Moon does not let simpletons stay focused, and in fact Valencia—the city in Spain which nourishes thousands of fools—feels her nip at their brains.

"Peasants, even though they are as thick as wood, nonetheless 51 watch the Moon so that they will know when to cut trees, since otherwise woodworms will spring up under the bark. Doctors observe the Moon so that they will know when to give their patients medicine that otherwise would make them shit out their intestines. When the moon is shining, witches rejoice and wizards dance around; they strip themselves naked under its horns and then smear their limbs with devilish salves. And after that they ride all night on rolling pins, three-legged stools, wool-winders, logs and chairs.

"The Moon makes nocturnal thieves despair, for she discovers 56 their illegal activities and brings them to light. She announces rain when her round face darkens; when her face reddens she announces a storm for sailors. She occupies this low kingdom of cold Olympus and is lit up at night by Apollo's horses. Yet, from time to time, Pluto drags her to Orcus, where she had been tricked with pomegranate seeds.

"Once in a while I see you too Mercury, who are a thief and a 69 burglar and foremost in the robbing arts. In fact, you are afraid that while you are ambling through the skies, Apollo may overtake you in his speedy chariot and hurl you down to break your neck. You have placed your dwellings above the Moon's abode, where there are six hundred sheep, and a thousand goats cry 'beh, beh,' with as many oxen, donkeys and asses, and a thousand domestic pigs and humped camels. You run throughout the world, stealing

mille casalenghi porci gobbique camelli.
Tu scorris mundum, facis hinc, facis inde botinos,
quos trahis ad coeli furacia tecta secundi.

80 Alatum portat semper tua testa capellum,
alatos portat semper tua gamba stivallos,
fatidicam portat semper tua dextra bachettam,
quando ambassatas huc portas patris et illuc.
Tu mercantiam traficans, vadisque redisque,

85 tu ventura canis, tibi multum musica gradat,
tu guerram, si vis, compagna in gente maneggias,
tu pacem, si vis, sdegnata in gente ritornas.
Heu! patrone meus, tibi me recomando ladrettum,
ne triplicem supra forcam me lazzus acoiet.

90 'Sed iam de Veneris coelo nunc sermo fiatur.
Ipsam mirabar Phoebi seguitare pedattas,
quando idem Phoebus Neptunia regna sotintrat.
Oh! quantas voltas plantavit cornua zoppo
ghiottoncella viro fusosque in vertice tortos!

95 Vulcanum siquidem Veneris patet esse maritum,
sed populi siquidem Venerem patet esse maritam.
Dum martellabat ferrum Vulcanus in antro,
Mars occulte suo vangabat semper in horto.
Oh! quot Vulcani, quot Martes, quotve bramosae

100 prevendae alterius mulae vaccaeque trovantur!
Ista Venus terzo casamentum fixit in orbe,
per quem, nympharum multis comitata brigatis,
it nitidas relegendo rosas violasque recentes,
mentam, garofilos, mazuranam, basalicoium.

105 Ghirlandas texunt, frescadas, serta, corollas,
diversosque canunt strambottos atque sonettos,
diversasque sonant arpas, manacorda, leuttos.
Hic semper saltant, ballant danzantque puellae,
seque lavant nudas in fontibus atque laghettis.

loot here and there, which you bring back to the thieves' den in the second heaven. Your head always bears a winged hat, your legs always bear winged boots, and your right hand always bears a divine caduceus when you bear your father's dispatches here and there. You come and go trafficking in goods; you foretell the future; you like music a lot. You stir up war between friendly peoples on a whim, and on a whim restore peace between hostile peoples. O my patron, I recommend my thieving self to you so that the noose will not welcome me on the three-beam gallows!

"But now let us discuss the sphere of Venus. I have marveled as 90 she follows the footsteps of Apollo, when Apollo dips into Neptune's reign. O how many times has this minx put horns on her lame husband's head and twisted his spindle! For it is clear that Vulcan is Venus's husband, but it is also clear that Venus is everyone's wife. While Vulcan was hammering iron in his cavern, Mars was secretly plowing the man's orchard, over and over. O how many are Vulcans, how many Mars! How many mules and cows there are lusting for one another's fodder!

"Venus established her residence in the third heaven, where she 101 is accompanied by large groups of nymphs, and goes gathering bright roses and fresh violets, mint, carnations, marjoram and basil. They weave garlands, canopies, wreaths and crowns; they sing various strophes and sonnets; they play harps, clavichords and lutes. Here the maidens continually gambol, dance and prance and bathe naked in the fountains and ponds. Soft little breezes frolic

37

110 Venticuli molles myrthorum frondibus atque
    floribus insultant, frescas ornantibus herbas,
    et straccatarum nympharum pectora mulcent.
    Hic fagi, pini, cedri, pomrancia, nespoi,
    spernazant umbras, ubi nymphae corpora possant.
115 Ad cazzam vadunt, arcos et stralia portant,
    discazzantque leves dainos agilesque caprettos.
    Non mancant boschi de cedris deque narancis,
    de myrthis, lauris, lentiscis atque ginepris.
    Non ibi villani terram vangare fadigant,
120 non ibi villanae stoppam filare videntur,
    non ibi plantantur ravanelli, porra, cipollae,
    non aium, capiti nocuum, tyriaqua vilani;
    non ibi sub spinis, urticis atque ruidis
    stant serpae, rospi, bissae turpesque ranocchi.
125 Hic est grata quies, hic pax, hic plena voluptas,
    hic sunt gentiles animi, gentilia corda.
    Dumque Venus tanto gaudet bellina diporto,
    expectat donec vult Sol equitare per orbem,
    quem leggiadra suis cupiens anteire carettis,
130 plus bellas mandat sibi retro venire puellas,
    quae impositis capiti ghirlandis, quaeve tenentes
    in manibus virides frascas madidasque rosada,
    compagnant dominam, saltantes atque canentes.
    Illa praeit recreatque polos et, plena rosarum,
135 vadit ad Oceani regnum, quo spumea nata est;
    cuius tirratur niveis carretta columbis,
    cumque propinquantem sentit succedere Phoebum,
    en scoprit rutilam tremulo de gurgite frontem,
    atque sui formam visi mortalibus offert.
140 Iamque omnes alias discazzat ab aethere stellas
    et modicis parvam generat splendoribus umbram.

in the myrtle boughs and the flowers which grace the fresh grasses and caress the breasts of the weary nymphs. Here beech, pine, cedar, citrus and medlar trees spread their shade where the nymphs may rest their bodies. They go hunting: they carry bows and arrows and drive forth graceful deer and agile young goats. There is no dearth of cedar and orange groves, of myrtle, laurel, mastic and juniper. Here, the peasants do not weary themselves plowing the earth; the peasant women are not seen spinning hemp; they do not plant turnips, leeks, onions or garlic, which is harmful to the head, but an antidote for the peasant. Here under the thorns, nettles and briars, there are no serpents, toads, snakes or loathsome frogs. Here there is pleasing tranquility, here peace and total delight; here souls are gentle and hearts are kind.

"And while enjoying such pastimes, charming Venus waits until 127 such time as the Sun chooses to ride over the earth; then this graceful lady, desiring to precede him with her fine carts, commands the prettiest girls to follow her. They accompany their mistress dancing and singing, some with garlands on their heads, others clasping bows that are verdant and moist with dew. She leads them and delights the heavens; laden with roses, she goes to Ocean's realm, where she was born from foam. Her chariot is drawn by white doves, and when she senses that Apollo is drawing near, behold, she lifts her shining visage out of the quivering waves and offers the beauty of her face to us mortals. Already she has chased all the other stars out of the heavens and now generates a faint shadow with her delicate light.

'Sat Veneri dictum; Solis veniamus ad orbem,
qui medios inter cerchios sua regna governat
atque suum quarta fabricavit sede palazzum.

145 Chortem banditam portis ibi semper apertis
Sol tenet et cunctis intrandi nulla temenza est.
Hic habitat vecchius barbatus, nomine Tempus.
Tempus, quo nihil hac rerum sub mole terendum
parcius, usque adeo rapidis se surripit horis.

150 Qui semper varios horatim parturit actus,
qui nec pensero manet umquam saldus in uno.
Nunc vult, nunc non vult bagatella, magisque legerus
quam busca aut folium, quod ventus in aëra menat.
Ille sibi quamdam tenet in cantone botegam:

155 pulveris orloios fabricat plenosque rodellis.
Matronam coepit propria pro coniuge bellam
nomine Naturam, quae centum mille fiolos
impregnata parit, nec maium tendit ad altrum
quam stimulare virum lecto, quam ventre pieno

160 disvulvare homines, castrones atque cavallos.
Praecipue tamen ipsa duos de Sole fiolos
atque duas habuit, Tempus cornando, fiolas.
Hos nondimenum pensaverat ipse bonhommus
esse suam prolem, quorum sic nomina fecit:

165 Primavera, Aestas, Autumnus denique Vernus.
Primavera fuit Veneris maridata putello,
qui gerit in spallis alas de more civettae.
Nudus it et nullis tegitur vergogna mudandis.
Fert arcum semper caricum plenamque guainam

170 stralibus innumeris adeoque sotilibus ut vix
fila sotila magis possint filare begatti.
Sunt tamen effectu variae, quas iste sagittas
slanzat osellazzus, varios quia spargit afannos;
cum quibus ad coccam plus centum millia cordas

"We have said enough about Venus; now let us come to the   142
sphere of the Sun, who rules his kingdom in the middle spheres
and has constructed his manor in the fourth heaven. The Sun
holds open court with the doors always open: all may enter free of
fear. A bearded old man lives here whose name is Time, which
should be spent more sparingly than anything in the universe,
since indeed he snatches hours away so quickly. He constantly
spawns new activities every hour and never remains fixed on one
thought. First he wants this, then he doesn't; he's lighter than a
straw or a leaf that the wind carries through the air. In a corner he
runs a kind of workshop and turns out timepieces full of cog-
wheels or sand. He has taken a beautiful lady named Nature for
his wife, who, impregnated, gives birth to a thousand children.
Nature never has any other concern than to stimulate her husband
in bed and disgorge men, rams, and horses from her fecund belly.
Above all, she cuckolded Time and had two sons and two daugh-
ters by the Sun. All the same, easy-going Time thought that they
were his own offspring, so he gave them names: Spring, Summer,
Autumn and Winter.

"Spring was married to Venus' boy, who bears wings on his   166
shoulders like an owl. He goes around naked and his privates are
not covered by underpants. He always carries a cocked bow and a
quiver full of countless darts which are so fine that silkworms can
scarcely spin threads any finer. However, they cause a variety of
effects, the arrows that this naughty bird shoots, because they sow
a variety of woes. With these at the notch, he wears out more than
a hundred thousand bowstrings every year, but the steel is not

175   dissipat ognannum, sed nil frustatur azalum.
      Una sagittarum sors est, cui puncta piombi,
      unde remucatur nescitque forare coëllum
      nec penetrare potest, nolente Cupidine, panzam.
      Unde travaiato gentes sub sydere natae
180   vel sibi colla tirant, vel ferro viscera passant.
      Nam quis homo non se vel desperatus apicchet,
      vel de praecipiti sibi rumpat turre colengum,
      si miser, infelix, tragicus, sprezzetur ab illa,
      quam solam pensat, cupit, ardet, laudat, honorat?
185   Haec venit a dardis plumbi desgratia: quod, quam
      meschinellus amas, ab eadem spretus odiris,
      unde necessaris fato te tradere forchae.
      Altra sagittarum species aurata refulget,
      quae scoccando oculos intrat filzatque magonem
190   trincerasque animi spezzat murosque rasonis.
      Hac feriente, cadunt ab honesto corda volero.
      Hac feriente, cito mentis spezzantur habenae.
      Hac feriente, iacent conseia salubria spallis.
      Hac feriente, bonos compagnos quisque refudat.
195   Hac feriente, Paris patriae fuit, oyme!, ruina.
      Hac feriente, patri taiavit Scylla capillum.
      Hac feriente, colo filavit claviger Hercul.
      Hac feriente, Iovem cornutum Europa cavalcat
      Ioque de vacca ficta fit vacca daverum.
200   Hinc veniunt irae, sdegni, mala quaeque diabli.
      Primavera tamen, cum sit "muliebre polenta,"
      non cernit plus oltra sui quam culmina nasi;
      unde Cupidineo godit maridasse marito,
      cui placitura suas rastellat pectine chiomas
205   atque cerudellos crespat ponitque belettum.
      Ghirlandetta, rosis violisque cusita galantis,
      bellificat trezzas usque ad calcagna volantes.

consumed. There is one type of arrow whose tip is lead, so it bends and isn't able to pierce anything; it cannot penetrate the breast unless Cupid wants it to. Thus people born under misaligned stars either string themselves up or eviscerate themselves with a sword. For what desperate man would not hang himself or break his neck by throwing himself off a tower if, miserable, unhappy and tragic, he is disdained by that one woman whom he contemplates, desires, burns for, praises and honors? This is the misfortune that comes from those lead-tipped shafts: you will be despised by the one you love, miserable wretch, and be forced by fate to mount the gallows.

"A second type of arrow shines with gold; once shot, it enters 187 the eye, pierces the chest and breaks apart the fortifications of the soul and the walls of reason. When it strikes, hearts abandon honest desire; when it strikes, the reins of reason are quickly broken; when it strikes, sound advice is thrown over one's shoulders; when it strikes, one turns away good friends. When it struck, Paris became the ruin of his homeland; when it struck, Scylla cut off her father's hair; when it struck, Hercules, the club-bearer, started weaving with a spindle; when it struck, Europa rode horned Jupiter, and Io from a metaphorical cow became a real cow. From this arrow come rage and disdain and all the devil's evils.

"Now, Spring, a polenta of a woman, does not see any further 201 than the end of her nose, so she enjoys being married to her husband Cupid. To please him, she rakes her hair with a comb, crimps her curls and puts on makeup. A dainty garland, sewn with fine roses and violets, adorns the tresses flowing down to her

Canzanti vestit soccam setaeque sotanam,
per quas innumeri flores recamantur et herbae.
210 Semper odorantes perfumos portat adossum:
muschium, zibettum, nampham centumque cigalas,
in quibus allicitur Veneris bastardus, et ancum
talibus in fraschis minus ille cinaedus amorbat.
Sed quoniam bella est et cunctis bellior altris,
215 non curat stoppam tereti deducere fuso
nec, post deductam, naspo convolvere filum,
at sese virdis sub frondibus illa stravaccat,
vel magis ad spassum per florida rura vagatur;
quam seguitant dulces oselini semper et omni
220 sorte melodiae faciunt cantando regattam.
Non luscina deest, frifolo quae gutture laudat
laeta lovertisii mores formamque morosi,
et centum foggias gorghezzat voce metrorum.
Cardellinus adest, qui annidat in arbore buxi,
225 dulcis ab auditu, sed visu dulcior et qui
sublatos natos retrovans gabiaque seratos,
non umquam lassat, sed miro pascit amore.
Non ibi franguelli mancant facilesque fanelli
atque caputnigri lodolaeque per aëra vaghae.
230 Hic, papagalle etiam, cifolos ad sydera mandas,
humanasque etiam praesumis dire parolas.
Iugiter hic gazae: 'Puta, porca, vaccato' cantant.
Primavera godit tam dulci accepta ricetto
poltronemque, fame morientem atque dapocum,
235 nomine Solazzum, nutrit pascitque panada,
quam condire facit latesinis atque caponum
pellibus, et magrum sibi praeparat illa bufonem.
'Altera Naturae proles, bona foemina certe,
Aestas dicta, godit multis sudare fadighis.
240 Nullam fert soccam sed solam nuda camisam,

heels. She wears an ever-changing skirt and a silk shift on which countless flowers and herbs are embroidered. She always wears intense perfumes: musk, civet, orange water and a hundred trifles to lure Venus's bastard; and yet even amid these frivolities that little catamite corrupts. However, because Venus is so beautiful, more beautiful than all the others, she does not concern herself with winding hemp on a polished spindle or, after it is wound, with spinning its thread on a spool. Instead she reposes under green leafy bows or rather wanders in flowery meadows. Sweet little birds follow her at all times and hold a contest for singing every sort of melody.

"The nightingale is not absent, who with its trilling throat gaily   221
praises the habits of the hop plant and the comeliness of the lover, and with its voice warbles a hundred kinds of songs. There too is the goldfinch, which nests in the boxwood tree, lovely to the ears but even lovelier to the eyes, and when finding its babies have been stolen away and locked in a cage, never leaves them, but nourishes them with admirable love. There one finds no lack of finches and flighty buntings, blackcaps or larks dipping through the sky. There you too, O parrot, send chirps to the stars; and even pretend to speak human words. There the magpies keep singing 'whore, wench, sow.' Spring enjoys being welcomed into such a sweet retreat and nourishes a good-for-nothing bum named Leisure, who is starving to death, by feeding him bread-soup that she seasons with veal and capon skins, and she tends the skinny buffoon herself.

"Nature's other daughter, a good woman for sure, is called   238
Summer, and she enjoys sweating in many labors. She does not wear a skirt, but only a blouse on her bare body, for she would

namque brusaretur nimio scaldore Leonis.
Ipsa lavorando granaria frugibus implet,
qua sine mortales omnino pane carerent.
Zaltrones facit ista nimis sudare vilanos.
245   Haec tamen est illis sat grata fadiga marassis:
nam quamvis asinina dolet schenazza cuchinis
atque caro veniat tibiando crevata ladronis,
omnia supportant memores quod tempore freddo
non nix dat panem, non dat sibi giazza fugazzam.
250   Semper Apollineo nigrefacta lusore fadigat
attenditque sitim crebro lenire botazzo.
Dum coquitur Phoebo, segetes dum falce trucidat,
dum quoque cum virgis gravidas dispaiat aristas,
numquam sbaiaffae cessant cridare cicadae,
255   quae cridando super vignas culamina menant.
Debilis est ventus nullumque movetur ab aura
foiamen tenui, sbadacchiat terra, nec herbae
se drizzare queunt, quoniam fugit humor ab illis.
Diximus assaium de magni tempore caldi,
260   Naturae terzi promatur usanza fioli.
      'Autumnum veteres Silenum dire solebant,
cui testam nudam dicunt picigasse tavanos.
Ipse praeest Bacchi domibus totaeque fameiae,
quem nos gastaldum, multi dixere fatorem.
265   Et quoniam gustat Sol vinum dulce libenter,
quem caricum musto semper damatina videmus,
gastaldum Bacchi et Bacchum diligit ipsum.
Hic Silenus habet quamdam pro coniuge nympham,
cui caput est grandis baghae, cui panza tinazzi.
270   Semper olet vinum, tandem Vindemia dicta est.
Ambo sunt adeo pingues adeoque pafuti,
ut minus in grassa positi tumuere boazzi,
ac velut inflati vento schioppare minazzant.

burn up in Leo's heat. It is she who by laboring fills the granaries with the harvest and without her, mortals would utterly lack bread. She makes the base peasants sweat a lot. And yet that work is actually pleasing to these snakes, because even though these boors have aching donkey backs, and their flesh is wasted from threshing, they tolerate everything; for they are aware that in the cold season snow does not give them bread nor ice focaccia. Blackened by Apollo's rays, she labors constantly and tries to slake her thirst by drinking frequently from a flask. While Phoebus bakes her, while she cuts the grain with a scythe, and too, while she knocks the swollen ears from the stalks with a stick, the chattering cicadas never stop screeching, and as they screech they wave their bottoms over the vines. The wind is weak; not one tiny leaf is moved by the slight breeze; the earth yawns; the grasses cannot stand up because all moisture leaves them. We've said enough about this time of great heat; now let's recount the customs of Nature's third child.

"The ancients used to call Autumn Silenus, whose bald head, 261 they say, is nipped by horseflies. He presides over the house and all the servants of Bacchus; we would call him a chief steward, others would say a butler. And since the Sun gladly sips sweet red wine (we always see him covered with must in the mornings), he likes Bacchus's steward as well as Bacchus himself. This Silenus has for his wife a certain nymph with a head as big as a goatskin and a belly as big as a vat. She always reeks of *vino*; therefore she is called 'Vin-demia' for Harvest.

"These two are both so very fat and so very plump that fat- 271 tened oxen are smaller, and they threaten to explode as though they were inflated with wind. At their sides, back, and front they

Semper habent lateri, de retro et ante, sonantes
275   mille fiaschettos, barilottos atque botazzos,
cum quibus andando, stando, saltando, canendo,
se recreant crebrisque caput sorbotibus implent.
Usant saepe etiam plures cantare sonettos
gorgadamque tirant vini, cessante sonetto.
280   Post potum saltant, post saltum pocula siccant.
Sic alternantes, laxis ebriantur habenis:
hisque volant circum montes, casamenta, paësi,
non quod eant circum, sed quod gyrare videntur.
Immo sibi parent tam presto currere cursu
285   ut barbarescos lassent post terga cavallos.
Non cessant trincare tamen tota agmina donec,
agmina zuccarum, buttentur voda tereno.
Somnus adest tandem, quorum nisi membra ligaret,
illi plus cocti quam crudi, dummodo gambis
290   currere pensarent, de coeli sede tomarent.
His nudis nudi fant guardam mille putini,
dum sornacchiantes porcorum more quiescunt;
cantant "ehu ohe," saltant faciuntque morescas,
pinguiduli forsanque habiles aptique guacetto.
295   Quisque caput rizzum vignali fronde coronat,
quisque tenet manibus botros uvaeque razinos,
quisque fiaschettum, parvo pendente loretto.
Morbezant, rident, celebrant baganalia patri,
inde sub uviferis vignis ebriantur et ipsi.
300   Ebria stat mater, pater ebrius, ebria proles,
sicve ebri omnes patefacto gutture boffant.
Bacchus habet magnum quodam cantone palazzum,
quo centum canevae, cantinae, quove rivolti
sub terra occulti, servant, ut stalla cavallos,
305   vassellos varios, tum grandes tumque minutos.
Hic semper grossas lato ventramine buttas

always have a thousand tinkling little flasks, small kegs and bottles with which — while walking, standing, dancing or singing — they refresh themselves and fill their heads with frequent swigs. Indeed, they often make it a habit to sing lots of sonnets, and when each sonnet ends, they take a gulp of wine. After drinking, they dance, and after each dance they drain their cups. Alternating thus, they get drunk and cast restraint to the winds: mountains, houses, towns fly all around them, not because they are actually going around, but because they appear to be rotating. Indeed, to these two it appears they are running in a race so fast that they would leave Berber horses in the dust. And yet they don't stop drinking, not until the entire army — the army of gourds — is thrown empty on the ground.

"Sleep finally arrives: if sleep did not bind their limbs, this cou- 288
ple, more baked than boiled, would think that they could run on their legs and would tumble from the sky. Watching over these naked ones while they rest, snorting like pigs, are a thousand naked *putti*. They sing 'Hey, ho, Bacchus!' and dance and perform morescas, the pudgy little dears, and perhaps are suitable and fitting for a stew. Each one crowns his curly head with a leafy vine; each holds in his hands bunches and clusters of grapes; each has a small flask with a little dangling spout. They prance, laugh and celebrate their father's bacchanals; then, beneath the grape-laden vines, they themselves get drunk. The mother is drunk, the father is drunk, the children are drunk; thus, all of them are drunk and pant with gaping throats.

"Bacchus has a grand palace in a certain region, where a hun- 302
dred cellars, canteens and hidden underground caverns hold a variety of receptacles (some large, some tiny), just as a stall holds horses. Here you see people putting rings around big wide-bellied

incerchiare vides amplasque restringere tinas.
Hicve travasantur de vezis deque barillis
vina propinari superum dignissima mensis,
310 namque hinc fornitur vinis asinaia deorum.
Non ita formichae vadunt redeuntque frequenter,
quando aliquem mucchium gratae catavere ceserchiae:
grandia tergoribus granorum pondera sburlant;
fervet opus populique nigri magna horrea complent,
315 ut per mustigeri facitur casamenta tyranni,
quando frequenter eunt carichi vodique retornant
mille putinelli gestantes tergore corbas,
cistas, cistellos, sportas grandesque cavagnos,
dulcibus impletos tribianibus atque gropellis,
320 seu moscatellis, seu Greghis, sive zubebis.
Pars ibi discaricat sommas caricatque tinazzos,
sed pars calcagnis follat calcantibus uvas,
pars quoque mox factum vinum cavat extra tinazzos
immittitque cadis, longe sbilzante borono.
325 Postea torchiantur graspae sub pondere travi,
unde fluit madidis sat goffa vinessa vinazzis,
quam sibi povertas coeli comprare bisognat.
Hic sunt carrari, sunt hic ter mille botazzi
atque mezarolae atque ingens squadra vasorum.
330 Non Autumnus abest, camisazzam vestit olentem,
semper vinosis de macchis undique carcam.
Ipse praeest operi, facit hic, iubet illic et omnes
contentare deos studiat, mandante patrono.
Gens Todesca suos dicunt hos esse patronos,
335 immo deos alios non Lanzchineccus adorat.
Prova tibi effectum monstrat, si dicta refudas.
Aspice, cum studiant desco tavolaeque paratae,
quomodo boccalum vodant per quemque boconem.
Mangiaguerra ruit per zaynas perque becheros,

barrels over and over, and tightening the ample casks. Here from casks and jugs they decant wines that are most worthy to serve in toasts at the tables of the celestial deities, for it is from here that the herd of gods is furnished with wines. Ants are no more industrious coming and going when they have found a cache of tasty little peas. They haul the heavy weights of granules on their backs; and working fervently, this black populace fills immense warehouses — such is the activity in the household of the Lord of Must, when a thousand *putti* go forth laden and return unburdened, carrying on their backs bushels, baskets, sacks, and large bags, filled with grapes for sweet Trebbiano, Groppello, Muscatel, Greco, or Zibibbo. One group empties the tubs and fills the vats, another group crushes the grapes by stomping them, and another takes the wine just made out of the vats: it gushes out the bungholes and they pour it into jugs. Next they press the grape-stalks under the weight of the beam, and from this oozing pulp flows a very thin *vinaccia*, which the celestial paupers must buy for themselves. Here, then, are long flagons and three thousand big bottles and half-barrels and an endless army of jugs.

"Autumn is never absent; he wears a stinking shirt, perma- 330
nently covered with wine stains everywhere. He oversees the operation: he works here, commands there and tries to satisfy all the gods, following the boss's orders. The German people say that these gods are their patrons; indeed, the Landsknecht worships no other gods. Experience proves this to you even if you deny the words. Look at how devoted they are at their tables and banquets, how they empty a goblet with every mouthful. Mangiaguerra cas-

340 fracassusque ingens per Greghi pocula fitur.
　　　Non aqua praesumit tales accedere mensas,
　　　quae, bandita, pedes salicum tantummodo bagnat.
　　　Estque vetus mottum: "Scelus est iugulare Phalernum."
　　　Mox ubi se retrovant tandem vacuasse barillam,
345 dant pugnos calzosque ipsi furibunde barillo,
　　　spezzatumque vasum, numquam reparabile, mandant.
　　　Chioccant inde sibi frontes culamine zayni,
　　　deque gravi mittunt redolentes gutture rottos.
　　　Per letram melius parlant quam ante bevandas,
350 nec nisi de vino tunc fit parlamen in illis.
　　　Semper enim vinum pensat loquiturque Todescus,
　　　somniat et piccam, dagam bragasque frapatas
　　　pro vino impegnat, vendit semetque pisonat.
　　　Si quid ei restat, quod nult lassare, celata est,
355 quae sibi tazza capax scusat, dum sorbet in illa.
　　　Dum trincher faciunt multus tartofen habetur;
　　　inde resurgentes ut eant, andare negantur,
　　　namque bogas pedibus vernazza iniecerat illis,
　　　quos numquam muro se discostare videbis.
360 Sunt vultu similes Phoebo damatina levanti,
　　　fumantesque oculos torquent centumque miaros
　　　efficiunt cerebro, quamvis stent in pede saldi.
　　　Inde movendo pedes, nulla ratione guidantur
　　　tantonesque abeunt, veluti de nocte solemus,
365 ac ubi nullus adest intoppus saepe trabuccant.
　　　Tandem se taccant manibus, se prorsus acostant
　　　aut muro, aut banco, seu trunco, sive pilastro,
　　　donec se buttent zosum, vel supra paiarum,
　　　vel medium in fangum porcino more volutent.
370　　'Nunc Invernus adest, Naturae filius ultim,
　　　de quo dum dicam, mihi da, Boccale, pelizzam,
　　　namque procul dubio me magrum giazza gelabit.

cades into tankards and glasses, and a huge massacre is made among the cups of Greek wine. Water does not dare present itself at such tables: having been banned, it only bathes the feet of willow trees. There is an old saying: 'It is a crime to cut Falernian wine.' And when at length they discover they have emptied the barrel, they furiously kick the barrel and beat it with their fists, and reduce this broken cask beyond repair. Then they smack the butts of their tankards against their foreheads and emit smelly belches from their heavy guts. They speak more eloquently than before drinking, since at this point, their discussion is only of wine.

"For indeed a German thinks, speaks and dreams always of wine, and for wine he hocks his pike, sword and fancy trousers and sells them and pawns himself! If one thing remains, which he does not wish to give up, it is his helmet, which serves him as an ample cup since he slurps from it. While they yell 'Trink!,' there's many a 'der Teufel!' Then getting up to go, they can't move, for the vernaccia has thrown their legs in irons; thus you will never see them detach themselves from a wall. Their faces look like the rising sun at dawn: they screw up their cloudy eyes and cover a hundred miles in their minds, even though they are standing stock still. When they do move their feet, they are not guided by reason at all, they move along haltingly, as one typically does at night. And where there are no obstacles, they keep tripping. In the end they hang on with their hands, sidling up to a wall, or a bench, or a tree trunk, or a pillar, until eventually they throw themselves down on a straw mat or rut about in the mud like pigs.

"Now comes Winter, Nature's last child. While I am speaking about him, give me a fur coat, Boccalo, because without a doubt, skinny as I am, the ice will freeze me. Winter is an emaciated

351

370

Vir macer Invernus, quo non plus magra Quaresma est,
non habet humorem venis bigolumque tacatum
375 fert schenae guanzasque cavas subtileque collum,
deque pede ad testam numerari ossamina possunt
ut Gonnella suo poterat numerare cavallo.
Semper habet fluvidos oculos in fronte latentes,
pallidus et smortus, stropiatus, rancidus, untus,
380 tamque malenconicus quod semper flere videtur;
cui ghiazzata colat de mento barba gelato,
ghiazzatique sonant per circum tempora crines.
Horrescunt magrae nimio pro frigore carnes
pocchettumque iuvat duplices gestare pelizzas;
385 cui nisi donaret soror Aestas atque Autumnus,
altera mangiandas spesas alterque bibendas,
gaioffazzus enim marza de famme periret.
Semper apud brasas sibi stesso crura boientat
nec miser ingegnat retro portare cadregam,
390 substizzatque focum, cogens bollire polentam.
It piger et strictus, cum vadit ad aëra, tantum,
integer ut posset per gucchiae intrare busolum.
Sunt albis semper sua tecta coperta pruinis
et candelotti giazzae de culmine pendent.
395 Non habet un minimum spassum, nisi quando dapocus
unghibus ante focum rognam sibi grattat aguzzis.
Omnis osellorum cantantum dulciter hymnus
hinc procul et quidquid Primavera tilata ministrat;
tantum cornacchiae "qua qua," corvi quoque "cro cro"
400 continuo resonant tacolantque insemma mulacchiae.
Provida non exit dulcem formica masonem;
clauditur in gusso limaca busumque muraiat.
In stabulis conduntur apes ad grepia mellis.
Non errare vides bissas freddosque lusertos.
405 Pastores mandris servant armenta stopatis.

man; even Lent is no thinner than he. He has no humor in his veins and his belly button sticks to his back, and he has concave cheeks and a scrawny neck, and from his head to his toes you can count all his bones, like Gonella could count the bones on his horse. His eyes, concealed in his head, are always rheumy; he is pale, lifeless, worn down, rancid and greasy. He is so melancholic that he always seems to be crying. An icy beard drips from his frozen chin; his icy hair tinkles against his temples. His lean flesh shivers from the excess cold; it does him little good to wear two furs. If Autumn and his sister Summer did not give him money, she for buying food, he for drink, the wretch would certainly die of brutal hunger.

"Winter is always broiling his own legs by the coals; the wretch   388 does not think to push his chair back, and he stirs up the fire imagining he is cooking polenta. When he goes outside, he moves sluggishly and so hunched up he could pass right through the eye of a needle. His roof is always covered with white hoar-frost and long ice-candles hang from the eaves. He has no entertainment whatsoever, except when the good-for-nothing scratches his scabies before the fire with his sharp nails. Every hymn sweetly sung by birds and all that delicate Spring prepares is far off; only the 'caw, caw' of the crows and the 'croak, croak' of the ravens echo continually, together with the chattering of the jays.

"The provident ant does not leave its lovely home; the snail   401 stays in its shell and walls up the opening; bees hole up in their little stables with their mangers of honey. You don't see snakes and cold lizards running about. Shepherds keep their flocks shut up in stalls. Only bums struggle about in the cold season, and not cov-

Tantum furfanti stentant hoc tempore freddi,
qui faciunt nulla tremolantos veste coperti.
Sunt tamen inverni gratae studiantibus horae,
longa quibus multa de nocte dat ocia semper.
410 Praticat has igitur Solis fameia masones
magnaque pro tantis bocchis fit spesa quotannis.
    'Sed tibi somniferam cerno, Leonarde, vedutam.
Tu male dormisti tribus istis noctibus et tu,
Balde, caput plumbi spallis portare videris.
415 Ergo repossemus; video ronfare Bocalum'.

Liber quintus decimus

    Corpora somnifero recrearat quisque riposso,
quae magis officio somni quam pane carebant.
Dum tamen attendit, Baldo mandante, coquinam
condere Boccalus magnumque ad prandia piscem
5 expedit inque brodo piscis caulata paratur,
ecce lyram spoliat rursum Giubertus eburnam
dulceque chordiculis carmen dyapenter acordat.
Vult etenim generosus homo gradire sodales
ut sibi mox etiam donetur banca scolaro,
10 in qua consideat cathedram sentire magistri
Cingaris et, secum percurrens almanach omne,
deveniat praticus passatas dicere cosas.
Praeterea non est placidi natura Giberti
qualis quorundam cantorum temporis huius,
15 qui, bene muschiati, petenati, benque politi,
non cantare volunt nisi sint a rege pregati.
Non sic Giubertus, non sic novus alter Apollo,
cui si dixisset mulier pinzocchera: 'Canta',
cantasset subito, minima ne in parte negasset.

ered by any clothes, they shiver. And yet winter hours are pleasing
to students: the long nights always give them a lot of leisure time.
And so the entire family of the Sun resides in these dwellings, and
every year, it costs a great deal to feed so many mouths.

"But I see that you are looking quite sleepy, Leonardo. You   412
have slept badly these past three nights, and you, Baldo, seem to
be carrying a lead head on your shoulders. Therefore, let us rest; I
see Boccalo snoring."

Book XV

With restful slumber, all of them had restored their bodies, which   1
had been more in need of the benefits of sleep than of bread.
While Boccalo, at Baldo's command, labors to set up the kitchen
and prepare a large fish for lunch and make cabbage stew in the fish
broth, there Gilberto once again uncovers his ivory lyre and sweetly
harmonizes a song in fifths on the delicate strings. Indeed, this
gracious fellow wants to please his companions so that shortly he'll
be given a student's desk where he may sit and hear Master Cingar
lecture, and become an expert in speaking about past events by pe-
rusing with him all the almanacs. In any case, gentle Gilberto's na-
ture is not like that of certain singers of our day who, nicely per-
fumed and coiffed and nicely preened, are loathe to sing unless they
are implored by a king. Not so Gilberto, not so the next new Apollo;
and if some sanctimonious biddy had said, "Sing!" he would have
started to sing right away and would not have refused in any way.

20 Dispositis ergo terzis quintisque, simulque
 vocibus octavis, tandem sic voce comenzat:
     'Heu quibus hoc mundi quantisque in gurgite monstris
 iactamur miseri! linguarum flatibus aequor
 nostrum hoc et tumidis cynicorum exaestuat undis.
25 Quid freta nugarum referam? quid fulmina pravi
 nominis et famae? quid saxa latentia tristis
 invidiae? Scillaeve canes gutturve Carybdis?
 Felices nautae, quibus apta peritia magnum
 hoc mare sulcandi Syrtesque Arasque cavendi.
30 Vos labor assiduus tantum indefessaque virtus
 monstrorum domitrix tolerantia reddidit aptos
 turgentis pelagi cumulos superare minaces,
 ponere seu sit opus, seu malo attollere vela'.
     Vix ea finierat Giubertus, mensa Bocalo
35 sternitur et lotis manibus disinare comenzant.
 Quattuor accumbunt tavolae, cui forma quadrata est:
 Baldus, Lonardus, Cingar scalcusque Bocalus.
 Non curat pro tunc stomachus mangiare Giuberti.
 Baldus amorevolo, velut est gentilis usanzae,
40 invitat sembiante omnes ad fercula mensae;
 quisque refudavit, seu pro viltate vilana,
 sive quod in multis stomacarat nausea gustum.
 Ponitur in centro scanni, trans littora mensae,
 grandis in amplifico basiotto forma varoli.
45 Quamprimum medio stetit haec impresa senatu,
 Cingar, habens gladium propter taiare paratum,
 dividit in solas tres partes ghelfice piscem:
 tres, inquam, partes uno de corpore fiunt.
 Prima caput, bustumque secunda est, tertia cauda.
50 Quattuor accumbunt ubi tres accumbere debent.
 Cingar, ochiolinum faciens, accennat amicis
 ut sibi, dum trapolam nunc praeparat, ambo secundent.

After tuning the lyre in thirds, fifths and octaves, at last he be-   20
gins with his voice, thus:

Alas, by how many and what sorts of monsters in the whirl-   22
pool of this world are we wretches flung! This ocean of ours
is roiled by squalls of tongues and swelling waves of cynics.
What shall I say about the eddies of nonsense? What of the
lightning bolts of a damaged name and reputation? What of
the hidden rocks of morose envy? What of the dogs of
Scylla and the maw of Charybdis? Happy are the sailors
whose skills are suited to furrowing the great seas and avoi-
ding the shoals of Syrte and Ara. Only assiduous labor, unti-
ring virtue and fortitude, that tamer of monsters, have made
you capable of overcoming the menacing swells of the turgid
depths, whether it is time to lower the mainsail or raise it.

Gilberto has scarcely finished with this when Boccalo lays the   34
table, and after they have washed their hands, they begin to dine.
There are four of them seated at a square table: Baldo, Leonardo,
Cingar and the steward Boccalo. At the moment Gilberto's stom-
ach is not ready to eat. With an affectionate demeanor, Baldo
beckons everyone to the dishes on the table, as noble custom re-
quires: they each refuse, either out of rustic reluctance or because
most of them had lost their appetites from seasickness. In the
middle of the tabletop, spanning the edges of the table, the large
body of the sea bass is served in a wide basin.

As soon as this matter reached the hub of the senate, Cingar,   45
with his sword ready for cutting, divides the fish in the Guelf
manner in just three parts; I mean that three parts are made from
one body: the head first, the trunk second and the tail third. Yet
there are four of them at table where there should have been three.
With a wink, Cingar signals his friends so that they will go along

Protinus ascorti cognoscunt id quod avisat,
namque fit aguaitus poverum trapolare Bocalum
55 ut nihil intuttum comedat de pisce tapinus,
cum cocus extiterit, cum fecerit ipse broëttum,
cum centum zacaras, melaranzas atque sapores
sparserit huic supra, circum ventremque per ipsum.
Cingar primus agit causam primusque retirat
60 testam varoli de piatto supra taierum,
fratantumque inquit sociis: 'Scriptura favellat:
"in capite libri de me scripsere prophetae,"
sic caput istud erit sanctae completio legis'.
Baldus, id advertens, ad libros mente recurrit,
65 nec fecit grattare diu sententia testam;
grafiat ut gattus partem quae meza vocatur,
scilicet ad sese traxit ventralia piscis
Lucanumque legit: 'Medium tenuere beati'.
Cauda manet iam iam toto soletta cadino;
70 non perdit tempus iuvenis Leonardus, at ipsam
caudam, cui dederat pridem Boccalus ochiadam,
extrahit e brodo, dicens: 'Nasone probante,
"exitus acta probat"; poterit nodare Bocalus,
cui iacet ante oculos pelagus brotaminis istud'.
75 Boccalus guardat nunc hunc, nunc turbidus illunc.
Quid facit? Advertens pro se non esse coëllum,
ni velit ut porcus sese voltare brodaiis,
protinus azzaffat vasum, pauloque moratus,
suspexit* coelum dixitque novissima verba:
80 'Asperges meme, Domine, mundabor isoppo'.
Sic dicens, illum gyrat spruzzatque panadam
vicinosque omnes, Baldum Baldique sodales
schittat aquis grassis ungitque brotamine barbas.
Oh! quis non risit? quis non ridendo crepavit?
85 Barba pluit Baldo, Cingar sugat ora maniplo,

with the trap that he is setting. At once, these clever men know what he is planning, for in fact an ambush is planned to trick poor Boccalo, so that the poor fellow won't get any fish at all, even though he not only served as cook, but made the broth and seasoned the fish inside and out with a hundred delicacies, bitter oranges and spices.

Cingar is the first to plead the case and the first to take the 59 head of the sea bass from the platter onto his plate, while he announces to his friends, "Scripture tells us, 'At the head of the book the prophets wrote of me,' and thus this head shall fulfill the Holy Law." Baldo catches on and quickly sorts through his mind for books and didn't have to scratch his pate long for a quotation. Like a cat, he pounces on the part called the middle, which is to say, he grabs the belly of the fish for himself and cites Lucan, "The fortunate held the middle." By now, only the tail remains on the platter; and the young Leonardo does not waste any time, but from the broth he pulls forth the tail that Boccalo had eyed earlier, saying, "As Nasone affirms, 'the end justifies the means.' Boccalo can still swim, this sea of broth lies before his eyes."

Boccalo glances here and there, frantically. What can he do? 75 Seeing that there is nothing left for him, unless he wants to wallow in the slop like a pig, he quickly seizes the serving tray, holds it up for a moment, raises his eyes to the heavens and says these latest words: "Purge me with hyssop, O Lord, and I shall be clean." Saying this, he swings the platter and sprays the stew, spattering the greasy liquid on all those nearby — on Baldo and Baldo's mates — and oils their beards with broth.

Who could keep from laughing? Who did not split with laugh- 84 ter? Baldo's beard is streaming; Cingar dries his face with a hand-

pars sua toccavit Giuberto parsque Lonardo;
quisque fregat vultum pectusque sinumque colantem.
Surgitur a tavola, prohibet mangiamina risus;
non cessat Baldus ridendo probare tal attum;
90   dicit enim: 'Merito piscem sua broda secuta est.
Non sine aqua piscis, nec aqua sine pisce manebit'.
'Ergo', Cingar ait, 'piscem mangiabimus ut qua
flumen abundavit sic illic piscis abundet.
Non Boccalus habet rombum, culamina gratet'.
95   Sic dicens, tornat tavolae masinatque molino.
Sic faciunt alii, sua quemque prevenda moratur.
Baldus at interea comedens tutavia ragionat:
'Miror enim, Boccale meus, cur quando, relicto
pisce, crepabamus risu, non protinus illum
100   prenderis, ut nobis resa sit pro pane fugazza'.
'Non', Boccalus ait, 'sine garbo et gratia et arte,
inter compagnos facienda est soia galantos.
Optime gabbastis, spartito pisce, Bocalum.
Transeat, et nullo guastetur beffa tumultu.
105   Sic et ego in vobis "Asperges" optime feci.
Transeat hoc etiam cronicisque notetur ad unguem.
Optima pro tuttis passarunt omnia rebus,
praeter quod surdas faciet pan suttus orecchias'.
Cingar ait: 'Poteris prigolo te opponere tanto,
110   cortellum cum pane licet mangiare famatis'.
'Sic faciam', respondit ei. Mox, dum modo panem
sic blotum sgagnat ut cardos mula Stopini,
quidam pauper homo, nimia pietate movestus,
nescio quot menolas freddas piscesque minutos
115   attulit involtos charta donatque Bocalo.
Non ea Boccalus poveretti dona refudat;
immo ait: 'Exiguum cum dat tibi pauper amicus,
incipe Dameta, lento tibi mittit Ulisses'.

kerchief; Gilberto gets his share, and Leonardo as well: they all wipe their faces, shoulders and dripping chests. They stand up from the table, and their laughter keeps them from eating. While laughing, Baldo keeps on praising the feat. And he says, "Justly has the broth followed its fish. The fish cannot be without water, nor the water without fish."

"Therefore," says Cingar, "let us eat this fish, so that where wa- 92 ter abounded, there too may fish abound. If Boccalo has no bass, let him scratch his ass." So saying, he returns to the table and grinds away like a millstone. The others follow suit, for a portion awaits each of them.

In the meantime, as Baldo eats, he speaks: "I am curious, my 97 dear Boccalo, why, when we were splitting with laughter, you did not quickly take the fish we had left, thereby rendering tit for tat."

"Among worthy friends," answers Boccalo, "we must not make 101 practical jokes without grace, style and skill. You played a good trick on Boccalo in dividing the fish. Let it go, and we won't ruin the joke by any quarreling. I, for my part, did a good job anointing all of you. Let it go, and may it all be noted in the chronicles in great detail. Everything went very well, except that plain bread makes your ears deaf."

Cingar notes, "You will be able to overcome this danger: starv- 109 ing people may eat the knife with the bread."

"I'll do that," Boccalo replies. Then, while he nibbles the plain 111 bread as the mule Stoppino nibbles thistle, a certain pauper, moved by great pity, brings over I don't know how many cold minnows and other little fish wrapped in paper and gives them to Boccalo. Boccalo does not refuse the poor man's gift; instead he quotes, "When a friendly pauper offers you a small thing, begin Dameta; she sends to you, Ulysses, slow as you are." Saying this, he pulls

Sic dicens, distrigat eos guardatque traversus,
120 ut guardare solet scottantem gatta menestram.
Denique pisciculum per caudam suscipit unum,
quem non in boccam sed orecchiam ficcat, et inde,
ad socios illum tornans, ita brancat et altrum
medesimumque facit; post illum tertius et post
125 hunc etiam quartus; post quartum quintus et omnes
denique per caudas presi porguntur ad aures.
Baldus, id advertens, parlat cum Cingare: 'Magnus
piscis cum bocca mangiatur, parvus orecchia;
si bene Boccali meditor documenta periti.
130 Ecquid hoc importat? quid habent cum piscibus aures?'
Respondet Cingar: 'Pan suttus stoppat orecchias,
fecit orecchinos de piscibus ille sotilis,
unde repurgat eas; aliam non penso casonem.
Pur, si aliam mentis tenet in forciria scosam,
135 dicat et ambiguos ab amicis toiat afannos'.
'Toio', Bocalus ait, 'dubium. Iam hebdomada quarta
est hodie, quando mea coniux ivit a nodum
aequoreque in medio calzas stringasque tiravit.
Nunc in mente mea stat prorsus grande talentum,
140 velle de illius statu sentire novellam.
Ergo meis alzo pescettos auribus istos
ut certum faciant ubi stet, si mortua prorsus
aut si solazzet illa cum gente dabassum.
At mihi respondent se natos esse pradessum,
145 unde negatur eis posse hoc agnoscere factum.
Sed maior natu seniorque varolus et ingens,
cum quo tres tacite compagni dente ragionant,
dire mihi poterit melius de uxore negata;
quapropter liceat secum chiachiarare pochettum'.
150 Quo dicto fremuere omnes: habet ille rasonem,
non inhonesta quidem talis domanda videtur;

64

out the fish and looks at them sideways, the way a cat looks at scalding soup. Next he takes one little fish by the tail and sticks it, not in his mouth, but in his ear. Then turning to its companions, he takes another and does the same thing; after this a third and even a fourth; and after the fourth, a fifth, so that finally he has held all of them up to his ear by their tails.

Observing this, Baldo speaks to Cingar: "Big fish are eaten with 127
the mouth, small fish with the ears, if I fully understand the teaching of our expert Boccalo. Is this what it means? What do fish have to do with ears?"

Cingar responds, "Plain bread can stop up the ears: he makes 131
ear wipes out of the little fish to clear his ears out again. I can't think of any other reason. Yet, if he keeps hidden another reason in the treasure chest of his mind, let him tell us and thereby relieve his friends of this troubling uncertainty."

"I'll settle the matter," said Boccalo. "Today is already the 136
fourth week since my wife went for a swim and kicked the bucket in the middle of the sea. I now have a great desire in my mind to hear news of her condition. Therefore, I raise these little fish up to my ears so that they may inform me where she is, if she is really dead or if she is enjoying herself with the people down there. But they all answer that they have just now been born, so it is not possible for them to know this fact. However, they add that an older fish, the mighty and elder sea-bass, with whom my three companions are conversing silently with their teeth, could better tell me more about my drowned wife. Wherefore, please allow me a moment's chat with him."

At this speech, they all roar. He is right, and such a request 150
does not seem inappropriate. He should be given the opportunity

detur ei merito parlandi copia: piscis,
piscis testa sua est, quae fert soletta loquelam;
panza loqui nescit, muta est quoque cauda, sed ipsa
155 testa ragionabit, cui format lingua parolas.
Sic vulgus strepitat, sic stat sententia Baldi,
sic licet; et dictum factum testazza varoli
sistitur avantum Boccalo, a Cingare tolta.
Cingar adirato similis, qui ridet ab intro,
160 smergolat haec: 'Esto! sublata est bocca varoli,
cuius lingua potest bramam complere Bocali;
esto! dat officium parlandi bocca; sed ipsi
cur oculi dantur? cur frons? cur coppa varoli?
grande mihi tortum faciunt. Appello Gibertum'.
165 'Sum contentus', ait Boccalus, 'chare Giberte,
te rogo per caput hoc, voias decidere litem'.
Suscipit impresam leta cum fronte Gibertus;
tum sedet in banca cunctisque oldentibus inquit:
'Dum rana et toppus faciunt insemma tumultum,
170 milvus ego hanc rixam dirimo'. Sic fatus agraffat
protinus in tavola testam, laudante brigata
esse satisfactum civilibus optime libris.
    Et iam finierant, tavolis trespisque levatis.
Cingar ad astrologas, Baldo mandante, facendas
175 tornat et ingenio stabat Leonardus ateso.
'Mars', ait, 'armipotens quinto versatur in orbe,
qui scorozzata semper cum fronte menazzat,
brasatos oculos guardando torcet adossum,
sanguineasque bavas sua labra colerica spudant.
180 Cristatam gestat galeam chiusamque viseram,
totus azalinis semper cazzatus in armis.
Targonus dextro galloni, spada sinistro
pendet et arzono taccatur mazza ferata,
quae centum libras pesat, non una demancum.

to speak: the fish, or the head of the fish, is his because it is the only part that possesses speech. The belly does not know how to speak, and the tail too, is mute; but the head will deliberate and its tongue will form the words. The people have spoken. This is Baldo's decree: It shall be thus; and no sooner said than done, the head of the sea bass is taken from Cingar and set before Boccalo.

Cingar pretends to be angry, although he is laughing inside, and 159 shouts, "So be it! The mouth of the bass has been taken away so that its tongue may satisfy Boccalo's wish. Fine then, it is the mouth's duty to speak. But why does he get the eyes? Why the top of the head? Why the neck of the bass? I appeal to Gilbert: they are doing me a great wrong."

"I agree," offers Boccalo, "Dear Gilberto, by this very head I beg 165 you to judge the case."

Gilberto accepts the task with a beaming face and then sits on 167 the bench and announces to the listening crowd, "While the frog and the mouse are fighting between themselves, I, the kite, shall resolve this dispute." And with this, he immediately snatches the head from the table, as the group praises him for having satisfied brilliantly the books of civil law.

Now they had finished and had cleared away the tables and 173 stools. At Baldo's command, Cingar returned to astrological matters, while Leonardo waited attentively. "Mars mighty in arms," he says, "occupies the fifth heaven, and always threatens with an angry brow; looking around, he fixes his fiery eyes on everything, and his choleric lips spit bloody foam. He wears a crested helmet with a closed visor and is always completely encased in steel armor. On his right hangs a large shield and on his left a sword; attached to his saddle is an iron-clad club that weighs a hundred pounds

185 Talem portabat iuvenum fortissimus ille,
ille gaiardorum columen Gonzaga Lovisus,
quem male consulto quidam Rodomonta vocarunt,
quem bene consulto poterant chiamare Rugerum,
aut magis Orlandum, si cum virtute gaiardi
190 corporis est animi virtus pensanda coëllum.
Mars ruit in pressam, grosso galopante cavallo,
et bastiones sua circum castra gaiardos
vadit adestrando, turres, casamatta, reparos.
Non ibi telorum generatio quaeque bramatur:
195 ronchae, alebardae, partesanae, scuta, celatae,
spontones, lanzae, picchae spadaeque daghaeque,
corsaletta, elmi, maiae, cossalia, guanti.
Stendardique volant, banderae; timpana pon pon
continuo chioccant sonitantque tarantara trombae.
200 Non mancant alii stromenti: cornua, cifoy,
gnacara, bussones, pifari pivaeque bitortae,
et quidquid tandem doperatur tempore guerrae.
Talibus in cosis sua Mars pensiria ficcat,
solum squarzones delectans cernere carnis.
205 Huic caedes soror est, lis coniux iraque mater;
huic livor pater est, rabies et stizza fiolae.
Hic hominum clamor strepitat, nitritus equorum.
Non ibi cagnones, bombardae, passavolantes,
non sagrae mancant, basilischi, non colubrinae;
210 suntque pavaiones, sunt tendae suntque trabacchae.
Polvificant nebulas pedibus repetando cavalli.
Celsa fracassatae conturbant sydera lanzae,
non quod conturbent, sed conturbare videntur,
gestarum quoniam sunt hic simulacra cosarum.
215 Armatas densasque vides concurrere squadras,
ordine quae nullo bottis se grandibus urtant,
squarzantes maiam, schiodantes arma pesocchis

and not a pound less. A similar one was carried by that immensely strong young man, that pillar of the brave, Luigi Gonzaga, whom the ill-informed called Rodomonte, but whom the well-informed could call Ruggiero, or rather Orlando, if strength of mind is to be considered together with the strength of a robust body.

"Mars charges into the fray on a huge galloping horse and strides about setting up staunch bastions to surround his fortress, towers, battlements and walls. No kinds of arms that one yearns for are missing: there are hooks, halberds, partisans, shields, sallets, spontoons, lances, pikes, spades, daggers, cuirasses, helmets, mail, cuisses and gauntlets. Banners and standards fly; the drums continually pound out 'boom, boom'; the trumpets blare 'tararan.' There are also other instruments: horns, pipes, recorders, castanets, fifes and double-reed bagpipes and everything else that is used during wartime.   191

"Mars fixes his thoughts on such things, delighting only in seeing huge shreds of flesh. Slaughter is his sister, strife his wife, wrath his mother, malice his father, and rage and anger his children. Here resound the shouting of men and the neighing of steeds. Cannon are not lacking here, nor bombards, long-range artillery, mortars, heavy guns or rifles. There are pavilions, tents and barracks. The horses make clouds of dust by kicking up their heels. Shattered lances disturb the lofty stars; they don't really disturb them but they seem to, since there are images there of past glories. You see dense armed squadrons rush together which, without any order, clash with huge blows, ripping apart chain   203

cum mazzis, stocchis, picchis partesaque nonis.
Marsque roversatos ibi gaudet cernere mortos,
220 subque cavallorum pedibus stentare misellos.
        'At rex cunctarum stellarum Iuppiter, alto
in solio residens, sextum delegit olympum.
Urbs ibi campagnae in medio spatiosa repossat,
martello Steropis Brontisque incudine nec non
225 arte Pyragmonica miris fabricata murais.
Non est calzinis, non est fundata quadrellis,
ceu Zenoa et Napoli, Florentia, Roma, Milanus,
sed tantum variis finisque gitata metallis
stampatur, veluti campanas Brixia stampat.
230 Merlos de duro gestat muraia diaspro,
possidet ignitum merlorum quisque rubinum.
Centum porfideae toccant ibi sydera turres,
fundamenta iacent duro de marmore bronzi
cristallumque nitent frisorum cingula schiettum.
235 Culmina sunt aurum purum, quibus alta volazzant
continuo vexilla aquilis recamata grifagnis.
Rupibus argenti videas hic stare colonnas,
sustentare arcus ad sydera summa levatos.
Hic thermae ingentes, hic magna palatia surgunt,
240 hicve colossaei gyramina larga tinazzi,
hic circi et campi, fora multa theatraque multa,
naumachiae, colles, aquaeducti, rostra, colossi,
archi, pyramides, templorum millia crustis
marmoreis fabricata, domusque casaeque deorum;
245 quas super aspicias ter centum mille caminos,
semper fumantes nunc myrrha et thure brusato,
nunc rosto et lesso atque alio nidore culinae.
Hic sua fundarunt omnes palatia divi,
in medio quorum sua Iuppiter atria struxit.

mail, demolishing armor with heavy clubs, staffs, pikes and large barbed spears. Mars enjoys watching how the vanquished die and how the pitiful agonize under the horses' hooves.

"Yet the king of all the stars, Jupiter, sitting on his high throne, chose the sixth heaven. There, in the middle of the countryside, resides a spacious city constructed with admirable walls made by Steropes' hammer, Brontes' anvil and Pyracmon's skill. It is not built with limestone or brick, as in Genoa and Naples, Florence, Rome and Milan, but rather is forged only with fusions of various precious metals, like the bells that Brescia forges. 221

"The walls boast battlements of hard jasper; each of these battlements displays a fiery ruby. Here a hundred porphyry towers touch the stars; the foundations are made of hard-fused bronze, and the cornices of the friezes shine with pure crystal. The gables are made of pure gold, and high upon them wave banners embroidered with rapacious eagles. On the cliffs there, you can see silver columns rising to support arches elevated to the highest stars. There are vast baths, magnificent palaces rise up there, and there are wide rings in the bowl of the colosseum. There are fields and circuses and many theaters and squares: sea battles, terraces, aqueducts, platforms, huge statues, arches, pyramids, thousands of temples covered in marble and the houses and dwellings of the gods. Above these you see 300,000 chimneys forever smoking, sometimes with burning frankincense and myrrh, sometimes with roasts and stews and other rich cooking smells. Here all the gods have built their palaces and in the midst of these, Jupiter has built his own home. 230

250 Dedalus, artificum columen primusque murator,
  atque marangonus primus primusque magister
  architectus, ibi perfectas condidit arces.
  Centum balcones alti centumque fenestrae,
  pars hac, pars illac, pars hoc, pars illoc apertae,
255 omnia lontano venientia semper adocchiant.
  Porticus in gyrum, sex centum fulta pilastris
  bronzineis, late circumserat omne palazzum.
  Mille dei totidemque deae nymphaeque galantae,
  semper ibi praticant, spatiantes ordine tondo.
260 Porta superba patet, quae numquam chiusa videtur,
  vestibulumque suas largum tenet ante vedutas:
  ponitur in quadro super octo pilastra levatum.
  Porphideus blanchis in postibus eminet arcus,
  circulo et in medio tria formidanda locantur
265 fulmina, quae magno sunt propria tela Tonanti.
  Continuo andatu divorum tota cavantur
  limina, sint quamvis alabastro condita duro.
  Suntque cadenazzi portarum, suntque seraiae,
  et chiodi, et cancri, de argento supra dorato.
270 Atria praeteriens, intras perystilia, centum
  qualibet in banda claustrorum longa cavezzos,
  ac diamantineis circum munita pilastris.
  Quaeque columna suam mira tenet arte misuram,
  quas proprio duras Vulcanus sanguine fecit.
275 Becchus erat, becchi sic sanguine reddidit ille
  mollia, quae nimium diamantis saxa rigescunt.
  Basilicae locus est amplissimus, undique cinctus
  sedibus ex auro, quo tractant numina causas,
  fata hominum, sortes, breve tempus, mille travaios.
280 Ad caput alta Iovis stat scragna levatior altris,
  quam deus argenti, deus auri omnisque richezzae
  fossor et inventor fabricavit, et omnia riccha

"Daedalus, that master artificer, foremost bricklayer, foremost   250
carpenter, and foremost architect, has made perfect works of art
here. One hundred high balconies and one hundred windows
opening on all sides — here, there and everywhere — constantly
survey everything coming from afar. Supported by six hundred
pillars, a circular portico amply surrounds the entire palace. Here
a thousand gods and as many goddesses and graceful nymphs visit
continually, strolling about in circles. A splendid doorway stands
open, which is never seen closed, with a large vestibule looking out
on the views; square-shaped, elevated on eight pillars. A porphyry
arch rises up on white posts, and in the middle of a circle there
stand three formidable lightning bolts, which are the distinctive
weapons of the great Thunderer. By the constant coming and go-
ing of the gods, the thresholds are worn down, even though they
are built of hard alabaster. And there are thick chains on the
doors, and there are locks, bolts and hinges gilded in silver.

"Passing through the atrium, you enter into a peristyle which   270
stretches for a hundred yards on each side, and is fortified all
around with diamond pilasters. Every column displays patterns of
admirable artistry; Vulcan solidified them with his own blood: as
a capon, he used his capon-blood to render them malleable, be-
cause diamond rocks grow too solid. The space inside the basilica
is immense and is encircled all round with chairs of gold, where
the gods deal with lawsuits, human fate, destiny, fleeting time, and
a thousand other woes. At the head stands Jupiter's throne, higher
than the others, which was built by the god of silver, the god of
gold, that miner and inventor of all riches, and he threw in every-

et pretiosa magis sic sic buttavit abunde,
ut spazzaduras buttat Vegnesa quotannis.

285 Pensa igitur, quam bella illic cadrega sedetur.
Diique deaeque omnes hic prendere iura frequentant,
Iuppiter his fatum trutinat sortemque misurat
Fortunamque super mattum facit ire cavallum.
Nulla datur deitas aliis ac nulla potestas,

290 ni Iovis annutu signentur brevia, bollae,
certa quibus pendet ratio de rebus agendis.
Iuppiter est etenim cunctorum papa deorum,
cui basare pedes inchinant imperatores,
dum centum rubeae circonstant agmine testae.

295 Quottidie divum grege cortezatur, at ille
suscipit exultans omnes; bona chiera brigatis
omnibus, aut poveris aut ricchis, semper ab illo est.
Laeditur interdum, cur non? deus alter ab altro:
Vulcanus de Marte dolet Veneremque ribaldam

300 esse cridat; vultu Ganimedem Iuno traverso
guardat; et ipsa Ceres raptam Plutone fiolam
lamentatur; agitque reum dea quaeque Priapum,
qui scherzat propriis cum nymphis absque mudanda.
Iuppiter ergo omnes utraque ascoltat orecchia

305 campanasque audit iudex utrasque sonantes,
inter quas tandem discrimine iudicat aequo.
Si tamen ipse deis fuerit quandoque noiatus,
fulmina ferre iubet, reboare tonitrua mandat
terrificatque homines, coelum cascare putantes.

310 Sed quando apparet Ganimedes oraque basat
blandidulisque illum codegonem scannat ocellis,
cui quoque dulciguli recat aurea pocula musti,
protinus ira cadit, fugiunt e pectore sdegni,
nubibus exonerat coelum, novus emicat et sol,

315 soleque sub claro surgit flos imbre cadutus.

thing rich and precious in greater abundance than the garbage Venice throws away every year. Imagine therefore, what a beautiful throne he sits on there!

"All the gods and goddesses frequent this hall to get sentences: Jupiter weights their fate and measures their destiny and sends Fortune off astride a crazy horse. No divinity is assigned to others, no power, unless the briefs and bulls are signed by a nod from Jupiter, on which a certain rule is predicated about how things are to be done. Indeed, Jupiter is the pope of the gods. Emperors bow down to kiss his feet while a hundred red-capped heads stand around in a group. Every day he is courted by a flock of gods, and he happily welcomes them all; he always has a pleasant face for all and sundry, whether rich or poor. On occasion, not surprisingly, one god gets insulted by another. Vulcan complains about Mars, and screams that Venus is a harlot; Juno gives Ganymede the evil eye; Ceres complains that her daughter has been kidnapped by Pluto; every goddess blames Priapus, who plays with their nymphs without his underwear on. 286

"Jupiter therefore listens to them all with both ears: as a judge, he hears both bells ringing and then in the end makes a just ruling between them. However, if sometimes he is perturbed by these gods, he calls for his lightning bolts and bids the thunder crash, and it terrifies humans who think the sky is falling. But when Ganymede appears and kisses him on the mouth and seduces the big fool with his fawning eyes and, what's more, brings him golden goblets filled with sweet must, suddenly his anger abates and irritation flees from his breast. He liberates the sky of clouds and a new sun appears; flowers bent by the storm perk up under this 304

Sic quandoque homines magni grandesque maëstri,
et qui dicuntur signores esse bachettae,
plus aliquando potest apud illos forma regazzi,
quam sapientiloqui sententia docta Catonis.
320 Insurgunt scalae regales culmen ad altum,
pars de corralo, pars marmore parsque dyaspro.
Quaelibet ipsarum scandit nonanta scalinos,
per quas semper eunt redeuntque deique deaeque.
Passant per cameras doras dorosque salottos,
325 quorum solari, nullo lignamine facti,
tantum ex argento tavolas auroque travellos
ostentant, multaque nitent ibi luce saphyri.
Hic illic famuli divum famulaeque dearum
diversis lectos bene cultos floribus ornant,
330 lenzolesque albos tendunt riccasque copertas,
quas mira nymphae recamarunt arte galantas.
Namque Minerva, Iovis cerebro nassuta, scolaras
hic habet ad studium spolae curamque conocchiae.
'Ultima Saturni fieri parlatio restat,
335 ultima namque illi regio lontana tocavit.
Hic habet uxorem, quae tres insemma fiolos
parturiit tales, quales peperisse dolebat,
namque patri proprio membrum genitale secarunt
bacchettamque sui regni perforza tulerunt.
340 Hic magrus est nimium vecchius bolsusque crevatus,
sbavazzatque sibi naso scolante bocazzam.
Oh! quis amorbator maior maiorque carogna?
Non unum retinet dentem massilla galosi,
atque omnes flatu putrido, cum parlat, amorbat.
345 Malpetenata grisis sordescit barba pedocchis
lendinibusque riget semper caviata molestis.
It gobbus terrae, numerat bastone pedanas,

bright sun. It is thus with great men, grand masters, those who are called sceptered lords—that sometimes the beauty of a boy can sway them more than the learned opinions of a wise and eloquent Cato.

"Regal staircases lead up to the high roof, one made of coral,   320 one of marble, one of jasper. Each one of these numbers ninety stairs, on which gods and goddesses come and go continually. They pass through golden chambers and golden salons whose ceilings are made with no wood; only planks of silver and beams of gold are showing, and sapphires shine with bright light. Here the man-servants of the gods and the maids of the goddesses decorate the well-fashioned beds with various flowers and lay out white linens and rich coverlets which the nymphs have elegantly embroidered with admirable skill. For in fact, Minerva, born from Jupiter's brain, has pupils here dedicated to the study of the spindle and the spool.

"The last lesson concerns Saturn, for the most distant realm   334 was his. His wife gave birth to three sons all at once, whom she was sorry to have birthed, for they cut off their own father's member and violently took the scepter of his reign. Saturn is very scrawny, old, broken down and creaking; he drools with his nose running into his gaping mouth. Who could possibly smell worse or be more putrid? The jaw of this old cock doesn't hold a single tooth; when he speaks he sickens everyone with his fetid breath. His gnarly beard is filthy with grey lice and his hair always bristles with bothersome nits. He moves along the ground hunched over,

de passu in passu bolsat spudatque macagnos;
fert sgarbellatos oculos nec sbercia mancat.
350 Pellizonus eum usque ad calcanea coprit,
sed tamen ille facit tremolantos tempore quoquo.
Eius bassa domus plorat pro humore nocivo,
plorant muraiae, plorant solaria, plorant
omnia Saturni quo non Saturnior alter.
355 Occupat et guastat rumatica muffa vivandas
namque ibi splendiferas non mandat Apollo fasellas.
Praticat hic semper nigris nox bruna tenebris,
qua barbagiani, qua guffi pippaquestrelli
strident noctivagi, qua locchi quaque civettae
360 semper gnao cantant, semper gnao nocte frequentant.
Tristitia hic habitat, macies, genus omne malorum:
angonaia, malum costae quartanaque febris,
mazzuccus, lancum, carbones, morbida pestis,
flegma, tumor ventris, vermes colicique dolores,
365 petra vesigarum, cancar, giandussa, bognones,
franzosus, fersae, cagasanguis, rogna, varolae,
defectus cerebri rabiesque frenetica, chiodus,
stizza canina, dolor dentorum, scroffa, puvidae,
phistula, galtones tumefactaque lergna cadentis
370 testiculi, brofolae tegnosaque codega, lepra,
schelentia, gulae sicitas et pectoris asma,
necnon tenconus, necnon morena, podagra,
muganzae, febres tysichae tardaeque pedanae;
infirmitates non totas dicere possum.
375 Ista fameia senem Saturnum semper honorat,
sed male fida quidem, nam bursa vodatur ab ipsa.
Hanc medici preciant, sed in altro corpore ficcam.
Ergo Saturnus supremo praesidet orbi,
de quo cascatus possit sibi rompere collum.

counting his shaky steps with a cane. Step by step he wheezes and
hawks up loogies; he has oozing pinkeye.

"A big fleece coat covers him down to his heels, and yet he   350
trembles in every season. His squat house weeps with noxious hu-
mors, the walls weep, the ceiling weeps, everything belonging to
Saturn weeps; no one is more Saturnine than he. A creeping mold
infects and destroys his food, for Apollo does not shine his splen-
diferous rays there. Dank night with its black shadows always
haunts this place, where night-flying barn owls, horned owls and
bats screech, and where little owls and tawny owls always sing
'hoo' and keep repeating 'hoo' all night long.

"Here dwells sadness, emaciation and every type of illness: in-   361
guinal swellings, flank pain, quartan fever, delirium, bovine pox,
carbuncles, the black plague, catarrh, stomach tumor, worms, coli-
tis, kidney stones, cancer, boils, buboes, the French pox, measles,
dysentery, mange, smallpox, microcephalia, rabies, encephalitis, ca-
nine rabies, toothache, scrofula, pip, fistula, mumps, swollen her-
nia in a fallen testicle, pustules, ringworm, leprosy, angina, dry
throat, bronchial asthma, as well as genital abscess, hemorrhoids,
gout, rhagade, tuberculosis and slow-foot ailment—I can't name
all these diseases! This servant clan always honors old Saturn, but
they can't be trusted, because they empty purses. The doctors ap-
preciate them, but only when they infect other peoples' bodies.
Therefore Saturn presides over the last planet: May he fall from
there and break his neck!

380　'En vobis coeli septem descripsimus orbes,
　　　quos male scripserunt veteres peiusque moderni,
　　　seu sit Aristotel, seu Ginus, sive Macorbi.
　　　Restat ut octavam veniamus dicere zonam.
　　　Sed quid ego (lassus!) video? num cernitis? ecce . . . .'
385　Talia dum parlat Cingar, cito gabia clamat:
　　　'Fustae! sunt fustae!'; quo dicto curritur armis.
　　　Astrologus Cingar subito se attrigat, oportet
　　　astrologare aliter quam nocte spiare Bootem.
　　　　Tuque tuas, Mafelina, satis, mea Lodola, stellas
390　cantasti, astronomis ignotas tempore longo.
　　　Nunc melius poterunt grossam ingannare brigatam.

Liber sextus decimus

　　　Togna caput mundi, Cipadae lampada, quam nunc
　　　quanta sit atque fuit quondam vel eritque futuro,
　　　ipsa ruina docet, quam fecit circa lasagnas;
　　　dum cantare parat stupidasque sonare bataias,
5　　ecce venit, venit ecce furens: guardate, botazzi,
　　　hinc sgombrate viam, zainae plenique barilli!
　　　Vestra ruina venit, bibet omnia more Todeschi,
　　　deinde fracassabit totos sdegnosa fiascos.
　　　Nescio quid referet. Vos ergo audite, brigata.
10　　Plura secuturus de primis deque secundis
　　　causis, ecce procul tres fustas currere Cingar
　　　viderat et sociis digito monstraverat ante.
　　　Non ita praecipitat coelo falconus ab alto,
　　　cum venit apiombum, cui bracca levaverit ocam,
15　　qualiter ecce ruit galeottis fusta gaiardis,
　　　qui stant ad remos, nulla religante cathena.

"There! We have described the seven heavens for you, about 380 which the ancient authors wrote badly, and the modern ones worse, whether Aristotle, Hyginus or Macrobius. The eighth sector remains for us to speak about. But what do I see, poor me, just look!" While Cingar is saying this, the watchman yells, "Ships, there are ships!" At this, they rush to their arms. Cingar, the astrologer, suddenly stops. It is necessary now to 'astrologize' in a different way than spying on Boötes at night.

And you, my Mafelina Lodola, have sung enough about these 389 stars, unknown to astronomers for a long time. Now they will be able to fool ignorant people more easily.

Book XVI

Togna *caput mundi*, light of Cipada! How great she is now, has 1 been in the past and will be in the future is demonstrated by the destruction she has made on all sides of the lasagne, while she gets ready to sing and recite stupendous battles. Here she comes, here she comes raving! Watch out, flagons, get out of her way! You kegs and full barrels, your ruin is at hand: she will guzzle everything like a German and then she'll shatter all the bottles in anger. I don't know what she will recount, so people, listen up!

As he was about to continue with many things relating to first 10 and second principles, look! Cingar saw three vessels racing from afar, the ones he'd just pointed out to his friends. A falcon, when it comes straight down from the pinnacle of the sky, just as a hunting dog is about to pick up its goose, does not plummet as fast as that vessel races here with hardy rowers, who stay at the oars un-

Intus piratae, corsari gensque ladrona,
qui seu non credunt in Christo sive negarunt.
'Vela!' cridant, 'heus! vela cito bassate! presones
20 vos estis nostri! navem smontate! sonata est!'
Vix ea finierant, altra huc bastarda galaea
altraque post illam veniunt infretta bravantes.
Hic vir magnus adest, gentis capitanus, et urget
remigeros fantes tamquam praesentia Turni.
25 Non fuit in mundo quidquam crudelius umquam,
quem ladrum ladrae gentes dixere Lyronum.
Ferreus aspectu, cui barba cruore recenti
semper olet carnesque hominum ceu bestia mangiat.
Tres igitur fustae veniunt demergere navem
30 et freta vorticibus retro spumantibus implent.
Baldus ad arma volat, sfodratum corripit ensem
imbrazzatque rotam scuti bassatque viseram.
Ipse Leonardus se Baldo firmat apressum
stansque parecchiatus stoccum tenet atque rodellam.
35 Viderat interea dispostos nauta barones,
nil timet, immo rotat timonem contra galaeas
seque parat guerrae, qua non prigolosior altra.
Chiozzotti et Schiavi, gens telis apta marinis,
arma piant animantque alios animositer omnes.
40 Implent sulphureo strepitosos pulvere schioppos
martinulosque rotant, curvas flectendo balestras.
Pars ratis ascendit gabiam, pars restat abassum,
quadruplicant forzam, Baldo praesente gaiardo,
totaque mercantum spes Baldum cascat in unum.
45 Iam venit una prior remis impulsa galaea,
circum circa fremens gyrat; tunc nauta timonem
praticus advolgit veluti si advolgat habenam.
Vidi Franciscum de Feltro saepe Mariam,
cuius in exiguo regnat dos maxima busto,

bound by chains. Aboard are pirates, corsairs, thieving sorts who either do not believe in Christ or have denied that they do. "The sails!" they cry out. "Lower the sails immediately! You are our prisoners. Get off the ship. Your time has come."

They have scarcely finished with this when another bastard galley, and after that yet another, rush forward, menacingly. A great man stands there, the commander of these people, and urges on the rowing infantry as though he were Turnus in person. There has never been anyone crueler the world over than this thief whom thieving people called Lirone. With an iron gaze, his beard always reeks of recent carnage, and like a beast, he eats human flesh. These three vessels come to sink this one ship, and behind them the sea is filled with foaming whirlpools.

Baldo flies to take up arms, grabs his unsheathed sword, straps on the disk of his shield, and lowers his visor. Leonardo plants himself firmly next to Baldo, standing equipped with his sword and buckler. Meanwhile, the helmsman, having seen these heroes at the ready, is not afraid and turns the rudder toward the galleys and prepares for war, the most dangerous kind there is. His crew of Slavs and Chioggiotti, people skilled in naval warfare, take up arms and courageously encourage all the others. They fill the noisy guns with sulfur powder and turn the windlasses, cocking the curved crossbows. Some of them take to the topsails, some stay on the deck; in the presence of fearless Baldo, they quadruple their force. All the merchants' hopes rest with Baldo alone.

Now one galley approaches propelled by its oars; it circles around threateningly; then the captain of the ship skillfully turns the rudder just as one might shift reins. I have often seen Francesco Maria da Montefeltro, in whose slight body there reigns

50 villanum Spagnae leviter manigiare poledrum:
    docta manus seu frena tiret, seu lenta remittat,
    ille statim redenae paret dominique volero;
    pirlat et a testa descernit nemo culattas,
    tam subito voltatur equus, tam praestus arancat.
55 Non minus ingentem barcam cito nauta maneggiat,
    semper habens zuffum prorae qua fusta menazzat.
    En cito schioppetti scaricantur ab igne tresenti
    milleque laxantur vertones extra nosellas,
    nemo sagittarum posset numerare bachettas.
60 Iamque comenzarant ad nubes surgere voces,
    innumeri quoniam primo piagantur asaltu.
    Saxa volant grossique trabes pegolaeque brusatae;
    artificiosus focus arma virumque squadernat.
    Tunc animosus aper, Baldus despiccat ab alta
65 prora terribilem saltum supraque galaeam
    hostibus in mediis balzat ferrumque cruentat.
    Cingar eum sequitur, magno targone copertus,
    atque samitarram toto conamine vibrat.
    Inde Leonardus de schena tollitur alte
70 ac super unius corsari tergora balzat,
    quem, feriendo alium stocco, trabuccat in undas.
    Baldus in introitu primo, velut impiger haeros,
    nocchiero fustae sese provistus acostat,
    pungentemque rotans stoccatam more trivellae,
75 ex una banda trippas sbudellat in altram.
    Corsari, magnis tunc urlis astra tocantes,
    intornum Baldo largam fecere coronam;
    at solitas barro furias in pectora chiamat,
    se totum lassat quo maior calca videtur
80 ac ibi principiat disquistellare piastras.
    Hi subito largam pavidi fecere piazzam;
    cui terit ille elmum, cui scudum cuique celadam,

great skill, easily guiding a young Spanish steed. Whether his expert hands pull back on the bit, whether they let up, the steed immediately obeys the bridle and its master's will; it spins around and you can't tell the head from the tail because the horse turns so swiftly and pulls ahead so rapidly. No less quickly does the helmsman maneuver the bark, always keeping the tip of the prow where the vessel threatens. All of a sudden, three hundred muskets are discharged by firing, and a thousand bolts are released from the catch of the crossbows, so that no one could count the arrow shafts. Soon voices have begun to ascend to the clouds, since in the first assault countless men are wounded. Rocks fly and heavy beams and burning pitch; the fireworks split apart arms and man.

Then, like a bold boar, Baldo launches a terrific leap from the   64 top of the prow and lands on the galley in the middle of the enemy and bloodies his sword. Cingar follows him, protected by a huge shield, and brandishes his scimitar with great force. Next Leonardo rears high up and jumps on the back of one of the corsairs, whom he pushes into the waves, while wounding another with his dagger.

As soon as he arrives on board, Baldo, indefatigable hero that   72 he is, carefully approaches the helmsman of the vessel and, twisting his pointed spear like a drill, disembowels his guts, passing from one side to the other. Then, with their great shouts reaching the stars, the corsairs form a large ring around Baldo; but the baron summons his customary fury and unleashes all his might where the crowd seems thickest and here begins to dismantle plates of armor. The enemy is frightened and hastily makes way. He crushes someone's helmet, another's shield, and another's sallet;

cui spezzat cufiam, spallazzum rompit et urtat
atque tridat carnes; nilque elmi nilque corazzae
85 stant saldae ad Baldi colpos Orlanditer actos.
Testas et bustos pariter dat piscibus escam;
et quod flamma facit, Borea sofiante, canellis,
id facit et Baldus stricto praedonibus ense.
Non scampare potest qui pugnat in aequore, sive
90 inveniet mortem per spadas, sive per undas.
Tantus afogatum Baldum furor incitat ut non
sancto Francisco potuisset habere riguardum.
Non illum Cingar pigritat seguitare, nec illum
forza Leonardi: dant sorbas ambo cotoras.
95 Hi tres compagni quid sit colpire maëstrant,
qui sint mandritti, quae puntae quive roversi;
totum sanguificant pontum terrentque diablos.
At Lyronus adest bastardam supra galaeam
fertque alebardam testasque superminet omnes:
100 non vir, sed paret grossi statura pilastri.
Hic iubet ad spallas navis gyrare galaeam,
dum se contra duas alias deffensitat illa.
Praestus obeditur, navem postremus asaltat;
hicve menans vastis alebardam forzibus, uno
105 truncavit fendente gravem de retro timonem.
Tunc se spazzatum iam cogitat esse paronus,
namque suo mancat frenum redinaeque cavallo.
Ille manu taccat navem crudelis et ipsam
iam montare parat, nec opinio fallit homazzum;
110 nam, licet obiciant Chiozotti saxa, travellos,
sulphureas faculas, pegolas rasamque fogatam,
ille valorosus, sociis seguitantibus, altam
se rapit in poppam mediosque ruinat in hostes,
quos cimigare facit sine brazzis ac sine gambis.
115 Non curat schioppos, non arcus atque balestras,

here he splits a bonnet, breaks a shoulder-plate, then presses forward and dices flesh. Neither helmet nor armor can resist Baldo's blows, delivered with Orlando's force. He feeds the fish both heads and torsos. And as fire acts on dry stalks when Boreas blows, so does Baldo act on the raiders with sword in hand. He who does battle at sea cannot escape: he will incur death either by the sword or in the waves.

Such fury incites the ardent Baldo that he would not have been 91 able to show respect even to St. Francis. Cingar does not hesitate to follow suit, nor mighty Leonardo; they both give meaty thwacks. These three companions teach what it means to strike, the essence of thrusts and slashes and backhands. They bloody the entire ocean and terrify the devils.

But Lirone approaches on the bastard galley, carrying a hal- 98 berd and towering over everyone's head. Not a man he seems, but rather the size of a massive column. He orders the galley to turn toward the side of the ship, while it is defending itself from the other two galleys. He is promptly obeyed and assaults the ship from behind; and wielding his halberd with vast force, he chops off the heavy rudder with one swipe. Their captain realizes he is already done for: his horse has no bridle, no reins. That brute grabs the ship with his hands and even now prepares to board. Nor does the awful giant fall short, for even though the Chioggiotti are throwing rocks, beams, sulfur torches, pitch and flaming resin, this valorous man, with his friends in tow, pulls himself high astern and plunges into the middle of the enemy, whom he makes crumple, without arms and without legs. He is

patronoque ratis colpo caput abscidit uno.
Fac, lector, contum, si quis intrando botegam
plenam pignattis, boccalibus atque scudellis,
incipit a circum grossam manegiare bachettam:
120   oh quantas facit ille scaias, facit ille menuzzos!
sic Lyronus agit, scapolantibus undique Schiavis,
quos taiat, strazzat, squarzat, sbudellat, amazzat.
Boccalus, qui forte uno cantone latebat
valdeque formidans strictum de retro tenebat,
125   nec scit nec maium curavit scire bataiam,
stabat ibi quacchius, spectans quid sortis acadat:
vel vincat navis, vel vincat fusta, quid inde?
arte bufonandi victorem vincere sperat.
At quando vidit grandem montare gigantem
130   longeque testarum coelo mandare borellas,
extemplo moruit; quid agat fantasticat amens.
Forte videt solitum schifettum stare paratum
ire, redire cito, nautis portare vivandas.
Providus hunc pelago buttat, iuttante Giberto,
135   amboque discostant sese, portante batello.
        Non erat hoc tanto de casu Baldus acortus,
scilicet ut navis Lyrono praesa fuisset,
sed magis arditus provas facit ense cruentas,
atque scadenatus tamquam leo rugit et omnes
140   vel penitus mortos lassat vel valde feritos.
Eius ab aspectu furibundo quisque paventat
ac in abandonum potius buttantur in undas
ut faciunt pisces, qui saltant extra padellam.
Hic illic taiat, hac illac pungit et urtat,
145   totus mortorum sbroiatus sanguine boffat.
Possanzam sed non basto contare Lyroni:
in qua parte suas dat brognas, stygmata parent.
Sanguinolenta cadens carnes alabarda staiezat,

not worried about muskets, bows or crossbows, and with a single blow lops off the skipper's head.

Imagine now, reader, if someone entering a shop full of pots, 117 jugs and bowls started to wheel a big club around, imagine how many shards, how many tiny fragments he would produce! This is just what Lirone does, with the Slavs fleeing in every direction: he slices, shreds, quarters, disembowels and kills them. Boccalo, who was hiding by chance in a corner and holding tight behind and panicking thoroughly since he doesn't understand combat and never bothered to learn, stayed there mutely watching what would happen. Will his ship win or will the galley, and what then? He hopes to vanquish the victor with his comic arts. But when he sees the huge giant climb aboard and dispatch head-balls way up to the sky, he suddenly feels dead. Frenzied, he plots what to do. By chance he sees the usual little skiff, standing ready to go back and forth quickly to bring supplies to the sailors. Cautiously, with Gilberto's help, he pushes it into the sea and the two of them are carried away by the boat.

Baldo was not aware of this important turn of events, that is, 136 that the ship had been taken by Lirone, so with still more daring, he does bloody deeds with his sword and roars like an unchained lion and leaves everyone utterly dead or badly wounded. Everybody panics before his ferocious countenance, and they prefer to throw themselves into the waves with abandon, like fish who jump out of the frying pan. He cuts here and there, stabs and strikes there and here; smeared with the blood of the dead, he grunts.

I cannot describe the power of Lirone: wherever he does his 146 pruning, stigmata appear. In its descent the blood-encrusted halberd minces flesh. Therefore everyone flees, but they leave before

unde omnes fugiunt ac post atque ante relinquunt
150 pulmones, milzas, ventres, redicella, figatos.
Nil nisi sentitur clamor fremitusque morentum
horrendique cridi stridoribus aethera fendunt.
Altri clamabant Christum sanctumque Nicolam,
altri cornutum Macomettum altrique diablum.
155 Non fuit auditus, postquam nascuntur orecchiae,
tam grandis rumor, strepitus guerraeque fracassus.
Parte alia Baldus, rabiosi fluminis instar,
quod, praeceps veniens alta de rupe, marinas
findit aquas aperitque maris vortigine schenam,
160 sic per Evangelii Baldus se ventilat hostes,
donec amazzavit cum Cingare cumque Lonardo
cotantos penitus coquantos fusta tenebat.
Plus quam barberii bacillus netta remansit.
Et iam Lyronus barzam acquistaverat omnem;
165 oh! quantum gaudet talem fecisse guadagnum!
Dumque repentinus consurgit flatus ab austro,
totos in navim piratas scandere mandat.
Et grossum ponens alium de retro timonem,
sgombrat iter liquidum, vento spirante secundo.
170 Succeduntque duae cantanti voce galeae,
quas tres esse putant Lyronus et altra brigata;
nam per alegrezzam mens nostra fit orba soventer.
Ergo volant hiniantque preso unusquisque botino.
Nulla sed in Baldo gaudendi causa relicta est.
175 'Heu quid', ait Cingar, 'sic sic incaute gabamur?
Saepe guadagnandi nos ingordigia fallit.
Balde, vides? en navis abit, quo presa menatur?'
Baldus, id aspiciens, se signat fronte rapata,
statque tacens, nescitque loqui, parlatque nientum.
180 Semet at incepit Leonardus battere pugnis:
'Ah! mala sors!', inquit, 'nimis es contraria nobis!

and behind them lungs, spleens, bellies, viscera and livers. Only the yells and laments of the dying are heard, and horrible cries pierce the heavens with their screams. Some were invoking Christ and Saint Nicholas; others, the cuckold Mohammad and yet others, the devil. Never since the birth of the ear has there been heard such tremendous noise, racket and din of war. On the other side, Baldo — like an angry river which, by gushing down from a high mountain and crashing into the marine waters, splits the back of the sea with its vortex — in this same way, Baldo ventilates against the enemy of the Gospel, until with the help of Cingar and Leonardo he has killed every single person on the vessel. It was left cleaner than a barber's basin.

Meanwhile, Lirone had conquered all of the main deck: How 164 thrilled he is to have made such a conquest! When a wind rises suddenly from the south, he orders all the pirates to board the ship. After securing a large new rudder in back, they take off on the watery road with a favorable wind at their backs, and two of the galleys follow with cheering voices. Lirone and his cohorts think that there are three, because our minds are often blinded by joy. So they fly off, every one of them whinnying at the booty seized.

But Baldo is left with no cause for celebration. And Cingar 174 wonders, "O why do we so rashly let ourselves be fooled? How often greed for gain trips us up. Do you see, Baldo? Look, the ship is leaving. Where is it going now that it has been captured?"

As he observes the departing ship, Baldo makes the sign of the 178 cross with his brow furrowed. He keeps silent and does not know what to answer and says nothing. But Leonardo begins to beat himself with his fists. "Ah, Bad Luck!" he says. "You are really

Surripiuntur equi tamque acres tamque galanti
quam numquam maium terrae pars ulla creavit.
Quos nisi vel per aquas retrovabo vel per abissum,
185   iuro deos omnes mihimet volo tradere mortem,
hancve coracinam numquam spoiabo da dossum,
donec ego inveniam ladrosque ducamque ladrorum,
quem vel amazzabo, vel ego amazzabor ab illo'.
Incagnatus erat Baldus coleraque brasabat,
190   nam seguitare ladros sese non posse videbat:
non est qui menet remos vacuamque galaeam.
Cingar ait: 'Gaude, spero scattare cavallos'.
Dixit at haec Cingar pro confortare Lonardum,
attamen interius dubiat mentemque burattat
195   quove modo aut guisa valeant uscire galaeam.
Damangiare nihil retrovant mancumque dabever,
littora nulla vident, non circum circa terenum;
omnia sunt oculis pelagus, sunt omnia coelum
estque marisellus faciens smaltire budellas,
200   unde fament vellentque famem scazzare nec ordo est.
Cingaris at cura Baldus premit atque Lonardus
cordoium ingentem ponuntque dabanda temenzam,
sperantes et quod destreros ille raquistet,
et quod in hac fusta quidquam mangiabile trovet.
205   Non ea barrones decepit opinio, namque,
dum Cingar totam buttat sotosora galaeam,
multa retrovavit de sub fundamine puppis,
quae consolarunt animos prius, inde budellas.
Dumque recordari sociis vult Baldus amicos
210   Giubertum iuvenem charumque insemma bufonum,
Giubertus iuvenis charusque insemma bufonus
ecce procul veniunt, remis fugiente batello,
et cridant tutavia: 'Oh! oh! aspettate fradelli!'
Aspettant laeti, nam quo partire volebant

against us! The horses have been stolen, our strong and noble horses, better than those produced by any region on earth. If I cannot find them on the seas or in the abyss, I swear by all the gods that I shall kill myself. I shall never remove my armor until I find those thieves and their leader, whom I shall kill, or be killed by him."

Baldo was infuriated and burned with anger, because it seemed 189 that they could not pursue the thieves, as there is no one to row and the galley is empty. Cingar says, "Rejoice! I hope to free our horses." However, Cingar said this to comfort Leonardo, even though he himself is wracked with doubt and straining his mind for a plan, for a way they might be able to get off this galley. They find nothing to eat, nothing to drink; they can see no shore, no land anywhere around; water and sky are all the eye can see. The water is choppy, making their innards churn, so they are hungry and want to drive away their hunger, but this is not in the scheme of things. Thanks to Cingar, Baldo and Leonardo repress their tremendous grief and set aside their fears, in hopes that he will recover their chargers and find something edible on this vessel. And their trust is not betrayed, for when Cingar turns the galley inside out he finds many things in the bottom of the hold, things which consoled first their spirits, then their bellies.

While Baldo entreats his companions to remember their 209 friends — the young Gilberto and the dear buffoon — behold! The young Gilberto and the dear buffoon come from afar, whence they have fled on the rowboat, and they yell continually, "O! O! Wait, brothers!" The others wait happily, for where could they expect to

215   si nullus remex et remi infrotta superchiant?
      Hos igitur picola cum barca insemma levatos,
      Baldi forza tirat sursum dentrumque reponit.
      Giubertus narrat qua fugerit arte Bocali;
      dumque alternatim passata pericla recordant,
220   Cingar formigat per fustae mille latebras
      et tandem reperit damisellum fronte galantum,
      qui iacet, a testa calcagnos usque ligatus,
      et lachrymans orat longo de carcere trari.
      Confestim accurrit Cingar miseratus, in illum
225   aspicit atque hominem quondam vidisse recordat.
      Ast in quo bosco, seu Fundi sive Bacani,
      nescit et in dubia sibi grattat mente tosottos.
      'Dic', ait, 'ecquis tu? quae patria? quaeve cathenae?'
      Respondet: 'Fuimus tres nunc insemma sodales,
230   Falchettus, Moschinus ego magnusque Fracassus,
      qui cum sex, carichis moresca gente, caracchis
      Italiam versus zephyris vela alta dabamus.
      Tanta sed alzavit montes tempesta marinos
      quod pars armatae rupta est, pars gita traversum,
235   ac ita tres charos mala sors divisit amicos.
      Verum ubi regressa est, Phoebo ridente, bonazza,
      ista ladronorum classis fuit obvia meque,
      non sine strage sua, capitanum gentis in ista
      nave cadenarunt, sperantes praemia taiae.
240   Caetera gens una cum nave perita negatur.
      Quo tendant alii caporales nescio; verum
      quam doleo, si nulla datur vindicta baronis,
      illius egregi barronis nomine Baldi'.
      Cingar id ascoltans, veluti cagiada tenellus,
245   deleguat dentrum; simulat tamen extraque tascam
      fidam compagnam limas trahit atque tenaias,
      unde, scatenatis, sic sic tuttavia loquendo,

go if they have not one oarsman, although they have piles of oars?
The two therefore are lifted up, together with the little bark;
Baldo's strength pulls them up and sets them down on board.
Gilberto narrates how he escaped by means of Boccalo's skill, and
while they take turns recalling the dangers they had overcome,
Cingar pokes about in a thousand hiding places on the vessel. In
the end, he found a handsome youth lying prostrate, bound hand
and foot, who begs, sobbing, to be freed from his long imprison-
ment. Cingar, feeling compassion, rushes to him at once. He looks
at him and recalls having seen this man before, but doesn't know
in which forest, whether that of Fondi or of Baccano, and he
scratches his stubble, unsure. "Do tell," he says. "Who are you?
Where do you come from? Why the chains?"

The man replies: "There were three of us boon companions: 229
Falchetto, Moschino (that's me), and the great Fracasso. With six
carracks loaded with Moors, we were heading full sail toward Italy
with a westerly wind. However, a great tempest raised up moun-
tains of water, so that part of our fleet was destroyed, part was dis-
persed, and thus bad luck separated three dear friends. Then,
when good weather returned, with Apollo smiling, a flotilla of
raiders overtook us and after considerable losses they shackled me
(the captain of the crew) in this ship, hoping to collect a ransom.
A throng of people was drowned when the ship went down. I
don't know where the other leaders ended up, but what really
pains me is if no revenge is to be granted that baron, that illustri-
ous baron named Baldo!"

Hearing this, Cingar melts inside as soft as milk curds, but   244
doesn't let on, and pulls his files and pliers out of his faithful
companion-pouch, unlocking the ankle irons while still talking,

compedibus ferri, quamprimum liberat illum.
Mox vocat huc Baldum, Baldus venit atque Lonardus.
250 Quid velit ignorant; Moschinum Cingar ad ipsos
praesentat, relevansque oculos, sic versus Olympum
alloquitur clamans: 'Oh laus! oh gloria mundi!
oh paladinus homo qui nostra aetate coruscat!
En tua nobilitas quales tibi, Balde, sodales
255 conciliat qualesque viros quantosque barones!
Per mare, per terras, perque hinc perque inde requirunt
te, cortesiae speculum, te, robur honorum;
nilque maris pelagum, nil Scillam, nilve Carybdim,
nilque ladronorum fustas timuere timendas:
260 quo te magnanimum, quo te sine fraude realem
aut presone cavent, aut pro te morte necentur.
Dico tibi, et replico bis, ter, quater octoque voltas:
tres te compagni cercant cagione trovandi
haud in ricchezzis Croesi, haud in Sardanapali
265 delitiis porci, non summa in sede levatum;
sed magis hoc faciunt compagni denique veri:
ut vel in obscuro cum tecum carcere stentent,
vel dent diabolo pro te dissolvere vitas.
Per montes, valles perque aequora perque travaios,
270 huc, illuc sese ficcant animasque refudant.
Numquid acquistandi robbam cagione vagantur?
numquid ut obtineant papae regumque favores?
Non, non! ast ut te longo de carcere ducant,
aut tecum ceppos turremque per aëra portent.
275 Ecce cadenantur miseri tristemque famati
sustentant vitam: quis tales trovet amigos?
Quot reperis, tot tu naso numerare valebis;
tempore disgratiae veri noscuntur amici.
Quid plus amicitia? valet esse beatior ipsa.
280 Quid melius mundo, quid plus agradat Olympo?

and frees him as quickly as possible. Cingar calls to Baldo, and Baldo comes with Leonardo. They don't know what he wants. He presents Moschino to them, and raising his eyes up to the heavens, exclaims loudly, "O praise, O glory of the world, O chivalrous man, who brightens our age! Behold, Baldo, what boon companions your nobility commends to you, what heroes, what barons! By land and by sea, this way and that, they seek you out: you, the mirror of courtesy, and you, the bulwark of honor. They did not fear the vast seas or Scylla or Charybdis or the terrible raiders' ships. They sought to free you from prison or else to be quenched by death for you—you the magnanimous one, you, guileless and loyal!

"I am telling you, and I repeat twice, thrice, four times and eight: three companions look for you, not with hope of discovering you amid the riches of Croesus, nor amid the delights of that pig Sardanapulus, nor raised on a high throne. Nay, your truest friends do this to suffer with you in a dark prison or to give up their lives to the devil to get you released. Over hill, over dale, across seas and travails, they thrust themselves this way and that, and risk their lives. And are they wandering in order to acquire goods? Or in order to obtain the favors of king and pope? No, no! Rather so that they can lead you out of your long imprisonment or else wear leg irons with you in the high tower. Look! These starving wretches are chained and live a miserable life. Who could get such friends? The number you find you could count on your nose. True friends are recognized when times are bad.

"What is better than friendship? Is anything more blessed than this? What on earth could be better? What is more pleasing to

262

279

Omnibus his cosis incago praeter amicis.
Quae gemmae possent, quae magni vena tesori
charum, secretum, fidum comprare sodalem?
Est poltronus homo, nec homo sed bestia basti,
285 qui magis apretiat trippas implere busecchis
quam reperire virum sua cui pensiria dicat.
Ecce tuus Moschinus adest, o Balde! Quid illum
cernis adhuc dubitans? Heu! tempore tempus obumbrat
vultum hominis memoremque minus distantia reddit'.
290 Sic referens Cingar, lachrymis sibi pectora bagnat
atque facit nimia tenerezza flere sodales.
Baldus in amplexum Moschini currit et inquit:
'Tune, meus Moschinus, ades? tune ille mearum
quondam curarum requies ac dulce levamen?'
295 Nec parlare valens plus avantum, strectus abrazat
atque basat iuvenem, cui tunc vix barbula spuntat.
Posthabitis demum lachrymis, Moschinus ad illos
omnia de sociis perdutis ordine contat.
Baldus ait: 'Retrovare meos dispono fradellos.
300 At quis nos istam deduxerit extra galaeam?
Non sunt qui menent remos, qui carbasa tendant'.
Doctus ad hanc artem Moschinus, qui maris olim
viderat ad Pietoli zuffum plus mille fiatis,
passaratque fretum San Zorgi ad Vasa Ceresi,
305 respondet: 'Pocam facio de hoc aequore stimam,
qui magnum oceanum Bugni golfumque Cipadae
sulcavi toties per drittum perque traversum.
Ne dubita; dum prosper adest Levantus ab Euro,
ad totam per trenta horas nos ibimus orzam.
310 Ergo spiegamus velam. Tu, Cingare, cordam
hanc tira. Leonarde, iuva! Tuque . . . hola! quis est hic?
Bon compagne, mihi fer opem distendere velam!'

heaven? I don't give a shit about anything except friends. What gems, what rich vein of treasure could purchase a dear, close, faithful companion? He is a worthless man — not even a man, but a beast — who would rather fill his intestines with tripe than find a good man with whom to share his thoughts. See, here is your Moschino, O Baldo. Why do you still look at him doubtfully? Alas, time dims the face of a man over time, and distance diminishes our memory of him!"

While stating this, Cingar bathes his breast with tears and makes his companions weep from a surfeit of tenderness. Baldo rushes to embrace Moschino and says, "Are you here then, my Moschino? You, who before were the repose and sweet solace of my burdens?" Unable to speak further, Baldo tightly hugs and kisses the youth, whose bit of beard is barely showing. Eventually brushing aside his tears, Moschino tells them the entire story of his lost companions. Baldo says, "I am ready to go find my brothers. But who will lead us off this galley? There is no one able to man the oars, no one to work the sails."

Moschino was an expert in these arts and from the hillock at Pietole had seen the sea more than a thousand times and had navigated the straits of San Giorgio to the Port of Cerese. He responds, "I'm not impressed by these waters, I who many times ploughed the great ocean of Bugno and the gulf of Cipada, back and forth. Do not fear, while this levanter is favorable, coming from the east, we will go downwind for thirty hours. Therefore, let us raise the sail. You, Cingar, pull this rope; Leonardo, help him; and you . . . Hey! Who is this? Good friend, give me a hand to inflate this sail."

Cui Boccalus: 'Ego? sum praestus, en, sia factus'.
Moschinus rursum: 'Sta tu istic, Balde, timoni.
315   Cingare, tira, tira! day day! tira, Cingare, tira!
Issa, Lonarde, issa! ih, oh! succurre, Giberte!
Iam satis est! Orzam scurta! Preme, Balde, timonem!
Bon compagne, sede! Satis es male praticus. Horsu!
Ad nomen Christi, cordam paulisper amolla,
320   Cingar! Hem, socii, qualis fortuna secundat!
Tu quoque, Balde, sede, lassa me stare timoni.
Labra mihi sunt aspra siti; quam bramo bocalum!'
'En', Boccalus ait, 'me vis?' Risere sodales,
et sic Boccalum tunc nomen habere Bocalum
325   novit Moschinus. Post coelum guardat et inquit:
'Quam bene velamen gaiardus gonfiat Eurus!
Sancte, precor, nobis esto Nicolaë benignus,
qui nos semper habes curam defendere nautas;
assassina licet sit barcarola canaia,
330   non tamen attendas haec mancamenta, sed omnem
tolle annegandi prigolum drizzaque caminum'.
Cingar ait: 'Quid tam sanctum chiamare Nicolam
ut tibi det ventum? potius prega det tibi panem,
namque affamato crepitant mihi ventre budellae,
335   magraque Boccali facies lanterna videtur'.
Cui cito Boccalus: 'Tua nec grassedine colat'.
At Cingar de more suo rugat huc, rugat illuc
biscottosque trovat quodam cantone latentes,
semimufolentos et avorum tempore natos,
340   barba quibus canuta riget corrosaque tarmis.
Post haec dulcis aquae mezarolam ducit et ollam
persutti ranzi secreta in parte catatam.
Haec sunt visa tamen sibi lac, sibi zuccarus et mel,
et giurant numquam similes gustasse bocones.
345   Omnia consumant, nec zanza fit ulla tralorum:

Boccalo answers, "Me? I am at your service. There—it's done."   313

Moschino continues, "Baldo, stay here at the helm; Cingar,   314
pull, pull! Come on, pull, Cingar, pull! Up, Leonardo, up! Hey,
ho, help out, Gilberto! That's enough now; trim the sail. Baldo,
bear the rudder. Ease up, good friend; you are really a novice.
Come on, in the name of Christ, give the rope some slack, Cingar!
Ah, mates, what a favorable wind! You too, Baldo, ease up; let
me take the helm. My lips are rough from thirst. How I wish I
had a jugful."

"Here I am, do you need me?" Boccalo responds. The crew   323
laughed, and so Moschino learned then that Boccalo is named for
a jugful, a *boccale*. Next, Moschino looks at the sky and says,
"How well gallant Eurus swells the sail! St. Nicholas, I pray you,
look favorably upon us, you who always take care to defend us
sailors. Even if the sea-faring rabble is treacherous, don't dwell on
these defects, but spare us the danger of drowning and steady
our way."

"Why are you praying so to St. Nicholas to give you a good   332
wind?" asks Cingar. "Pray rather that he gives you bread, because
my guts are grumbling in my starving belly, and Boccalo's gaunt
face looks like a lantern."

Boccalo quickly says, "And yours isn't dripping with fat." Yet   336
Cingar, as is his custom, pokes around here and there and finds
some biscuits hidden in a corner—half-moldy, born in the age of
our forefathers, now bristling with white beards and gnawed by
moths. After these, he brings them a half-barrel of water and a
crock of rancid prosciutto that he found in a hidden compartment.
These things seem to them milk, sugar and honey and they swear
they've never tasted such morsels. They consume everything; there

qui famet et comedit, si parlat tempora perdit.
Providus interea Cingar, post apta Molorco
fercula, se fustae gabiam rampavit ad altam,
rampatusque supra rodit tutavia fenocchios.
350 Hinc oculos per aquas largat lateque vedutam
spantegat, et stricto cilio freta larga traversat
si piet ex aliqua banda scopratve terenum.
Sed campos tantum immensos discernit aquarum.
Prosper erat ventus rapidae tunc forte galaeae.
355 Moschinus tendit nisi non guidare timonem,
saepe iubens nunc trare sogas, nunc solvere funes;
quam Baldus curam dexter facit atque Lonardus.
Cingar cantabat, lingua frifolante, vilottas.
Ecce propinquantem fustae procul aspicit unum
360 nescio quem, medias nodantem forte per undas.
Esse prius lignum pensat, mox esse cavallum;
alter ait: 'Butta est'; 'Non sic', ait alter, 'hic est bos'.
Inde vident chiarum non esse nec ista nec illa,
ast homo certus erat, vivus nodansque per undas.
365 Sed nodando tamen, solitam non servat usanzam,
scilicet ut pariter gambas et brachia menet;
brachia non menat, non spingit ab ore liquorem,
immo super fluctus apparet tota giuponi
forma, nec a bigolo sursum lana ulla bagnatur.
370 Tantum crura menat pedibusque per aequora solis
enatat, et dardum dextra scudumque sinistra
fert animosus homo; reliqua sed parte sotacquam
findit inaequalem, velut ales aquatilis, undam,
sive sit ocha Padi varcans nodando canalem,
375 sive folenga giocans fangosa in valle Comacchi.
Ille venit contra fustam veniensque menazzat,
namque ladronorum pensaverat esse galaeam,
quae sibi non pocum tulerat per alhora botinum.

is no chatting among them. A starving man who eats wastes time if he speaks.

Meanwhile, the ever-vigilant Cingar, after this meal worthy of   347
Molorchus, climbed up to the ship's tall crow's nest and, having climbed up, continued to gnaw on fennel seeds. From there, he casts his eyes across the waters, scans the panorama far and wide, and with his brow creased, criss-crosses the ample ocean to see if he can glimpse or discover land in any direction. But he only detects immense stretches of water. As luck would have it, the wind was favorable to the swift galley. Moschino is wholly intent on steering the rudder, often calling out orders now to pull in the cables, now to loosen the stays — orders which the able Baldo carries out with Leonardo.

Cingar was singing country songs with a trilling tongue. All of   358
a sudden, he spied something from afar, I don't know what, that approached the vessel, swimming by chance through the waves. First he thinks it's a log, next a horse. One man says, "It's a barrel." "Not so," says another, "it's an ox." Finally they see clearly; it was neither the one nor the other, but was undeniably a man, alive and swimming on the waves. Yet in swimming, he does not follow the usual manner — that is, moving his arms and legs together. He does not move his arms, or spit water out of his mouth. Instead, the whole shape of his torso appears above water, and from his belly button on up, not one hair gets wet. He moves only his lower limbs, and swims through the sea using only his feet. And this spirited fellow bears a spear in his right hand and a shield in his left. His submerged parts slice the waves unevenly, like a water bird — whether a goose crossing the Po channel or a coot playing in the muddy valley of Comacchio. He makes for the galley and threatens as he comes, for he thought this was the raiders' vessel

Obstupuit Baldus quod vir sub pondere ferri
380   tam facilis nodet nec brachia prorsus adopret.
Ast ubi Moschinus placidos gyravit ocellos,
clamat alegrus: 'Hic est noster Falchettus!' et 'Heus oh!
O Falchette, veni! Baldus te . . . Baldus, et ipse,
ipse tuus Cingar manet hic. Affretta, camina!'
385   Proh puta! quando suos compagnos sentit adesse,
quos partim mortos, partim praesone seratos
crediderat, scudum subito dardumque relinquit,
quattuor et gambis, pariter brazzisque duobus
enatat, immo volat, medius canis et medius vir.
390   Quando etiam Cingar Falchettum vidit in undis,
quem, Baldo excepto, super omnes semper amavit,
exuit extemplo faldam spoliatque camisam
et, stoppans nasum digitis, ex arbore navis
cum capite innantum se ficcat in aequora tuttum.
395   Sex brazzos descendit aquae; mox ecce videtur
desuper orecchias scorlare liquore pienas,
oreque boffanti salsos respingere potus;
dumque ferit palmis et crebris calcibus aequor,
scindit aquas rumpitque levi sub pectore pontum.
400   Denique iunguntur; Falchettum Cingar in undis,
ut valet, abbrazzat veniuntque insemma natantes
atque ragionantes, donec, manudante Lonardo,
unus post alium trantur de fluctibus ambo.
Absque ullo numero faciunt sibi mille carezzas,
405   passatos casus, passata pericula narrant,
perque susum guaios toleratos perque dabassum.
Talia dum parlant, chiachiarant unaque moteggiant,
insperata procul discoprunt culmina terrae,
horrentes nemorum sylvas montesque levatos.
410   Haec erat aut, dicam correctius, esse parebat
insula, quae pinis, fagis verdeggiat et ornis.

which had just taken no small amount of booty from him. Baldo
is amazed that a man weighed down with armor could swim so
easily and not even use his arms. But Moschino, turning his calm
gaze, exclaims joyfully, "Here is our Falchetto!" and "O hey! O
Falchetto, come on! Baldo . . . your Baldo is here and your very
own Cingar! Hurry now, get a move on!"

Just think! When Falchetto hears that his companions are   385
there, some of whom he had thought dead, some locked up in
prison, he immediately drops his shield and spear and swims on
all fours, using his arms too, or rather flies, half dog and half man.
And when Cingar sees Falchetto on the waves — Falchetto, whom
he has always loved above all others except Baldo — he instantly re-
moves his armor and takes off his shirt and, plugging his nose
with his fingers, dives from the mast headlong into the sea. He de-
scends six cubits into the water, but soon appears on the surface to
shake out his ears, which are full of water, and to puff the salt wa-
ter out of his mouth. At the same time he assails the ocean with
his cupped hands and quick kicks; he parts the water and cleaves
the sea with his buoyant torso.

At last, they are united. In the waves, Cingar embraces   400
Falchetto as best he can; and they proceed together, swimming
and conversing, until with a hand from Leonardo they are pulled
from the swells one after the other. Then they all greet each other
endlessly and tell about their experiences, the dangers overcome,
the hardships suffered high and low. While they are all talking and
chatting and joking at the same time, they spot unexpected peaks
of land in the distance, the bristling branches of a forest and
mountaintops. This was — or, to put it more correctly, this ap-
peared to be — an island, verdant with pine, beech and ash. Hav-

Hac visa, incipiunt laeti saltare barones.
'Terram!', Cingar ait, 'terram! Quin cernitis? Ecce!'
Huc celer, huc Baldus timonem torcere mandat
415 ad portumque facit versam inculare galaeam.
Anchoreus buttatur aquis rampinus et omnes
saltant armati de fusta supra terenum.
Tangere quisque solum gaudet damnatque marinam.
Ingrediunt boschos si qua mangianda catantur,
420 nam biscotellos satis est mangiasse trigiornos,
aut unxisse gulam ranzi pinguedine lardi.
Ecce duas capras, binis seguitantibus albis
capreolis, cernunt prolixis currere gambis,
saltibus et magnis culum monstrare biancum.
425 Se citat ad cursum Falchettus moreque veltri
pulverulentus abit pedibusque viluppat arenam,
unde brevi cursu caprettos strangulat ambos,
quos butat in terram mortos; caprasque secutus,
unam acquistavit tantum, scampante sorella.
430 Cingar ibi laetus matrem natosque gemellos
accipit et, factis solito de more cavecchis,
scorticat et capram, et caprettos scorticat ambos.
Non ibi Boccalus fuit ultimus: omnia versat,
omnia sollicitat, facit hoc, iubet illoc et omni
435 cazzat in impresa nasum, faciendo bufonem.
Baldus fraxinea detruncat ab arbore ramum,
optime quem sbroccat foliis et rendit aguzzum.
Hunc piat altandem Boccalus et ipsa caprarum
frusta, per hunc spetum sic factum, ponit arostum.
440 Ipse Leonardus iam traxerat extra galaeam
ignivomam petram, lescam durumque focile;
multiplicat colpos, dum saxum chioccat azalo,
scintillasque cavans, tandem flammarier escam
inspicit unde ignem pochetino sulphure brancat.

ing sighted the island, the heroes begin to dance with joy. "Land!" cries Cingar, "Land! Do you see it? Look!"

Straight away, Baldo orders that the rudder be turned toward   414
the island, and he has the galley berth in the port butt first. The grappling iron is thrown into the water and they all jump off the vessel onto the ground, armed. Each of them rejoices at touching the soil and curses the sea. They enter the woods to find something to eat because they are fed up with eating biscuits for three days and greasing their throats with the fat of rancid lard. Here they see two she-goats running on graceful legs, followed by two white kids, displaying their white butts as they leap high in the air. Falchetto gives chase, raising dust like a greyhound and whirls up dirt with his feet. After a brief chase, he strangles both of the kids and throws them, dead, on the ground. Then having followed the she-goats, he captures only one—her sister escapes. Cingar happily takes the mother and the twin kids, and with wood scrapers made in the usual way, he skins the she-goat and both the kids.

Boccalo is not far behind; he gets involved with everything,   433
gives advice, does this, orders that and sticks his nose into every affair, playing the buffoon. Baldo cuts a branch off an ash tree that he carefully strips of its leaves and sharpens. Then Boccalo takes the spit thus fashioned and puts the pieces of goat meat on it to roast. Leonardo had already taken the flint, tinder and steel from the galley; he redoubles his strikes as he hits the stone with the steel and makes sparks until at last he sees the tinder flare up, so with a bit of sulfur it catches fire. Once the flame is high,

445 Iamque altus focus est, Moschinus ligna trabuccat;
plurima tum Cingar fert instrumenta coquinae,
smenuzzat trippas, bis terque quaterque lavatas,
inque pignatonem, quem tunc aqua calda netarat,
cum sale cumque oleo ponit, faciendo menestram.

450 Boccalus rotolat spetum, iam fumat arostus,
supra quem Baldus lardi scolamina buttat.
Quasdam frondosas Giubertus praeparat umbras,
sub quibus est agium coctos mangiare caprettos,
namque cicala canit, giugno brusante terenum.

455 Denique iam omnes cocto refrescantur arosto.
Cingaris incoepit primus masinare molinus,
Boccalus mezam iam capram dente vorarat;
Baldus nil parlat, qui parlat tempora perdit.
Dat nunc Giuberto meliores nuncve Lonardo

460 boccones, quos saepe sibi Boccalus agraffat.
Moschinus frangit, nettum lassando, taierum,
quem sibi de fundo scatolazzae fecerat ante.
Quisque suas implet caprina carne budellas,
consydrant nec adhuc Falchettum prorsus abesse;

465 tanta famis quandoque citat possanza talentum
quod, quantumque supercharos, smemoramus amicos.
Non tamen hanc umquam Baldus servavit usanzam,
sed, qui dilectis procurat semper amicis,
sic ait: 'Heus socii, non hic Falchettus habetur,

470 quonam discessit? nostra est vergogna daverum.
Ille capram rapuit manibus rapuitque caprettos,
cui pars debetur maior meliorque boconus,
et nos mangiamus, non illo adstante, codardi?
Surge cito, Cingar, Moschini suscipe piccam,

475 vade per has macchias; compagnum cerca; camina!'
Surgit amorevolus Cingar gittatque taërum
corripit et piccam sylvamque subintrat opacam.

Moschino piles on firewood; Cingar then fetches several cooking utensils. He chops the tripe, after washing it two, three and four times. Then he puts it in a big pot—just cleaned with hot wa-ter—and adds salt and oil to make soup. Boccalo turns the spit; the roast on which Baldo pours melted lard is already smoking. In the meantime, Gilberto constructs a shady bower under which they can eat the cooked goats in comfort, for the cicadas are sing-ing, and June is burning the earth.

At length, they are all restored by the cooked roast. Cingar's 455 mill begins to grind first. Boccalo had already devoured half a goat with his teeth. Baldo does not talk, for he who talks wastes time. He gives the choicest morsels first to Gilberto, then to Leonardo, which Boccalo often snatches for himself. Moschino wipes clean the cutting board that he had fashioned for himself earlier from the bottom of an old box. Every one of them fills his gut with goat meat, and they do not yet realize that Falchetto is utterly missing. Sometimes such force of hunger stimulates the appetite that we forget our friends, even our dearest friends. But Baldo has never followed this custom. Rather, as one who always looks after his cherished friends, he speaks thus, "Hey, mates, Falchetto is not here. Where can he have gone? We should be ashamed. He caught the she-goat with his own hands and the kids too. So he should get the biggest portion, the choicest piece. Should we knaves be eating without him here? Get up quickly, Cingar! Take Moschino's pike, go into that thicket and look for your compan-ion. Move it!"

Solicitous, Cingar gets up and throws down his trencher, 476 grabs his pike and enters the dark wood. He shouted, "Hey ho,

'Heus oh!', cridabat, 'heus oh! Falchette!'; sed 'Heus oh!
Falchette!' respondet ei de rupibus Echo.

480 Interea iuvenis Leonardus prestiter escas
deserit et, cingens spadam ferrique brocherum,
terribilem boscum post gressum Cingaris intrat.
Texuerat sibimet tortam de fronde coronam:
nuper enim dixi raucas cantare cigalas.

485 Cingar abit magno spacio lontanus ab illo;
nescit heu!, nescit miserum seguitare Leonardum;
nam bene dicendus miser est, cui cruda paratur
mors, iuveni schietto, puro similique rubinis.
Et quae causa necis fuit huius? foemina. Mirum,

490 si quid monstrum aliud quam foemina rumpere possit
mentem tam sanctam castamque Deoque placentem.
Oyme Deus, quantis grassa est nunc terra bagassis,
tantarum quae pressa gemit sub fasce luparum.
Dic horsu, dic, Togna, mei possanza botazzi,

495 dic rofianarum trapolas soiasque rognosi
mille putanismi et Veneris cagatoria nostrae.
Non desdegneris, quamvis sis foemina, namque
teque tuasque pares fas est dabanda relinqui.
Parcite, signores, si forza colerica meme

500 straparlare facit bruttasve sfogare parolas.
Ah! nimis importat tam bellum perdere florem.
Credite non mancum Tognae, quod dire parecchiat,
quam si respondens ad messam proferat amen.
Non plus merda nocet naso, non morta carogna

505 quam mulier quae, se falsa beltate galantans,
cortigiana iubet pariterque signora vocari.
Oh! sporcum bruttumque nefas, oh! millibus umquam
non unctis, totoque orbis sapone lavandum!
Et quid agunt istaec porchae frustaeque lupazzae?

510 Heu iuvenes, audite, precor, sentite poëtam

Falchetto," but Echo answers back from the cliffs, "Hey ho, Falchetto." Meanwhile, the young Leonardo immediately leaves the meal and, strapping on his sword and iron buckler, enters the terrible woods in Cingar's steps. He had woven a crown twisted with twigs—indeed, as I just said, the raucous cicadas were singing. Cingar wanders quite a distance away from him. He doesn't know, alas! He doesn't know that the hapless Leonardo is following him. It is right to call him hapless, since cruel death awaits this guileless youth, pure as a ruby.

And what was the cause of his death? A woman. A wonder it would be if any monster other than a woman could break a heart so saintly and chaste and pleasing to God. O my God, how many harlots are there now on the fertile earth which groans, crushed under the weight of so many she-wolves! Speak up, Togna! Speak, O power of my bottle! Tell of the traps laid by these bawds and of the thousand tricks of scabby whoredom and of the shithouses of our Venus. You will not recoil, even though you are a woman, because it is only right that you and your peers be excluded. 489

Forgive me, sirs, if the force of my anger makes me rant and unleash ugly words. Alas, the loss of such a beautiful flower is too grave. Believe in Togna and what she is about to tell you no less than if, giving responses at Mass, she pronounced "amen." Shit is not more noxious to the nose, nor is rotting flesh, than a woman adorning herself with false beauty who demands that she be called a courtesan and a lady, too. O ugly foul abomination which can never be washed away by a thousand ointments and all the soap in the world! 499

And just what do these pigs and scruffy she-wolves do? Alas, young men, I beg you, listen to your poet and to the poetess 509

atque poëtissam Tognam quae, tacta bocali
fulmine, dovinat verum drittumque prophetat.
Sunt Romae, Napoli, Florenzae suntque Venecis,
Millano, Genoae, sunt Bressae suntque Bolognae
515   agmina vaccarum tantarum quod mare totum,
flumina, stagna, lacus borsaeque sugantur ab illis,
quas divas dominas, signoras atque madonnas
turba gazana vocat, scribit chiamatque fenestris,
atque madrigalibus, seu merdagallibus, illas
520   cantant humana cum voce sonoque lautti.
Has tamen aspernunt illae sbeffantque losingas,
atque pochifaciunt versus mancante guadagno,
quo veluti mulae ostinatae infine domantur.
Simplicium sed amor iuvenum visique galanti,
525   sinceri purique agni niveaeque columbae,
has faciunt nimia smaniare libidine cagnas.
Oybo quis ascoltans non nasum stopet et aures?
Ergo manus adhibent operi cercantve caminos
huc illuc varios, nunc donis nuncve sonettis;
530   denique fundatas nequeuntes flectere turres,
ut sua cunctivorans satietur aperta vorago,
quasdam consultant putrefactas tempore vecchias,
quae tabachinandi, quae dant documenta striandi.
Hae sunt carnivorae zubianae suntque beghinae,
535   quae bigamas sese iactant terzique sorellas
ordinis et sanctas Cittas dignasve beatis
pizzocaras fusis ornari supra sepulchros.
Has ego per gesias hinc inde recurrere cerno,
candelasque brusant a tota plebe videndas,
540   atque *Paternostros* talquales ore biassant,
saepeque tellurem basant leccantque matones,
saepe manu chioccant stomachum faciuntque sonare
pectus, tamburrum don don, per forzaque striccant

Togna who, struck by lightning from the bottle, divines truth and prophesies rectitude. In Rome, Naples and Florence and in Venice, Milan and Genoa and in Brescia and Bologna too there are such great ranks of these cows that entire seas, rivers, ponds, lakes and purses are sucked dry by them. These are the females whom the mass of simpletons calls goddesses, grand dames, ladies and madonnas and writes for them and beckons them to the windows, performing madrigals for them, or rather *merda-gals*, with the human voice and the sound of the lute.

But these women spurn and mock their attentions and belittle their verses unaccompanied by money; for being obstinate as mules, this is what finally dominates them. As for the love of simple youths and handsome faces and sincere, pure lambs, white doves — all these make the bitches crazy with lust. Phew! Who on hearing this would not plug his nose and ears? So they take up the task and try various approaches, here and there, sometimes with gifts, sometimes with sonnets. When at last they cannot bend sturdy towers to satisfy their voracious chasms, they consult old women putrid with age who give them lessons on pandering and sorcery. These are carnivorous witches, beguines who claim to be bigamists and Sisters of the Third Order and St. Zitas — sanctimonious churchwomen deserving to be honored with blessed spindles on their sepulchers. 521

I myself see them running here and there through the churches; they light candles in full view of the congregation and mutter what pass as *Paternosters*. They kiss the ground over and over and lick the bricks; they strike their breasts over and over with their palms and make their bellies sound 'boom, boom' like a drum. From 538

ex oculis lachrymas, guanzis aposta tacatas.
545 Sparpagnant instar Crucifixi brachia coelo,
barbozzumque menant sdentatum more caprarum
cum grattaculos sgagnant cardosque biassant.
Nunc gesias intrant in aperto seque videndas
omnibus ostentant, nec per loca scura pregantes
550 ut candelero sua det candela lusorem.
Nunc per mille busos, tanas latebrasque remotas,
perque tenebrosos cantones, postque pileros,
subque sepolturis, hae tygres haeque mulazzae
stant quacchiae, tum cum celebrant altaria missas.
555 Et quid ibi tractant poltronae, quidve cigalant?
quid sgarbellatae, rancae putridaeque crevellant?
Seu chiachiaris cercant niveam ammacchiare putinam
seu garzoncellum dictis corrumpere purum.
'Ah mal nate puer!', dicunt, 'mal nata puella!
560 Nam quid ego de te valeo pensare quod ullam
non tibi procuras, velut est bonusanza, morosam?
Non tibi de summo tenerum balcone morosum,
castroncella, tiras in lectum tempore noctis?
Scilicet est hominum de te grandissima cura,
565 si facias illud, quod non fecisse dolebis
mille dehinc voltas et bestia matta parebis.
Haec tua quid giovat tibi fazza galanta? Quid ista
frons calcedonii? Quid ocelli corda tirantes
ut tirat in boccam donolinam rospus apertam?
570 Quidve rapraesentant dentes albedine perlas?
Quidve coralicios frustra natura labrettos
contribuit niveasque genas insemmaque rossas?
Nonne lac et vinum vermeium fazza palesat?
Quid te, sic bellum, quid te sic esse galantum
575 cernimus indarnum, frustra nulloque guadagno,
quandoquidem nec vis, nec sofris amare puellas?

their eyes they squeeze tears which are cunningly applied to their cheeks. They extend their arms to the heavens like the Crucifix and move their toothless jaws like goats when they crunch thistles and gnaw on butt-thorn. They enter a church in full view, making sure everyone sees them; not praying in dark corners, but so that their candle giveth light on a candlestick.

Yet now, these tigresses, these ugly mules lurk in a thousand 551 niches, in lairs and hiding places, in shadowy corners, behind pillars and under sepulchers, while Mass is being celebrated at the altar. And what are these tramps up to, what are they humming about? What are they scheming, these red-eyed, rancid, putrid creatures? They hope to tarnish an innocent girl with gossip or to corrupt a pure young gentleman with their talk. They say, "O unfortunate boy! Unfortunate girl! What should I think of you, if you never take a girl for yourself, as is customary? And you, you little chick, if at night from your high balcony you don't lure a tender boy into your bed? To be sure, men care for you, and you will regret it a thousand times if you don't do it and will seem to be a crazy fool.

"What good does this pretty face do you? What good is this 567 brow of milky chalcedony? What good are those little glances that tug at heart strings, just as a toad pulls a small weasel into its open mouth? What good are teeth as white as pearls? Why has nature endowed you with those pretty little coral lips and those cheeks of rose and cream in vain? Doesn't your face look like milk and vermilion wine? And you, why are you so handsome? Why do we see you look so noble to no avail, in vain, for naught, since you don't want to love a girl and can't bear to? You are handsome so that you

Bellus es ut placeas, ut ames, ut ameris, ut uras,
urarisque simul, non in fornacibus Aetnae,
sed magis in dulci, mellato, nectare pleno,
580   atque zucarato tenerinae pectore nymphae.
Visne, giovenaster, sine fructu perdere florem?
Visne malenconicum sine gioia incurrere fangum?
Spernis amare puer? vecchius, sis certus, amabis.
Spernis amare puella? fies mulazza diabli.
585   Numquid vis fieri monachus fraterque vel alter
gentibus ex illis bufalazzis atque dapochis,
quos vel sempietas, vel desperatio duxit
ad fieri fratres, monachi goffique romiti?
Numquid lassabis te, menchionella, serare
590   grossibus in muris et ad aethera summa levatis
ut velut in paia nespol marcescere possis?
Nemo super terram sanctus, stant aethere sancti;
nos carnem natura facit quo carne fruamur
atque voluptates ingordo ventre piemus.
595   Nil Deus indarnum simul et natura crearunt.
Instituuntur aves, pecudes piscesque feraeque
ut cazzatores piscatoresque fiantur,
utque gulam variis saturemus ognhora guacettis.
Plantantur boschi, surgunt de marmore rupes
600   quo naves, barcas et tecta locemus et aedes.
Lana datur pegoris, gallinis pluma vel ochis
quo molles adsint lecti caldaeque pelizzae.
Sic etiam teneras mundo fecere putinas,
quas vos, o teneri, debetis amare, putini'.
605   Talia sic istae sgualdracchae propter aquistum
per cantonadas, loca per sibi commoda, chiarlant
utque damigellos inveschient utque puellas,
ut sua bocca rosam iuvenum disverginet albam.
Quorum si nequeunt solidatam flectere mentem

may please, so that you may love, so that you may be loved, so that you ignite fires and be ignited yourself, not in Etna's furnaces, but in the sweet, honeyed, nectar-rich, sugary breast of a tender nymph. Do you wish, young buck, to lose the flower without the fruit? Do you want to end in the mud of melancholy without bliss? So you spurn love as a boy? Then mark my words, you will love as an old man. And do you spurn love as a girl? Then you will become the devil's old mule.

"Do you wish to become a monk or a friar or one of those old 585 buffaloes and bums whom stupidity or desperation drives to become brothers, monks or ridiculous hermits? Will you allow yourself, you little schmuck, to be locked up behind thick walls reaching up to the sky, so you can rot like a crab apple packed in straw?

"No one on earth is a saint; saints live in heaven. Nature made 592 us of flesh so that we could delight in flesh and could take our pleasures with a full belly. God and nature have created nothing in vain. Birds exist, and sheep, fish and wild game so that hunters and fishermen may exist, and so that we might satisfy our palates all day long with various delicacies. Woods grow and cliffs of marble rise up so that we can construct ships, boats, houses and other buildings. Sheep give us wool, and hens and geese their feathers, so that we may have soft beds and warm furs. So too, tender lasses are made on this earth whom you, O tender lads, must love."

Such things these trollops say for gain. They babble in dark 605 corners, in places suited to them, so that they can ensnare young gentlemen and girls and so that their words deflower the white rose of youth. If they cannot manage to bend solid minds, which

117

610   idque trovant ferrum quod pensavere piombum,
      ad magicas veniunt artes chiamantque diablos;
      mille modos totidemque vias retrovare docentur
      a Satana et Belial: seu tandem vincere pugnam,
      sive suis miseros furtim guastare maliis.
615   Huc illuc scurrunt, secreta indagine cercant
      grappas piccati, nascentis sputa putini,
      cervellas gatti, cor talpae, stercora vulpis,
      terram quae sepelit mortos, duo membra ranocchiae,
      matricis lectum parientis quo latet infans.
620   Sed plures alias brevitatis causa fusaras
      praetermittit, habens altros ad texere filos.
      Hoc unum restat: quod tanta est voia nocendi
      ut lac gallinae inveniant fungique semenzam,
      campanaeque sonum capiunt, ragiamen aselli,
625   calcagnum tenchae, zenzalae in pectore costas,
      urinas ochae, gruis aurem melque tavani.
         Sed iam, Togna, casam redeas tornesque camino
      te modo lassato; de vacchis satque superque.
      Me dudum a studio chiamat fantesca: 'Patrone,
630   iam depone cito pennam, calamaria, cartam;
      coena parecchiatur, frigescit calda polenta,
      compagni totam iam mangiavere salattam'.
      Iste liber vobis finit, mihi coena comenzat.

they thought made of lead but find of iron, then they turn to magical arts and call upon the devil. They are taught by Satan and Belial to find a thousand ways and means either to win the battle eventually, or to secretly ruin the poor wretches with their enchantments.

They run around helter-skelter; they furtively search for finger- 615 nails from a hanged man, a newborn infant's saliva, cats' brains, the heart of a mole, fox droppings, dirt used to bury the dead, two frog limbs, the womb of a birthing mother in which the baby is hiding. But for the sake of brevity, other follies are omitted, as there are other threads to weave. One fact remains: their desire to harm is so great that they find hen's milk and mushroom spore; they capture the sound of a bell, the bray of a donkey, the heel of a tench, the ribs in a mosquito's chest, goose urine, a crane's ear and horsefly honey.

But now, Togna, go back home and return to the hearth you 627 just left. That's enough and more than enough about cows! The serving girl calls me now from my study: "Sir, quickly now, put down your pen, inkwell and paper. Dinner is ready and the hot polenta is getting cold; your companions have already eaten all of the salad." For you, this book ends; for me, dinner begins.

Liber decimus septimus

Ibat honestatis radius per coeca ferarum
lustra Leonardus quo mors violenta vehebat;
ipse, ubi boscaias sylvarum intraverat altas,
perdidit infelix drittae signalia stradae;
5   saepe vocat socios et clamans duplicat 'oh! oh!',
quas voces spargit Fortuna ribalda per auras.
Iam super innumeris depictum floribus agrum
improvisus adest, ubi dulcis ventulus eflat.
Hic medio in campo saxi fontanula vivi
10 perstrepit undiculisque suis nova gramina bagnat.
Circumstant fontem lauri myrtique virentes,
limones, garbique simul dulcesque naranci.
Cantant per frondes oselini mille vagantes
invitantque omnes peregrinos sistere passum,
15 seu currentis aquae vitreos haurire liquores,
seu genium somni freschis gioire sub antris.
Semper ibi arrident tremulae venientibus umbrae,
quas numquam splendore suo trapassat Apollo.
Huc igitur, sembiante loci tiratus amoeni,
20 forte Leonardus declinat apudque riveram
se cristallinam vernantes buttat in herbas
seque dat in praedam, disteso corpore, somno.
Ecce sed interea venit huc formosa puella
formosumque videt solum dormire puellum.
25 Se duplici sfogare siti cupit illa repente:
venerat ut biberet, sed eam sitis altera coepit.
Haec erat et meretrix et centum plena magagnis
doctaque carminibus magicis iurare diablos,
quam rofianorum Pandragam turba vocabat.
30 Non bene bellezzam comprenderat illa baronis,

Book XVII

That beacon of honor, Leonardo, strode past dark lairs of wild an- 1
imals where violent Death was leading him. The unfortunate man
lost track of the right path as soon as he'd entered the tall trees of
the forest. He calls to his companions over and over again and cry-
ing out, repeats "O, O!" Wicked Fortune disperses his cries into
thin air.

All at once, he finds himself in a meadow adorned by innumer- 7
able flowers, where a soft breeze blows. There, in the middle of the
field, a little fountain gurgles forth from a formation of rock and
with its tiny waves bathes the new grasses. Around the fountain
stand green laurels and myrtles and lemon and orange trees which
are sweet and sour at the same time. A thousand fluttering birds
sing from the branches; they are inviting all travelers to stay a
while, either to drink the clear liqueur of flowing water or to in-
dulge their inclination to sleep in the cool grottoes. Here dappled
shadows smile continually on passers-by, for Apollo never pene-
trates them with his splendor. Leonardo strays here by chance
and then, drawn in by the sight of the idyllic spot, throws himself
on the spring grasses along the crystalline brook; with his body
stretched out he surrenders to sleep.

Behold, in the meantime a beautiful girl comes along and sees 23
the handsome boy sleeping here all alone. Suddenly she yearns to
quench two thirsts: she had come to drink, but another thirst has
set her off. For she was in fact a harlot and full of a hundred vices,
an expert in summoning devils with magic spells. The throng of
pimps called her Pandraga. She had barely grasped the beauty of

non bene leggiadram faciem bustumque tilatum,
non bene puniceos imitantia labra coralos,
praesta dedit sporco squarzandum pectus amori.
Sed quid agat nescit; timor hinc, amor increpat illinc:
35 ne rompat somnum timor admonet, unde gelatur;
ne perdat gioias amor incitat, unde brasatur.
Saepe sibi parlat: 'Sum grandis pazza daverum.
Tempus non tornat, sordis quod transvolat horis'.
Mox animum capiens, se proximat ore nec audet
40 hunc toccare tamen, sed tamquam pegola brusat.
Deficit in solo visu, dare basia vellet;
dumque propinqua movet propter basare bochinum,
se rursum retrahit metuens distollere somno.
Attrectare manu frontem magis ausa comenzat;
45 ille nihil sentit: somnum strachedo profundat.
Interdum violas decerpit vacca propinquas
inque sinum ficcat, nihil oppugnante camisa.
His ausis, tandem facta est animosa nec ultra
perdere vult horas, sic sic scampare fretosas.
50 Ad latus angelici pueri finique gioielli
se butat, inde rosam vult infangare lavacchio,
laedammoque suo purum corrumpere fontem.
Protinus insuetos Leonardus senserat actus,
discutit a somno sibi mens castissima sensus.
55 Non aliter sese de floribus ille rebalzat,
quam cum tollit humo cifilantia pectora serpens,
qui, dum flammato godit sub sole iacetque
herboso in strato, fit pressus calce romeri.
Barro super sese mirans adstare puellam,
60 ut fugit ante lupum agnus, lepus ante livrerum,
sic puer ante magam, sic angelus ante diablam.
Infuriata, magis Pandraga stigatur ab oestro
luxuriae, veluti stimulatur vacca tavano.

this hero, barely seen the handsome features and elegant torso, his lips the image of crimson coral, when in that instant she let her breast be rent by an unclean love. But she does not know what to do; fear incites her this way, love that. Fear cautions her not to interrupt his sleep, so she cools down. Love goads her not to miss these delights, so she is rekindled. She keeps telling herself, "I am really quite crazy. Time, which flies by in unhearing hours, does not turn back."

Soon, summoning her courage, she brings her mouth close to   39 him yet does not dare to touch him, although she burns like pitch. Just seeing him, she falters and wants to give him kisses, and even as she moves closer to kiss his precious mouth, she pulls herself back, afraid to disturb his sleep. With growing audacity, she begins to stroke his forehead with her hand; he feels nothing, since exhaustion plunges him into deep sleep. Meanwhile, this cow plucks nearby violets and places them on his breast, his shirt offering no resistance. At length, she becomes impassioned by this boldness and does not want to waste any more time, which is fleeing so hastily. She throws herself alongside the fine, angelic jewel of a boy; next she wants to soil this rose with smut and corrupt this pure fountain with her manure.

Leonardo had immediately sensed these unusual acts, and his   53 chaste mind shakes his senses from sleep. He shoots up out of the flowers, just like a hissing serpent, lying on a bed of grass enjoying the blazing sun, raises its breast off the ground after being stepped on by a traveler's foot. The baron, seeing a girl stand over him, flees as a lamb before a wolf, a hare before a hound; just so, the boy before the sorceress, the angel before the devil. Infuriated, Pandraga is even more roused by lascivious passion, like a cow

'Ah! demens iuvenis!', parlabat, 'mene refudas?
65 Mene, puer tenerine, fugis? Sta, siste caminum!
respice quas habeo carnes, his utere liber,
dum prohibet nemo, dum sors dat pulchra favorem'.
 Non Leonardus eam scoltat, procul immo recedit,
cui minus una placet mulier quam trenta diavoi,
70 ac genus humanum miserum putat esse per istud,
quod pro sorte mala muliebri ventre caghetur.
Ergo viam scampat, veluti scamparet ab igne,
per quem mille brusant Troiae semperque brusabunt.
Dumque fugit, secum loquitur: 'Brevis illa voluptas
75 subripit aeternum coeli decus. O Pater, o Rex,
quem trepidant victi manes, cui coelica paret
militia, unum oro: da invictum pectus et arma,
daque triumphatis meme hostibus altius ire'.
Candida virginitas quam pulchro in corpore praestat!
80 At Pandraga vocat retro: 'Me aspetta puellam!
O puer, o formose puer, me aspetta puellam!
Non ego sum tigris, non sum leonissa nec ursa,
non draco; mi pulcher Narcisse, quid ah fugis? Ecce,
te seguito atque pedes rupi seguitando tenellos!
85 Et patis indignans tenerinae damna puellae?
Dispietate nimis, saltem me cernere voias,
et me, quam fugis, aspicito si sim fugienda,
sive sit apta tibi mea frons inferre pauram.
Deh moderare fugam! deh tantum respice quae frons,
90 quae mihi sit facies, aetas iuvenilis et ardor!'
Cor Leonardus habet diamante probatius omni;
quo magis illa vocat, surdis magis audit orecchis.
Hinc tumuit sfondrata Venus, bardassa Cupido.
Ambo simul removent Pandraghae a pectore flammam,
95 crudum ubi flant odium, serpas lacerante Megaera.
Praesta diabolicum traxit Pandraga quadernum,

stung by a horsefly. "Ah foolish boy," she said, "are you rebuffing me? O tender lad, are you fleeing from me? Stop, don't go! Look what a body I have! Make free use of it while no one forbids it, while pleasing fortune grants her favor!"

Leonardo does not listen to her; instead he retreats far away, for he finds a single woman less pleasing than thirty devils and considers the human race wretched for this reason: that unfortunately it gets shat from a woman's belly. Therefore he runs away, as one would run from a fire in which a thousand Trojan whores are burning and will burn forever. As he flees, he speaks to himself, "This brief pleasure snatches away the eternal glory of Heaven: O Father, O King, whom the vanquished shades of Hell fear, whom the heavenly troops obey, I beg of you one thing: Grant me an invincible heart and arms, and grant that I may ascend on high after triumphing over my enemy." How stainless virginity shines forth in a beautiful body! 68

But Pandraga calls after him, "Wait for me — your girl! O boy, O pretty boy, wait for your girl! I am not a tiger, not a lion or a bear, not a dragon. My handsome Narcissus, ah, why do you flee? Look now, I follow you, and while following you, I have hurt my tender feet, and will you haughtily allow a tender girl to suffer? You are too cruel; give me at least a glance and see if I whom you flee am to be fled, or if my face is likely to strike terror in you. Come, slow your flight! Come now, just look at my face, look at my appearance, my youth and ardor." 80

Leonardo has a heart more tried and true than any diamond: the more she calls him, the more he listens with deaf ears. Insatiable Venus and randy Cupid seethed at this. Together the two of them take the flame from Pandraga's breast and fill it instead with cruel hate, while Megaera tears her serpent-hair. At once Pandraga takes up the diabolical book and reading it, compels fierce bears 91

quem relegens ursos constringit adire feroces
atque comandat eis iuvenem squarzare tapinum.
Non fugit ille ultra sed firmat littore plantas,
100   imbrazzat scudum, stricto se praeparat ense,
atque facit testam, disposto pectore, bestis.
Ursa prior, rabiosa magis, levat aethere saltum,
rugit et hirsuto pillamine dorsa rabuffat.
Esse comenzatam cernens Pandraga bataiam,
105   sdegnabunda illos postergat et inde recedit.
    Cingar at interea Falchettum cercat et illum
saepe vocat: cifolat, blastemat, giurat, avampat.
Baldus item, reputans quod eorum nemo retornat,
ingreditur nemus ingenti targone copertus
110   Moschinumque iubet ladris guardare galaeam;
cum quo Giubertus remanet buffonque Bocalus,
qui tres, a somno victi, ronfare comenzant.
Septem igitur socii, quo tempore stare dunatos
mysterum fuerat nec ab uno abscedere groppo,
115   ecce squadernantur, sic sorte menante tapinos.
Phoebus contradas sensim callabat in altras
antipodisque suo giornum lusore ferebat.
Luna palesabat nobis ex aequore cornos
atque impraestatos a fratre gerebat ochialos.
120   Falchettus sentit vacuos in ventre budellos,
quippe ingoiaret totum cum pelle vedellum.
Se modo compagni caprina carne replerant;
non habet ipse voiam, stomacho rodente, canendi:
poenituit cantare lupus cum ventre famato.
125   Ergo trahens gambas, mastini more cagnazzi,
quando caristiae castigat sferza vilanos,
aspicit a longe modicam de nocte lucernam;
huc mandat pedibus ventrem portare famatum,
qui iacom iacom faciunt, mancante fiato.

to come forth and commands them to dismember the wretched youth. Leonardo flees no further; instead, he plants his soles on the ground, straps on his shield and readies himself, sword in hand. And with a staunch heart, he confronts the beasts. The first bear, the most rabid, makes a leap in the air, roars and bristles the stiff hair on its back. Seeing that the battle has begun, Pandraga disdainfully turns her back and departs.

In the meantime, Cingar is looking for Falchetto and calls him 106 often; he whistles, blasphemes, swears and fumes. Baldo, realizing that his companions are not returning, also enters the forest, protected by a huge plate of armor. He orders Moschino to guard the galley from the raiders. Gilberto and the buffoon Boccalo remain with him; but overcome by sleep, the three of them start to snore. Consequently the seven friends, at a time when they should have stayed together, not one withdrawing from the knot, lo! they are separated: thus does Destiny lead these poor fellows apart.

Apollo was rapidly descending to other regions and with his 116 light was bringing day to the Antipodes. The Moon was showing her horns to us from the ocean, wearing eyeglasses borrowed from her brother. Falchetto feels the empty entrails in his belly and could have eaten an entire calf with its skin. His pals had just filled themselves with goat meat; he has no desire to sing with his stomach gnawing, just as the wolf regrets singing on an empty belly. Thus, dragging his legs like an old dog when the whip of famine is punishing the peasants, he sees a dim light far away in the night. He commands his feet to bring his starving stomach toward it; but they buckle, for he is on his last legs.

130 Illius en tandem retrovatur causa lusoris,
    namque casuzza fuit crudis fabricata quadrellis;
    hanc sine chioccatu portae, sine dire coëllum,
    intrat et intrando spadam tenet atque rodellam.
    Invenit hic hominem scherzantem circa bagassam,
135 quae brutti vecchi temnit sdegnosa carezzas.
    Bruttus erat vecchius, quo non manigoldior alter,
    tergore delphini facieque colore safrani.
    Densque suis nullus massellibus extat apiccus
    nasazzusque colat tamquam lambiccus aquarum.
140 Interdum tamen illa senem cativella zelosum
    sustinet et basos tolerat poltrona bavosos,
    mellitisque piat cornutum vacca parolis,
    illeque per nasum, bufalazzi more, tiratur.
    Haec est illa quidem Pandraga malissima, qua non
145 altera vaccarum melius tibi cornua plantat.
    Quando igitur contra Falchettum movit ochiadam,
    protinus amplexu patefacto suscipit illum,
    ut solet optatum uxor carezzare maritum.
    Pro gentilezza tanta stetit ille balordus,
150 nescit menchionus quas uset porca taiolas.
    'Da', inquit, 'damisella, precor, mangiare famato.
    Sunt modo tres giorni quod trippam gesto vodatam.
    Te rogo per si qua est bellis compassio damis,
    da mihi tochellum panis, tibi schiavus habebor'.
155 Cui vecchius respondet: 'Habes duo mille rasones;
    arreca, Pandraga, cibos, succurre tapino'.
    Illa, sochinello vestita galantiter albo,
    se movet et, gestu, risu garboque putanae
    expediens epulas, huc se travaiat et illuc.
160 Nec bene finierat mensas onerare vivandis,
    in pede stans drittus, panem Falchettus agraffat,
    quem veluti pilulam, nil dente tocante, trabuccat.

Finally he finds the source of the light — a little cottage made of   130
crude brick. Without knocking on the door, without saying a
word, he enters and while entering grips his sword and round
shield. Here he finds a man sporting with a strumpet who dis-
dainfully spurns the ugly old man's caresses. The old man was re-
ally ugly; no one could be more repugnant. His back is hunched
like a porpoise and his skin is the color of saffron. Not one tooth
still hangs in his jaws and his big nose drips like an alembic. Now
and then, the hussy tolerates the jealous old man; the slut endures
his drooling kisses, and this cow baits the cuckold with honeyed
words; she leads him by the nose like a buffalo. In fact, this is
wicked Pandraga herself; no other cow plants horns on your head
better than she. Now as soon as her gaze lands on Falchetto, she
welcomes him at once with a wide hug, as a wife does when em-
bracing her longed-for husband. Falchetto was stunned by such
kindness; the rube is ignorant of the traps this sow uses. "I beg
you, mademoiselle," he says, "Give a famished man something to
eat. For three days now I have borne empty entrails. I beseech you,
if beautiful ladies have any compassion: give me a crust of bread,
and I will be your slave."

The old man responds, "You are so right! Pandraga, bring food,   155
succor the poor fellow." She, in her elegant white skirt, gets mov-
ing, and with the gestures, grace and smile of a whore, busies her-
self here and there preparing the dishes. She had scarcely finished
laying the table with food when Falchetto, still standing upright,
grabs bread and swallows it like a pill; it doesn't touch a single

Post illum binos alios, tres inde nec umquam
tregua fuit donec septem periere bufetti.

165 Non tamen hunc anchum stimulabat voia bibendi;
sed facit assaltum, celeri cum dente, cadino
quo, velut argentum spezzatum, millia vallis
Iosaphat ossa trovat non aspernanda famato:
colla gallinarum, gambas gelidosque magones.

170 Omnia Falchettus, servando silentia, mangiat.
Denique, non pochis saturato ventre boconis,
accipit ambabus manibus, sine forbere musum,
bottazzum ingentem quamvis sibi zaina paretur.
Ac miser, absorbens opiati pocula vini,

175 protinus ad terram somno devolvitur alto
distesusque iacet, tamquam si mortuus esset;
perque caput diversa volant pensiria noctis.
Tangarus ille senex, Beltrazzus nomine, ridet
ridendoque aperit sdentatas ore ganassas,

180 namque facit festam, vecchius malus iste Susannae,
sic trapolare suae peregrinos arte putanae.
Ipse quidem plus mattus erat quam trenta cavalli,
filius invidiae galloque gelosior omni,
tam incarognatus, tam presus amore bagassae

185 quod solo parebat eam trangluttere sguardo.
Si quandoque super guanzas frontemque puellae
musca reposabat nec scazzabatur ab illa,
ibat adulterium metuens cito pellere muscam;
dumque fugabat eam, dicebat: 'Guarda diavol!

190 mascula num musca est? an foemina? porca ribalda,
tu mihi cornarum, dubito, cimmeria ponis'.
Talia parlando, currebat protinus atque
moschettam brancare manu pulicemque studebat,
cercabatque inter gambas signalia maschi.

195 Ipsemet ergo ligat Falchetti membra cadenis

tooth. After this, he eats two more rolls, then three; there was no cease-fire until seven of them had perished. And yet the desire to drink still wasn't goading him; instead, he launches an assault with rapid teeth on a serving platter on which he finds thousands of bones from the valley of Jehosaphat, gleaming like pieces of silver, not to be turned down by a starveling: hens' necks, legs and cold gizzards. Falchetto eats all of it in silence. Finally, his belly satisfied by these considerable mouthfuls, with both hands (without wiping his muzzle) he grabs a huge keg, although he is offered a goblet. Then the poor thing, guzzling a drink of opiated wine, suddenly rolls to the floor in a deep sleep and lies there stretched out as though he were dead, and various night thoughts fly through his head.

The boorish old man, whose name is Beltrazzo, laughs and 178 while laughing, exposes the toothless jaws in his mouth, for this wicked elder of Susanna revels to entrap travelers thus with the whoring arts. He was without a doubt crazier than thirty horses, the offspring of Envy, more jealous than any cock and so bedazzled and so caught up in love for his strumpet that he seemed to swallow her with his gaze alone. If a fly alighted on the girl's cheeks or forehead and she did not chase it off, Beltrazzo, in his fear of adultery, would quickly drive the fly away and while chasing it, would say, "Look here, you devil! Is this a male fly? Or female? Bawdy sow, I think you are giving me a crest of horns." Talking like this, he would run fast and try to capture the fly in his hand and would search between its legs for signs of masculinity. For that reason he binds Falchetto's members all by himself; he does

nec vult officium per damam tale fiatur
ne dormentato stupretur adultera moecho.
Illa, diu sciocchi mattezzis usa mariti,
ridet et hoc risu dat pazzo intendere vecchio
200   in puteo lunam stellamque negare Dianam.
Beltrazzus ghignat pariter ghignante puella.
Quisquis troppus amat, cum ridet amasia ridet,
nec non, cum plorat, plorat menchioniter idem.
Tollitur ergo lapis, sub quo latet atra caverna,
205   in quam Falchettum longo cum fune calarunt;
inde, superposito saxo, bocca illa seratur
carceris; et numquam quisquis chiavatur in illo
hinc se posse putat dissolvi et cernere giornum.
Haec ea dum tali rerum vertigine passant,
210   scilicet ut vivus soteretur Falco, Lonardus
mortuus a nullis sit humatus fraude puellae,
hunc repetamus ovemque ursis buttemus edendam.
    Ursa, diabolicae rabiis uscita Megaerae,
valde travaiabat, maschio adiutante, Lonardum.
215   Ille, pudicitiae fidus defensor et acer,
mille daret vitas, si mille teneret, ob illam.
Cum leva obiectat scutum dextraque frequentes
stoccatas vibrat, nunc bassus nuncve levatus,
nunc retro nunc ante, pedes agitando legeros.
220   Ursa ferox et dira magis se cazzat inantum,
quae male formatos ursattos liquerat antro.
Cui punctam in ventrem torquet Leonardus, at illa
destra sinistrorsum balzat scansando repente,
inde super gambas derdanas ritta levatur
225   ongiatasque manus aperit panditque bocazzam.
Barro sed in medium mostazzi, dando roversum,
colsit eam tandem fecitque tomare stravoltam,
dentatamque simul spicavit ab ore ganassam.

not want such a job to be done by his dame, lest the sleeping fornicator rape the adulteress. Long accustomed to the antics of her crazy husband, Pandraga laughs, and her laughter makes the crazy old man think that the moon is in the well and that the star of Diana is about to drown. Beltrazzo grins together with the grinning girl. Whoever loves too much laughs when his beloved laughs, and when she cries, idiotically, he too cries.

After this, they lift up a rock under which a dark cavern is hidden, and they lower Falchetto into it with a long rope. Once the stone is put back, the mouth of the prison is sealed, and whoever gets locked in there thinks he can never be freed to see the light of day. While these things happen in such a flurry on account of this girl's treachery, namely, that Falchetto is buried alive and Leonardo, dead, lies unburied, let us return to the latter, and cast out this sheep to be eaten by bears. 204

With the help of her mate, the she-bear that was summoned by the wrath of Megaera is overpowering Leonardo. This faithful and ardent defender of chastity would give up a thousand lives for virtue, if he had a thousand. With his left arm he blocks with the shield and with his right he makes continual thrusts both high and low, shifting his agile feet forward and back. The ferocious mother bear rushes forward, all the more enraged since she has left her newborn cubs in their den. Leonardo aims a thrust at her belly, but dexterously she jumps, dodging rapidly to the left. Then she rears up on her hind legs, spreads her clawed hands and throws open her maw. But the hero lands a backhand in the middle of her snout that strikes her and makes her fall flat on her back and at the same time dislodges a toothy jaw from her mouth. 213

Ursus adiratur, sociam videt esse feritam,
230 sanguine quae largo flores malnettat et herbas;
unde Leonardo stizza maiore sotintrat
cumque manu dextra zampatam vibrat apertam,
quae, quantam gremiit faldam, de corpore squarzat
nudatumque forat duris ongionibus inguen.
235 Vulnere non tamen hoc persona gaiarda paventat.
Ursam, quae suberat rursus, fendente salutat,
sed levior gatto saltum facit illa dabandam
ipseque, dum colpus vadit fallitus, arenam
percutit ad manicum ficcans sabionibus ensem.
240 Hinc piat ursus atrox tempus, rapit unguibus ansas
elmetti, tum valde tirat iuvenemque fogabit,
ni celer huic casu provisio debita fiat.
Ergo valorosus, dum forte tiratur ab illo,
pungit abassato ferro panzamque trapassat,
245 et tamen absque elmo, nuda cervice, remansit.
Proh dii! Quando suum videt ursa morire maritum,
vivere dispresiat; nunc dextra nuncve sinistra,
nunc vicina fremens, nunc se lontana retirans,
tam celeri balzat studio quod apena videtur.
250 Est verum quod nulla suis in dentibus est spes,
stringere qui nequeunt, una mancante ganassa;
sola stat in duris sibi confidentia branchis;
cum branchis agit illa operam, furit illa per ongias.
At tribus e bandis iam versat barro cruorem,
255 nec mundi contornus habet cor firmius illo.
Se videt extinctum, nihil est tamen ille minutus
excellenti animo, nec mens sibi conscia recti
formidare potest niveam deponere vitam.
Semper adocchiabat nudam fera bestia testam,
260 huc acuit griffas, huc zampas drizzat aguzzas,
hanc tamen et scuto defendit et ense guererus.

The male bear is incensed when it sees that its mate is   229
wounded and that she stains the flowers and grasses with copious
blood. So it attacks Leonardo with heightened rage. With its right
paw it delivers a flat blow that rips from his body all the armor it
strikes and tears into the exposed groin with its big claws. Yet this
brave individual is not frightened by such a wound. The she-bear
had gotten back up, and he greets her with a downward blow, but
she jumps aside lighter than a cat. Missing his target, Leonardo
strikes the ground with his sword, driving it in up to the hilt. The
ferocious male bear seizes the moment and grabs the straps of Le-
onardo's helmet with its claws. Pulling hard, it will strangle the
youth unless a quick remedy is found for his plight. So while the
valiant man is being pulled hard by the bear, he thrusts his sword
underneath and pierces its belly. And yet he was left without his
helmet, his neck exposed.

O Gods! When the she-bear sees her mate die, she scorns liv-   246
ing and rages now from the right, now from the left, now rushing
forward, now pulling back. She moves rapidly with such zeal that
you can scarcely see her. It is true that she cannot rely on her
teeth, which cannot clench, for she is missing a jaw, and must rely
on her hard talons. She does the job with her talons; she rages
with her claws. By now our hero is losing blood from three
wounds, although no one in the world has a stauncher heart than
he. He sees that he is finished, but his excellent courage does not
diminish in the least. A mind conscious of its own rectitude is not
afraid to lay down its spotless life. The wild beast keeps eyeing Le-
onardo's bare head; here she aims her claws and here directs her
sharp mitts. However, the warrior wards her off with his shield
and sword.

Denique non patitur tam longius ire bataiam.
Proicit a brazzo targam manibusque duabus
incipit et colpos illi sine fine ramazzat.
265 Se movet ursa levis, nunc huc nunc emicat illuc
mandrittosque omnes paladini reddit inanes;
quem dum destituit sanguis, sed maxima crescit
et magis atque magis virtus animosa guerero,
spada, gaiardiam non sueta capescere tantam,
270 heu peccat medioque operae fit iniqua patrono.
Frangitur ad manicum, lamma cascante tereno,
infelixque puer dextram sibi sentit inermem.
Ambo statim currunt contra, se amplexibus ambo
fortibus abrazzant; premit hic, premit illa fiancos,
275 ut non dura magis stringantur ferra tenais.
Tandem affogantur pariter pariterque cadentes,
sic sic complexi, fato periere medemo.
Non tamen ad vitam seguitata medesima sors est:
ille volat coelo, iacet ista cadaver inane.
280 Aspicis, alme Deus, pro te quamque impia quamque
fert indigna puer tuus iste simillimus agno?
Iste tuus puer innocuus, puer iste fidelis,
aspicis ut pro te tam dira morte necetur?
Nonne hic expulsor Veneris columenque pudoris,
285 quo datur ad vitae, via, lux aditusque coronam?
Siccine mortales tanto nos munere fraudas?
Felices oh vitae hominum, felicia secla,
lapsa quibus coelo est animi praestantia tanti.
Cingar at interea sylvas peragraverat omnes
290 Falchettumque suum iam rauca voce cridabat.
Denique speluncam sancti trovat ille romiti
portellamque casae bussans petit: 'Heus, quis aloggiat?'
Ad quem vox intus sic rettulit: 'Ave Maria'.
Cui Cingar: 'Nobis semper laudata sit illa'.

At last he cannot suffer the battle to continue any longer. He 262
strips the plate from his arm and begins with both hands to de-
liver endless blows. The bear moves quickly; she darts here and
there and renders the paladin's forward thrusts futile. Although
his blood is running out, the warrior's spirited courage grows
stronger and stronger. But alas! His sword, unused to bearing
such bravery, fails and in the midst of these feats becomes its mas-
ter's foe. It breaks at the hilt; the blade falls to the ground, and the
unfortunate youth feels his right hand disarmed. Right at this mo-
ment the two combatants run toward each other; they embrace
each other in a strong hug: he presses her flanks, she presses his;
the hard iron of pliers does not grip more tightly. In the end they
are strangled together, and falling together thus embraced, they
perish by the same fate. However, in the afterlife a different des-
tiny pursues them each: he rises to heaven; she remains a lifeless
cadaver.

Do you see, gracious Lord, how many wicked things, how 280
many indignities your boy suffers, just like a lamb, this innocent
and faithful boy? Do you see how he dies such an awful death for
your sake? Isn't he the adversary of Venus, the pillar of decency
who shows us the path, the light, the way to the crown of life? Do
you thus defraud us mortals of such a gift? Happy are the lives of
men, happy the age, in which the greatness of such a soul has de-
scended from heaven.

In the meantime, Cingar had scoured the entire woods, calling 289
for his Falchetto with a voice already hoarse. At last he finds the
cave of a holy hermit, and knocking on the little door of the hut,
he asks, "Hello, who lives here?" A voice within responds, "Ave
Maria." To which Cingar rejoins, "May she always be praised."

295 Quo dicto, angustae crepuit portella celettae
canutusque senex, cui pectus barba covertat,
costumatus adest et quid vult ore domandat.
Cingar ait: 'Venerande pater, deh dicite, quaeso
(si mea verba tamen non dant fastidia vobis):
300 vidistine hominem medium mediumve catellum?
Quaero, per hunc boscum vidisti forsitan illum?'
Subridens senior dixit: 'Mi splendide Cingar,
quamvis non video te nunc (quia lumine privor),
te tamen interius cerno teneoque palesum.
305 Quaerere Falchettum frustra, tibi dico, laboras'.
'Me miserum!' clamat Cingar; 'quid, mi pater, inquis?
Mortuus an fors est? Morerer, si morte perisset'.
'Non', respondet ei vecchius; 'non ille morivit,
nam Beltrazzus eum tenet atro in carcere vinctum,
310 non certe mortum sed valde morire bramosum,
cui meretrix Pandraga dedit mala pocula somni.
Ille catenatus centri manet intra budellas;
non hunc inde trabis, nisi porcam fune ligabis,
nec meretricaeae gabberis fraude losinghae.
315 Illa spudat blando tantam sermone carognam
ut nimis incautos ad guisam pestis amorbat'.
Cingar ait: 'Deh quaeso, pater, monstrate caminum,
qui me scanfardam subito deducat ad istam.
Se teneat, si me scapolat, scapolasse diablum.
320 Verum, sancte pater, per barbam perque capuzzum,
per si qua est charitas hoc in gestamine sportae,
oro mihi vestrum voiatis dicere nomen.
Namque pur est grandis facenda stuporque mirabel
vos me, vosque meum socium, vosque omnia nosse.
325 Numquid vos Balaam? aut Balaae bona mula prophetae
vivit adhuc? vestraeque godit praesepia stallae?'

After this exchange, the small door of the narrow little cell creaks open and an elderly white-haired man appears, whose beard covers his chest, and politely asks what he wants. Cingar replies, "Venerable father, tell me, pray (if my words do not disturb you), have you seen someone who is half-man and half-hound? I am looking for him in these woods. Have you by chance seen him?"

Smiling, the elder says, "My wonderful Cingar, although I cannot see you now (for I am deprived of sight), I can still see you within and keep you in my mind. You struggle in vain, I tell you, to find Falchetto." 302

"O woe is me!" cries Cingar, "What are you saying, father? Is he perhaps dead? I will die if he has perished in death." 306

"No," the old man answers him, "Falchetto has not died, for Beltrazzo is keeping him chained in a dark prison; no, he is not dead, but yearning deeply to die. The harlot Pandraga gave him an evil sleeping potion. He remains chained up in the bowels of the earth. You will not be able to pull him out unless you bind that sow with a cord and do not get tricked by the enticements of that harlot. She spews forth such pestilence with her flattering words that she sickens unsuspecting men like the plague." 308

Cingar says, "O, I pray you, father, show me the way that will bring me immediately to this strumpet. If she escapes from me, she can claim to have escaped the devil. Yet now, I pray you, holy father, by your beard and cowl, if there is any charity in the purse you wear, please be so kind as to tell me your name. For it is indeed a great mystery, a stupendous marvel that you know me, this friend of mine and all these things. Are you perhaps Balaam? Is the prophet Balaam's good mule still living? Does he enjoy the manger in your stall?" 317

Respondet senior: 'Nostrum si nomen habere
vis ad noticiam, quod saxis dormit in istis,
huc prius ad meme velis deducere Baldum.
330 Inde tibi Baldoque meum volo pandere nomen'
Obstupuit Cingar vecchium cognoscere fratres
appelletque suo Baldum de nomine, seque
Falchettumque suum; magnum putat esse prophetam,
ad quem vult penitus compagnos ducere secum.
335 Ergo cuncta illi promittit et inde caminum
brancat eum proprium, sibi quem sant'alma palesat,
atque ad speluncam meretricis denique venit.
    Candentes lunae paulatim aurora colores
scurabat clarumque diem portabat Eous.
340 Cingaris adventum quando Pandraga spiavit,
protinus incontra saltaverat extra cavernam
fronteque rididula et brazzis currebat apertis.
Cingar, amorosos quando guardavit ocellos,
fat ter signa crucis, velut illa diabolus esset,
345 mancavitque pocum, tam pocum, tamque pochinum
quin trapolaretur ceu vulpes vecchia taiolis.
Sed cum Falchetti grandem rammentat amorem,
praestiter indretum scura se fronte retirat
et mostazzonem talem cito porrigit illi,
350 atque manu replicans roversa vibrat un altrum
quod duo denticuli cascarunt extra ganassas.
In terram cadit illa ruens squarzatque capillos;
arrabiata cridat stridosque ad sydera mandat
lamentisque petras montagnae spezzat aguzzis.
355 Ecce, senex crevatus, adest Beltrazzus: ad illum
currebat strepitum, si currere dicitur ulla
testudo, aut portans limaca in tergore stanzam.
De passu in passu tussit mollatque corezzam,
sbolsegat atque sonat magno cum murmure cornum.

The elder replies, "If you want information about my name, 327
which lies dormant in these rocks, please lead Baldo here to me
first. Then I will reveal my name to you and to Baldo." Cingar is
amazed that the old man knows his brothers, that he calls Baldo
by name and himself and Falchetto, too. He thinks that the man
must be a great prophet, and he eagerly wants to lead his compan-
ions to him. He promises to do these things and then sets out on
the path (which the holy man shows him) and comes at last to the
harlot's cave.

Little by little dawn was dimming the bright colors of the 338
moon; Eos was bringing in the clear day. As soon as Pandraga
spied Cingar approaching, she quickly sprang out from the cavern
and ran toward him with her arms open and her face smiling.
When Cingar looked at her amorous eyes, he made the sign of the
cross three times as though she were the devil; for he comes close,
very close, very close indeed to being entrapped by this vixen's
snares. But when he recalls Falchetto's great love, he immediately
pulls back with a darkened brow and quickly gives her such a wal-
lop on her muzzle and another with the back of his hand that two
small teeth fall from her jaw. She falls headlong to the ground and
rips out her hair. She bellows in anger and sends her screams up
to the stars and with her sharp laments shatters mountain cliffs.

And here comes decrepit old Beltrazzo. He came running 355
at that sound, if you can say that a tortoise runs or a snail carry-
ing its house on its back. With each step he coughs and breaks

360 Proh Satan! Ut vidit sub Cingare stare morosam,
quam male nunc pugnis nunc calcibus ille burattat,
atque ad misuram carbonum donat acerbas
Pandraghae sorbas asinamque melonibus ornat,
irruit atque hosti currit, ceu porcus, adossum,

365 dentibus et strictis, quorum pars maxima desunt,
vult ingiottitum tribus in bocconibus illum.
Cingar at in medium stomachi dat protinus urtam;
illeque, cascando, maroëllas rupit abassum,
saltaruntque foras lergnae, schioppante braghero,

370 et pover antiquus levasusum denique fecit.
Interea, similis rabiosae foemina cagnae,
se levat et raspis, ut gatta, lavorat aguzzis
Cingaris in fazzam et morsu talvolta canesco
multaque barbozzo streppat pilamina barbae.

375 Ille tamen miseram per trezzas corripit atque
perque vias fango perque invia plena rovidis
trat retro, veluti trat ladrum coda cavalli.
Prosequitur Beltrazzus eum: 'Manigolde!', cridabat,
'Ah! ladrazze, meam sic fers lacerare putinam?

380 Mille tuo nascant cagasangui ventre, gaioffe.
O mea mi, Pandraga, decus! tibi dura cruentant
saxa caput tenerum spinaeque insemma ribaldae?
Nec te tutari? nec te defendere possim?
He heu quanta meum desleguat doia magonem!

385 Candidulas rumpit cardorum copia guanzas,
blandidulos guastat campus lapidosus ocellos.
Sta, beccone, latro! Sta, furcifer! Oyme tapinus!
Oyade sum mortus, spazzatus et absque socorso.
Sum straccus, ruit ille latro, volat ille diavol.

390 Crudeles spinae, crudelia saxa, rubetis
siccine de tepido tam bellae sanguine damae?'
Talia dum creppat, plus avantum ire vetatur,

wind, wheezes and blows his horn with much fanfare. O the devil! When he sees his beloved mate under Cingar—who thrashes Pandraga first with his fists, then with his feet, then gives her a full measure of hard fruits and decks out the she-ass with melons—Beltrazzo races and rushes against the enemy like a wild boar with bared teeth, which for the most part are missing, and wants him swallowed in three bites. But Cingar promptly gives him a blow to the middle of his belly. As he falls, he ruptures his hemorrhoids, and when his truss splits, his hernias pop out and the poor old man finally runs away.

Meanwhile, the woman gets up like a rabid bitch and goes to 371 work on Cingar's face like a cat with her sharp nails and sometimes with dog-bites and tears a lot of hair from the beard on his chin. But he grabs the miserable woman by her tresses and drags her behind him through the mud in the roads and through the brambles alongside the road, just as the tail of a horse drags a thief. Beltrazzo follows him. "Rapscallion!" he yells. "O dirty thief, are you carrying away my dear girl to mangle her like this? May a thousand bloody stools begin in your belly, you scoundrel! O my dear Pandraga, my glory! Are those hard stones and wicked thorns bloodying your tender head? Can't I protect you and defend you? O! Ah! How much pain demolishes my chest! All these nettles gouge your sweet milky cheeks, and the rocky terrain disturbs your flirtatious eyes. Stop, you capon! You thief! You delinquent! O poor me! O good God, I'm dead, I'm ruined and without relief. I'm exhausted, but that thief rushes, that devil flies. Cruel thorns, cruel rocks, do you turn red with the warm blood of such a beautiful woman?" While he sounds off thus, he can go no

nam parit aegrotas aetas vecchiarda pedanas,
strassinatque pedes retro vecchiezza cavalli.
395 Se trigat ergo sedensque gravi spiramine boffat;
et velut antiquus seu bos, seu buffalus, ansat.
    Ecce sed interea strani persona gigantis
huc improvistus sylvarum sbuccat ab umbris,
qui nunc oymisonos Pandraghae senserat alte
400 rimbombare guaios, nec rem tamen ille sciebat.
Non erat in toto plus mordax bestia mundo
plusque asino similis; scopertis namque pudendis
ibat, iensque nigro siccabat semine flores.
Hanc monstri spetiem veteres dixere Moloccum,
405 quod rofianorum nec non puzzore luparum
miscetur: fitque atra simul corruptio grossi
aëris unde animal tale hoc deforme cavatur.
Est homini similis quantum quod drittus et alto
incedit vultu, sed totus bestia restum.
410 Dentiger ut porcus, cagnazzi more pilosus,
moreque serpentum vomitat simul ore venenum
flammatasque simul schizzat de retro corezas.
Illico Beltrazzus, visto de longe Molocco,
plus bove leggerus se drizzat apena cridatque:
415 'Day day! Para, pia! Fer aiutum, chare Molocche!
Chare Molocche, tuam tibi raccomando signoram;
ecce, cavester eam poverinam quomodo trattat!
quomodo malmenat, strassinat, quomodo pistat!'
Talibus admonitus, properat slanza ille foiada,
420 pestiferumque spudat patefacto gutture flatum,
post quem abbrasatam spruzzat culamine loffam.
Cingar, amorbatus nimio puzzore, bagassam
deserit et, tracto brando, petit alta gigantis
moenia; nec poterit cum scalis iungere testam,
425 sed tenet ad bassum: basso truncone taiato

further. Old age makes movement painful and in old age, a horse drags its legs behind. He pauses, therefore, and as he sits, he heaves with heavy panting and wheezes like an ancient ox or buffalo.

In the meantime, the figure of a strange giant emerges suddenly   397
from the shadows of the forest. He had heard just now Pandraga's woe-is-me shrieks echoing loudly; but he did not know what was happening. In the entire world there was not a beast more mordacious or more like an ass, for he walked around with his genitalia exposed and, while walking, withered the flowers with his black semen. The ancient ones called this sort of monster Molocco, who is concocted from the stench of pimps and whores; a black corruption forms in the dense air, from which such a deformed creature is fashioned. He is like a man in that he walks upright with his face raised, but the rest of him is all beast. He is fanged like a boar, hairy like a mangy dog, and like a dragon vomits venom from his mouth while he squirts flame-farts from behind.

The moment Beltrazzo sees Molocco from afar, he stands up   413
more nimbly than an ox and yells, "Come on, come on, stop him, grab him! Help me, dear Molocco! Dear Molocco, I urge you to aid your lady friend. Look how that gallows bird is treating the poor thing, how he mauls and pounds her!"

Hearing these exhortations, the noodle-gobbler rushes forth.   419
From his gaping gullet he spews forth a pestiferous breath and then spurts a fiery wind from his butt. Cingar is sickened by the strong stench and releases the trollop, and with his sword drawn he assails the high walls of the giant. Not even with a ladder could he reach the creature's head, so he stays low. Cut at the base, a tree

arbor it ad terram; bassis dat vulnera gambis.
At male provistus, dum punctam concite laxat,
tanta venenati sbrofantur flumina sputi
quod cadit attonita Cingar cum mente balordus,
430 atque velut mortus sese distendit in herbam.
Prestiter accurrit brazzis mastinus apertis,
impositoque levi conatu Cingare spallis,
ambulat ut sic sic tepidettum sicve recentem
deglutiat digitosque untos pinguedine lecchet.
435 Ipse sed interea Beltrazzus abrazzat amicam,
hancve quasi mortam plorat ploransque carezzat;
basat ei boccam, frontem, basatque biancum
pectus, et annorum centum puer omnia tentat,
quae tentare senex annorum trenta puderet.
440 Cingar fratantum de peso fertur in alto
tergore Molocchi, ceu fertur vulpe galina.
Nil sentit, quoniam tenet illum forza veneni.
Desdottum certe buttavit alhora tapinus,
namque desesettum buttaverat ante Moloccus,
445 dispositus mangiare tribus bocconibus illum,
ut quoque mangiarat, nec non mangiare solebat,
tot quot vacca suis captat Pandraga taiolis.
Illa gigantescas humana carne budellas
replebat, faciens ventronem saepe satollum
450 atque adeo plenum quod avanzum carnis et ossa
mille lupos ac mille canes corvosque cibabat.
Sed Molocchus eam numquam satiare valebat
carne sua propria, quae nocte dieque dabatur
ante lupam rabidam et nullo cozzone domandam,
455 quae stracca interdum, numquam satiata manebat.
Ergo desdottum Cingar buttavit alhora
sive gigantazzo pransus seu coena fuisset,
ni tunc, in puncto stesso spacioque medemo,

falls to the ground, so he wounds the lower legs. But he is caught off-guard while excitedly landing a jab; Molocco spews forth such rivers of poisonous spittle that Cingar falls stunned with his mind befuddled and sprawls on the grass as though dead. At once the beast runs up with arms open and, after placing Cingar effortlessly on his shoulder, ambles off so that he can devour him just like this, warm and fresh, and lick his fingers dripping with grease.

Meanwhile, Beltrazzo embraces his lady friend. He weeps for her as though she were dead and while weeping, caresses her. He kisses her mouth and forehead and kisses her white breast. This hundred-year-old boy tries everything that an old man of thirty would be ashamed to try. For the moment Cingar is being carried on Molocco's high back, as a hen is carried by a fox. He cannot feel anything because he is under the effect of the venom. At that moment the poor man must have drawn twenty-one, for Molocco has already shown twenty and was about to eat him up in three swallows, just as he has already eaten, and is used to eating, everything which that cow Pandraga captures with her snares. She always filled his gigantic entrails with human flesh, often making his stomach so sated and indeed so full that the leftover meat and bones would feed a thousand wolves and a thousand dogs and crows. And yet Molocco was never able to satisfy her with his own flesh, which night and day he put before this ravenous wolf, who, untamed by any tamer, was occasionally weary but never remained satisfied.

So, yes, Cingar drew twenty-one this time, or else he would have furnished dinner or supper for that nasty giant, if right now,

435

456

porrexisset ei subitum Centaurus aiuttum.

460 Est Centaurus homo medius mediusque cavallus,
qualis ab Ancroia paladina Ignarus et acer
Tarrassus fuit ammazzatus, teste Beroso.
Ipse gerit binos dardos targamque copertam
desuper azzalo et fodratam pelle draconis.

465 Ferrea dependet gallono mazza sinistro,
unde vocabatur Virmazzus nomine ficto.
Quando is Molocchum vidit, quem tempore multo
noverat et voltas cum secum mille provarat:
'Pone, lupazze, agnum!', cridat; 'volpazza, polastrum!

470 Non, renegate, tui cibus est ventraminis! Ola
cui dico, poltrone? Nimis coena illa stimanda est'
Sic dicens, torquet dardum vibrante lacerto,
cuius in hirsutum ficcatur puncta galonem.
Molocchus grandem smagonat vulnere cridum,

475 Cingareque abiecto terrae, stizzosus avampat
Centaurumque suis bellandi scontrat usanzis:
ignitam faculam culamine vibrat aperto,
nec puzzolentos curat spudare macagnos,
namque sciebat eos Centaurum laedere pocum;

480 qui sibi tum nasum, tum polsos, tempora corque
unguento ungebat multa virtute probato,
quod sibi donarat medicae doctissimus artis
Serraffus, qui gesta vigil paladinica curat.
Ecce autem dardum vasto rumore secundum

485 fulminat, idque volans sonat ipsa tonitrua coeli
per mediumque bigol post tergum prompsit acumen.
Ille ruit moriens veluti si quando vilanus
praticus officio agricolae contemplat in agro
stare pioppazzam vecchiam segetique nocivam:

490 hanc ad radices assaltat vulnere ferri
taiandoque facit volitare per aëra scheggias;

in that very moment, a centaur had not brought him help. This centaur is half-man, half-horse, like Ignarus and the fierce Tarrassus, who was killed by the paladin queen Ancroia (as stated by Berossus). He is carrying two javelins and an armored plate clad in steel and lined with dragon hide. From his left flank hangs an iron mace, for which he is called by the nickname Virmace. When the centaur sees Molocco, whom he had known for a long time and had fought a thousand times, he cries, "Put down that lamb, nasty wolf; that chick, nasty fox. You recreant, this is not food for your belly. Hey! I'm talking to you, knave! — this dinner is too refined for you." Saying this, he hurls a javelin, propelling it with the might of his arm, and the point pierces the giant's furry flank. The wounded Molocco lets forth a great cry; then having thrown Cingar to the ground, he flares up angrily and confronts the centaur with his usual methods of combat: he shoots a fireball from his open butt, but doesn't bother to spew his smelly gobs. For he knew they did little harm to the centaur, who covered himself — his nose, his wrists, his temples and his chest — with a strong unguent of proven efficacy, given to him by Seraphus, who was highly skilled in the medical arts and watched over the paladins' exploits.

And now with a tremendous noise he hurls his second javelin. 484 As it flies by, it sounds just like thunder from the sky and its tip passes through Molocco's bellybutton and comes out his back. He plummets dying, just as when a peasant, skilled in a farmer's tasks, contemplates a large old poplar standing in his field, harmful to his crops; he attacks its roots with ax-blows and with his chopping sends woodchips fluttering through the air. At last, the nuisance

illa cadit tandem stirpata disutilis arbor,
nec dapoca novas iam strangulat amplius herbas.
Bestia sic nostra haec, turpi concepta ledamo,
495 cascat morta solo, moriensque culamine bilzat
ut bilzare solent brodam chrysteria ballae,
Centauroque pilos barbae scintilla strinavit.
Nondum Cingar erat de somno redditus ad se;
hunc bonus imponit spallis Centaurus equinis
500 et, iactos relegens dardos, hinc cedit onustus
fontanamque aliquam nunc huc nunc quaeritat illuc,
ut bagnatus aqua tornet smemoratus acasam.
Pervenit ad rivum tandem campumque virentem,
infelix ubi stat mortus Leonardus et ursi.
505 Huc volgens oculos guardat relevatque, stupentum
more, supercilios rugaeque in fronte rapantur.
Formosum iuvenem squarzato gutture mirat,
qui quoque tunc ursam mortam brazzatus habebat.
Cingara deponit spallis prope littora fontis,
510 formam garzonis pulchri contemplat et annos;
cumque diu stupuit lagrymasque gittavit ab occhis,
hunc levat amplexu bramans donare sepulchro;
namque recordatur tumulum vidisse vetustum,
quem cercans peragrat sylvas portatque Lonardum.
515 Interea Cingar paulatim corde resentit,
ut solet a somno cum quis non illico surgit.
In pede saltatus, coram putat esse Molocchum,
dumque samitarram pugno se pensat habere,
hunc vibrat ventumque ferit pazzusque videtur.
520 Mox sibi medesmo rediens, circumspicit et nil
Molocchi prope stare videt nilque ultra puellae,
nil quoque Beltrazzi, neque scit cognoscere quare.
Dumque petit fontem, Leonardi retrovat ensem
atque duos mortos apud ensem conspicit ursos.

tree falls uprooted, and now the worthless thing no longer strangles the young plants. Just so, this beast of ours, conceived in filthy manure, falls dead on the ground and in dying, squirts a broth from his butt, like the squirt of an enema bulb, and a spark singed the hair of the centaur's beard.

Cingar had not yet regained consciousness. The good centaur 498 places him on his equine shoulders and, collecting the javelins he had thrown, starts out with this load. He looks here and there for a spring where the stunned Cingar can be bathed with water and brought back to his senses. Finally he reaches the stream and green meadow where the bears and the unfortunate Leonardo lie dead. Casting his gaze around, he looks bewildered and arches his eyebrows and wrinkles are creased on his brow. He beholds the handsome youth with a slashed throat who was still hugging the dead bear. He lowers Cingar from his shoulders near the edge of the spring and contemplates the beauty and years of the lovely young man. And after standing dazed for a long time and spilling tears from his eyes, he lifts him in an embrace, wishing to place him in a sepulcher, for he remembers having seen an old tomb. Searching for it, he carries Leonardo and traverses the woods.

Meanwhile, Cingar is returning to his senses little by little, as 515 someone does from sleep when he does not arise immediately. Jumping to his feet, he still thinks he's facing Molocco, and believes he still has his scimitar in hand, so he strikes and slashes at the wind and appears crazy. Soon, coming back to himself, he looks around and sees that Molocco is no longer there, and neither is the girl or Beltrazzo either, but he doesn't know how to explain this. While he is approaching the spring, he discovers Leonardo's

525 Protinus expavit, putat illum, non putat illum
    esse Leonardi stoccum; dumque omnia cercat,
    ecce videt carmen sic summo in fonte tacatum:
        'Quanta pudicitiae sit laus, hic morte probatur.
    Maluit occidi quam se violare Lonardus'.
530 Carminis authorem nymphae dixere Seraphum,
    qui modo se Phoebi, modo se Zoroastis alumnum
    ostentat famaeque ornat splendore barones;
    et memoravi illum, et mox memorabo frequenter
    tamquam praesagum rerum geniique ministrum.
535 Iam iam non dubitat, iam iam cognoscit apertam
    Lonardi mortem Cingar culpatque bagassam,
    namque bagassarum scit mores Cingar et artes.
    'Proh Deus!' exclamat, 'periit Leonardus! iniqua
    sic Fortuna tulit? morietur Baldus ob iram,
540 ob coleramque sui, puero quem portat, amoris.
    Heu quid agam tapinellus ego? quo me ultra reducam?
    O sfortunati socii, tot casibus acti!
    Exanimusne iacet Leonardus? Forte ferarum
    ventribus esca fuit? Non saltem cernere mortum
545 possumus? Obscuro Falchettus carcere stentat?
    Baldum non video? Moschinus longe moratur?
    Siccine dant forzas scanfardae sydera tantas?
    siccine propitiant cagnazzae fata putanae?
    Non tibi parco umquam! Non, non! Disponor ad omnes
550 iamdudum prigolos; mortem non estimo ravam'.
        Sic fatus Cingar, quamprimum corripit ensem,
    sylvas inde subit foltas leporumque coattos;
    de passu in passu meditat chieditque Lonardum,
    donec terribilem nemora inter frondea sensit
555 rumorem, quo terra tremit sonitantque riverae.
    Intrepidus cupiensque mori, quo murmur habetur
    portat iter speratque illic acatare ribaldam.

sword and next to it he sees two dead bears. Right away he is fear-
ful: first he thinks it is Leonardo's blade, then he thinks it isn't.
While he observes the scene, he sees a poem hanging over the
spring, which reads: "How praiseworthy chastity is, is proven here
by death. Leonardo preferred to be killed rather than violated."
The nymphs said that the author of this poem was Seraphus, who
variously claims to be a student of Apollo or of Zoroaster and
who honors heroes with fame and glory. I have already mentioned
him, and soon I will mention him frequently, both as a foreseer of
events and a guardian angel.

By now Cingar has no doubt, by now he truly knows that Leo-   535
nardo is dead, and he blames that harlot, for Cingar is familiar
with the practices and abilities of harlots. "Good God!" he ex-
claims, "Has Leonardo perished? And cruel Fortune allows this?
Baldo will die from anger and fury for the love he bears the boy.
What am I to do, poor wretch that I am? Where will I end up? O
my poor companions, driven by such calamities! Does Leonardo
lie lifeless? Did he really serve as fodder for the bellies of wild
beasts? Are we not even able to view him dead? Falchetto suffers
in a dark cavern? I cannot see Baldo? Moschino lingers far away?
And the stars grant such powers to a tart? Are the Fates thus pro-
pitious to a whoring bitch? I will never forgive you! No, no! I am
already prepared for every danger; I count death less than a tur-
nip."

So saying, Cingar quickly grabs his sword and makes his way   551
through the thick woods and rabbit warrens. With each step, he
thinks of Leonardo and calls for him, until he hears a terrible
sound in the leafy forest that makes the earth tremble and the
shores reverberate. Intrepid, seeking death, he directs his path to

Sed videt ecce duos tandem pugnare barones:
alter erat Baldus, summa canegiatus in ira,
560   qui modo Centaurum incontrans Leonarda ferentem,
crediderat tanti mazzatorem esse baronis;
unde smisurato vibrabat robore spadam
menteque ficcarat Centaurum opponere morti,
mox super occisum semet scannare Lonardum;
565   nam centum mortes nihil amplius aestimat haeros,
postquam compagni privatur imagine tanti.
Centaurus multo Baldum sustentat afanno,
quem sibi mazzatas cechi dare sentit et orbi.
Torserat indarnum dardos frustraque menabat
570   bastonem ferri; tamen alto corde repugnat.
Non procul in terra Leonardi busta iacebant,
quem quoties guardat lacrymoso lumine Baldus,
maiore in furia Centauro currit adossum
crudelesque illi rotolat sine fine stocadas.
575   Cingar adest plorans; quo viso Baldus, ab imo
pectore singultans, cordis superante dolore,
non manet at, sensus velut urget passio nostros,
tramortitus abit terrae sentitque nientum.
Quo casu horrenti, Centaurus constitit in se
580   atque suprasedit, reputans non esse belopram
(ut generosus erat) si lapsum vulnerat hostem.
Cingar ibi ad Superos lacrymantia lumina drizzat
atque cridat: 'Vos, o Superi, pietate carentes,
sufficiat vobis nostrum rapuisse zoiellum,
585   nostram virtutis perlam morumque tesoros!
Vultis quin etiam validum prosternere Baldum?
Si sic saevitis, si sic crudescere vultis,
eya age! quid statis? quid adhuc indusia tardat?
Me quoque Falchettumque meum sustollite mundo.

the source of the noise, hoping to catch that bawd. But then he sees instead two barons fighting. One is Baldo, infuriated and at the height of anger. He had just met the centaur carrying Leonardo and believed him to be the assassin of this great baron. So he wielded his sword with boundless strength and held fixed in his mind that he would fight the centaur to death, then slit his own throat over the slain Leonardo. For this hero, after being deprived of the sight of such a companion, values even a hundred deaths as nothing.

The centaur resists Baldo with great effort; he feels he's receiving blows from a wild man or a blind man. He had hurled his javelins uselessly and was wielding his iron mace to no avail, yet he still resisted with great courage. Not far off the remains of Leonardo lay on the ground, and every time Baldo looks that way with a tearful eye, he attacks the centaur with increased fury and whirls vicious thrusts at him over and over again. Cingar approaches in tears, and when Baldo sees him, he sobs from deep in his chest, overcome by the anguish in his heart. He cannot continue. Instead, as when suffering overwhelms our senses, he passes out on the ground unconscious and feels nothing. 567

At this dreadful event, the centaur stops and holds back (for he was kind-hearted), deeming it discourteous to wound a fallen enemy. And Cingar raises his tear-stained eyes to the gods and cries, "O gods in heaven, you are pitiless. Suffice it that you snatched away our jewel, our pearl of virtue, our treasure of decency! Do you want to bring down the worthy Baldo as well? If you are so fierce, if you choose to become so savage, then go ahead! Why stop here! What's holding you back? Take me from this world and 579

590 Quae mora? nunc rabies satietur denique vestra'.
Sic ait, et voltus Centauro turbidus inquit:
'Quae, Centaure, tibi fama est, quae gloria tanta
occidisse agnum, quo non mansuetior alter?'
Centaurus respondet: 'Ego? Te fallis, amice.

595 Non mea sed sola est Pandraghae culpa ribaldae.
Sicut apud fontem poteris cognoscere verum,
ad quem bagnandum cum te, barrone, tulissem
ut sbroffatus aqua posses cazzare venenum,
hunc reperi iuvenem, crudeli caede necatum;

600 quem quoque dum tumulo saxi tumulare parecchio,
affuit hic novus Orlandus, novus affuit Hector,
immo nec humanas tales volo dicere possas'.
Cingar suspesus paulum stetit, inde favellat:
'Quae, Centaure, tuas me sors buttavit in ongias?'

605 Tunc Virmazzus ei narravit cuncta per orden;
Cingar in amplexum fraterno currit afettu,
tercentumque illi basos in pectore stampat.
'Per te', inquit, 'mihi vita datur? Licet illa noiosa
posthac semper erit semperque bramosa resolvi

610 ossibus his, postquam tanto viduamur amico.
Iste valorosus, quem iecit doia tereno,
est Baldus; Baldi scio te sensisse prodezzam,
quam sensere poli terraeque maresque profundi.
Huic similem cunctos non est reperire per orbes,

615 dico gaiardiae similem saviique governi,
quem tibi germanum reddam fidumque sodalem.
At precor interea, per amoris vincla novelli,
fac mihi servitium neque me domanda vilanum'.
Cui Centaurus: 'Ego faciam quaecumque iubebor.

620 Manda, comanda mihi; dictum factumque putato'.
Cingar ait: 'Subito Pandraghae quaere capannam,
ne nostras scelerata manus evadere possit.

Falchetto too. Why wait? Let your rabid fury be slaked at last!" Cingar says this and with a scowl turns to the Centaur and asks, "What fame do you acquire, centaur, what great glory for having slain this lamb, the most gentle of all?"

The centaur responds, "I, slay *him*? You are wrong, friend. The 594 blame is not mine, but only the wicked Pandraga's. You will be able to learn the truth at the spring where I took you to bathe, O baron, so that sprinkled with water you could wash off the venom. Here I found this youth killed in violent death. While I was preparing to bury him in a stone tomb, this new Orlando arrived, this new Hector arrived whose strength I cannot even call human."

Cingar is still for a moment and after that exclaims, "What fate 603 has thrown me into your clutches?" Virmace then told him everything in order. Cingar hastens to embrace him with brotherly love and stamps three hundred kisses on his breast. "It is to you that I owe my life? Even though after this, my life will always be onerous and eager to be released from these bones, now that I am widowed of such a friend. This brave man who lies on the ground from grief is Baldo. I know that you have heard of the prowess of Baldo, which has been felt by the skies, the earth and the deep seas. His equal is not to be found anywhere in the universe, that is, his equal in bravery and in wise governance. I will restore him to you as a brother, as a dear friend. But for now I pray you, bound by this new affection, do me a favor, and do not call me a coward."

The centaur replies, "I will do whatever I am bid. Order, com- 619 mand me; whatever you say, consider it done."

Cingar says, "Look for Pandraga's hut right away, so that the 621 villain cannot slip through our grasp. Hold her until I come, and I will come right away."

Hanc teneas donec veniam; veniamque debottum'.
'Sic faciam', respondet ei; tunc illico sylvas
625   per densas strepitat cursu ramosque fracassat.
Cingar it ad Baldum, bassa qui voce gemebat.
Cingare mox viso, sic fletum sustulit altum:
'O Leonarde puer, sine te quid vivere prodest?
O Leonarde puer, sine me quid morte teneris?
630   O Leonarde, tuae sum solum causa ruinae!
O Leonarde, meae tua mors est causa gravezzae!
O Leonarde, tibi nimis improba fata procellant!
O Leonarde, mihi vita est odiosa tapino!
Sed quae dextra dedit tibi nunc saevissima mortem,
635   mortem non mancum mihi det saevissima dextra'.
    In pede saltatus, sic Baldus dixit, et ensem
perstringens manibus, Centaurum credit adesse
mandrittumque tirat (velut ingens forza doloris
insanire facit), quo antiquam tempore querzam
640   atque repugnantem valido per saecula borrae,
ad sabiam voltat, mozzo troncone, stravoltam.
Cingar eum, tamquam delapsum cardine mentis,
confortat parlans: 'Erat, o mi Balde, Lonardus
vassallus mortis, sic nos, sic ipse vel ille,
645   tertius et quartus, Martinus, barba Philippus.
Si lachrymae possunt huic toltam rendere vitam,
spargamus lachrymas, horsu, nosmetque pichemus.
Non tamen ignoras quod quidquid nascitur orbi
tam remanet vivum quam gonfius ille sonaius,
650   ille sonaius aquae, qui fitur tempore pioggiae:
hic cito comparet, citius disparet in unum
buf baf, et quod erat quidquam nil illico restat.
Non tibi bombardae pulver mage praestus avampat
quam volat ad mortem quidquid tutavia creatur.
655   Mors nulli parcit, nullum fert illa ritegnum,

"I will do this," he answers, and at once he crashes through the   624
dense forest at a run, breaking branches.

Cingar goes to Baldo, who was moaning in a low voice. As soon   626
as he has seen Cingar, he utters this profound lament: "O my
young Leonardo, without you, what good is living? O my young
Leonardo, why are you held in death without me? O Leonardo, I
alone am the cause of your ruin! O Leonardo, your death is the
cause of my affliction! O Leonardo, the all-too-relentless fates
buffet you! O Leonardo, life is hateful to me, I am forlorn! But if a
savage right hand caused your death, let the same savage right
hand cause my death as well."

Jumping to his feet, Baldo speaks thus, and gripping his sword   636
with his hands, thinking the centaur is there, he delivers a fore-
hand blow (the tremendous force of grief makes him crazy) which
cuts through the trunk of an ancient oak that has resisted the
mighty Boreas for centuries and topples it to the ground. Cingar
comforts him as one whose mind has come unhinged, saying, "O,
my dear Baldo, Leonardo was subject to death, as are we all — this
one and that, and a third and a fourth, a Martin and an uncle
Philip. If tears can bring back the life that was taken from him,
then let us cry, or better, let us hang ourselves! But you are aware
that whatever is born on this earth remains alive as long as a swol-
len bellflower — a bell formed by water when it rains, that appears
suddenly and even more suddenly disappears in a poof-paff! And
where there was something, now abruptly there is nothing. All of
creation continually races toward death as fast as a cannon's gun-

respectum nec habet temeraria personarum.
Omnes affattum proscribit, prendit, amazzat;
papas, caesareos, reges aliosque tyrannos,
furfantes, sguataros, sbirros aliasque canaias
660 mors ad sbarraiam menat, deque omnibus herbis
fat fascem, nec stanca piat quandoque ripossum.
Ne, mi Balde, fleas mortos, nam, teste Cocono,
fletur id indarnum quod scantonare nequimus.
Debemur morti nos nostraque, pulsat et aequo
665 mors pede nobilium turres inopumque botegas.
Non hac perpetuis in terra ducimur annis.
Patria, quae nostra est, in coelo constitit alto.
Non haec, quas mittunt lachrymas tua lumina, possunt
esse Leonardo gratae; non ista, gementi
670 pectore ducta, placent animo suspiria laeto.
Foemineum est plorare, virum decet esse virilem.
Mors haec vita fuit, numquam moritura, Lonardo,
qui, ne virginei tenebraret lumina solis,
coelestem accepit vitam mortemque peremit.
675 Sufficit has paucas tibi promulgasse rasones.
Non Centaurus eum, non, o mi Balde, puellum,
ut pensas, mazzavit: habes hoc crimine tortum'.
    His dictis, Cingar seriem narravit ad unguem
passatae impresae, tam quod Pandraga ribalda est,
680 quam quod Centaurus vir optimus ac bonamicus.
Baldus humi ficcos oculos tenet instar aheni
marmoreique viri, qui stat stabitque milannos
vel super altarum gesiae vel supra pilastrum.
Cingaris eloquium distesis brancat orecchis,
685 una parolarum non perditur onza suarum.
Mitior imprimis apparet, at inde solutis
ex improviso lachrymis, non fronte dolorem
dissimulare potest; nam quae frons schietta, lealis

powder takes flame. Death spares no one, death shows no restraint; it is brazen and respects no one. It arrests, condemns and kills absolutely everybody: Popes, emperors, kings and other tyrants, vagrants, scullery boys, cops and other riff-raff. Death brings them to ruin and harvests one and all alike and never gets tired and takes a nap from time to time.

"Do not weep for the dead, my dear Baldo, for, as Cocaio attests, we weep in vain over what we cannot avoid. We are bound to die, we and our possessions, and death's foot knocks impartially at the towers of nobles and at the huts of paupers. We do not last for eternity here on this earth. Our real homeland lies in the high heavens. These tears that your eyes are releasing cannot be welcome to Leonardo, nor can these sighs, drawn from a sobbing breast, be pleasing to a blessed soul. Crying is for women; men need to be virile. This death has become for Leonardo a life that will never die. Lest the light of his virgin sun be cast in darkness, he has achieved celestial life and cheated death. Let it suffice to have brought these few thoughts before you. The centaur did not, my dear Baldo, did not kill this boy as you believe; you are wrong about this crime." 662

After saying this, Cingar recounted the entire series of past events in detail, including how Pandraga was as wicked as the centaur was a wonderful man and a good friend. Baldo keeps his eyes fixed on the ground and remains like a man of bronze or marble that stands and will continue to stand a thousand years, either above the altar of a church or on a pedestal. He seizes on Cingar's speech with wide-open ears and does not lose a dram of his words. At first Baldo seems calmer and then suddenly dissolves into tears. His countenance cannot hide his pain, for what candid face does not display the heart's thoughts faithfully sculpted? His voice, which at first had been held back by a sense of shame, now erupts 678

non portat sculpita sibi pensiria cordis?

690 Vox, quae tenta prius fuerat cagione pudoris,
sic tandem erumpit, sic tandem erupta comenzat:
'Cor, qui curarum factum es mihi vena ferarum,
sis lachrymarum etiam, donec miserabile corpus
in lachrymas abeat totum! Cor perdite, plange!

695 Plange, nec a planctu per te cessetur amaro!
Quid maris interea confinia, quidve colonnas
quaerimus extremas terrarum? Vivimus ergo?
Vivimus an frustra suscepto vulnere mortis?
Spes mea dempta mihi, mea lux, mea gloria. Plange,

700 plange, nec a lachrymis tua, cor, precordia cessent!
O male felices socii, num vivere prodest,
si mors solamen vitae tulit improba nostrae?
O decus, o requies mea, mi Leonarde, vocanti
non mihi respondes? Sum Baldus, sum tuus ille,

705 sum tuus ille miser miserabilis, arca dolorum,
poenarum Phlegethon, lachrymarum flumen et aequor.
Proh Superi! Qualem voluistis perdere! qualem,
fata, trucidastis! Dolor! heu dolor! heu dolor! heu dol . . . '.
'Or' tacuit Baldus; sed iam nudaverat ensem

710 in se conversum, ferro iam pectus adhaeret.
Corripit hunc humeris Cingar spadamque repente
divellit manibus. Pavido cadit ille tremore,
fronsque repentinam contraxit pallida formam
mortis, at in somno mens consolata quievit.

Liber decimus octavus

Alta soporifero mens Baldi aspersa liquore
iverat in partes, quo se sua candida stella,

at last and, having at last erupted, begins, "My heart, you who have become a stream of fierce pains, become a stream of tears as well, until my miserable body disappears entirely in tears. O wasted heart, weep, weep, and do not cease from bitter weeping! Why should we go on seeking the ends of the ocean, why the furthest reaches of the earth? Are we really living? Or are we living in vain after receiving a mortal wound? My hope has been taken away, my light, my glory. Weep, weep, my heart, and do not let your heartfelt prayers cease from tears!

"O unhappy companions, is life worth living if vile death has 701 taken the consolation from our lives? O virtue, O my tranquility, my Leonardo, won't you answer my calls? It is I, Baldo, your friend, the miserable wretch, the coffer of suffering, the Phlegethon of pain, the river and sea of tears. Gods above, what sort of man have you seen fit to destroy? What sort of man have you cut down, O Fates? Such Anguish, O the anguish, the anguish, the ang. . ."

Baldo cannot finish the word, having already unsheathed his 709 sword and turned it against himself—his breast already touches the blade. Cingar grabs him by the shoulders and instantly strips the steel from his hands. Baldo fell with a frightening shudder, and his pale face tightened in the sudden look of death, yet his mind found rest in soothing sleep.

Book XVIII

Anointed with sleeping drops, Baldo's lofty spirit went off to re- 1 gions where it was led by its shining star, in conjunction with

auricomo coniuncta Iovi Venerique benignae,
traxit et in Fati secreto sistitit horto.

5   Hic sua docta fuit sors; inter caetera, quantum
futile sit studium titubanti haerere columnae,
scilicet in rebus quidquam sperare caducis.
Cingaris in gremio testam tenet ille chinatam;
amboque sub quercu, vigil unus, somnius alter.

10   Interea Centaurus, habens pro Cingare voiam
ad centum prigolos mortis deponere vitam,
it quacchius quacchius Pandraghae ad tecta ribaldae.
Quove potest picolo strepitu premit ille pedattas
ne sentire queat fugiatque cativa ruinam,

15   quam sibi cognoscit Leonardi morte parari.
Vidimus interdum toto cum corpore gattam
ire chinam, seu post macchiam, seu iuxta muraiam,
quae, dudum aguaitans oculis cativella tiratis,
servat osellinum per opacos ludere ramos.

20   Sic Centaurus abit pian pianum per nemus illud,
dormentemque trovans (oh gran ventura!) ribaldam,
dormentem, dico, Beltrazzum iuxta zelosum,
hanc citus aggriffat, portans levitate medema
qua portare lupum infreddatam cernimus ocham.

25   Sed quia sacratum fert iugiter illa quadernum
attritas inter mammas frustasque Moloccho,
id quoque Centaurus liquido cognorat avantum,
cercat eum, sotosora manu versando pelizzam.
Repperit altandem secreta in parte latentem;

30   quo tolto, magis illa cridat, magis illa cagnezat.
Cui Virmazzus iter vocis per guttura stoppat
viluppo herbarum ne chiamet forte diablos,
qui veniant infretta suae succurrere vacchae.
Se iam spazzatam, se iam tenet esse brusatam.

35   Beltrazzus sequitat, desperat, trat via bragas

golden-haired Jupiter and compassionate Venus, and came to rest in the secret garden of Destiny. Here his fate was made known to him: among other things, how futile it is to lean on a shaky column, which is to say, to place one's hope in transient matters. He rests his bowed head on Cingar's lap, the two of them seated under an oak, one vigilant, the other sleeping.

Meanwhile, the centaur (who is willing to lay down his life for Cingar in a hundred mortal dangers) goes very, very quietly toward the abode of the depraved Pandraga. He treads with the least possible noise, so that she cannot hear him and escape the nasty end which she knows awaits her on account of Leonardo's death. We've all seen at times a cat crouch with her whole body, either behind a bush or along a wall, as she wickedly waits in patient ambush with a fixed gaze and observes a little bird playing in the shady branches. Just so the centaur moves silently through the forest and (O great fortune!) finds the bawd asleep—asleep, I say, alongside the jealous Beltrazzo. The centaur quickly grabs her and carries her off with the same ease with which we see a fox carry off a stiff goose. But since she keeps her magic book between her breasts, withered and consumed by Molocco—this too the centaur knew clearly beforehand—he searches for it, moving his hand all around under her fur cloak. He finds it at last hidden in a secret place, and after he has taken it, Pandraga cries and howls all the more. So Virmace stifles her voice in her throat with a clump of grass, so that she cannot call the devils, who would quickly come to succor their cow. She considers herself already done for, already burned up. Beltrazzo follows in despair, rending his clothes, scratching his face and tearing the hair from his beard.

sgrafegnatque visum barbaeque pilamina streppat.
Senserat hunc pridem rumorem Cingar et ipsam
testam paulatim Baldi declinat in herbas.
Se levat in pedibus, trat spadam, mirat atornum,

40　expectat quaenam sit tanti causa fracassi.
En Centaurus adest, Pandragam portat adossum,
ut portat quaiam griffis sparaverus aguzzis
gallinamque velut fert vulpes extra polarum.
Cingar eum scontrat, cui cennat adire pianum

45　ne tantus rumor de Baldo somnia cazzet.
At Pandraga cridat mandatque ad sydera stridos,
unde, illi faciens boccam vi Cingar apertam,
sbadacchium ficcat, quo posse cridare vetatur.
Hanc ergo (ut nata est) dispoiant corpore nudo,

50　quam frustare volunt totamque scopare palesam
ut merito a cunctis puttana scovata cridetur.
Istud ad officium peragendum boia niunus
tunc aderat, nisi sors guidasset alhora Bocalum.
Ecce Bocalus adest, faciet galantiter artem.

55　Cingar ait: 'Centaure, precor (nisi forte molestus
sim nimis) ad corpus redeas exangue Lonardi,
quod potes in notam Pandraghae ferre masonem;
hic vestiga locos omnes sub, subter et infra,
presonemque trova sub saxi mole seratam.

60　Hanc aperi officio clavis, si clavis habetur;
ast ubi clavis abest, spezzari porta tenetur.
Rumpe fores ac tira foras de compede magnum
magnanimumque virum, Falchettum nomine dictum,
cuius forma tuam similat; pars ultima tantum

65　pars magni canis est, non, ut tua, groppa cavalli.
Inde Leonardum medesmo in carcere serva
ne retrovent guastentque lupi tam nobile bustum'.

Cingar had already heard the noise and gently sets Baldo's head   37
down on the grass. He stands up, draws his sword, looks around
and waits for whatever is causing this great ruckus. Behold, the
centaur arrives carrying Pandraga, as a hawk carries a quail in its
sharp talons or as a fox takes a hen from the coop. Cingar meets
him and motions to him to approach quietly, lest the great noise
drive off Baldo's dreams. But Pandraga shrieks and sends her cries
up to the stars, so that Cingar forces open her mouth and sticks in
a gag to stop her cries. Then they strip her body as naked as she
was born; they want to whip her and take a broom to her in public
so that she can justly be known to all as a caned whore. There
would have been no executioner present to carry out this office, if
chance had not delivered Boccalo right then. Here comes Boccalo;
he will do the job nicely.

Cingar says, "Centaur, I beg you, if I'm not asking too much,   55
return to the lifeless Leonardo and take him to Pandraga's house,
which you know. There, search everywhere — under, over and
within — and find the prison locked beneath a massive stone.
Open it by using the key, if you have the key. But if not, the door
will have to be broken. Break down the door and free from his
chains that great magnanimous man called Falchetto. His form is
similar to yours, except that his lower part is that of a big dog, not
a horse's back like yours. Next, secure Leonardo in that same
prison, so that wolves do not find him and ravage his noble
corpse."

Excipit hoc iussum Virmazzus; et inde recessus,
quo Leonardus erat sistit brazzisque levatum
70   portat, amorevolis bagnans humoribus occhios.
At Boccalus, ubi Centaurus abiverat illinc,
colligit ex aspris bronchis spinisque flagellum,
inde, sibi faciens digitis sine veste lacertos,
incipit in colera gabiazzam battere frustam,
75   ut nova peccatum purget penitentia vechium.
Qualis villanus, cui forza liquore botazzi
creverat, humectat palmas utrasque spudazzo,
bacchettasque menat crebro paiamque flagellat,
sic Boccalus equam Satanasi, fasce virentum
80   spinarum chioccat totoque labore sigillat.
Illa dolorisonas calcat sub pectore stridas,
sbadacchiata quidem prohibetur fortius oymos
vociferare suos, quapropter maxima doia est.
En rivat ad tempus multo Beltrazzus afanno,
85   quem procul ut vidit, Cingar de sede levavit
et male cappatum post vecchium currere coepit.
'Oh!', ait, 'ad tempus venistis, domine pater.
Quo sic in frettam pueritia vestra caminat?
Expectate, habeo plures ad dicere causas,
90   inque vicem nostros poterimus rendere contos'.
Cingar hoc improperans sequitur, miser ille scapinat.
Cernebas daynum tardam seguitare galanam,
quem tribus in saltis per collum prestus achiappat.
Ille pregat veniam, surdas dat Cingar orecchias,
95   sed secum tutavia menat retinendo cavezzum.
'Hunc', inquit, 'Boccale, tibi comendo zoiellum.
Nil fit in officio boiae magis utile quam si
puttanis humeros, vecchis culamina frustes.
Vecchius, amoroso qui damas corde vaghezat,
100 non aliam meritat castigam quam scoriadae;

Virmace accepts this order and then withdraws, stopping where   68
Leonardo lay, and lifting him up, carries him in his arms, his eyes
awash in loving tears. Then, once the centaur had left them,
Boccalo assembles a whip from sharp branches and thorns. Next,
freeing his arms from their sleeves with his fingers, he starts to
beat the shabby hussy so furiously that the new penance would
purge her old sins. Just as a peasant whose strength grows with li-
quor from a bottle wets both palms with a gob of spit and wields a
flurry of club-blows and whips the straw, just so Boccalo strikes
this Satan's mare with a bundle of green briars and brands her
with all his might. She suppresses the pain-wracked shrieks in her
breast, for being gagged, she's hindered from voicing her laments
any louder, so that her agony is extreme.

Just in time, Beltrazzo arrives gasping; as soon as Cingar saw   84
him in the distance, he got up from his seat and began to run after
the ill-fated old man. "O Lord father!" Cingar calls, "You have ar-
rived in time! Where is your boyhood rushing in such haste?
Wait, I have a lot to tell you, and we can settle our scores with one
another."

Cingar gives chase, insulting him; the wretch flees. You might   91
picture a deer chasing a slow tortoise: in three jumps he quickly
grabs him by the collar. Beltrazzo pleads for mercy, but Cingar
turns a deaf ear. Instead, he drags him along, holding him by the
scruff of the neck, saying, "Here, Boccalo, I recommend this jewel
to you. Among the duties of an executioner, there is none more
useful than whipping the back of a whore and the buttocks of old
men. An old man who courts women with a love-struck heart

namque inamoratus vecchius pariterque zelosus
est puer annorum centum dignusque cavallo
alzari et nudas chioccari supra culattas.
Ecce tuam, Boccale, scolam novus iste scolaris
105 ingreditur: tener est, praestissimus omnia discet.
Hunc per passivos doceas componere normas.
Non est discordans tam discordantia, quam non
hic puer ad sonitum scoriatae praestus acordet'.
Suscipit hanc curam Boccalus fitque pedantus,
110 fitque reformator, pedagogus, fitque magister.
Sbarbatum vecchium rimbambitumque gaioffum
dottorare parat, si qua est dottrina stafili,
si qua sculazzatis castigat mamma fiolum.
    Tolserat interea Centaurus ab ore cavernae
115 saxum ingens Falcumque foras cum fune tirarat.
Hic, exangue videns Leonardi forte cadaver,
flevit et, intesa mortis cagione, momordit
stizzosus digitum: caveat Pandraga ruinam,
partitas siquidem multas scontare tenetur.
120 Ergo, hic deposito Leonardi corpore, donec
congrua tanthomini fiat iactura sepulchri,
discedunt pariter veniuntque trovare sodales.
Paulatim Phoebus descendit ab aethere scalam
tresque appena horae giorni morientis avanzant.
125 Perveniunt tandem qua parte Bocalus afannat
se circum vaccam, dum pistat dumque repistat.
At Cingar, mirans Falchettum accedere, currit
obvius, abrazzant, stringunt lachrimantque Lonardum.
Post haec Falchettus, Boccalo dante flagellum,
130 incipit oh quantis, oh qualibus ille deratis
singentos numerare pilos relevareque crustas!
Nata Satanaso, mortem Pandraga vocabat;
verum sdegnatur portare diavolus illam.

deserves no other punishment than flogging. For an old man in love and jealous besides is a hundred-year-old boy who deserves to be set on a horse and pummeled on his bare butt. Here he is, Boccalo, this new student is entering your school; he is impressionable and will learn everything very quickly. You will teach him the rules for composing in the passive. There is no discord so discordant that this boy will not soon learn to be in accord with the sound of the whip." Boccalo assumes this duty, and becomes a pedant, a reformer, a pedagogue and a teacher. He prepares to 'indoctrinate' this beardless old man, this doddering scoundrel, if there is any doctrine in a strap or in the spankings with which a mother punishes her child.

In the meantime, the centaur had removed the immense stone 114 from the mouth of the cave and had pulled Falchetto out with a rope. Upon seeing Leonardo's lifeless corpse, Falchetto weeps, and after learning the cause of death, he bites his finger in anger: Let Pandraga beware of her own end, since she has many debts to pay. So then, depositing Leonardo's body here until a resting place worthy of such a man might be arranged, they depart together to go find their friends. Little by little, Apollo descends the stairway of heaven and now scarcely three hours remain in the dying day. They come finally to the place where Boccalo is working hard on that cow from all sides, as he beats her and beats her again. When Cingar sees Falchetto approach, he runs to meet him; they embrace, hug and weep for Leonardo. After this Boccalo gives Falchetto the whip and he begins — oh, with such lashings! — to pay out stripes one by one and raise welts. Satan-born Pandraga is begging for death, but the devil refuses to take her away.

Baldus adhuc mentem per vera insogna volutat.

135 En subito comparet homo sylvaticus illuc
extraque boscaiam saltat: cui barba diabli
sanguinolenta colat musumque imbrattat edacem,
perque pedes portat Giubertum more capretti,
aut cum fert ocham mercato vecchia ligatam.

140 'En', Centaurus ait, 'Furaboscus; hic iste Molocchi
est frater; proh dii! quae fex! quam sporcus amorbat!'
Vix ea complerat Virmazzus et arma piarat,
ecce incalzabat Moschinus iugiter illum
infestosque strales soriano scoccat ab arcu.

145 'Ah renegate!', cridat, 'deponas, ola, catellum!
Non est ille tuo pastus pro dente, lupazze!'
Sic clamans, tutavia facit strissare sagittas,
quarum nona caput per utramque trapassat orecchiam.
In pede Giubertus saltat, ruinante giganto,

150 ringratiatque Deum magnam scampasse ruinam.
Baldus eo instanti, discusso corpore sognis,
se levat. Accurrit Cingar, Falchettus et omnes
de se ghirlandam Baldo fecere loquenti.
'Oh!', dixit, 'quantum Deus est laudandus, amici,

155 cui plusquam humanos innotuit esse dolores,
quos modo pro dira Leonardi morte ferebam.
Hunc mihi per somnum demisit ab axe superno
oh quam forma alium, gestu fatuque Lonardum!
"Quid fles, Balde?" inquit; "quid fles temetque dolentas?

160 Te fortasse piget meme bona summa tenere?
Ah cohibe tepidos, quos fundis inaniter, imbres.
Non id flere decet per quod gaudere tenemur.
Summa bataiandi palma est superare seipsum.
Ista meum studuit meretrix violare pudorem,

165 fecissetque suum, me non obstante, volerum,
ni subito praesens mihi gratia summa fuisset,

Baldo's mind is still wandering through credible dreams. All of a sudden a wild man appears and jumps out of the woods; his bloody devil's beard drips, sullying his gluttonous muzzle. He carries Gilberto by the feet like a kid goat or as an old woman carries a trussed-up goose to market. "This," says the centaur, "is Furabosco, Molocco's brother. By the gods, what scum! How the foul thing reeks."   134

Virmace had scarcely finished saying this and grabbed his weapons when Moschino was already pursuing Furabosco, firing deadly arrows at him from his brindled bow. "You miscreant!" he yells. "Let that pup go! He is not fodder for your teeth, vicious beast!" While shouting thus, he continues to make his arrows hiss; the ninth one passes through Furabosco's head from one ear to the other. As the giant falls, Gilberto jumps to his feet and thanks God he has escaped the mighty fall.   142

In the same instant, Baldo shakes the dreams from his body and gets up. Cingar, Falchetto and the others come running and form a ring around Baldo as he speaks: "O how much God deserves our praise, my friends, for He knew that the anguish I was suffering right then for the cruel death of Leonardo had become more than a human could bear. And from the heavenly pole, He sent me a Leonardo quite different in features, gestures and speech. 'Why do you weep, Baldo?' the apparition asked. 'Why do you weep and cause yourself pain? Does it perhaps grieve you that I am in the arms of supreme goodness? Come now, restrain these warm showers that you pour out in vain. It is not right to weep for that which should cause us to rejoice. The greatest victory in battle is to conquer oneself. That prostitute tried to violate my chastity, and she would have gotten her wish, despite my resistance, if grace had not come promptly from above, after which she could sooner have leveled mountains than have tempted me even slightly to   151

qua magis in planum montagnas illa chinasset
quam neque tantillum coitu me inflectere lordo.
Sordidius nihil est quam se meschiare putanis."
170   Sic fatus, brancare manum mihi visus, in altas
coelorum gioias per totum vexit Olympum,
meque videre cosas fecit, quas dicere possem
si centum linguas vocemque azzalis haberem.
Ultima quae dixit tandem mihi verba fuerunt:
175   "Quaere tuum patrem, non longius ille moratur,
quem nunc sarcophago mecum soterabis in uno."
Ergo simul, fratres, concordi pace manentes,
simus torrazzi fortunae contra bataias,
quas haec amicorum stentando lega patibit.
180   Per mare, per terras, per fundamenta profundi
ibimus et nigri lustrabimus antra diabli.
Sed prius ad savios opus est andemus avisos
illius, qui me saeclo generavit in isto.
Quaerendus meus est genitor, quaeramus adunca,
185   quamvis nullus adhuc, ubi sit, comprenditur index'.
Cingar ad haec tostum facie respondit alegra:
'Penso tuum reperisse patrem, mi Balde; venite'.
Sic ait anteriorque aliis fretolose caminat,
perque hac perque illac boscos rammescolat omnes,
190   donec ad angustam venerunt denique grottam,
in qua solus erat sanctissimus ille romitus,
ad quem decrerat Cingar conducere Baldum;
et coniecturam nunc fecerat esse talhommum
patrem, quem Baldo suasit cercare Lonardus.
195   Introëunt ergo; surgit cito barbifer ille,
quem facies Pauli decorat veneranda romiti,
nec non Antoni, nec non pia chiera Machari.
Protinus in brazzos trepida dulcedine Baldum
suscipit et rivos tenerissime fundit ab occhis,

tainted intercourse. There is nothing more sordid than getting mixed up with whores.' Having spoken thus, he seemed to take my hand, and he led me through the lofty joys of heaven across all Olympus, and showed me things that I could only recount if I had a hundred tongues and a voice of steel. At last, the final words he spoke to me were these: 'Go find your father, who dwells not far from here; soon you will bury him with me in the same sarcophagus.'

"Therefore, my brothers, remaining together in harmonious peace, let us be as staunch towers against the battles of fortune, which this league of friends will withstand by persevering. We shall go by land and sea, through the depths of hell, and we shall inspect the caverns of the black devils. But first we must go and get wise advice from the man who brought me into this world. We must find my parent, so let us look for him, although we have no clue yet where he is." 177

Cingar promptly responds to this with a joyful face, "I think I've found your father, dear Baldo. Come!" He says this and walks rapidly ahead of the others. He churns up the entire woods going here and there, until they came at last to the narrow grotto where that most saintly hermit lived alone, the man to whom Cingar had promised to lead Baldo. By now he had figured out that this man was the father whom Leonardo had urged Baldo to find. They enter therefore, and the bearded man quickly rises with a venerable aspect like that of Paul the Hermit or of Anthony or the devout face of Macarius. Right away, he takes Baldo in his arms with trembling affection and lovingly pours forth rivers from his eyes, unable for a while to loosen his tongue. 186

200 nilque per un pezzum valuit dissolvere linguam.
Non potuit Cingar, non Falco et caetera turba
non lachrymare huius tanti spectacula facti.
Hic pater est (iam non dubitatur), filius ille.
Ambo abbrazzati pariter strictimque tenentes,
205 intenerant lapides non quod pia corda virorum.
Ut tandem potuere loqui, pater ipse sedendo
sic facit et natum natique sedere sodales;
mox ita, suspiciens coelum, parlare comenzat:
    'O gobbae in terris animae gentesque dapochae!
210 Per nos ah quantum facies humana brutatur!
Nonne canes sumus invidia, grassedine porci,
vulpes inganno, stizzosi morsibus ursi?
Nonne gula rabieque lupi, tumidoque leones
orgoglio, et gatti simiaeque libidine brutta?
215 Non est qui cerchet drittae vestigia stradae!
Quisque suam pleno seguitat ventramine voiam.
O bene nassuti mundo qui vana refudant,
sbrigatasque trahunt de terrae glutine mentes!
Nosco ego quid radiat coelum, quid terra virescat,
220 quid mare fluctivaget, quid denique Tartarus umbret;
nec capitis grisos, nec longa pilamina barbae
cernitis haec frustra; freddum caldumque provavi,
reddidit et finum me martellatio sortis.
Magna fui quondam Francorum gloria Guido,
225 Guido Rinaldesca natus de stirpe Sagunto.
Franza mihi testis, Germania, Sguizzera, Spagna,
Ongaria quibus giostris, quibus atque batais
vincitor et princeps toto cridabar in orbe.
Noverunt Itali, novit mala schiatta Gregorum,
230 Mori asini Turchique canes et caetera norunt:
quod ducis ingenium quondam, quod robur in armis,
quaeve manegiavi multis stratagemata guerris!

176

Cingar, Falchetto and the rest of the group could not help but   200
cry at the sight of such a great event. This is the father (it is no
longer in doubt), and this, the son. The two of them, embracing
and holding each another tight, could have moved stones to pity,
let alone the devout hearts of men. When at last they were able to
speak, while seating himself, the father seats his son and his son's
companions. Then looking up at the heavens, he begins to speak
thus: "O creatures bent toward the ground, people of little ac-
count, alas, how the human form is debased by us! Are we not like
dogs in our envy, pigs in our gluttony, foxes in our treachery? And
in our backbiting, like hot-tempered bears? Are we not wolves in
voracity and rage? Lions in our swollen pride? And cats and mon-
keys in our vile lust? There is no one who seeks the path of righ-
teousness. Everyone follows his own desires, with a full belly. O
the high-born in this world are those who refuse all that is vain
and who free their minds from earthly bonds! I know why the
heavens shine, why the earth grows green, why the sea fluctuates
and why the underworld is shadowy. Not for naught do you see
gray hairs on my head and the long strands of my beard. I have
known cold and heat, and the blows of fortune have sharpened my
wits.

"I was once Guido, the mighty glory of the French, Guido,   224
born of Rinaldo's lineage in Sagunto. France is my witness and
Germany too, Switzerland, Spain and Hungary, in whose jousts
and battles I was proclaimed victor and champion throughout the
world. The Italians knew, and that evil race of Greeks knew, the
Moorish asses and the Turkish dogs—they all knew what bril-
liance I had as a leader, what force in arms, what stratagems I car-
ried out in countless wars! And why should I go on? My main

177

Ut quid plura sequor? summa haec: mihi gratia tandem
tanta fuit rerum quod Franchi filia regis
235 me vidit, periitque simul, cepitque maritum.
At praestat reliquis donare silentia rebus.
Sufficit his paucis nostram concludere follam.
Ille furor rabiae, quem chiamat vulgus amorem,
qui tirare petras savios facit atque saputos,
240 atque altum, bassum, sicut sua voia talentat,
disponit, trattat, mundum sotosora travaiat,
nos de magnificis bassavit ad esse pitoccos,
esse vilanorum numerum, escas esse pedocchis;
ac ita furfantes nos nostra superbia reddit,
245 ac ita quid sit homo scitur: fanfugola quippe,
et giocola a ventis motu iactata pusillo.
Est homo stoppa foco, nix soli, brina calori;
non (ut se iactat) caesar, rex, papa, vel omnis
qui ferat in Roma camisottum supra gonellam.
250 Hac in sorte tamen misera gaiarditer egi.
Principio uxorem gravidam stancamve camino
non volui (hocve minus potuissem) ducere mecum.
Hanc bona suscepit miris persona carezzis
Bertus in hospitium fidum portumque segurum.
255 Ast ego dispostus vel amore vel impete ferri,
aut certam acquistare urbem aut perdere vitam,
protinus avisor praeclaro a vate Serapho
esse mihi fausto nassutum sydere maschium.
Quantum alegrezzae tulerit mihi nuntius ille,
260 scire potest nemo nisi patris amore calescat.
Sed mondanorum constantia nulla bonorum est.
Post malvasias arsenica saepe bibuntur.
En iterum gramo denuntiat ore Seraphus
esse mihi uxorem diro sub sydere mortam.
265 Heu quae non dixi toto convicia coelo?

point is this: in the end, I was so favored in everything that as soon as the daughter of the king of France saw me, she was done for and took me as her husband. But it is better to give over the rest to silence. Suffice it to conclude our fable with these few words.

"Passionate fury, which the common people call love, that 238 makes the wise and learned throw stones, orders and disposes the high and the low as its whim dictates, and flips the whole world upside down. It lowered us from being glorious to being beggars, to being numbered among the peasants, to being bait for lice. And thus our pride turns us into vagabonds, and thus one learns what a man really is, namely, an air bubble and a whirligig spun by the faintest wind. Man is kindling to the fire, snow to the sun, frost to heat, and not (as he considers himself) an emperor, a king, a pope, or one in Rome who wears a surplice over a cassock. But nonetheless, even in this sorry state, I acted bravely.

"First of all, I did not wish to take my wife with me, pregnant 251 and exhausted from the journey, nor would I have been able to do so. A good person, Berto, welcomed her with admirable affection into a stable home, a safe haven. Yet when I was determined either to conquer some city by love or by force of arms or to lose my life in the attempt, I was suddenly informed by the illustrious poet Seraphus that a son had been born to me under an auspicious star. What joy this announcement brought me no one can know who is not warmed by paternal love. But there is no constancy to earthly pleasure; after malmsey, we often drink arsenic. Behold, Seraphus with a sad countenance brings news a second time, that my wife has died under an inauspicious star. What abuse did I not heap on

"O mors, clamabam, mors, o correra diabli
atque Satanasi staffetta, citissima cunctis
at mihi tarda moves, ceu longa quaresma, pedanas.
Tira, gaioffa, mihi renegato falce roversum,
270 aut mihi da cordam, qua desperatus apiccher."
Hac igitur persa, rammingus et orphanus ibam
mille per aguaitos, per mille pericula vitae.
At bonitas divina, pii miserata doloris,
quem pro te, Balde, orphanulo, pro uxore ferebam,
275 fecit ut in melius sese mea voia tiravit.
Nil nisi stultorum gabiam mundum esse notavi,
at bene scire mori virtutum summa vocatur.
En quibus in bandis me solum, nate, catasti.
Usque modo, fugiens hominum consortia, pascor
280 herbarum crudis radicibus amneque puro.
Ipsa aetas, lachrymae, vigilantia sustulit occhios:
occhios corporeos, inquam, sed lumina cordis,
quo minus inspicitur terra haec, magis astra penetrant.
Ipse prophetandi docuit me iura Seraphus,
285 quae sunt digiunis longisque vegiare pregheris:
illius ante oculos Deus orbem donat apertum,
rerum aditus, mentesque hominum casusque futuri.
Hoc ego dignatus dono, tua semper in occhis
facta habui sensique tuos, o nate, travaios.
290 Mantua non modicos tenuit te carcere giornos;
passus es imbriferas, vento sforzante, ruinas,
post quas corsari bellum crudele tulerunt;
quo facto, tandem venisti ad littora patris.
Non vos disturbet magicas hic cernere burlas:
295 credite, sunt burlae, sunt baiae signa stryarum.
Insula non ista est, quae vobis insula paret,
non mons, non scoius, sed plurima schena balenae,
quam strya firmavit magicis Pandraga susurris;

the entire heavens? I cried out, 'O Death! O Death, messenger of the devil, Satan's courier, you are quick to reach others, but for me you move your feet too slowly, like tedious Lent. Cut me down with your scythe as an outcast, you scoundrel, or give me a rope so that I can hang my desperate self!'

"Having lost her, I wandered as an orphan through a thousand 271 dangers and a thousand mortal perils. But then divine goodness, moved to pity by the pious suffering I bore for you, my orphaned Baldo, and for my wife, caused my will to turn to better things. I realized that the world is only a cage of fools, and that the greatest virtue is called knowing how to die well. You see, my son, in what regions you found me. Until now I fled the company of men and fed on the raw roots of herbs and drank at pure streams. Age, tears and vigils have taken away my eyes — my physical eyes, I mean; but as for the eyes of the heart, the less one inspects the earth, the more they penetrate the stars. Seraphus taught me the rules of prophecy, which are fasting and vigils of long prayers. God lays the world revealed before the seer's eyes: the causes of things, human plans and future events. Having become worthy of this gift, I have kept your deeds in sight at all times, and I have felt your pain, my son. Mantua held you in prison for more than a few days; you have suffered the rages of winter storms driven by wind, after which pirates savagely waged war, and after all this, you have come at last to the land of your father.

"Don't let the magic tricks you see here disturb you. Believe me, 294 they are tricks and lies, these witches' mirages. What seems an is- land to you is not an island, nor is it a mountain or a cliff. It is the great back of a whale that the witch Pandraga arrested with her magical mutterings. On its broad shoulders and very wide back,

supraque spallazzas eius dorsumque peramplum,
300 arte diabolica fecit portare terenum,
montes, campagnas, boscos, animalia, fontes.
Sic ego, dum stabam solus solettus in antro
rupibus Armeniae, sensi me ferre per auras
cum grotta pariter, cum sylva et monte levatum,
305 hucve giusum poni pian pianum, more panarae,
quae sit vel freschis ovis vel plena becheris.
Tres modo sunt pestes, quibus aër, pontus et omnis
mundus amorbatur, tres saghae tresque diablae:
haec Pandraga una est, Smiralda secunda, sed altra
310 Gelfora, cunctarum pessissima, fezza stryarum.
Hae sempiterno se iactant tempore fatas
vivere, dante illis Demogorgone bevandam,
per quam mortalis vita haec sine morte trapassat.
Sic Fallerinam, sic dicunt esse Medaeam,
315 sicve Dragontinam, sic Circem, sicve sorocchiam
Morganae Alcinam, vel eam quae dicta Foletti
est uxor, Sylvana; stryas sic mille brusandas,
quas paladinorum forti virtute Seraphus
continuo impugnat, simul impugnatur ab illis.
320 Theseus, Orlandus, Iason, Tristanus et ille
Hector nigrae aquilae gestator, et ille bianchae
Ruggerus, qui sunt Tavolae fortezza rotondae,
talibus in studiis contentavere Seraphum.
Serraphus sacer est genius magiaeque bosardae
325 asper amazzator, sed fortis bastio verae.
Ille hic Serraphus, cui solo vivere dudum
concessit mens alta Dei, cui fusa probatae
sensa prophetiae magnique scientia coeli,
cui paladinaeos servandi cura barones,
330 ut quoque sint illi pro se giostrare parati,
quod sic usus habet pro iusto rumpere lanzas.

by her diabolical arts, she had soil brought here, and mountains, meadows, woods, animals and springs. While I lived all alone in a cave in the mountains of Armenia, I too felt myself being raised and carried through the air together with the grotto, forest and mountains, and then I was set down very carefully, like a basket full of fresh eggs or glasses.

"There are three types of pestilence that infect the air, the sea and the whole world, three sorceresses and three she-devils: this Pandraga is one, the second is Smiralda, and the third, Gelfora, who is the worst of all, the dregs of witches. She boasts that Fates live eternally because Demogorgon gives them a drink so that their mortal life continues without death. Such is Fallerina, they say, and such Medea and Dragontina and Circe and Alcina, the sister of Morgana, as well as Silvana, who is said to be the wife of Folletto. Such are a thousand witches who should be burned, whom Seraphus, with his courageous host of paladins, continually attacks and by whom he is in turn attacked. Witness Theseus, Orlando, Jason, Tristan and Hector (the bearer of the black eagle) and Ruggiero (the bearer of the white), who are the strength of the Round Table—all their exploits have served the aims of Seraphus.

"Divine Seraphus is a guardian, a keen destroyer of evil magic and strong defender of good magic. This Seraphus is the only one whom the lofty wisdom of God has allowed to live for a long time and to whom the understanding of true prophecy and knowledge of the great heavens is imparted. It is his job to take care of the paladin barons, so that they too are ready to do battle for him, because it is their custom to break lances for a just cause. Dead are

Mortuus est Orlandus, Aiax, Tristanus et altri,
quos supra dixi cavaleros esse doveri.
Sic ego nunc ligni meme vestibo giuponem
335 sub terramque ibo, mundi andamenta relinquens.
Et quoniam guerrerus eram barroque Seraphi,
haec impresa manet Baldum: te, Balde, ribaldas
desertare magas liceat, namque una soletta est
Manto Bianorei syncera Sibilla Seraphi,
340 qui tibi non poterit sese monstrare priusquam
Guido ego non abeam de mundo ad climata coeli.
Hic illum cernes, hic, inter busta baronum
et simulachra virum, rationis campio fies,
iustitiae, fidei, patriae Tavolaeque rotondae.
345 Qui melius brando guastabis regna stryarum
quam inquisitorum sex millia, quamque Magistri
Sacri Pallazzi cum centum mille casottis.
Eya age! ne timeas caput obiectare periclis,
perque ignem perque arma rue, virtutis amore!
350 Dixi ego. Destituor iam viribus istius aegri
corporis et moriens coelum peto. Nate, valeto'.
        Sic dicens, iunctis manibus, stetit altus et haesit
par statuae, sanctamque animam spudavit in auras.
Nox erat et tanta est lux circum fusa cadaver
355 quod quisquam dixit: 'Non nox hac nocte videtur'.
Confremuere omnes Baldumque in lumine guardant;
qui, postquam stupuit dudum, sic voce gementi
pauca refert: 'Saltem, pater o sanctissime, vivo
has tibi supremas potuissem reddere voces'.
360 Sic ait, et curvans toto se corpore, fixit
oscula per sanctos artus, quos fletibus omnes
lavit, et ah! quali ter patrem strinxit amore!
Tunc ibi Giubertus tetigit modulantia fila
taleque gorgisono modulavit gutture carmen:

Orlando, Ajax, Tristan and others, whom I just mentioned as dutiful cavaliers. So now I too shall dress myself in a wooden cloak and go underground, leaving the ways of the world. And since I was a warrior and hero of Seraphus, this enterprise now falls to Baldo. May you, Baldo, eliminate the bawdy mages. For Manto is the only authentic sibyl of Mantuan Seraphus; the latter cannot reveal himself to you until I, Guido, leave the world for the heavenly regions.

"Here you will see him, and here, amongst busts of barons and 342 statues of heroes, you will become the champion of reason, justice, loyalty, the homeland and the Round Table. With your sword you will destroy the witches' reign better than 6,000 inquisitors or than the Master of the Sacred Palace with 100,000 pyres. Take courage! Do not be afraid to throw yourself into dangers and rush into fire and into battle for the love of virtue! I have spoken. I am already abandoned by the strength of this ailing body, and in death, I seek heaven. Farewell, my son."

Speaking thus with his hands folded, he stood upright, frozen 352 like a statue, and spewed forth his holy soul to the heavens. It was night, but there was so much light flowing around his corpse that everyone said, "This night does not seem like night." They all tremble and look at Baldo in the light, who is amazed for a time, and then with a grieving voice offers a few words, "If only I had been able to speak these final words to you while you were alive." He speaks thus and bowing his whole body, places kisses on the holy limbs and washes them all with tears. And oh! with what love he embraces his father thrice!

Then Gilberto strummed his harmonious strings and with his 363 throat quivering, composed this song: "We are born and once

365 'Nascimur et nati morimur; sua quemque moratur
     iam praescripta dies: miser est quicumque cadaver
     et vitam pariter gelido sub marmore condit'.
     Haec appena quater moesta cum voce sonarat
     (namque pari numero manes et funera gaudent),
370 contremit intornum mediam locus ille per horam,
     qua stetit intrepidus firmato lumine Baldus.
     Quid sit hoc ignorant omnes tacitique vicissim
     aspiciunt sese, velut est usanza stupentum.
     En quidam usciolus crocat in cantone celettae,
375 seque da sestesso leviter movestus aprivit.
     Nulla tamen persona foras exivit ab illa.
     Hanc in mente venit Baldo discernere cosam.
     Intrat porticulam solus; quo intrante quievit
     ille tremor terrae Baldusque seratur in antro,
380 compagnique foras remanent ad busta Guidonis.
     Vix erat ingressus barro, post tergaque chiusae
     vix portae fuerant, se firmiter in pede trigat
     praestantique animo sint aut oracula, sint aut
     somnia, sint Phoebi responsa remirat atornum.
385 Stanza erat in forma quadrati facta salotti,
     cuius in umblico pendebat desuper ardens
     lampada, quae claro sedias lusore palesat.
     Trenta quidem sediae quadro stant ordine circum,
     quarum quae maior super omnes alta levatur.
390 Hic Guido, vel potius simulachrum grande Guidonis,
     constitit armatus seditque sedereque fecit
     barones totidem quotidem stant scamna senati.
     Guido stat in medio, stant circum circa guereri,
     quisque sua sedia, vestiti quisque corazzis,
395 atque inter sese vario sermone ragionant.
     In pede stat Baldus nec ab inde movetur un onzam.
     Si stupeat, pensare potes, qui vivere patrem

born, begin to die. For each of us the appointed day awaits. Wretched is he who buries his corpse and his life together under cold marble." He had scarcely finished singing this four times with a sorrowful voice (for shades and corpses prefer even numbers), when the area around them trembled for half an hour, during which time Baldo remained undaunted, his eyes steadfast. None of them knows what this means; they look at each other speechless, as people do who are stunned. Then a small door creaked in a corner of the little cell; and moving by itself, it opened slowly. However, no one came out. It comes into Baldo's mind that he should investigate this thing. Alone, he enters the small opening, and upon his entering, the earthquake calms. Baldo is sealed up in the cave, while his friends remain outside near Guido's remains.

The baron has scarcely entered and the doors scarcely closed   381
behind him, when he stands stock still and with extraordinary courage looks all around. Are these oracles or are they dreams or revelations from Apollo? The room was square, fashioned like a hall; in the center of the ceiling hung a burning lamp which lit up chairs with its clear light. Now around the four walls were arranged thirty chairs, one of which is raised far above the others. There Guido, or rather a large simulacrum of Guido, stands armed and then is seated and seats all the other barons, as many as there were benches in this senate. Guido was in the middle; the other warriors were on all sides, each in his own chair, each wearing armor, and they converse among themselves about various things.

Baldo stands stock-still and doesn't move an inch. You can   396
imagine how surprised he is to see his father here, alive and

armatumque videt stare hic, quem liquerat illic
inter compagnos mortum sub veste romiti.
400 Mirat ibi atornum fortissima busta virorum
atque gaiardiae flores fideique barones
ornantes armas sola virtute biancas;
qui sua, pro specchio, Baldo simulachra palesant.
Horum quisquis adhuc vivit cum corpore vivo,
405 rex hic efficitur, non re sed imagine rei.
Ut puta, quando Hector, seu Theseus, sive Ferandus
Gonziacus vivebat adhuc in carne davera,
ille guereggiabat re vera in corpore vivo,
nec fabat alcunas impresas contra rasonem;
410 sed sua fra tantum speties, vel imago, sedebat
intra gaiardorum princeps simulachra virorum,
qui certant solum pro dritto contraque tortum.
Ergo fin adessum regnarat imago Guidonis;
nunc, ubi complevit giornos simul atque fadigas,
415 est opus a prima sedia descendat abassum
succedatque sibi novus alter campio dritti,
quem paladinorum primum simulachra balottent.
Fitque balottandi ratio de mente Seraphi,
qui, quem proponit, talem a felicibus umbris
420 obtinet, et quidquid probat ipse, probatur ab illis.
Huc ergo ignarus causae similisque facendae
nescius, intrarat Baldus, guidante Serapho,
miraturque viros tam gaios tamque legiadros,
nunc hunc, nunc illum, nunc questum, nuncve quelaltrum.
425 Hector ibi largus spallis strictusque fianchis
exuperat, cui folta rubent pilamina barbae.
Nemo illo propius maiori stare cadreghae
cernitur Aeneasque ipsi vicinius haeret,
qui stetit et stat nunc et stabit semper alegrus
430 Virgilii meruisse tubam, quam nulla superchiat.

armed, whom he had just left with his companions, dead and dressed as a hermit. He marvels at the valiant figures of men around him there, flowers of chivalry, barons of the faith, adding luster to their white armor by their singular valor; they show their simulacra to Baldo as in a mirror. Whoever among them still lives in his body is here made king—not in reality, but as the image of a king. Just think! When Hector or Theseus or Ferrante Gonzaga still really lived in the flesh, he fought as a true king in a live body and did not do any deeds that ran counter to reason. Yet all the while his specter or image was seated as the leader of the images of these chivalrous men, who fight only for the right against the wrong. Until this moment the image of Guido had reigned; at this time when he has completed his days as well as his labors, it is required that he vacate the first seat, and that a new champion of the right succeed him, whom the simulacra of the paladins elect as their leader. The voting is done according to Seraphus's intention: whomever he proposes, prevails with the happy shades, and whatever he approves is approved by them.

So Baldo, ignorant of these matters and of their meaning, had 421 entered here guided by Seraphus, and he marvels at these men who are so cheerful and so charming, now here, now there, now this one, now that. There Hector is overpowering with his broad shoulders and narrow hips, with his thick whiskers glowing on his beard. No one is seen to be nearer to the highest throne than he. Aeneas stands closest to him, the man who once, now and forever takes pleasure in having merited the trumpet of Vergil, which no

Theseus et Iason, nec non fortissimus Aiax
succedunt, unus post altrum, seque carezzant.
Hic tenet in dextra cettam Torquatus aguzzam,
pro qua iustitiae durat per saecla ribombus.

435 Non procul est Brutus, simili qui laude triumphat,
nec tam degeneres fecit mazzare fiolos,
quam dedit exemplum populis scazzare tyrannos,
qui sic per dominum nostrum satiare golazzam
luxuriamque suam pensant, aliena robando.

440 Hic stat Fabricius, stat Cincinnatus, et ambo
paupertate sua godunt nausantque dinaros,
contentantque magis frustum portare gabanum,
malque petenati taconatis ire stivallis,
supraque deschettum coctae discombere rapae,

445 quam vestire togas de raso deque veluto
et bandisones centum pransare ciborum.
Bon compagnus adest laeta cum fronte Camillus,
qui nigras aquilas S.P.Q.R.que reportat.
Ipse comenzavit populis ostendere Francae

450 quod sibi sortiret melius remanere delaium,
quam tanto illorum damno passare dequaium.
Huic duo succedunt austera fronte Catones,
qui numquam parlant nisi sit parlare bisognum.
Scipio stendardum Spagnae Cornellus inalzat

455 cumque suo bassa fratello voce ragionat.
Maximus hic Fabius crespo stimat omnia vultu
subque suo mundi dominam targone covertat;
cui simul et brando nudo Marcellus acostat
et simul Aemilius vitae sprezzator apoggiat.

460 Hic est ille ducum primissimus, ille citellus
Scipio, qui mento spuntans appena peluzzos,
totam Africam sguerzumque Africae facit ire legeros,
dum se vantabant rerum spoiasse madonnam.

one surpasses. Theseus and Jason and mighty Ajax follow one after the other, touching each other. Here Torquatus holds in his right hand a sharp hatchet, on account of which his acclaim for justice endures through the centuries. Not far off is Brutus, who is celebrated with similar praise, not because he had his degenerate sons killed, but because he gave the people the example of driving off tyrants, tyrants who think that thus, with a simple *Our Father*, they can satisfy their gullets and their extravagances by stealing from others.

Here is Fabricius and here Cincinnatus. They both enjoy their 440 poverty and are nauseated by money; they prefer to wear worn cloaks and go unkempt with patched boots and sit and eat cooked turnips at a little table than to wear togas of silk and velvet and dine on a hundred sumptuously-prepared dishes. And that boon companion with his pleasant mien is there, Camillus, who bears the black eagles and the SPQR. He was the first to show the peoples of France how it would be better for them to stay over there rather than cross over here to their great harm. After them, with austere countenances the two Catos followed, who never speak unless they must. Cornelius Scipio raises the flag of Spain, and converses with his brother in a low voice. And here Fabius Maximus surveys all with a furrowed brow, and under his shield he protects the Mistress of the World. Marcellus too flanks him with a drawn blade, and Aemilius, disdainer of life, is also at hand. And here is the foremost leader, the young Scipio, who with his chin barely sprouting little hairs, drove off Africa and the one-eyed African, just as they were boasting of having plundered the Mistress of the World.

Cui tenet ipse suam scragnam Pompeius arentum
465 et facit et faciet diuturno tempore scusam,
non cagione sui sed Caesaris ambitione,
Romanos in se ferrum voltasse medemos.
Cassius et Brutus simili ratione ribaldam
Caesaris inculpant voiam stravisse senatum,
470 cui pugnalatas tres et viginta dedere.
Hic Lanzalottus rutilat, Tristanus avampat,
qui propria de sorte dolent mancasse pedantis
ut, velut hi spadam furibunda per arma menabant,
sic isti pennam libros fabricando menarent
475 multosque inchiostri possent vacuare bocalos.
Oh si Plutarcos, Livios Crisposque Rinaldus
Orlandusque ferox habuissent tempore Carli!
Hic tamen apparent alto cum vertice bravi,
struzzorumque albis umbrant sibi terga penazzis.
480 His prope Gonziacus Ferrandus et ille Rugerus
Estensis, ambo gentiles, ambo gaiardi,
ambo quos Carli auspicio tremet Africa semper.
Hic quoque Sordellus Godiorum maximus astat,
de cuius stupidis scitur per ubique prodezzis.
485 Ergo ubi comparet magni praesentia Baldi,
ecce senex intrat venerabilis ille Seraphus,
suscipit et Baldum primaque in sede repossat
Ipseque Guido pater Sordello venit apressum.
Baldus, honoratos se mirans intra signores,
490 non vivos quantumque viros discernit at umbras,
nondimenus eis parlans oravit un horam
seque minus dignum tanti accusavit honoris.
Quo facto, en iterum subito locus ille tremavit,
in fumumque abeunt sedes umbraeque sedentes,
495 quae tamen asportant secum pro rege creato
atque balottato Baldum, sed imagine tantum;

Pompey occupies the seat next to him, offering now and for 464
years to come this excuse—that it was not his fault but Caesar's
ambition that made the Romans turn their weapons against them-
selves. With similar reasoning, Cassius and Brutus blame Caesar's
bad faith for having destroyed the senate, for which they stabbed
him twenty-three times. Here Lancelot flushes with anger and
Tristan flares up. They curse their peculiar fate: while they were
wielding their swords in furious battle, they lacked pedants who
could have wielded their péns by creating books and emptying
many ink pots. O! If only Rinaldo and fierce Orlando in the days
of Charlemagne could have had their Plutarchs, Livys, and
Sallusts! Nonetheless, they appear proud with heads held high,
and they shade their backs with white ostrich plumes. Near them
stand Ferrante Gonzaga and Ruggiero of the Este family, both no-
ble, both courageous, under the auspices of Charles, still feared by
Africa. Here too stands mighty Sordello from Goito, whose stu-
pendous exploits are known everywhere.

Now then, when the figure of the great Baldo appears, behold! 485
Seraphus, that venerable ancient, enters and receives Baldo and
places him in the seat of honor, while his father Guido is seated
beside Sordello. When Baldo sees himself among such great gen-
tlemen, although he could tell that they were not live men but
shades, he addressed them nevertheless and pleaded for an hour
and declared himself utterly unworthy of such an honor. When he
had finished, suddenly the place trembles again, and all the seats
and the seated shades go up in smoke, yet they carry away Baldo
as their created and elected king, but only his image. For the true

verus namque manet Baldus cum corpore Baldi,
fictus namque volat Baldus sub imagine Baldi.
Qui redit ad socios atque illis omnia narrat,
500   seque valenthominum facies vidisse rubestas
vantat et illorum iussu brancasse bachettam.

Liber decimus nonus

Menter ego, in Berghem lauratus et urbe Cipada,
praeparor ad sonitum gringhae cantare diablos,
Fracassique provas horrendaque facta balenae,
altorium vestro, Musae, donate Cocaio.
5   Non ego frigidibus Parnassi expiscor aquabus,
ceu Maro castronus, quo non castronior alter,
dum gelidas Heliconis aquas in corpora cazzat
agghiazzatque sibi stomachum vinumque refudat,
unde dolet testam rumpitque in pectore venam.
10   Per quid? per quatros soldos; dum cantat in umbra
'Dic mihi, Dameta', tondenti braga cadebat.
Malvasia mihi veniat, non altra miora est
manna, nec ambrosiae, nec nectaris altra bevanda.
Scosserat a somno iam pulcher Apollo cavallos
15   portabatque diem tam bellum tamque tilatum
quam non portavit per multum tempus avantum.
Ne volet ergo dies tam candida sitque facendis
tota malenconicis consumpta, Boccalus ad ipsos
compagnos guidat Beltrazzum more scolari,
20   qui tremat atque cagat stopinos ante pedantum,
nam male cum numero casum grosserus acordat;
increpat hunc primo, facit inde levare cavallo:
Cingar equus, Beltrazzus eques spronatque Bocalus,

Baldo remains in Baldo's body, and the false Baldo flies away in Baldo's image. He returns to his companions and tells them everything, boasting that he has seen the ruddy faces of great heroes and has seized the scepter at their command.

Book XIX

While I, the poet laureate of Bergamo and the city of Cipada, prepare to play my guitar and celebrate devils and the exploits of Fracasso and the whale's terrifying actions, help your Cocaio, O Muses! I do not fish in the frigid waters of Parnassus, like Maro the castrated — no one is more castrated than he, given that he refuses wine and chugs the gelid waters of the Helicon into his body and freezes his stomach, so that his head aches and he ruptures a vein in his chest. And for what? For a lousy two bits. While he sings in the shade, "Speak to me, Dameta. . . ," the barber's breeches fell down. Let Malvasian wine come to me: no other manna is better, nor any drink of ambrosia or nectar. 1

Handsome Apollo had already shaken the horses from their sleep, and was now bringing on a day more gorgeous and perfect than he had brought for quite a while. And lest such a splendid day rush by spent entirely on melancholic things, Boccalo leads Beltrazzo to his companions like a student who trembles and shits bricks in front of the teacher, for the dunce is matching case and number poorly. First Boccalo berates him, next he puts him on a horse: Cingar is the horse, Beltrazzo the rider, and Boccalo spurs 14

qui dum bragarum sopraveste culamina scoprit,
25   ut queat impazzo menare stafilia nullo,
omnis in allegro versa est gramezza cachinno.
'Dic', Boccalus ait, 'Beltrazze galante: 'poëta',
quae pars est?' Respondet: 'Amen'. Boccalus ad illum:
'Optime respondes, si vellem dicere messam'.
30   Quo dicto, vibrat scuticam vibrandoque clamat:
'Non 'amen', ast 'ari' est! Pru sta! mala rozza, camina!'
Ille tremens poverellus ait: 'Perdona, magister,
nescio gramaticam'. Boccalus menat un altram,
unde cito respondet ei callante secunda:
35   'Ianua sum rudibus'. Risu tunc Baldus et omnes
se buttant herbae; seguitat sua coepta Bocalus
datque alias centum nudo sine fine quaderno;
sicve sculazzatus, Baldo mandante, fugatur
per sylvas, nec plus oltra comparuit ille.
40   Ast, ubi conditio patuit turpissima cagnae,
non disgroppantur Pandraghae vincula sic sic
per dominum nostrum, sed strictior illa tenetur;
ad cuius guardam stat Falco provistus in armis,
dum duo busta simul comites soterare parecchiant.
45   Centaurus nec non pariter Moschinus abirat
quaerere marmoreum, quem vidit nuper, avellum,
in quo binorum deposta cadavera stabunt,
donec iudicii giorno taratanta sonetur.
Giubertus Cingarque simul cum torzibus ibant
50   tollere Lonardum portareque iuxta Guidonem.
Baldus retro manet solettus et ossa parentis
componit pheretro, violas et lilia spargit
perque super corpus, perque altum, perque dabassum.
Ghirlandam lauri merito dat tempora circum;
55   inque manu eiusdem floret frons congrua palmae,
congrua victori tot guerris totque baruffis.

them while he bares Beltrazzo's buttocks of their covering of breeches so that he can wield the strap without hindrance; all sorrow is transformed into mirthful cackling.

Boccalo says, "Tell me, my gallant Beltrazzo, what part of   27
speech is 'poet'?" He replies, "Amen." Boccalo replies, "An excellent answer if I were trying to say Mass." After saying this, he cracks the whip and while cracking it shouts, "Not 'amen' but 'giddy-up' and 'hi-ya, old nag, move along!'" Trembling, the poor man says, "Forgive me, master, I do not know my grammar." Boccalo lands another, and as this second one is coming down, Beltrazzo quickly answers him, "I am the portal of ignorance." At this, Baldo and all the others throw themselves on the grass from laughter. Boccalo continues what he has begun, and endlessly gives him another hundred lashes on his bare notebook. And having been spanked thus on Baldo's orders, Beltrazzo is chased into the woods and never seen again.

On the other hand, once the truly base nature of the bitch has   40
been revealed, Pandraga's chains are not released just like that, in an *Our Father*. Instead she is restrained more tightly, and Falchetto stands guard over her, armed and ready, while the group prepares to bury the two bodies together. The Centaur had gone off (along with Moschino) to look for the marble tomb he had just seen, in which the corpses of both men will reside until the *tara-tanta* is sounded on Judgment Day. Gilberto and Cingar go off together with torches to get Leonardo's body and bring it alongside Guidone's. Baldo stays behind alone and arranges his father's bones in the bier and scatters violets and lilies over his body and all about, both top and bottom. As is fitting, he places a laurel crown around his head. And in his hand there rightfully blooms a palm frond, rightfully, that is, for the victor of so many wars and so many skirmishes.

Centaurus tumulum lactis candore biancum
reppererat, qui sic vasto fabricatur in antro.
Inter montagnas alias, quas nigra nigrorum
60   turba Sathanorum Pandraghae astretta parolis,
huc tulit, est Metrapas, quae lunam altissima toccat,
portat et in testa semper nebulosa capellum.
Ipsius in fundo scurissima tumba cavatur,
cuius in introitu primo suspenditur ingens
65   petra sepulturae, qua sic epigramma taiatur:
'Molchael et Bariel, alter magus, alter astrolech,
ambo governarunt isto sua membra sepulchro'.
Quo lecto, Centaurus ait: 'Ventura catata est.
Ut quid perditio haec, si non tenet urna coëllum?
70   Molchael, auditor Zoroastris, tempore Nini
floruit; an spatio tam longi temporis ossa
non sua putrescunt et tandem facta nientum?
Bramo videre provam'. Sic dicens, fortiter urnae
desuper annellos brancat pro alzare copertum.
75   En Moschinus adest, Baldo mandatus, et illi
porrigit altorium donec dabanda gitatur.
Quo vix cascato, niger ecce diavolus exit
atque super groppas Centauri balzat equinas.
Hic illum crebro pugnadis chioccat acerbis,
80   nec scortesus eum lassat repiare fiatum.
Hunc per curva tamen Moschinus cornua zaffat,
sed corlans testam muzzat levis ille per umbras.
Mox, revolans iterum, Centauri terga flagellat
atque iubet (si vult lassari) ponere librum,
85   librum quem tulerat nuper perforza puellae.
Centaurus reprobans certamen contra diablos,
illum proiectat terrae pacemque domandat.
Quem cito daemonium, nullo prohibente, rapinat
atque facit festam, velut esset laetus habere

The Centaur had relocated the tomb, as white as pure milk, 57
which had been erected inside a vast grotto. Among those moun-
tains which a black throng of black Satans brought to this place,
coerced by Pandraga's words, is one called Metrapas, so tall that it
touches the moon and always wears a cap on its cloudy head. At
its base there is hollowed out an extremely dark cavern, and over
its entrance a huge gravestone is poised, engraved with this in-
scription: "Molchael and Bariel, one a mage, the other an astrolo-
ger, both consigned their limbs to this sepulcher."

Having read this, the Centaur exclaims, "We're in luck! If the 68
urn contains nothing, why should it go to waste? This Molchael, a
disciple of Zoroaster, flourished in the days of Nineveh, and over
the space of such a long time, haven't his bones rotted and turned
at last to nothing? I want to see the evidence." Saying this, he grips
the rings of the urn firmly from above in order to raise the cover.
And here comes Moschino, sent by Baldo, and gives him a hand
until it is cast aside. As soon as it comes off, behold, a black devil
emerges and jumps on the Centaur's equine back. This ill-man-
nered creature pummels him with a volley of sharp fists and won't
even let him catch his breath. Yet Moschino seizes him by his
curved horns, but with a twist of his head, the devil deftly slips
into the shadows. Then, flying back at them, he flogs the Cen-
taur's back again and orders him (if he wants to be let go) to set
down the book, the book he had just taken from the girl by force.
The Centaur, disapproving of combat against devils, throws it
down on the ground and sues for peace. With no one to prevent
him, the demon snatches it up and starts to rejoice, as though he

90   scartafazzum illud, fuerat quo saepe domatus
et bastonatas susceperat ante cotoras.
Obstupidant illi; tum magno corde sedentes
constituunt penitus rerum cognoscere finem.
Ille super saxum levibus se balzat in alis,
95   nulla quibus forma est nisi quam gregnapola portat.
Quattuor ingentes stant alto in vertice cornae,
binae coperiunt montonis instar orecchias,
binae incastrati surgunt bovis instar aguzzae.
Mostazzus canis est Morlacchi, cuius ab ore
100   hinc atque hinc sannae vista panduntur acerba.
Non griphonus habet nasum harpyaque becchum
tam durum sodumque aptumque forare corazzas.
Barba velut becchi marzo de sanguine pectus
concacat et magno foetet puzzore bavarum.
105   Plus asini longas huc illuc voltat orecchias,
deque cavernosis oculis duo brasida vibrat
lumina, quae diris obscurant sydera sguardis.
Serpentis caput est pars vergognosa davantum,
codazzamque menat pars vergognosa dedretum.
110   Gambae subtiles pedibus portantur ochinis,
sulphureumque magro culamina spudat odorem.
Tunc ibi Virmazzus Moschino parlat in aurem,
orat et ut vadat sociis hanc dire novellam.
It via Moschinus, Baldum trovat, omnia contat.
115   Cingar erat giuntus tunc tunc tuleratque Lonardum;
sic Giubertus adest cum Cingare. Falco vocatur.
Itur et insemmam cupiuntque videre diablos,
si sit tam bruttus quam pingere vulgus avezzat.
Iamque subintrarant tacito cum murmure tumbam,
120   cuius in ore trovant vacuum sine tegmine saxum.
Centaurus latet hic quodam cantone copertus.
Surgit et incontra veniens cum calce legero,

were thrilled to possess this tattered tome, by which he had often in the past been mastered and had suffered so many ripe beatings.

Virmace and Moschino are stupefied; sitting down with great 92 courage then, they resolve to know in detail the conclusion of this affair. The devil springs up on a rock with light wings whose shape is just like those of a bat. Four enormous horns stand up on his head: two cover his ears like those on a ram, two stick straight up like those on a bull. His muzzle is that of a Molossian dog; from his mouth fangs hang out both sides, horrible to see. No griffin has a nose nor any harpy a beak as hard and as solid and as good for piercing armor. His beard, like that of a billy goat, befouls his chest with rotten blood and reeks with the foul stench of his slobber. He turns his ears — which are longer than an ass's — this way and that, and from his cavernous eye sockets he brandishes two eyes of burning coal that block out the stars with their fierce glares. The unmentionable part in front is the head of a serpent; and the unmentionable part in back wags a nasty tail. His spindly legs are borne on goosefeet, and he spews forth an odor of sulfur from his scrawny butt. At this moment Virmace whispers in Moschino's ear and urges him to go tell the others of this news. Moschino goes off, finds Baldo, and tells him everything. Cingar had just arrived carrying Leonardo, Gilberto is there with Cingar, and Falchetto is summoned. Then they all go off together, yearning to see if the devil is as ugly as the masses tend to paint him.

Now they have entered the tomb with a hushed murmur; in the 119 entrance they find an empty grave without a cover. The Centaur hides here, concealed in a corner. He rises and goes toward them

voceque summissa parlat: 'Guardate, fradelli!
Ad mancam guardate manum, niger ecce diavol!'
125   Sic dicens, illum digito monstrante, palesat;
qui, licet astutus sit spiritus atque sotilis,
non tamen a Baldo sese putat esse vedutum.
Ergo facit danzam, guardat sotosoraque voltat
librum sacratum Pandraghae; vixque videndo
130   esse putat verum quod sit liber ille tremendus,
quo rex Luciferus, quo gens inferna ligatur.
Quapropter saltis balzat mattazzus alegris
scambiettosque facit varios fingitque morescam.
Compagni rident inviti labraque chiudunt
135   saepe sibi stessis, propter retinere cachinnos,
unde fadigabat mandare silentia Baldus.
Non satis hic ridet Boccalus, at omnis in omnem
se Baldum ficcat, nec lassat apena fiatum,
nam timet atque tenet strictum busamen aparum.
140   Post longas festas, alter volat ecce diavol,
voceque cornacchiae passutae carne picati,
sic raucus stridet: 'Quid agis, Rubicane? Quid istic
te tenet impresae? Num aliquod grafiabile speras?'
Cui respondet: 'Ita est; venias, Libicocche galante!
145   Nos hodie talem noscum portabimus almam
qualem non maium sibi nostra Caina tiravit.
Ecce, viden? liber est nigromantibus ille sacratus,
qui tibi, quique mihi tantos dabat ante travaios;
an cosam nescis? de gratia, scolta pochinum.
150   Quinque cavalleri fortes, quos Taula rotonda
nuncupat errantes, capitarunt partibus istis
et potuere dolos Pandraghae rumpere nostrae.
Illa quidem stat fresca; modo ter mille picatas
sive scoriatas pro avanzo nuda tiravit,
155   unde magis vellet penitus meschina brusari,

with light steps, whispering, "Look, brothers! Look to the left, see the black devil!" Saying this, he points him out with his finger, and the devil, although clever and of a discerning mind, still does not notice that Baldo is watching him. Therefore, he does his dance, looks at Pandraga's magic book, turning it every which way, and seeing it, can scarcely believe it's real—that this is the terrible book which harnesses King Lucifer and the people of the underworld. Because of this, the silly fool skips about with happy leaps and cuts a variety of capers and improvises a *moresca*. The companions laugh despite themselves and keep covering their mouths to hold in their guffaws. Baldo strains to impose silence. But Boccalo does not laugh much; instead he attaches himself completely to Baldo, scarcely letting him breathe, for the buffoon is frightened and keeps his hole shut tight behind.

After this long merriment, another devil flies over, and with the voice of a crow fed on hanged-man's flesh, raucously shrieks, "What are you doing, Rubicane? What endeavors keep you here? Are you hoping to find something to snatch?"   140

The devil answers him, "Yes, indeed! Come, my gallant Libicocco!   144 Today we will carry off a soul the likes of which our region of Cain has never dragged in. Do you see? This is the sacred book for necromancers that has given you and me and many others such trouble in the past. You don't recognize the thing? Well then, listen up, please! Five strong knights (whom the Round Table calls "errant") happened upon this place and were able to break our Pandraga's spells. She's done for now: she's naked and has taken 3,000 beatings or whippings, so that the poor thing would prefer to be com-

quam sic squarzari, quam toto in corpore frangi.
Perdidit en librum, quo damno se tenet esse
spazzatam penitus, quia nos portabimus illam'.
Tunc Libicoccus: 'Heu! squarza, Rubicane, quadernum!
160   Heu squarza! ne forte illum magus alter acattet
et mala sint nobis peiora prioribus ancum'.
'Non', Rubicanus ait, 'liber est squarzandus adessum,
sed res a nobis facienda est ante galanta.
Omnes quippe volo baratri giurare diablos,
165   aut si non omnes almancum trenta miores.
Oh! quantae (cernis?) picturae! Quaeso, pochettum
has, Libicocche, vide: plus centum plusque milanta!
En Salomonis habet primum pentacula foium;
aspice quam multis sunt compassata righettis,
170   quadratis, punctis, numeris, centumque facendis!
Pingitur en primo Zoroaster persa registro,
qui prior Inferno misit perforza cavezzam:
tu scis, ipse scio, scit Pluto sciuntque diabli,
quos nunc ad virgam traxit posuitque cadenae,
175   nunc bastonavit fecitque vogare tapinos.
Ecce magus Thebittus adest, destructio regni,
atque Picatricis sculpita tabella magistri,
per quam cum numeris ad amorem quisque tiratur.
Picta Michilazzi patet hic proportio Scotti,
180   qua sex effigies cerae, mox una piombi
fingitur, influxu Saturni ac daemone Martis,
unde per incantum miracula tanta fiuntur.
Ecce idem Scottus qui, stando sub arboris umbra,
mille caractheres circo designat in arcto.
185   Quattuor inde vocat, magna cum voce, diablos:
unus ab occasu properat, venit alter ab ortu,
dat mediusque dies terzum, septemtrio quartum.
Consecrare facit fraenum conforme per illos,

pletely burned up than to be lacerated like that, than to be broken in every part of her body. Here's the book she lost; she considers herself to be utterly ruined by this loss, since we shall carry it off."

Thereupon Libicocco says, "Well then, Rubicane, tear up the 159 book! Come on, tear it up so that another magician doesn't find it by chance, and make our woes even worse than before."

"No," says Rubicane, "the book shouldn't be torn up just now, 162 because first we need to do something fun. In fact, I want to conjure up all the devils from the underworld, or if not all of them, at least thirty of the best. O, do you see how many drawings there are? I beg you, Libicocco, look at some of these! There are more than a hundred, more than a gazillion! Look, the first page has the pentacles of Salomon; notice how many fine lines there are drawn with a compass: squares, points, numbers, a hundred things! Look, Zoroaster of Persia is pictured in this first section, the one who earlier forced a harness on Hell. You know, I know, and Pluto and the devils know whom sometimes he summoned to his wand and threw into chains, while at other times he clubbed the poor things and put them to the oar.

"Here is the sorcerer Thabit, destroyer of our realm, and here's 176 the table engraved by Master Picatrix, with which anyone can be drawn into love by the use of numbers. Here lies 'de-picted' the proportion of Michael Scotus, by which six statuettes of wax and one of lead are fashioned under the influence of Saturn and the daemon of Mars, so that many wonders are created through enchantments. And here is Scotus again, who, while staying under the shade of a tree, draws a thousand symbols in a tight circle. Then with a loud voice he calls four devils: one hastens from the west, one comes from the east; the south sends the third and the north, the fourth. He has them charm a bridle suitable for re-

cum quo fraenat equum nigrum minimeque vedutum,
190   quem quo vult tamquam Turchesca sagitta cavalcat.
En quoque designat magus idem in littore navim,
quam levat in nubes octoque per aëra remis
navigat et magnum tribus horis circuit orbem.
Humanae spinae suffumigat inde medullam,
195   atque docet magicis cappam sacrare parolis,
quae dum sacratur, sentita per aëra strident
murmura spirituum, quia nos perforza tiramur.
Hanc igitur cappam, seu mantum, sive gabanum
quisquis, seu maschius seu foemina, mittit atornum,
200   non vedutus abit quocumque talentus avisat.
Artaus en gladius, qui atrigat flumina, siccat
pascola, grandineat fruges et amazzat osellos.
En cessat calamita sibi coniungere ferrum,
si baptizatur, sed cor de pectore scarpat
205   atque hominum carnes in amoris vincula groppat.
Cernis Apollonium Thianaeum? mox saracenum
incantatorem Granatae? deinde Magundat
quomodo chiamatis satiat sua vota diablis?
Hic Paduanus adest, cernis? Petrus Abanus ille,
210   ille Petrus, physica doctor, sed in arte magorum
doctior; hic, comprans quae sunt mangianda vel altrum,
spendet abundanter scudos buttatque ducatos;
inde casam rediens spesos sua borsa dinaros
ad sese revocat; sed qui modo vendidit, unum
215   nec minimum retrovat bezzum solumque baioccum.
Immo putat clausam pugno retinere monetam,
quando vero aperit, plenus carbone catatur,
seu buschis potius, seu moschis, sive saiottis.
En tibi cuncta patent, bellis depincta figuris;
220   ut quid ego indusio? Iam sconzurare parecchio'.
    Sic ait, et circhium designat more magorum,

straining a black horse, completely invisible, that gallops as fast as a Turkish arrow wherever he wishes. See how the same sorcerer also draws a ship on a beach that he raises into the clouds, where it navigates through the air with eight oars and encircles the entire globe in three hours.

"Next, he suffumigates marrow from a human spine and 194
teaches how to enchant a cape with magic words. While the cape is being enchanted, the howls of the spirits are heard screeching through the air, for we are drawn in by force. As a result, anyone who puts on this cape or coat or cloak, whether male or female, goes without being seen wherever his fancy takes him. See Arthur's sword, which stops rivers, dries meadows, hails down on crops, and kills birds. See how a magnet, if baptized, ceases to conjoin itself to iron, but it plucks the heart from the breast and binds human flesh in chains of love.

"Do you see Apollonius of Tyana and then the Saracen En- 206
chanter of Granada? And after that, how Magundat satisfies his own wishes by calling the devils? Here is the Paduan, do you see? He is the famous Pietro d'Abano, that Pietro who is a learned physician, but even more learned in the magical art. When he is buying things to eat or other stuff, he spends *scudos* abundantly and throws around ducats, and upon returning home calls back into his purse all the money he has spent, and the person who has just sold him things can't find even a penny, not a single cent. Quite the contrary: he thinks he's holding a coin closed in his fist, but when he opens it, he finds it full of carbon or else straw or flies or grasshoppers. There, you have seen everything depicted in beautiful drawings. But what am I waiting for? I'm ready to conjure now."

As he says this, he draws a circle as magicians do, and com- 221
mands Libicocco to stand in the middle of it. Next, he opens the

in cuius medio Libicoccum stare comandat.
Mox aperit cartas, legit has, relegit simul illas,
in terramque facit virga ter mille figuras.
225 Magnum Semiphoram vocat audax: 'Aglaque ya ya',
et quascumque magi faciunt, facit ille pregheras.
Ecce fracassatas per sylvas impetus ingens
advenit atque facit totum tremolare paësum.
Barbarizza venit, secum baiante Cagnazzo.
230 'Quid, Pandraga', cridant; 'quid nunc, Pandraga, comandas?'
Verum sbeffatos sese Rubicane videntes,
oh qualem faciunt schioppanti ventre risaiam!
Procedit Rubican folios voltare quaderni.
Tres quoque terrisono veniunt stridore diabli:
235 Calcabrina prior, quem Gambatorta sequebat,
terzus adest Malatasca, focum qui naribus eflat.
'Quid, Pandraga, iubes? quid nam, Pandraga, rechiedis?'
Uriel et Futiel magno huc rumore galoppant.
'Quid, Pandraga, vocas? ad quid, Pandraga, domandas?'
240 Farfarellus adest, illi Draganizza secundat.
Hi quoque ridentes se noscunt esse gabatos.
Vix quibus adiunctis, Malacoda ruinat et ipsum
insequitur Marmotta furens Satanasque tricornis.
'Quid, Pandraga, petis? quid nos, Pandraga, molestas?'
245 Cum vero nullam Pandragam adsistere cernunt,
sed tantum magiae Rubicanem stare magistrum,
oh! puta si rident scherzantque insemma gaioffi!
Astaroth in furiam properat, sic Belzebub unum
portat forconem, seguitat Malabolza, nec asper
250 Grafficanis, habens rascum, succedere tardat.
'Quid, Pandraga, spias? ut quid, Pandraga, ruinas?'
Asmodeus adest, Alchinus, Molchana, Zaffus,
Taratar et Siriel, omnes facto agmine sbraiant:
'Quid, Pandraga, novi est? ad quid, Pandraga, vocamur?'

pages, reads some, rereads others as well, and makes three thousand drawings on the ground with his wand. Boldly he calls the great Semiphora with "Agla and ya-ya." And he says all the prayers that magicians say. Then, behold, a huge disturbance advances through the fractured woods, making the whole countryside tremble. Barbarizza appears, and with him barking Cagnazzo. "What, Pandraga?" they cry. "What do you command now, Pandraga?"

However, seeing themselves duped by Rubicane, O how they 231 burst their bellies laughing! Rubicane keeps turning the pages of the volume. Three more devils come with a terrifying shriek: first Calcabrina, followed by Gambatorta; the third is Malatasca, who blows fire from his nostrils. "What are your orders, Pandraga? What do you require, Pandraga?" Uriel and Futiel gallop up with a tremendous noise, "Why do you call, Pandraga? What do you ask of us?" Farfarello arrives; and Draganizza follows. Laughing, these too as well recognize that they have been tricked.

After they have joined the group, Malacoda rushes forth, fol- 242 lowed by raging Marmotta and three-horned Satanasso. "What do you seek, Pandraga? Why, Pandraga, do you bother us?" When they see that Pandraga is not actually present, and that Rubicane is the only master of magic, O just think how these rascals laugh and joke together!

Astaroth hastens in a frenzy; so too Beelzebub, who carries a 248 pitchfork; Malabolgia follows, and fierce Grafficane advances slowly, holding a big fork. "What are you looking for, Pandraga? Why are you in such a rush, Pandraga?"

Here too are Asmodeus, Alchino, Molchana, Zaffo, Taratar 252 and Siriel, and having formed a unit, they all bellow, "What's up, Pandraga? What are we being called to do, Pandraga?

255   Stizzaferrus item, Melloniel, Acheron adsunt,
       quos Malabranca sequens Ciriattum guidat apressum.
       Magnum quisque facit tenebrata per aëra murmur:
       'Quid, Pandraga, iuvat? quid te, Pandraga, talentat?'
       Zaccara, Scarmilius, Paymon, Bombarda, Minossus
260   denique concludunt festam dicuntque medemum:
       'Quid, Pandraga, iubes? quid nam, Pandraga, comandas?'
       Postea, scoperta Rubicani fraude, cachinnis
       talibus urlabant quod terrae motus et ipsum
       nimborum tonitru coelique ruina videtur.

265   Unde viri virtus Baldi generosa repente
       se levat et, tollens animos in corde feroces,
       irruit in medios, brando rutilante, diablos.
       Belzebub, ut princeps aliorum, baiat in auras
       more canis bruttamque aciem restellat in unum.
270   Tamburrinus adest gobbus Garapellus et, ipsum
       tamburri ad lypitop, 'Arma, arma' cridatur ubique.
       Belzebub a tombis, solo sofiamine corni,
       evocat armatos sex centum mille diablos.
       Lucifer ignorat causam, spiat omnia vultque
275   scire quid importat cotantum fare parecchium.
       Respondetur ei non altras esse casones
       maiores ista, quae tantos possit avantum
       spingere diavolos tantumque levare bagordum:
       ille bravus, bravus ille diu sentitus abassum
280   et menzonatus tenebrosa per atria Baldus,
       qui, velut in libris Serraphi Parca menazzat,
       debeat Inferni per forzam rumpere muros,
       est nunc perforzo cuncti prohibendus Averni,
       ne veniat giusum, scalisque ad bassa trovatis,
285   Tartara descendat te nosque ruinet afattum.
         Baldus at Inferni sbirros tutavia cridantes
       urlantesque simul, sbraiantes atque tronantes,

Stizzaferro too, Melloniel, and Acheron are present, followed   255
by Malabranca, who leads Ciriatto close behind. They each make
a rumbling in the darkening air. "What do you demand,
Pandraga? What is your pleasure, Pandraga?"

Zaccara, Scarmiglione, Paymon, Bombarda, and Minossus   259
bring the party to a close at last, and say the same thing, "What
are your orders, Pandraga? What do you command?" Then, upon
discovering Rubicane's hoax, they whoop with such guffaws that it
seems like an earthquake or thunder in storm clouds or the col-
lapse of the heavens. So the valorous spirit of the heroic Baldo
suddenly awakens, and drawing on the fierce courage in his heart,
he rushes into the middle of the devils with his sword gleaming.
Beelzebub, as the leader of the others, howls into the wind like a
dog and musters his hideous troops. Hunchbacked Garapello is
the drummer, and shouts of, "To arms! To arms!" are heard far
and wide to the boom-da-boom of his drum.

With one blast of the horn Beelzebub calls 600,000 armed   272
devils from the cavern. Lucifer does not know the reason for this;
he sees everything and demands to know the meaning of such
preparations. He is told that only one great reason could rouse so
many devils and raise such a ruckus: that brave man, that brave
man Baldus who has long been mentioned there below and talked
about in the shadowy halls. He is destined to destroy the walls of
Hell by force, as Fate threatens in the books of Seraphus, and so
should be hindered forcibly by all of Avernus lest, having found
the stairway, he comes down and descends into deepest Tartarus
and utterly destroys you and all of us.

Yet the indefatigable Baldo was dispatching infernal cops with   286
his sword, now from this side, now from that, as they kept shout-

ense sbaratabat nunc huc, nunc impiger illuc.
Illi cum forchis, forconibus atque tenais,
290   oncinis, graffis, ungis cornisque fogatis,
inforcant Baldum, grafiant et cornibus urtant.
Illico Centaurus sibi stesso terga flagellat,
namque cavallus erat retro, paladinus avantum;
evolat et Baldo succurrere prestus afrettat,
295   ingentemque travem fert pro bastone gaiardus.
Falchettus currit, Cingar, Moschinus; at ipse
Giubertus properat Pandraghae mittere guardam,
rizzatosque metu portat sua testa capillos.
Ast animi Boccalus inops et privus aiuto,
300   implerat muschio, nimia formidine, bragas.
Hic illic quaerit latebras, huc illuc afrettat,
nec retrovare locum scit sconderolibus aptum,
et quamvis aptum semper tenet esse palesum.
De passu in passu se signat mille fiatas,
305   optat aquam sanctam, quae scazzet longe diablos,
mille *Paternostros* barbottat *Aveque Marias*,
Salveque reginas, sed nescit dicere *Credo*.
    At iuvat alquantos Baldi describere colpos,
qui diavolorum facit ire ad sydera cornas.
310   Maximus illorum squadronus pugnat atornum:
qui ferit in bandis, qui dretum, qui ferit ante;
nil tamen ille ungias, nil dentes nilque rapaces
aestimat oncinos, forcas rascosque tricornes,
et quascumque usant illi schittare corezas
315   sulphureas pettosque olidos puzzore carognae,
qui nigras habitant Malabolgias, quique Cainam.
Fulminat ensigero Baldensis forcia brazzo
et cum mandrittis, et cum fendentibus, et cum
diversis guerrae tractis, at maxime puntis,
320   spiccat ab Inferni soldatis brachia, gambas,

ing and yelling all at once, bellowing and roaring. They stab Baldo with hoes and pitchforks and pliers, hooks, grapnels, flaming claws and horns, and scratch and jab him with their horns. Right then the Centaur whips his own back, for he was a horse behind and a paladin in front; he flies off and quickly hurries to help Baldo and bravely carries a huge beam for a club. Falchetto, Cingar and Moschino come running, while Gilberto hastens to stand guard over Pandraga, and the hair on his head stands straight up from fear. But Boccalo, lacking in courage and without help, in excess of fright had filled his breeches with musk. He searches for hiding places here and there, scurries to and fro, but can't manage to find a good cranny; even a good one he always considers too exposed. Step after step, he makes the sign of the cross a thousand times; he wishes he had holy water to chase the devils away. He mutters a thousand *Our Fathers* and *Ave Marias* and *Salve Reginas*, but he doesn't know how to say the *Credo*.

Yet it is satisfying to describe some of Baldo's blows which 308 make the devils' horns rise up to the stars. A huge squadron of them fights in a circle around him, some wounding his sides, some behind, some in front. But he disdains their claws, teeth, shredding hooks, spikes, three-pronged pitchforks and all those sulfurous farts that those who dwell in black Malabolge and Caina are in the habit of spurting, and the gas-bombs that reek of carrion stench. The might of the Baldensian sword arm strikes like lightning, with thrusts, slashes and various battle strokes. With the point of his blade, he lops off the arms, legs and horned heads of these infernal soldiers and makes them flap through the skies.

cornutasque facit volitare per aëra testas,
quas qui longe vident, non testas, brachia, gambas,
sed cornacchiones credunt nigrasque mulacchias.
Cagnazzus, cui testa canis grossissima baiat,
325   dentibus assannat Baldo post terga galonem.
Ille roversonem, subito gyramine, tirat,
cui cornas cum fronte duas levat ense politas;
atque sub istesso colpo Malatasca trovatus,
accipit in testam satis amplo vulnere crostam.
330   Ambo viam fugiunt implentque cridoribus auras.
Barbarizza subit, magno forcone paratus,
et forconadam toto conamine lassat.
Baldus vero manu manca piat illico forcam,
dumque piat, stringit spezzatque ladiniter illam,
335   atque tut an trattum callat sua dextra roversum
cinquinumque facit naso largumque silacchum.
Uriel et Futiel scampant, quos Baldus atrigat,
namque, manudritto, sine gambis ambo caminant.
Farfarellus eos cito vendicare parecchiat
340   rampinoque suo barronem taccat in elmo,
strassinare putans illum seu tollere pesum.
Baldus ei rotolat versus ventralia punctam,
quae per vergognas de pisso ad stercora passat.
Sed quid agit Cingar? quid Falco? quidve Vimazus
345   Moschinusque simul? Levius certamen habebant,
namque supratuttos vult solum Lucifer illum,
qui dare (si scampat) grandes sibi debet afannos.
Cingar abrazzarat se cum Rubicane, diuque
nunc gambarolis, nunc forza, nuncve rasone
350   exercet lottam, tentans deponere sottum.
Sunt ambo astuti, sunt cimae lanaque fina,
pettenanda (velut dicunt proverbia) saxis.
Falchettus bruschis Libicoccum pascit ofellis,

Those who view them from afar do not think that these are heads, arms and legs but rather big crows and black ravens.

Cagnazzo, whose huge dog's head barks, sinks his teeth into   324 Baldo's flank from behind. With a sudden twist, Baldo delivers a backhand blow, and his sword lifts the two horns clean off, together with the forehead. And Malatasca, struck by the same blow, receives a crack on the head with quite an ample wound. They both run off, filling the air with their cries. Barbarizza, armed with a huge pitchfork, pushes forward and unleashes a fork-thrust with all his might. But Baldo immediately snatches the pitchfork with his left hand, and in so doing, squeezes and easily breaks it; at the same time his right effects a backhand and makes a coin from the devil's nose, and a wide scar. Uriel and Futiel are escaping, but Baldo stops them with a forward thrust that leaves them both walking without legs. Farfarello quickly prepares to avenge them, and with his grapnel, hooks the baron by the helmet, thinking to drag him or to raise him up. Baldo twists the sword point into his entrails, which passes from the shame of piss to that of shit.

But what is Cingar doing? And what about Falchetto? What   344 about Virmace and Moschino, too? They had a lighter skirmish, because Lucifer was interested primarily in Baldo alone, who (if he escapes) would cause great problems for him. Cingar was engaged with Rubicane for a long time: he fought the battle first with leg thrusts, then with might, then with tactics, trying to bring him down. They are both clever, both shrewd, both the finest wool to be combed with rocks, as the proverb says. Falchetto feeds Libicocco some tough sweetmeats, and once he is well fed with

qui bene passutus nimio lignamine boschi,
355 vult scapolare viam, sed non scapolare dabatur.
Falco manu laeva tenet hunc dextraque sedazzat
burrattatque illi solido bastone farinam.
Huic dare se provat Sathanas quandoque socorsum,
cum tamen extra pilos polvinum surgere guardat,
360 quantum stare potest stat dislongatus ab illis.
Zaffus afrontarat Centaurum fortibus ungis,
at valeat Virmazzus eum stimare nientum,
si duo diavoli non illum semper agrezent.
Calcabrina retro, falsus traditorus, aferrat
365 per caudam firmumque tenet, nec senza casonem:
nullos namque potest sic calzos trare cavallus.
Dum tirat ergo unus retro, multum alter agraffat,
tertius en daemon fert Gambatorta tenaiam
Centaurumque omnem nunc hinc, nunc inde tenaiat.
370 Ille sed, a tali muscarum sorte feritus,
dum sentit streppare codam, picigare culattas,
sentit et ad nasum pariter montare senapram:
cum bastone giocat caudamque rescodit ab illo,
dansque manum Zaffo per cornu buttat aterram,
375 unde tenaiarum tantummodo restat arengus.
Non procul hinc Moschinus erat Draganizzaque secum
affrontatus habet multo sudore travaium.
Hoc tamen in medio Malatascam Baldus amazzat,
qui mortus fugit huc, fugit illuc absque corada,
380 fertque suam testam, quam troncam Baldus habebat.
Inde Malacodam per caudam praestus achiappat
et cazzafrusti de more volutat atornum,
inde manum slargans hunc lassat abire per auras,
qui procul octo mios vadit cascare deorsum.
385 Quo saltu, Marmotta fugit, fugit Astaroth, atque
Belzebub ipse prior longe calcanea menat.

plenty of timber from the woods, he tries to run away but is not permitted to run away. Falco holds him with his left hand while his right sifts and winnows his flour with a solid club. From time to time Satan tries to aid Libicocco; however, when he sees the dust rising from his hair, he stays as far away from them as possible.

Zaffo had attacked the Centaur with his strong claws, but Virmace would have paid him no heed if the devils did not always assault him in pairs. The devious traitor Calcabrina seizes his tail from behind and holds it tight, and not without reason, for in this way, the horse can't unleash any kicks. So while one pulls on the Centaur from behind and another claws him repeatedly, a third demon, Gambatorta, carries pincers and tears at the Centaur here and there. Having been wounded by such flies, when he feels his tail being torn off and his buttocks nipped, the Centaur also feels the mustard mount to his nose: he plays with his club, shakes his tail free from Calcabrina, and getting a hand on Zaffo's horn, he throws him to the ground, so that only the matter of the pincers remains. Not far off are Moschino; and Draganizza, who is challenging him, labors with much sweat.

Nevertheless, in the middle of this, Baldo slays Malatasca, whose corpse runs about here and there without its innards, carrying its head which Baldo had lopped off. Next Baldo quickly grabs Malacoda by the tail and swings him around like a sling. Then opening his fist, he releases him into the air, and off he goes to fall down eight miles away. Seeing this flight, Marmotta flees, Astaroth flees, and Beelzebub is the first to take to his heels far

361

378

Ecce gravem tundis bolzam Malabolza balottis
baiulat et lanzat crudas boiazza nosellas.
Non tamen ad Baldum timidus manigoldus acostat;
390   sat sibi quod feriat nec non lontanus amazzet,
ut nunc qui schioppos, ut nunc qui tempore guerrae
archibusa ferunt, moschettos paraque moscas.
Nonne saguratus quisquam sguatarusque bisuntus,
atque pedocchiorum plenus, destructio panis,
395   nonne retro muro latitans et quattus adocchians,
lontanusque pians miram stringensque ribaldam
mozzandamque manum, resonansque per aëra tut tof,
solus amazzabit, passabit pectora solus,
aut tibi, de Medicis fortissime Gianne brigatis,
400   terribilem cuius forzam scit mundus atornum,
aut, Borbone, tibi, Francorum gloria prima,
cuius consilio nostra aetas floret et armis?
aut tandem Gonzaga tibi, Gonzaga Loyse,
cuius magnanimum pectus forzamque leonis,
405   grandezzamque animi, provas sine fine parandas
omnibus Orlandis, immo Sansonibus illis,
qui spezzant montes portantque in tergore scoios,
scit Carlus Carlique duces, scitque ipse diavol,
cui saepe intrepida cartellum mente dedisti?
410   Sic Malabolza procul, nunc sub, nunc supra volando,
dardeggiat valido pomranzia ferrea brazzo,
quae tam praecipiti mandantur fulgure Baldo,
quam si bombardis ruerent scoccantibus arcem.
Baldus, ab impazzo tali retenutus, adirat,
415   dumque parat sese vindictae, dumque cotalum
vult sibi de pedibus omnino levare travaium,
ille manigoldus scampat, scampandoque monstrat
pro scherno guanzas culaminis; inde revoltus
trat de carnero ballam slanzatque, nec umquam

away. And now Malabolgia lugs a bag heavy with round cannon-balls, and the blackguard launches tough nuts. But the cowardly rapscallion doesn't go near Baldo; he is content to wound and kill from a distance, like those who nowadays carry rifles and during war-time carry arquebuses, muskets, and "fly-swatters."

Isn't it true that any knave, any lice-ridden, greasy scullery-boy, any bread thief hiding behind a wall, watching quietly, taking aim from afar and squeezing the trigger with a rogue hand that should be cut off, can make "toof, taff" echo through the air. Such a one will kill you all by himself and penetrate your chest all by himself—even yours, O most stalwart Giovanni delle Bande Nere of the Medici clan, whose tremendous strength is known throughout the world! Or yours, Bourbon, supreme glory of the French, by whose wisdom and prowess in arms our age flourishes! Or even yours, Gonzaga, Luigi Gonzaga, whose magnificent heart and lion's strength, greatness of spirit and endless deeds—to be compared to those of all Orlandos, or rather to those of the Samsons who break mountains and carry cliffs on their backs—is known to Charles, and to Charles' generals and to the devil himself, since you have often fearlessly sent him a challenge!

And so Malabolgia from a distance, flying now low, now high, hurls iron oranges with his robust arm, which are fired off at Baldo with lightning speed, like bombards destroying a fortress. Blocked by this obstacle, Baldo is angered; but as he prepares his revenge, and hopes to get this nuisance out of his way once and for all, the rapscallion escapes, and while escaping scornfully displays his butt-cheeks. And then, turning back around, he takes a ball

393

410

420 fulminat indarnum, sed chioccat semper in elmo.
Qua re non opus est ut stet dormire guererus:
nunc saltu schivat, nunc sese chinus abassat,
poenitet et nullam secum portasse rodellam.
Belzebub hac sola bellandi sorte guadagnum
425 sperat, et hoc fieri Malabolzae munere victor.
Providus at Baldus, cernens non ultra cotantis
posse canonatis obsistier absque riparo,
Belzebub affrettat brancare manuque sinistra
fortiter afferrat per folta pilamina ventris,
430 inde levans stesumque tenens cum robbore brazzum,
sic sibi daemonium scuti facit esse reparum,
opponitque illum Malabolzae contra balottas.
Belzebub ergo, ducum princeps, archive diavol,
quantos discaricat Malabolzae barca naranzos,
435 tantos per schenam panzamque invitus anasat;
unde comandatur quamprestiter archibusero:
ut caveat regis personam laedere tanti.
At nihil attendit simili Malabolza comando,
immo capit pomum, quo quondam stravit Adamum,
440 pomatamque tirat, non quam vibrare iuventus
Napolitana solet, sed quam colubrina Milani.
Stridulat illa volans ducitque fogata lusorem,
Belzebub hanc recipit, Baldo reparante, ceresam,
meschinusque duas sentit sibi rumpere costas.
445 Tunc ea militibus praesumptio troppa videtur,
totus in un solum Malabolzam exercitus arma
vertit, et hunc iam iam facient in mille bocones,
ni det ei aiuttum Baldus. Dat Baldus aiuttum,
perque pedes ambos ambabus Belzebub ipsum
450 azzaffat manibus, fodrumque reponit in ensem.
Incipit (o bellam festam giocumque galantum!)
hunc diavolorum capitanum supra diablos

from his sack and launches it. He never fires in vain, but always hits Baldo's helmet. Hence, our warrior must not be caught sleeping: first he dodges with a leap, then he bends down low and regrets having brought no buckler with him. Only with this sort of warfare does Beelzebub hope for an advantage and, with Malabolgia's aid, to be the victor.

Yet Baldo is shrewd: realizing that he cannot further resist such 426 cannon fire without protection, he hastens to grab Beelzebub. With his left hand, he grasps tightly the thick pelt on his stomach; then, raising and keeping his arm distended by sheer strength, he turns Beelzebub into a protective shield and holds him to ward off Malabolgia's cannonballs. So Beelzebub, the foremost leader and arch-devil, must unwillingly savor on his back and belly all the oranges that Malabolgia's bark expels. So the arquebusier is ordered at once to take heed lest he harm the person of such a king.

However, Malabolgia pays no attention at all to such an order 438 and instead takes up the apple with which he had once felled Adam and throws an apple-bomb, not like those usually fired by Neapolitan youths, but like those from a Milanese cannon. It screams as it flies by, and its flame sheds light. Beelzebub, still acting as Baldo's shield, receives this cherry-bomb, and the wretch feels two of his ribs break. At this, the outrage seems too much for the soldiers; the entire army turns its weapons on Malabolgia alone, and would already be chopping him into a thousand morsels if Baldo did not help him. Baldo does help him: as he puts his sword back in its sheath, with both hands he grabs Beelzebub by both feet. He begins (O what a party! what noble merriment!) to swing this captain of the devils down on the demon hordes

valde menare giusum totumque, per ipsa suorum
cornua, forcones, grafios, lacerare tapinum.

455 Sed tamen Alchinus, Siriel, Malabranca, Minossus,
quattuor egregii caporales, arma piarunt
atque piare suos faciunt insemma guereros
ut sint auxilio Malabolzae quippe cusino,
namque cusinus erat germanus quattuor illis.

460 Trenta miara ruunt 'Arma, arma' cridantia coelo;
atque ad un trattum se totus inordinat ordo,
scinditur in partes geminas exercitus omnis,
quisque suam repetit banderam, quisque suumque
persequit alpherum, capitano quisque secundat.

465 Fama sub Infernum properat ferturque per aures
anxia Luciferi: gentem, cridat, esse levatam
in se medesimam, ducibus scordantibus ipsis.
Lucifer in mula, nullo sine tempore vecchia,
huc salit et dictum factum desopra venivit.

470 Sentit longe sonos, tamburros, cornua, trombas,
aëra quae turbant sursum, Phlegethonta deorsum.
Asmodeus, apro similis, Melloniel urso,
cum sex mille lupis Stygiis totidemque cruentis
singiaris porcis, adversa per arma feruntur

475 praecipites, guerramque nigram manegiare comenzant.
His Acheron Paymonque simul squadraeque suorum
cornibus obsistunt, ronchis, ronchonibus atque
dentigeris grugnis, quibus ossa miara teruntur.
Taratar ante alios celsis se cornibus effert,

480 provocat atque hostes si voiant prendere gattam.
Stizzaferrus aprit bocchae bene quinque cavezzos,
sannutusque vomit meschias cum sanguine bavas;
Molchana non tardat, nec Zaccara, nec Graficanis;
signa movent raptim, octo mille sequentibus illos.

with all his might and to lacerate the wretch on their horns, pitch-forks and hooks. But four excellent corporals, Alchino, Siriel, Malabranca and Minossus, take up arms and bid their troops to take up arms to aid their cousin, for Malabolgia is in fact a first cousin to these four. Thirty thousand of them charge, crying to the heavens, "To arms, to arms!" Yet suddenly all order becomes disorderly and the whole army breaks into two equal parts; each follows its own flag, each follows its own standard bearer, and each heeds its own captain.

Rumor rushes down to Hell and is brought all atremble through the ears of Lucifer. His people are fighting against themselves, she cries, with the generals quarreling. Upon hearing this, Lucifer mounts a mule as old as time and in a trice has come up to earth. He hears sounds from afar—drums, horns and trumpets—which disturb the air above and Phlegethon below. Asmodeo like a wild boar and Melloniel like a bear, with six thousand Stygian wolves and as many vicious wild hogs, ride precipitously against the enemy ranks and start to wage their black war. They encounter Acheron and Paymon with their squadrons, who oppose them with horns, hooks, pikes and boar-toothed snouts, by means of which thousands of bones are crushed. Taratar charges in front of the others with his long horns and challenges the enemy, seeing if they want to skin the cat. Stizzaferro opens his mouth a good fifteen cubits, and his fangs vomit foam mixed with blood. Molchana does not delay, nor Zaccara and Grafficane; they move the battle flags immediately with eight

465

485 Hos Malabranca prior, post quem Ciriattus afrontat,
denique terribili veniens Bombarda fracasso.
    Iamque spaventoso miscentur cuncta bagordo:
scopius auditur cornarum maximus, atque
sentitur grugnire sues, nitrire cavallos,
490 mastinos baiare canes mugiolareque tauros,
exurlare lupos, tygres squillare, leones
ruggere, sed diros alte cifolare dragones.
Baldus atrigarat se iam, non dante veruno
amplius impazzum seu forchis sive balottis,
495 namque bimembris erat contentio nata fralorum.
Nil tenet in manibus, quo plus combattere possit;
spada quiescit enim nec vult exire guainis.
Belzebub, officio mazzae iam functus un horam,
iverat in centum settanta miara bocones,
500 inque manu Baldi tantummodo manserat unus
pes ochae; sed membra quidem sua caetera, partim
arboribus pendent, ut milza, corada, budellae,
partim, per Baldi brazzum tridefacta minutim,
aspersere nigram faciem cuiusque diabli,
505 unde tapinellus, sua quo desgratia menat,
ibat membrorum quaerens fragmenta suorum.
Certamenter habet pro doia plangere causam,
sed quae membra sibi doleant nessuna trovantur,
non qui bagnentur pietosis fletibus occhi,
510 non quae lingua cridet magnis urlatibus 'Oyme',
non qui cum gemitu tampellent pectora pugni.
Cingar cum sociis Baldo retirantur apressum
stantque simul stricti nigram guardare bataiam.
Quale Cremonesis plenum caldare fasolis,
515 quando parecchiatur villanis coena famatis,
seu quale in giorno mortorum grande lavezum
impletumque fabis, subiecto brontolat igne,

thousand following them. First Malabranca confronts them, then after him Ciriatto, and lastly, with a terrible ruckus, comes Bombard.

By now everything is jumbled together in a frightening skir-   487 mish. One hears a massive crash of horns and the snorting of swine, the neighing of horses, the barking of guard dogs, the bellowing of bulls, the howling of wolves, the screeching of tigers, the roaring of lions and the loud hissing of ferocious dragons. Baldo had already stopped himself, for since a two-member struggle had arisen between them no one has bothered him at all with pitchforks or cannonballs. He has nothing in his hands to fight with any longer; in fact, his sword rests in its sheath and does not want to leave it.

After an hour of serving as a club, Beelzebub is reduced to   498 170,000 bite-size pieces; only one of his goosefeet remained in Baldo's hand, but some of his parts, like the spleen, the offal and the intestines, hang from trees; the rest were minced into tiny particles by Baldo's arm and sprayed onto the black face of each devil. Thus the poor creature went looking for fragments of his body parts, as his misfortune guides him. He certainly has good cause to cry in pain, but the parts that could weep for him cannot be found. There are no eyes that might moisten with piteous tears; no tongue which might cry out, "Woe is me!" in loud shrieks; no fists which might hammer at a chest with a hollow sound.

Cingar and his companions pull back near Baldo and stand   512 close together watching the black battle. Imagine a caldron full of beans from Cremona, when a dinner is being prepared for famished peasants, or when on the Day of the Dead a large pot full of

magna fasolorum confusio, magna fabarum
est ibi, dum saltant, tomant sotosoraque danzant;
520   tale diabolicum rupto certamen Averno
mescolat insemmam bruttissima monstra baratri;
scilicet: absque coda vulpes, cum cornibus ursos,
mastinos tripedes, porcosque suesque bicornes,
atque quadricornes tauros, atque ora luporum
525   inficata super spallas et colla gigantum,
montones caprasque magras, simiotta, schirattos,
maimonesque gatos, baboinos et mamotrettos,
semileonazzos griphes, aquilasque dragonum,
semique gregnapolas, civetones, barbaque zannos,
530   et qui rostra ferunt guffi sed brachia ranae,
quique asinorum sub orecchis corna becorum.
Haec ea garbulio vilupantur monstra medemo,
diversumque sonum, neque talem forsan uditum
seu per passatum, seu praesens, seu futurum,
535   fant simul; atque simul sex millia mille fit unum.
Et nisi rex baratri veniat, magnusque monarcha
regnorum Inferni praestissime Lucifer adsit,
cuius maiestas, cuius praesentia, cuius
Caesareus decor irarum brusamen amorzet,
540   de se, deque suis est actum, terminat aula,
terminat imperium, res publica persa ruinat.
      Ergo venit, venit ille ingens, immensus et altus
mille quaranta pedes, horrendus, bruttus et asper
Lucifer, atque facit per postas currere mulam,
545   octoque post illum proceres galopando stafezant.
Grugnifer est primus, cui regis filia coniux,
Mosca, Cutiferrus, Dragamas, Ursazzus et illi
tres secretari: Calacrassus, Sesmilo, Poffi.
Murmura bellantum sentibant inter eundo.
550   Sed per aventuram cappant ubi forte Bocalus,

legumes grumbles over the fire and there's a tremendous confusion of beans and legumes that jump and tumble and dance in all directions. Just so as Avernus erupts, the diabolical battle mixes together the ugliest monsters of the underworld, namely, foxes without tails, bears with horns, three-legged mastiffs, two-horned pigs and sows, four-horned bulls, muzzles of wolves stuck onto the shoulders and necks of giants, big sheep and scrawny goats, monkeys, squirrels, chimpanzees, baboons and marmosets, griffins that are half-lion and eagles from dragons and barn owls and hooded owls that are half-bat and those that have the beak of a horned owl and the arms of a frog, and any creature with goat horns under donkey ears. These monsters are all entangled in the same snarl; they make a strange new sound, the likes of which was perhaps never heard in the past, the present or the future, and six million act as one. And if the king of the underworld is not come, if the great monarch of the infernal reign, Lucifer, be not there, whose majesty, whose presence, whose Caesarian seemliness quenches the fires of anger, then it is all up with him and his subjects, their kingdom is at an end, their empire is at an end and their lost republic collapses.

Therefore, he comes — huge, immense, one thousand and forty 542 feet tall, horrible, repulsive and fierce. Lucifer comes and makes his mule run the posts, and after him hurtle eight galloping leaders. The first is Grugnifer, who is married to the king's daughter, then Mosca, Cutiferro, Dragamas, Ursazzo and three secretaries: Calacrasso, Sesmilo and Poffi. They heard the din among the combatants as they rode. But coincidentally, they turn up not far from Guidone's cell, where Boccalo was hidden by chance under a thorn bush, making tremors and shivers in the boiling month of

non procul a cella Guidonis, fasce sub uno
spinorum nascostus erat, fabricando tremantos
atque tremolantos in zugni mense boienti.
Tum vero ut sensit strepitum post terga novellum,
555   respicit angustam per bucam quacchius in umbra.
Ecce diavolazzum, toccantem sydera cornis,
cernit in ingenti mulazza currere postam.
Oh puta, quando videt monstrum tam granditer altum,
monstrum horrendum, ingens, deforme superque mulazzam
560   horrendam, ingentem, deformem stringere gambas,
quae passando pedes grevos sibi ponat adossum,
deque sua panza stampet fortasse fritaiam,
protinus, ut vacuo surgit leporetta coatto,
quam braccus bau bau latrando catavit anasum,
565   sic levat attonitus sbuccatque fratonibus illis;
per sortemque malam, spinas in veste tacatas
machionemque illum, quo se perforza ficarat,
retro tirat fugiens nec tempus habere videtur
tantum quo possit se distriggare viluppis.
570   Quondam ego Merlinus portabar supra mulettum
sat male cingiatum, velut est dapocago regazzi,
sat bene passutum, velut est man larga famei.
Dum fossum volui sprono saltare ficato
in costis muli, se bestia matta levavit
575   sellaque sub panza cingis mollantibus ivit.
Ipse ego sub maltam teneram caput omne ficavi.
Sed veluti mulettus, habens sub corpore bastum,
se magis et magis ad cursum stimulabat, et alto
cum collo nec non drittis currebat orecchis,
580   sic, sua strassinans post terga Bocalus id illud
intricum duris de spinis deque rovidis,
se magis incalzat, punctus sperone timoris,
vestigatque locum, seu pozzum, seu cagatorum,

June. But when he hears a new clamor at his back, from his shaded spot, he quietly peeks out from a narrow opening. And here he sees a huge devil, his horns reaching the stars, riding hard on an enormous mule. O just imagine, when he sees such an incredibly tall monster, an enormous, terrifying and loathsome monster, clinching his legs on an enormous, terrifying, loathsome mule, which in passing could trample upon him with its heavy feet and could maybe even flatten his belly like a pancake! At once, like an agile hare leaping from its empty hole when a hound barking "bow wow" finds it by sniffing, Boccalo rises up dazed and springs out of the brambles. Unfortunately, the thorns stick to his clothing, and as he flees, he pulls behind him that bush into which he'd thrust himself, and there didn't seem to be enough time for him to extricate himself from the tangles.

Once upon a time I, Merlin, was riding on a mule that was 570 quite poorly harnessed due to the stable boy's negligence and quite well-fed due to the groom's generous hand. When I tried to jump a ditch by digging my spur into the mule's flanks, the crazy beast reared, and the saddle with its loose straps slipped under the mule's belly, and I jammed my whole head into the soft mud. Now just as my little mule with the saddle under its body spurred itself to race faster and faster and ran with its neck held high and ears erect, so too Boccalo, dragging that clump of harsh thorns and briars behind him, goaded himself faster with the spur of fear and looked for a place, either a well or an outhouse, where he can be buried in the musk and amber of shit; he has no qualms, doesn't

in quo non dubitat, non spicam stimat aietti,
585 zibetto merdae soterarier ambraque cano,
dummodo tanta suis de spallis susta levetur.
Grugnifer, hoc viso, post illum protinus urtat
sprone cavalazzum sine testa et corpore magro,
cui fiaschi possent ab utroque galone tacari.
590 Boccalus cazzat se stricta in limina cellae,
mortus ubi et positus cadelaeto Guido iacebat.
Illeque spinorum mansit defora viluppus,
namque per angustum poterat minus ire foramen.
Grugnifer hunc seguitat dentrum. Boccalus achiappat,
595 sic improvistus, crucifixum praestiter illum,
qui pedibus morti, velut est usanza, tenetur;
non quod eum pro se deffendere vellet aposta,
verum nescio quae bona sors dat saepe socorsum
improvisa bono, qui nil pensabat, homazzo.
600 Prohque Deum atque homines! Nam quae maravilia maior
esse potest? Quae cosa magis tradenda librazzis
historiatorum? Quod opus mage nobile dandum
est scarpellinis, pistoribus atque poëtis?
Grugnifer, ut vidit sanctos in imagine vultus
605 illius aeternique Boni, summique Tonantis,
qui se consortesque suos castigat in igne,
illico ronzonem voltat calcagnaque menat,
smergolat altisono clamore petitque socorsum.
Boccalus, cui sors ad casum presa riescit,
610 cum signale crucis properat post terga diabli.
Lucifer imbattit, voltat quoque Lucifer atque,
quanta cum furia datur illi currere, currit;
instat Boccalus, 'Day day' que cridando menazzat,
vexilloque Dei regem propulsat Averni.
615 Cornutam Ursazzus toccat sperone giraffam,
Mosca sequens trepidus groppas bastonat Echydnae,

give a turnip about it, as long as this scourge is lifted from his shoulders.

Seeing this, Grugnifer quickly rushes after him, spurring a huge 587 horse with no head and a body so thin that jugs could be hung from each side of its ribs. Boccalo ducks into the narrow entrance of the cell where Guido lay dead on a bier. But the tangle of thorns remains outside since it could not fit through the narrow slit at all. Grugnifer follows him inside; and without thinking, Boccalo at once snatches the crucifix that is customarily placed at the feet of the dead. Not that he deliberately planned to defend himself with it; indeed I know not what good luck brings the good man help out of the blue, without his planning it.

Then, O God and men! What marvel could be greater? What 600 could be more exalted in the fat tomes of the chroniclers? What nobler subject could be offered to stone-cutters, paint-mixers and poets? As soon as Grugnifer sees on the cross the holy face of the Eternal Good, the Supreme Thunderer who punishes him and his consorts by fire, he immediately turns his horse, digs in his spurs and bellows in an ear-splitting clamor, begging for help. Boccalo, whose luck, seized by chance, succeeds, hastens after the devils with the sign of the crucifix. When Lucifer runs into him, he too turns and races off with all possible fury. Boccalo pursues and threatens him, crying, "Get him, get him!" — and with the banner of God, he drives off the king of Avernus.

Ursazzo spurs a horned giraffe, and behind him fearful Mosca 615 beats the back of Echidna. Next Cutiferro forces a Chimera to

inde Cutiferrus cogit trottare Chimaeram,
fertque Minotaurus Calacrassum, fert Briaraeus
Sesmilon, et Poffi portante Geryone muzzat;
620   ultimus est Dragamas, crocodili terga flagellat.
Sic omnes insemma ruunt vellentque tapini
cuncta magis tormenta pati quam cernere Christum.
At nihil indusiat Boccalus currere dretum,
donec arivarunt ubi grossus praelia campus
625   mescolat et nigri currebant sanguinis amnes.
Ecce, crucifixo procul apparente, diabli
protinus inque uno subito, miliaria mille
stridentes abeunt in fumum, tantaque puzza
linquitur ut prosit nasos stopare nientum.
630   Omnes andati sunt in malhora, nec unus
munere Boccali malspiritus ultra videtur.
Ergo Boccalus vivat vivatque botazzus,
vivat et antiquae domus inclyta nostra Folengae.

Liber vigesimus

Postquam, excazzatis Crucifixi ad signa diablis,
Baldus avantarat longo sermone Bocalum,
inque sua dixit non pocas laude parolas;
postquam sarcophago patrem sepelivit in illo,
5   quem modo reppererat Centaurus eoque medemo
condidit appressum genitori busta Lonardi,
haec dicta in facie tumuli sculpita relinquunt:
'Guido pater Baldi iacet hic'. Quod nempe motivum
est breve, sed maior stat eorum notio seclis.
10   Ipse tamen vates, Baldo rogitante, Gibertus,
postquam cuncta super tumulum suspensa fuerunt

trot; a Minotaur carries Calacrasso, Briareus carries Sesmilo, and Poffi darts off carried by Geryon. Last comes Dragamas, who whips a crocodile's back. Thus they all rush off together, and the wretches would rather suffer all manner of torments than look at Christ. And yet Boccalo does not hesitate in the least to run after them, until they arrive where the battle was being fought in a large field, and the waters ran dark with blood. Behold, the moment the Crucifix appears from afar, instantly a thousand times a thousand devils go up in smoke shrieking, and such a stink is left that it does no good to stop one's nose. They have all gone to ruin; thanks to Boccalo, not one evil spirit is still to be seen. So long live Boccalo, long live the bottle, and long live the illustrious house of our age-old Folengos!

Book XX

After the devils had been chased away by the image of the Crucifix, Baldo commended Boccalo in a long sermon and spoke not a few words in his praise. After that, he buried his father in the sarcophagus discovered earlier by the centaur, the same one in which he interred Leonardo's remains next to his father's. They leave these words sculpted on the front of the tomb: "Guido, father of Baldo, lies here." Undoubtedly, the inscription is brief, but longer endures their renown through the ages. And after all of Leonardo's weapons had been hung above the tomb and the customary trophy had been made, the poet Gilberto, at Baldo's request, sang thus, adding to the stone many new verses: "These arms,

arma Leonardi, et factum de more trophaeum,
sic cecinit, sic plura dedit nova carmina saxo:
    'Haec ea, vestibulo quae primo adfixa, viator,
15 suspicis arma, piis quaeso venerare susurris.
Ipsa Leonardo decori, Leonardus et armis
ipse fuit; viguere simul, simul ecce quiescunt.
Martia Roma suis semper gratetur alumnis,
hinc ornata Ursis, illinc suffulta Columnis'.

20   Talia finierant, ut ut potuere barones;
nam, rogo, quae frifolis est convenientia trombis
cum campanarum sonitu *Chyrieque lysonis?*
Quid piccas manegiare leves, disponere squadras
cum *Requiem aeternam, Misererereque, Deque profundis?*
25 Basta quod almancum, devota mente pregantes,
signentam flexis genibus dixere coronam.
        At restat pagare suum Pandraga doverum,
quam tenet arbor adhuc cum soghis membra ligatam.
Parvum de stipulis secchis fecere casottum,
30 in quo, mandato Baldi, gabiazza brusatur.
Ipse tamen generosus abit lontanus ab illis,
cernere non passus miseri spectacula facti.
Ac ita finivit Pandraghae vita putanae,
ac ita finiscant tot quot retrovantur in orbe
35 sgualdracchae similes, ruptaeque utrimque gaioffae.
Sed vix Tartareis descenderat illa paësis,
ecce repentino sese movet insula cursu,
spaventatque animos sic improvista gaiardos.
At mox pensantes, memorant hanc esse balenam,
40 quam modo Guido senex Baldo praedixit et altris,
quod, postquam Stygias scanfarda calarit ad umbras,
ipsa teneretur non amplius insula monstro;
quae liquidas currit tam praesta per aequoris undas,

234

traveler, which you see hanging by the main entrance, I entreat you to venerate with reverent sighs. They did honor to Leonardo, and Leonardo did honor to them. Together they flourished; together they rest here in peace. Martial Rome shall forever rejoice in her children, distinguished on this side by the Orsini, sustained on that by the Colonnas."

The knights had concluded these rites as best they could, for I ask you, what harmony exists between blasting trumpets and the sound of bells and the *Kyrie Eleison?* What between the management of light infantry, the stationing of troops, and the *Requiem aeternam,* the *Miserere* and the *De profundis?* Let it suffice that each of them at least prayed the rosary, praying with a devout mind and bended knee.

But it remains for Pandraga to pay her due; her limbs were still tied to a tree with ropes. On Baldo's orders they made a little pyre of dry straw on which the strumpet is burned. This noble man, however, walks far away, unable to view the spectacle of this wretched event. So ended the life of the whore Pandraga, and so may all such slatterns end, and all the trollops found on earth who have been violated both in front and behind.

She had no sooner descended to the land of Tartarus than behold! suddenly the island moves forward by itself, and this unexpected turn frightens the brave souls. But then, thinking about it, they recall that the island is really a whale. Old Guido had just predicted to Baldo and the others that, as soon as the tart had fallen into the Stygian shadows, the island would no longer be retained by the monster. It races so fast through the watery waves of

quod non bombardam velocius ire videmus,
45 et iam motu oculi complerat trenta mearos.
Cingar desperans loquitur: 'Qui trenta diavoi?'
Centaurusque stupet, quia sic non fecerat ante.
Falchettusque alios animat lassare pauram,
cernere namque novas plus fit laudabile cosas,
50 ireque per mundum variosque patire travaios,
quam semper proprio panzam grattare paëso,
nec bastare animum pagnoccam linquere dretum.
At Baldus reticens novitatem masticat illam
commandatque omnes in littore stare sedentes.
55 Boccalus buffonus ait: 'Gaudere bisognat,
mysterumque facit, socii, quod stemus alegri.
Non poterit pedibus nostris mancare terenus.
Quid dare travalii tempesta marina valebit,
si mare passamus, sub plantis stante tereno?'
60 Hinc non poca quidem sociis est orta voluptas,
qui sbalzare vident de boschis deque cavernis,
ursos, cingiales, leopardos atque leones,
quos novitas rerum cogit se tradere ponto.
Inde reguardantes aliam videre facendam,
65 quam Virmazzus eis, digito monstrante, palesat:
Guidonis post terga vident remanere sepulchrum,
atque super scopulum mediis fundarier undis.
Quin etiam anchoreo detenta est fusta bidenti
in mediaque maris campagna sola remansit.
70 Ast alia en maior visa est maravilia longe,
namque super grossam navem persona gigantis
apparet, drittusque haerens, sese arboris instar
erigit et brazzis velam sparpagnat apertis:

the sea that we don't see a cannonball fly more quickly. Already in the blink of an eye, it has gone thirty miles.

Despairing, Cingar asks, "What the devil is this?" The centaur   46 is amazed because the island had never done this before. Falchetto encourages the others to lay aside their fears, since seeing new things and going around the world experiencing various trials is more praiseworthy than remaining forever in one's own country and scratching one's belly, lacking the courage to leave one's supper behind. But Baldo silently chews over this novelty, and orders everyone to stay seated on the shore. Boccalo the buffoon says, "We need to keep our spirits up, and it's our duty to stay happy, friends. The ground under our feet will not disappear. What sort of trouble can a tempest at sea cause us, if we cross the sea with the ground beneath our soles?"

Indeed, the companions take no small pleasure when they see   60 bears, boars, leopards and lions jump out of the woods and caverns, for the strangeness of the situation drives the beasts to throw themselves into the sea. Next, looking around, they see another thing which Virmace points out with his finger. They see Guido's sepulcher remain behind them, settled on a reef in the middle of the waves. Their boat too is held back by its two-pronged anchor and remains alone in the middle of the sea-meadow. But then, behold! a greater marvel is seen in the distance, for upon a vast ship the figure of a giant appears, standing upright and holding fast like a mast, and he spreads open the sails with his arms stretched

namque mari et vento proprius cascaverat arbor.
75 Dico quod antennam scusant duo brachia longam,
    estque arbos bustum torrazzo firmior omni.
    Flent venti, si flare sciunt, saltentque per undas,
    si saltare volunt, castrones aequoris albi:
    tam poterunt magnum fortemque movere gigantem,
80 quam calzus moschae roccam murosque Trevisi.
    'Doh diavol', ait Cingar, 'quae cosa videtur?
    Nonne gigantonem, compagni, cernitis illum?
    Nonne tenens velam stat saldus more pilastri?'
    Cui Boccalus: 'Amen. Oh infelix illa taverna,
85 in qua tanta quidem se machina ventris aloggiat!
    Integer huic minimum bos implet apena budellum'.
    Ast etiam ipse gigas, veniens incontra, stupebat:
    cur sic illa, velut navillius, insula currit?
    Hi mirantur eum, qui praestat ut arboris instar;
90 ille stupet, quondam firmam, nunc currere terram.
    Denique iungentes medio se gurgite, sicut
    fit quando Paduae per flumen, nomine Brentam,
    nunc andando rates, nunc se redeundo salutant,
    incipiunt occhis sese guardare ficatis.
95 Falchettus subito laeta cum voce favellat:
    'O Deus, insogno? Estne hoc phantasma? Fracassus!
    Ecce Fracassus adest! Ille est qui carbasa tendit!'
    Moschinus dictum confirmat: 'Certe, daverum!
    Illa gigantaei tota est persona Fracassi.
100 O Deus, en quali foggia retrovamur amici!
    Ire sub Infernum tuti poterimus adessum,
    postquam nobiscum venit haec montagna gigantis'.
    Cingar alhora vocat laetus cifolatque deinde.
    Sed cum Fracassus sese chiamare Fracassum
105 audiit, abiectis velis, ex tempore saltat,
    supraque currentem summa de nave terenum

wide, because the actual mast had been toppled by wind and wa-
ter. I mean that his two arms function as a long yard-arm and his
body as a mast, stronger than any solid tower. The winds can blow
if they know how to blow, and the whitecaps can break over the
waves if they want to break: they are able to move the big strong
giant as little as a fly's leg can shake the citadel and walls of
Treviso. "What the devil? What do we see here?" exclaims Cingar,
"Don't you see that huge giant, friends? Doesn't he hold the sail
standing firm as a pillar?"

Boccalo answers him, "Amen! O it's an unlucky tavern where   84
such a massive stomach is lodged! An entire ox could barely fill his
small intestine." But meanwhile, the giant himself, coming closer,
was amazed — why was the island racing away like that, like a fast
little boat? These people are marveling at him, as he looks like a
mainmast, and he is amazed that what had been *terra firma* is now
racing along. Finally, meeting in the middle of the sea, just as
barks on the river Brenta in Padova greet each other coming and
going, they begin to look at each other and stare. Falchetto sud-
denly exclaims in a delighted voice, "O God, am I dreaming? Is
this a phantom? Fracasso! Look! Fracasso is here! He's the one
holding that canvas."

Moschino confirms this. "There's no doubt. That really is the   98
gigantic Fracasso in person! O God! Look in what manner we find
our friends! Now we will be able to go down to Hell safely, since
this mountain of a giant is coming with us."

After that, Cingar happily calls out and then whistles. But   103
when Fracasso hears himself called Fracasso, he lets go of the sails,
and immediately jumps down from the top of the ship onto the

saltat, et ipsius magno sub pondere salti
insula balenae pene est anegata sub undis.
Currere quae coepit maiori percita cursu,
110 nam sibi spezzantur costae saltante giganto.
Quin etiam navis Zenovae grossissima, de qua
sustulerat saltum, retro ivit quinque mearos.
Naturalis enim mos est respingere barcam,
quando quis in terram se buttat navis ab orlo.
115 Illum quamprimum Baldus et Cingar abrazzant;
abrazzant, inquam, gambas vix supra cavecchias;
nec non Falchettus, nec non Moschinus et altri
strinxerunt illum et multas fecere carezzas,
nam bon compagnum se vultu monstrat alegro.
120 Boccalus, saltu tremefactus, fugerat inde;
mox redit et longam fert scalam forte catatam.
Id rident fratres, nec scitur causa facendae.
Ut fuit inter eos, magnum petit ante Fracassum,
vultque suis spallis scalam accostare tamagnis,
125 quod nisi cum scala sursum montare valeret.
'Quid facturus', ait Baldus, 'Boccale galante?
Scala quid importat? Visne altam prendere roccam?'
'Non', Boccalus ait, 'sed orecchiae dire parolam'.
Risit amichevolam Boccali quisque novellam,
130 ac nihil altaerus comportat cuncta Fracassus,
ut bona cum schiettis compagnis semper usanza est.
Attamen ipse stupet, crispata fronte, stupendam
rem tantam, sensuque illam submaginat alto,
quodve videt propriis occhialis credit apenam.
135 Miracli bramat tamen huius cernere causam
vultque quod effectum penitus sua vota sequantur.
En se dispoliat nudum retinetque mudandam
ut nodare queat speditus, agente bisogno.
Stant ibi perplexi, quid voiat inire Fracassus;

racing land. Under the great weight of this jump, the whale-island is almost drowned in the waves. As if spurred onward, it starts to race with a faster course, for its ribs were broken when the giant jumped. What's more, the massive Genovese vessel from which he had leapt is pushed back five miles. Indeed, it is a law of nature for a boat to recoil when someone throws himself off the side of it onto land.

Baldo and Cingar embrace him as soon as possible; they em- 115
brace his legs, I mean, just above the ankles. And then Falchetto and next Moschino and the others hugged him and made a fuss over him, for his joyful face shows him to be a good friend. Boccalo, terrified by his leap, had run away; now he comes back carrying a long ladder he'd found somewhere. His companions laugh at this; they don't understand the reason for his actions. After he reaches the group, he faces the great Fracasso and wants to bring the ladder up to his mighty shoulders because only with a ladder can he get up there. "What are you doing, my dear Boccalo?" asked Baldo. "What's the ladder for? Do you want to assault a high fortress?"

"No," says Boccalo, "I just want to say a word in your ear." 128
They all laugh at this friendly joke, and Fracasso is not at all haughty and accepts everything, as is the good custom among true friends. Nevertheless, he is amazed. With furrowed brow, he ponders such a wonder in his lofty mind and scarcely believes what he sees with his own eyes. But he yearns to know the cause of such a miracle and wants his undertaking to be fully attained. So he strips naked, keeping only his underpants, so that he can swim freely should the need arise. The others stand there perplexed: what does Fracasso plan to accomplish? He begs them to strip

140   quos pregat ut pariter cum secum corpora nudent.
     Id faciunt omnes, metuentes forte negari.
     Ergo gigas, duro qui magnas corpore forzas
     altus habet, nec se putat Herculis esse minorem,
     extirpat vecchiam manibus de littore querzam.
145   Hinc tirat e fodro cortellum, panis ad usum
     semper adopratum, cui brachia quinque misura est.
     Hoc totam querzam disfrondat, more stropelli,
     moreque flexibilis virgae qua vigna ligatur;
     et faciens partem, quae grossior extat, aguzzam,
150   ingentem fustum calcans in littore ficcat,
     ut ficcare solet steccos oselator in agris,
     seu cum pernices, seu cum vult prendere quaias.
     'En', Boccalus ait, 'porros mangiare bisognat!'
     Baldus cum sociis ridet multumque Gibertus
155   miratur tantis de forzibus esse gigantem.
     Ecce magis fretolosa ruit prestezza balenae,
     namque suis sentit costis intrare cavecchium.
     Quo facto, longam drittamque rafrontat abetem;
     hanc quoque tam facilem, ruptis radicibus, extrat
160   quam facilis tenero scalogna cavatur ab horto.
     Undique dispennat tronconem frondibus, atque
     vult habeat formam remi vogare parati.
     Haec abies scusat remum; haec querza, tereno
     inficcata, dabit forcam, cui remus apoggiat.
165   Tum bene fundatis pedibus, distendere schenam
     incipit et vogat balenae contra viaggium.
     Contra, inquam, cursum balenae remigat et non
     onziolam lentat; magis immo magisque reforzat
     terribiles tanto schenae conamine brazzos
170   ut per nervigerum strepitent ossamina corpus,
     deque alto caschet vultu larghissimus imber.
     Confessat numquam similem tolerasse fadigam.

themselves naked along with him. They all do it, perhaps terrified of drowning. Next the lofty giant, who has great strength in his hard body and does not consider himself inferior to Hercules, uproots a mature oak from the bank with his hands. Then from its sheath he pulls a knife that measures five cubits in length which he always uses to cut bread. With it, he strips the entire trunk as if it were a twig or a flexible stick for binding vines. Having sharpened the thicker end, he jabs the immense trunk into the shore, just as a bird catcher will jab stakes into a field when he wants to capture grouse or quail. "It looks like we'll be eating leeks," says Boccalo. Baldo and his companions laugh, and Gilberto is much astonished that the giant has such strength. And behold, the whale rushes with even greater speed when it feels that peg penetrating its ribs.

Having done this, Fracasso turns to a tall straight fir tree and 158 this too he extracts easily, breaking its roots as easily as one would pull a leek from a tilled garden. On all sides he strips the large trunk of foliage and gives it the shape of an oar ready for rowing. Thus this fir serves as an oar, and the oak stuck in the ground will serve as an oarlock on which the oar will rest. And now, with his feet planted firmly, he begins to stretch his back and row counter to the whale's direction. I mean to say, he rows against the whale's course, and does not let up for an instant. Instead, he plies his tremendous arms with such exertion of his back that the bones in his muscular body complain and a torrent of rain falls from his lofty face. He swears he has never endured such an effort. Seeing this

Baldus, id aspiciens, aliis comitantibus, ultro
altoriare parat, quem scridat valde Fracassus:
175 'Desine, Balde, precor: totum sic ducere mundum
dat mihi nunc animus; rogo te, mi Balde, recedas'.
Illico cessavit Baldus, sermone Fracassi,
qui magis impellit spallas gambasque manusque.
Sudat et horrendo repiat cum pectore laenam.
180 Nil per tres horas balenae cursus atrigat,
nil tam praecipitem valet ille siare caminum;
concita namque nimis cavat undis bestia fossam,
et sforzata magis properat nescitque trigari.
Hinc sdegnata quidem mens est altaera gigantis.
185 Tres ibi puntadas tanto dat pectoris urto,
unam post aliam, quod naso tangit arenam,
sic basso, sic ille chino se corpore slongat.
Denique consequitur votum, iuxtaque talentum
sistitur, immo retro cursum balena reflectit.
190 Obstupuere omnes tam fortis robur homazzi:
quando hic sufficiens fuerit voltare caminum
tam magni piscis, qui regnum tergore portat.
Gambarus indretum sic sic andare videtur,
ut nunc retrogrado praeceps ruit insula passu.
195 Non tamen interea cessat vogare Fracassus,
vult per despresium naturae vincere guerram.
Navigat ingentesque facit, dum navigat, undas.
Sed tamen impatiens tolti balena viaggi,
et quod per forzam retro sua poppa tiretur,
200 ecce improviso longam super aequora caudam
exerit, atque illa colpos menare comenzat
tam grandes crudosque simul, tam valde sonantes
ut strepitum nuper diabolica guerra minorem
fecerit, et, nisi succurrat possanza gigantis,
205 non poterunt certe nostri scampare barones.

with the rest of the group, Baldo gladly offers to help, but Fracasso scolds him soundly. "Stop, Baldo, I beg you: my mind now gives me the power to lead the whole world this way. I ask you, dear Baldo, stand back."

Baldo immediately yields at the words of Fracasso, who rows ever harder with his shoulders and legs and hands. He sweats and catches his breath in his awesome chest. For three hours the whale does not slow its course at all, nor is Fracasso able to overcome such a precipitous trajectory, for the overly agitated beast carves a trough in the water and, being constrained, hurries faster and will not be stopped. Thus the giant's sense of pride is offended. He tugs three times in a row, pushing his chest so hard with his body bent so low that his nose touches the ground. Finally, he gets what he wants, and in accordance with his wishes, the whale stops and actually reverses its course. They were all amazed that the giant's strength was enough to change the path of a fish so huge that it carries a kingdom on its back. Just as one sees a crab going backwards, so now the island rushes headlong in retrograde motion. But in the meantime Fracasso does not stop rowing; he wants to win the war in defiance of nature. He rows ahead, and as he rows, makes immense waves.

But the whale is frustrated by its thwarted voyage and because its tail is being drawn back by force. Behold! It suddenly lifts its long tail over the waters and begins to deliver blows so great and ferocious, resounding so loudly, that the diabolical warfare which had just now taken place made less noise. And if the giant's might does not aid them, our knights will certainly be unable to escape.

Cauda erat (ut referunt annalia nostra Cipadae)
longa quatercentos, nullo mancante, cavezzos.
Hanc menat huc, illuc, per drittum perque traversum,
inque infinitos nodos aliquando viluppat,
210   ut fit quando piat truccum villanus aguzzum
dormentemque viae serpam traditorus asaltat.
Dextriter ad testam punctam bastonis acostat,
inde premit schiazzatque illi, velut ova, cerebrum;
dumque tenet fixum, nitens in littore, palum,
215   illa nihil rehavere potens ab acumine testam,
dimenat reliquum prolixi corporis, et nunc
dat baculo formam thyrsi, nunc chioccat arenam.
Sic tampellat aquas balena, tiratque roversos
terribiles, spezzatque ornos vecchiasque cipressos,
220   ipseque gran strepitus sentitur otanta miaros.
Tum quoque parte alia grossissima testa levatur
fluctibus e mediis et boccam sbarrat edacem.
Proh! quam magni oculi, quam larga foramina nasi!
Cui montagna caput, cui frons campagna videtur,
225   dentorumque altos pinos longhezza somiat.
Non, Fracasse, tamen brazzos arcare rafinas;
et magis atque magis duplicatur fortia schenae.
Hunc animat Cingar, dicens: 'Fracasse gaiarde,
nunc te nassutum Morgantis semine monstras.
230   Sta saldus stagnusque simul, paladine valente!'
Talia dum stimulat Cingar, balena coazzam,
fulminis ad guisam, tanto conamine vibrat
quod, veluti paias, tridat plus trenta cipressos,
altaque truncones volitant per sydera virdi.
235   Mox venit ad spallas medesima botta Fracassi,
quae cantare animam facit illi in corpore vasto.
Protinus, abiecto remo, Fracassus aferrat
codazzam strictis manibus retinetque gaiardus,

The tail (as our annals of Cipada record) was no less than four hundred cubits long. He swings it here and there, right and left, and every now and then it gets tangled in endless knots, just as happens when a peasant takes a pointed club and sneakily assaults a snake asleep in the road: with his right hand, he brings the point of the cudgel close to the reptile's head, and then pushes it and splatters its brain like an egg. And while he holds the stake firmly, pressing it into the ground, the serpent, utterly unable to get its head back out from under the point, thrashes the rest of its long body. At times the snake makes the club resemble a thyrsus, and at times it smacks the ground. Just so, the whale thumps the water and lashes back violently, breaking apart ash trees and full-grown cypresses, and the loud crashing is heard eighty miles away.

Right then, from the other end, its enormous head rises up 221 from the middle of the swells and throws open its voracious mouth. O, the eyes are so big, the nose holes so wide! Its head is a mountain, its forehead a field; its teeth are so long they resemble tall pines. But nevertheless you, Fracasso, do not stop arching your arms and redoubling the force of your back again and again. Cingar takes courage, saying, "Gallant Fracasso, now you show that you were born of Morgante's seed. Be brave and hold fast, valiant paladin!"

While Cingar cheers him on with words like these, the whale 231 thrashes its big tail like a bolt of lightning, with such force that it crushes thirty cypresses as if they were straw, and the big green trunks fly up to the lofty stars. Soon the same blow strikes Fracasso's shoulders and rouses the spirit in his huge body. Swiftly throwing away the oar, Fracasso seizes the huge tail in his tight

cui tales donat streppos talesve tiradas
240 quod mugire facit grossasque molare corezas.
'Strictam', Baldus ait, 'strictam, Fracasse, coazzam
detineas: pulchrum faciam tibi cernere colpum'.
Quo dicto, spadam de taio fortiter urget
ut possit taiare viam de netto coazzam.
245 At nihil offendit, retro quia spada resaltat,
nam squamis passim duris erat illa coperta.
Presta caput, tractum medio de gurgite, voltat
obscurasque aperit multo sofiamine boccas,
et parat, incutiens sannas, mordere gigantem;
250 cui pede dat calzum tam grandem tamque gravosum
ut smassellaret tres dentes extra ganassas.
Illa boans reboansque simul stridensque per auras,
aequora mugisonis coelumque revulnerat echis.
Inde, cruentosos vomitans super aethera spudos,
255 Iunonis bellas imbrattat stercore damas.
Mox iterum, dum sentit adhuc sibi stringere caudam,
testonem volgit propter boccare gigantem;
at Virmazzus erat brazzo dardoque paratus:
hunc iacit et dextrum sfronzando ficcat in occhium,
260 punctaque cervellas intrans penetravit ad imas.
Cingar, Falchettus, Moschinus tela frequentant
conglomerare procul: festucos, saxa, quadrellos,
spinarum fasces, vulsos cum gramine cespos,
omnia convolvunt ridentque insemma novellum
265 hoc genus armorum, nec non risibile bellum.
Assaltare lupum vidi talvolta vilanos,
quando fame ductus quaerit quem devoret agnum.
It bassus bassus per sulcos perque ruidas,
donec aquistatur quidquid sua voia bramabat.
270 Ecce fugit portatque agnum cunctisque palesat.
Turba vilanorum, velut est usanza gaioffis,

grip and courageously holds it; he gives it such yanks and tugs that he makes the whale grunt and let loose heavy farts. "Hold tight, hold that big tail tight, Fracasso!" calls Baldo. "I will show you a handsome blow." So saying, he vigorously swings the blade of his sword, trying to cut the tail clean off. Yet he does no harm: the blade bounces back, because the whale is covered all over with hard scales. Quickly the whale lifts its head from the middle of the sea and turns it, opening its cavernous mouth with great blowing. It tries to bite the giant by striking with its fangs, but Fracasso gives the whale such a great and violent kick that he knocks three teeth from its jaw. Bellowing back and forth and shrieking through the air, it rends the sea and sky with its echoing groans. After that, vomiting bloody sputum into the heavens, it befouls Juno's lovely maidens with filth.

Then, once again, feeling its tail still being grasped, it turns its 256 head to swallow the giant, but Virmace is ready with his arm and javelin. He throws it, and with a whistling sound, it sticks in the whale's right eye, its point penetrating deep into the brain. From a distance, Cingar, Falchetto and Moschino continue to pile up projectiles: sticks, rocks, bricks, bundles of thorns, uprooted bushes and grasses. They roll these all up and laugh together at this new kind of weaponry and at this ludicrous war. I have on occasion seen peasants assault a wolf, when, driven by hunger, it looks for a lamb to eat. The wolf slinks very, very low to the ground, moving through ditches and briar patches, until it gets what it craves. Then it flees, carrying the lamb and showing it to everyone. The mob of peasants, as is the custom of scoundrels, rushes forth

sparpagnata ruit, coelum sbraioribus implet,
cumque ruginosis spuntonibus occupat illum;
qualem rumorem dictis factisque viluppant,
275 talem barrones misturant contra marinum
monstrum illud magnisque auras clamoribus implent.
Baldus habet voiam prorsus taiare coazzam,
non cessat punctas, mandrittos atque roversos,
sed quo plus chioccat, plus mancum vulnerat ensis.
280 Ergo viam gittat spadam plenusque furore
se parat expectans quod maxima testa resurgat.
En iterum stizzosa menat cum dentibus unum
terribilem morsum, sperans sorbere gigantem;
sed Baldus, qui nudus erat tunc corpore, tostus
285 saltat, orecchionem manibus prendendo duabus,
fortiter hunc retinet; subitus quoque Falco subintrat,
atque aliam sudando prius zaffavit orecchiam;
cui tamen altorium donat Moschinus; at illa
granditer exululat stridisque assordat Olympum,
290 fatque sibi forzam pro se retirare sotacquam;
sed non posse datur, caudam retinente Fracasso,
nec sua testa sibi est in libertate primaia.
Illa tirat giusum, susum retirantibus istis:
quod fieri non posse tibi fortasse videtur;
295 accascasse tamen sic sic monimenta recordant.
Talia dum fortis Baldus sociique maneggiant,
ecce iterum sprovistus adest pirata Lyronus.
Hic simulac persam cognoverat esse galaeam,
quam sibi sustulerat Baldus Baldique sodales,
300 hos quaerit giuratque illis mangiare coradam.
Et iam sex centum leucas passarat aquarum,
atque Zibeltarri per stricta canalia corsus,
ire per Oceanum spretis praesumpserat austris,
et voltans proram contra Afros parte sinistra

helter-skelter, fills the skies with yelling and attacks the wolf with rusty pikes. Their words and deeds create a commotion like that our heroes are stirring up against the sea monster, and they fill the air with great shouts.

Baldo wants to cut the whale's tail off completely. He continues his thrusts, forward cuts and backhands, but the more he strikes, the less his sword wounds. So he throws aside the sword, and full of fury stands ready, waiting for the huge head to re-emerge. Meanwhile, the infuriated beast lands another terrible bite with its teeth, hoping to gulp down the giant. But Baldo, who was naked then, quickly jumps and grasps one large ear with both hands and holds it tight. Falchetto immediately steps forward as well and, sweating, grabs the other ear. Moschino helps him too, and the whale roars ever louder and deafens Olympus with its cries and makes an effort to retreat under the water but is not able to, with Fracasso holding its tail and its head not at liberty as it was before. The whale pulls downward as they pull upward. This may not seem possible to you, but documents record that it happened just like this. 277

While mighty Baldo and his companions are thus engaged— behold! the pirate Lirone comes back unexpectedly. As soon as he realized that he'd lost the ship that Baldo and his companions had taken from him, he went looking for them and swore he would eat their hearts. He had already traveled six hundred leagues by sea and had passed through the narrow straits of Gibraltar. Despite the west winds, he dared venture on the ocean and, turning his prow towards Africa on the left, had come upon a sea never 296

305 venerat in pelagum non ante vogabile maium,
     cui sedet oppositum montagnae culmen adustae;
     quae, quia sustentat cervice solaria lunae,
     mons Lunae dicta est, quae busa est tota dedentrum.
     Has Lyronus aquas sulcat cercatque nemigos,
310 blasphemat coelum, quoniam non retrovat illos.
     Armatas secum numero fert trenta galaeas,
     in quibus ad remos noviter perforza ligarat
     mille Zenovesos, Colicutti ad littora presos,
     quos Mutinae princeps Philofornus duxerat illuc,
315 perque tradimentum fuerat dux captus ab illis.
     Fecerat et taiam Lyrono mille medaias,
     quas Pretus Iannus fino stampaverat auro.
     Lyronus tamen hunc solum cortesus honorat,
     ast aliis nervo ventosat terga bovino.
320 Trenta vehit fustas (seu fustas sive galaeas)
     namque, volens pelagi diversas quaerere bandas,
     suspicat aguaitos inimica per aequora tesos.
     Illum praecipue multi per regna tyranni
     cercant denariis multis trapolare pagatis,
325 namque diavol erat non lassans vivere quemquam.
     Huc igitur properans, celerantibus ante galaeis,
     praecipit ad littus Schiavones flectere proras;
     sed stupet aspiciens caudam testamque tamagnam,
     nec minus ingentem bustum possamque Fracassi,
330 qui smisuratam tenet alto corpore caudam.
     Clarius hoc factum meliusque videre talentat;
     egreditur primus mandatque uscire seguaces,
     mandat et adduci sibi magnum Spezzacadenam
     (Spezzacadena fuit Leonardi quippe cavallus,
335 quem navali olim tulerat certamine Baldo).
     Saltat in arzonem armatus, sine tangere staffam,
     destrerumque acrem nullo sperone maneggiat.

before able to be navigated. In front of him stood the peak of a scorched mountain whose peak supports the sphere of the Moon. Hence it is called Moon Mountain, and is totally hollow inside. Lirone plows these waters looking for his enemies; he blasphemes the heavens because he doesn't find them. He brings with him thirty armed galleys in which he had forcibly chained a thousand Genoese sailors recently captured near the shores of Calicut. Philoforno, prince of Modena, had led them there, and this leader had been betrayed into captivity by the pirates and had made a payment to Lirone of a thousand coins that Prester John had minted in fine gold. Hence, Lirone treats only Philoforno courteously; on the backs of the others he raises welts with a rawhide strap. He sails with thirty vessels (whether vessels or galleys), because he intends to explore various regions of the sea and suspects ambushes have been laid in enemy waters. Many tyrants in different kingdoms try to entrap him by paying a lot of money, for he was a devil who let no one live in peace.

Thus, while speeding along with the galleys out in front, Lirone 326 instructs the Slavs to turn their prows toward shore, but is amazed to see the whale's huge head and tail, and then the equally immense torso and might of Fracasso, who is holding that immeasurable tail with his great body. Lirone wishes to see this matter more clearly and distinctly. He is the first to disembark, and he orders his men to leave and orders the great Spezzacadena to be brought to him (Spezzacadena was in fact Leonardo's horse, which Lirone had taken from Baldo earlier during the naval battle). He jumps into the saddle armed, without touching the stirrups, and guides the spirited charger without spurs.

Cingar ait Baldo: 'Num cerno Spezzacadenam?
Balde, viden? Num somnus hic est? Num visio falsi?
340 Ille quidem latro est, ille, inquam, boia diabli,
qui nostram rapuit navim secumve cavallos'.
Impatiens ullum Baldus stimare periclum,
protinus accurrit contra brancatque cavallum
per frenum, bravans quamvis sit corpore nudo:
345 'Sta, latro, saldus!', ait; 'Non altro nomine scirem
te nomare! Latro es! Dignus quem forca guadagnet.
Iste tuus non est, meus est. Desmonta cavallum!'
Quando Lyronus equi briliam videt esse piatam,
obstupet in prima facie pensatque pochettum
350 quomodo vir nudus sic possit usare brauram;
attamen in fianchis destrerum calcibus urget
ut quatris pedibus paladino balzet adossum.
At Baldus, gatto similis, dabanda levatur
cum salto, pariterque tirans in pectora stoccum,
355 fecit ei mancare lenam, quae appena ritornat.
At mille interea veniunt infrotta latrones,
quos praecedit atrox quidam capitanius, Hippol,
qui frater Lyronis erat, corsarus et ipse:
scaltritus, guerraeque avidus, famaeque sititor.
360 At cum Centaurus bellum videt esse paratum,
armis armatur subito fulgentibus, atque
it celer ad fustas, armato milite vodas,
quos menat, exceptis cinquanta, citissimus Hippol.
Caudam balenae non audet linquere prudens
365 ipse gigas, dubius ne se velut ocha trapozzet.
Baldus ataccarat se fortem contra Lyronem,
quem trovat expertum guerrae validumque guererum.
Circum circa illum, tamquam leonessa, regirat,
cui facit, existens nudus, sudare camisam.
370 Nudus osat certare, tamen non dextera nuda est,

Cingar says to Baldo, "Do I make out Spezzacadena, Baldo, do   338
you see? Is this a dream? Is this a mirage? That's the thief, I
say, that's the devil's henchman who stole our ship and our horses
with it."

Too impatient to weigh the danger, Baldo quickly runs up and   342
grabs the horse by the bridle, threatening despite his naked body,
"Stop right there, thief! I know no other name to call you—you
are a thief worthy for the gallows to claim! That horse is not
yours, but mine! Get off my horse!" When Lirone sees him seize
the horse's bridle he is at first amazed and wonders a moment how
a naked man could be so menacing. But then he prods the steed in
the flanks with his heels to make it trample the paladin with all
four feet. Yet Baldo springs like a cat and at the same time lands a
blow to Lirone's chest, making him lose his breath, which comes
back with difficulty.

But meanwhile, a thousand other raiders arrive in swarms, led   356
by their savage captain, Hippol, who was Lirone's brother and a
corsair himself; he is shrewd, hungry for war and thirsty for fame.
But as soon as the centaur sees that a battle is imminent, he arms
himself at once with gleaming arms, and races to the galleys,
empty of armed soldiers, all but fifty of which the extremely quick
Hippol is leading. Wisely, the giant does not risk letting go of the
whale's tail, wary lest it dive like a goose.

Baldo attacks the mighty Lirone, whom he finds an expert in   366
war and a powerful warrior. He circles around him like a lioness,
and although he is naked, makes him sweat through his shirt. He
dares to fight naked, but his right arm is not naked—it is armed

sola sed armatur solito spadone, nec omnem
aestimat hic mundum tanti sub tegmine ferri.
Cingar alhora timet, sortem maledicit iniquam;
Falco sed hunc scridat dicitque morire batais
375   esse decus magnum; quo dicto, fulminis instar,
arma piat ferroque omnem se providet, atque
it retrovare ladros, quos mille haud stimat ofellam.
Dumque ruit praeceps, cridat: 'Mora! Taia! Retaia!
Gens maladetta, cave! Non gens, sed merda diabli!
380   Non solettus ego vos unum stimo lupinum'.
Et iaculans dardum, tres uno in vulnere passat.
Mox alium lanzat, quo corpora bina tramazzant
mortua sanguineasque animas per guttura buttant.
Inde pians mazzam, cum qua bellare solebat,
385   incepit spezzare elmos, spezzare corazzas;
incepit schiazzare ossos, smaccare cerebros.
Qua plus folta videt gentem sibi flectere piccas
se iacit hastarumque facit de pulvere fustos.
Nemo suam spectat mazzam, vult nemo rosadis
390   se bagnare suis, vult talia nespola nemo.
Illi donat opem Cingar qui, armatus et ipse,
efficit in terram currentes sanguine rivos.
Non discostus ei, Moschinus fortiter urtat;
sanguificantque omnes forbitas sanguine spadas.
395   Centaurus miseros buttabat in aequora ladros
trentaque vodarat nigra de gente galaeas.
Non quod solsolus tam sanctam fecerit opram,
sed, qui praeson erat, Philofornus viderat omnem
pro se proque suis tandem succedere sortem,
400   si Baldo et sociis compagniter addat aiutum.
Ergo valorosus trat spadam, menat et urtat
seque provat factis et verbis esse fidelem
Centauro socium; squarzat laceratque budellas.

with his usual sword, and he counts the whole world for naught under the protection of such a blade.

Cingar at this point is fearful, and curses his adverse fate, but Falchetto scolds him and says that to die in battle is a great honor. Having said this, Falchetto takes up arms as fast as lightning and girds himself all over with armor and goes off to find the raiders, a thousand of whom he values less than a fig. As he rushes forth, he cries, "May you die, slash and slash again! Beware, damned people! Not people, but the devil's turds. Even by myself I wouldn't count you as worth a bean." And hurling a spear, he pierces three of them with one blow. Then he launches another and two bodies drop dead, and their bloody souls spurt forth from their throats. Next, grabbing the club with which he usually fights, he begins to shatter helmets and shatter breastplates and begins to crush bones and smash brains. He throws himself into where the crowd is thickest, where he sees people turn their pikes against him, and he pulverizes the shafts of their spears. No one looks at his club, no one wants to be bathed in its dew, no one wants welts like these.

Cingar gives him a hand, and having armed himself, he makes rivers of blood flow on the land. Not far from him, Moschino drives forward bravely; all of them bloody their blades, already polished with blood. The centaur was throwing the miserable raiders into the sea and had emptied the thirty galleys of the black people. But he did not accomplish such holy work all alone, for the prisoner Philoforno saw that fortune would at last smile on him and his men if he aided Baldo and his companions. Therefore he valiantly pulls out his sword, swings it and drives forward. His words and deeds prove him to be a loyal friend to the centaur as he rips and lacerates

373

391

Inde Zenovesos Christi de gente cathenis
405   eripit, ac extra ferros trat mille tapinos.
Tunc data libertas animosos efficit illos:
'Arma!', vocant, 'Arma, arma!', cridant, simul arma requistant,
inque illos rabiem porcos e pectore sfogant.
Nam bastonatas vecchias bussasque receptas
410   seu mescadizzi loris, seu fuste bovino,
valde recordantes, reddunt pro pane fugazzam.
Hos Philofornus enim deduxerat extra galaeas
contraque mille ladros Zenovesi mille bataiant.
Portat inhastatam modo toltam forte gianettam
415   Cingar, et altorium cernens, animositer omnes,
quotquot scontrantur, sbudellat, seque coralo
fecerat aequalem rossedine sanguinis, atque
magna suae memorat celebratae facta Cipadae.
At se Boccalus, sese Boccalus in antro
420   sconderat, utque lepus quacchiarat membra coatto,
nam qui non scampat mortem putat esse bachioccum.
    Dudum mirarat zuffam fortissimus Hippol;
obstupet armigeros tanta virtute barones.
Nescit enim generosus homo deducere spadam
425   cortice corammi brazzumque intexere scuto;
namque voluptatem tacito sub pectore sentit,
dum Baldum Baldique viros cum caede suorum
Orlandis guardat similes similesque Rinaldis:
despiccant etenim testas brazzosque manusque,
430   inque poco spatio tam multa cadavera fundunt
tota quod e mortis campagna coperta videtur.
Quisque facit provas ingentes, corde gaiardo,
purgantes miseram ladrorum stercore gentem.
Oh! quis vidisset barbutas, quisve celatas,
435   scheneras, faldas, nec non spezzarier elmos,

guts. Then he tears the Genoese prisoners (Christ's people) from their chains and pulls a thousand wretches out of their shackles.

Their newfound freedom now makes them courageous. "To arms!" they cry. "To arms, to arms!" they yell, as they win back their arms and vent the anger in their breasts on those pigs. For they remember all too well the former clubbings and wallops they suffered from leather straps and cowhide whips, and they give tit for tat. Philoforno had led them out of the galleys, and a thousand Genoese fight against a thousand raiders. Cingar carries a pike he has just seized. Seeing reinforcements, he spiritedly disembowels everyone he meets, turning himself coral red with blood and recalling the great deeds of his illustrious Cipada. But what of Boccalo? Boccalo had hidden himself in a cavern and like a rabbit had retracted his limbs into his abode, for he thinks that anyone who doesn't flee death is a dumbbell.

The powerful Hippol had been admiring the skirmish for some time, amazed by warring barons of such excellence. In truth, this magnanimous man is unwilling to draw his blade from its leather sheath and strap a shield on his arm, for, in fact, he feels a secret pleasure in his breast as he watches Baldo and Baldo's men—like so many Orlandos and so many Rinaldos—slaughtering his people. For indeed they sever heads and arms and hands, and in a short while cast away so many corpses that the whole field seems completely covered with dead people. Each of them does tremendous deeds with a brave heart, cleansing wretched people of the scum of thieves. O, if anyone had seen the faceplates, the sallets, greaves, back-pieces and helmets all shattered, he would certainly

406

422

dixisset certe: 'Nihil est horrentius orbi!
Non terremoti, non fulmina voxque tronorum!'
Sed tardare tamen nimium se viderat Hippol:
impetuosus equum Rocafortam stringit, et ensem
440 targonemque ferens, it aquosi turbinis instar.
Cingar, id addocchians: 'Guarda, Falchette!', cridavit;
'Ecce ruina venit! Sta saldus, non tibi manco!'
Dixerat, et veluti nocchierus praticus undam
prospiciens magno venientem murmure venti,
445 hanc spezzare parat ferrato pectore navis,
sic Cingar contra furibundos Hippolis ausus
firmus aparecchiat sese, nec ab impete scampat.
Hippol ad un trattum quod arivat fulminat ense,
Cingaris ac tanto cervellum robore chioccat
450 ut bene non sapiat si nox vel giornus adesset.
Cum tamen oltraggium vidit Falchettus amico
sic fieri, colera succenditur ultra misuram.
Ferratam stringit mazzam, ferit Hippolis elmum,
ac dishonesta quidem fuit illa nosella barono.
455 Nec sorbam interea Falchettus tardat un altram;
maiori, quam prima fuit, botta ipsa valore
iungit et ad terram pennazzum buttat ab elmo.
Mox ait: 'Attenta, si nostra panada saletur!',
Atque menat colpum terzum pur semper in elmum,
460 unde coactus equi collum ferus Hippol abrazzat,
et bene tres voltas cascandi signa fuerunt.
Non Mongibellus tanto vampatur in igne,
quanto inflammatur collericus Hippolis ardor,
dumque furit boffans, tempesta marina someiat.
465 Exulutat ferrumque manus perstringit ad ambas,
fendentemque gravem tantis cum forzibus offert
quod, nisi Falco statim balzasset alhora dacantum,
in geminos illum squartasset nempe mezenos.

have exclaimed, "Nothing in the world is more horrifying! Neither earthquakes nor lightning nor the voice of thunder!"

Yet now Hippol realized he'd delayed too long; impetuously he spurs his horse, Roccaforte, and carrying both sword and shield, rides like a white tornado. Spotting this, Cingar cries, "Look, Falchetto! Here comes our ruin. Stand fast, I will not abandon you!" Thus he spoke and, as a skilled helmsman foresees an approaching wave driven by a howling wind and prepares to break it with the iron prow of his ship, so Cingar readies himself firmly in the path of Hippol's furious onslaught and does not run away from the impact. As soon as Hippol arrives, he strikes like lightning with his sword and smites Cingar's brain with such force that he no longer really knows if it's night or day.

438

As soon as Falchetto sees the outrage thus inflicted on his friend, he is inflamed with anger beyond measure. He grips his iron mace, hits Hippol's helmet; that blow was quite a disgrace for the baron. Meanwhile Falchetto does not hesitate to give him another wallop, and this clout arrives with greater force than the first, knocking the plume off his helmet and onto the ground. Then he says, "Just see if our bread isn't salty!" and delivers a third blow, once again on the helmet, so that the proud Hippol is forced to hug his horse's neck, and three times there are signs he's about to fall. Mount Etna does not burn with as much fire as Hippol's angry ardor is inflamed; as he huffs in his fury, he resembles a storm at sea. He cries out and, gripping his sword with both hands, delivers a heavy slash with such force that if Falchetto had not instantly jumped aside, he would have undoubtedly sliced him into twin halves.

451

Non tamen interea cessat dopiare feritas,
470   nam, vix fendentem complerat, protinus altrum
atque altrum lassat stizzosa voce roversum.
Non potuit Falchettus eam schifare ceresam,
quae sic brusca fuit, quae sic fuit illa gaiarda
ut smemoratus humo caderet, guanzale tridato.
475   Viderat hoc Cingar, currit furibundus in illum
atque super brazzum dextrum, qui deserat ensem,
percutit ut strato Falchetto porgat aiutum.
Falchettus tamen ecce levat se saltibus altis,
dumque Hippol voltans brancat cum Cingare guerram,
480   dumque ferire parat, canto Falchettus ab altro
mazzatam donat; cui voltus, Cingare licto,
dum dare parecchiat, Cingar succurrit amico
atque fiancalem spiccatum ad littora mandat.
Sic leo terribilis cunctisque superbior usat
485   intra duos ursos rabido combattere morsu,
qui vix tempus habet spatiumque piare fiatum;
dum squarzare unum quaerit, mordetur ab altro,
dumque istum retrovat, subito retrovatur ab illo:
sic erat in medio fratrum validissimus Hippol.
490   Tanta ibi corripitur rabie tantoque furore
ut focus ob nimiam stizzam vamparet in elmo.
Ergo, dum Cingar nimium se cazzat inanzum,
dat piatonadam toto conamine talem,
non supra schenam sed supra Cingaris aurem,
495   ut campanellos audiret mille sonantes.
Sbalorditus humo cascat calzasque tirare
apparet, ranaeque instar se stendit arenae.
En cruor a naso, cruor ore cruorque fluebat
auribus, et rubeum mandat per gramina rivum.
500   'Ah ladrone!', cridat Falchettus, 'Brutte ribalde!
Bastardone! Virum talem tantumque necasti?'

Nonetheless, Hippol does not stop redoubling his strikes, for scarcely had he completed one downward slash, when quickly he lands one backhand after another with a furious expression. Falchetto was unable to deflect such a plum hit, which was so rough and so vigorous that he fell down unconscious, his faceplate shattered.

Seeing this, Cingar rushes at Hippol in a fury and smites his right arm, which releases its blade so that Cingar can succor the fallen Falchetto. Yet see now! Falchetto rises up with high jumps, and while Hippol turns to engage Cingar in combat and prepares to strike, Falchetto bashes him from the other side. Hippol lets go of Cingar and turns toward Falchetto to strike him when Cingar comes to his friend's aid and severs the pirate's breastplate, which falls in the sand. Just as a ferocious lion, prouder than all the other animals, will fight between two bears with rabid bites, scarcely having the time or the space to take a breath — for while the lion strives to tear one, it is bitten by the other, then while it attacks the one, it is immediately attacked by the other — such was the superb Hippol in the middle of these brothers-in-arms. He is overcome with such rage and such wrath that fire could have blazed in his helmet from his extreme fury. So when Cingar drives too far forward, he gives him such a thwack with all his might — not on Cingar's back but on his ear — that he heard a thousand tinkling bells. Stunned, he falls to the ground and seems to be kicking the bucket and like a frog stretches out in the sand. There was blood flowing from his nose, blood from his mouth and blood from his ears, and he poured out a river of red through the grass.

"Ah, thief!" Falchetto cries out. "You beastly villain, you bastard, have you slain so great a hero?" Thus he spoke, and gripping

475

500

Dixerat, et stricto manibus bastone duabus,
se levat in guisam balzantis ad aethera pardi.
Mox ferit hunc tanta possanza desuper elmum
505   quod, quamvis Hippol se sub targone covertet,
targonem tamen hunc spezzatum mandat ad herbas;
tamque pesenta gravat durae tartuffola mazzae
quod Roccafortae groppas cervice flagellat
Hippol, et in sella stando portatur apertis
510   huc illuc brazzis magno galopante cavallo.
At corsarorum fratantum huc advolat agmen
surgentemque suas in plantas Cingara trovat.
Non aliter rugit leo cazzatore feritus,
quando canes inter seu corsos sive molossos
515   unguibus et morsu carnarum frusta minuzzat,
sicut alhora facit Cingar; quem Falco secutus
mazzatas orbis nunc huc, nunc dirrigit illuc.
Hi duo ben stretti simul agmina grossa fugabant,
ante suamque iram voltabant terga ladrones.
520   Baldus at interea distemperat ense Lyronem,
atque sui similem iam nudum fecerat armis
et nisi Fracasso trarupta haec gara fuisset,
absque ullo dubio finisset vita Lyronis.
Moschinus, Centaurus item, Philofornus in uno
525   groppetto stricti spegazzant sanguine terram
atque coradellas milzasque ad sydera iactant.
Nullus alhora quidem remanebat supra galaeas,
omnes in terra, tam Mori quam Zenovesi,
combattunt multosque alios Centaurus in undas
530   iecerat, inde suis tornarat ferre socorsum.
Verum Giubertus, spatians in littore solus,
se viat ad fustas, intrat nullumque retrovat,
et velut imbellis nec usatus in arte scrimandi,
cernit et horrescit tantam guardare bataiam.

his club in both hands, he rises like a leopard leaping into the air. Then he strikes him on the helmet with such force that although Hippol protects himself with his armored plate, the plate itself is dispatched in splinters to the grass, and the beating from the hard cudgel weighs so heavily that Hippol lashes Roccaforte's crupper with his neck. Although he stays in the saddle with his arms spread, he is carried hither and thither at a gallop by his great horse.

In the meantime a squadron of corsairs races this way and finds 511 Cingar rising to his feet. Just as a lion roars when wounded by a hunter and shreds hunks of meat with its claws and jaws while surrounded by Corsican or Molossian hounds, so Cingar does at this moment. Falchetto, who is right behind him, directs drubbings hither and thither like a wild man. Close together, these two drove off whole squadrons; facing their wrath, the raiders turned their backs.

By now Baldo had undone Lirone with his sword and had 520 left him stripped of arms like himself, and if this contest had not been interrupted by Fracasso, Lirone's life would no doubt have ended. Drawn together in a tight knot, Moschino, the centaur and Philoforno smear the earth with blood and fling tripe and spleen up to the stars. By now no one remained on the galleys; they are all fighting on land, both the Moors and the Genoese. The centaur had thrown many others into the waves, then he had turned back to bring help to his friends. Gilberto in turn was walking alone along the shore, heading toward the boats. Going onboard, he finds no one, and being unfamiliar and unused to the art of war, he looks out and shudders to gaze upon such a battle.

535 Per nubes ingens hastarum fractio bombat,
    perque sinum ponti vocum fragor altus eechat.
    Fiunt squarzones carnis fiuntque cruoris
    flumina, de mortis hinc inde fiuntur acervi.
    More bechariae pulmones, viscera, trippae,
540 atque coradellae, panzae, ventralia, milzae,
    arboreis ramis pendent herbasque cruentant.
    Oh crudas bottas, oh vulnera digna Rinaldo!
    Millibus oh doctis cantanda Maronibus acta!
    Hic ferit, hic reparat, taiat iste, sed ille taiatur.
545 Squarzatas maias tridasque omnino piastras
    cernebas avibus similes volitare per auras.
    Ad bassum volucres tanto pro murmure crodant,
    seque trabucantes fasso meschiantur in uno.
    Et cervi et lepores extra boschalia saltant
550 piscesque attoniti bacchantur in aequoris imo.
    Et iam corsari voltant calcagna fugaces,
    instant nostrates miseram cazzare canaiam.
    Non tamen interea laxatur cauda Fracasso,
    qui clamans socios commandat linquere guerram,
555 atque ad vodatas raptim properare galeas:
    nam fare vult bellum tractum dignumque corona.
    Tunc omnes rati non posse tenere Fracassus
    amplius ingentem codam, quae lubrica muzzat,
    ut muzzat manibus nequiens anguilla teneri,
560 concurrunt veluti cernis concurrere gentem
    quae, versus Paduam cupiens andare per amnem
    Brentae, qualcunam mirat discedere barcam,
    de cuius prora navarolus cridat: 'Apava!'
    Baldus mandatum negat exaudire Fracassi,
565 spernit ab impresa guerrae se tollere fortis
    campio, nec mortem curat mercator honoris.

A tremendous breaking of lances resounds in the clouds, and a   535
loud clash of voices echoes in the bay. There are hunks of flesh
and there are rivers of blood and there are piles of corpses on all
sides. As in a butcher shop, lungs, viscera, tripe, offal, stomachs
and spleens hang from the branches of trees and bleed on the
grass. O harsh blows! O wounds worthy of Rinaldo! O deeds de-
serving to be sung by a thousand learned Virgils! This one strikes,
that one parries; this one cuts, but that one gets cut. You could see
shredded chain mail and plates of armor chopped to bits flying
through the air like birds. Winged creatures cascade down because
of all the noise, and tumbling into one another, they merge into
one pile. Deer and hares leap from the woods, and the shocked
fish wiggle in Bacchic frenzy at the bottom of the sea. And the
swift corsairs already turn tail; our men press on, chasing the mis-
erable curs.

Meanwhile, Fracasso has still not released the whale's tail.   553
Shouting, he orders his companions to forsake the battle and to
hasten at once to the empty galleys, for he is planning to pull a
good one, worthy of a crown. They all think that Fracasso can no
longer hold the enormous tail, which is slippery and slithers as an
eel slithers from the hands of someone who doesn't know how to
hold it. They all come running, just as you see people come run-
ning who want to go toward Padua on the Brenta River when
someone spots a boat approaching from whose prow a boatman
cries, "A Pava!"

Baldo refuses to execute Fracasso's order; the brave hero dis-   564
dains to withdraw himself from a wartime exploit: as a merchant

Si cum destrezza valeat fortezza coëllum,
decrerat contra Lyronem vincere pugnam.
Iamque gigas tanto caudam conamine torquet
570   quod, dum torta caput voltat balena Fracassum
boccatura, velut boccat bona cagna leprettum,
illico dimittit caudam, caput illico brancat;
inde pedes mittens, veluti si strangulet ocham,
quattuor in crollis testam de tergore spiccat.
575   Ecce mari medio pigritatim littora circum
incipiunt callare, simul surgente profundo.
Insula disparet, quam portat bestia secum,
et quisquam pedibus sentit mancare terenum;
dumque bisognat aquis mergi, desiderat alas,
580   in moia quoniam se trovat habere culamen.
Iam maris in fundo sese balena stravaccat,
boscorumque trahit secum sex mille biolcas,
per quos discurrunt pisces, novitate gioiscunt,
saepe cachinnantes rident: pars incubat ulmis,
585   parsque capellutas mangiant de robore giandas.
Miranturque capros, lepores cervosque negatos,
nec minus humanas facies bustosque taiatos
et carnes, modo quas Baldi fecere sodales.
At super innumerae testae sofiare videntur,
590   arma, trabes, tavolae, capannae, millia rerum.
Antea saltarant barrones supra galaeas,
atque Zenovesi, quanti de caede supersunt.
Hi cuncti pariter fustas insemma tenebant,
ad quarum spondas, dum se attaccare volebant
595   corsari miseri pietosa voce cridantes,
seu respingebant urtis et calzibus illos,
sive trabant susum per orecchias perque capillos,
donec complessent remos bancasque vodatas,

of honor, he has no fear of death. If strength combined with skill can achieve anything, he is resolved to win the fight against Lirone.

By now, the giant is twisting the tail with such force that the twisted whale turns its head to take Fracasso in its mouth, just as a good retriever takes a small hare in its mouth. But Fracasso abruptly lets go of the tail and grabs the head. Next, placing his feet as though about to strangle a goose, in four jerks he detaches the head from the body. Behold! in the middle of the sea, the shores all around begin to sink lazily while the swells surge upward. The island disappears; the beast takes it with him and everyone feels the ground give way under his feet. And since sinking into the water is inevitable, now that they find their butts in the brine, they all want wings. {.margin} 569

The whale already sprawls on the bottom of the sea and pulls with it six thousand acres of woods through which fish roam: they enjoy the novelty, often bursting into giggles. Some recline in the elms and some eat the capped acorns off the oaks. They marvel at all the drowned goats, rabbits and deer and also at the human faces, truncated torsos and chunks of flesh produced recently by Baldo's friends. On the surface, one sees countless heads breathing and armor, planks, tables, huts — a thousand things. The barons and the Genoese sailors who survived the slaughter have already boarded the galleys. Together they held the vessels in equal measure and when the wretched corsairs wanted to grab hold of the sides, crying out with piteous voices, they either pushed them away with shoves and kicks or pulled them up by their ears or by their hair until they filled the empty benches with rowers. And {.margin} 581

      atque cadenatis pedibus statuere nodaros,
600 qui tam desconcis usantur scribere pennis.
      Fracassus menat piscosa per aequora brazzos
      ingentesque facit cumulos, dum nodat, aquarum;
      scindit eos manibus gambasque racoltus inarcat,
      inde viam faciens calcagnis aequora pulsat,
605 et puntando pedes sofiandoque gutture pleno,
      non tempestatem pelagi facit ille minorem
      quam Borra et Gregus sibi contrastante Sirocco.
      Dumque natat, casu vel sorte guidante, Bocalum,
      qui nil mangiarat, retrovat sine fine bibentem,
610 cui quasi tripparum compleverat unda misuram.
      Protinus hunc mittens in summo vertice campat,
      nec mancum Boccalus erat securus alhoram
      quam castellanus seu Mussi, sive Salei.
      Hippol fertur equo gaiarditer extra profundum,
615 sustinet aequor equum, sed equus quoque sustinet ipsum
      Hippola, cui tantum schinchae bagnantur ab undis.
        Cingar in excelsa maioris puppe galeae
      stabat et ad Baldum frezzosa mente cucurrit.
      'Me miserum!', clamat, 'Num Baldus forte sotacquam
620 piscibus esca fuit? Proh dii, qui fata guidatis,
      iustitia haec vestra est? Tali ratione guidantur
      fata hominum? Non, non, stellis incago ribaldis;
      incago Marti, Phoebo totaeque canaiae!
      Et mihi recrescit non scribere posse corezas,
625 in vestrum quoniam dispregum grande volumen
      dictarem, plenum de centum mille corezis.
      Non dii, sed potius vos estis merda diabli.
      Est sine cervello populus, qui pazzus adorat
      vos, seu beccones ravaiosos, sive bagassas,
630 aut imbriagos, homicidas, aut rofianos.
      Nonne Venus meretrix totius publica gentis?

having chained their feet, they set them up like notaries who are used to writing with awkward pens.

Fracasso thrashes his arms through the fishy sea. He makes   601 huge mounds of water as he swims and cuts through the waves with his hands, and having gathered himself together, arcs his legs, then thrusts with his heels, making a path in the water. And kicking with his feet and blowing at full force, he causes a storm at sea no less than Boreas and Greco when Sirocco opposes them. And while he is swimming, whether guided by chance or destiny, he finds Boccalo, who has eaten nothing but is drinking continuously; the waves had almost completely filled the capacity of his guts. Quickly placing him on top of his head, Fracasso saves him, and Boccalo was as secure as the lord of the castle of Musso or San Leo. Hippol is bravely borne above the water by his horse. The water holds up the horse, but the horse also holds up Hippol, who gets only his shins wet in the waves.

Cingar is on the highest poop deck of the largest galley, and his   617 mind races frantically to Baldo. "Woe is me!" he exclaims. "Did Baldo perhaps feed the fish underwater? O gods who guide our fate, is this your idea of justice? Are the fates of men controlled by such principles? No, no, I don't give a shit about treacherous stars, or about Mars, Apollo and all that riff-raff. And I regret that I cannot write farts, because to show my contempt for you, I would dictate a large volume full of a hundred thousand farts. You are not gods, but rather devil's shit. Brainless is the mob that insanely adores you—you who are rabid cuckolds, harlots, drunkards, assassins or pimps. Isn't Venus a public prostitute for the entire pop-

Nonne Iovis soror est Iuno, contraria Troiae?
Iuppiter accepit tamen hanc pro uxore gaioffam?
An poterant bastare Iovi de mille puellis
635   cinquantae numero? centae? tandemque tresentae?
Bestia matta fuit, qui te laudavit, Homerus,
menchionusque Maro nec non scola caetera vatum.
Ecce tibi ficcas facio stronzisque ledammo.
Cancar te mangiet, penitus restante niento,
640   qui totum tantis implesti fecibus orbem.
Dic mihi, merdipotens o Iuppiter, ut quid ab omni
gentili vulgo totius factor Olympi
esse putabaris? Cum sit quod adulter, avarus,
quod stuprator eras castarum boia sororum?
645   Taiasti patri genitivos, ladre, sonaios
ut non stamparet plures tribus ille fiolos.
Stuprastique tuam post haec, manigolde, sorellam.
Sforzasti Alcmenam propter fabricare gigantem,
qui palmam semper vastis in rebus haberet;
650   hunc tamen una uno stravit muliercula sguardo,
ac in guarnello fecit filare gazanum.
Tu quascumque tuis oculis, gaioffe, placerent
seu consanguineas seu non, sine iure puellas
turpabas, faciens asinaliter omnia secum.
655   Ergo (si vivis) possis tibi rumpere collum,
postquam sic nobis crudelia fata ministras,
postquam virtutum Baldus candela stuatur'.
    Talia dum Cingar iactat renegatque batesmum,
Fracassus guardans coelum sic ore braveggiat:
660   'Iuro per hunc sacrum quod porto in fronte batesmum,
perque illum ventrem qui me sborravit in orbem,
tantum cercabo per montes, saxa, cavernas,
per sylvas, boscos, per valles, flumina, terras,
mox diavolorum per tecta, per antra, per amnes,

ulace? Isn't Juno, who was hostile to Troy, Jupiter's sister? Didn't Jupiter take this tramp as his wife anyway? Of a thousand maidens, could fifty be enough for Jupiter? One hundred? Or even three hundred? Homer who praised you was a crazy fool, and Vergil a schmuck just like all the others in the school of poets. Look, I give you the finger and spread turds on you. May cancer eat away at you so that nothing at all remains of you who filled the whole world with crap.

"So tell me, 'omni-shit-ent' Jupiter, why were you considered   641
the creator of all Olympus by all the pagan masses, since you were an adulterer, a miser, a rapist, and the murderer of your chaste sisters? You cut off your father's genital bells, you thief, so that he couldn't stamp out more than three children? And after that you raped your own sister, you rapscallion! You forced yourself on Alcmena in order to produce a giant who would always take the prize in his great labors. And yet one little woman weakened him with a single glance and made the wimp spin, wearing a petticoat. You, scoundrel! Whatever girls pleased your eye, whether they were relatives or not, you unjustly defiled, doing all sorts of asinine things with them. Therefore (if you exist), may you break your neck, since you administer fate to us so cruelly and since Baldus, the candle of virtue, has been extinguished."

While Cingar hurls these words and renounces his baptism,   658
Fracasso, examining the sky, boasts thus, "I swear by this sacred baptism that I wear on my forehead and by the belly that spat me out into the world, I will search hard, through mountains, cliffs and caverns, through forests and woods, through valleys, rivers, and fields, then through the devils' dwellings, through hollows and

665 et si conveniet per celsa palatia coeli,
donec seu vivum, seu mortum, sive malatum
inveniam Baldum, cum quo vel vivere semper
in coelum statuo, vel sub Stigialibus umbris.
Sed prius arripiam Plutoni regna gaioffo,

670 cuius de testa pavidam streppabo coronam,
subque meo stabit sceptro diabolica proles'.
Mox ait: 'O comites, animum deponite moestum.
Ut vindicemus Baldum tantummodo restat.
Me seguitate, precor, nigrumque calemus ad Orcum'.

675 Dixerat, atque omnes capitanos chiamat in unam
maiorem fustam reliquasve seguire comandat.
Egressique undas finaliter, aequora lassant,
Fracassusque rapit sumpto bastone viaggium.
Moschinus seguitat, Falchettus et altera turba.

680 Cingar vult solus cighilinum stare dedretum,
si mare fortassis tret morta cadavera ripis,
ipsius ut Baldi det membra negata sepulchro.
Centaurus remanet cum Cingare, caetera squadra
non sine ploratu vadunt post terga gigantis.

685 Quisque suam vitam non binas stimmat ofellas.
In qua parte via est magis aspera, tenditur illuc;
nil curant spinas, nil curant saxa, ruinas,
nil tempestates, pluvias, nil frigora, caldum,
nil tigres, apros, nil serpas atque ladrones.

690 Omnibus his, quae saepe trovant, gaiarditer obstant.
Si retrovant, mangiant; si non, 'Patientia!' dicunt.
Ad grandis tandem radices montis arivant,
quem appena queant ertum superare camozzae.
Non saliunt illum, tenebrosa sed ora cavernae

695 intrant impavidi montagnaeque antra busatae.
Cercat iter pedibus, vadens Falchettus avantum,
insegnatque alios quo debent ponere plantas.

streams, and if it is allowed, even through the noble mansions of
the skies until I find Baldo—whether dead or alive, or ailing—
with whom I am determined to live forever in Heaven or in Sty-
gian shadows. But first I will strip that scoundrel Pluto of his
kingdoms, I will rip the fearful crown from his head, and the dia-
bolical race will remain under my command." Then Fracasso adds,
"O comrades, set aside the sadness of your souls. The only thing
left for us is to avenge Baldo. Follow me, I beg you. We will go
down into black Orcus."

Having spoken, Fracasso calls all the captains onto the largest   675
galley and orders the rest to follow. Having emerged from the
waves at last, they leave the sea. Fracasso heads out with club in
hand. Moschino follows along with Falchetto and the others in the
band. Cingar wants to stay back alone a bit, in case the sea should
carry dead bodies to shore, so that he could place Baldo's drowned
limbs in a sepulcher. The centaur stays with Cingar; the rest of the
squadron, not without tears, walks behind the giant. Each values
his life less than a couple of pastries. Where the path is most diffi-
cult, that's where they head; they heed neither thorns nor rocks
nor crags nor storms, rains, cold or heat, nor any tigers, boars, ser-
pents or thieves. All these things, which they encounter repeat-
edly, they confront bravely. They eat if they find something; if not
they say, "Pazienza!"

At last they come to the base of a great mountain, whose   692
steep slopes even mountain goats can scarcely conquer. They do
not climb this, but fearlessly enter into the tenebrous mouth of
the cavern and the caves of the hollow mountain. Going ahead,
Falchetto feels for a path with his feet and shows the others where

Est opus ut gobbo Fracassus tergore vadat,
nam grandazzus homo daret ipsa in saxa zucadas.
700 Cingar at interea per longam solus arenam
ibat, passeggiando pedes grattandoque testam,
et ficcans oculos in terram plorat amicum,
quo sine scit certe non vivere posse quatrhoras.
Saepe sibi stesso cazzasset in inguina stoccum,
705 praesens Virmazzi nisi tunc persona fuisset.
At tandem gravis ecce venit de longe cavallus,
ille cavallorum meliorum maximus, ecce
Spezzacadena venit, portans se fluctibus extra
fortiter, inque suo (quis baiam non vocet istam?)
710 inque suo dorso duo grandia corpora gestat,
scilicet in groppam Baldum, arzone Lyronem.
Nam Baldus, cum sensit aquas subcrescere, cumque
Lyronus subito voltasset fraena cavallo,
non se curarunt coeptam finire bataiam,
715 quod nimis importat barronibus ire negatum.
Baldus it in groppam saltu brazzatque Lyronem,
cui Lyro datque manum, dat verbaque dulcia, dat cor,
amboque contraris fiunt in rebus amici,
hostes quippe facit fratres commune periclum.
720 Spezzacadena ruit, cuius tantummodo musus
apparet testaeque hominum modo supra videntur,
et modo sub latitant velut usat mergus et ocha.
Peiorem sed Baldus habet, stans retro, pitanzam;
saepe trapozzatus gorgadas tirat aquarum.
725 Is tamen alto animo divinum sperat aiuttum.
Cingar, id aspiciens, sperat clamatque sodalem,
monstrat ei digito cosam de longe nodantem.
Quid sit enim, nescire datur, quia copia vistae
deficit humanae tam longos currere tractus.

they must place their soles. Fracasso has to walk like a hunchback because otherwise this oversized fellow would bean himself on the rocks.

In the meantime, Cingar paced the shore alone, moving his 700 feet, scratching his head and staring at the ground. He weeps for his friend, without whom he knows for certain he cannot live another four hours. He would have repeatedly driven his sword into his own groin if Virmace had not been present in person. But at last from afar arrives a weighty horse, the very best of excellent horses—here comes Spezzacadena, carrying himself strongly above the swells. On his—who will not call this a tall tale?—on his back he bears two large bodies, namely, Baldo on the crupper, and Lirone in the saddle. Because as soon as Baldo felt the waters rising and as soon as Lirone had swiftly turned the horse's reins, the two of them didn't bother to finish the battle they'd begun, since these barons took drowning very seriously. Baldo jumps onto the crupper and puts his arms around Lirone, and Lirone gives him his hand and offers him kind words and his heart. And the two of them became friends in adversity, for a common danger truly makes enemies into brothers. Spezzacadena plummets, only his muzzle appears, and the men's heads are sometimes seen above and sometimes they disappear below, as does a goose or merganser. But Baldo, being in the back, has the worst lot; often submerged, he swallows gulps of water. Yet, in the depths of his soul, he hopes for divine intervention.

Seeing this, Cingar is hopeful and calls to his companion and 726 points out to him the thing swimming in the distance. What it is, indeed, one cannot know, because the range of human sight is too weak to travel such long distances. However, the centaur quickly

730 Centaurus tamen ipse cito se cazzat in aequor,
parte cavallina nodans; tandemque rivatus
gurgite qua medio iam Spezzacadena fiatum
spingebat grossum nimiae sub pondere somae,
suscipit extemplo Baldum supraque groperam
735 hunc tirat, allevians straccati dorsa cavalli.
Prospicit haec Cingar sentitque per ossa medullas
discolare suas ut cera liquescit ad ignem.
Gustat enim tantam dolzuram intrinsecus ut non
in brenta mellis voluisset habere culamen.
740 Denique perveniunt omnes ad littus arenae,
fit novus hic gustus basorum, fit nova festa,
mille carezzinae fiunt plus zuccare dulces.
Baldus amorevola sic sic piat arte Lyronem,
ut Lyro disponat Baldum seguitare per ignem.
745 Venerat ad ripam nec non gaiarditer Hippol,
cui iacet appressum sellis Rocaforta bagnatis.
Hunc Lyronus adit strictumque abrazzat, et inde
supplicat ut sortis voiat incagare travaio
seque valenthomini penitus committere Baldo.
750 'Sum contentus', ait, 'faciam quaecumque comandas'.
Quo dicto, ad Baldum brazzis currebat apertis.
Baldus eum subito sembiante apprendit alegro
germanosque sibi forti charitate cadenat,
pro quorum forzis non mundum prezzat un aium.
755 In Roccafortae post haec se arzone piantat.
Lyronus charum non lassat Spezzacadenam,
Hippol it in sellam Pardi, Philofornus at ipse
Centauri iussus groppas montavit equinas.
Cingar nil curans, stafferi more, pedestrat.
760 Iamque recedebant, quando sibi trenta galeae
in mentem veniunt, quas sic sine rege relinquunt.

throws himself into the water, and swimming with his equine part, he arrives at length in the middle of the raging sea where Spezzacadena was already struggling for breath under the weight of the heavy load. He picks Baldo up at once and pulls him onto his rump, relieving the horse's tired back. Cingar watches this from afar and feels the marrow in his bones melt, like wax liquefies in fire. Indeed, he feels such sweetness deep inside that he would not prefer to have his butt in a vat of honey. At last they all reach a landing place on the shore and there is new gusto in their kisses, there's new merriment; there are a thousand caresses sweeter than sugar. Baldo clasps Lirone so lovingly that the man would be ready to follow Baldo into fire.

Hippol too had jauntily come ashore, and Roccaforte lies along-   745
side him with his saddle soaking wet. Lirone goes up to him and hugs him tight and then urges him not to give a shit about the trials of destiny and to pledge himself entirely to the gallant Baldo. "I agree," he says, "I shall do whatever you command." So saying, he runs to Baldo with open arms. Baldo welcomes him at once with a happy countenance and binds the two brothers to him with strong love. If he has their support, he counts the world less than a clove of garlic.

After this, Baldo plunks himself into Roccaforte's saddle. Lirone   755
does not leave dear Spezzacadena, Hippol mounts Pardo, and Philoforno, at the centaur's request, climbs onto his horse-back. Cingar walks along like a page, not minding in the least. They are already moving away when they recall the thirty galleys which they

279

Baldus Lyronem, fratrem quoque saepe pregavit
ut classem tantam, pro seque suisque, nequaquam
prorsus abandonent: satis est quod ametur ab illis.
765 At nec Lyronus vult hoc audire nec Hippol,
ac minus hanc voluit Philofornus prendere curam:
tanta sodalicii calamita tiraverat illos.
Ergo abeunt fustasque omnes gentemque relinquunt,
nam nimis importat mistatem linquere Baldi.
770 Solus it ad staffam Cingar solusque pedestrat,
donec villanum qui binos menat asellos
obvius incontrat pensatque robare coëllum.
Ast ille, ut vidit soldatos, protinus altrum
brancat iter sylvaeque asinos per devia cazzat.
775 Cingar eum chiamat: 'Quo, quo? Sta! Scolta, gazane!
Scolta parolinam solam! Sta! dico, bonhomme!'
Cui respondet homo: 'Blabla, chiz, felchena, gozca'.
Sic parlans, cursum duplicans calcanea menat.
'Quo diavol abis?' respondet Cingar: 'Adessum
780 te faciam gustare tuam, villane, paciam!'
Quo dicto, insequitur clamans tutavia: 'Vilane
tangar, ni smontes, pentibis! Scende, gaioffe!
Lege comandatur nostra quod quisquis habebit
sive duas tunicas in dossum sive gabanos,
785 det male vestito seu quellum sive quelaltrum.
Non aliter quicumque duos menat ante somaros,
iure viandanti donare tenetur asellum'.
Rusticus exurlat neque vult smontare iumentum.
Non inthesus ait: 'Flep, chelp, cocozina, boaster'.
790 Dumque suas similes baias sbraiando frequentat,
Cingar eum currendo rivat caudamque somari
corripit, inde trigat fossumque gaiardus in unum
patronem ac asinum, sociis ridentibus, urtat.

are leaving behind, just like that, without a commander. Baldo repeatedly begs both Lirone and his brother not to abandon a fleet so important to them and to their mates; Baldus is content to be loved by them. But neither Lirone nor his brother wants to hear this, and Philoforno is even less willing to take this on, for the magnet of solidarity had so drawn them together! Hence they depart and leave behind all the ships and people because their friendship with Baldo is too important to forsake. Cingar acts as sole page and is the sole pedestrian until he comes across a peasant who is leading two donkeys and he decides to steal something. Yet as soon as he sees the soldiers, the peasant promptly takes another path and drives the asses on a detour through the woods. Cingar calls to him, "Where are you going? Stop! Listen, you oaf! Just listen to one little word! Stop, my good man! I'm talking to you!"

The man answers, "Bla-bla, chiz, felchena, gozca." Speaking   777
thus, he quickens his steps and scampers off.

"Where the devil are you going?" responds Cingar, "Now I'll   779
give you a taste of your foolishness, peasant!" Saying this he follows him, still yelling, "You peasant lout, if you don't dismount, you'll be sorry. Now get off, you scoundrel! Our law demands that anyone who is wearing two tunics or two cloaks must give one or the other to an ill-clad wretch. Likewise, anyone who is leading two donkeys is obliged by law to give one ass to a man on foot."

The rustic swears and does not want to dismount from his   788
mule. Incomprehensibly he says, "Flep, chelp, cocozina, boaster." And while he keeps shouting similar gibberish, Cingar reaches him at a run and snatches the donkey's tail, then stops and heartily shoves the one ass and its master into a ditch, to the laughter of

Quo facto, subitum spiccat de littore saltum
795 supraque colaltrum balzat leggiadrus asellum.
Iam non Francesum sub se voluisset ubinum,
non orecchiutas quas mulas Roma cavalcat,
nam portantino passu trampinat asellus,
foiadasque paret pedibus taiare minutim:
800 tichi tich et tichi toch resonat per mille lapillos;
ponitur in fallum pes numquam parvulus et non
pontigero suffert costas sperone tocari;
nam subito calcem laxat pariterque corezam.
Miraculum si asinus tret calzos absque corezis!
805 Ergo inter comites orta est non poca voluptas;
dum spronat Cingar, mollat celer ille fiancum
et caput in gambas ficcans de retro levatur,
unde bisognabat Cingar tommare deorsum,
atque super littus maiores prendere bottas
810 quam si frisonis caderet de arzone cavalli.
Talibus in festis compagni tempora passant,
donec arivarunt ubi maxima surgitur alpa;
alpa columna poli, quae saxi culmen aguzzi
ficcat in aethereas sedes ac sustinet astra.
815 Haec Lunae montagna quidem chiamatur et illic
ad fundum socii magnam reperere cavernam,
totaque per circum grottis montagna busatur.
Centaurus norat vestigia pressa Fracassi,
terribiles quoniam mostrabat arena pedattas.
820 Cuncti gaudentes statuunt seguitare gigantem.
Baldus smontat equum, smontat Lyronus et Hippol.
Cingar asinaster, reliquis derdanior, inquit:
'"Qui stat retro seret portam", proverbia dicunt'.

his companions. Having done this, he quickly launches himself off the ground and jumps nimbly onto the remaining ass. And now he would not want a French hobby under him, or the big-eared mules that Rome rides, for the little ass keeps up a good pace and seems to chop the underbrush into tiny pieces with its feet. "Tick-tick, tick-tock" resounds on a thousand pebbles; the ass never makes the tiniest misstep, but it does not tolerate being poked in the side with a sharp spur, for it will instantly let loose a kick and also a fart. What a miracle it would be if an ass could give kicks without farts!

As a result, considerable amusement arises among Cingar's 805 companions: when Cingar spurs the flank, the ass toots right away and, sticking its head between its legs, lifts up in back so that Cingar is forced to fall forward and to take a harder knock on the ground than if he'd fallen off the saddle of a Frisian steed. The friends spend their time in such merriment until they arrive where a huge crag surges up, a crag that is like a column to the sky, with its sharp crest of rock sticking into the heavens and holding up the stars. This, indeed, is called Moon Mountain, and the friends find at its base an immense cavern, and the mountain is pierced all round with grottoes. The centaur had recognized Fracasso's trail, because the ground revealed humongous footprints. Joyfully they all decide to follow the giant. Baldo dismounts, as do Lirone and Hippol. Riding the nasty ass behind the others, Cingar says, "As the proverb goes, 'Last one in, close the door.'"

Liber vigesimus primus

Venimus ad pavidum Malamocchi denique portum,
gurgite qui medio fert centum mille diablos
naviculamque meam fluctu sorbere menazzat.
Contra fortunam grandis matezza videtur
5   spingere schirazzum, quando est garboius in undis.
Ergo ego quid faciam? Spicchetur ab arbore velum
butteturque giusum maioribus ancora soghis.
Non bastat nobis animus transcendere passum,
passum tam durum, tam horrendum tamque cativum,
10   in quo multoties barchae gentesque negantur.
Non mihi sufficiens cor est, non circa coradam
aes triplex ut grande velim tentare periclum.
Impegolata pocum sub fundo navis, ab omni
parte forata, cagat stuppas aperitque fenestras.
15   Ergo, inquam, quid nunc faciam? Timidusne redibo?
Semper difficilis est scortegatio caudae.
At quia non modicum video mihi nascere scornum,
qui iam vogarim tercentos mille miaros,
non formidarim cagnae latramina Scillae,
20   non me terruerit rabies ingorda Carybdis . . .
et Malamochaeos trepidem tentare diablos?
Fac animum paveasque, Striax mea togna, nientum.
Grandis erit (confesso quidem) straccatio schenae,
dum contra pegoras opus est intendere brazzos.
25   Ergo sub infernas Baldum sociare masones
est opus, o Musae, populosque catare stryarum,
quos maris in fundo strya Gelfora sola governat.
    Ibant obscuri Baldus Baldique seguaces
nigra cavernosae peragrantes clymata tombae.
30   Nec mirum si dant crebras per saxa zucadas

Book XXI

We have come at last to the terrifying port of Malamocco, which 1
in the midst of the maelstrom hosts a hundred thousand devils
and threatens to swallow up my little ship in its surges. It seems
sheer folly to force a square-rigger counter to fate, when the
waves are in turmoil. So what shall I do? Haul down the sail from
the mast and cast the anchor with stronger ropes. Courage is
not enough for crossing over this passage — a passage so hard, so
horrible and so vicious, that many times boats and people are
drowned in it. My heart is not equal to the task, for it has no tri-
ple coating of bronze around it so that I would choose to attempt
a great danger. The ship has a poorly pitched keel, is punctured on
all sides, craps straw and opens wide its windows.

So what shall I do now? Am I to turn back in fear? It is always 15
difficult to skin the tail. Yet since I see considerable scorn aris-
ing — I, who have already rowed three hundred thousand miles,
who did not fear the barking dog of Scylla, who did not allow the
ferocious eddy of Charybdis to terrify me. And I should tremble
to confront the devils of Malamocco? Take courage, my silly
Striax, and fear nothing! There will be great strain on our backs (I
admit it), since we must exert our arms against the white-caps.
Now it is necessary to accompany Baldo down to the infernal
dwellings, O Muses, and find the nations of witches that the witch
Gelfora governs alone at the bottom of the sea.

They continued in the dark, Baldo and Baldo's followers, scour- 28
ing the black regions of the cavernous tomb. It's no wonder that
they keep banging their heads on the rocks and bumping their

ac per inaequales petras si schinchibus urtant.
Quapropter rident animoque feruntur alegro,
et bon compagni sua damna libenter abrazzant.
Non procul ante meant alii duo tracta balestrae,
35　scilicet insemmam quattri post terga Fracassi,
qui testam ruptam banda portabat in omni.
En sentit tandem post se pistare cavallos;
quid sit avisatur; cridat: 'Ola, manete pochettum!
Audio cum ferris contundere saxa cavallos.
40　Numquid erit Centaurus, equi cui forma dedretum est?.
Vix ea finierat, Cingar veniendo cridabat:
'Oh oh, Falchette! Oh oh, Fracasse! Bocale!'
Giubertus fatur laetus: 'Vox Cingaris illa est.
Expectemus eum'. Tunc illi firmiter adstant
45　conveniuntque omnes, nec se discernere possunt.
Fracassus voluit brazzis amplectere Baldum,
sed tulit in saxo magnum cum fronte garofol.
Tum quoque Boccalus Baldum toccare volebat,
et quasi cum digito steso sibi vulsit ocellum.
50　Cingar ait: 'Properate ultra, videamus abyssum.
Ipseque Falchettus praecedat, guida, caminum'.
　　Quattuor in voces post haec cantare comenzant;
nam (velut accascat tal volta) fuere tralorum
quattuor insemma voces cantare scientes.
55　Accipit ut gracili sopranum voce Gibertus;
suscipit at firmum Philoforni bocca tenorem;
gorga tridans notulas prorumpit Cingaris altum;
trat grossum Baldus extra calcanea bassum.
Quattuor hi varios ita sic andando motettos
60　cantant et simili nihilant dulzore fadigam.
Gorgula Phoebaei frifolat magis alta Giberti
deque 'ci sol fa ut' modulanter surgit ad 'ela'.
Semicromas minimasque notas sic ille menuzzat

shins on the jagged boulders. And so they laugh and bear it with bright spirits, and the good friends cheerfully embrace such mishaps. Not far ahead — some two crossbow shots — others are moving along; to be precise, four of them together behind Fracasso, whose head was bruised on all sides. Lo! At last he hears horses pounding behind him and guesses who it is. He shouts, "Hey, wait a bit! I hear horses crushing the rock with their horseshoes. Could it be the centaur who has the form of a horse behind?"

He has scarcely finished this when Cingar, coming closer, shouted, 41 "O, O, Falchetto! O, O Fracasso! Boccalo!"

Gilberto happily exclaims, "That's Cingar's voice! Let's wait for 43 him." At that, they stand still, and all the others join them, even though they can't see each other. Fracasso wanted to put his arms around Baldo, but instead got a big carnation on his forehead from the rocks. Next, Boccalo too wanted to touch Baldo, but with his finger almost tore out Baldo's eye. Cingar says, "Hurry along. Let's go see the abyss. Let our guide Falchetto lead the way."

After this, they began to sing in four parts, for (as sometimes 52 happens) there were four different voices who knew how to sing together. Gilberto takes the part of soprano with his falsetto voice; Philoforno's mouth takes the melody in the tenor; Cingar's throat, mincing the notes, breaks out as an alto; Baldo pulls a deep bass up from his heels. So the four of them sing various motets as they walk along, and with such entertainment obliterate their exhaustion. Like Phoebus Apollo, Gilberto with his fine throat trills higher, and from *ti sol fa do* he rises harmoniously up to *la*. He subdivides the sixteenth notes and half notes, just as an expert carver ut pratichi frollam trinzantis dextra vacinam.

65   Longas atque breves Philofornus pectore squadrat
sustentatque omnem relevata voce camoenam.
Interdum pausas expectat quattuor, octo,
viginti, et trenta, velut est usanza tenoris,
dumque silet, ternis resonat modulatio linguis.

70   Non minus aure canit Cingar quam voce peritus:
nunc usque ad coelum vadit retrovare sopranum,
nunc usque ad baratrum scalam descendit ad 'are'.
Nulla quidem vox est aliorum promptior et quae
plus notulas nigras crevellet more farinae.

75   Baldus at educit tremulo de gutture bassum,
hunc quoque Flamengum iurares esse canonem,
nam fundans simulat cannam, velut organa, grossam.
Est sibi pochettum gamautti tangere cordas,
bassior at giusum canevae descendit in imum.

80   Plus ascoltantum sopranus captat orecchias,
sed tenor est vocum rector vel guida canentum;
altus Apollineum carmen depingit et ornat,
bassus alit voces, ingrassat, fundat et auget.
Cantus Flamengos, Talianos atque Todescos

85   hi cantant, quia sic passatur inutile tempus.
Sunt tamen insani quidam pazzique balordi,
sunt quidam stronzi, dico, bis terque cagati,
qui tam dulcisonis plenam concentibus artem
esse legerezzam dicunt tempusque gitatum,

90   plusque volunt aut esse asinos aut esse cavallos,
et tamen attracta reputari fronte Catones.
Plusque suam boriam preciant et, ventre pieno
lardatisque gulae paffis vultuque botazzi,
praelati insignes dici quam scire coëllum

95   seu sit parlandi, seu sit doctrina canendi.
Immo macer quidam bos Chiari, tortus et omnes

dexterously slices tender beef. Philoforno measures the long and short notes in his chest and supports the entire melody with a strong voice. At times, he pauses for four, eight, twenty, even thirty beats, as tenors will do, and when he is silent, three-part harmony is heard. Cingar sings as skillfully with his ear as with his voice: first he soars up to heaven to visit the soprano, then he goes down the steps to the depths of *re*. Indeed, none of the others has a more agile voice, or one that can sift through more little black notes like flour. Yet Baldo produces a bass from his tremulous throat that you'd swear was a Flemish cannon, for while holding the low notes, it imitates the large pipes of an organ. It is easy for him to sing a whole gamut of notes, yet, as a bass, he descends to the bottom of the cellar. The soprano is the most captivating to the listeners' ears, but the tenor is the rector of the voices and the leader of the singers. The alto colors and ornaments the Apollonian song. The bass nourishes, fortifies, anchors and augments the other voices. They sing Flemish, Italian and German songs, for this is how they pass their free time.

There are, however, certain madmen and crazed idiots — there 86 are certain turds, I mean, shat out two or three times, who say that an art so full of beautiful harmonies is frivolous and a waste of time. They prefer to be asses or horses, but want to be regarded as Catos with furrowed brows. They give more value to their own self-importance, a full belly and greasy orgies of food, and their wine-red faces and their reputation as distinguished prelates, than learning anything, whether the art of speaking or singing. Indeed, there is a certain lean ox from Chiari, excommunicated and having

scomunicatus habens materno a lacte diablos
in gobba, hypocritus, gnato vecchiusque crevatus,
est qui sbaiaffat, gracchiat de hac arte canendi.

100 Musica continuo versatur in ore deorum,
musica concordi fert circum cardine coelum,
musica nascendo humanos compaginat artus.
Cur hymnos, psalmos, cur cantica tanta vetusti
disposuere patres gesiis cantanda per orbem?

105 Cur, dico, antiqui doctores atque magistri
ornavere libros responsis, versibus, hymnis,
Kyrie leysonis, *Introitibus* ac *Aleluis?*
Ite genus pecudum, pacchiones, ite gazani!
Vos quicumque fero laceratis dente Camoenas.

110   Cessarant comites cantu, nam Cingaris ipse,
Cingaris ipse asinus firma cum voce comenzat
canzonem cantare suam, mostrare volendo
non minus esse bonam sibi vocem, non minus esse
cantandi garbum lingua gorgaque palesum,

115 quam fuit Agricolae quondam magnoque Bidoni.
Vox asini grata est asinis, neque gratior altra
esse potest, quamvis frifolet Philomena per umbras.
Ingentem interea strepitum sentire comenzant.
'Auditis?' Falchettus ait. Tunc quisque tacendo

120 stat chetus ac longis rumorem brancat orecchis.
Cingar ait: 'Seguita quo te via praevia guidat.
Fortasse invenies quo causa cridoris habetur'.
Falchettus paret tastatque andando petrarum
passibus intoppos sociisque annuntiat illos;

125 et quem Cingar ait, curat captare viazzum,
namque vias quandoque trovant velut ypsilon ire.
Quo magis accedunt, sonitus magis ille rebombat,
et iam vix unus parlans auditur ab altro
tam strepitus rumurque ingens assordat orecchias.

the devil in his hunched back ever since he drank his mother's milk; this hypocrite and decrepit old Gnatho bellows and squawks about this art of singing.

Music is the constant conversation of the gods; music makes 100 the heavens go round on their harmonious axis; music knits our human limbs at birth. Why were our ancestors disposed to sing hymns, psalms, and so many canticles in churches all over the world? Why, I ask, did scholars and teachers of old adorn their books with responsorials, verses, hymns, the *Kyrie Eleison*, the *Introit* and the *Halleluiah*? Be gone, you herd of sheep, you gluttons, go, you bumpkins, all of you who lacerate the Muses with your savage teeth.

The companions had stopped their singing because that ass of 110 Cingar's began to sing its own song with a sure voice, trying to prove that its own voice was just as good, and its talent in singing with tongue and throat just as evident as that of Agricola or the great Bidone in times past. An ass's voice is pleasing to asses; no other can be more pleasing, not even Philomena warbling in the shade. Meanwhile, they begin to hear a tremendous noise. "Do you hear that?" asks Falchetto. Then each of them keeps silent and listens for the sound with outstretched ears.

Cingar says, "Follow where the path leads you. Maybe you will 121 find the cause of those cries." Falchetto obeys, and as he walks he feels with his steps for obstructions of rock, and warns the others about them. He is careful to take the trail that Cingar tells him to, for sometimes they find that the paths split like a Y. The further they proceed, the louder the sound reverberates; soon they can't hear each other speaking, for the noise and clamor is so loud it deafens the ears. Although they have staunch hearts, they are all

130 Horrescunt omnes, quamvis sint pectore franco,
seque putant venisse nigri Plutonis ad umbras.
Denique per quandam fissuram splendulus ignis
apparet modicoque viam dat lumine claram.
Huc Baldus celerans alios restare comandat;
135 elevat hinc oculos quantum lux parvula monstrat;
ecce videt portam, vario quae sculta metallo est.
Accurrunt, placet ire intus; Fracassus in illam
ter pede chioccavit portam, sed tanta ruina
fit martellorum quod nil sentitur ab intro.
140 Impatiens Fracassus eam bis tergore crollat
atque cadenazzis rutpis sine chiave recludit.
Conticuere omnes martelli ferra domantes
nec sonat ulterius tich toch incudine pulso.
Stant ibi ferrari centum totidemque gaioffi,
145 qui carbonorum portant in tergore saccos,
qui quoque manticibus ventosis semper afogant,
quique domant ferrum martellis atque tenais.
In pede saltatus, vir grossus alhora pigrezzam
fert testudineam, et tamquam bosaccarus inflat
150 ingentem panzam et plenum fece botazzum;
tresque gulae cascant de mento ad bigolis imum.
Is Baffelus habet nomen primusque boteghae
stat faber, e zoppi Vulcani semine zoppus.
Introit en Baldus, coetu seguitante, bravosus
155 ut soldati intrant albergos tempore guerrae.
Cui Baffellus ait: 'Nimium, compagne, superbis.
Tune meam sic sic audes intrare fosinam?'
Baldus respondet ghignans: 'Te affretta, magister,
expediasque bonas armas, comprabimus illas';
160 sic parlans rugat buttatque sosopra botegam.
En rursum fabri nudo cum corpore menant
martellos magnos, candentia ferra domantes.

terrified and think that they have arrived at the shades of black
Pluto. At last, a splendid fire appears through a fissure and with
its modest glow lights the way. Rushing up, Baldo orders the oth-
ers to stop. He raises his eyes to what the faint bit of light is show-
ing, and sees a door sculpted in various metals. They all come
running and decide to enter. Fracasso bangs the door three times
with his foot, but there is such a fury of hammers that nothing is
heard within. Becoming impatient, Fracasso slams his shoulder
into it twice and breaking the heavy chains, opens it without a key.

The hammers shaping metal fall silent: "tick, tock" no longer   142
resounds on the anvils being struck. There are a hundred black-
smiths here and an equal number of scoundrels. They carry sacks
of coal on their backs and keep stoking the fire, too, with windy
bellows, and they shape iron with hammers and tongs. Jumping to
his feet, a big man then moves like a lazy tortoise; he puffs out his
huge belly like an old ox or a barrel full of feces; he has three chins
that fall down to his bellybutton. His name is Baffello and he is
the head craftsman in the shop; he is lame, from the race of lame
Vulcan. And here comes Baldo blustering, with his gang be-
hind him, as soldiers enter an inn during wartime. Baffello says to
him, "Companion, you are too bold! How dare you enter my forge
like this!"

Baldo responds, sneering, "Hurry up there, maestro! Get some   158
decent weapons ready and we'll buy them." As he says this, he
rummages through the shop, turning it upside down. And once
again the naked blacksmiths swing their great hammers, shaping

Pars facit huc, illuc vivas saltare favillas;
pars cum manticibus, pars cum carbone fogato
165 abbrasant durum venti sofiamine ferrum;
pars elmos limat cristatos parsque corazzas,
agroppantque tridas circum bragalia maias.
Sunt qui multifores, velut ars merscalca docetur,
excudunt ferros pro ramponare cavallos.
170 Dumque lavoratur, Baffellus praesidet illis,
dat quibus interdum crustas bastone cotoras.
Sunt omnes nigri, ruginentes, absque savono,
malque petenati, nudi plenique pedocchis.
Nec Baffellus eis lassat mancare bocalum,
175 nam male ferrari martellant absque bocalo.
Dumque ita perficitur parlantque insemma fradelli
de penitus finis sese fornire piastris,
velleque vestiri rutilis perforza corazzis,
ecce suum Baldus sentit nitrire cavallum,
180 Lyronusque suum, quos nunc deffora ligarant,
atque asinus bis sex pontadis protulit 'a a'.
Quid sit nescitur; currunt ad cernere causam:
Spezzacadena magis nitrit raspatque terenum,
Roccaforta simul magno rumore balanzat,
185 calzibus et duris cum Pardo marmora spezzat.
Vult Baldus saltare foras denantior altris;
sed pede vix posito super aerea limina portae,
maximus hunc spingit ventus drentumque rebuttat.
Obstupuere omnes; iterum vult bravus apertas
190 transpassare fores, at flatus fortior urtat,
quem simul et socios alios sotosora butavit.
Ter sic tentavit, ter sic indreto tomavit.
Tunc Baffellus ait: 'Grandis desgratia vestra est.
O sfortunati, vos nempe morire bisognat!
195 Sic sic ausi estis secreta subire deorum?

the glowing iron. Some of them make hot sparks fly here and there; some work the bellows; some use burning coals to make the hard iron glow under the blowing air; some file crested helmets and others breastplates; still others fit fine chain mail around breeches. There are some who pound out many-holed pieces of iron for shoeing horses, as taught by the farrier's art.

While they work, Baffello supervises and gives them some   170
meaty wallops with a club. They are all black, sooty, unwashed and unkempt, naked and full of lice. However, Baffello does not spare the jug, for blacksmiths hammer badly without a jug. So, while they work, and the brothers talk about furnishing themselves from top to bottom with fine armor and about wanting to wear shining breastplates at all costs, Baldo suddenly hears his horse neigh, and Lirone hears his (they had been tied up outside). And the ass offers his twelve-tone scale of "haw haw." They don't know what it is; they run to learn the cause. Spezzacadena neighs more loudly and paws the ground; at the same time Roccaforte rears up amid a great racket and together with Pardo breaks rocks with hard kicks. Baldo plans to jump out ahead of the others, but as soon as he places a foot over the threshold of the bronze door, a tremendous wind pushes him and throws him back inside. They are all stunned. Again, the brave man tries to pass through the open doors, but the wind blows even harder and knocks him down along with his friends. So he tried a third time and a third time he toppled. Then Baffello says, "This is a great disgrace for you. O you poor fellows, obviously you need to die. So you dared to

Nec formidastis grottas intrare dearum?
Non hic mortales fas est calcare pedattas,
ni dea concedat vobis Smiralda caminum'.
Fracassus dixit: 'Qui dii, quae Smerdola, quod fas?
200 Est Deus in coelo, quo lux nitet absque tenebris.
Vos mage diavoli brutti lordique stryones,
qui fugitis radios giorni, qui semper in umbris,
more civettarum, gufforum, gregnapolarum,
vivitis; et vosmet divos divasque vocatis?
205 Iuro tibi quod non discedam partibus istis,
donec iter retrovem quod nos deducet ad Orcum,
Luciferumque tibi patrem fratresque diablos
discornare volo totosque relinquere pistos.
Dic: quod nomen habes?' Respondet: 'Tune Tiphoeus?
210 Tune Briaraeus, quia me deitate segurum
sgomentare putas? Ego sum, qui fulmina magno
condo Iovi praesumque istis sine fine cavernis.
Iuro deos: faciam vestras pentire pacias.
Hinc uscite foras, praestum! Quid statis? An anchum
215 vultis ego dicam bis vobis? Ite deforas!
Vos altramenter tot porcos totque cavallos
cangiabo, veluti dii transformare cativos
malvagiosque solent homines in turpia rerum'.
Cui Fracassus: 'Habes magnam, confesso, rasonem,
220 dummodo, qui faciant illam, retroventur adessum.
Attamen invenias seu divos sive diablos,
qui te, quive tuam possint defendere causam;
non aliud ius nos, aliud non numen habemus
quam cor magnanimum, spadam mazzamque feratam.
225 Ergo, quid indusio? Nimium parlare codardos
arguit. Arma meis da compagnonibus! Ut quid
me sguerzis guardas oculis? Da praestiter arma!'
Sic dicens, calcem calidum vibravit eidem,

slip into the haunts of the gods, just like that? You weren't afraid
to enter the grottoes of the goddesses? No mortals are permitted to
trespass here if the goddess Smiralda does not grant you passage."

To this Fracasso says, "What deities? What Smerdola? What
permission? God is in heaven where the light shines without shad-
ows. You, though, are ugly devils and filthy sorcerers who flee the
sun's rays, who live in shadows forever, like tawny and horned owls
and bats — and you call yourselves gods and goddesses? I swear to
you that I will not forsake these regions until I have found the
path that will lead us to Orcus. I want to dehorn your father Luci-
fer and your brother devils, and I want to leave them all pum-
meled. Speak: what name do you have?"

He answers, "Are you then Typhon? Are you then Briareus,
that you think to frighten me when I am protected by my god-
hood? I am the one who fashions thunderbolts for great Jupiter
and I preside over these endless caverns. I swear by the gods, I will
make you regret your folly! Get out of here, now! What are you
waiting for? Do you really want me to tell you again? Get out of
here! Otherwise I will change you all into so many pigs and so
many horses, just as the gods are wont to transform wicked and
evil men into vile things."

Fracasso answers him, "You are quite right, I admit, as long as
you can find someone now to help you. Go ahead; look for gods or
devils who can defend you and your cause. We have no other law;
we have no other deity than a magnanimous heart, a sword and an
iron mace. What am I waiting for? Talking too much is a sign of
cowardice. Give my companions arms! Why are you looking at me
squint-eyed? Give us arms immediately!" So saying, he lets fly a

199

209

219

quem smagazzavit rafioli more tenelli
230 merdaque corporeis cunctis de partibus exit.
Hinc alius, terrere putans bravegiando guereros:
'Praesti', ait, 'o famuli! Quid statis? Prendite tela
scazzemusque istos temeraros extra fosinam.
Exite, o tristes asini gentesque ribaldae!'
235 Ac ea dum parlat, martellum corripit unum
et martellatam dat Baldo supra cerebrum.
Quando fabri nudi zuffam videre comenzam,
expediunt raptim martellos atque tenaias,
parsque graves limas, chiodos et azale fogatum,
240 hisque armis audent mastris se opponere guerrae.
Ridebat Baldus, nec fodro educere stoccum
se dignat, quamvis nesplum gustaverat unum.
Quamprimum festinus eos Boccalus asaltat,
seque valenthomum nuda inter corpora monstrat.
245 Sed poco in spatio cuncti periere ferari;
sunt etenim nudi, ceu fresca povina taiantur,
nec per miracolum mansit, qui viveret, unus.
Spezzacadena intrat per apertas denique portas
ruptaque de collo pendebat soga cavezzae;
250 sese cum Pardo cantonem tirat in unum.
Roccaforta tamen sentitur calcibus extra,
qui pistando petras frangit, qui boffat et hinnit
more cavallorum quando fit gara tralorum.
Tunc Fracassus, equo cupiens praestare socorsum,
255 vult exire foras, sed grandis ventus in illum
ecce ruit vastumque facit retro ire gigantem.
Baldus ait: 'Certe guastabitur ille cavallus'.
Respondet Cingar: 'Si sic fortuna repugnat,
quid nostras ultra cercamus rumpere testas?'
260 Hoc dicens, sotosora domum voltare comenzat.
Giubertus ponit carbones, excitat ignem

mighty kick at him which splatters him like tender ravioli, and shit comes out every part of his body. Then another devil, hoping to terrify the warriors by threats, says, "Quick now, servants, what are you waiting for? Take up arms and we will drive these foolhardy men from our forge! Get out now, you sad asses and scurrilous folk!" And while he is saying this, he grabs a hammer and gives Baldo a hammer-blow to the head.

When the naked smiths see that the battle has begun, they swiftly snatch up hammers and tongs; some take up heavy files, nails and red-hot steel, and with these weapons they dare to oppose the masters of war. Baldo laughed and did not deign to pull his sword out of its sheath, even though he had tasted a plum hit. As quickly as possible Boccalo assaults them, and proves his valor amid these naked bodies. Before long, all the smiths perish; they are nude, after all, and are cut through like fresh ricotta. No one is left who miraculously survives.

In the end, Spezzacadena enters through the open doors; the strap of his halter hangs from his neck. He withdraws to a corner with Pardo. Outside Roccaforte could still be heard by his kicks: he is breaking rocks with his stomping, and snorts and neighs as horses do when there's a fight. Then Fracasso, wanting to help the horse, attempts to go out, but lo! the great wind drives against him and makes the immense giant go backwards. Baldo says, "That horse will ruin himself for sure."

Cingar responds, "If Fortune thwarts us thus, why should we keep trying to break our heads?" Saying this, he begins to turn the place upside down. Gilberto adds coal, fans the fire with bellows and makes the glowing embers give off light. Lirone finds a hunk

237

248

258

    manticibus rossasque facit dare lumina bronzas.
    Lyronus retrovat vivo de marmore saxum,
    quod removet speratque aliquem accatasse thesorum.
265 Ecce repentinus fit terrae motus et antra
    undique tota sonant faciuntque stupire barones.
    Attamen interea saxum Lyronus abrazzat,
    mox levat et buttat per portas extra fosinam.
    Ecce drago (horresco referens) longhissimus intrat,
270 intratusque ruit propter squarzare Lyronem,
    qui sic arditus fuerat scoprire cavernam,
    qua latet haeroum pretium palmaeque ducarum.
    Tunc causa hic patuit quare tres ante cavalli
    saltabant fremitu, quos luridus anguis agebat.
275 Hunc tamen accensi tractique insemma cavalli
    calzibus assaltant, morsu pedibusque davantis.
    Nil drago deffendit se fortes contra cavallos,
    immo venenoso cercabat dente Lyronem
    sternere, dum grottam vult ille intrare scovertam.
280 Baldus et Hippol ei currunt praestare socorsum,
    qui contra bissam crebro deffenditur ense.
    At focus interea morzatur flamine venti,
    quo tenebrae totum penitus rapuere lusorem,
    nec possunt socii proprias cognoscere fazzas.
285 Baldus ibi clamat: 'Nihil, heia!, timete, barones!
    Nostra quidem virtus magicas non extimat artes.
    Sed precor intantum (quia sic lusore caremus):
    nemo menet spadam ne mutua vulnera dentur.
    Sola cavallorum sit guerra incontra dragonem'.
290 Sic ait, atque animat stimolanti voce cavallos
    ut stimulare canes in porcos saepe solemus;
    qui, nunc mordendo nunc calzos trando, domabant
    foetentem dragum, quamvis non vistus ab illis;
    quaeritur ad nasum solummodo, namque cavalli

of bare rock which he moves, hoping to find some treasure. But suddenly there is an earthquake and all the caves resound from every side, leaving the barons stunned. Yet at the same time Lirone puts his arms around the hunk of rock, then lifts it and throws it out the doors of the smithy. And behold! an extremely long dragon (I tremble to tell the tale) enters, and as soon as it has entered, rushes to dismember Lirone, who had been so foolhardy as to uncover the cavern that hides the elite of heroes and the crown of leaders.

And now it is clear why earlier the three horses had reared in a 273 frenzy: this ghastly serpent had stirred them up. Nevertheless, inflamed and drawing together, the horses assault it with kicks and bites and their front hooves. The dragon does not protect itself at all against the powerful horses but rather tries with its poisonous tooth to lay Lirone low, since he wants to enter the exposed grotto. Baldo and Hippol run to help him as he defends himself against the snake over and over with his sword. Yet meanwhile, the fire has been snuffed out by a blast of wind, so that the shadows completely snatch away all brightness, and the friends can no longer recognize each other's faces. Then Baldo cries out, "Have no fear, barons! Our courage does not bow to magical arts. But I beg you, for now (since we are thus without light) let no one wield his sword; let us not wound each other. Let the battle against the huge dragon be fought by the horses alone." Saying this, he goads the horses with rousing words, as we often rouse dogs against pigs. The horses, first biting, then kicking, were overcoming the fetid dragon even though they cannot see it and can only find it with

295 nil penitus possunt tenebris discernere foltis.
Pardus agit calzis nec lassat prendere flatum;
Roccaforta tenet portam prohibetque volenti
se scampare fugam, tenet ac perforza dedrentum.
Ille sed interea, nigrum vomitando venenum,

300 sibilat et sese tumefacto gutture gyrat.
Porrigit attentas quisquam compagnus orecchias,
interdumque suas per gambas ire tralorum
sentit, eumque procul sospingit calce Fracassus.
Omnes coguntur nasum stoppare, nec oybo

305 dicere tempus habent, tantus iam puzzor amorbat.
Tandem non potuit plus Spezza tenere cadena;
Spezzacadena dragum lassat scampare tirantem.
Ille viam liber scapolat seguitantque cavalli:
alter cum calzis agitat, sed morsibus alter.

310 Ille fatigatus sibi iam ingrossare fiatum
sentit, et intornum bassis volat anxius alis.
Fracassus validum menaret saepe tracagnum,
sed timet aut socios aut desertare cavallos.
Pardus, habens animum furiatum contra nemigum,

315 dum tirat calzum, percusso Cingare, fallat.
Cascat humi Cingar Pardusque retornat et ipsi
Boccalo supra schenam saltavit adossum.
'Heu!', Boccalus ait, 'succurrite! Namque butavit
me sotosora draco; magis immo diavolus extat'.

320 Respondet Cingar: 'Patientia! contra doverum,
contra meam voiam, patientia!, chara brigata.
Me quoque nunc fecit saligatam rumpere culo'.
Giubertus ridet. 'Rides, Giuberte, facendam
istam?', Cingar ait, 'Mihi nulla est voia grignandi.

325 Scilicet hic habeo ventosas atque cirottos,
cum quibus acceptam possim medegare schenadam'.

their noses, as they can make out nothing at all in the thick shadows. Pardo lets fly with kicks and doesn't let it catch its breath; Roccaforte guards the door, prevents it from escaping should it wish to flee and keeps it inside by force. But meanwhile, vomiting black venom, it hisses and gyrates with its puffed-out throat.

The friends perk up their ears attentively and feel it move 301 among them time and again between their legs. Fracasso propels it far away with a kick. They are all forced to plug their noses and don't have time to say "Yuck!" as the stench already makes them sick. Finally Spezzacadena is no longer able to hold fast, and allows the bucking dragon to escape. As it runs away the horses follow it; one attacks it with kicks, another with bites. Exhausted, it feels its breath grow heavy and circles anxiously on drooping wings. Fracasso would have wielded his mighty cudgel many times, but he worried about laying low his friends or the horses. Pardo, with his spirit infuriated against the enemy, lets fly a kick, misses, and strikes Cingar. Cingar falls to the ground and Pardo turns around and jumps on Boccalo's back. Boccalo cries, "Help me, for the dragon has thrown me upside down; indeed it is worse than a devil."

Cingar answers, "Patience! Contrary to justice, dear friends, 320 contrary to my own wishes—patience! I, too, was just forced to smack the gravel with my butt."

Gilberto laughs. "You are laughing at this matter, Gilberto?" 323 asks Cingar. "I myself have no desire to snicker. Of course, I have bandages and cups with which I could medicate that blow to the back."

Talia dum placidis mottis baronia solazzat,
egreditur cifolans oficinam denique serpens,
quem Rocaforta suis calzis prohibere nequivit.

330 Ille cavernosas vadit stridendo per oras;
dumque seguire parant guereri, protinus ecce,
ecce fores bronzi portaeque serantur apertae.
At pede cum dextro, Vasconum more, Fracassus
currit et ad terram, scarpato cancare, mandat

335 cuncta sotosopram, clamans sic voce tonanti:
'Me seguitate ducem! Quo nobis nostra codardis
forcia smarrita est? Ubi nostra prodezza, diavol?'
Sic ait et signans sese, ruit extra botegam,
quem non ulterius ricolavit forcia venti.

340 Tunc illi imbrazzant scudos brandosque filatos
disfodrando, foras armato pectore balzant;
hos quoque destreri drittis seguitantur orecchis.
Mortifer at dragus tenebrosa per antra vagatur,
tumbarumque cavas cifolis ingentibus explet.

345 Ad quorum strepitum socii vestigia drizzant
tantonesque abeunt quaeruntque per orba draconem,
quem vel habere volunt mortum vel perdere vitas.
Tum novus exoritur rumor tantusque bagordus
ut non esse putent nisi centum mille diablos.

350 Vox confusa procul loca per scurissima bombat,
quae venit innantum sensim crescitque gradatim.
Est id cunctarum rabidissima schiatta ferarum;
quaeque suas reddit voces ut usanza ministrat:
dat leo rugitum horrendum, lupus elevat urlos,

355 bos bu bu resonat, bau bau mastina canaia,
nitrit equus nasoque bufat raspatque terenum;
sgnavolat et gattus, et adirans eiulat ursus,
mula rudit mulusque simul, tum ragghiat asellus;
denique quodque animal propria cum voce favellat.

While the barons relax thus with playful rejoinders, the serpent 327
comes hissing out of the workshop at last; Roccaforte was unable
to block it with his kicks. Shrieking, it goes through the cavern
openings, and just as the warriors get ready to follow, behold, the
bronze gates and the opened doors are closed. Now Fracasso runs
up and with his right foot, Gascon-like, unhinges the door and
sends everything topsy-turvy to the ground, yelling with a thun-
derous voice, "Follow my lead! Why have we lost our might, cow-
ards that we are? Where the devil is our prowess?"

Saying this and crossing himself, Fracasso rushes out of the 338
shop and no longer recoils from the force of the wind. Then the
others strap on their shields, and, unsheathing their sharpened
blades, leap out with armored chests; their steeds too follow them
with ears erect. But the death-dealing dragon roams about the
dark caverns and fills the hollow vaults with its massive snorts.
The friends direct their steps toward this noise, groping along,
searching in the darkness for the dragon which they want to have
dead or lose their lives.

And now a new din arises, such a ruckus that they think there 348
must be at least a hundred thousand devils. A confusion of voices
reverberates from afar through the murky regions; it gets closer
and closer and grows louder and louder. It is an extremely fero-
cious conglomeration of wild animals. Each one expresses itself as
custom dictates: the lion lets out a horrible roar, the wolf raises
howls, the ox echoes "moo moo" and the mastiff "bow wow." The
horse neighs and snorts from its nose and paws the ground; the
cat meows and the angry bear wails. The she-mule bawls and her
mate does too; then the donkey brays. To sum up, each animal
speaks with its own voice. All together they race toward the un-

360 Hi pariter celerant incautos contra guereros,
      duraque cum rabidis afferrant morsibus arma.
      Si manegiare volunt spadas, est grande periclum
      ne sibi medesimis mortalia vulnera figant.
      Quisque suum corpus sentit morderier atque
365 per tenebras ullam nescit comprendere cosam.
      Longa cavernarum via, nigris plena latebris,
      tomboat istarum vario cridore ferarum.
          Fantasticarat multo iam tempore Cingar
      quam retrovare guisam possit dare lumen ad orbos.
370 Invenit ascortus, gratans sibi denique testam,
      commenzatque petras azzalo tundere spadae;
      quae, quia spagnola est finissima lama, favillas
      per caecos passim busos facit ire micantes
      et pocho alquantam praestat lusore vedutam;
375 unde avisantur saltem gnarique fiuntur
      compagni si stent sibi retro aut ante diabli;
      namque diabli erant, induti membra ferarum.
      In quorum medio Baldus se primus afrontat,
      ignudoque feras brando smembrare comenzat.
380 Fracassus pariter, longe bastone butato,
      cum manibus tantum brancat, perstringit, afogat,
      atque caneggiatos duris necat unguibus apros.
      Cum manibus, dico, tantum, cum dentibus atque
      squarzat, et in tepido se totum sanguine sbroiat.
385 Virmazzus, nec non iunctus Philofornus apressum,
      contra duos tauros magnam coepere baruffam.
      Cingar crebra menat per duras vulnera cotes,
      quem drago predictus post schenam falsus asaltat
      vultque vetare illum ne sic det lumen amicis.
390 Clamitat altorium Cingar; Moschinus aiuttat
      et, spadam abiciens, illi se buttat adossum
      per collumque tenens, manibus stringendo, cavalcat.

prepared warriors and seize their hard weapons with ferocious bites. If the men wish to draw their swords, there is great danger that they will inflict mortal wounds on each other. Each man feels his body being bitten, but in the darkness no one can get a handle on anything. The long stretch of caverns, full of the blackest hiding places, rumbles with the diverse yowling of these animals.

For some time, Cingar has been ruminating how to find a way 368 to give light to the blind. Scratching his head, the astute man figures it out at last and begins to hack the rock with his steel sword: This fine Spanish blade sends glittering sparks here and there into the blind holes and with a bit of brightness offers a little sight, so that the companions can at least be warned and made aware whether the devils are ahead or behind—for these were devils who had taken on the bodies of animals. Baldo is the first to advance among them, and stripped of his blade, he begins to dismember the beasts. And Fracasso likewise, having thrown his club far off, grabs only with his hands, squeezes, suffocates and kills the mutated boars with his hard nails. With only his hands, I mean, and tears them apart with his teeth and soaks himself thoroughly in the warm blood.

Virmace, with Philoforno right beside him, began a huge brawl 385 with two bulls. Cingar keeps making strikes on the sharp crags, but the aforementioned dragon treacherously attacks him from behind and tries to stop him from giving light to his friends. Cingar shouts for assistance. Moschino helps, and flinging down his sword, he throws himself on top of the beast, holding it by the neck; and gripping tight with his hands, he rides it like a horse.

Serpa, viam currens, Moschinum tergore portat.
Viderat id factum Falchettus, donat aiutum
395 insequiturque cridans: 'Quo te, Moschine, diavol?
Quo, Moschine, drago te portat? Smonta, miselle!
Namque tuae timeo vitae! Cito, salta deorsum!'
Moschinus non audit eum, sed fertur ab angue,
quem validis pugnis semper ferit inter orecchias.
400 Ecce ambos raptim volucer Falchettus arivat,
ut giusum balzet, crebro clamore monendo.
Moschinus vero, post se cum sensit amicum,
quadruplicans animos, tam fortiter ilia serpae
stringit ut illa cadat terrae, mancante fiato.
405 Falchettus subito per dextram zaffat orecchiam,
serpentemque retro nunc huc, nunc protrahit illuc;
Moschinus stat firmus equo calcagnaque menat,
cumque manu armata guanto tampellat et urtat;
se retrahit serpens nec vadere curat avantum.
410 Non aliter cum vacca neci sit tracta becaro,
plus redit indretum quo plus guidatur inanzum,
squartatas quoniam cernit de longe sorellas,
inque cruentatis pendentia membra cavecchis.
Cingar ibi assistens totum dentaverat ensem,
415 qui iam non brandus sed dentea sega videtur.
Non tamen e saxis flammas excudere cessat
exiguosque suis sociis praestare lusores.
Ipse drago noscit se mortum, protinus altram
vertitur in spetiem, quoniam (mirabile dictu)
420 quae nunc anguis erat, formosa putina videtur,
cui nomen Smiralda fuit, de gente luparum.
Cascat Moschinus, dum sub culamine longa
schena deest formamque piat drago ille novellam.
Falchettus stupuit, cuncti mirantur in illam,
425 a capite ad plantas indutam vestibus albis;

Running away, the serpent bears Moschino on its back. Falchetto
had seen this take place; he brings help and gives chase, crying
out, "Where, Moschino, where the devil is that dragon taking you,
Moschino? Get off, you wretch, I'm afraid for your life! Quickly
now, jump down!"

Moschino doesn't hear him, but is carried away by the snake,   398
which he keeps pummeling between the ears with mighty fists. Yet
fleet Falchetto rapidly reaches them both, and with a volley of
shouts warns him to jump down. But when Moschino feels that
his friend is right behind him, redoubling his force, he squeezes
the serpent's flanks so hard that it falls to the ground out of
breath. Falchetto immediately grabs the serpent by the right ear
and from behind drags forward this way and that. Moschino sits
firm in the saddle and digs in his heels; and with his hand pro-
tected by a glove, punches and pounds it. The serpent pulls itself
back and does not want to advance. It is no different when a cow is
dragged to its death by the butcher; the more she is driven ahead,
the more she goes backward, for she sees her sisters in the dis-
tance, gutted, and their parts hanging from bloody hooks. Cingar,
standing nearby, had notched teeth along the length of his sword:
it no longer looks like a sword but a saw-toothed blade. However,
he does not stop striking sparks from the rocks and offering his
friends meager brightness.

The dragon knows it is dead. At once it changes into another   418
species—what was just now a snake (marvelous to relate) appears
to be a shapely young girl, whose name was Smiralda, of she-wolf
stock. Moschino falls, since the long back under his butt disap-
pears and the dragon takes on a new form. Falchetto is amazed; all
the others are looking at her. Dressed head to toe in white cloth-

quae manibus librum retinet mussatque parolas
seque coprit latitans ne sit compresa baronis.
Sed rapit in socca Falchettus praestiter illam,
cui fugit e manibus vestis; Falchettus, osello
430 praestior, hanc iterum per trezzas illico zaffat
medesimoque actu scarpat de pectore librum.
Admiranda nimis comparuit ecce facenda:
vix Falchettus eam raperat librumque serarat,
omne repentinas animal se scampat in umbras,
435 immo abeunt infrotta simul sex mille chiapini.
At Smiralda cridat planctumque comenzat amarum,
Falchettumque rogat supplex sicve: 'Ayme!', losingat,
'Ayme! Ego, non curans hominum consortia, vitam
his teneo castam grottis servoque pudorem.
440 Ah miserere tuae famae, Falchette! nec istud
dignum laude putes, teneram offendisse putinam.
Quid facias de me, quae sum muliercula? de me,
quae sum de numero nympharum Palladis una?
Ergo, precor, voias toltum mihi rendere librum
445 perque meam me andare viam permittere fas sit'.
Talibus ingannans, Falchettum porca carezzat
barbozzoque eius digitis putanella duobus
fat squaquarinellum, velut est ars vera piandi,
sive carezzandi menchiones atque dapocos.
450 Venerat huc Baldus, Cingar, cunctique barones,
hique simul quantum sit bella fiola stupescunt.
Alter ait: 'Scelus est bellam ammazzare putinam';
alter ait: 'Scelus est bruttam scapolare putanam'.
Dum tamen hanc Falco, mossus pietate, parecchiat
455 linquere, quae vadat quo se sua voia comandat,
dumque putat secum proprii dishonoris afettum,
ecce procul vox alta tonat cum voceque lumen

ing, holding a book in her hands, she mutters words and covers herself, hiding so she won't be seized by the barons. Falchetto instantly snatches her by the skirt, but her clothes slip out of his hands. Falchetto, faster than a hawk, grabs her again at once by her locks and with the same motion, strips the book from her chest.

Then an extraordinary thing happened: as soon as Falchetto had grabbed her and had closed the book, all the animals rapidly flee into the shadows; or rather a swarm of six thousand hellions flees simultaneously. Smiralda cries out and begins a bitter lament; and kneeling, begs Falchetto thus: "Poor me!" she pleads, "Poor me! Not caring for the society of men, I lead a chaste life in these grottoes and preserve my modesty. Ah, have mercy on your own good reputation, Falchetto, and do not think that this is worthy of praise — to assault a tender maiden. What will you do with me, I who am only a little woman and a nymph of Pallas Athena? So I pray you, please give me back the book you took and let me be allowed to go on my way." Tricking him with such words, the pig caresses Falchetto; the little whore takes his chin between two fingers and gives it a small tug, in accordance with the true art of getting and stroking dolts and low-lifes.

Baldo, Cingar and the other barons had arrived. Together they marvel at how beautiful the girl is. One says, "It's a crime to kill a beautiful girl." Says another, "It's a crime for an ugly whore to escape." But while Falchetto, moved by pity, is planning to release her so that she can go where her fancy dictates, and while he ponders the result of his own dishonor, behold, from a distance, a

432

450

apparet radians, quae clamat: 'Prendite rursus!
Prendite, barrones, lordam foedamque bagassam!
460 Mundus namque omnis tali pro peste ruinat'.
Lyronus repiat subitus per colla puellam,
quae se de teneris Falchetti solverat ongis,
hancve tenet firmam, donec barbatus arivat
illuc vecchiardus, similis gravitate Catono,
465 qui primum laeta compagnos fronte salutat.
Mox iubet ut voiant magicum sibi tradere librum;
illa statim cridat: 'Ne des, Falchette, quadernum!
Iste malus vecchius vos ingannare parecchiat'.
Cui senior conversus ait: 'Strya pessima, iam iam
470 tempus avicinat, quo debes rendere contum
de tot perdutis animis, ad averna gitatis
pro te, proque tuis paribus de prole stryarum.
Dic, meretrix Satanae; dic, concubina Chiapini:
dic 'nunc' quae pars est? Dicis te Palladis unam
475 de nymphis, cum sis Porta ipsa Comasna Milani,
per quam tot gentes vadunt redeuntque frequentes.
Oh! nimium tete passa est vindicta Tonantis;
quam dare iam poenas, quam iam decet ire sub orcum.
Eice nunc, Falchette, librum, nunc eice pestem
480 carrognamque orbis totius et aetheris oybum!'
Falchettus Baldum guardat, cui Baldus acennat
barbato parere seni. Falchettus arenae
librettum gittat; nec apena butaverat illum,
ecce repentinus strepitus motusque tereni:
485 turba diavolorum properant zaffantque ribaldam,
quae meschina cridans tunc strassinatur ad orcum,
cumque putanabus aliis, sex millia voltas
per quamcumque horam cibus est et fezza diabli.

voice thunders loudly and with the voice appears radiant light. "Hold on to her, barons, hold on to that filthy, loathsome trollop! The entire world is being ruined thanks to that plague of a witch."

Lirone promptly recaptures the girl by the collar, for she had 461 freed herself from Falchetto's tender talons. He holds her tight until a bearded man appears there, an old man similar in gravity to Cato, who greets the companions right away with a happy countenance. Then he orders them to hand over the magic book. At once Smiralda cries out, "Don't give him the volume, Falchetto! This wicked old man is planning to trick you."

The elderly man turns to her and says, "Worthless witch, now 469 the time is approaching when you must answer for all the lost souls, all those who were thrown into Avernus on account of you and your peers among the progeny of witches. Speak, slattern of Satan! Speak, concubine of the Devil! Do tell, what part of speech is "now"? You say that you are one of Athena's nymphs, when really you are the Porta Comacina of Milano, through which so many crowds of people come and go. O far too long has the revenge of the Thunderer passed you over; now it is high time that you pay your penalty; it is fitting that you descend to Orcus. Now, Falchetto, throw down that book! Throw down the plague and the carrion of the entire planet, the stench of the skies!"

Falchetto looks at Baldo, and Baldo gives him the sign to obey 481 the bearded old man. Falchetto tosses the book on the ground, and no sooner had he thrown it when instantly there is a loud noise and an earthquake. A gang of devils rushes forth and grabs the harlot, and the wretch is dragged screaming into Orcus, and with the other whores, six thousand times every hour, is made the food and feces of the Devil.

Liber vigesimus secundus

Nunc bastum caricare tuum, mea mula, gravoso
est opus incarico, sub quo sudando cagabis,
atque fachinando foenum speltamque padibis.
Tu mihi monta susum, tu mecum, Grugna, cavalca,
5   namque necessamur coeptum complere viaggium.
Malferrata licet pedibus sit chiucchia davantis,
importanza tamen multa est acatare poëtam,
illum barbatum, vecchium grassumque poëtam,
quem praecedentis sub fine voluminis esse
10 dixisti apparsum Baldo Baldique brigatae.
Ut tamen ad plenum vatis chiarezza cotanti
nota sit, historiam primo repetamus ab ovo.
    Est lagus Italiae, Degardam nomine dicunt,
quem mea cantavit soror olim Gosa Maderno,
15 tempore quo Gardon vastabat regna Monighae
inque Rivoltella cathedrabat papa Stivallus.
Hoc de ventre laghi grandis flumara cavatur,
quae, qua Pescheriae rocchae fortezza menazzat,
trottat praecipiti per pascola virda camino.
20 Menzus habet nomen, qui fregat moenia Godi,
donec Mantoae muros circumfluit urbis
parque fit Oceano, cum vastis calcitrat undis.
Ast ubi perque urbem properat circumque muraias,
ventronesque menat zosum, cagatoria purgat,
25 en iterum stringit ripas, fit flumen et ancum
currit ad ingentem retrovare Governolis arcem.
Primius ille tamen quam tornet currere, factus
de pelago flumen, binas trovat ecce nemigas
per scontrum terras, quas inter Mintius ipse
30 defluit atque tenet spartitas more luparum,

Book XXII

Now, O mule of mine, it is necessary to load your saddle with 1
heavy baggage, under which you'll sweat and poop, and while
drudging along you'll digest hay and spelt. Mount and ride with
me, Grugna, for we must finish the journey we have started. Al-
though my molly is poorly shod on its front feet, still, it's impor-
tant to find that poet, the fat, bearded old poet, the one you said
appeared to Baldo and Baldo's gang at the end of the preceding
book. Yet, so that the brilliance of such a bard may be fully
known, let us recount the story from its origins.

There is an Italian lake they call by the name of Garda, which 13
my sister Gosa sang about earlier in Maderno, at the time when
Gardone was devastating the kingdoms of Moniga and Pope Stivallus
was enthroned in Rivoltella. From the belly of this lake, where the
mighty fortress of Peschiera threatens, there runs a large waterway
that trots along a steep path through green pastures. It is called
the Mincio; it rubs against the bulwarks of Goito until it flows
around the walls of the city of Mantua and becomes like an ocean
thrashing with big waves. Yet as it hurries by the city and around
the ramparts and carries off entrails and purges outhouses, lo! it
narrows its banks again, becomes a river, and courses finally to-
ward the immense stronghold of Governolo. But before it returns
to flowing, changed from sea into river, behold! it reaches two op-
posing enemy territories. Between them the Mincio descends and
keeps them apart, as though they were wolves who would like to

quae rabido vellent addossum currere morsu.
Sic Hosthya Padi Revero spartitur ab undis,
sic Stellata sedet Figarolo sgiunta per amnem.
Illas ergo inter terras sua flumina Menzus
35 fert vaga ne vastis meschientur cuncta ruinis,
et male dispostos rabies diabolica stighet.
Altera stat valli, chiamata Pyetola, dextrae;
altera stat monti, chiamata Cipada, sinistro.
Illa bravat contra totos, ut Roma, paësos;
40 ista suas spresiat, veluti Cartago, brauras;
unde piat forzam capitalis guerra tralorum.
Sed quia Virgilium studiosa Pyetola vatem
gignerat et sese decorarat nomine tanto,
morsibus invidiae marcebat flegma Cipadae.
45 Omnibus impresis nolebat cedere mundo,
hoc solo in factu sibimet Cipada corozzat,
quod nullis esset penitus fornita poëtis.
Quid facit? Eligitur, sancto mandante senatu,
ambassator habens lettras magnumque saperum,
50 qui doctoratus totum messale sciebat.
Is Curtatonis de portu ad regna Gregorum
pervenit, et claram Nigroponti fertur ad oram.
Protinus accurrunt gentes magnumque Cipadae
ambassatorem multo sumpsere triumpho.
55 Postea, quid tandem vadat faciendo rechiedunt.
Ille sibi poscit guidam, qua ductus arivet
mons ubi Parnassus forat alto vertice Lunam,
namque habet ut Phoebo parlet Phoebique sorellis.
Praestiter admissus fuit ambassator ad undas
60 Belorophontaeas et, factis mille carezzis,
ambassariam scoltavit Apollo Cipadae.
Quae fuit: ut, veluti de vate Pyetola tanto
Virgilio godit, sic magna Cipada poëtam

rush against each other with rabid bites. In this same way Ostiglia
is separated from Revere by the waves of the Po, and thus Stellata
sits divided from Ficarolo by the current.

The Mincio, therefore, keeps flowing between these two lands,   34
lest all things get mixed up in tremendous destruction, and diabol-
ical rage stirs up their embittered spirits. One place, called Pietole,
lies in the valley on the right bank. The other, called Cipada, lies
on a slope to the left. The former, like Rome, blusters against all
the other towns; the latter, like Carthage, scorns her blustering, so
that a deadly conflict gathers momentum between them. And yet
because the learned Pietole had brought forth the poet Vergil and
had ennobled herself with such a great name, Cipada's humors
were festering from the pangs of jealousy. She refused to yield in
all enterprises in the world; only in this one matter Cipada gets
vexed with herself—that she has not been provided with any poet
whatsoever.

What is to be done? By mandate of the holy senate, an ambas-   47
sador is elected possessing learning and great knowledge, whose
doctor's degree had acquainted him with the entire missal. From
the port of Curtatone, he reaches the kingdom of the Greeks and
the famous shores of Negroponte. At once people run up and wel-
come the ambassador of renowned Cipada with great pomp. Af-
terwards, they finally question what he's doing there. He asks for a
guide to lead him to where Mount Parnassus pierces the moon
with its peak, for he needs to speak to Phoebus Apollo and to his
sisters.

Straight away the ambassador was admitted to the Bellero-   59
phontic waters and there, after a thousand welcoming gestures,
Apollo listens to the petition from Cipada. And it was this: Just as
Pietola thoroughly enjoys such a poet as Vergil, so too great
Cipada should possess a poet that might overthrow with the

317

possideat talem, qui nervo carminis ipsum
65   non tam Virgilium sed Homerum buttet abassum,
qui nec sint digni sibi nettezare culamen.
At Phoebus, reputans cosam maturiter omnem,
sic tandem responsa dedit: 'Diversa metalla
sunt, quae diversis soleo partire poëtis.
70   Cui datur argentum, cui stagnum, cui datur aurum,
fluxile cui plumbum, cui tandem cagola ferri.
His de materiis magazenus noster abundat,
praeter quod solos per Homerum perque Maronem
scattola vodata est auri, nec dragma remansit.
75   Illi poltrones sicophantae cuncta vorarunt,
nec migolam fini liquere nepotibus auri.
Si mihi Pontanum proponis Sanque Nazarum,
si Fracastorium, si Vidam, sive Marullum,
crede mihi, alchimia est quidquid dixere moderni.
80   Quapropter nostrum ne spernas carpere sanum
conseium, si vis impresae talis honorem.
I magis ad sguataros et clara trovare procazza
regna lasagnarum, felix ubi vita menatur,
ocharumque illic verax paradisus habetur.
85   Sicut ego hic cytharam pulso danzantque Camoenae,
intornumque mihi faciunt saltando coronam,
sic illic pivam Tiphis sonat intra sorellas,
quae sibi pancifico faciunt infrotta morescas.
Huc fretolosus abi, ne migam tarda caminum:
90   nullus adhuc illa praecellit in arte novella,
prima manet siquidem macaronum palma Cipadam'.
His ambassator sentitis, masticat alto
cuncta supercilio Phoebumque rigratiat; inde
per Zibeltarri strictum canale trapassat,
95   Oceanumque secans per drittum perque roversum,
cercat, vestigat, petit hic, interrogat illic,

power of his verse not only Vergil but Homer as well, who are not worthy of wiping his butt. And Apollo, after mature reflection on all this, at last gave this response: "There are different metals which I usually distribute among the poets. One is given silver, another tin, one gold, another malleable lead, and lastly, iron filings. Our storehouse is full of these materials, except for the box of gold, which has been emptied by Homer and Maro alone—not a dram remains. Those worthless sycophants have devoured everything; they have left not even a glint of fine gold for their grandchildren. If you suggest Pontano to me, or Sannazaro or Fracastoro or Vida or Marullo, believe me, what these moderns have spoken is alchemy.

"For this reason, do not disdain to take our wholesome advice, 80 if you want honor in such an enterprise. Go instead to the scullery boys and try to find the illustrious kingdom of lasagna, where happy lives are led; the true paradise of geese is found there. Just as here I strum the lyre and the Camenae dance and form a circle around me leaping about, so there Tifi plays the pipes among those sisters who dance the *moresca* in swarms around the paunchy fellow. Depart in haste for this place; do not delay your trip one little bit. Up until now, no one has excelled in this new art, so that the first prize for macaroni awaits Cipada."

After hearing these things, the ambassador chews them over 92 with a raised eyebrow and gives thanks to Apollo; then he passes through the narrow strait of Gibraltar, cuts back and forth across the ocean—searches, investigates, inquires here, questions there,

319

donec acattavit montes finaliter illos,
gens ubi salsizzis vignas ligat, omnis et arbor
talibus in bandis tortas parit et tortellos.
100 Hic patrem alloquitur Tiphim Tiphisque sirocchias,
grataque praestata est tanto udientia messo.
Ergo novam tandem tulit hinc Cipada recettam,
per quam trippiferum valet aquistare poëtam,
cui Maro sit zagus et mulae striggiator Homerus.
105 Ergo putinellus clara de stirpe Folenghi
eligitur patribus, populoque insemma dunato
ponitur in medium, quem publica spesa Cipadae
nutriat, et tassis nemo scusetur ab illis;
utilitas quoniam cunctis est publica, quando
110 sit comunis honor cunctis nutrire poëtam,
qui sonet et cantet cum piva gesta Cipadae.
Mox fuit apparsum toto miracol in orbe,
quale aiunt magno quondam evenisse Platoni,
quem pascebat apum squadronus melle putinum;
115 sic quoque quottidie passabat nigra frequenter
merla Padum, portans infanti pabula becco;
quapropter nomen Merlini venit ab inde,
mottivumque frequens coepit celebrarier illud:
'Merla Padum passat propter nutrire Cocaium'.
120 Traditur inde viro savio doctoque pedanto
Merlinus puer, et versu prosaque peritus
cum sociis multis ivit studiare Bolognam
et philosophastri baias sentire Peretti;
unde comenzavit super illas torcere nasum
125 inque Petri Hispani chartis salcicia coxit.
Ad macaronaeas potius se tradidit artes,
in quibus a teneris ungis fuit ille Cocaio
praeceptore datus pinguisque poëta dicatus.
Dum Pomponazzus legit ergo Perettus et omnis

until finally he finds those slopes where people tie up vines with sausages and every tree in those parts produces cakes and pies. Here he addresses father Tifi and Tifi's sisters, and a welcome audience is given to this great ambassador. In this way Cipada got a new recipe at last, and with it she can acquire a tripe-filled poet whom Vergil may serve as an altar boy and Homer as a groom for his mule.

In this way, a little boy from the illustrious Folengo clan is cho- 105
sen by the nobles and placed in the middle of the assembled people. He is to be nourished by Cipada at public expense, and no one is to be excused from these taxes, since it is a public benefit for everyone, since it is an honor shared by everyone to nourish the poet who will play the pipes and sing the deeds of Cipada.

Then there appeared a miracle across the whole region which 112
they say had happened earlier to the great Plato, who, as a boy, was fed by a squadron of bees. In the same way, a merle crossed the Po several times a day carrying baby pabulum in its beak, and consequently, the name Merlin came from this; and that popular saying began to gain fame, "The merle passes the Po to nourish Cocaio."

Next, the lad Merlin is delivered to a wise man and learned 121
pedant. And when he had become skilled in verse and prose, he went to study in Bologna with many companions and to hear the whoppers of the philosophaster Pomponazzi. He started to turn his nose up at these, and cooked sausages in the pages of Petrus Hispanus. He preferred to dedicate himself to the macaronic arts, for which he was given at a tender age to the tutor Cocaio, and consecrated as a plump poet. So while Pomponazzi lectures and

130 voltat Aristotelis magnos sotosora librazzos,
     carmina Merlinus secum macaronica pensat
     et giurat nihil hac festivius arte trovari.
     Ergo per obscuras dum praticat ille cavernas,
     ecce hic apparet Baldo, velut ante notatur,

135 Smiraldamque magam iubet hinc portare diablos.
     Mox acarezzanter Baldum Baldique sodales
     stringit et abrazzat, ducitque in tecta fabrorum,
     quos super adstantes faciens residere cadregas,
     sic favoleggiat eis: 'Bene nunc veniatis, amici.

140 Sunt anni centum, sex menses octoque giorni
     quattordesque horae, quod ego Merlinus in istis
     vos attendo busis terrae grottisque diabli.
     Sors bona me fecit tales meritare barones,
     qui vadant penitus, magno guidante Serapho,

145 Gelforeas guastare casas, scornare diablos.
     Conveniet grandes vobis passare travaios
     ut desperati vitae quandoque saritis.
     Gratia sed coeli, quae voscum semper habetur,
     non aberit vobis, nec vos possanza diabli

150 offensare potest, si rerum Factor aiuttat.
     Attamen, ut Giesiae vetus est retrovatio sanctae,
     nuntio vos omnes: mihi confessare bisognat,
     namque pretus sacratus ego sum lectus ad istam
     legitime impresam, per quam peccata lavantur.

155 Nec confessandi vobis vergogna sit ulla,
     namque bonum talis meritum rossezza ministrat'.
     Cingar, id ascoltans, toto se corpore stringit:
     oh quam dura cosa est homini confessio pravo!
     At Baldus, cui semper inest syncera voluntas,

160 laetus ait: 'Nobis parlatio vestra gradivit;
     sic, Merline pater, tibi confessabimus omnes.
     Dudum coelestis nota est clementia Patris,

turns all of Aristotle's books inside out, Merlin thinks to himself about macaronic verse and swears that nothing can be found more fun than this art.

So then, while he frequents those dark caverns, he suddenly appears to Baldo, as noted above, and commands the devils to take the sorceress Smiralda away. Then he hugs Baldo and his friends affectionately and leads them into the smith's abode. Having them sit on the benches there, he spins these yarns: "Welcome to you today, friends! For one hundred years, six months, eight days and fourteen hours, I, Merlin have been waiting for you in these holes in the earth and grottoes of the devil. Good fortune has made me deserve such barons, who will go deep inside, under the guidance of the great Seraphus, to destroy the houses of Gelfora, to scorn the devils. You will have to endure great hardships, such that at times you will be in despair for your lives. But you will always have with you heavenly grace; it will not leave you, nor can the might of the devil harm you if the Creator of all things helps you. However, according to an ancient discovery of Holy Church, I declare that you all must confess to me, for I am a consecrated priest legitimately chosen for that action by which sins are washed away. And let there be no shame for you in confessing, for such blushing earns you good merit." 133

Upon hearing this, Cingar's whole body stiffens. How difficult it is for a corrupt man to confess! But Baldo, whose good will is always sincere, happily says, "Your sermon pleased us. Hence, Father Merlin, we will all confess to you. For a long time the clemency of our heavenly Father has been known, who does not mea- 157

qui non misurat quantum peccamus in illum,
sed nos optat, amat, tirat salvatque ribaldos;
165 nos immo elegit, nos immo vocavit ad esse
iustitiae invictos soldatos atque barones.
Spondeo sic igitur, per iusti pignora dritti,
ille sibi fidos nos cheros semper habebit.
Vos agedum, socii, mentem brancate gaiardam:
170 quisquam nostrorum sua nunc malefacta sedazzet,
discutiatque suum veteri de sorde gabanum'.
Tunc omnes taciti subito loca singula prendunt,
seque sibi testam grattant cerebroque travaiant:
utque sciunt, aut scire queunt, peccata recordant.
175 Cingar plus aliis habet unde tapinus ab imo
pectore suspiret: nescit qua in parte galonem
voltet pensandi montes pelagumque malorum.
Dum memorare studet, scelerum confusio surgit,
dumque malum putat hic, subito domenticat illic.
180 Baldus adest primus, deponit cingula spadae,
fronteque summissa curvoque utroque ginocchio,
incipit et miro sua facta sub ordine narrat.
Post quem Falchettus quidquid commiserat ipse
parte viri (ut naso, gustu visuque) fatetur,
185 sed quae parte canis tacuit tenuitque budellis,
namque canes Gesiae non confessare tenentur,
et Falchettus erat vir ante canisque dedretum.
Crimina Fracassi multum pochetina trovavit,
namque bonus certe semper fuit ille polaster.
190 Sat Lyronus erat caricus, sat plenus et Hippol,
corsarus quoniam fuit hic, fuit ille ladronus.
Moschinus sequitur cantorque Gibertus; et ambo
defectus dixere illos illasque fusaras,
quas aqua sancta lavat, quas pulsio pectoris arcet.
195 Centauri non longa fuit confessio, nam quod

sure how much we sin against him, but who chooses us, loves, attracts and saves rogues like us. In fact he has chosen us, and in fact has called us to be triumphant soldiers and knights of justice. So therefore, I promise, by a pledge of the right path, that he will always have us as faithful defenders. Come now, friends, take hold of your valiant minds! Each of us must sift through his misdeeds and shake out the old debris from his cage."

Thereupon, they all silently seek solitary niches at once, and 172 scratch their heads and work their brains so that they know or are able to know and recall their sins. Cingar has more than the others, so the poor fellow sighs from deep in his breast. He doesn't know where to turn while considering his mountains and seas of wicked deeds. While he endeavors to remember, a confusion of crimes surges up and while he thinks of one bad deed here, right away he forgets one there.

Baldo goes first; he sets down his sword belt and, with a bowed 180 head and both knees bent, begins narrating his deeds in admirable order. After him Falchetto discloses whatever he had done with his human part (like his nose, taste and sight), but keeps silent those things of his canine part and holds them in his guts, since dogs are not required to confess themselves to the Church, and Falchetto was a man in front and a dog behind. Merlin finds that the crimes of Fracasso are very few, for indeed he was always a good young buck. Lirone was quite loaded down, and Hippol is quite full—since one was a corsair and the other a pirate. Moschino follows and the singer Gilberto, and both of them recount those defects and follies that holy water washes and a simple beating of the breast repels. The confession of the centaur was not

parte cavallina peccatur culpa niuna est.
Inde satisfecit Philofornus et inde Bocalus,
quem sibi quamprimum Merlinus ab ante levavit,
cogebatur enim gravitatem rumpere risu.

200 Casus quos dixit, censuras quas memoravit,
non *Pisanella* tenet, non *Summa Rosaria* versat,
non *Deffecerunt*, non altri mille libelli.
Manserat extremus Cingar, chiamatur ad ultim,
it velut ad forcam, montagnam portat adossum.

205 In primis nescit signum formare crosarum;
postea confundens simul omnia, quidquid in ore
concipitur spudat clausisque eructuat occhis.
Baldus id advertit, suspiria Cingaris audit,
et mussando suis cum compagnonibus, inquit:

210 'Em em! stat freschus, colmus est saccus et arca'.
Illi non possunt non risum promere, quando
Cingaris advertunt, dum se confessat, afannum.
Quem suspirantem, quem fazzam saepe sugantem
contemplant poverum stanchisque dolere ginocchis.

215 Confessus tandem, fuit assolvestus ab illo,
cui datur, ut potuit credi, penitentia grandis.
Omnia promittit Cingar; gran cosa parebit,
si de promissis attendet forte mitadem.
Illico se tollens a confessore, scapavit

220 promittitque Deo posthac, dum vita manebit,
non confessandi plus oltra piare fadigam,
qua non est maior, qua non stentatior altra.
Talibus exactis, surgit Merlinus et inquit:
'Eya cavalleri, quae vos indusia tandem?

225 Non est tardandi, cum tempus habetur agendi;
vos estis mundi, vos netti benque sgurati,
quae tardanza trigat? Tantum peccare cavete.
Peccantes iterum grandissima poena moratur'.

long, because where he sinned with his equine part, there is no blame. Next Philoforno made amends, and then Boccalo, whom Merlin dismissed as soon as possible, as his confession made him laugh and break the solemnity of the occasion. The incidents he told, the transgressions he remembered, the *Pisanella* does not contain, the *Summa Rosaria* does not discuss, nor the *Defecerunt*, nor a thousand other manuals.

Cingar had remained last and is called at the end. He goes 203 as though to the gallows; he carries a mountain on his back. To begin with, he doesn't know how to make the sign of the cross. Then jumbling everything together, whatever he conceives in his mouth he spits out and spews with his eyes closed. Baldo notices this; he hears Cingar's sighs, and whispering to his friends, observes, "Hmm, hmm! He's in big trouble now, his bag and box are full up." They can't contain their laughter when they notice Cingar's discomfort in confessing. They watch the poor man sighing and wiping his face over and over; his weary knees are causing him pain. Having finally confessed, he is absolved by Merlin, who gives him, as one can imagine, a large penance. Cingar promises everything, and it would be really something if he should keep even half of these promises. Immediately withdrawing from his confessor, Cingar runs off and promises God that henceforth, as long as he lives, he will never make the effort to confess again, for there is nothing greater or more difficult.

Having finished all this, Merlin rises and says, "Hey there, 223 knights, what are you waiting for? You should not delay; it's time to act. You are purified, you are clean and well-scrubbed; what's stopping you? Just beware of sinning. A very grave punishment awaits anyone who sins again." Having spoken, he places cookies

Dixerat, et nullo biscottos zuccare factos,
230 persuttumque satis ranzum modicasque nosellas
apponit tavolae cunctosque sedere comandat,
excusamque facit de rerum paupere mensa.
Denique post epulas et aquati pocula vini,
hos menat introrsum petramque levare molini
235 praecipit; huic paret fortissima schena Fracassi:
dimidiam removet montagnam vastaque rupis
bocca scovertatur, per quam datur ire facultas.
Tunc Merlinus ait: 'Tombam rugate per ipsam.
Nil dubium, magna hic ventura catabitur. Ite!'
240 Baldus it in prima, descendit mille scalinos;
succedunt alii, solo remanente Cocaio.
In fundum scalae porta ingens clausa trovatur,
cardine quam rupto cum calce Fracassus aprivit.
Introëunt altam, longam largamque masonem,
245 lux ubi tanta nitet tantoque lusore coruscat,
ut iurare queas ibi Solis stare palazzum.
Lucis causa petra est, petrarum maxima, carbon,
quae non gallinae, sed struzzi grandior ovo est,
et subterranae scurezzam noctis agiornat.
250 Protinus huc trahitur Baldus splendore rubini,
fulguritas cuius vistam sibi tollit ab occhis.
Circum circa salam sunt arma tacata murais,
pulchra nimis, totum nec talia vista per orbem.
Stant omnes stupidi, veterum gestamen honorant,
255 relligioque sibi est tales toccare facendas.
Ad caput ipsius camerae stat maximus elmus,
elmus Nembrotti longo surgente penazzo.
Baldus ait: 'Nembrottus erat persona gigantis
tuque gigantescam portas, Fracasse, staturam;
260 ergo gigas cum sis, caelatam sume gigantis'.

made with no sugar, some rancid prosciutto, and a few little nuts on the table and orders them all to sit down, apologizing for his table's poor offerings. Finally, after the food and cups of watered-down wine, he leads them inside and commands them to move a millstone. Fracasso's powerful back obliges: he removes half a mountain and a huge opening in the cliff is uncovered through which they may pass. Now Merlin says, "Search this tomb. Doubt-less you are in for a real adventure, so get going!" Baldo is the first to enter. He descends a thousand steps; the others follow, with Cocaio remaining alone.

At the bottom of the stairway they find a huge closed door, 242 which Fracasso opens by breaking the hinges with a kick. They enter into a great, long and broad hall, where so much light shines and sparkles with so much brightness that you could swear you were in the palace of the Sun. The light is coming from a gem, the grandest of gems, a ruby bigger than an egg—not a hen's, but an ostrich egg—and it brings daylight to the darkness of the subter-ranean night. Baldo is drawn at once by the splendor of the ruby, whose radiance takes the sight from his eyes. All around the room there are weapons fixed on the walls, so very beautiful that the like has not been seen anywhere in the world. They are all stunned; they respect whatever was worn by the ancients, and religious awe prohibits them from touching such matters. At the head of the room is an enormous helmet, the helmet of Nimrod, with a long, rising plume. Baldo says, "Nimrod was a gigantic person, and you, too, have the stature of a giant, Fracasso. Therefore, since you are a giant, take the giant's sallet."

Paret Fracassus ferrique in vertice brettam
calcat, et altanum despiccat in aëra saltum.
Hectoris arma, nigris aquilis ornata, manebant
fixa similmenter muro, quae fina metallo
265 argento ac auro duroque azzale coruscant.
Temporis haec spatio godivit Roma totanto,
quotanto tenuit mundi signora bachettam.
Ast ubi se stessam nimis alta superbia stravit,
arma retornarunt sub terram Brontis in antrum.
270 Quae modo magnanimus merito sibi Baldus adobbat.
Sunt ibi quae Greghi stiparunt corpus Achili;
sunt quae fortis Aiax, quae Theseus atque bravazzus
Pirhus adobbabat, quae Orlandus, quaeque Rinaldus,
quaeque Durastantus, Rodomontus, quaeque Gradassus,
275 Zanque Picininus, Nicoloque et Gattamelada,
Barthoquelomeus quem gens dixere Coionem.
Pendula stat travis etiam corrazza Goliae,
ipsaque Sansonis dentata ganassa gigantis,
ipseque Morgantis de pesis mille bachioccus;
280 Fracassus piat hunc, licto bastone, sonaium,
cum quo campanas Inferni rumpere sperat.
Baldus ait: 'Nulla hic armorum copia mancat.
Quae viltas animi, vel quae reverentia trigat
vestros nunc sensus ut non bona tela pietis?'
285 Tunc ibi compagni, nudato corpore vecchis
protinus arnesis, ferro sese undique fino
circumdant fibiantque auro gemmisque corazzas.
Inde piant scudos, targas tondasque rodellas
affectantque atris iam se meschiare baruffis.
290 Verum Boccalo non ullam contigit armam
proposito retrovare suo: butat omnia, versat
omnia, nec penitus, quod passim cercat, acattat.
Tandem vista sibi fuit unica cosa volenti:

Fracasso obeys, and presses the iron hat onto the top of his   261
head and takes a leap high in the air. Hector's arms remained like-
wise affixed to the wall, decorated with black eagles, and the fine
armor shimmers with silver, gold and hard steel. Rome enjoyed
the use of these for the entire space of time that she held the scep-
ter of the world. However, when she destroyed herself through
overweening pride, the arms returned to the subterranean cave of
Brontes. And now the magnanimous Baldo decks himself out in
them, and rightly so.

Here too are the arms that encased the body of the Greek   271
Achilles, and those that the mighty Ajax and Theseus sported,
and the bully Pyrrhus, and Orlando and Rinaldo and Durastante,
Rodomonte, and Gradasso, and Gianni and Niccolò Piccinino,
Gattamelata and Bartolomeo, whom people called Colleoni. Also
hanging from a beam were the breastplate of Goliath, the tooth-
filled jaw of the giant Sampson, and Morgante's thousand-stone
clapper. Having let go of his club, Fracasso grabs the ringer with
which he hopes to break the bells of hell. Baldo says, "Here there
is no dearth of arms. What cowardice of spirit, what reverence
dulls your instincts and prevents you from taking up these excel-
lent arms?" Right then, the companions, having stripped their
bodies at once of their old gear, cover themselves all over with fine
mail and buckle on breastplates of gold and gems. Next they take
up shields, plates and round bucklers and pretend already to clash
in fierce skirmishes.

To be sure, it turns out that Boccalo does not find any armor   290
that fits his needs: he flings everything and tosses it about, but he
truly cannot find anything suitable no matter where he looks.

Margutti squarcina, olim cantata Loyso,
295 in quodam cantone iacet sine cortice fodri,
unde refulgebat multo rubiginis auro.
Hanc avidus brancat, basat cingitque galono,
incusatque alios compagnos esse fachinos
atque insensatos, omnique rasone carentes
300 clamitat ut, nullis qui possint ire gravezzis,
en voiant sic sic ferri portare valisas,
sicve fachinales usare ad pondera spallas.
Baldus, id ascoltans, inquit: 'Boccale, quid armis
non te sicuras? En aspice quanta superchiant!'
305 Respondet: 'Non me ferrum natura creavit.
Sum de carne caro, sic sic de carne manebo'.
Cui Baldus: 'Dagam Margutti quid geris ergo?
At Boccalus: 'Ego sensi credoque quod ipso
sub Phlegetonte bonas anguillas illa brigata
310 peschet et inflatas multa grassedine ranas.
Si tibi mancabunt illic, menchione, vivandae
dic: quid mangiabis? Qua guisa quove modello
anguillis poteris, vel ranis tollere pellem?
En ad propositum nostrum squarcina trovatur,
315 quae cavet anguillis soccam ranisque camoram.
Suntque illic oleo caldaria plena boiento,
ut Bariletta docet predichis fraterque Robertus;
frizere padellis quis ranas posse vetabit
anguillasque illas ad arostum ponere speto?'
320 Talia dum rident socii compagniter, ipse
Baldus in aspectu magno se lanzat in auras,
leggiadrusque cavans brandum scrimire comenzat
intornumque agilis ventos colpizat inanes.
Cingar in istanti trat de gallone spadettam
325 verdugumque habilem cum cappa ferre stocadas,
subque rodelletta se totum curvus abassat.

Finally he saw the only thing he wants: Margutte's dagger, celebrated once upon a time by Luigi Pulci; it lies in a corner without its sheath, so that it glowed with the rusty color of much gold. He grabs it eagerly, kisses it and straps it to his side. He accuses his companions of being boors, and declares that they are mindless and lacking all reason, for they could go without any weight and yet they choose to carry iron baggage like that and use their shoulders for weights suited to a porter.

Hearing this, Baldo asks, "Boccalo, why don't you protect yourself with armor? Just look at how much remains!"   303

He answers, "Nature did not make me out of iron. I am flesh made of flesh, and thus I will remain flesh."

Baldo to him, "Why then do you carry Margutte's dagger?"

Boccalo answers, "I have heard and do believe that down in   308 Phlegethon, people catch good eels and frogs puffed up with a lot of fat. If you don't have these foods there, idiot, tell me, what will you eat? In what manner, in what way will you be able to skin eels or frogs? So this dagger is found to fit our needs, which can take the skirt off an eel and the dress off a frog. And there are caldrons full of boiling oil there, as Barletta and Fra Roberto teach in their sermons; who will forbid us to fry frogs in pans and put eels on a spit to roast?"

While the friends are laughing amiably at these things, Baldo in   320 all his glory launches himself into the air and, extracting his blade deftly, begins to scrimmage and thrust agilely about at empty space. Cingar in the same instant draws a little sword from his side and a Spanish dagger, good at landing blows, when with a cape he crouches all curved up behind a small round shield. "What are

'Quid tu', inquit, 'bravas? Pentibis forte; pochettum
stimo bravamentum rofiani. Guarda! Sta saldus!'
Sic dicens, tractum tres colpos fecit in unum,
330   mandrittum, puntamque statim, celeremque roversum.
Baldus cuncta schivat, nec semet aretrat un onzam;
ridet et it circum, nec adhuc tirat, immo repossat
miratque attentus quod Cingar porrigat unum
ante pedem; quod si faciet, sotosora tomabit.
335   Ergo piatonadam distesam denique menat,
et pede supra pedem posito simul, ecce repente
Cingar humi cascat culoque sigillat arenam;
namque, pedem proprium calcatum sub pede Baldi
dum retirare putat propter scansare roversum,
340   non potuit subito, Baldi sub calce retentus;
inde statim, Baldo plantam relevante retrorsum,
in schena tomavit humi iacuitque stravoltus.
Omnes quam subito laetos movere cachinnos!
Cingar et ipse ghignans, sursum levat illico, cridat:
345   'Eya cito, fratres, quid statis? Ducite spadas,
atque simul mecum Baldo chiocchemus adossum'.
Tunc omnes pariter brandos in fretta cavatos,
menant de piatto Baldumque tocare procazzant:
qui ferit in fianchis, qui retro, qui ferit ante.
350   Ast ita non pirlat, cum foemina fila revolgit,
guindalus, aut naspus, vel petra rotonda molini,
ut rotat hic Baldus nunc huc, nunc praestiter illuc
arduus atque parans sibi muscas undique brando.
Denique toccavit cunctos, intactus at ipse
355   constitit et scrimmae ludique reportat honorem.
Tunc Cingar gemmam, cui par cum sole lucerna est,
despiccat muro Baldique reponit in elmo.
'Hunc tibi victori', dixit 'largimur honorem;
per baratrique domos tali nos luce guidabis'.

you swaggering about?" yells Cingar. "Perhaps you shall regret it: I have little regard for a ruffian's swagger. En garde!"

Saying this, he delivers three blows in just one movement—an upper cut, then straightaway a thrust and a quick backhand. Baldo dodges them all without stepping back in the slightest. He laughs and circles, but does not yet strike. Instead, he pauses and watches attentively to see if Cingar steps forward, for if he does, he will fall head over heels. So then Baldo strikes at last with the flat of his blade, at the same time placing his foot on top of Cingar's, and lo! Cingar suddenly drops to the ground and stamps the dirt with his butt. For when he tries to withdraw his own foot, which is wedged under Baldo's foot, at first he couldn't move it to ward off a backhand, for it was held fast under Baldo's foot; then the instant Baldo pulls his sole back off, Cingar falls to the ground on his back and lies there bewildered. How they all shake at once with merry chuckling! Right away Cingar gets back up grinning and cries out, "Quickly now, brothers, what are you waiting for? Draw your swords and together, let's beat up on Baldo." 329

So with their swords readied in haste, they all lead together with the flat of the blade and try to touch Baldo; one strikes at his flanks, one behind, another strikes in front. But Baldo twirls faster than a skein-winder or reel when a woman spins yarn or than a round millstone. Baldo rotates here and then instantly there, invincible, driving the flies away on all sides with his blade. Eventually he touched them all, but remained untouched and won the prize in the fencing match. Then Cingar detaches the gem (whose luminosity equals the sun) from the wall and puts it on Baldo's helmet. "On you the victor we bestow this honor; you will guide us with its light through the abodes of the abyss." 347

360 Annuit huic barro scalamque salire comandat.
Iamque superveniunt, stippati corpora ferro.
Tum Merlinus eis ita paucula dicta favellat:
'Dux eris atque pater sociorum, Balde, tuorum.
Nulla superstitio poterit te vincere solum.
365 Sic tibi disposuit savii mens alta Seraphi.
Ite viam tandem, vos tandem lasso, valete!'
Dixerat, et clauso restavit solus in antro.
    Cingar it allegrus balzatque legerus ad auras:
sustulerat spallis vastum confessio pesum.
370 Bertezzat, burlat, soiat *Titaloraque* cantat.
Aures Falchetto tirat nasumque Bocalo,
qui quoque Merlino salsa de carne mezenum
robbarat, quamvis confessus alhora fuisset.
Et licet ad grepias restarant retro cavalli,
375 quos promittebat Merlinus pascere foeno,
seu Demogorgonis spelta, seu Pinfaris orzo.
Ipse tamen Boccalus, habens quod habere bisognat,
menabat caricum multis de rebus asellum.
Increpat hunc Baldus poverum spoliasse romittum.
380 Cui Boccalus ait: 'Deh! mangia in pace biavam!
Et tu non portas in bocca forte molinum?
Scilicet, ad baratrum poteris retrovare tavernam?'
At Baldus: 'Plenae bastant de pane sachozzae'.
'Immo', respondet Boccalus, '*Norma* recordat
385 quod "solo non pane potest homo vivere mundo."
Nonne 'caro' 'carnem' facit, attestante pedanto
Doctrinale meo, declinans nomina terzae?
Nonne flagellabat mihi saepe culamina propter
'rectis as es a'? qui mattus nascitur, umquam
390 non guarrire potest, etiam medegante Galeno'.
His mottis allegra ibat brigata per umbras.
Quisque piat festam pro Cingare proque Bocalo,

The hero accepts this and commands them to climb the stair-   360
case. Soon they have come back up, their bodies encased in iron.
Then Merlin speaks a few words to them: "You will be the leader
and the father of your companions, Baldo. You alone will not be
overcome by superstition. The lofty mind of wise Seraphus has ar-
ranged this for you. Go your way at last, at last I leave you. Fare-
well!" Having spoken, Merlin stayed alone in the closed cave.

Cingar goes happily and jumps lightly into the air; confession   368
had lifted a vast weight from his shoulders. He jests, jokes, teases
and sings *Titalora;* he pulls Falchetto's ears, and Boccalo's nose—
the latter had even stolen a side of salted meat from Merlin,
although he had just confessed. And even though the horses
had stayed behind in the stall (Merlin promised to feed them hay
or Demogorgon's spelt or Pinfar's barley), Boccalo had what he
needed and was leading an ass loaded with many things. Baldo
scolds him for having fleeced a poor hermit. Boccalo counters,
"Well then, eat your fodder in peace! I don't suppose you are car-
rying a mill in your mouth? Do you think you will be able to find
a tavern in the abyss?" But Baldo says, "Sacks full of bread are
enough."

"On the contrary," rejoins Boccalo, "as the Good Book reminds   384
us, 'man cannot live by bread alone in this world.' Is it not true
that flesh begets flesh, as shown by my learned teacher in the
Doctrinale, when declining nouns of the third declension? Didn't
he flog my behind often enough for *rectis, as, es, a?* He who is born
crazy can never be cured, not even with Galen treating him." With
these quips the happy group travels through the shadows. Every-
one is entertained, thanks to Cingar and Boccalo, for they are

nam concurrentes sunt ille, vel ille magistri
arte Bufalmacchi, Neli mastrique Simonis.
395 Vadunt praeterea follas narrando facetas
ut via longa nimis videatur curta brigatis.
Baldus in excelso carbonem baiulat elmo,
qui nihilat grossas radianti luce tenebras.
Iamque caminarant miliaria multa per umbras,
400 quando novus rumor post terga auditur ab illis.
Stat Baldus pariterque alii, drizzantur orecchiae.
En vox multa sonat: 'Sta! Guarda! Vade! Ritorna!'
Quali cum guisa regem sociare videmus
mille alebarderos inter totidemque barones,
405 per quos huc illuc dabandam stare iubetur,
dicitur et 'Largum! Largum!' baculique menantur;
tali vicinat sese barronibus agmen,
qui non contra venit, sed post sua terga caminat.
Baldus ait: 'Mirum! quo nascitur ista novella?
410 Disfodrate cito brandos! Date brachia targhis!'
Dixit, et ad bandas stradae cito dividit omnes.
Fit via per puntas spadarum, utrimque paratas
sforacchiare illos, qui ultra passare menazzant;
sic sic per piccas seu Guizzer, sive Todescus
415 trapassare solet, crudeli morte necandus.
Ecce rivat tandem multae confusio gentis,
nulla sub alphero quos ordinanza coërcet,
sed variis foggis Franceso more cavalcant.
It fretolosa cohors spronatque trotone serato
420 non miga zanettos, curtaltos atque frisones.
Sed proh!, num dicam? quis credat? Nempe cavalcant
quadrupedes ligni scannos tripedesque scanellos,
fornari gramolas, descos misasque farinae,
concas, telaros, conocchias, guindala, naspos,

competitors in this—both are masters in the art of Buffalmacco, Nello and Maestro Simone. Besides, they go along narrating silly stories so that the very long journey will seem short to the group. Baldo carries the ruby high on his helmet, which cancels the dense shadows by radiating light.

They have already walked many miles through the darkness 399 when they hear a new sound at their backs. Baldo stops and the others likewise; they prick up their ears. Suddenly many voices sound, "Halt! Look out! Go! Come back!" Just as we see a king joined by a thousand halberdiers and as many cavalry who command people here and there to keep their distance and say, "Make way, make way!" and wield staffs, just so this squadron approaches our barons, which does not come against them but walks backwards. Baldo says, "Look! Where is this novelty coming from? Unsheathe your swords quickly! Strap on your shields!" So saying, he quickly divides them all onto both sides of the street. A path is made between the points of their blades, both sides ready to riddle with holes those who threaten to pass by, as when a German or a Swiss goes through a line of pikes, to be killed in cruel death.

So finally there arrives a confusion of many people; they are 416 not organized behind a flag bearer but ride helter-skelter as the French do. The cohort moves hastily and in a close trot spurs not jennets or *curtaldi* or Frisians, but . . . O shall I tell you? Who will believe me? In fact, they are riding four-legged wooden chairs, three-legged stools, bakers' kneaders, tables, breadboards, basins,

425 cadregas, cassas, cophinos, lettiria, scragnas,
    barrillos, secchias, gratarolas, mille novellas.
    Omnes ingentem faciunt per saxa tumultum,
    trentaque para sonant, dum tirant retro per umbras
    schiodatas tavolas, dum stringunt ilia buttis.

430 Per medios passant muti tacitique guereros.
    Unde prior Cingar sbroccat de pectore risum,
    postea conclamat: 'Quae gens? ola, ola, quo itis?
    quae vos fretta menat? nobis parlate coëllum'.
    At nemo respondet ei tutaviaque passant.

435 Rident compagni factum, tamen omnia cauto
    stant mirare oculo, brandos menare parati,
    si qua sibi forsan tunc noia fiatur ab illis.
    Falchettus loquitur: 'Longa est ea tira virorum;
    credo tirintanam penitus hanc esse stryonum.

440 Est hodie giornus zobiae giovedique triumphus.
    Ad Demogorgontem properant cursique madonnam.
    Non tamen ulla mihi certezza; domanda, Bocale'.
    'Non', Boccalus ait, 'faciam; tu stesse domanda.
    Fortunam tentare nocet spessissime multis.

445 "Quando canis dormit, noli distollere somno"'.
    Vix et finierant, extremior ecce ruebat
    atque stafezabat magrazzam supra cavallam,
    scilicet in dorso magni grossique botazzi;
    dumque ultra passat per spadas undique nudas,

450 Cingaris extremo toccavit pollice nasum;
    quo facto ad totam briliam dat fraena botazzo.
    Res miranda statim comparuit ante vedutam:
    Cingaris en sese nasus gonfiare comenzat,
    ut fit cum flatu porci vesica repletur.

455 Iamque fluens giusum barbozzi ad menta calabat,
    iamque bighignolus lambicchi paret aguzzus,

looms, distaffs, skein winders, reels, armchairs, trunks, coffers, bed frames, benches, barrels, buckets, graters, a thousand novelties. Together they all make a huge din on the rocks and sound like thirty devils, while they drag behind broken tables through the shadows, squeezing their thighs on kegs. They pass through the middle of the warriors in mute silence. Cingar is first to uncork a laugh from his chest, then he cries out, "Who are you? Hey you, hey, where are you going? What's the rush? Come on, say something to us!"

No one answers him, and they keep passing by. The friends laugh at this, and yet they continue to survey the whole scene with a cautious eye, ready to use their swords if any harm should come to them from those passing by. Falchetto remarks, "That's a long train of men. I actually think this is a long line of witches. Today is witches' day, and Thursday's cavalcade; they are hurrying to trot to Demogorgon and to their lady. But I am not at all sure. Ask them, Boccalo!"—"I will not!" says Boccalo. "Ask them yourself! Tempting fate almost always hurts lots of people. 'Let sleeping dogs lie.'"

434

They had scarcely finished and, lo! the last rider was dashing by, mounted on a scrawny horse, which is to say, on the back of an enormous keg. As he passed the barons' naked blades, he touched Cingar's nose with the tip of his thumb, and having done so, gave full rein to his keg. Instantly a wondrous thing appeared before their eyes. Behold! Cingar's nose begins to swell, as when a pig's bladder is blown up with air. Already it droops over and reaches

446

quo stillare solet bozas spetiarus aquarum.
Obstupet hic Cingar nescitque movere parolam;
nescio quid monstri pensaverat esse, vel umbram,
460   unde manu reparare volens urtavit in ipsum
nasazzum, qui iam terrenum longus arabat.
'Me miserum', clamat, 'quae cauda? quis iste budellus?
Unde mihi magnus subitano tempore nasus?
Cernitis, o socii? Quo tanti copia nasi?
465   Qua mihi de banda nasorum maximus exit?
Numquid totus ero crescendo denique nasus?
Deh per amore Dei! deh non permittite, fratres,
ut sit opus tanti mihi nasi ferre valisam!'
Baldus non potuit non fata dolere sodalis.
470   'Ne timeas', inquit, 'ne fle: mozzabimus istum
nasonem petito, cui pristina forma redibit'.
Hinc Boccalus ait: 'Nescis, marzocche, coëllum.
Immo tibi invideo de longi munere nasi.
Nonne manens drittus poteris nasare melones?
475   Nec peponessarum plus oltra chinabis odori?'
Quo motto risit Cingar. 'Patientia', dixit,
'me iam per nasum bufali de more tirabis.
Sed quia trenta pedes iam nasi forma trapassat,
andantique mihi gambarum crura molestat,
480   hunc volo prolixum dare circum circa colengum,
deque meo naso triplicem formare colanam'.
Sic ait atque facit: collum ter nasus abrazzat.
Sed quia continuo crescens humore pesabat
tamquam bos Chiari, nec eum ferre ultra valebat
485   Cingar cum spallis propriis, nisi detur aiutus,
illico Falchettus, dulci compassus amico,
illius a collo nasum distorthiat omnem,
supra suosque humeros nasonis pondera gestat;

his chin, and soon it looks like the pointed spout of an alembic in which an apothecary distills flagons of water. Cingar is stupefied now, and he is unable to utter a word. I don't know what monstrous thing or shadow he thought it was. Trying to ward it off with his hand, he ran into his own gigantic nose, which was already plowing the ground.

"O poor me!" he cries, "What tail is this? What tripe is this? 462 Where did I get such an enormous nose in so short a time? O friends, do you see? Whence this abundance of nose? From what part of me is this greatest of noses emerging? If it keeps growing will I end up all nose? O for the love of God! O please don't leave me, brothers, and oblige me to carry such heavy nose-baggage!"

Baldo could not help but grieve at his companion's fate. "Don't 469 worry!" he says, "Don't cry! We will chop off this huge nose if you so desire, and its former shape will return."

At this, Boccalo says, "You don't know anything, birdbrain! On 472 the contrary, I envy you for this gift of a long nose. Won't you be able to sniff melons while standing upright? And no longer bend over for the aroma of little muskmelons?"

Cingar laughs at this quip. "Good grief!" he says. "Now you 476 will be pulling me by the nose like a buffalo. But because the shape of my nose already exceeds thirty feet and trips up my shanks as I walk, I want to wrap this ample thing around my neck and fashion a triple necklace of my nose." He says this and does it: his nose embraces his neck three times. But since it had grown continually with fluid and weighed as much as an ox from Chiari, Cingar could no longer carry it on his own shoulders without help. So Falchetto, in compassion for his dear friend, immediately unwinds the whole nose from his neck and bears the weight of it

cui, mutando vices, succedunt saepe sodales.
490   En pater interea veniebat alonge Seraphus
garzonesque duos uno menat agmine secum.
Alter erat mulus, Greghesco patre creatus,
cui mater Calabresa fuit: pensate, fradelli,
quae mistura brodae, quae messedanza salattae!
495   Barrus erat, giottus, latro, fur, forca, trufator.
Quid restat? Stradiottus erat; queo dicere peggium?
Sed quia per guerras stradiotica semper usanza est
ferre scaramuzzas, aut appizzare baruffas,
inde attaccatis armis se trare dabandam,
500   Pizzacapellettus seu Pizzaguerra vocatur.
Hac hominis spetie sibi servit cura Seraphi
impresasque novas ad efettum mandat ob ipsum,
sicut certa monet sibi constellatio cosas.
Alter erat iuvenis, quo non formosior umquam
505   Narcissus fuerat, non castior ipse Iosephus.
Is nihil omnino mangiat pissatque cagatque,
sed fortunato semper nutritur amore.
Bellus amat bellum, bello redamatur amante,
nec zelosiae squarzatur dentibus umquam,
510   namque fit a stellis bene iunctis certus amari.
Haec quoque gratificat complexio diva Seraphum
egregiasque facit, prout chiedunt tempora, provas.
Cui Rubinus erat nomen, cognomen Ubaldus.
    Ergo hic Serraphus traxit de pectore librum,
515   dumque legit, magni tres cervi protinus adsunt.
Ore brias, ut equi, gestant et tergore sellas.
Hos montare iubet redinasque molare Seraphus;
unde simul strictis calcagnibus oreque chiuso,
menteque raccolta, per opaca silentia trottant,
520   immo volant, quoniam portantur supra diablos.

on his own shoulders, and taking turns, his companions frequently relieve him.

Meanwhile Father Seraphus was coming from a distance, leading two young men in single file. One was a mule; he was born of a Greek father and a Calabrian mother. Just think, brothers, what a mix of soups, what a tossed salad! He was a paladin, a glutton, a bandit, a thief, a gallows' bird, and a swindler. What else? He was a mercenary. Can I name anything worse? Now since it is the practice of mercenaries to start skirmishes during wars or spark a brawl and then, once the fighting is under way, to withdraw, he is called Pizzacapelletto or Pizzaguerra. Seraphus uses this kind of man with care; through him, he carries out novel exploits, as certain heavenly conjunctions advise him to do. 490

The other was a youth whom even Narcissus did not surpass in beauty nor Joseph in chastity. This young man eats and pees and shits nothing at all, but rather is always nourished by fortunate love. Handsome himself, he loves a handsome man, and is loved by a handsome lover. He is never tortured by the pangs of jealousy, for due to a favorable conjunction of stars, he is certain to be loved. This divine combination is also pleasing to Seraphus, and he performs important deeds as the times require. Rubino was his name, Ubaldo his surname. 504

So Seraphus now pulls a book from his breast, and as he reads, three large stags suddenly appear. Like horses, they carry bridles on their muzzles and saddles on their backs. Seraphus orders them to mount and to loosen the reins, so that spurring with their heels, their mouths shut with concentration, they trot through the opaque silence or rather they fly, since they are carried on devils. 514

Itur ad orbescam quocumque guidatur ab illis,
inque oculi motu post Baldi terga fuere.
'Sistite!' tum dixit Serraphus, 'sistite cervos!
ecce mihi Baldi grottas illuminat elmus'.
525 Tunc dismontatur cervosque andare iubetur.
Inde petras upupae signentas quisque stupendas
collocat in bocca; quo facto nemo videtur,
ast invisibilis vadit neque cernitur usquam.
Ergo simul properant: alios comprendere possunt,
530 at non comprendi, velut est essentia rerum.
Inter compagnos Baldi compagniter intrant,
quo muti, taciti, cheti nulloque veduti,
incipiunt menare manus ac ludere pugnis.
'Oyme!', cridant omnes, 'quid enim novitatis habetur?'
535 Serraphus ridens Boccalo tirat orecchiam:
'Oy!', ait, 'oy! Quis erit tantum indiscretus ut aures
de testa streppare mihi . . .'. Dum dicere 'voiat'
ille parat, chiappa culi picigatur in una.
'Vah cagasanguis! Ego non possum vivere? Cancar,
540 Balde, tibi veniat! Quo me in bonhora guidasti?'
Pizzacapellettus gambam transversat inanzum
Lyrono, qua se simul ille intoppat et ancum
it simul in terram rumpitque cadendo ginocchium.
Hippol ait: 'Nihil hic giovat portare lucernam,
545 cum sit quod nobis tollatur vista videndi.
En ego tampellor pugnadis, Balde, cotoris,
nec prorsus video, sed tantum sentio goffos.
Attamen esse tibi pazzus fortasse videbor'.
Sic ait, et colera tractus, chioccante Rubino,
550 incipit ad ventum palmas vibrare seratas,
morsibus et calzis foltas bussare tenebras.
Saepe menat gambas picigatus ubique Fracassus

They proceed blindly wherever the stags lead and in the blink of an eye they're right behind Baldo. "Halt!" says Seraphus then in mute silence. "Halt the stags! See how Baldo's helmet illuminates the grottoes for me now." Then they dismount and the stags are dismissed. Next, one by one, they place the magical stones of the hoopoe in their mouths. After this, they are seen by no one, but move invisibly and are not detected anywhere. Thus they hurry along together; they can perceive others and not be perceived, as is the essence of things. They enter among Baldo's friends in a friendly way, where mute, silent, soundless and seen by no one, they begin to strike with their hands and sport with their fists.

"Ouch!" they all cry. "What is this strange novelty?" Laughing,   534
Seraphus pulls Boccalo's ear. "Ow!" he yells. "Ow! Who is so indiscreet as to want to yank the ears off my . . ." While he is about to say "head" he gets nipped on one butt cheek. "Bloody hell! Can't I live in peace? I hope you get cancer, Baldo. For goodness sake, where have you led me?"

Pizzacapelletto thrusts his leg out in front of Lirone, who trips   541
and hits the ground all at once, breaking his knee in the fall. Hippol says, "A lantern does us no good here, since something is taking away our ability to see. I am being pummeled by fists, Baldo, pounding fists! And I can't see anything. I can only feel the blows. But maybe I just seem crazy to you."

Thus he speaks, and overcome by anger as Rubino strikes him,   549
he starts to swing his clenched hands in the air and to trounce the shadows with bites and kicks. Fracasso is nipped all over and

villanusque paret, qui scalzus tempore caldi
non valet a moschis gambas reparare caninis,
555 aut a zenzalis duram deffendere pellem.
Serraphus subito Falchetti e tergore nasum
Cingaris abstulerat passimque menabat ut orbum.
Ille cridat: 'Ducor per nasum buffalus, et quo
et quis me ducat, minimum non cerno cotalum.
560 O gran cosa quidem! Pazzi qui talia cercant'.
Vult illi Moschinus opem conferre, sed unum
accipit in fianchis punzonem, retroque factus
vindicare parat schiaffumque roversat acerbum
ut tres de bocca dentes smassellet ab umbris;
565 at rigidum colpit saxum recipitque figuram
iuxta materiam, et meritum mercede pagatur;
namque super digitos sofiat, velut assolet ille
qui nimium caldam properat mangiare polentam.
Multoties huc se voltat Giubertus et illuc,
570 dum sponsonatur pugnis ab utroque galono.
Ipse similmenter trahitur Philofornus, et ictus
dum recipit stranios, banda se torquet in omni.
Denique post aliquod susceptum utrimque solazzum,
Serraphi iussu de bocca quisque lapillos
575 extrahit, et clari cunctis patuere visaggi.
Oh puta, si rident ac laeto corde solazzant!
Noscunt Serraphum, cui chinans Baldus honorem
rendit et abrazzat Pizzam iuvenemque Rubinum.
Supplicat inde: voiat, si alcuna potentia libris
580 est magicis, contra praestrigia tanta stryarum,
Cingaris a vultu tam grossum tollere nasum.
Cui Serraphus ait: 'Bene si consydero cosam,
Cingar habet tortum proprium nec ad utile guardat,
dum bene fornitum cercat deponere nasum.

shakes his legs incessantly. He looks like a peasant who goes bare-
foot in hot weather and is unable to protect his legs from horse-
flies or defend his leathery skin from mosquitoes. Seraphus had
quickly taken Cingar's nose from Falchetto's back and led him all
over like a blind man. Cingar yells, "I am being led by the nose
like a buffalo, and I can't make out who is leading me. This is re-
ally something, and people who go looking for things like this are
crazy."

Moschino wants to aid his friend, but he takes a powerful jab in   561
the flank. Stepping back, he gets ready to avenge himself and un-
leashes a harsh backhand that could knock three teeth from the
shade's jaw. But he hits solid rock, and gets a shape that suits its
matter, and is paid justly for his efforts. He blows on his fingers
like someone in a rush to eat very hot polenta.

Gilberto turns this way and that over and over again, since he   569
is being pummeled by fists from both sides. Philoforno is treated
similarly and as he receives strange blows, he twists in every direc-
tion. At length, after both sides have had some fun, on Seraphus'
orders, each man takes the stone from his mouth, and their faces
appear clearly to all. O just imagine how they laugh and en-
joy themselves with cheerful hearts! They recognize Seraphus, to
whom Baldo bows in homage, and he embraces "Pizza" and young
Rubino. Then he beseeches Seraphus: If there is any power in
magic books against such witches' spells, would he take the huge
nose from Cingar's face?

Seraphus says to him, "If I consider the matter carefully, Cingar   582
is mistaken and ignores his best interest if he wants to get rid of

585 Si bene quidquid agat nescit retinere cerebro,
ad nasum faciat tres, quattuor octoque groppos'.
Cui Cingar: 'Serraphe pater, non curo quatrinum
esse parum memorem cerebrumque ostendere gatti,
dummodo tanta mihi scarichetur sarcina nasi.

590 Nam quis rinoceros naso nasutior isto?
Deh, per amore Dei, pactum veniamus ad istud:
tollite vobiscum nasum totumque cerebrum;
tantum, quos habeo dentes, serventur in ore
ut mangiare queam; si non memorare, quid inde?'

595 Tunc Serraphus, habens plenam de nescio quidnam
tascazzam, cavat inde, velut chirugicus, unam
ampollam unguenti mira virtute pieni.
Ungit utramque manum sibi stesso, deinde perungit
nasonem leviter pressatque tirando deorsum,

600 ut pressare solent qui mungunt ubera vacchis.
Ille calat sensim, candelae more brusantis,
quae venit ad virdum, parvo remanente mochetto.
Dumque redit primum guttatim nasus ad esser,
stat Cingar prontus raptimque se ab ungue Seraphi

605 eripit, ut vidit sgrossatam denique codam.
Nec fuit ordo umquam posthac sibi tangere nasum,
addubitans etiam prigolos incurrere nasi,
de quibus exierat sola mercede Seraphi,
cui grates reddit, docto sermone, galantas.

610 Inde vale dicto se compagnia diremit:
Baldus it ad bassum, Serraphus tornat ad altum.

his well-endowed nose. If he can't remember something he must do, he can tie three or four or eight knots in his nose."

Cingar says to him, "Father Seraphus, I don't give a hoot about my poor memory or exhibiting the brainpower of a cat, as long as this great burden of a nose is unloaded from me. For what rhinoceros is nosier than this nose? O for the love of God, let's make a deal: Take the nose with you and my whole brain too, as long as you leave me the teeth I have safe in my mouth so I can eat. If I can't remember, so what?" Seraphus has a pouch full of who knows what, from which, like a surgeon, he takes out a vial of a miraculous ointment. He rubs both his hands with it, then rubs the big nose gently and squeezes while pulling down, as people generally squeeze when they milk cows' udders. It goes down gradually, like a burning candle that recedes to its core, leaving a little stub. While the nose is returning to its previous state drop by drop, Cingar stands ready, and as soon as he sees his tail finally shrunk, he quickly pulls himself away from Seraphus's fingertips. And from then on, he made it his practice never to touch his nose; he remained fearful of incurring nose dangers, from which he had escaped thanks only to Seraphus, to whom he expresses cordial gratitude in a learned discourse.

Then, having said goodbye, the group separates. Baldo goes down and Seraphus goes back up.

587

610

Liber vigesimus tertius

Iamque caminarant giornatas quinque per umbras,
donec ad extremum fines reperere cavernae.
Non datur ulterius procedere posse pedattas,
nam smisurato trarumpitur orbita saxo.
5   Hinc sibi destranium paret reflectere gambas
et replicare viam tanta stracchedine factam.
Ergo impazzati restant, velut usus habetur
quando formicae spatiantes ordine longo,
sive super murum seu vecchiam supra nogaram,
10   vadunt et redeunt se crebro insemma basantes;
at si per medium squadrae transversa notetur
linea carbonis, faciunt ibi protinus altum
agmina nigrorum seque omnis campus adossat.
Denique sub pedibus sibi petram Baldus adocchiat
15   hancve alzare iubet; datur haec impresa Fracasso,
qui speditus eam, firmis in littore plantis,
elevat et pozzum sub retrovat esse profundum.
Apponunt aures, si quid sentitur ab imo:
hinc auditur aquae strepitus per saxa sonantis;
20   cernere nil possunt in fosso valde cavato.
Cingar confestim pensat descendere bassum:
taccat se manibus pedibusque ad saxa cavernae,
tandemque in fundo se repperit esse calatum.
Hic trovat undantem lagum sentitque per atras
25   montagnae tombas liquidum properare canalem.
Tunc ibi compagnos vocat alta voce deorsum:
'Oh!', cridat, 'oh!, socii, baratri descendite scalam'.
Quo vix audito, spadarum cingula, nec non
cavezzam et cingias asini simul undique groppant,
30   perque sogam similem descendunt unus et unus;

Book XXIII

For five days now they had walked through shadows until they'd   1
reached the farthest limit of the cave. It is impossible to proceed
further on foot, for the trail is blocked by an enormous rock. It
seems irksome to turn their legs around and go back along the
path traversed with so much effort. So they stand there stymied,
just as ants do when moving in a long line freely, either along a
wall or on top of an old walnut. They come and go at the same
time, one after another, kissing each other, but if a line of charcoal
is drawn across the middle of their troop, the black army comes to
a halt there at once, and the whole field piles up.

Eventually, Baldo notices a stone slab under his feet and orders   14
it to be lifted. This task is given to Fracasso, who gets a firm foot-
hold on the ground and easily lifts it and discovers a deep well be-
low. They cock their ears near it to listen for any sound below:
they hear the roar of water resounding against rock, yet they can
see nothing in this very deep pit. Right away, Cingar wants to go
down into it: he clings to the rock walls of the cave with his hands
and feet, and at last finds he has climbed down to the bottom.
Here he finds a seething lake and hears a canal of water rushing
through the black caverns of the mountain. Loudly then he calls
his friends down there. "O!" he cries, "O companions, descend the
steps of the ravine."

As soon as they've heard this, they knot their sword belts and   28
the donkey's halter and straps together, and using this as a rope,
descend one by one. The ass goes first, then Boccalo, and at last

de quibus ipse asinus prior extitit, inde Bocalus,
tandem se quisquam retrovat cum Cingare giusum.
Baldus ibi stagnum rutilo fulgore palesat:
elmus enim, cui petra nitet, fugat undique noctem.

35 Hic lagus ingenti grembo se largus alagat,
quo magnum egreditur flumen, neque magnius altrum
est reperire quidem, si flumina tota misuras.
Compagni ad longum ripae perque arginis orlum
ire comenzarunt, ceu flumen currit abassum.

40 Ecce procul medio cernunt in gurgite vecchium,
vecchium cui pectus longhissima barba covertat,
supraque longa sedet crocodili terga nodantis,
quem quoque tres alii crocodili pone sequuntur,
gestantes strato bellas in tergore nymphas.

45 Ut videt ille senex lumen procul atque brigatam
ire solazzantem, brandos targasque ferentem:
'Quae nova res?' inquit 'Delibero noscere quare'.
Mox contra Baldum brava sic voce comenzat:
'Quo te, matte, pedes? Quae vos per littora Nili

50 Trentapara guidat? Praesti reflectite gambas.
Guarda gaioffazzos, quae, quanta superbia menat!'
Baldus respondet: 'Coelo cascamus ab alto,
imus ad Infernum, nobis insegna caminum'.
Cui vecchius: 'Facilis cosa est descendere bassum,

55 sed tornare dretum bragas sudare bisognat.
Attamen has nostras per stradas ire dolebis,
et nisi tantostum tornare fretabitis istinc,
dat mens quod veniet grandis desgratia vobis.
Vosne, hominum stronzos, sanctum imbrattare paësum?

60 Ergo retornetis vestrasque reducite plantas!
poltrones qui vos estis, bastonibus usi.
Ad quos parlo modo? Num terzam dicere voltam
me vultis? Asini, porci, gens plena pedocchis!'

everyone finds himself down below with Cingar. Baldo lights the lake there with a red glow, for his helmet with its shining gem chases the darkness away on all sides. Here a broad lake widens into a huge basin from which flows a great river, indeed no greater can be found, even if you measure all the rivers.

The companions began to walk along the shore and on the edge   38
of the bank, as the river runs downward. Then, in the distance, they see an old man in the middle of the torrent. An old man whose breast is covered by a very long beard sits on the long back of a swimming crocodile, while three other crocodiles follow him, carrying beautiful nymphs on their long backs. When the elderly man sees a light in the distance and the band coming along joking and carrying swords and shields, he asks, "What's going on? I want to know the reason for this." Next, facing Baldo, he begins in a menacing voice, "Where do your steps lead you, fool? What pack of devils brings you to the shores of the Nile? Turn your legs around immediately! Look what great arrogance leads these wretched scoundrels!"

Baldo responds, "We have fallen from on high, and are going   52
into Hell. Show us the way!"—The old man says to him, "It's an easy thing to go down, but to come back you will have to sweat through your breeches. However, it will cause you pain to travel our roads. Unless you hurry and go back soon, I reckon a great misfortune will come to you. You human turds dare to defile the holy land? Therefore, go back! Retrace your steps, knaves that you are, slaves of the lash. Do you hear me now? Do you want me to say it a third time? Asses, swine, lice-ridden rabble!"

Omnia supportat Baldus prenditque solazzum
65 de rimbambito vecchio, cui flegma superchiat.
At non Fracassus dentrum tenet amplius iram,
sed crollans testam scridat: 'Numquid deus es tu?
Aut dii cornuti tombis versantur in istis?
Archidiavol eris potius baratrique carogna'.
70 Cui vecchius, dictis alquantum mitibus, inquit:
'Gelfora diva mihi regnum dedit istius amnis,
hasque per aeternum tempus iam subdidit undas.
Nilus habet nomen, qui drizzat in aequora septem
undantes rivos, nec quo nascantur in orbe
75 scitur Aristotolo, Piatone aliisque pedantis,
qui sua de innumeris scripsere volumina frappis.
Vos tantum nunc mente mala, nunc corde cativo,
nascimenta huius superis ascosa trovastis
et pede mortali calcastis littora divum.
80 Ista galantarum servit mihi squadra dearum
sublimemque deum fluvii me Gelfora fecit;
quae maris in fundo sibi maxima regna locavit,
distribuitque suis barronibus atque vasallis
flumina, stagna, lagos, fontes, cannalia, rivos;
85 deque deum numero sum dictus nomine Ruffus.
Ergo, velut deus et plenus deitate deorum,
impero, commando, iubeo, scomunico, giuro,
desgratiae sub sorte meae, sub crimine forchae,
tollite carneros praestique netate scapinos.
90 Et quibus haec mando? Via, protinus! Ite, ribaldi!'
Baldus ait: 'Deus es merdosae forte latrinae;
si tamen, ut gracchias, tutus deitate probaris,
en te scanfardasque tuas deffende ruinis'.
Sic dicens, chinus tollit de littore saxum,
95 quod iacit et testam crocodili spezzat in undis.
Ruffus it ad nodum frustraque negando repettat;

Baldo puts up with all this and is actually amused by the child- 64
ish old man overflowing with bile. But Fracasso can no longer re-
strain his anger, and shaking his head, he scolds, "And I suppose
you're a god? So do cuckold gods live in these caves? More likely,
you are an arch-devil, carrion of the abyss."

With somewhat milder words, the old man answers him, "The 70
goddess Gelfora gave me the kingdom of this river; she gave me
command of these waters for all eternity. The name of the river is
the Nile, and it sends seven rivers flowing into Ocean. No one
knows where on earth they come from, neither Aristotal nor
Playtoe nor the other pedants who filled their books with infinite
nonsense. You alone now, with evil minds and wicked hearts, have
found their source, hidden from the gods above, and have trodden
with mortal feet on these holy shores. This multitude of charming
goddesses serves me, and Gelfora has made me the supreme god of
the river. She placed her greatest kingdom at the bottom of the
sea, and to her barons and vassals she distributed rivers, ponds,
lakes, springs, canals and streams. I am one of these gods and am
named Rufus. Therefore, as a god and full of the godhead of the
gods, I decree, command, order, excommunicate and swear, on
pain of my displeasure and under a charge of the gallows: Clear on
out of here, hit the trail! Hey, I'm talking to you! Away now, get
going, you rogues!"

Baldo says, "You may be the god of a shitty latrine, but if, as 91
you squawk, you are protected by your divinity, defend yourself
and your wenches from ruin." So saying, he bends over and picks
up a stone from the shore which he throws and breaks the head
of the crocodile in the water. Rufus goes into the water and strug-

extra tenet musum veluti ranazza lavacchio.
Turba puellarum commenzat battere palmas
confugiuntque super crocodilos valde fugatos.
100 Intrarat sed iam medium Fracassus in amnem
et Ruffo veluti pollastro colla tiravit.
Baldus it ulterius, facit altris lampade scortam
multaque ragionant de Nili fonte latentis.
Dumque simul tempus simili sermone trapassant,
105 ecce nigram boccam montis reperere forati,
quae totum largo sorbet sbusamine flumen.
Hic mancant ripae Nilo totumque meandi
hic vanescit iter, drittas fluit unda per alpes.
Compagni fixas sabiae tenuere pedattas,
110 nulla pedestrandi conceditur ultra facultas,
nec datur andandi senterus euntibus illuc,
ni sibi sint pennae, seu nandi sive volandi;
sed nec habent ullam barcam, nec Daedalus illic
ullus adest, qui tunc incoeret brachia pennis;
115 nec nodandi etiam modus est, aut tempus et ordo,
namque sub armorum peso traherentur ad imum.
Ergo hic Fracassus medias se balzat in undas,
quas spruzzare facit ter centum brachia sursum;
et licet ingentis bustum manifestet homonis,
120 sgozzolat ipsa tamen madefactis braga culattis,
per moiamque menat grossos andando galones.
'Heus!', vocat, 'O socii, cunctis provisio rebus
semper adest, modo sit cordi prudentia nostro.
Supra meam schenam saltate gaiarditer omnes:
125 sum dispostus ego vos totos ferre per amnem'.
Baldus ait ridens: 'Poteris, Fracasse? Quid audes?'
Respondet: 'Non vos, minimi qui ponderis estis;
verum, si sit opus, populum portabo Milani.
Herculus, ille gigas, fertur portasse cadregam

gles in vain while drowning; he holds his nose out like a bullfrog in a swamp. The throngs of nymphs begin to clap their hands and flee quickly atop the fleeing crocodiles. But Fracasso had already reached the middle of the river and wrung Rufus' neck like a chicken's.

Baldo moves further along, acting as guide for the others with 102 his light, and they discuss at length the source of the hidden Nile. While they are passing the time together in similar conversation, lo! they find the black mouth of the cleft mountain, which absorbs the whole river in its great, wide hole. Here the banks of the Nile disappear, here the trail vanishes and the water flows straight through the cliffs. The friends hold their footsteps immobile in the sand. There is no further way to proceed on foot and no path to travel for those going along here unless they have wings for flying or swimming. But they have no boat, nor is there any Daedalus who could smear wax on their arms for feathers. There is no means, time, or method for swimming, since they would be dragged to the bottom by the weight of their armor. So Fracasso bounds into the middle of the waves, which he makes shoot up three hundred feet. And although he displays the torso of a huge man, nonetheless with his buttocks soaked, his britches drip, and as he walks, he swings his huge thighs through the water. "Hey!" he calls. "O friends, there's always a solution for all problems, if only there is wisdom in our hearts. All of you gallantly jump up on my back. I am ready to ferry all of you across the river." — Laughing, Baldo says, "Can you, Fracasso? Do you dare?"

He replies, "Not only you, who are of minimal weight, but if 127 necessary I could carry the populace of Milan. It is reported that Hercules, the giant, carried Jupiter's throne, upon which the entire

130 Iuppiteris, qua tota sedet fameia deorum.
Nec pulmonus ego saldus sub pondere stabo
octo putellorum, qui nostris forzibus estis?'
Tunc omnes saliunt schenam spallasque gigantis
ac si cum scalis fortezzam prendere voiant.

135 Lyronus dextrum caricat sine pondere tergus,
cui frater sese manibus tenet Hippol apressum.
Baldus at, e contra, laevae se brancat orecchiae,
Giubertumque tenet retro iustatque bilanzam.
Nec somae, ut solitum, fuit addere saxa bisognus.

140 Calzarum stringhae Boccalus nectitur uni,
rampat in orecchiam Philofornus, rampat in altram
Moschinus camerasque illic habuere patentes.
Cingar sopra caput se rampegat altius altris.
Centaurus non vult adeo caricare gigantem:

145 sicut parte canis Falchettus crura dimenat,
sic quoque Virmazzus gambettat parte cavalli.
Solus retro manens, asinellus raggiat et orat
non ita destitui solettus in ore luporum.
Ire per undosum cursum male semet arisgat

150 nec sibi vult nulla guisa bagnare gonellam.
Hunc piat ergo gigas leviter cubitique sub ala
collocat et striccat faciens lentare corezas.
Sic facitur cum piva sonat ventrone pieno,
quae cubito dum stricca canit dat musica versum;

155 sic bona dat chiaros asini proportio cantus.
Tot passarottos Fracassus ferre videtur
totque graves pesos iurat pesare nientum.
Quo sustentatur portat sua dextra bataium,
ac ita prolixis cum passibus ille viatur.

160 Se per gallonem quandoque revoltat eundo
saepeque terribili sfrantummat saxa bachiocco,
nam trovat intrigos per stricta canalia multos,

family of gods was sitting. Am I a weakling then, unable to stand firm under the weight of eight little boys, which is all you are for my strength? They all climb up to the back and shoulders of the giant then, as though they planned to storm a fortress with ladders. Lirone gets on his right shoulder as though weightless; his brother Hippol holds himself next to him with his hands. On the other side, Baldo grabs onto Fracasso's left ear. Gilberto holds on behind, adjusting the balance, so there was no need to add the usual rocks for ballast. Boccalo is attached to a lace on his breeches. Philoforno climbs into one ear, Moschino climbs into the other, and they had spacious chambers there. Cingar scrambles on top of his head and is higher than the others. The centaur does not wish to overburden the giant. While Falchetto moves the legs of his canine half, Virmace kicks with his equine half.

Remaining behind alone, the little ass brays and begs not to be   147
abandoned all by itself to the mouths of wolves. It's a bad risk to swim through the waterway seething with waves, and the ass doesn't want to get its skirt wet at all. So the giant gently takes it and places it under his wing and squeezes, making it release farts. The same thing happens when bagpipes sound with a full bladder: as it is squeezed by the elbow it sings and gives harmony to the music. Thus the ass's fine counterpoint makes excellent songs.

Fracasso seems to be carrying a lot of sparrows, and he swears   156
that so many heavy weights weigh nothing. His right hand carries the bell clapper by which he is supported, and so he hikes with lengthy strides. As he walks, he sometimes turns to one side and smashes boulders again and again with the tremendous clapper,

transversasque petras azali stipite rumpit.
Tandem post longos tractus multosque miaros,
165 ecce procul giornum cernunt finemque cavernae.
Incipiunt cantando simul dissolvere linguas,
canzonesque iubet cantari Baldus alegras:
Forselament, De tous, Dungaltre merque, Petite.
At Cingar tandem cecinit cotale motivum:
170 'Postquam de coeca sumus hac praesone cavati,
Tur lu cantemus, *Tur lu capra mozza* sonemus.
Quid Ramacina facit? quia non venit illa marito?
Cantemus *tararan,* cantemus *tantara taira'.*

Denique perveniunt ubi giorni lusor habetur,
175 ac ibi discarigat se pondere schena gigantis.
Non tamen extemplo potuerunt cernere lucem,
sed fecere velut facimus cum mane iacentes
poltronizamus nolentes surgere lecto,
quamvis ad mezam sol spargat lumina gambam;
180 sed cum fanteschae veniunt aperire fenestram,
slongamus cordas, asinorum more, lautti,
nilque lusimentum giorni guardare valemus.
Sic isti, egressi tenebris, vix lumen inalzant
sursum oculorum, barbaiati lampade solis.
185 Sed mox vezzati, mirantur quomodo possit
esse sub hac terra, aut terrae in viscere, giornum.
Hic alium siquidem mundum catavere novellum,
hicve novum solem, nova saecla novasque posadas.
Artibus at magicis memorant ea facta sotacquam,
190 nam maris ad fundum noscunt se denique giuntos.
Hic absque arboribus grandis campagna videtur,
qua non est maior per longum perque traversum
Veronae campagna vetus, campagna vel illa
qua se menchiones Godii super aethera iactant.

for he finds many impediments in the narrow channel and with his steel club breaks through the obstructing rocks.

Finally, after long stretches and many miles, behold! in the distance they glimpse the light of day and the end of the cavern. They begin to loosen their tongues and sing together, and Baldo bids them sing cheerful songs like *Fors seulement*, *De tous biens*, *D'un aultre amer* and *Petite camusette*. Yet in the end, Cingar sang this tune: "After we've been sprung from this blind prison, let's sing, *Tur lu!* Let's play *Tur lu, la capra è mozza*, and *Che fa la Ramacina, che la non vien dal marito?* Let's sing *Tararan*, let's sing *Tararan taira*." 164

At last, they come to where there's daylight, and here the giant's back unloads its burden. However, they could not look at the brightness right away. They did as we do when lying in bed in the morning: we act lazy and don't want to get out of bed, even though the sun spreads its rays up to the calf. When the maids come to open the windows, we stretch the strings of our lute like asses and are unable to look at the brilliance of daylight. Just so, these men: having left the shadows, they raise their eyes up a bit and are dazzled by the sunlight. But once they are used to it, they wonder how there could be daytime underground in the bowels of the earth. If indeed it is possible they found there a different new world, a new sun, a new era and new seasons. But they recall that these things are created underwater by magical arts, and they realize that they've reached the bottom of the sea at last. Here a vast treeless meadow appears: the old *campagna* of Verona is no greater in length and breadth, nor is that field which dolts from Goito praise to 174

195 In medio campi magnus petit astra palazzus,
de quo mille vident longe fumare caminos.
Illic scroffa suam plantarat Gelfora sedem
banditamque tenet semper maga pessima chortem;
perque suum regnum multas fabricarat Arenas
200 atque Colossaeos, qualem Verona theatrum
nunc habet, atque illic tenet omni tempore vaccas
ut simili tota urbs semper stet netta ledamo.
Sed magnum factum mirandaque folla videtur,
quod pelagi fundus stet in altum more solari
205 nec fluat abassum, quamvis agitetur ab Austris;
per quem sol radios spargit penetratque liquores
ac si per vitrum brusans candela trapasset.
Unde novus paret mundus nova vitaque gentis.
Compagni tutavia stupent clamatque Fracassus:
210 'Doh, diavol! Erit numquid tibi tanta potestas
ut naturales possis voltare statutos?
Sicine tu pelagi fundamina pendis in altum?
Aut, velut aër, aquae per te gravitudine mancant?
Non, non! Quid facimus? Nimium tardata ruina est'.
215 Respondet Boccalus: 'Habes, maruffe, ragionem.
Sed quod mangemus nihil ultra portat asellus'.
Cingar ait: 'Fameo'. Sequitur Moschinus: 'Ut orbus
nil video'. Centaurus item: 'Mihi brontolat intus
panza fame'. 'Mangemus', ait Fracassus, 'asellum'.
220 Quo dicto, piat hunc pedibus, colloque tirato
strangolat antrattum, veluti massara galinam.
Scortigat huic gambas Cingar, Boccalus adoprat
Margutti dagam dum spaccat pectora dumque
ventre cavat trippas, rognones atque figatum.
225 Baldus azalino de saxis ense favillas
accipit in ferulam, festucos aggerat omnes
Hippol, et altandem Lyronus suscitat ignem.

364

the skies. In the middle of the field a great palace reaches for the stars, from which at a distance they see a thousand chimneys smoking.

It was here that the sow Gelfora had established her base; this evil witch always kept an open house. Throughout her kingdom she had built many arenas and Coliseums, like the arena that Verona still has where she keeps cows year round so that the rest of the city always stays rid of such filth. But in truth it seems a great phenomenon and a marvelous fable that the bottom of the sea stays high up like a ceiling and doesn't pour down even when blown by winds from the south. The sun spreads its rays through it, penetrating the liquid as a burning candle passes through glass. So it seems like a new world, a new way of life for people. The friends continue to be amazed and Fracasso exclaims, "The devil, I say. Do you really have such great power that you can turn upside down the laws of nature? Can you hang the bottom of the sea up high like that? Or is it that you make the waters weightless like air? No, no! What should we do? The collapse so long delayed is coming!" 197

Boccalo answers, "You're right, stupid. But the donkey no longer carries anything for us to eat." Cingar says, "I'm hungry." Moschino adds, "Like a blind man, I can't see." The centaur agrees, "My belly grumbles deep inside from hunger." Fracasso says, "Let's eat the donkey!" Having said this, he grabs it by the feet and strangles it in one motion, with a snap of the neck, as a farm wife strangles a hen. Cingar skins its legs and Boccalo uses Margutte's dagger to split the chest, then takes out of the gut the tripe, the kidneys and the liver. Baldo uses a fennel stalk to catch the sparks his steel sword makes from the rocks; Hippol piles up all the straw, and 215

Fert Philofornus aquam nec non Giubertus in elmis,
diversosque lavant asini de corpore quartos,

230 qui partim lessus, partim mangiatur arostus,
et tandem saturi vadunt incontra palazzum.
Nec bene finierant andando trenta cavezzos,
en procul occurrit vecchius sciancatus et una
it secum mulier vultu peregrina zoioso.

235 Gestant ambo manu bordones atque capellos
parvaque dependet baculo de utroque tabella,
qua sua depicta est facto desgratia voto.
Immantellati breviter cinctique fiaschis,
seque fadigatos monstrant longo esse camino;

240 quapropter, stratis umbrosa in valle gonellis,
membra solo buttant forzasque sedendo raquistant.
Illuc conveniunt socii, pietate moventur;
namque viandantus cent'annos tempore monstrat,
cui reposare magis quam circum ire bisognat.

245 Tum peregrina virens facie tenerinaque multum
ad prigolum vadit ne sole scoletur eundo.
Blandidulos oculos in terram semper abassat,
quos aposta levat quandoque tiratque saëttas,
deque balestranti vista dardeggiat acutas.

250 Praecurrens socios hanc primius Hippol adocchiat
et iam, sicut erat solitus, veschiatur in illa.
Baldus amorevolo vecchium sembiante salutat;
mox ait: 'Unde venis? quo vadis? quod tibi nomen?'
Respondet: 'Venio Paradisi e partibus alti,

255 vadoque ad Infernum, Pasquinus nomine dicor'.
Baldus ait: 'Quis te Paradisum linquere fecit?
Nonne bonum bravumque illic tu tempus habebas?
Cambius iste tuus malus est, lassare beatos,
ire ad damnatos; miror quae causa sit ista'.

lastly, Lirone ignites the fire. Philoforno and Gilberto bring water
in their helmets and wash the various quarters of the donkey's
body, which they eat, part boiled and part roasted, until sated at
last, they head off toward the palace.

They had scarcely traversed thirty yards when there in the dis- 232
tance a crippled old man moves toward them, and with him comes
a pilgrim woman with a joyful face. Both wear hats and have walk-
ing sticks in their hands, and a little picture hangs from the end of
each staff, on which is depicted the transgression for which their
vow was taken. Dressed in short coats with flasks on their belts,
they appear to be weary from the long journey, and thus they
stretch out their cloaks in a shady valley and throw their limbs
down on the ground and rest to restore their strength.

The companions arrive there and are moved by pity, for the one 242
traveler seems a hundred years old and should rather be resting
than taking a trip. The pilgrim maiden, with her young and tender
face, runs the risk of melting as she walks in the sun. She continu-
ally lowers her charming eyes to the ground, but intentionally
raises them from time to time and shoots arrows and sharp darts
from her crossbow-like gaze. Running in front of his companions,
Hippol notices her first and, predictably, is already ensnared by
her. Baldo greets the old man in a friendly manner, then asks,
"Where do you come from? Where are you going? What's your
name?"

He responds, "I am coming from the lofty regions of Paradise 254
and am going to hell. I am called by the name Pasquino."

Baldo says, "Who made you leave Paradise? Weren't you having 256
a jolly good time there? This change of yours is bad: to leave the
blessed and go to the damned. I wonder what the reason is."

260 Respondet malvecchius: 'Ego sum pratica mundi
    nec tegit indarnum mihi barba grisissima pectus.
    Crede mihi experto: te stessum fallis, amice;
    ingannatur homo, Paradisum qui putat esse
    deliciis plenum, allegrezzis atque solazzis.

265 Sunt cinquanta anni quod ego plantando tavernam
    ostus eram Romae, tam toti cognitus urbi
    ut mea perpetuis ibi stet nomanza diebus,
    meque patres statua decorarint, sicut usatur
    de signalatis fieri dignisque triumpho.

270 Non est poca tibi virtus aquirere famam
    talibus in rebus, quales gradire videbis
    regibus et papis, mitris rossisque berettis.
    Quapropter studium tribus artibus omne trovavi:
    arte coquinandi, buffonis, tum rofiani.

275 His ego pro meritis larghissima dona rochettis
    saepe guadagnavi multosque insemma placeros;
    unde sciens hominum tantorum facta, prodezzas,
    artes, virtutes, meritos et caetera vitae,
    solus ego toto possum de his omnibus orbi

280 rendere bon contum secretaque pandere genti.
    Si praestanda fides sanctis est ulla prophetis,
    credite Pasquino schietto savioque prophetae;
    quidquid ait *Credo* est, quam sancta Ecclesia cantat.
    Iam mihi decrepito moriendi venerat hora,

285 pro me tota simul monstrabat Roma gramezzam.
    Supplicat ad Patrem Sanctum me voiat, onustum
    bullis et brevibus, coelo mandare beato.
    Collegium subito pro me papa ille radunat,
    postque ragionamen varium quod, cive tamagno

290 sic sic perduto, grandis iactura sequetur
    cortesanorum iuvenum cortesaquenarum,
    ecce mihi tandem datur indulgentia talis:

The bad old man answers, "I am Worldly Experience; not for 260 nothing does this full gray beard cover my chest. Believe me, I'm an expert, and you, friend, are wrong: anyone who thinks Paradise is full of pleasures, joys and amusements is deceived. It was fifty years ago that I set up a tavern and became an innkeeper in Rome. I was so well-known throughout the city that my fame there will last for all eternity, and the senators honored me with a statue, as is done for those who become illustrious and worthy of glory. You need no small amount of skill to acquire fame for things that you see are pleasing to kings and popes, miters and red birettas. For this reason, I placed all my efforts in three arts: the arts of cooking, buffoonery and pimping. For my merits in these arts, I often earned many gifts from the surplices, together with many favors. Hence, knowing so much about these great men — their deeds, abilities, skills and merits, and about the rest of their lives — I alone can give a full account of them to the world and divulge their secrets to everyone.

"If one should place any faith in the holy prophets, then believe 281 in Pasquino, a wise and sincere prophet. Everything he says is like the *Credo* sung by Holy Church. Now I was already decrepit, the hour had come for me to die; all Rome together was grieving for me. They besought the Holy Father to send me, loaded with bulls and briefs, to blessed Paradise. Immediately the pope convoked the College of Cardinals on my behalf. After a long discussion about how the loss of such a great citizen would entail misfortune to many young courtiers and courtesans, in the end I was granted this indulgence: that I should go to establish a tavern in front of

369

ante ussum coeli vadam plantare tavernam
ut quando venient Paradisi ad regna godentis,
295   supra suas mulas ben grassi benque pafuti
praelati Gesiae, sim praestus simque paratus
hos mihi bon meritos pingui recetare taverna,
quae cameras habeat fornitas more Todesco;
sed meus in Roma genius stet semper in una
300   marmoris effigie, qua non magis altra catatur
digna maraviliis, si sit pensata brigatis.
Nunc tibi sum maschius, nunc sum tibi foemina Romae,
nunc ego Relligio, nunc sum Victoria, nuncve
sum tibi Pasquinus slancatus et absque mudanda,
305   fazzaque merdifluens privatur munere nasi.
Haec mihi contingit saxo desgratia propter
civem Marphoium, cui cuncta archana paleso;
nosque ragionamus nisi non heroica miris
diversisque modis; neque deest facundia nobis,
310   quamvis abstulerint puerilia saxa loquelas.
Ergo super limen Paradisi nostra tre annos
ostaria fuit modico celebrata guadagno.
Namque cadenazzis chiusae stanghisque seratae
semper erant portae nulloque intrante mufosae,
315   et sua taccarant gambati lintea ragni.
Passabant giorni vel sex tal volta vel octo,
nemo foresterus bandas veniebat ad illas.
Si tamen ullus erat tandem qui accederet illuc,
vel zoppus, vel gobbus erat, vel lumine sguerzus,
320   vel cantans borsis coram latrone vodatis.
Nemo qui scottum posset pagare tavernae,

the gates of Heaven. In this way, when Church prelates would come to the happy kingdom of Paradise on their plump, well-fed mules, I would be ready and eager to host these well-deserving souls in a rich tavern, with rooms stocked in the German manner. But my essence remained forever in a marble statue in Rome — the most marvelous thing possible, if people think about it.

"In Rome, I am sometimes male, sometimes female; once I was 302 Religion, once Victory; and now I am your Pasquino. Deformed and without underwear; my face is flowing with shit and deprived of the use of its nose. This misfortune was caused by a stone thanks to my fellow citizen Marforio, to whom I reveal all my secrets. We speak only of heroic matters in diverse and admirable ways. Eloquence is not lacking despite the fact that the boys' stones have taken away our voices.

"So, for three years our tavern was famous for doing poorly at 311 the entrance to Paradise. Indeed, the moldy doors were always chained shut and bolted with bars; nobody entered, and long-legged spiders had hung up their linens there. Sometimes six or eight days would pass by and not one visitor would come that way. If, however, someone did finally come near there, he would be lame or hunchbacked or one-eyed or with bags so empty he could sing in front of thieves. There was no one who could pay a tavern bill or who wanted a room, a bed or fodder. They were all without

qui vellet cameram, qui lectum quique biavam:
quisque carens soldis, soliti dormire paiaris,
strazzati tunicis, cercantes atque pecentes
325   deque pitocatis implentes viscera tozzis.
Raro pontifices vidi, regesque ducasque,
raro signores, marchesos, raro barones,
raro capellutos, mitratos, raro capuzzos,
qui mihi scudiferas possent aperire crumenas,
330   quique zafranatos vellent pagare capones,
splumatosque toros, dulces garbasque caraffas.
Hi sunt qui riccas faciunt pinguesque tavernas;
hi sunt qui spendunt et possunt spendere scudos.
Procuratorem si quemquam forte videbam,
335   sive potestatem, advocatum, sive nodarum,
vix illud credens clamabam: "Oh grande miracol!"
Hac ego pro causa sdegnatus ab inde scapavi;
sed tunc praecipue quando Demogorgon abbas,
cui brocoli, sardae, fighi, fava frantaque curae,
340   affuit in mula tam magra tamque stryata
ut fiascos posses duris taccare galonis.
Non habuit marzum pro me sua borsa quatrinum,
quo vasum calidae posset pagare polentae.
Accedit clausae Paradisi denique portae,
345   qua pregat introrsum recipi fierique beatus
cittadinus ibi, aut aliquo cantone locari.
At Petrus in colera miserum de limine sburlat,
mox ait: "Hinc abeas, destructio favamenadae!
non es, nec maium fueris dignatus Olympo,
350   donec apud chiericos madonna Simona manebit;
quam dum permittit mundo sic vivere Luscar,
nec tu, nec tua stirps poterunt intrare chidentrum.
Vade! nec ultra chioches portam, ne forte chiocheris".

money, accustomed to sleeping on straw; beggars and mendicants in torn tunics who filled their bellies with crusts of begged bread. Rarely did I see popes, kings and dukes; rarely lords, marquises or barons; rarely cardinals, bishops or monks, who could open coin-laden purses for me, who wished to pay for saffroned capons or fine feathered beds or carafes of sweet and dry wine. These are the ones who can make a tavern prosperous and rich; these are the ones who spend and can keep spending coin.

"If by chance I spotted any sort of solicitor or magistrate, lawyer or notary, scarcely believing my eyes, I would cry, 'O what a miracle!' And so for this reason I fled from there incensed, specifically at the time when an abbot, a Demogorgon who loved broccoli, sardines, figs and split beans, came riding up on a mule so thin and bony that you could hang flasks from its ribs. His purse held not one rotten coin for me, even to pay for a platter of hot polenta. At last he approached the closed gates of Paradise, where he asked to be welcomed within and to become a beatified citizen or to be put in a corner somewhere. But Peter angrily shoved the wretch away from the door and said, 'Get away from here, devourer of bean soup! You are not and never will be worthy of Olympus, as long as Madame Simony remains a friend of clerics, as long as Luscar allows her to live in the world like this, neither you nor your race will be allowed to come inside here. Go now, and don't knock on the door again, or you could get knocked out.'

334

Talia dum fierent, exibant extra seraium,
355 deque schola coeli guizzabant mille putini,
qui male vestiti, qui nudi malque politi,
malque petenati, magri tegnaque coperti,
intravere meam nullo prohibente tavernam.
"Oh!", dixi, "troppa est praesumptio vestra, citelli!"
360 "Nos angeletti sumus", aiunt: "trade merendam!"
Quo dicto, coepere meas sbandare pignattas
et mihi cassonem fresco de pane vorarunt,
tresque simul porcos, vaccam unam, trenta capones,
gallinas totidem, cum becco sex quoque capras,
365 octoque persuttos, plenumque saluminis urzum.
Quid plura? et gattas, asinum, mulamque magrazzam
mangiarunt, et plus post mangiamenta famebant;
unde nisi raptim scapolassem nudus ab illis,
meque meamque simul cazzassent ventre fiolam.
370 Pensa mo, post mortem quae consolatio restat!'
Talia mal vecchius dum chiachiarat, Hipol acostat
sese dongellae vultque illam tollere secum.
Cingar ei scaltritus opem donare parecchiat,
qui tenet abbadam, scortam facit atque subocchiat
375 Falchettum; tandemque omnes favere sodali.
Id solum ignorat magni prudentia Baldi,
tempore qui simili vult castos esse barones.
En subito tremefit totum campagna per orbem,
disfantat vecchius sese ingannator ut umbra.
380 Obstuperantque pedes Baldi steterantque capilli,
quando repentina se volta repperit illic
solum solettum, neque coram vidit amicos.
Quid faciat, seu quo stampet vestigia pensat,
mente Deum clamat, Serraphum voce domandat.
385 Denique Gelforeas meium putat esse masones
vadere, smarritos ubi forte catabit amicos.

374

"While this was happening, a thousand little cherubs were leav-   354
ing the seraglio, skipping out of heaven school. Ill-clad, naked,
dirty, unkempt, skinny and covered with ringworm, they entered
my tavern with no one to stop them. 'O!' said I. 'Your presump-
tion is too much, little ones.'

"'We are angels,' they said. 'Give us lunch!' Then they began to   360
toss around my pots and pans, and devoured a huge bin of bread,
along with three pigs, a cow, thirty capons and as many hens, as
well as a billy goat and six she-goats, eight hams and a crate of sa-
lami. And what else? Well, they ate the cats, the ass and that old
skinny mule. Yet after this feast, they were hungrier than before,
so that if I had not quickly escaped from them, practically stripped
naked, they would have shoved my daughter and me into their
bellies at the same time! Just think what joy awaits us after death!"

While the nasty old man blathered about these things, Hippol   371
cozied up to the girl, hoping to take her with him. Wily Cingar
gets ready to come to his aid and holds the old man at bay, stick-
ing by him and winking at Falchetto; eventually the whole group
helps out. Only the wisdom of great Baldo ignores all this: at such
times, he wants his barons to be chaste. Behold! all of a sudden
the countryside trembles on all sides and the old swindler vanishes
like a shadow. Baldo's feet are stunned and his hair stands on end,
when he turns around and unexpectedly finds himself all alone
and doesn't see his friends before him. He wonders what he
should do, where he should place his footprints. He calls to God
with his mind and to Seraphus with his voice. Finally he decides
that it's best to go to Gelfora's palace, where he might find his
missing friends. But he had scarcely begun to go with slow-moving

375

Sed vix tardigradis cum passibus ire comenzat,
Pizzacapellettus procul obvius ecce ruebat,
qui super amblantem, stradiotti more, zanettum
390   currit et altivolam giavarinam sustinet armo.
Baldus eum norat, vocat: 'Heus! o Pizzacapelle!
angelus es numquid Gabriel, qui forte novellas
portes zoiosas? Ubi stat spes nostra Seraphus?'
Respondet: 'Non, barro, novas may porto cativas.
395   En cape scondificam Serraphi munere petram.
Hanc Optalamiam dicunt; hanc nemine vistus
ore ferens, intra stanzas ubi Gelfora praesul
vaccarum albergat mandrasque governat earum.
Ille senex, qui se Pasquinum dixerat esse,
400   non est Pasquinus, verum Demogorgon ille,
qui solet ut cauda vivaces battere fadas,
atque stryas ipsas asinarum more cavalcat.
Teque tuosque viros veniebat fallere, sed tu
solus es immunis tanta de fraude rimastus.
405   Compagni tolerant meritorum facta suorum,
quos tamen altandem cum tecum laetus habebis'.
Dixerat, et subitus campagna sgombrat ab illa.
Baldus in ore petram claudit neque cernitur usquam.
Versus Gelfoream se drizzat protinus aulam,
410   multas incontrat comitivas saepe stryarum,
per medium quarum subtilis ut umbra trapassat;
atque voluptatis causa tirat hic, tirat illic
guarnellos calzosque menat goffosque frequentat.
Pervenit ante fores palazzi semper apertas;
415   omnia sunt aurum: cornisia, limina, voltae.
Introit armatumque videt lanzonibus agmen,
guardam reginae quod iudicat esse probatam.
'Gaude', Baldus ait, 'mi brande! Cibaberis esca
carnis et aethereum guazzabis sanguine vultum'.

steps when, look! in the distance Pizzacappelletto rushes toward him. He rides on a smooth-gaited jennet like a light-armed mercenary and holds a high-flying javelin on his shoulder. Baldo recognizes him and calls, "Hey there, Pizzacappelletto, are you now the angel Gabriel, who is perhaps going to bring glad tidings? Where is our great hope, Seraphus?"

He answers, "No, Sir Knight, I never bring bad news. Here— 394 accept this invisibility gem as a gift from Seraphus. They call it 'opthalamia.' Carry it in your mouth, seen by no one, and enter the rooms where Gelfora lives as pastor of the cows and governs their herds. That elder who said he was Pasquino is not Pasquino, but is in fact Demogorgon, who likes to beat the immortal fates with his tail, and ride witches as though they were asses. He came to trick you and your friends, and you alone remained immune to his deception. Your companions are getting what they deserve; however, in the end, you will happily have them with you."

Having spoken, he clears out of that field at once. Baldo puts 407 the gem in. He heads straight away toward Gelfora's palace. He keeps meeting many groups of witches, but passes through their midst like a shadow. For the fun of it, he tugs here and there at their robes, giving them kicks and frequent blows. He reaches the doors of the palace, which are always open. Everything there is made of gold—cornices, lintels and vaults. He enters and sees a squadron armed with heavy lances, which he decides is the queen's chosen guard. "Rejoice, my blade!" Baldo says. "You will feast on a diet of flesh and spatter your ethereal countenance with blood."

420 Transit ad obcinctum largo gyramine claustrum,
    quod decorant circum centum cinquanta columnae.
    Omnia splendificant auro mirisque richezzis;
    aurum pillastri, frisi, capitella, peduzzi.
    Quos Baldus mores trovat illic quasve bruturas,
425 quos bordelliacos actus deshonestaque facta
    utile non posset scribi, si scribere vellem;
    nam neque simplicibus sunt omnia danda palesa.
    Ostia per gyrum camerarum plurima iusto
    discompagnantur discrimine, semper aperta,
430 semper et andantum discursibus et redeuntum
    trita pedum, veluti patet esse palatia regum.
    Cuncta sigillatim latitans vult cernere Baldus.
    Se viat ad primam spatioso intramine portam,
    de qua non pocam videt ire redire brigatam.
435 Intus tictocchant duri mortaria bronzi,
    nam speciariae locus est et pharmapotechae.
    Intro ascosus abit, vult omnia scire gradatim.
    Obstupet innumeras ibi vecchias esse dunatas,
    quae simul innumeros homines, magis immo stryones,
440 semper amaëstrant in rebus mille nefandis.
    Sunt Itali, Greghi, Spagnoles atque Todeschi;
    et ricchi et poveri, laici fratresque pretique,
    matronae et monachae, tandem genus omne brigatae.
    Sollicitant varias basso cum murmure cosas
445 multaque conficiunt unguenta, cerumina, pastas,
    unctos, impiastros, pilulas, confetta, cirottos.
    Mille serant, reserant scatolas, voltantque, revoltant,
    urceolosque tegunt, retegunt, solvuntque, resolvunt
    vasa triacarum, bozas, magnosque bocalos.
450 Pars mensurat aquas varia de sorte bilancis,
    pars chioccat pavidas crebris pistonibus herbas:
    taxum, cambrossen, squillas, aconita, cicutas;

He crosses through to an enclosed cloister with a wide perimeter, adorned all around by one hundred and fifty columns. Everything is resplendent with gold and surprising riches: gold are the pilasters, friezes, capitals, and pedestals. What low actions Baldo finds here, what shameful things, what bordello-like activities, what immoral deeds, cannot suitably be described. For even if I wanted to describe them, not all things should be revealed to the simpleminded.

The many doorways of the surrounding rooms are spaced apart 428
at pleasing intervals. Always open, they are continuously worn underfoot by people running back and forth, just as a royal palace remains open. Baldo, still invisible, wants to see everything bit by bit. He approaches the first door with its spacious entryway where he sees no small crowd entering and exiting. Inside, mortars made of hard bronze clatter, because this place is the herbalist's shop and a pharmacy. He enters hidden; he wants to learn about everything little by little. He is amazed that so many old women are gathered there, continually schooling so many men — or rather sorcerers — in a thousand nefarious things at the same time. There are Italians, Greeks, Spaniards and Germans; rich and poor; laymen, brothers and priests; matrons and nuns; in short, every sort of person. With a low murmur, they are stirring various things and concocting many unguents, cataplasms, pastes, rubs, poultices, pills, sugarcoated tablets and plasters. They open and close a thousand boxes, turning them around and back; they cover little jars, then uncover them; they open and close pots, casks and big jugs of cure-alls.

Some of them measure various liquids on various kinds of 450
scales; some pound frightful herbs with heavy pestles: yew, privet, squill, aconite, and hemlock. Others fill vials with black syrups,

electuariis pars implet bissola nigris,
compositis noctu quintae sub lampade lunae,
455 de spuma rospi, de ladri carne picati,
de pulmone asini, de virdi pelle ranocchi,
de lue matricis, de argenti sulphure vivi,
deque cadaveribus violenta morte peremptis,
de sudore lupi rabiosi, deque sagina
460 viperea, de felle upupae, de lacte cerastae.
Praeterea fingunt miscentque sacrata prophanis:
paschalis caerae candelas, chrismatis unctum,
baptismique salem multasque insemma novellas,
quas praeti dant saepe mali poltronibus istis.
465 Quas uti componant, fors fors describere possem;
sed dubito ne, dum errores reprendere vellem,
errorum fierem praeceptor meque Thomistae
dignum censerent mitra Christique cavallo,
ac asini, de more briae, mihi cauda daretur.
470 Talia pro magno nec haberent forte lavoro,
namque oratores, physicos strologosque, poëtas,
fratres et praetos, et qui dant iura brigatis,
omnibus in zobiis ad cursum vadere trovant.
Sed quia rispetto cedit drittezza rasonis,
475 atque solent grossi pisces mangiare minutos,
disventuratae quaedam solummodo vecchiae
sunt, quae supra asinos plaebi spectacula fiunt;
sunt, quae nobilium culpis velamina tendunt;
sunt, quae sparagnant claris incendia femnis.
480 Baldus it ascosus, consyderat omnia, versat
inscriptasque legit scatolas urzosque notatos:
non nisi mortiferum passim legit esse venenum.
Librazzos aperit, vel apertos lectitat omnes:
non nisi letales consyderat esse recettas;
485 scilicet: ut pueri faturentur odore marassi,

brewed at night by the beams of the fifth moon, from toad spittle, from the flesh of a hanged thief, from a donkey's lung, from green frog skin, from womb fluid, from quicksilver sulfur, from corpses slain by violent death, from the sweat of a rabid wolf, from the fattened body of a viper, from the gall bladder of a hoopoe and from the milk of a horned viper. In addition, they transform and mix the sacred with the profane: Easter wax candles, confirmation oil, baptismal salt and many other novelties as well which bad priests often give to these scroungers.

Perhaps I could describe how they combine these things, but I   465
fear that, while trying to rebuke these misdeeds, I might become a master of misdeeds, and the Thomists could judge me worthy of the miter and of Christ's steed and would give me the tail of an ass as a bridle. Perhaps they wouldn't consider my actions of such importance, since they find that diplomats, physicians, astrologers, poets, brothers and priests and those who make the laws for all the people go riding on Thursdays. But since the justice of reason yields to reverential respect and because big fish usually eat little fish, only certain unlucky old women end up on donkeys for public spectacle: it is they who shield the crimes of the nobility; they who spare illustrious women from the fire.

Baldo moves invisibly; he examines everything, scrutinizing all   480
sides, turns and reads the labels on boxes and the notations on jars. Everywhere he finds only mortal poisons. He opens heavy books or examines all those open already. He uncovers only lethal recipes, such as how to bewitch boys with the scent of vipers; how

quomodo stuprandi causa dormitio fitur,
uxorisque suae vir fusos noscere tortos
possit et in facto proprio retrovare ribaldam;
quomodo formosae cogantur amare puellae
490   sinceraeque harum mentes perforza tirentur;
quomodo non pregnet cum drizzat foemina cornas,
quomodo si pregnat fantinum pisset abortum,
quomodo vix natum corrumpant fascina puttum,
quoque modo siccent odiati membra mariti;
495   quomodo de birlo mentem, de corpore vitam
brutta stryazza cavet puero teneraeque puellae.
Foetentes ibi sunt, inquam, vecchiaeque beghinae,
quae vadunt redeuntque, ferunt referuntque novellas,
scilicet urzettos, scatolas et multifacendas.
500   Has sequitur Baldus vultque omnia tangere visu.
      Est locus alter ibi, ter centum brachia longus,
bis centum largus centumque sofitta levatur.
Hic amaestrantur partim partimque maëstrant
tot streghae quot arena micas, quot sylva Bacani
505   dat foias, quot Puia nigras parit arida muscas.
Sunt ibi scarcossae, sdentatae et lumine sguerzae
pinzocarae mediaeque sores, quas Gelfora doctas
esse pedantrices statuit satrapasque senati.
Quae pedagogarum de more galantiter artem
510   dispensare sciunt, dantes praecepta stryandi
atque per unguentos operandi multifacendas:
qualiter hae furiant moveantque tonitrua coeli
ut segetes vignasque simul tempesta ruinet;
qualiter huc lunam tirent perforza deorsum,
515   qualiter et stellae schegnent reflectere gambas,
qualiter et detrum voltent cava flumina spallas
deque mari ad proprios referant carneria fontes;
qualiter in formas diversas corpora mutent,

to induce sleep before a rape; how a husband may discover his wife's twisted spindle and catch the hussy *in flagrante delicto;* how to force beautiful girls to love and how to control their innocent minds by force; how a woman can keep from getting pregnant while giving her husband horns; how, if she does get pregnant, she can piss out the aborted baby; how enchantments can harm a newborn baby; how to dry up a hated husband's member; how an ugly hag can deprive the mind of sanity and the body of a youth or a tender young maid of life. There are, as I was saying, fetid old biddies there who come and go, carrying notions back and forth, such as little bottles and boxes and other such things. Baldo follows them and wants to touch everything with his eyes.

Next, there is another room, three hundred feet long and two 501
hundred feet wide, with a ceiling that rises a hundred feet. Here as many witches teach as are taught, as many as there are grains of sand on the shore or leaves in the forest of Baccano or black flies in arid Puglia. There are scrawny, toothless, squint-eyed bigots, lay sisters, whom Gelfora has declared to be learned pedantettes and satraps in her senate. Like pedagogues, they know how to dispense the art in a courtly way, giving lessons on witchcraft and on achieving many undertakings with ointments: how to rage and stir up thunder in the sky so that a storm will ruin the crops and vines; how to pull the moon down by force; how to make the stars turn their legs around, how to turn back the shoulders of deep rivers, and have them flow back from the sea to their own sources. And how to change bodies into different shapes: turning men into

inque lupos voltent homines ursosque canesque,
520   sequemet in gattas, in monas inque civettas,
augurium quae triste canant per tecta casarum;
qualiter et praetos doceant faturare comadres
atque malos fratres mulas equitare diabli.
    Nunc hic, nunc illic Baldus praecepta stryarum
525   audit et advertens si quam cognoscat in illis,
Cingaris uxorem mirat Bertamque magistras
esse puellarum; traxit quasi turbidus ensem,
at circumspiciens ibi multas esse madonnas,
nobilium uxores hominum pluresque papessas,
530   mucchiachias Sathanae, se prostituisse diablis,
bassavit coleram, tacuit latuitque libenter,
confortumque piat secum semetque reprendit
velle per un nihilum cotalas prendere gattas.
    Namque videt chiarum quod quas hic esse putamus
535   Harsilias, illic Thaydarum squadra trovantur.
Sed laudavit eas, quae furta coprire sciebant:
semiremissa quidem culpa est quam coltra covertat.
Tecta nitent aurum, muri, pavimenta, cadreghae,
strataque coltrinis variis; lectique parantur
540   argento, raso, samito, canzante, veluto.
Conspicit hic iuvenes circum scherzare puellas,
leggiadros motu, bellos facieque galantos,
stringatos, agiles, semper saltare vedutos;
quos Baldus cernens cito iudicat esse diablos,
545   humanum vestisse caput moresque virorum.
Quas gestent auri vestas brettasque veluti,
praetereo, et calzas ostri rensique camisas;
quin etiam petras pretiosas pono dacantum,
muschium, perfumos, zibetti vascula, namphas.
550   Sentit et ad nasum storacis aquaeve rosadae
spiramenta, quibus sbrofatur saepe palazzus.

wolves and bears and dogs, and themselves into cats, monkeys and owls that intone gloomy omens from the rooftops of houses. And how to teach priests to bewitch housewives and wicked friars to ride the devil's mules.

Now here, now there, Baldo listens to the witches' precepts, and looking to see whether he recognizes any of them, he wonders that Cingar's wife and Berta are teachers of the younger girls. As if in a daze, he pulled out his sword; yet seeing there are many ladies all around — the wives of noblemen, numerous popesses, Satan's *muchachas* who have prostituted themselves to the devils — he calmed his anger, kept silent and preferred to stay hidden. He takes comfort and chides himself for having wanted to go after these cats for nothing. For now he sees clearly that those whom we consider Hersilias are in fact a throng of Thaises. But he praised them because they knew how to hide their crimes: half-forgiven is any fault that stays hidden under the covers. 524

The rooftops shine with gold, the walls, floors, benches, and the various layers of bedcovers and beds are made of silver, satin, samite, shot-silk and velvet. Baldo observes youths here joking around the girls: elegant in their movements, with handsome and charming faces, well-dressed, agile, always seen dancing. As soon as he sees them, Baldus judges them to be devils that have put on human heads and manly manners. I won't describe their golden clothes and velvet hats and their purple stockings and fine linen shirts. And likewise I'll omit the precious jewels, the musk, perfumes and little vials of civet and orange essence. He feels rising to his nose spirals of storax and rose, with which the palace is often 538

Florida profidicos ornant spalleria muros,
in quibus adfixi dant specchi lumina circum.
Illic meschinae stant se doniare puellae,
555 imponuntque genis, fronti colloque biaccas;
atque coralinos faciunt parere labrettos,
increspantque comas ferro, ciliique tosantur,
streppanturve pili; strazzis stuppaque dedentrum
ingrossant humeros slargantque ad pectora mammas
560 ut, quam pensamus sembianzam Palladis esse,
sit saccus paiae, vel forma sit illa puvoni,
qui discazzandos ad osellos ponitur hortis.
Pono da banda lyras, flautos atque organa, cethras,
scambiettos, danzas: guantos de Spagna, morescas,
565 et ballum qui fit cum torza cumque capello.
Ipsa voluptati praestat maga Gelfora tantae,
quae super auratam stat salae in fronte cadregam.
    Talia dum crespo consyderat ore baronus,
ecce cadenatum grandi rumore Bocalum
570 huc strassinari, calzis pugnisque domari
prospicit a vulgo sguataro turpique canaia.
Undique, guardandi causa, populazzus adibat,
undique concurrunt poverumque offendere cercant.
Spingitur ante thronum reginae calzibus, urtis,
575 pugnadis, goffis, schiaffis persona Bocali,
qui cridat et chiamat, perdonum saepe rechiedit,
inque fededium giurat fecisse nientum.
Gelfora capturae causam tumefacta domandat.
Respondetur ei quod pessimus iste giotonus
580 intrarat furtim propter robbare cucinam,
et iam fardellum de caso deque botiro
fecerat, inde duos guataros bastone gratarat;
nec quod scriptus erat regalis servitor aulae,
nec quod sallarium bruttus manigoldus habebat,

doused. Floral draperies decorate the walls of porphyry, on which mirrors hang to give light all around. In that place pathetic girls stand about admiring themselves and put makeup on their cheeks and foreheads and necks. They make their precious lips seem the color of coral; they curl their hair with irons and trim their eyebrows, plucking out stray hairs, and with rags and straw they pad their shoulders and enlarge the breasts on their chests. So what we think to be the image of Pallas Athena is a sack of straw or one of those scarecrows we place in an orchard to chase away birds. I set aside the lyres, flutes and organs, the citterns, spins and reels, the Spanish gauntlets, the morescas, the dance one does with torches and hats. The mage Gelfora herself presides over these delights, seated on a golden throne at the front of the hall.

While Baldo contemplates these things with a furrowed brow,   568
behold! he witnesses Boccalo dragged in chains with great commotion and subdued with kicks and fists by a gang of knaves and vile riff-raff. From all sides, the rabble approach to view the spectacle; from all sides they come running and try to injure the poor man. Pushed in front of the queen's throne with kicks, shoves, fists, blows and slaps is the body of Boccalo. He cries out and yells; he begs repeatedly for mercy and swears to God he's done nothing. Gelfora arrogantly demands to know the reason for this capture. They answer her that this despicable scalawag had entered the kitchen by stealth in order to rob and that he had first made a bundle of cheese and butter and had then roughed up a couple of servants with a club. And the vile rapscallion would not

585   nec qua venisset banda parlare volebat.
      Gelfora sdegnoso voltat sembiante visaggium,
      et pariter spudans veluti stomacata, locuta est:
      'Hinc via! hinc, oybo, procul hunc menate gaioffum!
      Hinc cito! quae indusia? me mastinazzus amorbat.
590   Oh quam poca fuit discretio vestra, balordi!
      Vosne meis oculis hanc praesentasse carognam?
      Ite viam rozzamque eius voltate figuram'.
      Protinus hoc iussu streppatur ab inde tapinus,
      totaque turba retro seguitat: 'Day dayque!' frequentat.
595   Extrorsum trahitur suffertque in corpore bottas
      quales non asini comportat schena pigrazzi.
      Baldus apena tenet sese: bis, terque, quaterque
      spadonis manicum propter sfodrare cavarat.
      Pur tamen alquantum patitur pro cernere finem,
600   ut qui diversas optat cognoscere provas.
      Denique nescio quo Boccalus tingitur uncto.
      Ecce statim longas paulatim stendit orecchias
      mostazzumque procul mandans quasi toccat arenam;
      brachia deventant gambae, quae quattuor extant;
605   tandem tota pilos vestit persona bretinos
      efficiturque asinus is qui fuit ante Bocalus.
      Iam non 'oyme' cridat, tantum pronuntiat 'a a'.
      Cursitat huc, illuc, bastonibus undique toccus;
      vult trare non solitos, pro se deffendere, calzos,
610   sed cadit et duros piat ille cadendo tramazzos.
      Se stupet in semet, mirans non esse Bocalum,
      ast asini bustum, quo non bertinior alter
      raggiat in Arcadia, dum portat grana molino,
      dumque revolteggiat sibi tosto in pulvere schenam.
615   Nunc strassinatur per caudam, nunc per orecchias,
      excutiturque aspris pulver de pelle tracagnis.

say for what service he was enlisted in the royal halls, nor what salary he received, nor where he came from. Gelfora turns her face with a disdainful look, and at the same time, spitting in disgust, she says, "Away with him! Away, fie! Take the scoundrel away! Away, quickly! What are you waiting for? This nasty cur is making me sick! O what poor judgment you show, you dolts! To present this carcass to my eyes? Go away now and change his base shape."

At her command the poor fellow is dragged away from there at   593
once and the whole crowd follows behind, shouting, "Let him have it!" Dragged outside, Boccalo suffers blows to the body that the back of the laziest ass could not bear. Baldo can scarcely control himself: twice, three times, four times, he had pulled out the hilt of his sword to unsheathe it. Yet nevertheless he tolerates this for a bit in order to see what happens, since he wishes to experience a variety of events.

At last Boccalo is anointed with some sort of ointment. Be-   601
hold! at once his ears begin to grow long little by little and he sprouts a big mug that almost touches the ground; his arms become legs, so that he has four of them. Lastly, his entire body is covered with gray hair, and the person who had been Boccalo now becomes an ass. Already he cannot cry "Woe is me!" but can only utter "Hee-haw." He runs helter-skelter and is struck with clubs on all sides. He wants to let fly unusual kicks to defend himself, but he falls and in falling takes more hard whacks. He is amazed at himself, perceiving that he is not Boccalo, but the figure of an ass, and no grayer ass brays in all of Arcadia, while carrying grain to the mill and while rolling its back in the warm dirt. First he is dragged by his tail, next by his ears, and then the dirt is shaken from his skin with harsh drubbings.

Baldus at oltraggium tandem non sustinet illud:
scorzat de fodro saturandum sanguine brandum,
irruit in caecam lapidis virtute catervam,
620   ac velut undicolas falco secat ungue folengas,
sic Baldus miseram distemperat ense fameiam.
Quisque sibi membrum, seu brazzum, sive galonem
spiccari sentit, nec ferrum cernitur ullum.
Deserit extemplo gens haec malnata Bocalum,
625   atque per albergum latitans fugit huc, fugit illuc.
Fama novellatrix reginae accepit orecchias,
quae transmutavit fazzas in mille colores.
Pensitat esse magos, seu Coclen, sive Seraphum,
quos sibi mortales semper provat esse nemigos.
630   Introit a cameris aliis penetrale remotum,
exercere solet magicos ubi porca susurros.
Baldus at interea solus straviaverat omnes,
deque cadaveribus compleverat atria multis.
Manserat in tuttum clauster de gente vodatus,
635   quae se per stanzas ficcando seraverat ussos.
Baldus it, atque asinum vult secum trare Bocalum,
quem stimulo pungens solitum pronuntiat 'ari':
'Ari la! rozza, pru, sta!' Sic dicens, factus agaso,
extra fores claustri cogit trottare somarum.
640   Bestia Boccalus nescit quis retro goiolet,
nec comprendit adhuc qualis molinarus agrezzet;
saepe caput voltat si factum cernere possit,
nempe videt stimulum, sed non videt ille biolcum.
Ut procul astarunt, trat Baldus ab ore petrellam,
645   cum qua per gentes prius invisibilis ibat,
atque suam charo faciem scovertat asello;
qui, licet exterius beretina pelle tegatur,
signorile tamen Baldi cum prospicit actum,
protinus alzatis se gambis rizzat, ut ille

Yet finally, Baldo can bear this outrage no longer: he unleashes   617
his bloodthirsty blade from its sheath. He rushes into the throng
that is blinded by his gem's power; and as a falcon shreds water
coots with its talons, so Baldo destroys these wretched servants
with his sword. Each of them feels some part being lopped off—
an arm or a flank—but can't make out any sword. This ill-born
clan immediately lets Boccalo go and flees here and there, hiding
in the mansion. News-bearing Rumor reaches the queen's ears,
and transforms her face into a thousand colors. She thinks it must
be a wizard, either Coclen or Seraphus, whom she had always
found to be mortal enemies. From the outer chambers she enters
an inner sanctum, where the sow normally works her magical
mutterings.

Yet in the meantime, Baldo alone had routed all the others and   632
had filled the foyers with many corpses. The cloister was left com-
pletely emptied of people, for they had thrust themselves into the
rooms and locked the doors. As Baldo leaves, he wants to take the
ass Boccalo with him. Poking him with a stick, he utters the usual
"Hyah!" as in "Hyah, beast, giddy up now!" So saying, he be-
comes a mule-driver and makes the jackass trot out through the
cloister gates. Boccalo the animal does not know who is pricking
him from behind and can't understand which miller is driving
him. He keeps turning his head around trying to figure it out, but
although he sees the prod he does not see the plowman. When
they were far away, Baldo removed the small gem from his mouth
that had made him invisible to everyone, and he shows his face to
his dear little donkey. Even though he is covered on the outside
with gray skin, when the ass realizes what noble deed Baldo has
done, he quickly stands with his legs raised, as though intending

650 rumpere qui voiat cum mula virginitatem.
     Brachia dat Baldi collo musoque bavoso,
     discretus velut est asinus, dat basia bocchae.
     Non potuit Baldus non magnum rumpere risum,
     quando tanta sibi tunc machina venit adossum;
655 attamen, ut cunctis erat ille benignior altris,
     qui cortesiae causa discommoda nescit,
     saepeque vilificat semet gentilis ad omnes,
     sustinet amplexus atque oscula foeda Bocali,
     et quater eiusdem per se desgratia fleta est.
660 Postea, de sociis si sciret forte coëllum
     chiedit; at ille asini cum bocca raggiat et urlat,
     nec brancare potest Baldus quid ragget et urlet.
     Ergo dum lingua, manibus quoque, dicere nescit,
     annuit almancum scossisque moteggiat orecchis
665 ut Baldus, sese quo praeparat ire, sequatur.
     Baldus it a tergo plantasque observat aselli.
     Non procul ecce iterum venit obvia pulchra puella,
     quam modo cum secum falsus Pasquinus habebat.
     Ipsa quidem tunc sex animalia fune ligarat:
670 taurum, aprum, lyncem, simiam vulpemque, cavallum,
     retroque tirabat, posita feritate, tot agnos.
     At propius Baldo venienti quando propinquant,
     protinus incipiunt calzis et cornibus atque
     morsibus obniti, cercantes rumpere cordas.
675 Miratur Baldus, remanensque interrogat illam
     quae sua vel virtus vel fraus animalia vincat.
     Nil maga respondet, sed nectit in arbore funem
     contraque barronem turpis meretricula currit.
     'Mecum (si sapias)' dicebat, 'splendide barro,
680 mecum balneolos venies intrare paratos.
     Utere me liber; formosula, respice, quam sum.
     Candidulas habeo genulas rubeosque labrettos.

to breach his virginity with a she-mule. He throws his arms around Baldo's neck and with his drooling muzzle, as discreet as any ass, kisses him on the mouth. Baldo could not help bursting into laughter when such a huge thing comes on to him. Yet Baldo was always very obliging with all the others; out of graciousness he ignores discomfort and being kind often humbles himself to everyone. He endures Boccalo's hugs and repulsive kisses and weeps for his misfortune four times.

Afterwards Baldo asks if perhaps he knows anything about   660
their companions, but Boccalo brays and neighs with his donkey's mouth, and Baldo cannot grasp what he brays and neighs. Therefore, unable to speak with his tongue or his hands, Boccalo at least nods and talks with flapping ears so that Baldo will follow him where he intends to go. Baldo walks behind him and follows the donkey's footsteps.

Not far from there, behold! the pretty girl meets them again,   667
the one that had been with the false Pasquino. This time she had bound six animals with a rope—a bull, a boar, a lynx, a monkey, a fox and a horse—and as they had laid aside their ferocity, she was leading them behind her like so many lambs. Yet as soon as they get closer to Baldo, who is approaching, they begin immediately to resist the girl with kicks, bites and butting horns, trying to break the rope. Baldo is amazed and holding back, questions her: What power of hers or what trick subdues the animals? The sorceress doesn't answer, but secures the rope to a tree. Then the vile little trollop runs up to him, saying, "Come with me (if you know how), my splendid knight, come with me into the baths which await us. Have your way with me; gaze on how beautiful I am. I

Fessulus es, nec ego minus exto lassula: mecum
languidulos foveat noster tibi lectulus artus'.
685 Sic ait, et Baldo sinulum lassivula solvit,
et dare basiolum celerat putanella baroni.
Baldus eam subito cognoverat esse puellam,
quam nuper vidit peregrinam cum peregrino.
Transmutasse suos compagnos iudicat illam
690 inque animalorum fazzas voltasse tapinos.
Ergo manu celeri per trezzas corripit atque
mobilior gatto saltat cum graffat osellum.
At desdegnatur fragilem vir battere sexum;
sat sibi bastat enim quod primum tornet ad esse
695 illa sibi socios, et vadat postea quo vult.
Nudam ergo spoiat, sed, dum spoiatur, in unam
coepit converti vecchiazzam, dentibus orbam,
sguerzam calcagnis, oculis et lumine gobbam.
Baldus, garofolum qui se brancasse putarat,
700 hanc ubi prae manibus miravit habere carognam,
protinus obsoenam stomacosa fronte relinquit.
Illa cito scampat, nudatis undique membris.
Dumque stat in pedibus Baldus mirare quo ibat,
adfuit huc subito facies veneranda Seraphi
705 expediensque suas magicis cum versibus artes,
circulat in sabia numeros, quibus omne trematur
protinus Infernum veniuntque infrotta diabli.
Hic magus astringit cornutos carmine porcos
tollere praestrigium nostrasque reducere formas
710 humanis oculis et res monstrare prout sunt.
Spingitur extemplo simiae de corpore Cingar,
de bove Fracassus balzat, de linze Lyronus,
Hippol singiarum disvestit protinus aprum,
de toto Centaurus equo fit mezus, et ipse

have pure white cheeks and red lips. You are worn out, and I am just as weary. Our little bed will warm your languid limbs with me."

Having said this, she lasciviously bared her small breasts to   685
Baldo, and then the little whore hurried to give the baron a kiss.
Baldo had immediately recognized her as the pilgrim girl he'd seen earlier with the pilgrim man. He deduces that it is she who transformed his companions, changing the appearance of the poor men into that of animals. So, he jumps and instantly snatches her by the hair with his hand, faster than a cat when it snags a bird. Yet as a man he disdains to defeat the weaker sex: suffice it that she restores his companions to their former selves; after that, she can go where she will. So he strips her naked, but as he strips her, she starts to turn into an old hag, blind in her teeth, cross-eyed in her heels and hunchbacked in the light of her eyes.

Baldo thought he'd grabbed a carnation, but, seeing that he   699
held carrion in his hands, with a look of disgust he lets go of this obscenity at once. She quickly runs off, her limbs completely naked. While Baldo stood there watching where she was going, the venerable figure of Seraphus promptly appeared. Drawing on his skill with magic formulas, he encircles numbers in the sand, and thanks to these, all hell instantly trembles and devils arrive in hordes. With his spell the sorcerer compels these horned pigs to dispel the enchantment and to restore our forms to the human eye and to show things as they really are. Forthwith, Cingar emerges from the monkey's body; Fracasso leaps from the ox; Lirone from the lynx; Hippol quickly strips himself of the wild boar; from a full horse the centaur becomes a half; Falchetto throws off the fox

715 Falchettus vulpem reicit, Boccalus asellum.
Mutavere pilos, si vezzum nescio certe.

At quia candela est ad virdum usque culamen,
at quia consumpsit vodata lucerna stopinum,
multa per adessum dixi, damatina venito.

Liber vigesimus quartus

Iamque suae gentis satis amplam Gelphora caedem
audierat nec non propriis aspexerat occhis.
Obstupet, ac facti dum cercat scire casonem,
ecce supragiungit nudis vecchia illa culattis,
5 quae Baldi artilios peradessum fugerat uncos.
Qualis multoties vulpazza fugita taiolis,
cui sex turba fugam dederit villana miaros
scridaritque retro: 'Day, day! pia, para, repara!'
ipsaque scaltra ferens caudam de retro levatam,
10 indeque puzziferas vomitans culamine loffas,
fecerit assaium sanam portasse gonellam,
anxiat et brazzum linguae butat extra ganassas;
talis vecchia quidem, vecchiarum stronzus, arivat,
gentis amorbatrix, quae nunc ita bella parebat.
15 Ansat et ansando narrat vidisse legiadri
zuffum hominis, quo non vultu rubestior alter;
forte cavallerum unum de errantibus esse,
qui velut Orlandus veniat destruggere fatas;
octoque cum secum armatos guidare barones,
20 qui possent solis coelum confundere sguardis.
Hos tamen in vistas varias cangiasse ferarum,
rendere qui secum voluere libidinis actum.
Illius at castos mores animumque baronis

396

and Boccalo the ass. They have changed skins; as for their vices, I'm not certain.

Yet, since the candle is right down to its butt, and since the empty lantern has consumed the wick, for now I have said plenty. Come back tomorrow morning!

Book XXIV

By now Gelfora had heard about the full-scale slaughter of her people, and had even seen it with her own eyes. She's astonished, and while she tries to learn the cause of these events, lo! an old woman with naked buttocks shows up—the one who had for the moment escaped Baldo's sharp claws. She was just like a wily fox that has evaded traps many times, pursued by peasant mobs, shouting behind it, "Come on, come on, get it, stop it, corner it!"—and the clever thing, holding its tail raised in back and vomiting foul-smelling gas from its butt, does well enough to carry off its hide in one piece; it pants and sticks out a foot of tongue from its jaws. Just so the old woman, truly a turd among old women, arrives—a plague on the people now, she who before seemed so beautiful. She wheezes and while wheezing recounts how she has seen the face of a handsome man whose face is ruddier than any other. Perhaps he is one of the errant knights who like Orlando comes to destroy the sorcerers and to lead eight armed knights with him, a man who could confound the heavens with a mere glance. Those knights, however, were changed into various animal shapes for wanting to commit a lustful act with her, but the courage and chaste conduct of the one knight had restored them all

1

ad propriam subito cunctos tornasse figuram.
25 Nil pulchras valuisse sibi nudasse mamillas,
nulla superstitio quippe illum, nulla lusinga
ingannare potest; hunc forsitan esse Seraphi
aguaitum, qui semper habet pensiria calda
ut ruat omnino felicia regna stryarum.
30 Quapropter fieri debere provisio talis
qualis multorum faciat pentire pacias,
qui sic praesumant cum diis committere pugnam.
    Gelfora quam primum facier cotalia sensit,
praesta suam mandat sibi retro currere guardam.
35 Fit cridor armorumque sonus crepitusque tubarum,
campanae ad don don fitur concursio gentis
intornumque suae calcatur squadra reinae.
Sed diavolorum legiones mille tresentae,
quae simul hic inter miseros squaquarare solebant,
40 protinus (experti quondam quae forcia Baldi est)
inde levant campum cercantve altronde loginos.
Senserat hunc Baldus strepitum. 'Seguitate, sodales'
dixit, et adversus palazzum dirrigit ormam.
En procul apparens maga Gelfora, fortius urlat
45 bestia, cum Baldum vidit, comitantibus altris.
Haec super auratam celerat tirata carettam,
quam seguitant etiam nympharum quinque barozzi.
Non umquam regina fuit pomposior ista.
Quattuor albentes palafreni, terga coperti
50 drappibus ex auro, strassinant retro quadrigam.
Ipsa tenetque manu sceptrum doramque coronam
in testa, et rutilo trezzas diademate calcat.
Praecedunt famuli centum totidemque staferi;
quisque galone tenet seu spadam sive fachinum.
55 Longa sequit series hominum muschiata zibettis,
qui cortesanos se vantant esse tilatos;

to their proper appearance. It had done no good to bare her beautiful breasts to him, and of course no enchantment, no flattery could deceive him. Maybe this was an ambush from Seraphus, who at all times nurtures fervent hopes of completely overthrowing the happy kingdom of the witches. Therefore, measures should be taken so that all those who presume to do battle thus with the gods will repent of their folly.

As soon as Gelfora has heard what's happening, she immediately commands her guard to follow her in haste. A cry goes up, the din of arms, the clash of horns, and then, at the ding-dong of the bells, there was a convergence of people, and the army pressed in around its queen. But the 1300 legions of devils that usually sported among these wretches had now felt Baldo's might—and had straightaway decamped to look for lodgings elsewhere. Baldus had heard this commotion. "Follow me, companions!" he says and directs his tracks towards the palace. 33

Behold, in the distance, the sorceress Gelfora appears; the creature screams more loudly when she sees Baldo with the others accompanying him. She races off, drawn on a golden carriage, followed by five coaches of nymphs. There was never a queen more pompous than she. Their backs covered with golden trappings, four white palfreys drag her carriage behind them. She carries a scepter in her hand and a gold crown on her head, and presses down her locks with a glittering diadem. 44

A hundred servants precede her and as many grooms; each of them keeps a sword or dagger at his side. A long line of men follows: perfumed with civet, they claim to be refined courtiers; but 53

quorum si videas mores rationis ochialo,
non homines maschios, sed dicas esse bagassas.
Cortesanus erat tunc verus tempore vecchio,
60 cum rex ille produs, rex ille bonissimus Artu,
egregiam tenuit chortem tavolamque rotundam.
Quis fuerit scitur Tristanus Lanzaque lottus,
quis quoque Galvanus, nec non bella altra brigata,
quae regis fameia fuit, pulchraeque Ginebrae.
65 Tunc Amor indossum seu faldam sive corazzam
portabat, colpisque spadae acquistabat honorem.
Cui sudoris aquae, cui siccae pulvis arenae
muschius et ambracanus fuerant storaxque Levanti.
Tunc cortigiani facies fuit apta placendi
70 et molzinandi rigidae praecordia damae,
quando lavabatur solo sudore celatae,
quando nigrabatur sabiis sub sole boiento.
Tempore sed nostro, proh dii!, secloque dadessum,
non nisi perfumis variis et odore zibetti,
75 non nisi seu sazarae petenentur sive tosentur,
brettis velluti nec non scufiotibus auri,
auri cordiculis, impresis atque medais,
millibus et frappis per calzas perque giupones,
cercamus charum merdosi germen amoris.
80 En modo, dum celerem castigat Gelfora cocchium
subsequitantque aliae vaccarum quinque carettae,
has veluti nymphas, divas charasque madames,
cortesanelli sociant illisque ragionant
nescio quos sognos, passata in nocte vedutos;
85 et portantinas properantes supra mulettas,
dente bachettinas vadunt rodendo politas
mentitosque focos narrant recitantque sonettos
sat male stringatos ac parlant mille baianas,
menchionasque suo dicunt in amore fusaras.

if you were to examine them with an objective eye, you would say that they are not virile men, but harlots. A true courtier existed back in the olden days, when that valiant king, the most excellent King Arthur, held an illustrious court and Round Table. One knows who Tristan was and Lancelot and who Gawain was too, and all the other good men who were in the service of the king and of beautiful Guinevere. Back then, Love wore a cuisse or a breastplate and acquired honor with sword blows. Love regarded rivulets of sweat and dust from the dry arena as amber and musk and storax from the Orient. Back then, the face of a courtier was able to please and to soften the heart of a stern lady when it was bathed only in the sweat of a helmet, or blackened by dirt under a burning sun. But in this day and age of ours, ye gods, only with various perfumes and the scent of civet, only with manes that are styled or trimmed and with velvet hats and caps of gold, with gold brocade and emblems and medallions and a thousand other decorations on trousers and coats, do we seek the precious seed of a shitty love.

And so it is now, while Gelfora whips her rapid coach, and five 80 other carts of cows follow behind her, darling courtiers accompany them as if they were nymphs, divas and lovely ladies, and speak to them of I don't know what dreams seen the night before. And they go bustling along on quick little mules, gnawing smooth little sticks with their teeth and reporting phony passions and reciting sonnets quite poorly strung together and telling a thousand fibs and uttering idiotic twaddle about their own loves.

90   Baldus ab altano tumulo procul omnia visu
    coeperat et ridens ita raggionabat amicis:
    'Cernite, compagni: de tantis millibus unum
    non hominem video, non qui lignaminis ensem
    disfodrare sciat, peius tirare stocatam.

95 Hi sunt, quos tantum manifestat barba viriles,
    caetera conveniunt muliebribus apta conocchis.
    Sed volo quod pulchram faciamus horhora prodezzam:
    fingamus, quaeso, fingamus habere pauram
    de meretrice ista, per quam cuncta omnia puzzant.

100 Stemus et attenti, quae nobis damna parentur'.
    Talia cum sociis dum sic sic Baldus acordat,
    ecce propinquabat tandem regina stryarum
    Gelfora, quae cernens armatos stare barones:
    'Ola! quid', inquit, 'adest? Oh res non cognita maium!

105 Cernitis humanam (quo tanta pacia?) brigatam?
    Qui sunt hi porci? Qui sunt hi brutta somenza?
    Numquid habent animo tam grandem prosopopeiam
    ut mea praesumant intrare ad regna gaioffi?'
    Dixerat, et spazzat trombettam protinus unum

110 ut sciat unde hominum veniat baldanza malorum,
    qui bastent animum sic tecta subire deorum.
    Ille galoppando non spiccat ab ore canoram
    ton tararan frifolo trombam, fin donec arivat
    Baldus ubi comitesque manent finguntque pauram.

115 Ad quos his parlat dictis trombetta superbis:
    'O poltronzones, quae phantasia guidavit
    sic vos per dominum nostrum, sic absque riguardo,
    huc ad clausuras et loggiamenta deorum?
    An fors nescitis haec esse palatia divum?

120 Tantane vos vostrae tenuit fidanza canaiae?
    Maturate fugam subitique levate trabaccas!
    Siccine bastardi, zaltrones gensque tegnosa,

Baldo had witnessed all this at a distance from a high mound   90
and, laughing, spoke thus to his friends: "Note, companions:
among all those thousands, I don't see one real man, not one who
might know how to unsheathe a wooden sword, much less make a
thrust. They are the kind that only a beard shows to be men; oth-
erwise they are like women suited to the spindle. But I want us to
try a neat trick right now. Let's pretend, I urge you, let's pretend to
be afraid of this whore who makes everything stink. And let's
watch out for the losses they are planning to inflict on us."

While Baldo arranges these things with his companions, the   101
queen of the witches was drawing near at last. Seeing the knights
standing there armed, Gelfora says, "Ho, what's this? Such a thing
is unheard of! Do you see this gang of men? Whence such mad-
ness? Who are these pigs? Who are these offspring of a nasty
race? Do these scoundrels really have such effrontery that they
presume to enter my reign?" Having spoken, she immediately dis-
patches a trumpeter to learn the source of such boldness in bad
men that gives them courage to enter the dwellings of the gods.
Galloping forth, he does not take from his mouth the trumpet
that sounds "tan-tararan" until he arrives where Baldo and his
companions wait, pretending to be afraid. Then the trumpeter
speaks to them with these haughty words: "O you big oafs, what
whim, by Our Lord, has brought you thus thoughtlessly into the
cloisters and lodgings of the gods? Are you perhaps unaware that
these are divine palaces? Have you so much faith in rabble like

gensque spelorza, sacrum venistis tangere limen?
Ad vos me mandat venerabilis illa virago
125 (Cingar ait tacitus: 'Venerabilis illa putana')
quae tenet imperium sub se regnaminis huius.
Aut vos ire iubet lontanos partibus istis,
aut scorrozzatam chini veniatis ad illam:
forte sacrificium meritabitis esse beatum,
130 humano quoniam placatur diva cruore'.
Baldus ait: 'Oh! nos istuc male nempe capati!
Cur, quando matres nostrae de ventre cagarunt,
non potius mundo tantos peperere navones?
Andemus miseri sanctum componere numen,
135 numen adoremus coeli, quod forte pregheris
spegnitur humanis natura colerica divum'.
Compagni risu tacito sub pectore creppant,
fazza tamen magnum simulat defora dolorem.
Omnes cum testis bassis andare comenzant
140 ac si, post schenam manibus colloque ligatis,
ad scalam forchae conducat boia picandos.
Tunc trombetta illos dominae praesentat et inquit:
'Ecce, prophanarunt hi vestrae regna coronae'.
Gelfora contremuit bustum tam grande Fracassi,
145 interpellat eum: qui sit, quo sanguine venit.
Respondet tremulus: 'Sturlonus nomine dicor,
Bressa mihi patria est, mea razza gigantibus illis
descendit, qui trare Iovem voluere deorsum
atque inter sese regnum partire deorum'.
150 Gelfora plus dentrum tremuit, cum talia sensit.
Postea fattezzam Baldi vistamque legiadram
dum guardat, latosque humeros strictumque fiancum,
protinus in paniam vischumque Cupidinis intrat.
Ad quem sic placidis loquitur cortesa parolis:

yourselves? Get a move on and pull up your tents right away! So you bastards, you slobs, you wormy, miserable beggars, have you come to touch the sacred threshold? I've been sent to you by that venerable virago (Cingar says *sottovoce*, 'That venerable slut') who holds sway over this kingdom. She commands that either you go far away from this realm or that you bow before her wrath. Perhaps you deserve to be a blessed sacrifice, for the goddess is placated by human gore."

Baldo says, "O, we are really unlucky to have ended up here!   131
Why, when our mothers shat us from their bellies, did they not instead bring so many turnips into the world? Let us wretches go appease this sacred divinity. Let us adore this heavenly divinity, since perhaps the angry nature of the gods can be quelled by human prayers."

The companions burst with silent laughter in their breasts, yet   137
outwardly their faces simulate great sorrow. They all begin to walk with their heads down, as though, with hands and necks tied behind their backs, the henchman is leading them to the steps of the gallows to be hanged. The trumpeter presents them to his lady and declares, "Here are those who profaned the kingdoms of your crown."

Gelfora shudders at the great size of Fracasso and asks him   144
who he is and from whom descended. He answers, trembling, "I am Sturlone. Brescia is my homeland; my race descends from those giants who wanted to pull down Jupiter and divide among themselves the kingdom of the gods."

Gelfora trembles inside even more when she hears this. After-   150
wards, when she looks at Baldo's physique and handsome face,

155 'Tu quoque, qui sensum te prodis habere superbum,
da prolem nomenque tuum, genus atque tuorum'.
Baldus respondet: 'Caposeccus nomine dicor,
natus adulterio monachae fratrisque Caponis,
qui conceperunt me chiesae retro pilastrum.
160 Postea diabolo de me fecere sigillum.
Sum devotus ei, cui dono in corpore vitam.
Unde meum patrem vado retrovare Chiapinum.
Me mare, me tellus, me sydera celsa refudant;
si non esse Dei possum, decet esse diabli'.
165 Has desperati stupuit regina parolas.
'Eya, sacerdotes', inquit, 'nunc sacra parate,
atque mihi altaros holocausti condite tantos
quantos nunc istos homines mactare bisognat.
Hunc mihi solettum tamen asservate legiadrum,
170 quem volo sit primus regali eunuchus in aula'.
Haec ea dicebat de bello corpore Baldi.
Praestiter obedit famulorum turba suorum
lignaque portantur multusque accenditur ignis.
Ecce preti et frati, cum cottis cumque capuzzis,
175 cantantes veniunt infrotta boatibus altis:
'Eu oe iach iach, eu oe, pirila, buf baf'.
Quorum qui prior est puvialem portat adossum.
Turribuli pinguem mittunt ad nubila fumum,
incensaeque faces crepitant altaria circum.
180 Gelfora supra caput montaverat alta pilastri,
ut solet in summa plantari mole colossus;
hic dea chiamari vult, hic dea porca vocari.
Trombarum clangor rauca cum voce frequentat
tarara ton tarara, ton ton tara, tantara taira.
185 Cor brillat sociis spadas rancare guainis,
quos ciet ad carnes squarzandas musica trombae.
Ipse prior Cayphas insemmaque vescovus Annas

his broad shoulders and narrow hips, she at once steps into Cupid's birdlime and viscous mistletoe. She speaks to him courteously with these gentle words, "And also you, who display a proud spirit, tell me your name and lineage and the position of your family."

Baldo responds, "I am called Dryhead, born of the adultery of a   157 nun and Brother Capon, who engendered me behind a church pillar. Afterwards, they dedicated me to the devil. I am devoted to him, and offer the life in my body to him. Hence I am off to find my father, Hellion. The sea, the earth and the heavenly stars reject me. If I can't be God's, I should be the devil's."

The queen is amazed by these words of a desperado. "Come   165 now, priests," she says, "prepare for the sacrament and build me as many altars for the holocaust as there are men who must now be sacrificed. However, save this one lovely man for me: I want him to be the number-one eunuch in the royal palace." She was saying this because of Baldo's gorgeous body.

The multitude of her servants promptly obeys: wood is brought   172 and a large fire is lit. And here are brothers and friars with their surplices and their cowls: swarms of them come singing in loud croaks, "Euhoe, yack yack, euhoe, pirila, boof baff." The one who is their prior wears an alb. Thuribles send up greasy smoke to the clouds, and incense burners crackle around the altars. Gelfora has ascended to the top of a pillar's high crown, like a colossal statue placed above a pedestal. Here she wants to be called goddess, here a sow is to be hailed as goddess! The clash of trumpets repeats with a raucous voice: "Tarara ton tarara ton ton tara tantara taira."

accedunt, iugulumque parant scannare Fracasso,
inque satis largo tepidum addunare cruorem
190 vase parecchiatur, meschiandum pane stryarum.
Praecipitur curvos illi bassare ginocchios,
quem prius ut vaccam cum caetta cumque securi
discopare volunt, mox collo immergere cultrum.
Ille sed impatiens clamavit: 'Balde, facenda haec
195 it nimis avantum, nimis haec indusia durat'.
Talia dum memorat, se drizzat in aëra praestus
pontificemque piat digitis durosque restringit
artilios schiazzatque illum de more boazzae,
dextraque de merdis et sanguine tincta remansit.
200 Baldus adocchiarat guerram iam esse comenzam:
'Heus! Seguitate!', inquit, sfodratque celerrimus ensem.
Currit ad urtandam, quam diximus ante, colonnam,
cuius in excelso capitello Gelfora stabat.
Cum caput innanzum ruit illa simulque pilastrum,
205 quam piat extemplo Baldus per colla cridantem,
cui dare soccorsum gens infinita ruebat.
Sed Cingar comitesque alii, facto agmine, currunt
inque illas squadras intrant ut fulmen et ignis.
Ipse gigas clamat: 'Nunc est et tempus et hora
210 sacrificare Deo vacchasque hircosque petulcos'.
Sic dicendo, probat qualis sit tempra bachiocchi.
'Ah porcinaiae!' cridat Falchettus; et Hippol:
'Vosne putavistis nos qualchos esse maruffos,
scilicet agnellos pegorasque trovastis et haedos,
215 ut pensaretis sic nos mactare diablo?'
Talia bravando feriunt tutavia, nec ullum
sparagnant colpum testasque ad sydera mandant.
Septem mille homines sunt, qui sua ferra cavarant
et Baldum assaltant propter riscodere porcam.
220 At celer altorium dat Falco et Cingar et Hippol,

The comrades' hearts burn to snatch their blades from their   185
sheaths, for the music of the trumpets incites them to shred flesh.
The prior Caiaphas comes forth together with the bishop Annas,
and they prepare to slit Fracasso's jugular vein. Quite a large vessel
is readied to gather the tepid blood that will be mixed with
witches' bread. He is instructed to lower himself on bended knees,
because they want to slaughter him like a cow with a hatchet and
an ax first, then plunge a knife into his neck. But he called out im-
patiently, "Baldo, this matter is going too far, this delay is too
long!" Uttering these words, he quickly straightens up in the air
and grabs the pontiff with his fingers and, tightening his hard tal-
ons, squashes him like a cow pie; his right hand is now stained
with blood and shit.

Baldo recognized that war had already begun. "Hey, follow   200
me!" he says, and very swiftly unsheathes his sword. He runs to
knock down the column, which we mentioned above, on whose el-
evated capital Gelfora was standing. She plummets head first,
along with the column. Baldo seizes the screaming woman in-
stantly by the neck as countless people rush to her aid. But Cingar
and his comrades, having formed ranks, run up and penetrate
these squadrons like lightning and fire. The giant yells, "The time
and the hour have come to sacrifice to God cows and butting billy-
goats." Saying this, he measures the temper of his clapper.

"Ah, you herd of pigs!" yell Falchetto and Hippol. "Did you   212
think we were just some clods? That you'd found lambs, sheep and
goats, so that you thought you'd sacrifice us just like that to the
devil?" Blustering thus, they continue to strike and spare no blows,
dispatching heads up to the stars. There are seven thousand men

Moschinusque aliique simul, qui tempore curto
mortorum ingenti fabricarunt aggere montem.
Turba puellarum fractis fugit inde carettis,
smarritaeque sinus lacerant rumpuntque capillos.

225   Non bonus hic perdit Boccalus tempus, at illas
protinus inseguitat chiamando: 'State ribaldae!
state putanellae, quia vos frustare bisognat.
Quo? quo? State! Inquam; ola! Spettate! quo itis?
quove scapinatis? Mea nunc vendetta fietur.

230   Siccine me nuper vacchae fecistis asellum?
siccine grattastis mihi schenam pectine boschi?'
Haec referens, portat scoriadam forte trovatam
qualem Vegnesae vidi, cum boia putanas
per Merzariam frustat frustandoque currit;

235   tandem arrivatas chioccat tozzatque tapinas,
attamen alquantum sferzam leggerius offert,
dum capat in teneras damas niveasque putinas;
tantum scarcossas vecchias lippasque stryazzas
et rofianazzas stafilatis tozzolat aspris,

240   terga quibus parere facit persutta Labruzzi.
Non 'Pietas!' valet hic, non 'Perdonanza!' cridari,
nam mercadanti Boccalus fecerat aures.

    Baldus at in brazzis reginam portat et illam
continuo gens tota ruens riscodere cercat;

245   unde travaius erat certando baronibus ingens,
tanta superchiabat calcatim zurma bravorum.
Personat incircum campagna cridoribus altis
unde maris pisces veniunt atterra balordi,
namque super pendet pelagus de more solari.

250   Tunc homines superi (nec enim scio dire bugiam)
audivere illam liquido sub gurgite guerram.
Iamque striam Baldus multo sudore ligarat
inque suis spallis quoddam portarat in antrum.

who'd pulled out their weapons and attacked Baldo in order to res-
cue the sow. But Falchetto quickly succors him and Cingar and
Hippol and Moschino and all the others, too; in short order they
fashion a mountain with a huge pile of the dead. Then, with their
coaches shattered, the throng of girls flees and forlorn, tear at their
breasts and pull out their hair. The good Boccalo does not waste
any time now. He promptly chases them, calling, "Stop, you hus-
sies! Stop, you little whores, because you need to be flogged! O
where, where are you going? Stop, I say! Hey, wait, where are you
going? Where are you running off to? Now I will have my re-
venge. So you cows made me into an ass, did you? So, you beat
my back with a wooden rake?"

As he says this, Boccalo wields a strap that he'd found by   232
chance. I once saw such a strap in Venice at the time when the ex-
ecutioner flogs whores in the Merceria, and in order to flog them,
runs after them; reaching the poor things at last, he batters and
flays them. However, he applies the lash a bit more gently when
dealing with tender young ladies and snowy-white girls. But he
thrashes only bony old women, cross-eyed witches and ugly bawds
with harsh slashes, and makes their backs look like prosciutto
from Abruzzo. It does them no good now to cry "Have pity!" or
"Have mercy!" for Boccalo had turned a merchant's ear to them.

Baldo in turn carries off the queen in his arms, and all her peo-   243
ple try to rescue her, rushing forward over and over, so that it was
a huge struggle for the barons to fight, so overwhelming was the
team of guards pressing in. The countryside all around reverber-
ates with loud cries, and the fish in the sea wash ashore stunned,
for their ocean is suspended above like a ceiling. It was at that time

Non gens ultra sequit, vel mortua vel stropiata,
255   parsque fugae studiat cercatque per abdita scampum.
Gelfora, iam tristo portu guidata, diablos
invocat ut veniant promissam tollere vitam.
Sic igitur dum stridet adhuc, malnata piatur
unguibus innumeris diavolorum forte cridantum
260   umbraque in Infernum cum corpore fertur ab illis.
       Iamque fracassandi domicilia sporca Fracassus
coeperat impresam longisque ut passibus ibat;
quo iam Gelforeos de fundo ad tecta palazzos
sterneret ac mundum tanto privaret afanno.
265   Ad primam subito giuntam de marmore grossum
chioccat pillastrum, quod stat cantone palazzi.
Rumpitur in centum volitantes undique pezzos
fitque ingens strepitus de travis deque quadrellis,
magnaque terreno camerarum banda ruinat,
270   calzinaeque leves malnettant astra volando.
Replicat horribiles colpos geminatque bataium,
trita columnarum fit rutpio, deque supernis
machina muraliis reboans descendit abassum.
Indorata cadunt meschiatis tecta matonis
275   riccaque picturis vadunt solaria terrae.
Dumque gigas manibus turrim furibundus aferrat,
ecce Seraphus adest in fretta vocatque cridatque:
'Parce, gigas, iam parce, gigas! Sic poena soluta est.
Integra stet turris pro nunc, quae quando ruatur,
280   illico quae cernis pelagi fundamina sursum
pendula cascabunt, veluti natura chinarat,
vosque negabimini piscesque cibabitis omnes.
Si nescis, turri septem clauduntur in ista
fatales statuae, sex coerae, septima plumbi,
285   quas simul ad quintam lunam, sub monte Tonalo
composuere striae septem: Madoia, Catoia,

that people living on the earth above (I don't even know how to tell a lie) heard this war under the watery depths. By now, with a lot of sweat, Baldo had tied up the witch and carried her on his shoulders into a cavern somewhere. Her people are no longer in pursuit, for they are dead or maimed; some of them attempt flight, and look for escape in secret places. Gelfora, having been led to this tragic port, calls to the devils to come and take the life promised them. In this way, therefore, still screaming, the doomed woman is grabbed by the countless claws of devils shouting loudly, and her shade, with her body, is taken by them to hell.

Fracasso had already begun the task of raising a fracas among the filthy abodes. He walked with long strides now to destroy Gelfora's palaces from the foundations to the rooftops and free the world from great torment. To begin with, he immediately knocks down a solid pillar of marble that stands in a corner of the palace. It breaks into a hundred pieces that fly everywhere, making a tremendous crash of beams and bricks; and a large suite of rooms crashes to the ground as flying plaster dust soils the stars. He intensifies and redoubles the horrible blows of his clapper. There is a collapse of splintered columns and the whole structure comes rumbling down from the high walls. The gilded ceilings collapse amid sundry bricks, and the richly painted vaults fall to the ground. And just as the furious giant seizes a tower in his hands, behold, Seraphus hastens forth and calls out and shouts, "Stop, giant! Stop already, giant! The crime has been punished. Let the tower stand intact for now. If it were destroyed, the bottom of the ocean, which you see hanging there, would instantly crash down, as nature dictates, and you would all drown and feed the fish. If you don't know, there are seven enchanted statues en-

261

Stanaque, Birla soror, Sberliffaque, Cantara, Dina.
Quam primum frangas turrim guastesve figuras,
postizzus locus hic in fumum protinus ibit,
290 vosque bibetis aquas plus quam sit voia bibendi'.
   Venerat huc Baldus, mazzatis denique cunctis,
conciliumque suis cum compagnonibus edit
et quid sit tandem faciendum voce domandat.
Cingar ad infernas suadet callare masones,
295 quas Serraphus ait non multum longe catari.
Haecve relinquatur Serrapho impresa ruendi
regna stryanismi, turrem statuasque levandi.
Tunc omnes favere manu, favere parolis
Cingaris arditae menti laudantque talentum
300 hunc animi, quo non mundo generosior alter.
Attamen ipse manet, Baldo mandante, Gibertus,
quem retinet secum Serraphus amatque galantum.
Ad Phlegethontaeas igitur cascare cavernas
voia stat, una quidem Baldo paret horula centum
305 posse diabolicas rursum assaggiare prodezzas.
Ecce iterum scuras animoso corde latebras
introëunt callantque magis per clymata centri.
Gemma tamen fulget, quam Baldus servat in elmo,
qua cernunt aditus et multa pericula schivant.
310 Semper ad in giusum facili labente camino
frettantes abeunt, Baldi praeeunte lusoro.
Centum stradiculas centumque viacula iam iam
incipiunt reperire simul cuncurrere in unam
ingentem stradam variis venientia bandis.
315 Dico quod innumeras retrovant hinc inde viettas
derivare suos fines ad grande viaggium,
quem spatiosa menat Stygiis contrada paësis.
Quales in Veneta nos cernimus urbe canales
undique menantes barcas, descendere in unum

closed in this tower—six of wax, and the seventh of lead. They were built on the fifth day of the moon at the base of Mount Tonalo by seven witches: Madoia, Catoia, Stana, her sister Birla, and Sberliffa, Cantara and Dina. The moment you would shatter the tower and smash the statues, this artificial place would instantly go up in smoke and you would drink more water than you'd want to."

Having at last killed all the rest, Baldo arrives and forms a 291 council with his companions and asks what should be done at the last. Cingar suggests they go down to the infernal dwellings, which Seraphus says are found not very far away. And they should leave to Seraphus the task of destroying the kingdom of witchcraft and of razing the tower and statues. Then they all show support by hands and words of Cingar's daring ideas, and they praise his force of mind, for there is no nobler man in the world. Nonetheless, by Baldo's command, Gilberto remains behind; Seraphus keeps this gallant man with him and loves him. So then, a desire is expressed to descend to the caves of Phlegethon; and even a brief hour seems like a hundred to Baldo until once again he can sample diabolical deeds.

Behold, they enter again the dark shadows with brave hearts 306 and descend further along the slopes of hell. The gem that Baldo keeps in his helmet is still glowing, and lets them detect the pathway and avoid many dangers. Always heading downward, they hasten along a smooth and easy path, preceded by Baldo's light. Soon they start to discover a hundred little streets, a hundred little roads coming from all sides to flow together into one immense street. I mean that they find innumerable alleys from this side and

320 maiorem bravumque nimis grossumque canalem,
tales stradiculae, calles, sentiria mille
conveniunt monstrantque notas ea singula scriptas,
unde potest sciri qua quisque caminus ab urbe
huc descendat agatque suas huc illa brigatas.
325 Est via quam drizzat Florentia, Roma, Milanus,
Zenova, Neapoli, Vegnesia, Parma, Bologna,
Lyon, Avignonus, Parisus, Buda, Valenza,
Constantinopoli, Cairus, sedesque Cipadae.
Denique quodque solum, quaeque urbs, arx, villa, caminum
330 huc drizzat portatque suas ad tartara pravas
malnatasque animas, quarum tot milia nigrum
continuo ingombrant baratrum, quot milia toto
muscarum mundo nascunt in millibus annis.
Quo magis ante itur, magis orbita largior umbras
335 excipit innumeras, tacito rumore gementes.
Baldus compagnis nulli parlare comandat;
dumque illi parent, dumque alta silentia servant,
ecce caput stradae sese dilatat in amplam
campagnam, horribilem et cinerum de pulvere carcam.
340 Subterrana illic ventorum flamina regnant,
pro quibus efficitur mundo teremotus in isto;
impetuosa ferunt cineres agitantque savornam
per largos campos, redolentes sulphuris oybo.
Gaudet in hac rerum Baldus novitate, Lyronem
345 admonet atque alios nulla de sorte pavere.
'Quid?' Falchettus ait, 'dum te, mi Balde, videmus,
non sgomentabit nos quanta canaia sub orco
stat diavolorum, nec quanta sub aëre stridet'.
Dixerat et saltans animo se monstrat alegro
350 contraque terribiles ventos ruit huc, ruit illuc.
Cingar eum sequitur scherzando trufantque vicissim;
ambo simul rident, saltant vaduntque reduntque.

that, redirecting their borders into a great thoroughfare, which leads into the spacious regions of Stygian lands. As we see in the city of Venice, canals carrying boats from every direction, which then flow down into one Grand Canal, very mighty and wide, just so, a thousand little streets, lanes and corridors converge. And each one displays a written sign to make known from which city each pathway comes down to this place and leads its people here. Florence directs a road there, and Rome, Milan, Genoa, Naples, Venice, Parma, Bologna, Lyon, Avignon, Paris, Budapest, Valencia, Constantinople, Cairo and the settlement of Cipada. In short, every land, city, fortress and villa directs a pathway here and carries its corrupt, doomed souls to Tartarus: there are as many thousands of these incessantly encumbering the black depths as there are thousands of flies born all over the world in a thousand years.

The further one goes ahead, the wider is the roadway that receives the countless shades groaning with a hushed sound. Baldo orders his companions to speak to no one. And while they obey, while they keep deep silence, behold! the top of the road is expanding into a broad field, horrid and covered with the ash of embers. Subterranean blasts of wind reign there, which cause earthquakes in this world. These blustering winds carry ashes and stir up dust across the broad fields that emit a stench of sulfur. 334

Baldo delights in this novelty of events, and counsels Lirone and the others not to fear anything of the sort. "So what?" says Falchetto. "As long as we can see you, my Baldo, we will not be daunted by all the devil hordes that live in Orcus, nor all that 344

Quales agnelli fugiunt matremque relinquunt
quattuor et pedibus guizzant et in aëra pirlant;
355 ast ubi sentitur lupus exurlare propinquus,
confestim pavidi se matris ad ubera tornant;
pastor adest grossumque canem sibi chiamat apressum;
talis Falchettus laeto cum Cingare spassum
grande piat curruntque ambo lontanius altris;
360 ast improvisos prigolos si forte catabant,
praestiter ad portum Baldi remeare videbas,
inde sub illius combattere fortiter umbra.
Qui, velut avvezzat caporalis providus, ipse
de se non curat, tantum risguardat amicos.
365 Ad caput interea campagnae scurus et asper
boscus adest ac sylva pavens, non consita myrthis,
non lauris, platanis, ulmis altisque cipressis;
at nigrae taxus, aconita malaeque cicutae,
grandilitate pares alpino in culmine fagis,
370 toxica mortiferi sudant de cortice sughi.
Introit ante alios Baldus, nova cernere gaudet
perque venenifluas nihil aestimat ire latebras.
Incipiunt iam longe gravem sentire bagordum,
murmur et insolitum, tamquam tempesta petrarum,
375 vel magis ad guisam pelagi battentis arenam,
quando fremit vastasque polo subgurgitat undas.
In finem boschi retrovant intramina grandis
portazzae, numquam chiusae, sed semper apertae,
per quam trenta pares intrant insemma carettae,
380 verbaque sic duro saxi frontale notantur:
'Regia Luciferi dicor, bandita tenetur
chors hic, intrando patet ast uscendo seratur'.
Fracassus ridet: 'Subeamus adunca, sodales!
Non regrediendi dabitur, ut cerno, facultas'.

scream through the air." After saying this, he jumps about and shows himself in a happy mood, rushing this way and that against the terrible winds. Cingar follows him, joking around, and they play pranks on each other; they laugh together and gambol, going back and forth; like lambs that run off and abandon their mother, they spring up on their four legs and twirl in the air—but when a wolf is heard to howl nearby, in sudden fear they return to their mother's teats, for the shepherd is there and calls a big dog to his side. In the same way, Falchetto has a romp with the joyful Cingar, and both run off far from the others. But if perchance unforeseen dangers occurred, you saw them rowing rapidly into the port of Baldo, and then fighting bravely under his shadow. And Baldo, as is the habit of a skilled leader, does not care about himself, but only watches out for his friends.

Meanwhile, at the end of the field is a dark and harsh wood and 365 a frightening forest, not planted with myrtle, laurel or plane trees, elms and tall cypresses, but rather with black yews, aconite and poisonous hemlock, which are as tall as beech trees on a mountaintop and from whose toxic bark ooze deadly juices. Baldo enters ahead of the others; he enjoys seeing new things and considers it nothing to walk among venom-dripping shadows. They begin to hear a dull tumult now from afar, an unusual noise like a tempest of rocks or rather like the sea beating against the shore when it shudders and disgorges vast waves skyward. At the edge of the forest, they find the entryway to a massive portal, never closed but always open, through which thirty pair of carts could enter at the same time. And on the lintel these words are inscribed in hard stone: "I am called Lucifer's kingdom. An open court is held here;

385 Introëunt igitur, tenebris appena resistit
    carbonus Baldi; sed folta in nocte tumultant,
    horrisonasque tonant scurissima regna querelas.
    Ecce tavernarus tandem barbatus in illos
    obvius accelerat vivosque in corpore mirat.
390 'Oh!', secum parlat, 'quae cosa novella videtur?'
    Sic ait et, mulcens foltos ad menta pelazzos,
    stat pensorosus, stupidus sensuque revoltat
    debeat an similes scotto invitare brigantes.
    Tandem guarnazzam cingens, brotaminis unctam:
395 'Vultis', ait, 'nostram, compagni, intrare tavernam?'
    Boccalus raptim responsum primior affert.
    'Quid cercandum aliud? Bona si tibi caneva primum,
    inde bonae quaiae, bona lonza bonique capretti,
    ecce parecchiamur simul omnia ventre locare
400 et pagare simul patefactis omnia borsis'.
    Ostus ait: 'Mecum veniatis, non mihi desunt
    et pernicones et frolla carne fasani
    et vinum garbum et vinum dulce Reami'.
    Sic ait, ingrediens, mensasque parare comandat.
405 Hunc omnes seguitant, sed Baldus inanzior altris
    compagnisque facit per opaca silentia scortam,
    donec eos salam conduxerat ostus in amplam,
    in qua mille animas epulis catavere sedentes
    mangiantesque instar porcorum dente famato.
410 Sunt etenim magrae vultu nigraeque colore,
    sunt sguerzae, gobbae, slancatae suntque carognis
    omnibus aequandae nimio puzzore malorum.
    Irruit ad mensam iocunda fronte Bocalus,
    inque piatellum dum vult extendere griffum,
415 protinus indretum vultu pallente retirat;
    qui pensando aliquem forsan gremire caponem,
    gremiturus erat scurzum turpemque marassum.

it lies open to anyone entering, but is closed to any who would depart." Fracasso laughs, "Let's go in then, comrades. As far as I can see, we won't be allowed to come back out."

So they enter, and Baldo's ruby scarcely resists the shadows; but 385 in the dense night horrible-sounding lamentations reverberate and thunder in the darkest realms. At last, a bearded tavern-keeper hastens to meet them. Seeing them alive in their bodies, "O!" he exclaims to himself, "What marvel is this?" He speaks thus and, stroking the dense bristles on his chin, he remains thoughtful and, in a quandary, turns over in his mind: should he invite such brigands to be his customers? Finally, putting on a nasty apron greasy with gravy, he asks, "Would you like to enter our tavern, fellows?"

Boccalo rapidly offers the first response, "What more could 396 anyone look for? If, to begin with, you have a good cellar and good quail, good beef and good goat, then we are prepared to fit it all into our bellies and at the same time to pay for it all with wide-open purses."

The innkeeper says, "Come with me. I have no lack of par- 401 tridge and tender cuts of pheasant, or dry wine and sweet Neapolitan wine." Thus he speaks as he enters and orders a table to be laid. They all follow him in, with Baldo in front of the others, for he serves as guide for his companions through the opaque silence, until the innkeeper had led them into a large hall in which they found a thousand souls seated at a banquet and eating like pigs with famished teeth. And yet they are thin in the face and black in color; they are cross-eyed, hunch-backed, lame and in every way resemble carcasses with a strong stench of disease. Boccalo rushes to the table with a happy mien, but when he goes to put his mitt

Accedit propius, factum discernere, Baldus.
Quali cum guisa gattum rosegare codaium
420 aspicias, quando sibi retro cauda tiratur
striccaturque simul, manibus perforza retentus,
qui fremit et faciens gnao gnao se ingordus anegat;
illas sic animas contemplat Baldus edentes
vipeream carnem, rospos variasque vivandas,
425 unde venenorum mors invitabilis exit.
Praeterea aspideo completas sanguine tazzas
sorbebant oculosque foras sorbendo butabant,
ut solet infirmus cui ierae pocula dentur.
Corripit interea rigidam post fercula sferzam
430 ostus et intornum menando licentiat illas,
namque novas alias quoque pasturare bisognat.
Impetuosae igitur abeunt subeuntque novellae,
quas etiam cogit putridis accumbere mensis.
Mox ait ad Baldum sociosque: 'Sedete, bricones,
435 seu vos mangietis, seu non mangiare voiatis,
omnino faciet mysterum solvere scottum'.
Sic dicens, alzat scoriatae quinque catenas,
hinc menat et zif zaf resonando percutit Hippol,
quem male provistum tollit de peso levatum
440 atque suo fratri Lyrono buttat adossum,
amboque schenadam pariter cascando piarunt.
'Illa quidem vestra est', Boccalus parlat; 'habetis
praevendam vestram; tamen hanc non curo biavam'.
Sic ait, et scapolat cantoneque delitet uno.
445 Baldus arostitum rapit improviste dragonem,
inque tavernari mostazzum concite iactat
manserit ut medio faciei stigma notatum.
Non tamen hoc tantum colpo fuit ira baronis
sat contenta; tirat cum rosto insemma saporem
450 ingentis pugni, qui dextram tozzat orecchiam,

on a plate, he snatches it back instantly, pale in the face. He thought he would grab some capon perhaps, but he found himself almost grabbing a viper or a loathsome snake. Baldo moves closer to study the matter. If you observe a cat gnawing a head of garlic when it is pulled back by the tail and squeezed and held tight in your hands, it shakes and, crying "meow! meow!" the greedy thing chokes. In just the same way, Baldo contemplates the souls eating viper flesh, toads and other foods whose poison inevitably causes death. What's more, they were drinking entire goblets of asp blood, and while sipping it, bulged out their eyes, as a sick person will do when given cups of bitter aloes to drink.

After this meal, the innkeeper snatches up a sturdy whip and,   429 cracking it around the room, drives these shades off, for there are new ones who also must graze. Hence they leave precipitously, and the new shades enter and are likewise forced to sit at the disgusting mess. Soon he speaks to Baldo and his companions, "Sit down, rascals! Whether you eat or whether you prefer not to eat, you'll still have to pay the bill in full." At this, he raises the five chains of his whip and cracks it with a *ziff-zaff* — smiting the unwary Hippol, whom he lifts straight up and flings on top of his brother Lirone; and as they fall, they both land on their backs.

"That stuff's for you," Boccalo exclaims. "You have your provi-   442 sions. I, however, am not interested in this fodder." He says this and runs off and takes refuge in a corner.

Baldo abruptly snatches a roasted dragon and hurls it violently   445 against the tavern-keeper's ugly mug, where it leaves a mark stamped in the middle of his face. Yet the hero's rage is not fully satisfied by

unde tramazzanti chioccat quoque terra sinistram.
Cingar ait ridens: 'Nondum mangiavimus, et tu,
Balde, comenzasti scottum pagare tavernae'.
Respondet Baldus: 'Sic Hippolis esca soluta est'.

455   Interea Virmazzus eas interrogat umbras:
cur veniant illam sic albergare tavernam,
curque venenosas ingoient atque tracannent
has victuarias plenosque cruore becheros.
Cui maior sic umbra gemens suspirat et inquit:

460   'Quaelibet infernis cruciatibus alma ferenda,
corpore cum primum posito descendit ad orcum,
anteque quam vadat grottas habitare statutas,
hoc diavolazzo prius invitatur ab osto,
quem Griffarostum diabolica zurma domandat.

465   Nec tamen invitum contemnere possumus istum:
nolentes etenim ferri scoriada coërcet.
Quapropter quantas animas ingombrat Avernus
iste tavernarus marzo mangiamine pascit'.
Dixerat haec; alias en rursus adire videbant,

470   unde iubet propter fastidia Baldus ab illa
compagnos betola stomacosa cedere tandem.
Protinus egressi, denso sese agmine stringunt,
namque illic adeo grossa est fuscatio noctis
ut valeas etiam gladio taliare tenebras,

475   perdere vel sese potuissent unus ab altro.
Iussu ergo Baldi modicum fecere drapellum
atque capellettis similes insemma dunantur;
namque stradiotti leggeras supra pedrinas,
quando coreriam faciunt inimica per arva,

480   non se spernazzant veluti poltrona canaia,
verum groppetto strictim calcantur in uno,
donec aquistatis parlent sperone botinis,
atque 'Cavalla, grisa! bre bre!' vel 'Pospodo' dicant.

this lone blow, so together with the roast, he throws in the sauce of a huge fist, which wallops the innkeeper's right ear so that he crashes down, smacking his left one on the ground. Laughing, Cingar says, "We haven't even eaten yet, and you, Baldo, have already begun to pay our tavern bill."

Baldo answers, "So, Hippol's supper's paid for."   454

In the meantime, Virmace is questioning the shades. Why do   455 they come thus to lodge at this tavern? And why do they swallow and gulp down these poisonous victuals and glasses full of blood? Groaning, the largest shade sighs and tells him, "Every soul that is brought to infernal suffering, as soon as it has left its body, descends to Orcus; and before it goes on to inhabit its assigned locale, it is first invited by this devilish innkeeper, whom the diabolical hordes call Griffarosto. Nor indeed are we able to disregard this invitation, for he coerces the reluctant ones with his iron whip. In this way, all the souls that encumber Avernus this tavern keeper feeds with rotten food."

He had just said this when they saw others again arriving. So in   469 disgust Baldo orders his companions to withdraw from that nauseating dive at last. Outside, they quickly pull together in close ranks, for the murkiness of the night is so dense there that you could actually cut the shadows with a blade, and they could lose each other. Therefore, on Baldo's orders, they form a small squadron and group together like mercenaries, because soldiers for hire, riding their light mounts, do not scatter like cowardly rabble when they make incursions into enemy territory, but rather press tightly

Baldus praecedens sfodratum baiulat ensem,
485 at se Boccalus numquam lontanat ab illo,
seque volunteram, dum corde tremante cacabat,
vellet in illius totum se abscondere costis.
Saepe agnusdeos faciebat fronte revolta.
Iam procul ascoltant strepitum rumoris aquosi,
490 non aliter quando laxatur brena molinis.
Baldus ad hunc sonitum tendit drizzatque pedattas,
arrivantque illuc nigras Acherontis ad undas,
qui semper, veluti Porrettae balnea, fumat.
Illic circa suas testas hinc inde volazzant
495 innumerae flentes animae vocitantque Charontem,
quas ille ad ripam debet passare sinistram;
sed non, transactis iam giornis octo, videtur.
Cingar in hoc tantum sociis longatur ab altris,
namque coactus erat natura figere termen,
500 sive super littus fungum plantare novellum,
vel potius dicam Lombardam promere quaiam.
Iamque bragas implens huc illuc ibat anasum
ut brachetta solet, quae leprem china sausat.
Sed non hic leporem, sed non trovat ille caprettum,
505 sed iuvenem mortum, quo sic improvidus urtat
quantos unde pilos habuit per corpus arizzat.
Nec destringatis bene tunc in littore calzis
sese bassarat, fosso nascostus in uno,
totum per calzas se repperit esse zibettum:
510 nam cagarella metu procedit saepe gaiardo,
immo paura magis poterit bastabilis esse
destiticare cito stiticas in ventre budellas
quam per chrysterii pivam decoctio malvae.
Cingar se retrahit, ceu qui pede presserit anguem,
515 et iuvenem attonita guatabat mente galantum,
qui stramortitus re vera, non ibi mortus

into a single knot, until they can talk about the booty they acquired with their spurs, saying, "Giddy-up now, horse! Hyah, hyah!" or "Gospodin!"

Leading the way, Baldo carries his sword drawn. Boccalo never   484
willingly leaves his side; while beshitting himself with a trembling heart, he wanted to hide himself completely inside Baldo's ribs. He kept repeating *Agnus Dei* with his head turned down.

Now in the distance they hear the crash of rushing water, just   489
as when a mill sluice is opened. Baldo turns toward the sound and directs his steps there, and so they arrive at the black waves of the Acheron, which like the baths at Porretta are always steaming. Countless wailing souls flutter about their heads this way and that and call to Charon. He is supposed to transport them to the left bank, but eight days have passed since he's been seen.

For the time being, Cingar distances himself from the other   498
companions, for nature was calling him to drive in a post, or rather to plant a new mushroom on the shore or, as I might say, to produce a Lombard quail. He was about to fill his britches when he wandered off with his nose down like a hound sniffing out a hare. But he does not find a hare here or a kid goat, but instead a dead youth, whom he bumps into so suddenly that all the hairs on his body stand up. He had not yet squatted to the ground with his trousers fully loosened, hidden in a ditch, when all over his trousers he found there was an odor. Indeed, the runs are often caused by a strong fright; and fear will be able to unconstipate constipated

ut parebat, erat lachrymisque bagnarat arenam.
'Ayme', Cingar ait, quaenam fortuna guidavit
te, puer, huc? aut quo, sic vivo corpore, vadis?'
520 Dixerat, et sese paulatim proximat illi
vultque experiri si vitam liquerit istam.
Praestiter amotis sbarrattat pectora pannis,
cercat et un pocum tastat sub corde calorem,
unde datur sciri nondum spudasse fiatum,
525 nec *Requiem aeternam* fuerat cantare bisognus.
At pensare nequit foggiam, quae suscitet illum.
Non ibi credat aquis vultum sbrofare rosatis,
non ibi odorifero venas fregare cirotto,
non ibi speret aquam de flumine tollere frescam,
530 namque venenosis Acheron ibi fluctibus ardet.
Per mancum ergo malum caldam spinavit orinam
et iuvenis venas, polsos et tempia bagnat.
Ille pudicino pissamine Cingaris unctus,
paulatim forzas revocare per ossa comenzat;
535 en bellam frontem, bellos en schiudit ocellos
hasque parolinas inspecto Cingare parlat:
'Sis benedictus homo, tal qualis barro fuisti,
qui medio morto transtullum tale dedisti.
Non hoc fecisset medicinae inventor Apollo'.
540 Cingar eum tollit de terra et talia profert:
'O formose puer, quaenam desgratia tanta est?
Quaeve locis istis te sors adversa butavit?'
Cui sic responsum magno facit ille dolore:
'Est mihi de schiatta Cipadae pessima mater;
545 ipsa patrem Baldum praesenserat esse negatum,
unde novum subito zaffavit vacca maritum,
de quo quamprimum tres fecit scroia fiolos.
Meque simul fratremque meum, de sanguine Baldi,
contempsit propriamque casam nos linquere fecit.

bowels more quickly than an infusion of mallow in an enema bag. Cingar pulled himself back like someone who has stepped on a snake, and he looked at the handsome youth with astonishment — he was actually unconscious there, not dead as he'd seemed, and he had bathed the ground with his tears. "O my!" Cingar exclaims. "What fate has brought you here, boy? And where are you going with a live body like that?" So he spoke, and then gradually approached, wanting to ascertain if he'd left this life. Quickly Cingar removes the boy's clothes, baring his breast, and looks and feels for a little warmth left in his heart. From this, he can tell that the lad has not yet spit out his last breath, and there was no need to sing the *Requiem aeternam.*

Yet he's unable to think of a way to revive him. In that place   526
Cingar can't consider sprinkling the boy's face with rose water or rubbing his veins with a fragrant poultice; he can't hope to get fresh water there from a stream, for the Acheron burns there with poisonous currents. Consequently, as the lesser evil, Cingar taps his warm urine and bathes the youth's veins, wrists and temples. Anointed with Cingar's humble piss, he begins to regain some strength in his bones. Look at his lovely brow! Look, he's opening his lovely eyes! And after looking at Cingar, he speaks these sweet words: "Bless you, man, whatever knight you are, who gave someone half-dead such refreshment. Apollo, the inventor of medicine, would not have done this."

Cingar picks him up from the ground and offers these words,   540
"O handsome lad, what great misadventure is this? What adverse fate has thrown you into these places?"

With great sorrow, he replies to him: "I have a horrible mother   543
of the race of Cipada. She heard that my father Baldo had drowned,

429

550 Grillus ego dicor, fratrem dixere Fanettum.
    Amboque nassuti sumus, uno ex ventre, gemelli.
    Ambo universam mundi cercavimus oram
    dilectum patrem Baldum cagione catandi.
    Post mare, post terras multo sudore vagatas,
555 post assassinos, ladros pelagique travaios,
    ad desperatam (velut aiunt) fecimus ambo:
    Tartaricas nobis placuit cercare masones,
    mancum stimantes vitam quam quinque lupinos.
    Ast ubi nos fortuna locum deduxit ad istum,
560 nos, inquam, medios longa stracchedine mortos,
    affuit ecce Charon, praesentis nauta riverae,
    qui tenet officium curvo transferre batello
    damnatas animas et ademptas morte secunda.
    Ergo rogabamus si nos trascendere vellet,
565 sponentes illi causam pietatis, amoris
    et fidei, quam nos patri debere tenemur.
    Ille ribaldonus, crestosus vecchius et omni
    fraude sat impressus, velut omnis nauta catatur,
    promisit nos velle quidem passare delaium,
570 sed non insemmam, dicens quod transiet unus
    post alium fietque duplex vogatio nostra.
    Et causam tulit hanc: "ne scilicet ipsa periret
    gundola, corporibus sic sic onerata duobus."
    Hac igitur ratione meus germanus abivit
575 nec per sex giornos ultra mihi barca retornat;
    absque meo charo dilecto fratre remansi,
    ducitur in baratrum, sine quo iam vivere nolo'.
    Cingar, id ascoltans, exiverat extra seipsum,
    fecerat et veluti faciunt qui nocte vaneggiant.
580 In pueri facie fixissima lumina tendit
    et Baldi chieram sembiante notavit in illo.
    Immaduere statim scolato pectore guanzae

so right away the cow snatched up a new husband, by whom as soon as possible the sow had three children. She scorned both my brother and me—from Baldo's blood—and made us leave our own home. I am called Grillo and my brother is called Fanetto. Twins, we were both born of one belly. We have both searched the ends of the world in order to find our dear father Baldo. After roaming the land and the sea with considerable sweat, after assassins, thieves and troubles on the high seas, we were both reduced to despair (as they say) and we decided to explore the abodes of Tartarus, considering our lives not worth even five beans.

"But when Fortune led us to this place—we who were half- 559 dead, I mean, from our prolonged exhaustion—suddenly Charon arrived, the pilot on this river, whose job it is to transport on his curved vessel the souls that are damned and have been carried away by the second death. We asked, therefore, if he would transport us, explaining to him the reason for the piety, love and faith which we are bound to owe our father. This great scoundrel, this puffed-up old man, deeply stamped with every fraud, like every boatman one finds, promised he would take us over to the other side, but not together, saying that he would take one after the other, and ours would be a double crossing. And he presented this reason: 'So that the gondola won't founder, of course, weighted down like that by two bodies.' For this reason, my own brother went off, and for six days the boat has not returned for me. I am left without my dear beloved brother, who is led to the depths, and without whom I no longer wish to live."

ac adolescentis fronti dedit oscula centum.
'Pone, puer', dixit, 'spaventum; pone travaium,
585   pone doiam cordis, nec fle, tibi prospera barca est.
Non procul esse tuum patrem, tibi nuntio, Baldum'.
Dixerat, et versum ripas Acherontis afrettat,
ut referat Baldo solatia tanta parenti.
Qui vocat interea bravosa voce Charontem,
590   et giurat quod vult sibi pugnis rumpere schenam
ni subito ad prodam veniat cimbamque reducat;
qua tot debentur ripae passarier altrae
tardantes animae, quarum stant littora plena.
At bravat indarnum ac indarnum semet adirat.
595   Unam namque Charon nympharum regis Averni,
nomine Thesiphonam, totus brusefactus amabat,
nec quid speraret tamen ancum pazzus habebat.
Sed postquam puerum, nulla mercede, Fanettum
donat Thesiphonae, quae vult concedere noctem,
600   ille stat indarnum, stat mattus statque balordus,
seria postponens carnali cuncta desio:
cui propria utilitas, cui barchae puzzat aquistus,
et quod aquistatur seu stento sive salaro
dilectae tribuit, velut est usanza, bagassae.
605   Tantae huc ergo animae de mundo semper arivant
ut Baldi carichent humeros comitumque suorum.
Ignorant etenim miserae qua in parte repossent,
unde super spallas illorum mille quiescunt.
Harum fert plenas iam iam Fracassus orecchias,
610   nec non et nasum, barbam capitisque tosonos.
Ille frequens crollat testam, stranutat, arascat;
sed post stranutum redeunt iterumque sotintrant
antra cavernosi nasi testamque busatam.
Impatiens tamen ille humeros scossare frequentat;
615   sed quo plus scossat plus turba molesta ritornat.

Hearing this, Cingar was beside himself and acted as people 578
do who sleepwalk. He held his eyes firmly fixed on the boy's face
and recognized Baldo's features in that countenance. As his heart
melted, his cheeks at once grew moist, and he gave the adolescent
a hundred kisses on his forehead. "Set aside your fears, my boy,"
he said. "Set aside your worries; set aside the sorrow in your heart.
Don't cry, your ship has come in. I tell you that your father, Baldo,
is not far off."

Having spoken, he hurries toward the shores of the Acheron to 587
bring great solace to Baldo the parent. Meanwhile Baldo is calling
to Charon in a menacing voice and swears that he will break his
back with blows if he doesn't come to the shore immediately and
bring back his ferryboat in which the tarrying souls ought to be
transferred to the other bank, a great many of whom stand along
the shore. But he threatens in vain and in vain gets angry. For
Charon loved one of the nymphs of the king of Avernus, named
Tisiphone, and was completely on fire, even though the fool had
no cause for hope. After he gives the boy Fanetto free of charge to
Tisiphone, who wants to grant him a night, he stays in vain; he
stays crazy and stays befuddled, postponing all serious matters for
carnal desire. His own welfare and the income from his boat
stinks to him, and whatever he earns by hard work and his salary,
he bestows, as is customary, on his beloved strumpet.

As a result, so many souls keep arriving down here from the 605
world that they pile up on the shoulders of Baldo and his gang.
The wretches don't know where to settle, so a thousand of them
rest on the men's backs. Fracasso already has his ears full of them,

Hinc examen apum cunctis sua testa videtur,
agmine quae denso se circa foramen adossant.
Vel potius Fracassus erat bos tempore vecchius,
cuius sbercigeros oculos musumque bavosum
620   rodere contendunt hinc moschae ac inde tavani;
quos ut discazzet calzis et dente molestos,
absque intervallo pendentes crollat orecchias;
sed quo plus crollat, plus illi ad pascua tornant.
       Cingar at interea Grillum deduxerat illuc,
625   quem praesentando patri sic parlat et inquit:
'Nosce, pater, natum; genitor, cognosce nepotem.
Hanc tua, Balde, rosam generavit fronda galantam.
Protulit hunc nobis tua vivida planta garoflum.
Carpe tuae fructum, pater, arboris: haec tua proles,
630   hic tuus est Grillus, quem parvum liquimus orbi'.
Baldus ibi stupida mirabat fronte puellum
visceribusque diu motis stetit extra seipsum;
denique nil dubitans, illum indolcitus abrazzat
deque suo sic sic brazzando fratre domandat.
635   Cingar hoc incaricum narrandi suscipit, at nil
dicere tunc voluit de uxoris crimine Bertae.
Talia dum stabant una parlare barones,
ecce venit sbraiando Charon chiamatque bravazzus:
'Papa Satan, o papa Satan, beth, gimel, aleppe.
640   Cra cra, tif taf noc, sgne flut, canatauta, riogna'.
Canutam mentozzus habet sine pectine barbam,
quae bigolum distesa coprit tangitque ginocchios.
Non habet in calva solettum fronte peluzzum,
ac si cum rasa testa penitusque pelata,
645   vellet in aspectu populi mazzare gatuzzam.
Strazzolenta sibi carnes schiavina covertat,
quam saltimbarcam Chiozotta canaia domandat.
Navigat in fretta super orlum navis adunchae,

434

and his nose, beard and tufts of hair. Repeatedly he shakes his head, sneezes and clears his throat, but they come back after each sneeze and enter again the cavernous hollows of his nose and the holes in his head. Impatiently he keeps shrugging his shoulders but the more he shrugs, the more the bothersome crowd returns. To the rest of them his head looks like a swarm of bees that cluster in a dense squadron around a fissure. Or rather, Fracasso was an old ox whose rheumy eyes and drooling muzzle are bitten here by house flies and there by horseflies. Trying to chase them off with their irritating teeth and feet, he shakes his dangling ears constantly, but the more he shakes them, the more they return to the pasture.

Meanwhile Cingar had led Grillo to them and, presenting him 624 to his father, speaks as follows: "Father, know your son! Parent, recognize your offspring. Your branch has produced this noble rose, Baldo. Your lively plant put forth this carnation for us. Gather the fruit of your tree, father. This is your child, here is your Grillo, whom we left still little on earth."

With a stupefied face Baldo gazed at the boy and stood for a 631 long time with his innards in turmoil. At last, with no uncertainty, he embraces him tenderly and while so embracing him, he asks about his brother. Cingar undertakes the job of telling the story, although for now he prefers to say nothing about the crime of Berta, Baldo's wife.

While the barons were discussing the matter together, here 637 comes Charon bellowing, and he calls out menacingly, *Papa Satan, O papa Satan, beth, gimel, aleppe. Cra cra, tif-taf noc, sgne flut, canatauta riogna.* His big chin sports a white beard, never combed, which is so extensive that it covers his bellybutton and reaches his knees.

stansque pede in sponda paret cascare deorsum,
650 nec cascare tamen metuit quia praticus ille est.
Sic barcarolos Venetam vogare per urbem
multoties vidi, quibus ars est propria remus:
stat super ordellum barchae pes unus, at alter
pendulus huc illuc vadit stimatque negottam
655 si quandoque super fluctus extraque batellum,
nil penitus toccans audax cum morte solazzat;
per strictos tamen illa volat barchetta canales,
illeque schiavonus, vel morus, vel sarasinus,
cifolat et cridat: 'Barca!', 'Premi!'que, 'Stalium!'
660 nec mancant uno tria milia cancara giorno.
Iamque propinquabat ripae mala fazza Charontis
cumque bravariis animas terrebat acerbis.
Baldus at in furia poltronem nuncupat illum,
nec vult intrando barcam restare dedretum,
665 sed vix ad prodam fuit anchora ficca lavacchio,
ecce implent animae busos et transtra carinae.
Sed Charon, aspecto Baldo sociisque, cridabat:
'Quae vos in partes nostras ventura guidavit?
Ola! quibus dico? si barcam scandere vultis,
670 ponite corpoream somam carnisque valisam.
Una mihi cura est animas transferre solutas,
non altramenter fluvium passabitis istum'.
Baldus ait: 'Taceas, taceas, scornute diavol!
ad caput inchinum nisi vis andare sotacquam.
675 Nonne hic Meschinum varcasti corpore ficcum?
Nec mihi communem poteris concedere passum?
Cui dico? Dicone tibi, parone bugiarde?
Huc accosta ratem nobis, huc volge timonem.
Quo premis in laium? in quaium dico, maruffe'.
680 Non Charon ascoltat, sed navem praestus aretrat,
quam caricatam animis largum dilongat in amnem.

He doesn't have a single hair on his bald pate, as though with his head completely shaved and smooth he wanted to play "bat the cat" in front of the people. A ragged traveling cloak covers his flesh, which the Chioggian rabble calls a *saltimbarca*. He sails rapidly, standing on the edge of the curved boat, and with one foot on the rim he looks as though he'll fall backwards, but being experienced, he is not afraid of falling. I have seen boatmen rowing through the city of Venice like this many times. Rowing is their own special art: one foot rests on the brim of the boat and the other swings back and forth, and he doesn't care if it's over the water beyond the gondola, touching nothing at all; the bold fellow plays with death. Nonetheless, that little bark flies through the narrow canals, and a Slav or a Moor or a Saracen whistles and yells, "Boat! Shove off! Stay there!" and there are at least three thousand clashes a day.

And now Charon's nasty face approached the bank, and he 661 terrified the souls with bitter threats, although Baldo in a rage calls him a bum and refuses to keep back from boarding the boat. The moment the anchor sticks in the mud near the shore, the souls fill the niches and cross-beams of the hull. But Charon, having seen Baldo and his companions, yells, "What adventure brought you to our region? Hey, I'm talking to you! If you want to come aboard, lay down the burden of your bodies and the baggage of your flesh. My only responsibility is to transport released souls; there's no other way you will cross this river."

Baldo says, "Silence, silence, you cuckolded devil, unless you 673 want to go underwater head-first. Didn't you ferry *il Meschino* while he was still stuck in his body? Won't you grant me the usual passage? I'm talking to you. Aren't I talking to you, you lying boat-

Oh! puta si Baldus rodit furiando cadenam,
at sibi vendettae concessa est nulla facultas.
Tunc Fracassus ibi largum saltare canalem
685   praeparat, et spudans manibus se retro retirat,
discorsamque piat vel tres vel quinque cavezzos;
inde movens passus longones, inde galoppans,
inde citum corsum, de ripa saltat in altram;
quo saltu intornum graviter campagna tremavit
690   terribilemque omnes balzum stupuere barones.
Baldus mandat ei, tota cum voce cridando,
ut voiat barbam nautae streppare pilatim,
rumpere cervellum ac totos corporis ossos;
mox provet an possit barcam guidare dequaium.
695   Sed Charon, attonitus factus saltante giganto,
iam rivat ad portum cunctasque licentiat umbras,
quae sfortunatae de navi ad littora saltant
praecipitesque volant se confessare Chyroni,
ut confessatae vadant quo andare bisognat:
700   sive in boientae caldaria plena resinae,
sive in fornaces vitri fluxique piombi,
sive in giazzatum borea cifolante profundum,
sive inter flammas, basiliscos atque dragones.
Sed Charon interea non vadit tollere Baldum,
705   immo tremat guardans splendentis corpora ferri.
Non procul in stipulis fluvialibus atque canellis
se Fracassus erat nascostus, ut inde piato
tempore comprendat pian pian de retro Charontem;
qui dum burchiellum reficit pluresque facendas
710   expedit indusiatque aliae se reddere ripae,
Fracassus tacite se densis tollit ab ulvis
et, quacchius quacchius veniens post terga Charontis,
nil strepitat digitisque pedum vix signat arenam.
En cito per collum, sociis plaudentibus, illum

master? Bring the raft here close to us; turn the rudder this way. Why are you pushing over there? I said over here, you idiot!"

Charon doesn't listen, but quickly backs the ship out; loaded   680
with souls, it moves off on the wide river. O just imagine how fu-
riously Baldo chomps at the bit, yet is granted no possibility for
revenge. At this moment Fracasso prepares to jump across the
wide canal, and spitting on his hands, he steps back and takes a
running start of three or five yards. Then, first taking very long
steps, next galloping, and then running fast, he jumps to the other
bank. The whole countryside around shakes violently from this
jump, and all the barons are stunned by the tremendous leap.
Yelling with all his might, Baldo commands the giant to pull the
boatman's beard out hair by hair and to break his neck and every
bone in his body and then to see if he can steer the bark back
to them.

But Charon, stunned by the gigantic leap, now reaches the   695
other shore and dismisses all the shades, and the unfortunate dead
jump from the ship to the shore. They fly off in a rush to confess
themselves to Chiron so that, having confessed, they go where
they must go: whether to vats full of boiling resin, or to furnaces
of glass and molten lead, or to the depths frozen by blowing
Boreas, or amid the flames, basilisks and dragons.

But Charon, meanwhile, does not go to take Baldo; instead, he   704
trembles, looking at these bodies of glittering iron. Not far away,
amid the river reeds and stalks, Fracasso was hiding, so that at just
the right moment he can sneak up and capture Charon from be-
hind while he repairs his little craft and tackles lots of other tasks,
delaying his return to the other bank. Silently Fracasso raises him-

715 zaffat, et intornum bis terque quaterque volutans,
    ut solet ongiutum clamans strozzerus osellum,
    slanzat eum forti tenebrosa per aëra brazzo.
    Ille volat nigras, veluti cornacchia, per auras,
    qui nisi dextra Dei festina dedisset aiuttum,
720 certe fracassasset quanta ossa in corpore gestat.
    Sed per aventuram cascans in inania centri,
    adiutus levitate fuit sanusque remansit.
    Interea magnus barchettam intrare pusillam
    vult gigas, et pensat bonhomazzus posse teneri
725 ac sustentari tam parvo in ventre batelli.
    Sed pede vix posito, liquidis schiffettus in undis
    vult ire ad fundum, nec fert tam grande pilastrum.
    Anne pulex grossum poterit gestare cavallum?
    Anne super spallas saccum formica Bolognae?
730 Tunc discreta retro sese persona gigantis
    balzat et alterius foggae passamina cercat.
    Grattat quippe caput, capitis grattatio guisam
    en aliam retrovat, quam tunc tunc fare parecchiat.
    Cum pede dat calzum retro in culamina barchae,
735 quae, velut in poppa sofio percussa Sirocchi,
    evolat et ripam tam velox fertur ad altram
    ut nisi iuvissent hastas porgendo barones,
    se spezzasset enim duris in littore saxis.
    Cingar eam retinet curvumque ad littus apoggiat,
740 montat et accipiens remum cridat: 'Ola, sodales!
    intretis, quoniam passabimus absque Charonte'.
    Conscendunt igitur navim sub Cingare cuncti,
    non tamen insemmam, nimium quia pressa negaret.
    Unum post alium portat septemque fiatis
745 de ripa ad ripam guidata est Cingare barca.
    Baldus ridebat dicens: 'Mirate, sodales,
    quantus ad officium nocchieri Cingar habetur.

self from the dense swamp grass and comes up behind Charon's back very, very quietly—he makes no noise, and his toes barely make tracks in the mud. All of a sudden he grabs him by the neck and, with his friends applauding, swings him two, three, four times around—as a falconer does, calling his sharp-clawed bird—and then launches him with his mighty arm through the shadowy air. Charon flies through the black winds like a crow, and if the right hand of God had not helped him in time, he would have smashed every bone in his body. However, falling by chance into the emptiness of hell, he was rescued by the lack of gravity there and remained unharmed.

Meanwhile, the great giant wants to board the tiny boat—the 723 simple colossus thinks he can be held and sustained in the belly of such a small boat. But as soon as he has set down his foot, the little skiff is ready to sink to the bottom, unable to bear such a huge column. Would a flea be able to carry a hefty horse? Could an ant carry a Bolognese hogshead on its shoulders? At this moment the gigantic figure prudently leaps back and looks for another means of crossing. So naturally he scratches his head and in scratching, behold! he discovers another way, which right away he prepares to execute. With his foot he kicks the back end of the boat, and it flies as though the stern has been hit by a blast of Sirocco and is carried to the other shore so rapidly that, if the barons had not helped by poling, it would certainly have splintered on the hard rocks of the shore. Cingar holds it and, poised against the curved shoreline, climbs in and takes up the oar, crying, "Hey there, comrades, get in, for we will cross over without Charon."

Certe hic nec forma nec discrepat arte Charonti.
Cernite terribiles oculos magramque figuram.
750 Quis nam illum guardans non dixerit esse diablum?'
Cui Boccalus: 'Ita est, Chiozzotti fazza videtur.
Per quem si nummos voias mandare Venecis,
quam foret impresam speditus et aptus ad istam!'
Cingar respondet: 'Nec tu, Boccale, biolchi
755 officium cazzando boves conducere scires.
Namque volunteram grassum carnemque salatam
dum robbas codigasque omnes in guttura mandas,
non umquam lardo fregares fusta rotarum,
et tua continuo male uncta caretta cridaret'.
760 Baldus ait: 'Vos ambo estis lemosina sancta'.
    Tangite iam ripam; passato hoc flumine, iacta est
alea; tuque, Striax, tam longo parce labori.

Liber vigesimus quintus

    Per sabionigeros ad longum fluminis agros
ibant compagni nigram Plutonis ad urbem.
Ecce procul iuvenem lachrymosa voce cridantem
scampantemque vident ac dantem brachia coelo.
5   Hunc vecchiazza sequit stimulisque incalzat aguzzis.
Non aliter manzola truci picigata tavano,
praecipitosa ruit reboansque per invia fertur,
cui bonus altorium properat donare biolcus;
ut puer infelix nunc huc, nunc cursitat illuc,
10 dum sibi post humeros vecchiazzam currere sentit.
Haec habet ad ventum sparsos de vertice crines,
immo veneniferos angues turpesque cerastas,
quae arrectae cifolos horrendaque sibila mandant.

They all get on board the ship with Cingar as captain, but not   742
all at once lest they submerge and sink it. It carries one after the
other, and seven times the bark is guided by Cingar from shore to
shore. Baldo laughed and said, "Look, comrades, how suited Cingar
is to the job of pilot. In fact he does not differ from Charon in fea-
tures or skill. Observe that thin face and those terrible eyes! For
who looking at him would not say he is a devil?"

Boccalo replies, "So it is! His face looks like someone from   751
Chioggia. So therefore if you wish to send cash to Venice, how
quick he would be, how apt for this undertaking!"

Cingar responds, "And you, Boccalo, wouldn't know how to   754
perform the farmer's job of driving oxen. Since you're so quick to
steal lard and salted meat and shove all the pig rinds down your
gullet, you'd never take care to rub the hubs of the wheels with
grease and your poorly oiled cart would constantly squeak."

Baldo says, "You are both angels of mercy."   760

Touch the shore now. With the crossing of this river, the die is   761
cast; and you, Striax, forgive such a long labor.

Book XXV

Across the sandy terrain along the river, the companions advanced   1
toward Pluto's black city. All of a sudden, they see a youth fleeing
in the distance, crying in a tearful voice and holding his arms up to
the skies. A nasty old woman is chasing him and goading him
with sharp jabs. Just as when a young heifer, bitten by a cruel
horsefly, rushes precipitously and is carried off the path mooing,
while the good farmer hurries to help it, just so the unhappy lad

Vipereos retinet sua dextraque levaque bissos,
15 quos iacit in costas pueri laceratque fiancos.
Grillus in hoc subito magnum sic exprimit urlum:
'Me miserum! Misero tostum succurrite fratri!
Balde pater, pateris tam diram cernere cosam?
Ille est Fanettus, tibi filius et mihi frater.
20 Oyme, vide, quaeso, quantis laceratur afannis!'
Est Fanettus enim, quem pessima vecchia dolentat.
Intumuere patris praecordia tacta dolore
retroque Thesyphonam se cursu avventat equino.
Illa, videns Baldum post se furibunde volantem,
25 deserit impresam seguitandi terga Fanetti,
cazzat et incautos Baldi sese inter amicos
aspideasque illic trezzas laniare comenzat.
Proh dii! quanta illis coepit scaramuzza tralorum!
Quantosque horribiles pugnos et verbera menant!
30 Cingar Falchetto dat magnum fortiter urtum,
quem simul ad terram buttat sotosora balordum.
Fumigat in facie sguardo Falchettus amaro
datque manum mazzae, captans cum Cingare guerram,
et qui nunc fuerant ter centum mittere vitas
35 alter in alterius cosis et honore parati,
ecce coradellas cercant mangiare vicissim.
Moschinus tortis Philofornum guardat ochiadis,
cui Philofornus ait: 'Quid guardas? Sfodra, vilane!'
Hisque bravariis comenzant ambo duellum.
40 Armipotens Hippol rixat cum fratre Lyrono
seque rebruscabant ambo tegnamque gratabant.
Fracassus ferri bacchioccum menat abassum
ut de Centauro fratorum torta fiatur.
At Centaurus, habens nervos velut ova metalli,
45 non dare materiam poterit rostire fritadam;
attamen huc illuc slanzat colposque gigantis

darts here and there while he feels the old woman running behind him. She has hair flying in the wind from the top of her head, or rather venomous serpents and disgusting snakes, standing straight up, that send out horrifying hisses and whistles. She holds vipers in her right hand and water snakes in her left, which she flings at the boy's side, lacerating his flanks.

Abruptly, Grillo emits a tremendous shout: "O poor me! Help 16 my poor brother at once! Baldo, father, can you bear to see such a terrible thing? That is Fanetto, your son and my brother. Alas, I beg you, see how he is lacerated with such torments!" And indeed it is Fanetto whom the dreadful old woman is hurting. Touched by a father's anguish, Baldo's heart swelled, and he bolts after Tisiphone with the speed of a horse. And when she sees Baldo racing furiously behind her, Tisiphone abandons her aim of chasing behind Fanetto and charges into Baldo's unwary group of friends and there starts to tear out her poisonous tresses. Ye gods, what a brawl breaks out among them now! What horrible blows and lashings they inflict! Cingar vigorously gives Falchetto a great wallop, which immediately knocks him dazed head over heels to the ground. Falchetto's face clouds as he glares bitterly and puts his hand on his club, yearning for war with Cingar. Those who before had been ready to sacrifice three hundred lives for the interests and honor of the other now try to eat each other's hearts.

Moschino looks at Philoforno with sullen eyes and Philoforno 37 says to him, "What are you looking at? En garde, coward!" With these threats the two of them begin a duel. Hippol, strong in arms, brawls with his brother Lirone; they bruise each other and

saepe facit vanos et dat pro pane fugazzam.
Grillus afrontarat se fratrem contra Fanettum,
qui nihil in manibus gestantes saxa tirabant
50 sfronzantesque petras fraterna in corpora trabant.
Sed quia Boccalus contrastum non habet ullum,
incipit en solidos sibi stesso tradere goffos
unguibus et propriis testae squarzare peluccam.
Non tamen ipsius fuerat dementia tanta
55 quin prius in quodam tegeret cantone botazzum.
Baldus, id aspiciens, stabat ceu petra stupendo,
postea vult guerram penitus partire nocivam;
trat spadam atque cridat, quali cum voce cridamus
dum cortellantes bravazzos mangiaque ferros
60 dividimus stanghis, spadis multisque parolis.
'State retro!', clamat Baldus, 'Retro state, diavol!
Cui dico? Guarda! non! horsu! retro! menabo!
O Deus, hi certe mazzabunt intra seipsos!'
Sic Baldus, tutavia parans reparansque feritas,
65 insultabat eis, nunc huc, nunc providus illuc,
nec tamen accensum valet attrigare bagordum.
Hi sibi dismaiant sbergos, cossalia, faldas
spallazzosque tridos brandis ad littora buttant.
Cingar Falchettum, Falchettus Cingara pistat,
70 non parcit fratri Lyrono fervidus Hippol,
nec Lyronus ei lassat repiare fiatum:
sunt ambo nati de matris ventre medemae,
id tamen ut matti smemorant pacemque refudant.
Fracassus mugit Centaurum contra gaiardum
75 atque bachioccatas sine possa menat acerbas,
quas nisi Virmazzus saltans hinc inde schivaret,
saepe fracassatis cecidisset littore membris.
Boccalus spennata quidem iam chiozza videtur,
tam sibimet pazzus lacerat rumpitque capillos.

scratch their mange. Fracasso brings down the iron clapper in or-
der to flatten the centaur into a friar's pie. But the centaur, having
muscles like metal eggs, cannot supply the ingredients for frying
an omelet. Instead, he ducks here and there, so that the giant's
blows often go amiss, and he gives as good as he gets. Grillo had
gone up against his brother Fanetto, and since they carried noth-
ing in their hands, they threw stones and hurled whistling rocks at
their fraternal bodies. Boccalo does not have an opponent, so he
begins to smite himself with solid thwacks, and tears the scalp
from his head with his own nails. His madness was not so great,
however, that he did not first hide his bottle in a corner.

Observing this, Baldo stood stupefied like a rock, then reso-   56
lutely decides to break up the damaging war. He draws his sword
and shouts, as we do when separating with poles and swords and
lots of words knife-fighting thugs and tough guys. "Stay back!"
yells Baldo. "Stay back, devil! Who's listening to me? Look! No!
Come on! Get back! I'll clobber you! O God, they are going to
kill each other for sure!"

So Baldo, still deflecting and re-deflecting their thrusts, was   64
carefully jumping between them this way and that, but is not able
to stop the heated skirmish. They dismantle each other's mail—
hauberks, cuisses and faulds—and they flip pauldrons to the ground
after shredding them with their blades. Cingar pulverizes Falchetto;
Falchetto, Cingar. The fiery Hippol does not spare his brother
Lirone, nor does Lirone let Hippol catch his breath; although they
were both born from the belly of the same mother, yet, as though
crazed, they forget this and refuse to make peace. Fracasso roars
against the hardy centaur and ceaselessly delivers harsh clapper

447

80 'Cedite!', clamabat Baldus, 'iam cedite fratres!
Dicite cagionem cur vos discordia burlat.
Ne ferias, Cingar! Mazzam, Falchette, reponas!
Nexus amicitiae sic vester frangitur ergo?
Vade retro! Ne fac! Guarda, Virmazze, bataium!
85 Horsu, Lyrone, mane! Sic sic feris, Hippole, fratrem?
Ola! quid insanis, fraschetta Fanette? Quid et tu,
Grille, furis? Sic vos inter vos? Linquite petras!
Quid tibi Moschinus fecit, Philoforne? Quid ola!
mi Moschine, furis tam dulcem contra sodalem?
90 State retro cuncti brandosque reducite fodris!'
Talia sed frustra dum parlat, corripit ensem
cumque piatonadis sforzat partire baruffam;
saepe minazzat eis, nisi se pistare rafinant,
menabit spadae iam colpos absque riguardo.
95 Quisque erat ob nimium factus iam stancus afannum;
nil tamen ascoltant Baldum, nunc dulce rogantem,
nunc blasphemantem, nunc rauca voce minantem.
Qui tandem, cernens guisa prodesse niguna,
se post Tesiphonam, stantem guardare baruffas,
100 providus avventat: fors fors ita briga calabit.
Illa fugit stridens nigrasque cridoribus auras
spezzat et interdum, Baldo conversa, menazzat.
Mox grignat dentes et acerbos pandit hiatus.
An vidisti umquam rabiosam currere cagnam,
105 quae dum incalzatur bastonibus atque cridore,
fert inter gambas codam testamque revoltans,
candentes ringit dentes bau bauque frequentat?
Sic mala vecchia facit, Baldo seguitante dedretum.
Ipse volans iam iam sperat zaffasse, sed illa,
110 spiritus, ante fugit, cui se male corpus adaequat.
Versus montagnae culmen rapit illa caminum,
quo circum circa vallis spatiosa seratur;

blows; and if Virmace did not dodge them jumping this way and that, he would have sunk to the turf many times with his limbs splintered. Boccalo already looks like a plucked chicken, so madly does he lacerate himself and tear out his hair.

"Stop!" yelled Baldo. "Stop already, brothers! Tell me the rea- 80 son why discord makes sport of you. Don't strike, Cingar! Put down your club, Falchetto! So then, is the bond of your friend-ship to be broken thus? Get back! Don't do it! Watch out for the clapper, Virmace! Come on, Lirone, wait! Do you wound your brother like this, Hippol? Hey, why do you rage, wayward Fanetto? And you, Grillo, why so furious? Is this how to act towards each other? Put down those rocks! What has Moschino done to you, Philoforno? And why, my good Moschino, why are you enraged against such a sweet comrade? Stand back, all of you, and put your blades back in their scabbards!"

Even while speaking these words to no avail, he seizes his sword 91 and with the flat of his blade makes an effort to break up the fray. He keeps warning them that if they don't stop pounding each other, he will wield his sword with no restraint. They were ex-hausted by their tremendous efforts, but they do not listen to Baldo at all: not to his gently pleading, not to his cursing, not to his raucous threats. Finally, when he sees that he is getting no-where, he wisely goes after Tisiphone, who is standing there look-ing at the fray: maybe in this way the fighting will cool down.

She flees screaming and shatters the black winds with her cries 101 and, turning around now and then, threatens Baldo. Next she bares her teeth and opens wide her horrid chasm. Have you ever seen a rabid bitch run? While being chased with clubs and shouts, she carries her tail between her legs, and turning her head, snarls with her white teeth and repeats "bow-wow." So does the nasty old woman, as Baldo pursues her from behind. Flying, he hopes to

istaque flamiferos vomitat montagna vapores
sulphureisque facit nasum obturare latrinis.
115 Vecchia ribalda, nihil curans ascendere montem,
rampegnat et capras ita rampegnando superchiat.
Insequitur Baldus quo se viat illa, nec aspros
tunc guardat steccos, spinas rupesve petrasve;
destinat illius numquam lassare pedattas.
120 Dum sic urget eam, desertum callat in unum,
quo non strada fuit mundo saxosior umquam.
Nunc guidat ad bassum, nunc coelum scandere paret.
Cuius plena nigro puzzant confinia fango,
qui supportantem vix Baldum fangus amorbat.
125 Non illum curat, clauso sed lumine drentum
saltat et in putrida se totum fece volutat.
Numquam porcellus pantano pulchrior exit
ut desdegnatus tunc fango Baldus ab illo
se cavat, et multum portat paladinus afannum.
130 At paladinorum labor est preciosior auro.
Praeterea post terga sibi pluviosa ruinant
nubila, quae mista cum grandine cuncta fracassant.
Fulgurat intornum densis caligo tenebris
turbineosque movet nunc hinc, nunc inde balenos.
135 Tantis cum poenis barro tantisque fadighis
evolat et prigolos semper gaiardior exit.
Smontat in obscuram tandem mala vecchia paludem,
pallentes ubi stant boschi macchiaeque draconum.
Inter eas subito vanescit nympha Charontis
140 lassat et in petolis Baldum non ultra sequentem;
qui tunc non aliter se trigat et alzat orecchias
ut canis incalzans, musum distesus acutum,
aut caprum aut leporem vecchiam plenamque magagnis;
non per scopertas campagnas illa salutem
145 quaerit, at umbrosos intrat cativella fratones,

grab her at each moment, but she, a spirit, flees before him: his body is no match for her.

She races along a path to the top of a mountain, where a spacious valley is enclosed all around; this mountain vomits flaming vapors, and its sulfurous latrines makes one plug one's nose. The old bawd, ascending the peak effortlessly, scrambles up, scrambling even faster than a mountain goat. Baldo follows where she goes and pays no attention then to the sharp twigs, thorns, cliffs and boulders; he is determined never to leave her trail. While he gains on her, he descends into a wilderness; there was never a rockier road in the world: first it leads downward, then it appears to scale the sky. The region stinks, full of black mud that sickens Baldo; he can hardly stand it. Yet he pays no heed, but with his eyes closed, jumps in and rolls around in the putrid waste. Never has a little pig emerged from a bog more beautiful than Baldo who, at this moment, disdainfully pulls himself from that one, and the paladin bears many trials. Yet the labor of paladins is more precious than gold. What's more, rain clouds rush at his back which, mixed with hail, smash everything. A miasma of intense darkness flashes all round and sends forth spiraling lightning bolts on this side and that. The hero escapes amid great pains and struggles and always emerges more valorous from dangers.

At last the evil old woman descends toward a murky swamp where there are bleak woods and serpentine thickets. Into these, Charon's nymph suddenly vanishes, leaving Baldo in a fix, no

atque revoltellos quosdam facit hic, facit illic,
donec ab ungue canis videat se denique toltam.
Ergo velut canis aggabbatus drizzat orecchias,
quattuor in pedibus firmus, sic barro repente
150 constitit, ammittens Furiam Furiaeque pedattas.
Mox tamen, intrando sylvas, cercare comenzat
nunc hunc nunc illum, chioccans bastone, coattum;
cuncta tacent circum nec vento foia movetur,
unde it ascoltans pariter pariterque caminans.
155 Ecce videt tandem medio vallone casazzam,
semiruinatis quae stat scoperta quadrellis;
nullus adest custos nec oportet battere portam.
Introit et mentem nudo tenet ense paratam.
Discalcinatis domus humet ubique murais
160 deque carolentis crodat mufolenta solaris
fezza, velut vidi privata lusoribus antra.
Dum vadit Baldus, firmat saepissime plantas,
mox levis ascoltat si quid strepitescere sentit.
Nil sonat unde illic habitare silentia iurat.
165 De passu in passu, dum per pavimenta caminat,
ventrosos zattos armato calce tridabat
atque smagazzabat calcagni pondere vermes.
Saepe dragonazzos, largo ventrone tumentes,
invenit inque duos facit illos ense cavezzos.
170 Denique collegium reperit, quod vecchia Charontis
fecerat, et stabat deformis ubique senatus.
Baldus in introitu primi stat liminis, ultra
nec meat et tensa quod dicitur accipit aure:
namque inter populum sentit parlare ribaldam.
175   Hic erat in quadrum grandis spatiosaque sala;
stant ubique circum putrefacta sedilia ligni;
talia sunt quales longo post tempore capsae
mortorum trantur marzae de viscere terrae.

longer able to follow. He stops and pricks up his ears, just like a dog with its pointed muzzle extended, chasing a goat, or a hare that is old and full of tricks and does not seek safety in open fields, but rather hides, the naughty thing, in shady bushes, making quick turns here and there until she sees that at last she's free from the dog's claws. He therefore perks up his ears, like a dog that has been tricked and stands still on all four legs; just so, the hero stops abruptly, losing the Fury and the Fury's tracks. But soon, entering the forest, he begins to search first one hiding place and then another by striking them with his club. Everything is silent; not one leaf is moved by the wind, so he goes along listening and walking at the same time.

Then finally he sees a run-down house in the middle of a valley, 155 which sits exposed with dilapidated walls; there is no custodian present and no need to knock on the door. He enters with his blade drawn, keeping his mind alert. The house oozes moisture from its decaying walls and moldy dregs drop from the worm-eaten ceiling, as I have seen in caverns where no light shines. As Baldus moves along, he often stands still and listens for anything making a slight noise. Nothing makes a sound, so that one would swear Silence lives here.

Step by step, while he walks along the floor, he crushes paunchy 165 toads with his ironclad feet, and squashes worms with his heavy heels. He often comes upon big, mean dragons with their wide bellies swollen, and chops them into two hunks with his sword. At last he finds the gathering that Charon's old woman had summoned, where a misshapen senate stood all about. Baldo stands at the first threshold of the entrance; he doesn't pass beyond and

In medio salae stat maxima scragna metalli,
180   scragna cruentatis he heu circumdata spadis.
Hic sedet Ambitio sembiante tyranna superbo,
quae coeli, terrae, maris optat habere bachettam.
Spada taienta tamen filoque tacata sotilo
stat super illius testam casumque menazzat.
185   Non procul huic chiachiarat centum Discordia linguis,
mussat, sbaiaffat, mentit, movet ora manusque,
millibus et zanzis reginae tentat orecchias,
nec traditora suo partit quandoque galono.
Tres Furiae parent illi referuntque per orbem
190   ambassarias, quibus omnis terra ruinat.
Quottidie vadunt, redeunt portantque novellas
reginae: quantasve animas in Tartara mersas
arte sua trassent, solita vel fraude necassent.
Impietas alia frendens in parte cruentat
195   sanguinolenta locum guardatque cagnesca traversum.
Hic Vindicta fremit stimulisque agitatur aguzzis;
quam regina inter populos mundique brigatas
mittit et ingenti pagat mercede ribaldam
si pugnale suo turpantur sanguine regna,
200   non parcat frater fratri, non sora sorocchiae,
non mater nato, non uxor porca marito.
Seditio ignavum populazzum possidet illic:
Lis, Luctus, Rabies, Odium, Timor, Ira, Travaius
sunt ibi concilium baratri Mortisque senatus.
205   Ambitio praesul nulli vult esse secunda;
anteque conspectum eius desformataque monstra,
Thesiphone, Alecto, nec non germana Megaera
tunc altercabant simul ascoltante senatu.
Sed quid rixabant porchae magraeque lupazzae?
210   Huc huc, mortales, huc vestras currite provas,
tam bellas provas audire et plangere mecum.

with his ear extended, he grasps what is said, for he hears the bawd speaking among her people.

There was a big, spacious, four-sided hall; all around the room 175 are seats of rotting wood: these are just like the putrescent caskets of the dead pulled out of the bowels of the earth after a long time. In the middle of the hall stands a massive metal throne, a throne surrounded, alas, by gory swords. Here sits the tyrant Ambition with a haughty countenance, who yearns to wield her scepter over the heavens, earth and sea. However, a sharp blade hanging from a tenuous thread hangs over her head and threatens her with calamity. Not far off from her, Discord prattles with a hundred tongues: she whispers, rants, lies; moves her mouth and hands; and with a thousand quibbles tempts the queen's ears. Treacherous Discord never leaves her side. The three Furies obey her, and deliver her messages throughout the world, by which every country is destroyed. Each day they come and go and carry news to the queen. How many souls that have sunk into Tartarus were dragged there by her skill, or killed by her customary fraud?

Nearby, blood-stained Cruelty, gnashes her teeth, splattering 194 the place and glowering balefully. Here Vengeance growls and is vexed by sharp jabs. The queen sends her among the nations and peoples of the world and pays the bawd a huge salary if her dagger pollutes these realms with blood and if a brother does not spare his brother, nor a sister her sister, nor a mother her child, nor a swinish wife her husband.

There Sedition subjugates the base rabble: Strife, Mourning, 202 Rage, Hate, Dread, Wrath, and Agony, who form a council of the depths, a senate of death. The leader, Ambition, wants to be second to none. In her presence and before the other deformed mon-

Adsit condicio, sors, stirps, genus omne virorum,
humanasque velint miserasque audire pacias,
errorumque simul tantorum noscere causas.

215   Iusserat Ambitio totam reticere fameiam,
unde quis attentas subito porrexerat aures.
Foetida vermifluam scorlans bis terque Megaera
canitiem, sic sic primera comenzat et inquit:
'Audite, Inferni patres satrapique Magoghae.

220   Illa ego quae nigrum doceo meschiare venenum,
nec mea guarriri possunt aconita triachis.
Scragna mihi curae Petri est et mitra papalis
saepeque gardineos butto sotosopra capellos.
Cernite quam laceram caviatam vertice porto!

225   Hinc mihi perpetuis debetur palma triumphis.
Maxima pontificum libertas, maxima rerum est
pernicies! Si quando meam tramittere codam
possim ne sanctis precibus nutuque Columbae
ad sublime aliquis culmen tollatur honoris.

230   Oh venturatos nos tunc, oh vota secutos
dulcia, cum nostro fabricatur papa favore!
Ingrassamur enim de carne et sanguine schietto
armenti, sguerzo si sub pastore guidatur.
Per me mitratus capras pegorarus amazzat

235   mangiandasque lupo tribuit scampatque codardus.
Pilat oves avibusque cavat de corpore pennas.
Per me semirutis squalent altaria templis,
Chiesia tota cadit, ruit alto a culmine mater,
mater quae nutrit bastardos atque cinaedos;

240   quam nisi pontificis consolet gratia iusti,
mox Alcorano soterabitur illa tereno.
Veh nobis et guai, nec non malanaza tapinis,
tali si fuerit Christi concessa cadrega,
qui non cardineas voiat plus vendere brettas,

sters, Tisiphone, Alecto and their sister Megaera quarreled among themselves while the senate was listening. And what were these sows and scrawny she-wolves fighting about? Here, here, mortals! Run to hear these deeds of yours, such wonderful deeds, and weep with me! Let men of every condition, fortune, family and race be present, and let them hear shameful human follies and together learn the causes of so many errors.

Ambition had ordered all of her servants to keep silent, so they had all promptly perked up their eager ears. Fetid Megaera, shaking her wormy gray locks two or three times, begins thus to speak, saying, "Hear me, senators of Hell, satraps of Magog. I am the one who teaches how to mix black poison: my aconite cannot be cured with treacle. The papal mitre and the see of Peter are my concern; often I throw the cardinals' hats upside down. Just look at what a mangled baldness I wear on top of my head! For this, I should get the victory palm with continual parades. 215

"The maximum of liberty for the popes is the maximum of danger to our affairs! If I ever manage to insert my tail, it will not be by holy prayers and the Dove's consent that someone will be raised to the sublime pinnacle of honor. O how lucky we would be then! O sweet prayers fulfilled when a pope is made through our influence! For we get fat on the flesh and pure blood of the flock when it is guided by a squint-eyed pastor. Because of me, the mitred shepherd kills goats, presents them to the wolf to be eaten and runs off, the coward. He skins the sheep and plucks the feathers from the bodies of birds. Because of me, altars turn squalid in half-ruined temples and the entire Church topples. The Mother plummets from her lofty pinnacle, the Mother who nourishes 226

245   qui levet a spallis populorum mille gravezzas,
      qui renovet Chiesae itas in malhora facendas,
      inque malum punctum cascantia cuncta redrizzet.
      Quales nunc habeat sanctos Ecclesia patres,
      sat bene cognostis dudum, quam digne sacratos,
250   quam bene panzutos, quam lissos quamque tilatos,
      quam bufalos sensu, quam doctos ludere chartis,
      pascere garzonas et eas chiamare sorellas,
      pascere garzones et eos chiamare nepotes,
      spargere perfumis zazaras, portare capettas
255   undique Spagnolas calzisque frapare velutum,
      falcones nutrire, canes, sparaveria, braccos.
      Chiesa sed interea strazzata famataque lagnat.
      Quando intras portam, nil non malnetta catantur;
      porcilli effigies, non templi forma videtur.
260   Usque ad zenocchios paiae cum pulvere crescunt
      summaque strapluviant ruptis solaria cuppis.
      Longipedesque suis ragni lenzolibus ornant
      undique muraias. Crucifixo brachia mancant
      inque sui capitis nido vel noctua, vel mus
265   parturit et rodit tam dignae crura figurae.
      Hostia sancta parit, vecchia putrente farina,
      vermiculos, quae vase vitri lignive tenetur;
      namque tabernaculos auri postribula robbant.
      Nullum vas olei per honorem Numinis ardet,
270   nulla cesendilo sanctas brusat ante figuras
      lampada, namque oleum, quod curae linquitur isti,
      vertitur ad sanctam, luzzo stridente, padellam,
      lampredasque magis quam Christi corpus honorat.
      Nil coprit altarum, vel, si quid, strazza videtur,
275   quae bona non esset magro panadora cavallo.
      Campanile iugi foetet pissamine praeti
      saepeque commadres huc confessare tirantur.

bastards and catamites, who, if the grace of a just pontiff shall not console her, will soon be buried in the land of the Qur'an.

"Ah, woes and troubles and misery for us wretches, if the seat 242 of Christ is yielded to someone who no longer wants to sell cardinals' birettas, someone who would lift a thousand heavy burdens from the shoulders of the people, someone who would repair the matters of the Church that have gone awry and would put right everything that is falling to ruin. What sort of holy fathers the Church now has you have known quite well for some time. How admirably consecrated they are, how big-bellied, how smooth and how elegant, as intelligent as buffaloes! How learned in the art of card playing, in feeding their girlfriends and calling them 'sisters,' in feeding their boyfriends and calling them 'nephews,' in sprinkling their flowing manes with perfume, in wearing little Spanish capes everywhere, in·tricking out their shoes with velvet and in feeding falcons, dogs, sparrow hawks and bloodhounds!

"The Church, meanwhile, whimpers, famished and tattered. 257 When you enter her door, you find everything filthy: the picture of a pigsty it seems, rather than the image of a temple. Straw and dirt pile up to your knees, the ceiling leaks rain water from above through broken tiles. Long-legged spiders trim the walls on all sides with their linens. The Crucifix has no arms, and in the nest on its head, a bat or a mouse gives birth and gnaws the legs of this hallowed image. The sacred host, made with putrefying old flour, breeds maggots and is kept in a chalice of glass or wood, because brothels strip the tabernacles of gold. Not one oil lamp glows in honor of the Deity; not one votive candle burns in front of the statues of saints. For the oil offered up for these rites is turned over to the holy frying pan for sizzling pike, and honors the lamprey rather than the body of Christ.

Vel mancat corda, vel habet campana cavezzas
iam frustas mulae, groppis insemma tacatas.
280 Caetera quid referam? Scitis, o bella brigata,
quam sim giotta meis, quam sim saccenta, facendis.
His igitur causis, alias anteire sorocchias
debeor Alectoque mihi iam cedat honorem'.
      Talia parlanti surgit sdegnosa cadreghis
285 Alecto, meretrix Malabolgae, vacca Chiapini,
drizzat et innumeras bissas nigrosque marassos,
horribilemque cavat sic sic pulmone fiatum:
'Non ego sum mancum de te dignissima ferri
supra triumphalem, populo acclamante, quadrigam,
290 quae in mundo sparsi plus sanguinis atque cruoris,
quam nec aquam recipit nec volvit pontus arenam.
Illa ego Falsettae quondam puttana diabli
concepi et grossum portabam ventre botazzum.
Iamque propinquabat pariendi tempus et hora;
295 en mihi Luciferi coniux materque Lupazzi,
vacca Satanasi veniunt insemma comadres
ut mihi succurrant parienti tollere prolem.
Dumque fadigabant illam sterpare davantum,
scilicet ex vulvae, velut est usanza, latebris,
300 ecce duos natos culi sporchissima bocca
retro cagat foedumque simul diffundit odorem.
Qui bene nec nati, bene qui nec ab ore cavati,
incepere statim se parvis battere pugnis
atque ganassiculas ungis graffare tenellis.
305 Gaudebam, fateor, mecum quod brutta somenza
sic portendebat regum terraeque ruinam.
Illos semper ego serpentum lacte cibavi
atque dedi pueris basiliscas suggere mammas.
Iam tum certabant quis dextram quisve sinistram
310 ebiberet sizzam, dantes sibi calzibus urtas.

"Nothing covers the altar or, if there is something, it looks like   274
a rag that wouldn't make a good dab cloth for a skinny horse. The
bell tower stinks from the priest's ever-flowing piss, and the wom-
enfolk are often pulled in here to confess. Either the bell is missing
its cord or it is made of worn mule halters tied together with
knots. What more can I say? You all know, my dear people, how
cunning I am and how clever in my affairs. For these reasons,
then, I should have precedence over my sisters, and let Alecto
yield the place of honor to me."

Having spoken these words, Alecto rises indignant from her   284
seat—the whore of Malabolgia, the cow of Chiapino—and raises
up her countless serpents and black snakes, and draws from her
lungs a horrible breath: "I am no less worthy than you, Megaera,
to be born on a triumphal cart to popular acclaim, for I have
spread more bloody gore in the world than all the water the ocean
receives and all the sand it churns up. I am Falsetta, formerly the
devil's whore, and I conceived and carried a huge keg in my belly.
It was getting near the time and the hour to give birth, and Luci-
fer's wife came to me and the mother of Lupazzo, Satan's cow—
these midwives came together to help me bear my child. While
they were trying to excavate it from the front, that is, from the
hidden reaches of the vagina, as is customary, behold, my filthy
butt-hole in back shat out two infants and at the same time sent
forth a putrid odor.

"These infants, though not entirely born yet nor fully removed   302
from the orifice, began at once to hit each other with their small
fists and to scratch each other's delicate cheeks with their tender
little nails. I rejoiced, I confess, because this wicked brood thus

Uni nomen erat Ghelphus unique Gibellus,
qui mox, cressuti bis senos circiter annos,
numquam altercari noctuque diuque finabant.
Accidit una dies ut se pistare feroci
315 lite comenzarent ongis rictuque canino;
Ghelpus adentavit morsu, canis instar, aguzzo
Gibelli digitum grossum nettumque taiavit,
proque triumphato spolio portabat ubique
ut diuturna foret proprio vergogna fradello.
320 Ille similmenter digitum, qui dicitur index
dentibus abscindit Ghelpho prorsusque revulsum
devorat et portat palesum more triumphi.
Dextra manus Ghelphi pulices cum pollice mazzat,
laeva Gibellini mortaros indice leccat.
325 His ego prostravi totum giottonibus orbem,
hisque macellariis rubefeci sanguine terram.
Dicite: quid nostra haec praesens brigata valeret,
si mea non adsit proles, quae spezzat, aterrat,
quae sotosora trahit totque urbes totque governos?
330 Ghelphus vult dextra banda gestare penazzum,
ast e converso Gibellus parte sinistra.
Hic per traversum taiat quaecumque taiantur,
illeque per longum penitus vult cuncta taiari.
Millibus in fraschis, bagatellis atque fusaris,
335 cuius sit sectae studiat gens pazza videri.
Oh bene gens pazza! oh insani et absque sapero!
Hinc melius quam vos animabus tartara persis
repleo, nec lasso veram succrescere sectam,
atque fidem Christi, quae totum subderet orbem,
340 mille ruinasset Turcos, si mille fuissent,
quando assassinus Ghelphus et ladro Gibellus
non tantae in mundo sparsissent semina pestis.

foretold the destruction of kings and of the earth. I nursed them always with serpent's milk and gave these infants the breasts of basilisks to suckle. Already at that time they fought about who got to drink from the right breast and who from the left, giving each other blows with their feet. One was named Guelf, the other Ghibelline; and having grown to nearly twice six years, they never stopped quarrelling, day and night.

"It happened one day that they began to pound each other in 314 a ferocious fight, with nails and open jaws like dogs. Guelf sank his teeth into Ghibelline's thumb with a sharp bite, like a dog, and cut it clean off; then he carried it everywhere like victory spoils to perpetuate his brother's shame. And Ghibelline in turn tore off Guelf's finger (the index finger) with his teeth, and gnawed on the wholly detached member, carrying it in full view like a trophy. Guelf's right hand kills fleas using his brother's thumb, and Ghibelline's left wipes mortar bowls clean using his brother's index finger.

"With these scalawags I laid waste the entire world and with 325 these butchers I made the earth run red with blood. Tell me, what would this group of ours here be worth if my offspring didn't exist, who fracture, who demolish, who overturn so many cities and so many governments?

"Guelf insists on wearing his plume on the right side, but in 330 contrast Ghibelline wears his on the left side. The one wants to cut crossways everything that can be cut; the other insists on cutting absolutely everything lengthwise. With a thousand inanities, bagatelles and follies, these crazy people try to show to which sect they belong. O crazy people, you are truly insane and brainless! This is how I fill Tartarus with lost souls better than you

Ergo per umbrosum facienda est danza baratrum,
quod via reperta est per me tutissima tandem
345 unde fides Christi paulatim lapsa ruinet;
dum gentes Italae, bastantes vincere mundum,
sese in se stessos discordant seque medemos
vassallos faciunt, servos vilesque fameios
his, qui vassalli, servi vilesque famei
350 tempore passato nobis perforza fuere'.
    Talia dum memorans Alecto superba loquebat,
Thesiphone sdegnata pedes sese alzat in altos,
ac ita principiat, trarumpens dicta sororis:
'Baldanzosa nimis, demens, temeraria, nugax,
355 semper es, Alecto, nec te parlando misuras.
Optime quam fieret tecum, si meza palato
lingua tuo a nobis dudum taiata fuisset!
Nos fortasse magis de te ragionevola verba
saepe audiremus, non sic temeraria, non sic
360 insulsa et nullis penitus trutinata balanzis.
Dic mihi: quid populus, quid plaebs, quid vulgus inane
cum claris saviisque viris plenisque governo?
Nil populo levius, nil plaebe insanius et nil
vulgo mobilius toto reperitur in orbe.
365 Quisquis se iactat seu Ghelphum seu Gibilinum,
hunc dic villanum villano stercore natum.
Et quamvis habeat brettam scarpasque veluti,
et quamvis equitet celerantibus ante staferis,
si sectae unius sese ingerit esse sequacem,
370 lumine si torto guardat contrarius altram,
dic illi in facie: "Non es de sanguine claro,
non es signorus, dux, marchio, barro, nec es tu
gentilhomo quidem, quia nemo prorsus eorum
has vilacarias centum seguitabit in annos."

two do, nor do I allow Christ's true sect and faith to grow, which could subjugate the universe and bring a thousand Turks to ruin (if there were a thousand), if the assassin Guelf and the thief Ghibelline did not sow so much pestilence in the world.

"There should therefore be dancing throughout the shadowy   343
depths, because at last I have found the surest way by which the faith of Christ, slipping little by little, will collapse — so long as the peoples of Italy, capable of dominating the world, fight among themselves and make themselves vassals and menial servants and lackeys to those who in times past were forced to be vassals, menial servants and lackeys to us."

While proud Alecto spoke and called these things to mind,   351
Tisiphone indignantly lifted herself to her full height and, interrupting her sister's speech, began, "You are always too bold, crazy, reckless and frivolous, Alecto, and you show no restraint in speaking. How well you would have fared if long ago we had cut half your tongue from your palate! Perhaps we would then more often hear reasonable words from you, not rash and stupid ones, weighed in accordance with no scales.

"Tell me, Alecto, what are the people, what are the masses,   361
what is the inane rabble, compared to wise nobles and men full of political experience? Nothing in the world is more capricious than the populace, nothing more insane than the masses, nothing more fickle than the rabble. If anyone fancies himself a Guelf or a Ghibelline, call this man a peasant, born of peasant dung. And although he has a biretta and shoes of velvet, and although he gallops forth with pages running before him, if he forces himself to be the follower of one sect, if he looks askance at another with

375 Scilicet acquistas bellae praeconia laudis,
teque potes vantare meos superare triumphos,
quae totum penitus mundum sotosora butasti.
Una tuis tamen est intacta Cipada colubris.
Ast ego, quam nec tu, nec vacca Megaera Cipadam
380 dismembrare umquam potuit, vel dedere liti,
sola modo feci facioque ferociter arma
in se, inque suam propriam convertere panzam.
Quis credat potuisse umquam me rumpere pacem,
tam firmam pacem saldumque ligamen amoris
385 unius egregiae, clarae magnaeque Cipadae?
Quae, postquam cunctas mundi sibi subdidit urbes,
venit in Infernum Plutoni tollere sceptrum.
Baldus, Baldus adest! Ille, ille Rinaldicus haeros,
cui tam ghelpha placet quam pars gibilina realo,
390 sit modo vel ghelphus, modo vel gibilinus, amator
nominis insignis propriique sititor honoris.
Sunt hominum quidam stronzi fraschaeve legerae,
qui regem Francae praesumunt dicere ghelfum,
quique gibellinum promulgant imperatorem,
395 nec tamen illorum prudentia summa pigatur,
talibus ut gnacaris voiant intendere mentes'.
    Baldus id audierat dudum; celer arripit ensem
spezzatasque aperit portas introque ruinat.
Quo viso sic sic intrare superbiter, ecce
400 concilium deforme fugit linquitque cadregas.
Quales cum rubeos rutilans aurora colores
scoprit et aurato mortalibus axe ritornat,
gregnapolae scapolant noluntque videre lusorem,
et semper "gnao gnao" facientes nocte civettae,
405 sic inferna cohors, Baldo subeunte, scapinat,
nec valet aspectum tanti sofrire baronis.
Mansitat hic solus, vacuas videt esse cadregas,

hostility, tell him to his face, 'You are not of noble blood, you are not a lord, a leader, a marquis, a baron, you are certainly not a gentleman, since none of these would abide such incivilities in a hundred years.'

"Of course you deserve encomia of excellent praise, and you 375 may brag of surpassing my triumphs, you who threw the entire world into turmoil; still Cipada alone was untouched by your snakes. But neither you nor that cow Megaera could ever dismember Cipada or bring it into conflict; only I have made it, and continue to make it, violently turn arms against itself, against its very own belly. Who would believe that I could ever shatter the peace (a peace so firm!) and the solid bond of love of the unique, distinguished, great and noble Cipada? She who, having subjugated all the cities of the world, comes to Hell to take away Pluto's scepter. Baldo, yes, Baldo is here, the very man, that Rinaldo-like hero, the loyal one to whom the Guelf party is as acceptable as the Ghibelline — as long as both Guelf and Ghibelline love a glorious name and desire their own honor. There are some turds of men, mere twigs, who presume to say that the King of France is a Guelf, and some who proclaim that the Emperor is a Ghibelline. But their supreme wisdom is not so weakened that they would waste their thoughts on such trivialities."

Having listened to this long enough, Baldo quickly snatches 397 up his sword, opens the broken doors and rushes inside. Seeing him enter like this so confidently, the deformed council runs off and abandons the benches. Just as when glowing Aurora reveals her red tints, returning to mortals on her golden chariot, bats fly

unde corozzatus disquistilat omnia brando.
Dum studet huic operi, facies en grata Seraphi
410 apparet, qui saepe redit Baldumque revisit,
cuius compagnos retrovaverat ante furentes,
quos ad notitiam cordis cerebrique reduxit,
placatosque illos post se menaverat illuc.
Inde cito partit superasque retornat ad oras.
415   At comites iterum scuras peragrare cavernas
incipiunt. Fracassus abit primarior altris,
cui fera voia bulit cornas streppare diablis.
Parlabant variis sic sic de rebus eundo:
est qui Boccalum soiat; qui narrat Averni
420 vatibus effinctas follas; unusque ricordat
quid de Guerrino Meschino legerit olim.
Dum quoque Falchetto recitabat Cingar amico
Virgilii sextum . . . Res o miranda! quis istam
audiat et credat propriis nisi viderit occhis?
425 Ecce loqui cessat medio sermone retentus
Cingar, nil parlans, et imaginat omnia praeter
Virgilii sextum, nec se parlasse ricordat.
Falchettus pariter, quid Cingar dixerit illi
nescit et attonitus fantasticat omnia praeter
430 Virgilii sextum, nec id auscultasse rimembrat.
Centaurus curas cervello mille revolvit,
vult hoc, vult illoc, nec quid velit eligit umquam.
Castellos fabricat Fracassus in aëre multos;
sic sua lingua tacet, si semper muta fuisset.
435 Iam salis in zucca nihil amplius Hippol habebat,
passat per centum sua mens vilupata chimaeras.
Fantasticanti Lyronus mente tenebat
sublatos oculos coelo frontemque rapatam.
Moschinus pazzus, Philophornus pazzior extat,
440 multae namque homines faciunt stultescere curae.

off to avoid seeing the light, as well as the owls going "hoo, hoo" in the night, just so the infernal cohort, as soon as Baldo enters, runs off, unable to bear the sight of so great a baron. He remains here alone and sees the benches emptied, he furiously dismantles everything with his blade. As he concentrates on this task, behold! the welcome face of Seraphus appears, who often comes back and visits Baldo again, whose companions he had earlier found raving. These men he had brought back to consciousness in mind and heart, and once they were calm, he had led them here behind him. Then he quickly departs and returns to the upper regions.

Yet the comrades begin to wander again through the dark caverns. Fracasso walks in front of the others, boiling with a fierce desire to tear off devils' horns. They were talking thus of many things as they went along. Someone plays tricks on Boccalo; another narrates tall tales of Avernus completely made up by poets; and one recalls what he'd once read about Guerrino Meschino. And also, while Cingar was reciting Vergil's sixth book to his friend Falchetto . . . O what a miracle! Who will hear this and believe, if they do not see it with their own eyes? Lo! Cingar ceases to speak, checked in the midst of his recitation, saying nothing, and he thinks about everything except Vergil's sixth book, nor does he recall that he'd been talking. Falchetto likewise, does not know what Cingar said to him, and bewildered, fantasizes about everything except Virgil's sixth book, nor did he remember having listened to him. The centaur ponders many concerns in his head: he wants this, wants that, and never decides what he would like. Fracasso builds numerous castles in the air and his tongue is as silent as if it had always been mute. Hippol no longer had a grain of

415

Fanettus Grillusque simul pergendo tacebant,
sequemet admirant oculis in fronte tiratis.
Boccalus, veluti fantasticus, ante caminat,
labra movet parlatque nihil, manibusque duabus
445   ad moram secum ludit, sine voce cridando.
At Baldus, liber labiis atque ora solutus,
inter compagnos infesta silentia sprezzat.
Dumque illis quandoque loquit, responsa domandat,
sed facti elingues illum tantummodo guardant.
450   'Oh!', ait, 'est magna haec novitas! O Cingar! Apuntum!
O Lyrone! Hippol! Nil vos parlatis? Et unde hoc?
Num, velut in claustris, servare silentia vultis?
Dicite qualcosam, ne nos via longa recrescat.
Vestro num Baldo respostam ferre negatis?'
455   Talia compagnis vir parlamenta movebat,
sed melius poterat muros audire loquentes;
quapropter, stancus iam factus in arte rogandi,
non vult indarnum mutas tentare loquelas.
Ad strabucconem sguerzis cum passibus ibant
460   ut lanzchinecchi suescunt andare Todeschi,
quando plus cocti quam crudi vina padiscunt.
Tunc huius causam vult Baldus scire negoci;
se gerit ante alios, cosam trovat ecce novellam:
sub pede namque suo sentit mancare terenum,
465   nec iam qua figat calcagnos terra videtur,
immo suspensus menat per inania gambas,
totus et andandi labor est sublatus ab illo.
Se retro convertit, compagnos mirat eadem
cum levitate sequi tenuesque volare per auras.
470   Huic parlare volunt, sed tantum labra moventur,
et veluti muti ciliis manibusque loquuntur.
Quisque suum sentit corpus properare legerum,
per quoddamque vodum tacitumque feruntur agalla.

salt in his pumpkin; his mind goes off entangled in a hundred chimeras. Lirone held his eyes raised to the sky with his brow furrowed, his mind fantasizing. Moschino is crazy, Philoforno even crazier, because excess worries make men grow stupid. Going along together, Fanetto and Grillo were silent; they look in amazement at one another, with their eyes wide open. Boccalo walks ahead like a lunatic; he moves his lips but says nothing; he plays morra by himself with both hands, calling out voicelessly.

Yet Baldo, whose lips are free and whose mouth is unrestrained, 446 scorns the infectious silence among his companions. And although, whenever he speaks to them, he demands a response, nevertheless, as though they've been made tongueless, they only look at him. "Oh!" he says. "This is a great novelty! O Cingar! Precisely! O Lirone, Hippol, you have nothing to say? What's this about? Surely you don't want to keep silence as though you were in a cloister? Say something, so the journey won't seem so long. Do you deny your Baldo an answer?"

The hero urged his companions with such arguments, but he 455 could sooner have heard the walls speak. So, tiring of the art of questions, he does not want to attempt mute speech in vain. They went along stumbling with steps askew, as German Landsknechts usually walk when, more cooked than crude, they are digesting wines. Now Baldo wants to know the cause of this situation, so he places himself at the head of the others and suddenly discovers something new. He feels the terrain give way under his feet and already it seems there is no ground where he can dig in his heels. Suspended, he moves his legs in a void, and all the labor of walking has vanished. He turns himself back around and watches his companions follow with the same lightness, flying through the

Gaudent sic nulla gambas andare fadiga
475 donec ab exiguo flatu sopiantur in antrum.
Hic phantasiae domus est, completa silenti
murmure, vel tacito strepitu motuque manenti,
ordine confuso, norma sine regula et arte.
Undique phantasmae volitant animique balordi,
480 somnia, penseri nulla ratione movesti,
sollicitudo nocens capiti, fantastica cura,
diversae formae spetiesque et mentis imago.
Gabia stultorum dicta est; sibi quisque per illam
beccat cervellum pescatque per aëra muscas.
485 Hi sunt gramaticae populi pedagogaque proles;
nomen adest verbumque simul, pronomen, et illud
cum quo participant, reliqua seguitante brigata;
scilicet huc, illuc, istuc, hinc, inde, deorsum
atque sinistrorsum cum tota gente cuiorum.
490 Argumenta volant dialectica, mille sophistae
adsunt baianae: pro, contra, negoque, proboque.
Materies non mancat ibi, non forma, lyhomo,
ens, quiditas, acidens, substantia cum solegismo.
Omnis haec assaltat compagnos illico turba
495 ut moschae assaltant seu burum sive ricottam.
Me reperi, fateor, vino quandoque refectum
(quamvis nec modo sim sat liber satque speditus)
ire cavalaster sub sole, canente cigala;
ecce meam circum testam sex mille pusilli
500 moscini volitant, sicut volitare suescunt
borrono intornum buttae spinaeque vaselli.
Sic phantasiae tenues sensusque bizarri
dant simul assaltum sociis picigantque cerebros,
intrantesque caput sotosora silentia mandant.
505 Baldus at intactus remanet, guardatque, stupetque,
ac tandem ridet prenditque a Cingare festam

thin vapors. They want to speak to him but only their lips are moving, and like mutes they speak with eyebrows and hands. Each of them feels his body rushing and light, and they are carried floating through something empty and silent. They are glad that their legs walk without effort, until they are blown by a slight breeze into a cave.

This is the house of Fantasy, full of silent murmuring, of tacit   476
clamor, of movement in repose, of chaotic order, of a norm with neither rules nor art. All over the place phantasms flutter, and there are dreams of a daft spirit, thoughts stirred by no reason, anxiety hurting the head, implausible concerns and diverse forms, aspects and images of the mind. It is called the Cage of Fools. Everyone here pecks at his own brain and fishes for flies in the air. These are the people of Grammar, and the offspring of Pedagogy: the noun is here, and the verb too, the pronoun and the participle, with the rest of the gang following, namely, *huc, illuc, istuc, hinc, inde, deorsum* and *sinistrorsum* and the whole clan of *cuius*. Dialectical arguments fly around, and there are a thousand silly sophistries: *pro, contra, nego* and *probo*. Matter is not absent, nor form, *ly homo*, being, quiddity, accident, substance with the syllogism. This whole throng assaults the companions, just as flies assault butter or ricotta.

I found myself one day, I confess, refreshed by wine (and for   496
that matter am not really free or liberated from it now), going on horseback under the sun with the cicadas singing, and all at once there were six thousand little flies buzzing around my head, like the ones that buzz around the bunghole of a barrel and the tap of

qui, dum phantasmae nunc hinc nunc inde volazzant,
has seguitat manibusque piat, sed deinde tenendi
huic destrezza deest retrovatque piasse nientum.

510 Vidisti forsan pueros quandoque giocantes
velle piare manu moscas praesone ficandas,
scilicet in charta bis terque quaterque plicata?
Saepe quidem capiunt retinentque in carcere pugni,
sed quando allentant digitos panduntque pochinum,

515 ni cito scaltritas capiat manus altera, scampant,
et sic sic oleum, sic sic consumitur opra.
Cingar ita et comites, Baldo ridente, menabant
hic illic palmas propter brancare coëllum.
Attamen, ut tandem stracchae lassaeque fuerunt

520 hae similes notolae seu guffi sive civettae,
has zaffare queunt deque his implere besazzas.
Cingar de Paulo Veneto Petroque Spagnolo
mille baias recipit, subitoque in guttura mandat,
ac si mandaret coriandola zuccare facta.

525 Protinus it contra Falchettum, trenta debottum
argumenta facit; sed Falco logicus illi
respondet, chiachiarat, cridat hic, cridat ille, nec umquam
in centos annos pivam accordare valebunt.
Id quoque Lyro facit, facit Hippol et ipse Bocalus.

530 Omnes altandem tanto rumore volutant
ethican et phisican, animam centumque novellas
ut sibi stornito Baldus stopparet orecchias.
Zorneiam Scotti Philofornus retrovat illic,
quam rapit et giurat libros squarzare Thomasi.

535 Alberti Magni Centaurus somnia zaffat,
vult fieri cunctis gratus gnarusque futuri,
tollere cervellum cornacchis, prendere pisces
cum manibus, nec non sine clavi aprire seraias.
Fracassus quasdam saltantes undique ranas

a keg. In this same way, vague fantasies and bizarre feelings launch
an assault on the companions and nip their brains and, entering
their heads, turn the silence upside down. But Baldo remains in-
tact and he observes and marvels and finally laughs and takes de-
light in Cingar who, while the phantasms flutter here and there,
follows them and grabs them with his hands, but then, unable to
hold them, finds he has grabbed nothing.

Have you perhaps seen boys playing at times when they want to   510
catch flies in their hands and throw them "in prison" — that is to
say, into a piece of paper folded two and three and four times? In
fact, they often capture and hold them in the prison of their fist;
but when they loosen their fingers and open them a little, if the
other hand does not quickly trap the clever things, they escape,
and in this way both time and effort are wasted. Just so, Cingar
and his comrades, as Baldo laughed, were waving their hands in
every direction, in order to grasp nothing at all. However, when
these creatures, like little owls or tawny owls or barn owls, were fi-
nally worn out and tired, they are able to nab them and fill their
saddlebags with them.

Cingar gets hold of a thousand whoppers of Paolo Veneto and   522
Petrus Hispanus and gulps them down his throat at once as
though he were gulping candied confetti. And then he promptly
goes up against Falchetto and instantly makes thirty arguments,
but Falco responds like a logician and chatters. The one yells, the
other one yells, and never in a hundred years would they be able to
tune their pipes together. Lirone does the same thing; Hippol
does it and Boccalo as well. Eventually all of them turn ethics,
physics, the soul and a hundred novelties inside out with so
much noise that in a daze Baldo plugs his ears. Philoforno finds
there the cloak of Scotus, which he snatches, and he swears he'll

540 pissantesque retro manibus graffare laborat,
dumque unam pugno stringit, fugit altera longe.
Boccalus normas Epicuri nescio quantas
absque labore capit, complectitur, inque botazzum
claudit ne fugiant stoppatque cocamine busum.

545 Has inter follas scoperta est bestia tandem,
cui caput est asini, cui collum more camelli,
mille manus ac mille pedes, ac mille volantes
fert alas ventremque bovis gambasque capronis;
quae si non caudam simiae de retro teneret,

550 cum qua dattornum nequeat scazzare tavanos,
toccaret summo coeli testone solarum,
atque vorare uno vellet boccone Minervam.
Sed quia quidquid agit, cauda mancante, lasagna est,
ducitur in nihilum meritoque Chimera vocatur,

555 quae parit, oh!, magnos montes nascitque fasolus!
Hic quoque monstrum aliud duplici cum ventre videtur
qui sustentatur binis tantummodo gambis;
sic tenet impressos tacuini charta gemellos
Castora, Pollucem, monstrans signalia lunae.

560 Non aliter formatur ibi vir corpore duplo,
sive viri duplices coëuntes inguine tantum.
Dicitur hic Utrum; Utrum forma ista vocatur,
qui sibimet diris semper dat verbera pugnis,
scilicet alterutrum pars haec, pars illa flagellat.

565 Haec probat, illa negat, tandemque venitur in unum.
Attamen interea socii tolluntur ab uno
nescio quo motu, spinguntur et extra cavernam.
Quisque suis pergit iam gambis, quisque caminat,
nec penitus meminit quidnam vidisset adessum.

570 Phantasiae abeunt, quas in carneria nuper
sustulerant, redeuntque loco prius unde recedunt.

demolish the books of Thomas. The centaur grabs the dreams of Albertus Magnus: he wants to please everyone, to have knowledge of the future, to remove crows' brains, to catch fish with his hands and open locks without keys. Fracasso struggles to catch some frogs that jump every which way and piss from behind: while he grips one in his fist, another flees far away. Boccalo seizes I don't know how many maxims of Epicurus without any effort; he takes hold of them, and closes them in a bottle lest they escape, stopping the hole with a cork.

Among these illusions at last is found a beast, whose head is   545 that of an ass, whose neck is like a camel's. It has a thousand hands, a thousand feet, and a thousand flying wings. It has the belly of an ox and the legs of a billy goat; and if it did not possess the tail of a monkey behind, with which it could not chase away the horseflies, it would touch the ceiling of the sky with the top of its big head, and would like to devour Minerva with one swallow. But since whatever it does, without a tail, is a joke, it is considered nothing and is justly called Chimera — she who produces, O! great mountains, and gives birth to a bean!

Here too, another monster with a double belly appears, who is   556 held up by only two legs, just as an almanac chart showing the phases of the moon bears a print of the twins Castor and Pollux. In precisely this way a man is formed there with a double body, or rather two men joined only at the groin. This figure is named Whether; and its form is called Whether. It constantly strikes itself with dreadful fists, that is, both this part and the other part pummel each other. This states, that negates, and finally comes to one conclusion.

However, in the meantime, the companions are lifted by I don't   566 know what force and are expelled from the cavern. Now each one

Hi tamen et medii pazzi mediique balordi
grande manent spatium, tandemque accasa ritornant.
Oh menchionazzi, qui fraschis tempora perdunt
575 talibus atque suos credunt sic spendere giornos
utilius quam qui macaronica verba misurant,
quam qui supra humeros Pasquini carmina taccant!
Isti nempe sua tandem levitate recedunt,
vos ad Nestoreos semper stultescitis annos.
580 Ergo abeunt et Baldus eis passata recontat;
nec procul abscedunt, en quidam saltat avantum
buffonus, mattusque magis, magis immo famattus:
namque cavalcabat cannam de more citelli,
cumque manu laeva corseri fraena regebat,
585 cumque manu dextra giostrabat fuste canelli,
in cuius summo gyrabat giocola quaedam,
quam, dum currit homo, ventus facit ire datornum.
De panno fert ille duas, quas drizzat, orecchias,
quasve capuzzino fratesco sopra tacarat,
590 cusitumque tenet strepitosum quaeque sonaium.
Saltat hic atque facit manibus pedibusque morescam,
inde, manum porgens Baldo, danzare comenzat.
Baldus amorevolo non hunc sembiante refudat,
it secum ballans et iens quocumque menatur.
595 Compagni rident optantque videre quid istud
tandem importabit, danzam tutavia sequentes.
Nil pazzus loquitur, sed atezat saepeque cascat,
quem levat e terra Baldus nec tendit ad altrum
quam relevare susum cascantem saepe bufonem.
600 Post aliquod spatium, comparet machina grandis,
grandilitas cuius montem superabat Olympi.
Et quid erat moles tanta haec? Erat una cococchia,
sive vocas zuccam, seccam busamque dedentrum,
quae, quando tenerina fuit, mangiabilis atque,

478

can move along on his own legs; each of them walks and can scarcely remember what he has just seen. All the phantasms that they had just placed in their game bags go off and return to their previous place and slip away from there. And yet the men remain half-crazy and half-bewildered for a long time, but they come back at last to their senses.

O, the big dolts, who waste time on such trivialities, yet think   574
that they spend their days more profitably than those who count out macaronic words or attach poems to the top of Pasquino's shoulders! For such poets eventually abandon their frivolity, but you are stupid forever, right up to the age of Nestor.

Thus they depart, and Baldo tells them what has happened.   580
They have not gone far, when lo! a buffoon jumps in front of them, or rather a fool, or even more correctly, one who plays the fool. Like a little boy, he rides on a stick with his left hand guiding the reins of his courser and with his right hand jousting with the stalk of a reed, on whose tip twirls a kind of pinwheel that the wind spins as he runs. He sports two ears made of cloth that point upwards; they are attached to the top of a friar's cowl and have noisy bells sewn onto them. He dances, performing a *moresca* with his hands and feet. Next, stretching out a hand to Baldo, he begins to dance. Baldo fakes an amorous expression and does not refuse him; he goes off dancing and marching with him and is led every which way. The companions laugh; still following the dance, they are eager to see what this will finally mean. The fool says

605 certe omni mundo potuisset fare menestram.
  Ad latus ipsius, pro porta grande foramen
  panditur; hincve intrat buffonus, Baldus et altri.
  Stanza poëtarum est, cantorum, astrologorum,
  qui fingunt, cantant, dovinant somnia genti;
610 complevere libros follis vanisque novellis.
  Sed quales habeant poenas, audite, poëtae;
  audite, astronomi, cantores et chyromanti!
  ac quoque vos tantas caveatis fingere baias,
  ut parasythiaca placeatis in arte Signoris,
615 quos castronatis, quos menchionatis ad unguem,
  dando ad intender stellarum mille fusaras
  ac ea, quae possunt indovinare fachini
  cum coniecturis rerum cosisque vedutis,
  dicere cascari coniunctionibus ac in
620 ascendente Iovis cum Virgine cumque Leone.
  Zucca levis, sbusata intus similisque sonaio,
  in qua sicca sonant huc illuc semina dentrum,
  astrologis merito, cantoribus atque poëtis
  est domus; ut, veluti petra iacta retornat abassum,
625 utque focus per se supremum tendit ad ignem,
  sic leve cum levibus meschientur vanaque vanis.
  Stant ibi barberi, numero tres mille, periti,
  est quibus officium non dico radere barbas,
  sed de massellis dentes stirpare tenais,
630 hisque per ognannum sua dat sallaria Pluto.
  Quisque poëta, uni, seu cantor, sive strolecchus,
  barbero subiectus, ibi saepe oyme frequentat.
  Barberus, dum complet opus, stat supra cadregam
  atque rei testam tenet inter crura ficatam.
635 Hic numquam cessat nunc descalzare tremendis
  cum ferris dentes, nunc extirpare tenais,

nothing, but spins and falls often. Baldo lifts him up from the ground and spends his time lifting up the frequently falling buffoon.

After a short distance, a huge thing appeared, whose great size   600
surpassed Mount Olympus. And what was this great mass? It was a gourd, or you may call it a pumpkin, now dry and hollow inside, which, when it was tender and edible, could certainly have made soup for the whole world. In its side, a huge hole opens like a door, and the buffoon, Baldo and the others enter here. This is the abode of poets, minstrels and astrologers who invent, sing and interpret people's dreams; they have filled books with fables and worthless novelties. But hear now, you poets, what pains they suffer! Listen, astronomers, minstrels and palm readers, so that you too may avoid making up so many whoppers and pleasing your masters by the parasitic art — those whom you emasculate, whom you diddle quite thoroughly, by making them believe a thousand tall tales about the stars. And such things that porters could predict by reasoning and personal experience you say are the result of stellar conjunctions and of Jupiter in ascendance with Virgo and Leo.

This light pumpkin, scooped out inside like a bell, within   621
which dry seeds rattle this way and that, is a suitable home for astrologers, minstrels and poets. For just as a rock tossed upwards comes back down and as a flame by itself tends to rise to the highest fire, thus levity should be mixed with levities and vanity with vanities.

Here, there are skilled barbers, three thousand in number,   627
whose job it is, I do not say, to shave beards, but to pull teeth out

unde infinitos audis simul ire cridores
ad coelum; numquamve opera cessatur ab ista.
Quottidie quantas illi fecere bosias,

640 quottidie tantos bisognat perdere dentes,
qui quo plus streppantur ibi, plus denuo nascunt.
    Ergo sorellarum, o Grugna, suprema mearum,
si nescis, opus est hic me remanere poëtam:
non mihi conveniens minus est habitatio zucchae

645 quam qui Greghettum quendam praeponit Achillem
forzibus Hectoreis; quam qui alti pectora Turni
spezzat per dominum Aeneam, quem carmine laudat
"moeonia mentum mitra crinemque madentem."
Zucca mihi patria est; opus est hic perdere dentes

650 tot quot in immenso posui mendacia libro.
Balde, vale; studio alterius te denique lasso,
cui mea forte dabit tantum Pedrala favorem
ut te, Luciferi ruinantem regna tyranni,
dicat et ad mundum san salvum denique tornet.

655   Tange peroptatum, navis stracchissima, portum!
Tange! quod ammisi longinqua per aequora remos!
He heu, quid volui, misero mihi? Perditus Austrum
floribus et liquidis immisi fontibus apros.

of jaws with pliers, and Pluto gives them their annual salary. Each poet or minstrel or star-gazer there, when subjected to a barber, often repeats "woe is me." The barber finishes his job standing on a chair and holds the head of the culprit stuck between his legs. He never stops exposing teeth with his tremendous iron tools, then extracting them with his tongs, so you hear endless cries rising together to the sky, and he never rests from this labor. As many lies as they have told, so many teeth must they lose, day after day, and for every tooth pulled out there, another grows back.

Therefore, O Grugna, the utmost of my sisters, if you don't   642
know already, it is necessary for me, the poet, to remain here. In-habiting the pumpkin is no less fitting for me than for he who champions the Greekling Achilles over Hector's strength, or for he who splits the breast of proud Turnus by means of lord Aeneas, whom he praises in the verse, "with his chin and oiled tresses in a Lydian headdress." The pumpkin is my homeland, here I must lose as many teeth as the falsehoods I have put in this immense book. Baldo, farewell! I leave you in the end to the efforts of an-other, to whom perhaps my Pedrala will give so much favor that he may tell of you destroying the kingdom of the tyrant Lucifer, and return you at last to the world, hale and hearty.

Enter now the port you have yearned for, my exhausted ship,   655
enter! For I have lost the oars on the long trip across the seas! Alas! What did I want, wretch that I am? Reckless man, I have let loose the south wind into the flowerbeds and wild boars into crys-tal fountains.

Principal Characters

⁂

Names in parenthesis are nicknames or alternative versions of the character's usual name.

ALECTO: one of the Furies who boasts of having sown discord among the Italian peoples and of having destroyed the Catholic Church by means of her twin sons, Guelf and Ghibelline.

BAFFELLO (Mafelino): cheeky boss of the naked underworld blacksmiths; killed by Baldo.

BALDO (Baldino): the eponymous hero of the epic, son of Guido and Baldovina.

BALDOVINA: Baldo's mother and the daughter of the French king, she falls in love with Guido and elopes with him.

BELTRAZZO (Gilbecco): insanely jealous old man who lives as a consort to the witch, Pandraga; he is flogged by Boccalo and released.

BERTA (Bertola): Baldo's wife, mother of Grillo and Fanetto. She fights with Lena, humiliates Tognazzo, and tricks Zambello into thinking she has been killed and resuscitated.

BERTO PANADA: a generous peasant who hosts Baldo's parents; Zambello's father, he also acts as Baldo's step-father.

BOCCALO: one of Baldo's friends, he is a magician and cook from Bergamo; he throws his wife overboard (Book 12); is associated with the Folengo family (Book 19); is turned into a monk-colored ass that tries to mount Baldo (Book 23).

CENTAUR: see Virmazzo.

CHIARINA: a cow owned by Lena and Zambello whose misadventures occupy Book 8.

CINGAR: a clever and ruthless man, and Baldo's best friend.

CINGARINUS: see Grillo.

COPINO: see Jacopino.

CULFORA: see Gelfora.

DEMOGORGON: a creator of gods and demons, a master of witches and warlocks; in Book 23 he poses as Pasquino.

FALCHETTO (Falco): half-dog, half-man, one of Baldo's companions.

FANETTO: one of Baldo's twin sons, given as a gift by the besotted Charon to Tisiphone.

FOLENGO: the author's family name, referred to in Books 5.407 (Folengazzo), 11.455, 19.633, 22.105; and as a common noun, for watercoot: see 16.375, 23.620.

FRACASSO: giant friend of Baldo; carries a bell clapper like Pulci's Morgante.

FURABOSCO: a savage man-beast, brother of Molocco, killed by Moschino when he tries to eat Gilberto.

GAIOFFO: tyrannical mayor of Mantua; he has Baldo arrested and imprisoned, but later is kidnapped by Baldo, then mutilated and tortured to death by Cingar.

GELFORA (Culfora): queen of the witches; her kingdom is infiltrated then destroyed by Baldo and his men.

GILBECCO: see Beltrazzo.

GILBERTO (Giubertus): pacifist musician and song-writer, one of Baldo's friends, dear to Seraphus.

GRIFFAROSTO: infernal tavern host; he also appears in Folengo's *Orlandino* 8.

GRILLO (Cingarinus): one of Baldo's twin sons, brother of Fanetto.

GUIDO (Guidone): Baldo's father, a knight and later a blind prophetic hermit; descendant of Rinaldo (Renault de Montauban).

HIPPOL: like his brother Lirone, he is a pirate leader who fights against Baldo but later joins his band.

JACOPINO, FRA' (Copino): illiterate, lusty priest who purchases Zambello's wife, Lena, and participates in Cingar and Berta's miraculous knife scheme.

LENA: Zambello's long-suffering wife, she is attacked by Berta, swindled by Cingar and killed by her husband with a faux miraculous knife.

LEONARDO: handsome young nobleman who worships Baldo and joins his band; is killed defending his virginity from the witch Pandraga.

LIRONE: flesh-eating leader of the pirates who attack Baldo, but later joins him with his brother Hippol. (Hippol-Lirone mimics the sound of *Il Polirone*, the name of the Benedictine monastery where Folengo resided off and on.)

MAFELINO: see Baffello

MANTO: a Fate who gave her name to Mantua; she advises the heroes in Book 13. The name is also used as a personification of Mantua.

MARLOCCO: see Molocco.

MEGAERA: first of the three Furies to boast of having ruined the Church (by getting a bad pope elected).

MERLIN COCAIO: poet, priest, prophet and putative author of the *Baldus*, who also appears as a character in the text; he recites his own autobiography and continually compares himself favorably to Vergil.

MOLOCCO (Marlocco): a grotesque beast who comes to the aid of Pandraga and attacks the heroes; the name recalls the Biblical devil Moloch.

MOSCHINO: one of Baldo's friends and companions.

NARDUS: see Rufus.

PANDRAGA (Nocentina, Muselina): a vicious witch who has Leonardo killed for rebuffing her advances; Beltrazzo's mate, she enslaves devils and turns a whale into an island.

PASQUINO: a character based on an antique Roman statue displayed near the Piazza Navona in Renaissance Rome. Satires were affixed to the statue, hence the term "pasquinade." See also Demogorgon.

PHILOFORNO (earlier called Philotheus): an exemplary knight and prince who is held captive by pirates and later joins Baldo.

PIZZACAPELLETTO (Pizzaguerra): his name is formed from *appizzare*, to incite, and *cappelletto*, mercenary (or *guerra*, war); he is used by Seraphus for unusual missions; while invisible, he pinches Baldo and his friends.

RAFFUS: see Rufus.

RUBICANE: the hideous devil who emerges from what had been Merlin's tomb; he steals Pandraga's magic book, reads aloud the exploits of great wizards and playfully summons devils with it.

RUBINO (Ubaldo): with Pizzacapelletto, one of Seraphus' agents for mischief. Another Rubino who is a friend of Baldo's drops out after the second edition, together with Malaspina, and brothers Malfatto and Ircano.

RUFUS (Nardus, Raffus): an underworld river god in the employ of the queen witch Gelfora; drowned by Baldo.

SERAPHUS: a wizard, prophet and poet who aids the heroes but also plays tricks on them; he composes a poem on the death of the cow Chiarina.

SINIBALDO: a friend of Guido's who pleads with him on behalf of the French king to rejoin the joust.

SMIRALDA (Smerdola): a witch; in the form of a dragon she terrorizes the men, but is ordered by Merlin to be taken away by devils.

SORDELLO: prince of Goito. He has the same name as the famous thirteenth century troubadour. He is a knight and statesman who stands up for young Baldo and takes him into his household as a valet; Gaioffo may have ordered him murdered.

TISIPHONE: one of the Furies, she boasts of having sown discord on earth by setting the Cipadense against each other.

TOGNAZZO: a ruling elder of Cipada. He tries to help Zambello against Baldo and ends up humiliated and later slaughtered by Cingar.

VIRMAZZO (Vinmazzo): centaur and friend of Baldo; most often called merely "the centaur."

ZAMBELLO: son of Berto and Dina, a peasant whom Baldo mistreats and eventually kills although he is raised as his brother; he also suffers from Cingar's schemes.

Note on the Text

The text of the *Baldus* reproduces that found in the edition prepared by Mario Chiesa for the series "Bibliothèque Italienne" (directed by Yves Hersant and Nuccio Ordine) published by Les Belles Lettres with the support of the Istituto Italiano per gli Studi Filosofici. Volumes 1–2 (Books I–XV) of this edition appeared in 2004–2007. The author is grateful to Professor Chiesa and Alain Segonds of Les Belles Lettres for permission to publish. An earlier version of Prof. Chiesa's edition was published in Turin with the Unione tipografico-editrice Torinese in 1997. Readers interested in a fuller account of the textual tradition and the variants among editions should consult vol. 1 of Les Belles Lettres' edition. The author also gratefully acknowledges Prof. Chiesa's Italian translation and notes, which were very useful in preparing her own translation and notes.

The abbreviations used below to indicate the various editions (see Introduction to vol. 1) are as follows:

P   Paganini, 1517.
T   Toscolano, 1521. References are to the book and page number of the anastatic copy of 1994.
C   Cipadense, no date (but c. 1536).
V   Venice, 1552 (formerly known as VC). This edition forms the base text for Mario Chiesa's edition and this I Tatti text.

Full citations may be found in the Bibliography.

Notes

BOOK XIII

13.11. Anguillina (Lady Eel) as Triton's mother seems to be Folengo's invention. In Hesiod and other early writers, Triton is the son of Poseidon and Amphitrite; he is not mounted on a dolphin, but himself has the tail of a fish.

13.27. Deiopea is the sea nymph Juno promised to Aeolus for unleashing the winds against the Trojans; see Vergil, *Aeneid* 1.71–75.

13.35. Chiesa suggests that "sniffs at the smoke of the roast" may refer to the fact that Aeolus's reign is made up of smoke and no fire (i.e. just wind), and sees in Neptune's rebuke echoes from *Aeneid* 1.32–42.

13.117–121. Chiesa notes a similar passage in Ariosto's *Orlando Furioso* 20.20.7–8.

13.123. *Stirpe maronorum:* a play on Vergil's name; see note at 8.220.

13.155–165. Apelles is the renowned Greek painter of the fourth century BCE. For Manto and Folletto see the note at 6.12. Barigazzo is a Mantuan family name; there is also a Barigaccio in Boiardo's *Orlando Innamorato*. Grandonio in Pulci's *Morgante* is a Saracen king killed by Roland at Roncesvalles. Bufalco seems to be a humorous rendering of the name of Alexander's horse, Bucephalus. The others, Alexander the Great, Xerxes, Hannibal, etc., are well-known historical figures; note that Folengo refers to Achilles with the epithet, *capelletto* (mercenary); Albanian mercenary cavalry in the service of the Republic of Venice were called this because of the small red caps they wore: see 1.309, 10.153, 22.500 and 24.477.

13.220–31. *Althalac,* glossed as *sal* (salt) in T 12 p. 386; *alphatar* as *argentum vivum* (quicksilver) in T 12 p. 134r; *sal Liei* as *tartarum* (tartrate). The latter is the salt that forms in wine bottles and wine barrels, hence the name "salt of Bacchus," Lyaeus being an epithet of Bacchus, the god of wine.

13.240. Geber is the Latin name of the famous alchemist Abu Musa Jabir ibn Hayyan (c.721-c.815).

13.268. *Lypercol* is unknown; it is possibly a formation from *ly* + *percol(are)*, i.e. the filtering (Chiesa); in 25.492 *lyhomo* is listed as one of the sophistic lies (*ly* being the definite article, barbarously introduced into Latin by medieval logicians). See also *Chyrieque lysonis* at 20.22 and 25.488–93.

13.270. Possibly an allusion to John 14:6: "I am the way (*via*), the truth and the life."

13.291. *Conzalavezus*: Lombardian dialect word for someone who repairs vessels, from *conciare* to cure (and also to castrate) and *laveggio* (L *lapideum*, vessel).

13.293–8. The language used here points to layers of meaning having to do with sin, bodies, and being "de-albed" (= whitened, but the *de-* is also perhaps to be understood privatively as "deprived of one's alb," i.e. the vestment worn by priests at Mass). Note *peccat* and *peccatum* at 294, 297; *corpora nigra, corpus* and *ne corpora scilicet ipsa frangat* at 293–8; *dealbat* at 293.

13.316–8. Manto and Ocno belong to the Etruscan origins of the city; see also 6.12 and 18.339; and see Vergil, *Aeneid* 10.198.

13.328. Francesco Gonzaga (1532–1550), ruler of Mantua, son of Federico (1500–1540); the latter receives similar praise in C and T (T 12 p. 136). In fact the Gonzaga family had been ruling Mantua since 1328, so the reign of the *acerbo tyranno* (323) presumably occurred prior to this.

13.338. One could translate *quae toccare manu faciunt genitalia rerum* as "which cause them to touch with their hands the genitals of things."

13.376–95. Gilberto's song, which first appears in C, is in humanistic Latin rather than macaronic Latin, and seems particularly unmelodic.

13.391. *Iactura priorum* may be an allusion to Folengo's brother's fate: Ludovico was a prior and had been expelled from the Benedictine order in 1524, most likely due to charges trumped up by Ignazio Squarcialupi's faction. A similar poem is found in Folengo's *Varium poëma*, entitled "Metaphors for those who repent of having undertaken a magistracy" (VIII, pp. 16–19).

13.418. Mesue, also known as Mu'awiyah, was a Persian physician, 777–857 CE.

13.421–2. Borso d'Este, Duke of Ferrara (1413–1471); on Gonella see 6.6, above; Zaramella has not been identified.

13.471. All are related to the sun: Ptous was the name of a mountain temple in Boeotia in Greece that held festivals for Apollo; Horus is the Egyptian god of the sky; Pythias (serpent), is one of Apollo's epithets from classical mythology; Phos means light; Mithras was identified with the sun in ancient Persian religion; Myrinus may be the fortress of Myrina on the island of Lemnos, known for its fiery volcanic activity.

BOOK XIV

14.1. Memnon, the mythic son of Aurora and Tithonus, was killed by Achilles during the Trojan War; his mother's tears bring him immortality, so he lives on as the morning dew.

14.20–2. These are comically garbled references to Plato, Aristotle (as in 9.449 and 23.75), and the ancient Greek astronomer Ptolemy, as well as to the Old Testament figures Jonah, Melchisedech and the apocalyptic figures Gog and Magog.

14.49. As Chiesa explains, Valencia was known for having many clever prostitutes who (as Bandello says) knew how to dupe men; compare Ariosto, *Orlando Furioso* 8.553–4.

14.67–8. The Moon is identified here with Persephone (Proserpina), who according to Greek mythology was ravished by Pluto and constrained to spend one month in the underworld for each pomegranate seed she had eaten in his domain.

14.94. For *fusos tortos*, see note at 6.417.

14.167. The word for owl here is *civetta (carine noctua)*, which also means flirt and decoy, as it was used to lure other birds.

14.198–9. In Greek mythology Zeus assumed the shape of a bull in order to ravish Europa. Zeus also raped Io, an innocent maiden (not a cow!), and then turned her into a cow to hide her from his jealous wife; later she succeeded in writing her fate in the sand for her father to read

(Ovid, *Metamorphosis*, 1.583–746). For more on Io and Folengo, see the note at 23.660.

14.222. This was a popular fable, explained in T as follows: The hop plant, *humulus lupulus*, grew so quickly one night that it was able to imprison the feet of the nightingale, so from then on the nightingale sang all night to keep itself awake (T 13 p. 140).

14.232. In T, a gloss explains that birds say these words in imitation of humans.

14.270. This is in fact close to the accepted etymology of the Italian word *vendemmia*, meaning harvest: Lat. *vinum* (wine), *de* (from) and *emere* (obtain).

14.319–20. These varieties of grapes were known around the world: *groppelle*, red or white grapes, are grown in Lombardy; the *zibibbo* variety (from Arabic *zibib*, grape) is grown in Sicily and used primarily for sweet wines and is sometimes a synonym for muscat of Alexandria or muscatel. The other three were mentioned above, 1.503–8; *greghis*, Greek, as below, 340 and 1.503.

14.343. Martial, *Epigrams* 1.18.5.

14.356. *Trincher* appears to be from German *trinken*, to drink, and *tartofen* is probably from the expletive, *der Teufel!* (the devil!), used as an exclamation. Initially glossed in P simply as "German words," in T the gloss sends the reader to Suetonius: *Trincher et Tartofen quid significent lege Svetonium* (T 13 p. 142r).

14.377. For Gonella, see the note at 6.6.

BOOK XV

15.12. What one expects from a study of astrological almanacs is an ability to predict the future, not an expertise in talking about the past.

15.18. The word *pinzochera* (sanctimonious) is later used (23.501–22) to describe witches who are also panderers.

15.22–34. This song, also in humanistic Latin (as the previous one, 13.376–95), is new in V. The allusions to turbulent seas, monsters, a damaged reputation, etc., seem to be autobiographical and may recall

Folengo's difficult years outside the Benedictine monastery. It replaces a song in C, which was later published as no. 4 in the *Varium Poëma*. This earlier lyric is written in praise of Neapolitan humanist Scipione Capece (c. 1480–1551), who served as governor of Cosenza and later as head of the Academia Pontaniana. He was condemned by the Inquisition as a heretic in 1543.

15.29. Syrte Minor and Syrte Major were bays difficult to navigate on the Northern coast of Libya, now called the Gulf of Sidra (near the city of Surt); Syrte Major is also a dark region of Mars. Ara, the Altar, is a southern constellation, near Scorpio.

15.47. To cut things in the Guelf manner may have been a common saying; it is repeated in 25.311–50, where Alecto boasts of having sown discord between Guelfs and Ghibellines. Chiesa cites a precedent for this sort of division of food from Sacchetti, *Novella* 223.

15.62. A mangling of Hebrews 10:7: "In the volume of the book it is written of me, to do thy will, O God."

15.68. This hemistich is not from Lucan, but is a medieval Latin proverb.

15.73. Ovid, *Heroides* 2.85. Note the play on Ovid's name, Publius Ovidius Naso: *nasone* in Italian is a large nose.

15.80. Psalms 51:7. Boccalo's anointing of his friends here is a variation of *la benedizione del Pievano Arlotto*, named after the fifteenth-century Florentine priest Arlotto, known for his homely wit and practical jokes.

15.117–8. This jumble of nonsense-quotations has been untangled by Mario Chiesa as follows: first, a line from the *Disticha Catonis* (1.20), about acknowledging even small gifts graciously; then a famous phrase from Vergil's *Eclogues* 3.58; and lastly, an allusion to Penelope's letter from the first line of Ovid's *Heroides*.

15.132. This unusual meaning of *orecchino* is explained by a gloss: *Orecchino: auriscalpio* (T 4 p. 441).

15.186. Luigi Gonzaga da Gazzolo (1500–1532), nicknamed Rodomonte, was descended from a cadet branch of the ruling family of Mantua; he was celebrated not only for his strength (here and in 19.403–9), but also for his courtly virtues. See Ariosto, *Orlando Furioso* 26.50.5–8 and 37.9–11.

15.224–5. Steropes, Brontes and Pyracmon are the three Cyclopses who forged Jupiter's thunderbolt: see Hesiod, *Theogony* 139–46; Vergil, *Aeneid* 8.425.

15.274–6. It was thought that blood from a freshly slain capon could cut diamond; in *Orlandino* 3.7.1 Folengo cites Pliny the Elder in a gloss (*Natural History* 20.1.2, 37.15.59).

15.318–9. A similar observation is made in the autobiographical *Chaos del Triperuno*, in which two of the poet-selves tell of priests who kept many students subject (with implications of physical abuse), *e più li belli che li brutti* ("more the pretty than the ugly ones"): *Chaos*, pp. 275–8. See Introduction.

15.332–3. In T and C there followed twenty to thirty lines about weaving and embroidery, Minerva being the goddess of such arts.

15.382. 'Ginus' is probably to be identified with Gaius Julius Hyginus, a contemporary of Julius Caesar, who in the Renaissance was believed to be the author of a didactic poem *De astronomia*, now thought to be the work of a later compiler.

BOOK XVI

16.24. Turnus is the great opponent of Aeneas in the later books of the *Aeneid*.

16.26. The odd name Lyrone, when linked to Hippol, his brother's name, forms Hippol-Lirone, or Il Polirone, the name by which the large, important monastery of San Benedetto Po was known, where Folengo resided off and on. See the discussion in Otello Fabris, *Le Doctrinae cusinandi di Merlin Cocai: In coquina Iovis* (Nove [Vicenza]: Biblioteca Merliniana, 2005), 32–5.

16.38. Chioggiotti, men from Chioggia in the Veneto, famous sailors. The navigator John Cabot was said to be from Chioggia.

16.48. Francesco Maria I della Rovere (1490–1538), Duke of Urbino, nephew of Pope Julius II, was captain-general of the Papal States and later of the Republic of Venice.

16.147. Given what follows, about Christ, Mohammed and Baldo's battle with "enemies of the Gospel," and the earlier reference to St. Francis (16.92), the mention of stigmata here must allude to Christ's wounds; see note to 483.

16.264. Sardanapulus is the legendary Assyrian king from the seventh century BCE, infamous for living in decadent luxury.

16.304–6. These are all points along the river Mincio in or near Mantua; see the map on p. xiii.

16.335–6. An identical description of someone's face looking like a lantern and a similar retort are found in the *Mambriano* of Francesco Cieco da Ferrara (9.83.4–5 and 9.84.8).

16.347, 349. Molorchus is the poor laborer who offers Hercules hospitality on his way to and from killing the Nemean lion. Hard tack was often preserved with fennel seeds (*fenocchios*).

16.375. The word for coot is *folenga*: Folengo uses variations of his own name and those of various pseudonyms and characters throughout the text.

16.483. The implication seems to be that Leonardo is wearing a crown of thorns, like Jesus going to his death.

16.534–7. The Beguines were orders of religious women, sometimes married, and therefore denounced as heretics by elements in the Church. The Third Order of Saint Francis was set up for lay men and women. If the women being lambasted here claimed to be bigamists, this could point to women who joined a religious order and became brides of Christ despite being already married, or it could allude to witches being married to the devil. This passage first appears in C; see a similar passage in 23.497–537. Santa Zita is the patron saint of domestic servants whose liturgy was approved by Pope Leo X.

16.550. An allusion to Matthew 5:15–6.

BOOK XVII

17.29. Pandraga: "all dragon," a superdragoness. The *locus amoenus* recalls the forest where Venus finds Adonis in Book 10 of Ovid's *Metamorphoses*, and Alcina's island in *Orlando Furioso* 6.20–22. And see 14.90–141.

17.95. Megaera, one of the Furies, is associated with jealousy, as in 213 below. Megaera and her two sisters, Alecto and Tisiphone, are given important roles in 25.206–396.

17.124. Apparently a reference to Aesop's fable *The Kid and the Wolf*, also quoted in Folengo's *Orlandino* 1.6.8.

17.129. The Italian expression *fanno giacomo giacomo* is said of legs that are buckling from fatigue or fear.

17.180. Folengo retells the biblical story of Susanna in his *Umanità del figliuolo di Dio* 1.36.

17.199–200. To make someone believe that the moon is in the well means to dupe. Diana is usually identified with the Moon, although the latter is also associated with Venus.

17.280–89. In a paragraph included in V, entitled the *Argomento sopra il Baldo*, a friend of Folengo's, Francesco Donesmondi, is credited with being the inspiration for the epic, specifically for the character of Baldo. This young man (the son of Francesco Gonzaga's secretary of finance) was murdered in Bologna in 1515, as is proven by letters from Pietro Pomponazzi to Francesco Gonzaga and from Gonzaga to Annibale Bentivoglio. However, in Folengo's epic narrative, it is not Baldo, but his friend Leonardo who is killed and honored as a Christ-like figure. See Nora Calzolaio, "Dialogus Philomusi: edizione, attribuzione, commento," *Quaderni folenghiani*, 3 (2000–1): 57–106, at 93–5.

17.325. Balaam is a prophet in the Bible who appears at the end of the Book of Numbers; God's angel speaks to him through the donkey he is riding.

17.370. Chiesa interprets this line as a Macaronic rendering of the Italian expression *fece alto leva* (takes off), used by Luigi Pulci in *Morgante* 27.71.3.

17.404. Molocco: the name is otherwise unattested, but sounds vaguely biblical, and is perhaps meant to recall Moloch, the demon worshipped by idolatrous Israelites; the same figure is called Marlocco in P and T.

17.443–4. *Desdottom (diciotto)* is eighteen, the highest total of three dice, and as glosses in P and T explain, this is the luckiest draw.

17.461–2. *La Reine Ancroia* is a chivalric romance (cited above at 3.104) in which Ignarus and Tarrassus are centaurs. Berossus is a Babylonian historian of the third-fourth century BCE, whose work had been imitated in a popular fifteenth century forgery by Annius of Viterbo; it is cited here for comic effect.

17.531. Zoroaster (Zarathustra), a Persian philosopher-prophet (date unknown, possibly 700–900 BCE), in post-classical Europe was accredited with magical powers; he was considered by Renaissance Platonists the source of the most ancient tradition of pre-Christian theology. See also below, 19.70 and 171.

17.662. *Cocono*, like *cocaio*, is a dialect word for a bottle stopper, and hence refers to the author, Merlin Cocaio; see T 25 p. 245: *Cocamen et cocaius et coconus.*

BOOK XVIII

18.27. The centaur Chiron was noted for his prophetic ability, perhaps alluded to here.

18.35. For *trat via bragas* see the note at 11.25.

18.50–1. In Renaissance Italy witches were sometimes subject to public beatings with a bundle of switches.

18.196–7. For St. Paul the Hermit, see the note at 12.524–36; St. Anthony Abbot was one of Paul's disciples and also lived in the Egyptian desert, c. 251–356 CE; for St. Macarius, see the note at 10.51.

18.245. Chiesa suggests that *fanfugola*, not documented elsewhere, is a variation of *fanfaluca*, air bubble. The word for beggar, *pitocco*, is the surname Folengo uses for his authorial self in the *Orlandino*, Limerno Pitocco, who is also one of the main characters in Folengo's *Chaos del Triperuno*.

18.309–10. Pandraga was introduced above in Book 17, when she attempted to seduce Leonardo and then had him killed, and will be seen more below, in Book 19 and after. Smiralda has a prominent role in Book 21 (see note at 21.199). There is a witch named Smeralda in the anonymous chivalric epic, *La Reine Ancroia*. Gelfora appears in Books 22–24; in P and T she was named "Culfora" (perhaps from *culus*, butt, and *foro*, *-are*, to pierce).

18.312. Demogorgon is a creator of gods and demons, a master of witches and warlocks, and has been traced back to the creator-demiurge of Plato's *Timaeus*; he acquired a poetic persona in Boccaccio's *Genealogia deorum* and became popular as a character in chivalric romances.

18.314–9. These sorceresses fall into two categories: those of classical fame, Medea and Circe, and those who appear in Boiardo's *Orlando Innamorato*: Fallerina, Dragontina, Alcina, sister of Morgana, and Silvana or Silvanella. For Folletto see the note on 6.12, where he is the husband of the sibyl Manto, and 13.157.

18.320–3. For the story of the white and black eagles, see Boiardo, *Orlando Innamorato* 3.2; it is repeated below in 18.447–8 and 22.263–7.

18.339. *Bianorei*: Bianor, also called Ocno, is the mythological founder of Mantua; see the note at 6.12.

18.346–7. Master of the Sacred Palace is the title given to the pope's chief theologian, beginning with St. Dominic in 1218: the inquisitors were under his administration. "Pyres" here translates *casottis*, which were little structures, made of branches and twigs, for burning witches, as glossed in T 20 p. 207r.

18.359. In T, some two dozen lines followed, consisting of Baldo's address to his dead father (T 18 p. 176r).

18.406–7. Ferrante I Gonzaga (1507–1557), brother of Duke Federico, was a commander of the imperial army of Charles V and viceroy in Sicily during Folengo's stay there; he later fought against the Turks in Tunis and Algiers; see 18.480, below.

18.433–70. A list of famous Roman heroes. *Torquatus*: Titus Manlius Torquatus, fourth century Roman leader, had his son put to death for disobeying a military order not to engage in one-on-one combat with a Latin. *Brutus*: Lucius Junius Brutus, traditionally the founder of the Roman Republic in 509 BCE, following the defeat of the Etruscan king Tarquinius. When his sons plotted later to restore the Tarquins to power, he executed them. *Fabricius*: Gaius Fabricius Luscinus (d. 250 BCE), general and statesman, renowned for his simplicity of life. *Cincinnatus*: Lucius Quinctius Cincinnatus (c.519–430 BCE), statesman and dictator, famous for refusing the temptations of power and returning to his family farm. *Camillus*: Marcus Furius Camillus (c.446–362 BCE), general and political leader who among other achievements drove the Gauls out of the city of Rome, which they had occupied. SPQR stands for *Senatus Populusque Romanus*, the sovereign body of the Romans. *The two Catos*: Marcus Porcius Cato the Elder (234–149 BCE) and Marcus Porcius Cato Uticensis the Younger (95–46 BCE), his great-grandson, both symbols of republican severity. *Cornelius Scipio* and *his brother*: Publius Cornelius Scipio, father to the Scipio Africanus mentioned immediately below, was a Roman statesman and general. He fought the Carthaginians and died in battle in Spain in 211 BCE. His older brother, Gnaeus Cornelius Scipio Calvus, also fell in Spain the same year. *Fabius Maximus*: Quintus Fabius Maximus (c.280–203 BCE), hero of the Second Punic War, savior of Rome. *The Mistress of the World* is the city of Rome. *Marcellus*: Probably Marcus Claudius Marcellus (268–208 BCE), a hero the Second Punic War and the conqueror of Syracuse. *Aemilius*: Probably Lucius Aemilius Paullus Macedonicus (229–160 BCE), the general who won the Third Macedonian War at the Battle of Pydna. *Scipio*: Scipio Africanus (235–183 BCE), who defeated Hannibal in the Battle of Zama, arguably the most important battle in Roman history. The *one-eyed African* is Hannibal, who lost his left eye before the battle of Lake Trasimene in 217 BCE. *Pompey, Caesar, Cassius, Brutus*: all well-known political and military figures of the late Roman republic.

18.480–81. For Ferrante Gonzaga see 18.406 above; Ruggiero d'Este is the mythical chivalric founder of the house of Este, rulers of Ferrara, invented by Boiardo in *Orlando Innamorato* and used again by Ariosto in *Orlando Furioso*.

BOOK XIX

19.11. A quotation from Vergil's *Eclogues* 3.1 and a transformation of 1.28, *Candidior postquam tondenti barba cadebat* ("when my beard fell whiter from the barber's shears"). Folengo is playing on the similarity of *castronus*, castrated, with *castano*, chestnut-colored; *marrone* means chestnut and testicle and is also close to Vergil's *cognomen*, Maro. See the note on 8.220 in vol. 1 of this edition.

19.27–28. Chiesa reports that this is a standard question found in grammars of the day, the proper response being not "amen," but *nomen*, noun.

19.35. *Janua sum rudibus* ("I am the portal of the uninstructed"): the first words of the famous elementary grammar known as the *Janua*, falsely attributed in the Renaissance to the ancient grammarian Donatus.

19.61–68. Metrapas, Molchael and Bariel appear to be invented names. In P and T this tomb belonged to Merlin. In these earlier versions the tomb is uncovered not by the centaur, but by a blameless character named Philotheus (a transposition of Folengo's religious name, Teofilo); in the latter two versions Philotheus changes to Philoforno. See 20.311.

19.70. For Zoroaster see note at 17.531.

19.77–264. This devil, called Rubicane at line 142, is just one of a dozen or so devils about to appear whose name is identical or similar to one of Dante's devils in *Inferno* 21–22. See note at 229.

19.101. Mythological creatures: the Gryphon has the head and wings of an eagle and the body of a lion, while the Harpy has the trunk of a woman and the talons and beak of a bird.

19.133. The *moresca* was an exuberant and humorous dance, extremely popular in the Renaissance in all parts of Europe; it was known as the Morris dance in England.

19.146. Caina is the name of one of the four portions of the ninth circle of hell in Dante's *Inferno* (see 19.316 below). It is named after Cain who in the Biblical book of Genesis treacherously slew his brother Abel.

19.158. David Marsh suggests reading *illam* as *illum*, so that the referent is the book. Following Chiesa's text, one could translate: "since we shall carry her off."

19.176–7. Thebit or Thabit ibn Qurrah (836–901 CE) was a noted Arabic mathematician and astronomer; the *Picatrix* was the Latin name of a well-known Arabic treatise on magic, the *Ghayat al-hakim*.

19.179, 183. This play on the word *picta*, painted, for Pict (Scot) introduces Michael Scot (c.1175-c.1235 CE), scholar, necromancer and astrologer, cited by Dante, Boccaccio and others. See also 25.533 and note.

19.191. In T, Seraphus rows off with the handsome Gilberto in this ship conjured by Michael Scot (T 19 p. 192).

19.194. Glossed in T 18 p. 179r: *Suffimigium: quasi sacrificio diablo* ("fumigation from below, as though indicating a sacrifice to the devil").

19.206–18. Apollonius of Tyana, first century CE, was a famous Neo-Pythagorean holy man believed to have superhuman powers; the pagans often compared him to Jesus Christ. The Saracen enchanter from Granada has not been identified. Magundat is identified in a gloss, *Magundat, qui postea dictus est Anastasius* ("Magundat, who afterwards was called Anastasius"), as the Persian mage who was converted to Christianity after having witnessed the power of a relic of the Holy Cross (T 18 p. 180). He became a monk and was martyred in 628 by the Persian King Chosroes I for refusing to renounce his faith. Pietro d'Abano (1250-c.1316), a philosopher, astrologer and professor of medicine who worked at the university of Padua, was rumored to have possessed the Philosopher's Stone. He was brought up before the Inquisition on various charges, among them one of committing fraudulent transactions such as those specified in lines 211–218.

19.225. T 18 p. 180, glosses Semiphora as *dei nomen* ("the name of a god").

19.229–60. The thirty-some devil's names mentioned here come from a variety of sources, as noted above at 19.77. Identical or similar to names in Dante's *Inferno* are Alchino, Barbariccia, Cagnazzo, Calcabrina, Ciriatto, Draganizza, Farfarello, Grafficane, Libicocco, Malabranca, Malacoda and others. Malabolgia here is no longer the eighth circle of Hell (sins of fraud), as in *Inferno* 18–30, but together with the classical river, Acheron, has become a judge of the underworld (but see 19.316 below). Minos (Minossus) has become a devil. Other names are borrowed from the Bible: Beelzebub, Asmodeus, Astaroth, and the archangel Uriel. Formed like the latter name are a few of Folengo's inventions, Futiel,

Siriel, Melloniel. Others refer to people and things: Zaffus (cop, and also stopper for a bottle, like *cocaio*), Bombarda (cannon). Many of these names had made previous appearances in Luigi Pulci's *Morgante*, Boiardo's *Orlando innamorato*, and Cieco's *Mambriano*.

19.271. As noted by Chiesa, *lypitop* ("boom-da-boom") could be a play on the name of a fictitious personage, Lippo Topo; see his article in the journal *Lingua nostra* 32 (1971): 36.

19.334–6. *Ladiniter* is a Latinization of the Italian expression *latinamente*, meaning easily. A *cinquino* was a small coin; *silacchum* is from *silacq*, scar, attested in the in Modenese dialect.

19.351. Although *cima* is frequently used by Folengo with the meaning of top or peak (as in Italian), here, as in 4.82, it means one who is cunning, on top of things. The source of the proverb about wool has not been unidentified.

19.380. Legendary precedents for this behavior include not only Bertran de Born (*Inferno* 28.118–42), but also cephalopherous saints such as San Miniato and St. Denis of Paris.

19.392. The use of "fly-swatter" (*paramuscas*) as a weapon seems to play on the preceding word for musket, and *musca*, fly. Invectives against firearms were delivered by many contemporary authors, among them Machiavelli, *Arte della Guerra* 3, and Ariosto, *Orlando Furioso* 9.28–91 and 11.21–8.

19.399. Giovanni delle Bande Nere (1498–1526), the great Medici condottiere and father of Cosimo I de'Medici, died as the result of an artillery wound. Charles de Bourbon (1490–1527) was a distinguished general who passed from the French army of Francis I to the Imperial army of Charles V and was killed by an arquebus during the Sack of Rome. Luigi Gonzaga (nicknamed Rodomonte), in whose home Giovanni delle Bande Nere expired, was himself killed in 1532 (see note at 15.186).

19.480. "Skin the cat" : see note to 9.523 in vol. 1 of this edition.

19.495. *Bimembris* could also be translated as two-membered, especially given the sentence that follows.

19.529–31. For additional references to bats and owls on the attack, see 15.357–60, 21.203 and 25.404 and 520.

19.546–8. The names of the devils in this passage are thought to be Folengo's own inventions.

19.559. This description recalls Vergil's description of the Cyclops, *Monstrum horrendum, informe, ingens cui lumen ademptum* ("a frightful monster, ugly, huge, whose sight had been taken away") in *Aeneid* 3.658.

19.615–620. A variety of monsters culled from Greek mythology and from Folengo's imagination. Echidna is the mother of many monsters, among them Cerberus, the Sphinx and Chimera; the Minotaur had the head of a bull and the body of a man. Briareus is one of the Titans, and both he and the monstrous Geryon also figure in Dante's *Divine Comedy*.

BOOK XX

20.14–19. Written in standard Latin hexameters, not macaronic verse.

20.46. *Trenta diavoi*: as Zaggia and Chiesa have observed, thirty is not meant as a specific number, but rather as an expression meaning "many" (see also 3.364, 17.69, 22.428, 23.50).

20.153. As below (160), the image is of Fracasso as a gardener, pulling up leeks; see also 4.73–4.

20.175–6. Reminiscent of the famous statement of the ancient mathematician Archimedes, "Give me a place to stand and I shall move the world."

20.203. "Just now" : in Book XIX.

20.304. "On the left" : possibly an allusion to Dante's *Inferno* 26.126.

20.313. "Colicutti," as noted by Chiesa, is not to be confused with Calcutta, but instead, as in many sixteenth-century works, stands for a place that is incalculably far away.

20.314, 317. Philoforno (oven-lover?) in P and T was called Philotheus, a simple transposition of Teofilo. He was an exemplary knight, pure and valiant, and in these earlier versions he helped uncover Merlin's tomb (in the two later versions this tomb houses not Merlin, but unfamiliar mages, 19.63–7). Prester John is the mythical king of a Christian kingdom variously said to be located in India, Central Asia or Ethiopia.

20.319. *Ventosare* ("raises welts") in Italian can mean "to apply medical cupping glasses."

20.378. The meaning of these exhortations is not clear. *Mora* seems to be a third person imperative of *morire*, to die; and *taia* and *ritaia*, second person imperatives of *tagliare*, to cut.

20.390. *Nespola* are medlar fruits, but the meaning is extended to signify welts.

20.410–11. *Mescadizzo* is a Northern dialect form of *mascarizzo*, leather tanned with alum. *Pro pane fugazzam*, bread for focaccia, an Italian expression meaning to give tit for tat.

20.563. *Apava!* : "To Padua!"

20.600. Compare the reference to notaries who write *macaronica verba* in 2.11.

20.613. The castle of Musso is found on the western shore of Lake Como; San Leo is a fortress on a sharp precipice near San Marino, of Roman origins but enlarged in the fifteenth century by the famous condottiere Federico, Duke of Urbino; the steepness of this fortress is alluded to by Dante in *Purgatorio* 4.25.

20.638. For the sign of the fig (*ecce tibi ficcas facio*: "Look, I give you the finger"), see the note at 12.381.

20.646. The three children are Jupiter himself, Neptune and Pluto. The giant offspring of Alcmena and Jupiter is Hercules; the reference is to his labors and to the time he spent enslaved to the Queen of Lydia, later his wife, who made him weave and wear women's clothing.

20.777, 789. Rabelais would later elaborate on encounters with speakers of incomprehensible languages, for example, when Pantagruel meets the Limousin (2.6), and again when he meets Panurge for the first time (2.9).

BOOK XXI

21.1. Malamocco was an important port at the tip of the Venetian lagoon, near the mouth of one branch of the River Brenta; it was relocated a few miles north after suffering severe sea damage in the twelfth century. A gloss in T explains that the metaphorical meaning is that of mortal danger (T 23 p. 226). The following adventures in the underworld first appear in T, Books 23–25.

21.12. "Triple bronze" (*aes triplex*): a phrase from Horace, *Odes* 1.3.9: a triple bronze shield around his heart protects Horace's friend Vergil, sailing the Adriatic, from the terrors of the deep.

21.22. *Striax mea togna*. Striax (Grugnae Striacis Carossae: see 1.14) is the macaronic muse assigned to the final five books, as is made explicit in C. According to Chiesa, *togna* is used as an adjective, meaning silly (compare Tonella in 4.161). Carossa, defined by Folengo as *crapula*, is also the name of the second part of the *Chaos del Triperuno*.

21.24. *Pegoras* (sheep) was used for white-caps and as a metaphor for monks (12.105 and note). This invocation to the muse is reminiscent of a song sung by Gilberto at 15.22–33.

21.56. *Firmum* ("the melody"): i.e. the *cantus firmus*, the melody in polyphonic compositions, often used in motets, as here.

21.96. This seems to be a specific person: according to Chiesa (quoting Paolo Guerrini), this could be an allusion to Don Marco Cropelli di Chiari, an abbot of St. Eufemia, the Benedictine monastery in Brescia; or simply a more generic reference, as there was an important cattle market in Chiari (as referred to below, 22.484); but there, too, the context is ambiguous. For Gnatho see the note at 4.425. Ecclesiastical criticism of polyphony for its alleged sensuality and its tendency to make the text harder to discern went back to the twelfth century and was reiterated in certain canons of the Council of Trent.

21.115. Alexander Agricola (c. 1446–1506), a Franco-Flemish composer who worked in the French royal chapel and later for the Duke of Burgundy and King of Castile. Antonio Colabaudi da Asti, called Bidone (c.

1480–d. before 1520), sang at the d'Este court of Ferrara and later in Pope Leo X's chapel; he was praised by Castiglione in *The Book of the Courtier*, 2.37.

21.126. *Ypsilon* ("Y"). See Servius' commentary on Vergil, *Aeneid* 6.136; also Coluccio Salutati, *De laboribus Herculis* 3.7 (ed. Ullman 1: 182), with reference to Hercules at the crossroads.

21.142. *Conticuere omnes* is a Vergilian phrase (*Aeneid* 2.1), used also at 4.502 and 21.189. Similar echoes crescendo throughout the following descent into the underworld, including Cingar's repeated evocation of *Aeneid* 6 in 25.422–430, and ending with the last line of the poem.

21.174–5. The repetition of *boccalo* (jug) recalls the autobiographical juxtaposition of Boccalo and the Folengo family at the end of Book 19.632–3.

21.181. *Bis sex pontadis* ("twelve-tone scale"): the meaning is obscure. The reading of T is *bis septem pontadis*, glossed as *Quatuordecim pontadis asinus cantat; Valla quintedecim iungit*, alluding probably to the humanist Giorgio Valla, who published *Five Books of Music* as part of his vast encyclopedia of the sciences *De expetendis et fugiendis rebus opus* (1501).

21.199. Smerdola was the witch's name in T; here Fracasso changes Smiralda into Smerdola, bringing the name closer to *merda* (shit).

21.203. *Civetta*, translated as tawny owl, also means flirt in Italian; *gufo* is often translated as long-eared owl, but could also be a *bubo* or a great-horned owl and is so translated here, looking ahead to *discornare* in line 208. For references to bothersome nighttime creatures, see the analogous passage from the *Chaos del Triperuno* cited above, pp. 276 and 329.

21.208. The meaning of *discornare* could be either to shame or to scorn (as in 7.348, 355, 582 and elsewhere), or to de-horn (as in 22.145), take the horns off a *cornuto* or cuckolded husband.

21.209–10. Typhon (Typhoeus) is the monstrous offspring of Gaia and Tartarus, variously depicted with serpent legs and multiple serpent-fingered hands; he had the force of a hurricane. For Briareus, see the note at 19.615–20.

21.269. *Horresco referens*: the phrase is from Vergil, *Aeneid* 2.204.

21.333. "Like a Gascon" : like a braggart or show-off.

21.421. "Of she-wolf stock" : or "the offspring of whores."

21.435. In Piedmontese dialect (among others), *ciappin* means devil (see below at 24.162 and 25.285).

21.474. Compare 19.27–28, for a similar grammar game.

21.475. Porta Comacina or Comasina (*Porta Comensis* for the Romans) is near the present day Castello Sforzesco; it was a major entryway into the city.

BOOK XXII

22.4. For Grugna, see 21.22.

22.8. For the fat, bearded old man, now revealed as a poet, see 21.461–62. Later (105) the reader learns that the poet is Folengo himself.

22.13–16. Maderno and Gardone are found along the west coast of the Lago di Garda, together with Moniga and Rivoltella, mentioned above 5.99–101. Stivallus (Boots) is also the name given to one of Cingar's companions at 9.514. For the whole passage, compare Dante, *Inferno* 20.61–81.

22.28–29. "Two opposing enemy territories" : the unsuspecting reader would imagine that he means the Duchy of Milan and the *terrafirma* of the Venetian empire, traditional enemies divided by the Mincio, but Folengo soon reveals (37–38) that he has in mind the villages of Pietole and Cipada, comically compared to Rome and Carthage.

22.32–33. Ostiglia is situated south of Mantua, on the eastern bank of the Po; Revere is across the river on the west. Stellata is on the east bank of the Po further south, Ficarolo on the west (see Map in volume 1 of this edition).

22.42–43. Andes, identified with modern Pietole, was traditionally believed to be Vergil's birthplace.

22.51–2. Curtatone is a tiny village near the upper lake in Mantua (see Map); Negroponte in Euboea, much celebrated in the sixteenth century, is a town in the second largest of the Aegean islands; it was controlled by Venice from 1205 until captured by the Ottoman Turks in 1470.

22.58. The sisters of Apollo are the Muses.

22.60. Bellerophon was the mythological Greek hero who, mounted on the winged horse Pegasus, slew the Chimera (the Chimera appears below, 25.545–55).

22.77–8. The figures named are the leading Neo-Latin poets of the High Renaissance: Giovanni Gioviano Pontano (1429–1503), Jacopo Sannazaro (1455–1530), Girolamo Fracastoro (1483–1553), Marco Girolamo Vida (1485–1566) and Michele Marullo (1453–1500). Many of these poets were mentioned along with their works in a long roster of poets found at the end of T, where Vergil's preëminence is repeatedly acknowledged and lamented, *Namque vetusta nocet laus nobis saepe modernis*, "because praise of the ancients often hurts us moderns" (T 25 pp. 249–250r).

22.84. *Paradisus ocarum* (the paradise of geese) is an expression meaning a heaven that doesn't exist; see the note in Folengo, *Macaronee minori*, ed. Zaggia, p. 325 (note to *Moschaea*, T 1.162).

22.88. *Moresca*: see note at 19.133.

22.98. Compare Boccaccio, *Decameron* 8.3.9, and above, 1.37.

22.113–14. The information could be found in Guarino da Verona's popular life of Plato, found frequently in editions of Plutarch's *Lives*. The story of bees making honey on the lips is often told of other writers as well, including Sophocles, Vergil and St. Ambrose.

22.123, 125. Pietro (*diminutive*: Peretto) Pomponazzi (1462–1525), a controversial philosopher known for arguing against the immortality of the soul in defiance of a decree of the Fifth Lateran Council. Born in Mantua, he taught first in Padua, then briefly in Ferrara before ending up in Bologna, where he wrote his most famous work, *De immortalitate animi* (1516). For Petrus Hispanus see the note at 3.100 and below, 25.522.

22.132. Twenty lines followed in C, in which the poet mentions his other works (the *Moschaea* and the *Zanitonella*) and describes Baldus, a strong and skilled friend of Merlin's, *cui mens Balda fuit, cui cor virtute superbum*, "whose mind was brave, whose heart gloried in its virtue." He insists that *Baldo* was written during this youthful phase and not after he had become a monk, *non ut zentaia baiaffat / Quando cucullatae praticabat claustra brigatae* ("not, as people bruit it about, when he frequented the cloister of the hooded crowd"). He goes on to say, however, that before he had finished *Baldo*, a great tumult took place and he had to flee, and then he changed his mind and his habit under a strict law and relinquished the "inane" *Baldo*. (C 22.133–153). This autobiographical data in C is in keeping with information provided in a rare 1521 dialogue (see the *Introduction* to vol. 1, xvii and note), and with that given in peripheral materials added to the posthumous V edition.

22.145. For *scornare* (= *discornare*), see the note at 21.208.

22.156. Confession was a highly controversial subject in the early years of the Reformation; note that here (and below, line 186) it is said to be a practice of the Church, not of Christ or of the Gospel. The verb *retrovare* (to rediscover) is used about seventy times, but this is the only appearance of the noun form *retrovatio* and is believed to be a neologism. In Folengo's *Orlandino* (1526), Berta objects to confession because the priest gets too excited by her sins and ends up acting more like a pimp than a learned man (*Orlandino* 6.43–44). In T, it is said of the evil inhabitants of Cipada that they have never known what confession is: they eat priests *cum vertis*, i.e. with cabbage (or perhaps "converted priests") and frequently turn them into *mezenos*, side dishes of salted pork, but with a play on *mezzano*, a go-between or procurer (T, p. 48r).

22.168. The meaning of *cheros* is obscure: Chiesa suggests that the word could be related to *gherron*, shield and hence defender (see the review of scholarly opinion in Chiesa's edition of *Baldo* [1997], 2: 887).

22.201–2. *Pisanella* was the short name of the *Summa de casibus conscientiae*, a handbook for confessors compiled by the Dominican friar Bartolomeo di San Concordio of Pisa (c. 1338); the *Summa Rosaria* was a similar compilation of the Franciscan Battista Trovamala, published in 1484; *Defecerunt* is the incipit, hence an alternate title, of the *Summa moralis* of Saint Antoninus, bishop of Florence (1389–1459).

22.271–6. The first heroes are those whose arms were particularly noteworthy: Ajax, who among the Greek warriors was second only to Achilles, whose armor he rescued and who later lost these arms to Odysseus; Theseus, the great king of Athens, who as a youth had to move a stone to reclaim the arms of his father Aegeus; and Pyrrhus (son of Achilles). Orlando and Rinaldo are the heroes of chivalric epics; Durastante,

Rodomonte and Gradasso are their opponents. Niccolò Piccinino, Gattamelata (Erasmo da Narni) and Bartolomeo Colleoni were fifteenth-century *condottieri*, also mentioned at 5.403–12 (see note). Gianni (short for Giovanni) is possibly to be identified with Gian Giacomo Trivulzio (1441–1518), who fought for Milan and France, or with Giovanni delle Bande Nere (1498–1526), the Medici captain (see 19.399, above).

22.279–80. Chiesa identifies this as an allusion to a passage from Pulci's *Morgante* 2.11.1–3, in which there is a play on words with the expression *schiacciare un sognaglio* (to ring someone's bell).

22.294. See Pulci's *Morgante* 18.119.5. Chiesa identifies the *squarcina* as a dagger with a blade shaped like a scimitar.

22.315–17. Gabriele Barletta was considered a model Dominican orator. Two volumes of his sermons in a mixture of Latin and Italian were published in 1497. For Fra Roberto Caracciolo da Lecce see the note at 9.243.

22.370. *Titalora*: see 6.18.

22.376. Demorgorgon: see the note at 18.312. Pinfar has not been identified.

22.385. Compare Matthew 4:4.

22.387. *Doctrinale*: see the note to 3.97.

22.390. Galen: see the note to 6.183.

22.394. Buffalmacco, Nello and Mastro Simone are characters from Boccaccio's *Decameron*, known for playing practical jokes; they also appear together in 9.3.

22.428. *Trentapara* is an infernal threat, as in the "thirty devils" of 6.364; it is repeated below at 23.50, and see Folengo, *Macaronee minori*, ed. Zaggia, p. 336 (note to *Moschaea* T 2.23).

22.439. *Tirintanam* ("long line") has been traced to the Milanese dialect word *tirlindanna*, which is a long, baited fishing line.

22.440. *Zobias dies Jovis* ("Thursday is for witches") reads the gloss in T; the day is also known as Witches' Sabbath (compare *cursi madonnam*).

22.472. *Marzocche*: see the notes at 6.164 and 7.633.

22.484. *Bos Chiari* ("an ox from Chiari"): see note at 21.96.

22.498–500. The verb *appizzare* is to kindle (Folengo, *Macaronee minori*, ed. Zaggia, p. 705), *cappelletto* is synonymous with mercenary (see note at 13.164), and *guerra* is war, so the name means something like "warmongerer" or "provocateur."

22.526. In T, *lapides bubae* with the gloss, *Bubae latine upupae; avis est*. The hoopoe is a woodland bird with striking black and white markings and a high crest; when it walks along the ground, it can seem to disappear. Often revered as a celestial messenger, it was, however, considered an unclean bird in the Old Testament (Leviticus 11:19, Deuteronomy 14:18), and its nest has a strong odor of feces.

22.580. *Praestigia* (Latin for illusions, magic tricks) is the form that appears in V, but Chiesa rightly notes that in C this had been *praestrigia*, and this is the spelling which appears below (23.709) in both editions, so there is likely wordplay here on *strya* (witch).

BOOK XXIII

23.10. Compare Dante, *Purgatorio* 26.35.

23.54. A macaronic calque of Vergil's famous *facilis descensus Averno* at *Aeneid* 6.126.

23.75. For other playful references to Aristotle and Plato see 14.20.

23.89. As in 3.333, *tollite carneros* means to leave abruptly (and see below at 23.517).

23.106–110. "A great, wide hole" (*sbusamine*): Formed on the dialectal noun *buso* (*buco* in Italian, from medieval Latin *buca/bucca*: mouth, cavity), with the suffix *–men* and the intensifying *s-* prefix, *sbusamine* means a big hole. It is worth attending to the transformations of *buso* throughout the work (see Introduction). *Buso* appeared notably in the passage in which the mayor Gaioffo is castrated because his rogue member had entered *busos vetatos* ("holes forbidden by law," 11.534). The past participle form *sbusata* is used once when referring to the Folengo coat of arms, *sbusata* (dented) by a hundred blows (5.407), and again at the end of the epic when Baldo and everyone else must enter a pumpkin *sbusata intus* (hollowed out inside), in which *sicca semina* or dry seeds rattle, 25.621–2.

The heroes find their last adventures in Moon Mountain *quae busa est tota dedentrum* ("which is totally hollowed out inside," 20.308), and *tota . . . per circum grottis ... busatur* ("pierced all around with grottoes," 20.817). Another coinage used in this passage, *pedestrandi* (from Lat. *pes, pedes* foot), means going on foot, yet sounds like pederast (*paiderastes* in Greek); it is used as a verb form at 20.759 and 770, with noun variations at 1.347, 5.86, and 11.564.

23.168–173. These songs have been identified (see the notes to Chiesa's edition) as follows: three of them, *Fors seulement, D'un aultre amer* and *Petite camusette* were popular songs arranged in polyphonic settings by various Renaissance composers, among them Johannes Ockeghem (c. 1410–1497) and Josquin Des Prez (c.1456–1521). *De tous biens plaine est ma maitresse* (mentioned also in *Orlandino* 4.24.2) is the beginning of a chanson by Hayne van Ghizeghem (died after 1495) which was set as many as 28 times by various Renaissance composers (including Alexander Agricola, mentioned above at 21.115). The song began *Hors ch'io son de preson fora* has *Turlurù, turlurù* as the refrain; Cingar then uses the words to introduce *Tur lu la capra è mozza*, the beginning of a popular frottola by Bartolomeo Tromboncino (c. 1470–1535), who worked at the court of the Este in Ferrara. *Che fa la Ramacina* was a popular frottola set by Tromboncino, Loyset Compère (1445–1518) and other composers.

23.179. The expression *ad mezzam gambam*, up to the calf, is glossed in T as *Proverbium*, but the source of the proverb is not known (T 21 p. 215); it seems to have been used of people who rose late in the morning.

23.181. In the *Orlandino*, the ass thinks it is playing the lute when it is actually making farting noises, *e cosi' avvien che l'asino di lira / crede sonar, quando col cul sospira*, 1.29.7–8.

23.193. The *campagna* di Verona, is mentioned above 11.523; in T 21 p. 215, a gloss elaborates a known play on the words *menchione* (schmuck) and *mincione* (referring to the town of Goito's position on the river Mincio), found also in Matteo Bandello (*Novelle* 19).

23.199. Both locales were known for prostitution, as the gloss in T spells out: *Arenas postribula* (T 21 p. 215r); see also 8.523.

23.255. This, as the reader discovers below (23.400), is Demogorgon, posing as the famous Pasquino. Pasquino is the name given to an ancient statue which in 1501 was placed near the southwest corner of Piazza Navona (now Palazzo Braschi, formerly an Orsini family residence which Folengo may have visited while employed as a tutor by the Orsini family), and to which were affixed anonymous attacks in the Roman dialect (also in Latin and Italian), often against the Papal Court. These "pasquinades" were widely read throughout Europe.

23.275. The surplices: metonymy for prelates, though the word actually used by Folengo here is the less familiar term "rochet" (*rochettis*). The latter is a more elaborate form of surplice used by high prelates.

23.298. "In the German manner," i.e., with plenty to drink: see 14.334–69.

23.302–10. The statue of Pasquino suffered a number of mutilations, including a missing nose. Marforio is yet another classical statue to which were affixed satires, sometimes in dialogue with those attached to Pasquino.

23.351. Luscar is an anagram of Carlus, possibly a macaronic syncopation of the Latin Carolus, thus indicating the Holy Roman Emperor Charles V.

23.389. "Like a mercenary" : Chiesa explains that *stradiotti more* could mean either with swift and sudden movements, as in Folengo's *Moschaea* T 3.118 (in *Macaronee minori*, ed. Zaggia, p. 361), or with minimal armor, as in the work of a contemporary writer, Anton Francesco Doni's *Zucca*, ed. C. Cordié, *Folengo, Aretino, Doni*, 2 vols. (Milan: Ricciardi, 1976–77), 2: 603.

23.401–2. As Chiesa notes, Folengo reiterates the image in *Umanità* 6.114, 7–8, and Boiardo attributes similar activities to Demogorgon (for whom see the note at 18.312) in *Orlando Innamorato* 2.13.27, 7–8.

23.467–73. "Thomists:" i.e. members of the Dominican order, who in their capacity as inquisitors had charge of punishing witches and other heretics. Folengo alludes to the common custom of punishing witches by parading them about seated backwards on an ass, wearing a bishop's mitre. For "riding on Thursdays," see above, 22.440 and note.

23.487–507. *fusos tortos* ("in *flagrante delicto*"), as at 6.417 and 14.94, means to catch in the act of adultery. *Birlo* (495), is a dialect word meaning a spinning top, but as Folengo explains in a gloss, it is used here to mean *intelligentia*; see his *Macaronee minori*, ed. Zaggia, p. 146 (note to the *Zanitonella* T 989). *Beghinae* (497) is literally beguines, but is used by Folengo in a more general sense: see the note at 16.534 and below, 506–537. *Pinzocarae* (507) were lay women who belonged to the "third (lay) order" of the Franciscans, but were condemned for refusing obedience to ecclesiastical authorities.

23.535. Hersilia is the virtuous wife of Romulus in Livy 1.11 and Ovid, *Metamorphoses* 14.829–51; see also *Umanità* 1.38.2. Thaïs is the name of a courtesan in Terence's *Eunuchus*.

23.538. There seems to be a verse missing after 538: in T 21 p. 218r, this paragraph carried the section heading *Postribulum striarum* ("The witches' brothel") and began *Introit ulterius retrovans loca turpia tandem* ("He enters further, finding at last the vile dwellings").

23.602. The transformation of Boccalo into an ass is reminiscent of the *Metamorphosis* or *Golden Ass* of Apuleius (c. 125–180 CE). In this novel the protagonist Lucius becomes overly interested in magic, is transformed into an ass and has a series of picaresque adventures. The work became a model for the picaresque novel in the Renaissance; see Julia H. Gaisser, *The Fortunes of Apuleius and the Golden Ass* (Princeton: Princeton University Press, 2008).

23.605. The author persists in calling attention to Boccalo's transformation into an ass that is colored the gray of monks and Franciscan friars, *bretino*. He insists that of all the asses in Arcadia, Boccalo is the grayest, *quo non bertinior alter* (612), and he comes back again to *beretina pelle* (647). Further indications that we are to read Boccalo's transformation as allegorical are the piling up of names for authorial figures, for example the word *folengas* (620); note too that Gelfora (Culfora), upon hearing of Baldo's rout, speculates that it is the work of a mage, who in T is identified as Merlinus Cocai: *Extimet esse magum Serraffum, sive Cocaii/ fraudes Merlini* (T 21 p. 220). See the note at 660.

23.628. The name Coclen (which in T was Merlin Cocai) could be identified with Bartolomeo della Rocca, called Cocles or Coclenius (1467–1504), a contemporary expert on chiromancy and the art of physiognomy.

23.660–6. In T, when Boccalo cannot speak, he tries to write with his feet, and the gloss reads: *Io, quem* [sic] *in vaccam mutata fuit in arena scripsit nomen* ("Io who was turned into a cow wrote her name in the dirt"), a reference to Ovid, *Metamorphoses* 1.649–51. See also above, the note to 14.198–99.

BOOK XXIV

24.16. *Zuffo* : used here for face. Compare the expression *Han visto il lupo in zuffo* in Boiardo, *Orlando Innamorato* 3.2.50.5.

24.86. In the *Galateo ovvero de' costumi* (1558), a popular manual for good manners, Giovanni della Casa (1503–1556) chides those who get up from the table with a toothpick in their mouths, saying they look like birds building a nest.

24.106–7. With *brutta semenza*, Folengo echoes Ulisse's speech from Dante's *Inferno* 26.118–19: *Considerate la vostra semenza: fatti non foste a viver come brutti, ma per seguir virtute e canoscenza*, "Consider well your seed: you were not born to live as a mere brute does, but for the pursuit of knowledge and the good" (tr. Pinsky); see also below, 20.304 and 25.305. The word *prosopopeia* has two meanings in Italian, personification (as in English) and an air of self-importance.

24.117. "By our Lord" (*per dominum nostrum*): see the note to 3.466.

24.146. Chiesa suggests that the name Sturlone could be based on the dialectal *sturlòn*, a shove, a push (in keeping with *fracassare*, to smash).

24.162. *Chiapinum* means devil, as in 21.435, 473, and 25.285.

24.176. *Euhoe*, etc., seem to be nonsense syllables; compare *Euhoe, Bacche* in Vergil's *Aeneid* 7.389.

24.187. Caiaphas and Annas are the Jewish high priests mentioned in the New Testament who participated in the trial and condemnation of Jesus.

24.210. An echo of *oves haedique petulci* from Vergil, *Georgics* 4.10; *petulcus* also has the meaning of wanton, skittish. As elsewhere, *vaccae* connotes "whores."

24.234. The Merceria is a *calle* leading into St. Mark's Square in Venice, where the condemned were led to be whipped.

24.242. "Turned a merchant's ear:" turned a deaf ear. See 6.304.

24.260. In P (1517), the epic ended here with the final verse of the *Aeneid* (12.952): *vitaque cum gemitu fugit indignata sub umbras*, "and his offended soul fled groaning to the shades below." The ending was also borrowed and translated into Italian verse by Ariosto for the finale of *Orlando Furioso* (1516); in T this borrowed verse closes Book 22.

24.283–4. See 19.180.

24.303. "The caves of Phlegethon:" Phlegethon is a river of fire in Greek mythology and one of the five rivers of Hell. In Dante's *Inferno* it is a river of blood in the seventh circle (the circle of those guilty of violence against their fellow humans) that boils souls and is guarded by centaurs; see *Inferno* 11.34–39.

24.307. In Folengo's *Umanità* as well as in Dante, Pulci and Aretino, *centro* is used for hell.

24.342. The word *savornam* (from the medieval Latin *saburra*) means sand and gravel used as ballast. It calls to mind the Italian *zavorra* used by Dante in *Inferno* 25.142 to mean "deadweight," where the narrator implicitly compares the seventh *bolgia* to the hold of a ship, apologizing for his enigmatic language. Hence *zavorra* generally means a ship's hold or what is in it, but is used here for a circle in hell.

24.428. The word *ierae* is the short form of *gerapicra*, or *hierapicra* (the Greek words for sacred and bitter); it is a cathartic medicine made of aloes and canella bark.

24.464. Griffarosto (Roast-snatcher) is also the name of the abbot-gourmand who is the focus of the final *capitolo* of Folengo's *Orlandino*.

24.483. Luigi Messadaglia suggests that *pospodo* is for the Slavic *gospodo*, lord, in his *Vita e costume della Rinascenza in Merlin Cocai*, ed. E. and M. Billanovich (Padua: Antenore, 1974), 426–7.

24.493. The warm baths of Porretta are located about 60 kilometers southwest of Bologna.

24.499–501. The Lombard quail metaphor appeared above (7.460 and 8.532); a note printed in T tells us that an unbridled poet would have said, *Cingar cagare volebat*, "Cingar wanted to shit" (T 23 p. 230r).

24.550. Grillo (meaning cricket and whim in Italian) was named Cingarinus in T; his twin brother, here Fanetto, was named Marcellinus.

24.639–40. These two lines adapt and extend the nonsense syllables spoken by Pluto in Dante's *Inferno* 7.1. Note that Folengo uses *papa* (father or pope) instead of Dante's *pap(a)e*, in Latin an expression of alarm.

24.645, 647. In T, Folengo glosses this *ludus gattae* and mentions that he who killed the cat, *vel capite vel et caetera* ("with his head or with something else"), was called the *cavallerius gattae* ("Knight of the Cat"). The *Morgante* also refers to this game at 3.41.7. *Saltimbarca* means jump aboard.

24.675. Guerrin Meschino is the titular hero of the chivalric romance by Andrea da Barberino (c.1371–1431), whose adventure took him to Hell; in earlier editions of *Baldo* the example used is Aeneas.

24.698. Chiron was the centaur in Greek mythology who taught, among others, Achilles and Jason; see also the note to 24.303.

24.729. A *sacco* was a liquid measure; that of Bologna held approximately 157 liters, or forty gallons.

BOOK XXV

25.138. Chiesa cites *pallentes ... Morbi* from *Aeneid* 6.275; *macchiaeque draconum* could be serpent-like thorn bushes, or brush full of snakes.

25.221. The antidote treacle was much in vogue in sixteenth century Northern Italy; see the Introduction in volume 1 of this edition, ix–x.

25.224. C. F. Goffis, in his *L'Eterodossia dei fratelli Folengo* (Genoa: Pagano, 1950), p. 280, cited by Chiesa, notes that Erasmus also speaks of the Furies' baldness in his *Charon*.

25.228. "The Dove:" i.e. the Holy Spirit.

25.240, 243. In C these verses refer explicitly to a Pope Paul, presumably Pope Paul III: *quam nisi Romani consolet gratia Pauli; se fuerit Pietri Paulo concessa cadrega.*

25.285. Chiappin means devil, as above, 21.435 and note, 21.473 and 24.162; for Malabolgia, see the note to 19.229–60.

25.295. Chiesa notes that in Folengo's *Umanità* 4.58, Lupaccio is the name of the devil who tempts Christ in the desert.

25.339, 345. Alecto's emphasis on damaging Christ's faith appears first in C. In T, a long list of Italian towns follows that have been corrupted by the brothers Guelf and Ghibelline (T p. 242r); the 25 verses of baffling proper names and odd activities concludes with Alecto's regrets over the inability of her twins to seduce and defile Mantua and Cipada: *His tamen (heu) cur non seducta est Mantua nobis, / His tamen (heu) cur non potui violare Cipadae?* ("Alas, why have these brothers not seduced Mantua for me, why have I not, alas, been able to rape Cipada through them?").

25.366. Both in the *Orlandino* (5.57–8) and in C (2.381–2), Folengo presents this stercorous birth as a myth of origins.

25.401–6. In T, six verses follow verse 406 which explain why the *tenebrosa cohors* could not bear to look at Baldo: because of the gem he wears, not on his helmet, but in his heart, "the gem of purpose not puffed up by ambition, the gem of pleasure in the honor of virtue."

25.421. For Guerrino Meschino, see note at 24.675.

25.445. The game of morra, traced back to Egypt and still played around the world, is played by at least two players: the object of morra is to shout out the correct sum of fingers held up on one's own hand together with those held up by the opponent.

25.488–93. *Huc* (here), *illuc* (there), etc., are Latin adverbs; *cuius* the genitive relative pronoun. There follow terms used in philosophical disputation: *pro, contra, nego, probo. Ly homo* is a Latin noun preceded by a medieval French definite article. Such expressions were introduced by medieval philosophers to supply the lack of a definite article in Latin, but were mocked by humanist grammarians as barbarous neologisms; see also 13.268. The other terms – matter, form, being, quiddity, accident, substance – are terms used in the Aristotelian philosophy of the universities, satirized by Folengo here (in the humanist fashion) as empty verbiage leading to delusive ideas.

25.520. In a surprising (and perhaps allegorical) turn here, flies are compared to various kinds of owls; see the note above at 21.203. *Notolae* (Latin *noctua*, Italian, *nottola*) is synonymous with *civetta*, the *Carine noctua* referred to above (25.404). For *besazze* (Lat. *bisaccium*) see 6.240.

25.522. For Paolo Veneto see the note at 11.656; for Petrus Hispanus see the notes at 3.100 and 22.125.

25.533–9. *Zorneiam Scotti* ("the cloak of Scotus") probably refers to the whole apparatus of reasoning associated with John Duns Scotus, a famous Franciscan theologian (c.1266–1308) cited above, 8.709. Scotus's obscurity was a frequent target of humanist criticism. "Scotto" and St. Thomas are also coupled in *Orlandino* 3.20. The dialectal word for a cloak, *zorneiam* (Ital. *giornea*), also used of a judge's robes and a sailor's cloak, is used with a similar metaphorical meaning in 6.420 and 11.584; but note also the reference to magician Michael Scot and the bewitched cloak (*cappum seu mantum sive gabanum*) in 19.198–200. The other scholastics mentioned are St. Thomas Aquinas (c. 1225–1274) and his teacher Albertus Magnus (c. 1193–1280), both prominent Dominican theologians. In the later Middle Ages Albertus had a popular reputation as a magician, based on his supposed authorship of works on alchemy and the secrets of nature; it is these works that are alluded to in lines 536–39.

25.542–44. The maxims of Epicurus would have been known to Folengo from Latin translations of Diogenes Laertius' *Lives of the Philosophers*, but are probably here a generic reference to philosophical maxims of philosophers who contradict Christianity. A gloss in T states *Cocamen et cocaius et coconus*, meaning that all three words mean bottle-stopper; see the note to 17.662. The juxtaposition of Boccalo and the *domus Folengae* was seen in 19.632–3, and of (Merlin) Cocaio and Folengo in 5.403 and 407.

25.545–55. Chiesa aptly cites the passage from the *Orlandino* (3.16.1–4), in which the poet calls himself a chimera: *La stella di Saturno o sia pianeta / è quella che mi fa d'uomo chimera, / lo qual non ebbi mai né avrò mai queta / la mente, in fantasie matin e sera* ("The star of Saturn, or rather the planet, is that which turns me from a man to a chimera, who never had and never will have a calm mind, in fantasies night and day").

25.555. A transformation of Horace's *Parturient montes, nascetur ridiculus mus* ("The mountains shall give birth, and a ridiculous mouse shall be born"); see *Ars poetica* 139.

25.562. "Whether" (*utrum*). *Utrum* is the usual first word in a scholastic disputed question; for example, the first question in Thomas' *Summa theologiae* is "Whether it is necessary for there to be another discipline besides that of philosophy?"

25.577. For Pasquino, see note at 23.255.

25.597. Chiesa notes that the verb *atezare* is a technical term used for movements made by acrobats as well as by trained fleas (*atteggiare* in Italian is to strike a pose).

25.602. *Cococchia* is a long-necked gourd (presumably *Cucurbita lagenaria*); the word is still used in some Italian dialects (in the form *cocuzza*).

25.646–8. The citation (from *Aeneid* 4.216) is of course humorous because Folengo makes it sound as though Vergil praised Aeneas for being effeminate, whereas instead it is Iarbas, his rival, who describes Aeneas (4.215) as a Paris *cum semiviro comitatu* ("with an effeminate company").

25.657–59. The final verses are from Vergil's *Eclogues*, 2.58–9. Modern texts of Vergil read *Floribus Austrum / perditus* . . . . A version of these lines also concludes the *Chaos del Triperuno*, p. 333.

Bibliography

✿❦✿

EARLY EDITIONS

Merlini Cocai poetae Mantuani liber: Macaronices Libri XVII non ante impressi. Venice: Alexander Paganinus, 1517.

Opus Merlini Cocaii poetae Mantuani totum in pristinam formam per me Magistrum Aequarium Lodolam redactum. Toscolano on Lake Garda: Alexander Paganinus, 1521.

Macaronicorum poema. Baldus. Zanitonella, Moschaea, Epigrammata. Cipada: Magister Aequarius Lodola, undated (but c. 1536). Known as the Cipadense.

Merlini Cocalii [sic] poetae Mantuani Macaronicorum poemata. Venice: Heirs of Petrus Ravanus et Socii, 1552.

Anastatic copies of these editions have been issued by the Associazione Amici di Merlin Cocai, Mantua and Bassano del Grappa, 1991–1999.

COMPLETE MODERN EDITIONS

Il Baldo. Edited by Giampaolo Dossena and translated by Giuseppe Tonna. Milan: Feltrinelli, 1958. Revised translation only re-issued by Carlo and Teresa Tonna and Giorgio Bernardi-Perini. Reggio Emilia: Diabasis, 2004.

Baldus di Teofilo Folengo. Edited by Mario Chiesa. Torino: UTET, 1997. Critical text, translation, extensive notes, index and glossary.

Teofilo Folengo, Baldus. Edited Mario Chiesa with a French translation by Gérard Genot and Paul Larivaille. 3 vols. Paris: Les Belles Lettres, 2004–2007. With an extensive introduction, list of variants, and notes.

OTHER WORKS BY TEOFILO FOLENGO

Chaos del Triperuno. In *Opere italiane.* Edited by Umberto Renda. Bari: Laterza, 1911. Scrittori d'Italia 15.

Macaronee Minori. Edited by Massimo Zaggia. Turin: Einaudi, 1987. With extensive notes on prosody and metrics, and a glossary.

Opere di Teofilo Folengo. Edited by Carlo Cordié. Milan and Naples: Ricciardi, 1977. An annotated bilingual edition of much of the *Baldus,* the *Orlandino,* parts of the *Chaos del Triperuno* and other works, as well as Macaronic pieces by other authors.

Orlandino. Edited and annotated by Mario Chiesa. Padua: Antenore, 1991.

La Umanità del Figliuolo di Dio. Edited and annotated by Simona Gatti Ravedati. Alessandria: Edizioni dell'Orso, 2000.

La Palermitana. Edited and annotated by Patrizia De Corso. Florence: Olschki, 2006

Varium poema. Edited by Cesare Federico Goffis. Turin: Loescher, 1958.

SELECTED SECONDARY LITERATURE

Billanovich, Giuseppe. *Tra don Teofilo e Merlin Cocaio.* Naples: Pironti, 1948. Reprinted in *Teofilo Folengo: studi e testi,* as below.

Bonora, Ettore. *Le Maccheronee di Teofilo Folengo.* Venice: Neri Pozza, 1956.

Chiesa, Mario. *Teofilo Folengo tra la cella e la piazza.* Alessandria: Edizioni dell'Orso, 1988.

Chiesa, Mario e Simona Gatti. *Il Parnaso e la zucca: Testi e studi folenghiani.* Alessandria: Edizioni dell'Orso, 1995.

Cordié, Carlo. "Le quattro redazioni del *Baldus* di Teofilo Folengo." In *Memorie della Reale Accademia delle Scienze di Torino,* series 2, 68.1 (1935–6): 144–248.

Cultura letteraria e tradizione popolare in Teofilo Folengo. Atti del Convegno di studi . . . Mantova, 15–17 October 1977. Milan: Feltrinelli, 1979.

Goffis, Cesare Federico. *Roma, Lutero e la poliglossia Folenghiana.* Bologna: Pàtron, 1995.

Mullaney, Ann. "Teofilo Folengo: Ecce Homo." Ph.D. dissertation, Yale University, 1984.

Paoli, Ugo. *Il latino maccheronico.* Florence: Le Monnier, 1959. A shortened version of this work is printed in the Les Belles Lettres edition, vol. 1 (2004).

Quaderni folenghiani. Mantua: Tre lune, 1995-. Journal devoted to Folengo studies, with serial bibliographies.

Teofilo Folengo nel quinto centenario della nascita (1491–1991). Atti del Convegno di Mantova-Brescia-Padova. September 26–29, 1991. Edited by Giorgio Bernardi Perini and Claudio Marangoni. Florence: Olschki, 1993.

Teofilo Folengo: studi e testi. Edited by Luca Curti. Pisa: Libreria del Lungarno, 1994. Contains important studies on Folengo, including Billanovich's, as above.

Zaggia, Massimo. *Schedario folenghiano dal 1977 al 1993.* Florence: Olschki, 1994. Folengo bibliography.

Cumulative Index

ༀཨༀ

Two-part arabic numbers refer to book and paragraph of the English translation of Folengo's text, with the exception of note citations (e.g., 19.206–218n), which are keyed to book and line. Books 1–12 are found in Volume 1 of this edition (ITRL 25). Roman numerals refer to volume and page of the introductions.

Publication of this volume has been made possible by

The Myron and Sheila Gilmore Publication Fund at I Tatti
The Robert Lehman Endowment Fund
The Jean-François Malle Scholarly Programs and Publications Fund
The Andrew W. Mellon Scholarly Publications Fund
The Craig and Barbara Smyth Fund
for Scholarly Programs and Publications
The Lila Wallace–Reader's Digest Endowment Fund
The Malcolm Wiener Fund for Scholarly Programs and Publications